MW00562094

The Sweet
Blue Distance

ALSO BY SARA DONATI

The Gilded Hour
Where the Light Enters

THE WILDERNESS NOVELS

Into the Wilderness

Dawn on a Distant Shore

Lake in the Clouds

Fire Along the Sky

Queen of Swords

The Endless Forest

THE

Sweet Blue Distance

SARA DONATI

BERKLEY
New York

BERKLEY
An imprint of Penguin Random House LLC
penguinrandomhouse.com

Copyright © 2024 by Rosina Lippi-Green
Penguin Random House supports copyright. Copyright fuels creativity,
encourages diverse voices, promotes free speech, and creates a vibrant culture.
Thank you for buying an authorized edition of this book and for complying
with copyright laws by not reproducing, scanning, or distributing any part of it
in any form without permission. You are supporting writers and allowing
Penguin Random House to continue to publish books for every reader.

BERKLEY and the BERKLEY & B colophon are registered
trademarks of Penguin Random House LLC.

Library of Congress Cataloging-in-Publication Data

Names: Donati, Sara, 1956– author.
Title: The sweet blue distance / Sara Donati.
Description: New York: Berkley, 2024.
Identifiers: LCCN 2023042084 (print) | LCCN 2023042085 (ebook) |
ISBN 9781984805058 (hardcover) | ISBN 9781984805072 (ebook)
Subjects: LCGFT: Western fiction. | Novels.
Classification: LCC PS3554.O46923 S94 2024 (print) |
LCC PS3554.O46923 (ebook) | DDC 813/.54—dc23/eng/20231011
LC record available at https://lccn.loc.gov/2023042084
LC ebook record available at https://lccn.loc.gov/2023042085

Printed in the United States of America
1st Printing

Maps and interior image of cat by Rosina Lippi-Green

For Penny

Friends we are today

And friends we'll always be

For I am wise to you

And you sure see through me.

There are things that happen and leave no discernible trace, are not spoken or written of, though it would be very wrong to say that subsequent events go on indifferently, all the same, as though such things had never been.

—A. S. Byatt, *Possession*

Man is a being of varied, manifold and inconstant nature. And woman, by God, is a match for him.

—Dorothy Dunnett, *The Disorderly Knights*

Characters

THOSE FAMILIAR WITH the Wilderness series may realize that a few character names have changed. The online family tree should clarify things. You'll find it on my website at SaraDonati.com/sweetblue.

In Spain and the former colonies of Spain, including the southwest of what would one day be the United States, an individual's last name was, and to some extent still is, a composite of two names. Example: José Luis Bilbao-Luna. In this case the individual has two first names; his composite surname starts with Bilbao (his father's last name) and is followed by Luna (his mother's). This person would be addressed as Señor Bilbao because the father's surname is primary. The hyphen is included only to avoid misinterpretation of the first half of the surname as a middle name.

If there is a name in parentheses after a man's name, the two people are to be understood to be husband and wife. An asterisk indicates a historical character.

Paradise, Hamilton County, New York, 1840s Through 1860s

Lily Bonner Ballentyne, artist, widowed 1844.

Hannah Bonner, also known as Walking Woman of the
   Kahnyen'kehàka Wolf Longhouse, physician. Wife of Ben
   Savard, horse breeder and agent.

Daniel Bonner, teacher, hunter, trapper. Husband of Martha Kirby
   Bonner.

Gabriel Bonner, hunter, trapper, fur trader. Husband of Annie of
   the Kahnyen'kehàka Wolf Longhouse.

Blue-Jay of the Kahnyen'kehàka Turtle Longhouse, hunter, trapper,
   fur trader. Husband of Susanna Mayfair.

Blue Ballentyne, eldest child of Lily Bonner and Simon Ballentyne.
   Wife of John Young, miller.

Curiosity Bonner, physician. Youngest child of Nathaniel and
   Elizabeth Bonner. Wife of Henry Savard, physician, originally of
   New Orleans.

Greg Fisher, innkeeper. Husband of Martha Ballentyne Fisher.

Becca LeBlanc, widow, innkeeper.

Alois Bee, trading post proprietor.

New York City, 1850s Through 1860s

Lily Bonner Ballentyne (Aunt Quinlan) and her second husband,
   Harrison Quinlan, physician. Two of her children: Elizabeth
   Caroline Ballentyne, called Carrie, nurse and midwife; Nathan
   Ballentyne, student.

Anna Savard, student, an orphaned niece.

Sophie Savard, student, an orphaned niece. Originally of New
   Orleans.

Amelie Savard, midwife. Daughter of Aunt Quinlan's eldest half
   sister, Hannah.

Luke Scott Bonner, Aunt Quinlan's half brother, and his second
   wife, Rachel (Livingston) Wells.

Dr. Michael Colby, physician. Husband of Aurelia Markham Colby.

Margaret Quinlan Cooper, Aunt Quinlan's stepdaughter.

Henry and Jane Lee, groundskeeper and housekeeper for the Quinlans; in their own residence.

From New York to the Missouri

Eloise and Henrietta Conway, Marianne Worth, Candace Newton, ladies of good family.

Magleby family, Mormon emigrants bound for Utah.

Eli, Jules, and Mo Ibarra, brothers, sheep ranchers, New Mexico Territory.

Evangeline Roberts Zavala, widow, property and store owner, Santa Fe.

Captain Calvin Ashby (Constance), owner of the steamboat *Annabelle*.

Georgia Hamblin, widow, formerly of Santa Fe.

Herlinde Ratz, Gilbert Hotel housekeeper and cook, in Westport.

Esteban and Teresa Romero, horse breeders, in Westport.

Jose Romero and Maddalen Ibarra Romero, horse breeders, in Westport.

The Santa Fe Trail

Orwell and Joshua (Pate) Petit, brothers, Petit Overland Freight & Transport, based in Santa Fe. Their staff: Sol Taylor, Lionel Tock, Helmet, Liebling, Big Bull, Sam Wright, Bluey Brown.

Hugh Preston, merchant, and Kanti Ewell Chatham, a widow, passengers.

Titus Hardy, scout, guide, tracker.

Miguel Santos, Navajo, hunter, tracker.

Rainer (Rainey) Bang, German immigrant, trapper, tracker.

Bent Bow, chief, Kiowa.

New Mexico Territory / Territorial Government

*William W. H. Davis, secretary and acting governor.

David V. Whiting, postmaster.

Wilbur M. Pelham (Georgia), surveyor general.

Andrew Leroux (Helen), deputy surveyor.

Jesus Maria (Chucho) Sena y Baca, sheriff (or *alguacil*).

Thomas Bixby, attorney.

Henry Maddox Ford, circuit judge.

Eli Ibarra, surveyor, topographical engineer, cartographer, consultant.

United States Army

*Colonel Sterling Price, commander, Army of the West.

*Brevet Lieutenant Colonel George A. McCall, major, 3rd Infantry, Department of New Mexico.

Captain Jack Purdy, quartermaster, 3rd Infantry.

Captain Moses Brooks, 3rd Infantry.

*Lieutenant Amiel Weeks Whipple, U.S. Army Corps of Topographical Engineers (detached).

Santa Fe

PROMINENT CITIZENS / PROPERTY OWNERS

Don Diego Ibarra (*patrón*) (Doña Altagracia), sheep ranchers, Hacienda Catalan.

Don Pedro Zavala-Garza (*patrón*), sheep rancher, Hacienda Pontevedra.

Iñigo Guevara (Violante), Guevara Horse Farm and Livery.

Pío Ocampo-Cisneros (Carmen), burro breeders, trade, transport.

Primo Guzman-Macias (Alma), owners, fonda.

János Botka (Magda), president, First Territorial Bank.

Porfirio Muñoz-Ramos (Lena), publisher and editor, *Santa Fe Weekly Gazette*.

Evangeline Roberts Zavala, widow, proprietor, *cacharrería*.

Francesco Segura-Maldinado, wealthy landowner.

CLERGY

*Hiram W. Read (Alzina), Baptist missionary, Fort Marcy chaplain.

*Jean-Baptiste Lamy (1814–1880). Born and ordained in France, Lamy went to the fledgling U.S. as a missionary. The pope appointed him bishop (and later, archbishop) in the New Mexico Territory. He arrived in Santa Fe in 1851 and served there for the rest of his life.

Sisters of Loretto, Academy of Our Lady of Light.

Francisco Cortez-Chavez, parish priest, Te Tsu Geh Pueblo.

Marcel Jalbert, parish priest, Santa Fe.

*Antonio José Martinez (1793–1867), parish priest, Taos.

MEDICAL

Enzo Benenati, physician.

Maduhenía (Madu), Little-Foot, midwife, Te Tsu Geh Pueblo.

Samuel Markham (Indira Ewell), physician and surgeon.

John Edmonds, assistant to Dr. Markham.

Emilio Garcia-Lopez, apothecary.

Heinrich Hartmann, dentist.

OTHER RESIDENTS

Abram Goldblum (Chava), importer-exporter.

Adelina Gray Wolf, midwife, Ohkay Owingeh Pueblo.

Bonita Ruiz, prostitute, Casino Taquito.

Buzz Kelly, barber.

Carlos Guzman, Markham household help.

Chema Tejeda-Villalobos (Angela), barber.

Consuela and Lupe Cabrera-Cano, sisters, Leroux household help.

David Goldblum (Miriam), corn broker.

Diego Llabrés-Cisneros, undertaker.

Gustavo Aguilar-Álvarez (Inez), grocer.

Jean Paul Gillette, tailor. Husband of Roxanne Gillette, seamstress.

José Luis Bilbao, rancher.

Josefa Gray Wolf, Ohkay Owingeh Pueblo, Markham household help.

Levi Goldblum (Reizl), owner, Goldblum Bros. General Store.

Lucía Arrabal-Lopez, owner, Casino Arrabal and Four Aces Saloon.

Magdalena Luna-Ocampo, Carson household help.

Manuela Gray Wolf, Ohkay Owingeh Pueblo, Markham household help.

Mimi Torres, widow.

Nachín Justo-Maldonado (Leona), proprietors, Casino Taquito.

Pete Terney, barkeep, Pepperharrow Saloon.

Rick Carson (Tess), owner, hardware store.

Rocío Ramirez-Herrera aka Red Rosa or Rosita, owner, Cantina La Faena; and her father, Hugo, a widower.

Talli Ernesto Claw-Foot (Tewa name Póyo-taa), *cacique*, Te Tsu Geh Oweenge Pueblo.

Theo Agnew, barkeep, Four Aces Saloon.

Tom Samson, *cibolero*.

Yatzil Morales-Zapato, prostitute, Casino Taquito.

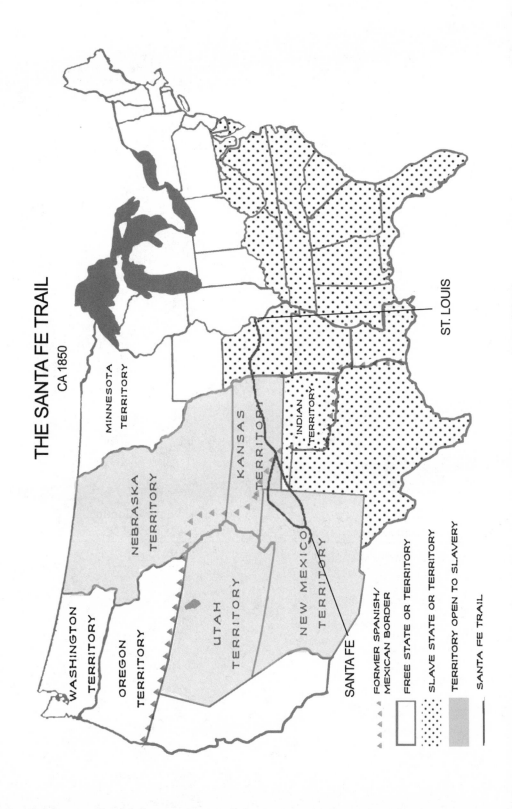

THE SANTA FE TRAIL
CA 1850

WASHINGTON TERRITORY

OREGON TERRITORY

MINNESOTA TERRITORY

NEBRASKA TERRITORY

UTAH TERRITORY

KANSAS TERRITORY

NEW MEXICO TERRITORY

INDIAN TERRITORY

ST. LOUIS

SANTA FE

▲▲▲▲ FORMER SPANISH/ MEXICAN BORDER

FREE STATE OR TERRITORY

SLAVE STATE OR TERRITORY

TERRITORY OPEN TO SLAVERY

SANTA FE TRAIL

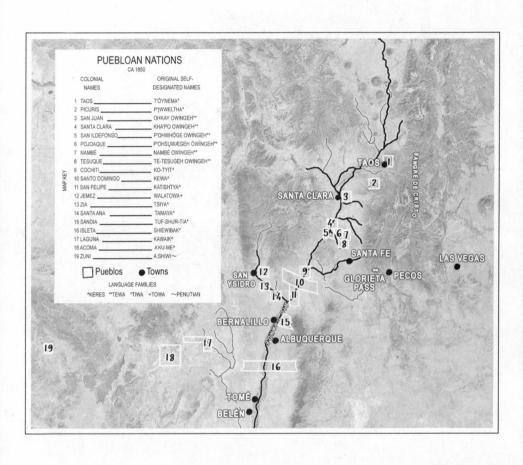

PUEBLOAN NATIONS
CA 1850

COLONIAL NAMES	ORIGINAL SELF-DESIGNATED NAMES
1 TAOS	T'ÓYNEMA*
2 PICURIS	P'ĮWWELTHA*
3 SAN JUAN	OHKAY OWINGEH**
4 SANTA CLARA	KHA'PO OWINGEH**
5 SAN ILDEFONSO	P'OHWHŌGE OWINGEH**
6 POJOAQUE	P'OHSŲWÆGEH ÓWÍNGEH**
7 NAMBÉ	NAMBÉ OWINGEH**
8 TESUQUE	TE-TESUGEH OWINGEH**
9 COCHITI	KO-TYIT^
10 SANTO DOMINGO	KEWA^
11 SAN FELIPE	KATISHTYA^
12 JEMEZ	WALATOWA+
13 ZIA	TSIYA^
14 SANTA ANA	TAMAYA^
15 SANDIA	TUF-SHUR-TIA*
16 ISLETA	SHIEWIBAK*
17 LAGUNA	KAWAIK^
18 ACOMA	A'KU-ME^
19 ZUNI	A:SHIWI~

☐ Pueblos ● Towns

LANGUAGE FAMILIES
^KERES **TEWA *TIWA +TOWA ~PENUTIAN

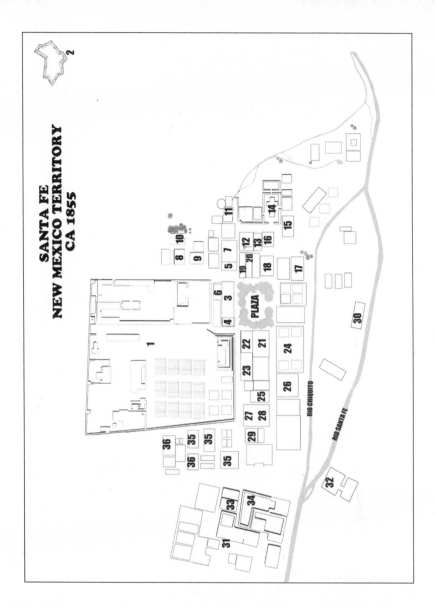

SANTA FE
NEW MEXICO TERRITORY
CA 1855

1. Fort Marcy Military Reservation
2. Old Fort Marcy
3. Palace of the Governors
4. Post Office
5. Courthouse
6. Jail
7. Fonda
8. Baptist church and academy
9. Bank
10. Leroux residence
11. Guevara Horse Farm and Livery
12. Markham residence
13. Dispensary
14. Catholic church with schools and convent
15. Bishop Lamy
16. *Santa Fe Weekly Gazette*
17. Zavala residence
18. Pharmacy
19. Barbershop
20. Bakery
21. Fancy dry goods
22. General store
23. Goldblum residences
24. Livestock, corn, and grain exchange
25. Grocer
26. Hardware
27. Surveyor
28. Ibarra residence
29. Cantina La Faena
30. Millhouse
31. Petit Overland Freight & Transport
32. Tannery
33. Blacksmith
34. Wheelwright
35. Saloons
36. Brothels

The Sweet
Blue Distance

PART ONE

Correspondence

Samuel Markham, M.D.
Physician and Surgeon
Calle del Convento Viejo de la Parroquia Principal
Santa Fe, New Mexico Territory

November 18, 1856

Michael V. Colby, M.D.
143 East 17th-Street
New York City

Dear Michael,
Many thanks for your letter dated 22nd September, and congratulations to you and Aurelia on the arrival of a healthy grandson. As our Lulu is so young, I can only hope I'll live long enough to be a grandfather, and so I count myself fortunate to have Matthew Markham Colby as a grandnephew.

Not sure if I should congratulate you on the directorship at the New Amsterdam. Of course you deserve it, but why would you want it? If you're tired of practicing medicine, maybe you should give it up and move to your place on Sag Harbor. Or better still, come out west. If Santa Fe doesn't suit, you could try your luck in the Sierra Nevada gold fields.

Our news: Indira is expecting again and due, if my calculations are correct, in July. She's more frightened than she is pleased, given three losses since. You have seen such anxiety—even hysteria—in your own patients, I know. Given all that and with the sincere hope I do not intrude too far, I must ask for your help.

Indira insists she must have a midwife, a woman of good family trained in Richmond, Philadelphia, or New York. She has a strong preference for an American midwife, but an English woman with excellent references would be acceptable to her. This person must be born in either the United States or England. I expect Scotland would pass muster, but Ireland would not.

I think I mentioned to you in my last letter that my assistant John Edmonds has been admitted to the medical school at Bellevue. When we first took him in, I said that if he did well and showed promise, I would underwrite his education, and that time has come. His maturity and intelligence indicate to me that he will do very well in medical school. With his departure imminent, I have to hire a nurse, and from that follows my decision to hire one person who is both nurse and midwife, and to get her here as soon as possible.

You will have noted that I have enclosed a draft of an advertisement. Would you be so good as to look it over and circulate it where you think it might catch the attention of suitable and qualified applicants? Make changes if you think I've been too blunt, but don't soften it up too much. New Mexico Territory isn't the place for gently reared women, as I have learned. If you are up to it, I'd be thankful if you could interview applicants briefly to weed out the inexperienced, unrealistic, or unsuitable ones, as time is of the essence. I am forever in your debt. Please give my love to Aurelia and your many offspring.

Your devoted friend and brother-in-law,
Sam

WANTED:
NURSE-MIDWIFE TO JOIN AN ESTABLISHED MEDICAL PRACTICE IN NEW MEXICO TERRITORY

Dr. Samuel Markham, originally of this city but resident in Santa Fe, New Mexico Territory, for the last ten years, is seeking a formally trained, experienced nurse and midwife to join his medical practice. This position requires someone who will see patients and assist in his Santa Fe dispensary, but who will also make home visits in the town and environs. Thus the successful applicant must be an experienced rider.

There is a great deal of unrest in the territory. Indian raids and attacks are not uncommon outside Santa Fe and less common within the boundaries of the town, due in part to the presence of the U.S. Army and the garrison. Thus the nurse who joins the practice must be courageous, quick-witted, and able to handle weapons. A truly excellent applicant who has no experience with firearms but is willing to learn will be considered.

To a well-trained, conscientious, compassionate, vigorous, and hardworking individual who is not afraid of the unfamiliar, Dr. Markham offers the following: all costs associated with relocation to Santa Fe; a weekly salary of $15; the use of a good horse and saddle; a private room and board; and services of the household staff. You will take meals with the family (which includes the doctor, his wife, and a young daughter) and be counted as one of their number.

Santa Fe's population is about one-quarter white, including the soldiers at the military garrison; the rest are Mexican, Indian, African, or mixed blood. There are very few Orientals. There are many different tribes in and near Santa Fe, including the Pueblo clans, the Apache, Navajo, and Ute. Other tribes pass through on a regular basis. As Spanish is the lingua franca, the person hired will be required to learn that language within a reasonable amount of time. Further, she must agree to set out for Santa Fe no later than the beginning of May, and to commit to a three-year period of service. In addition to a very liberal salary, Dr. Markham will consider an annual bonus for a person who becomes an asset to the practice and agrees to a longer contract.

Interested parties should first present themselves to Dr. Michael Colby at the New Amsterdam Charity Hospital. If that interview is successful, he will ask you to send a letter of application to Dr. Markham, in which you provide information about your background, your training, and experience.

Dr. Michael V. Colby, Director
New Amsterdam Charity Hospital

notice dated December 15, 1856

BALLENTYNE TO MARKHAM

E. C. Ballentyne
18 Waverly Place
New York, New York

January 4, 1857

Samuel Markham, M.D.
Physician and Surgeon
Calle del Convento Viejo de la Parroquia Principal
Santa Fe, New Mexico Territory

Dear Dr. Markham,
Dr. Michael Colby, a friend of my family, visited on New
Year's Day to tell us about a recent letter he had from you.
*   As a fully trained and qualified nurse and midwife, I listened*
with great interest to the description of the position you are now
trying to fill. Please consider this letter my application for that
position. You will soon receive letters of reference from Dr. Colby,
Dr. Elizabeth Blackwell, and the midwife Amelie Savard, a highly
regarded and respected practitioner, who happens also to be my
cousin, and with whom I apprenticed and trained in midwifery.
*   I was born on January 31, 1831. I attended school from age six to*
sixteen, first in the town where I was born upstate, and then at
Mrs. Highsmith's Trivium here in Manhattan. At age sixteen I
graduated and then began my training at the New Amsterdam. At
eighteen I began my apprenticeship with the midwife Amelie
Savard. Three years later I began attending births without
supervision. Since that time I have attended on average four births
a week, some at the New Amsterdam, but more often at the mother's
home. I also make home visits when physicians on staff are
otherwise occupied and the complaints are not life threatening.

I believe you will find me to be highly capable, clearheaded, decisive, self-possessed in the most chaotic of situations. My first concern is always for the patient's comfort and recovery.

Dr. Colby explained that you seek a midwife and nurse who will not mind living and working away from the conveniences of a city. I assure you that I would welcome such an opportunity. When my mother, then recently widowed, moved us away from the village of Paradise in the Adirondack wilderness to New York City, I was just twelve. My life here in Manhattan has not been lacking in any way, but I have never felt truly at ease here.

Further, I am in good health and capable of working long hours, and I am an accomplished horsewoman. Riding out to see patients is something I would look forward to.

I understand that the person you hire must be willing to work with and among Mexicans, Africans, and Indians of many different tribes. This is for me a very familiar way to live. My upbringing was unusual, as my family includes members of the Kahnyen'kehàka (Mohawk), Seneca, and Seminole tribes as well as many who have both Indian and African ancestors. Add to this my work with the poor and indigent, and you will see that I am more than comfortable with peoples and cultures other than my own.

My teachers have all remarked that I have an aptitude for foreign language, and I believe that I will be able to learn Spanish in a reasonable amount of time.

If my life or the life of someone nearby is in danger, I can and will take up weapons.

On one point I must ask for confirmation. Dr. Colby told us that you have never owned slaves and that you are an abolitionist. If this is not the case, please do not hesitate to tell me so; I could not in good conscience join your household or practice if you own slaves or are a supporter of slavery.

A simpler and less crowded life is what I want, but I need and welcome challenges and hard work as a midwife and nurse.

From Dr. Colby I understand that time is of the essence as your wife will have need of a midwife midsummer. In fact I am ready to travel west at any time. My brother Nathan will accompany me for my safety and then return to New York once he can assure my mother that I am well situated. He will, of course, pay his own travel costs.

Please accept my best wishes for you and your family. I hope to hear from you as soon as the mails allow.

Sincerely yours,
E. Carrie Ballentyne

PS You and Dr. Colby were students of my step-father's, Dr. Harrison Quinlan, at the same time. Dr. Quinlan remembers you well and asks me to send his best regards.

COLBY TO MARKHAM

Michael V. Colby, M.D.
Director
The New Amsterdam Charity Hospital
New York, New York

January 1, 1857

Samuel Markham, M.D.
Physician and Surgeon
Calle del Convento Viejo de la Parroquia Principal
Santa Fe, New Mexico Territory

Dear Sam,
I believe I have found you an excellent nurse and midwife.
Elizabeth C. Ballentyne (called Carrie, apparently) trained at the
New Amsterdam and as an apprentice to Amelie Savard. You may
remember Savard, a mixed-blood midwife with extraordinary
skills. She is related somehow to Miss Ballentyne, who is, I hasten to
say, of Scottish and English ancestry.

You may well receive her letter of introduction and application
along with this letter. References will follow. You will not be
disappointed.

I was going to write soon, anyway, as the enclosed books have
been sitting here for weeks now. You were not the most enthusiastic
student of anatomy, as I have good reason to know, but I am
determined to engage your interest and curiosity at long last. I found
Bennett's Clinical Lectures on the Principles and Practice of
Medicine well put together and informative, but I think that
Bernard's Illustrated Manual of Operative Surgery and Surgical
Anatomy will be especially useful in your practice. It has just been
translated from the French and the reviews are excellent.

With all my love to Indira and Lulu. Aurelia and I will keep you all in our prayers for a happier outcome—a healthy mother and child—sometime in the summer.

In haste (as usual, and also as usual, my apologies)
with best wishes your friend,
Michael

BALLENTYNE TO MARKHAM

E. C. Ballentyne
18 Waverly Place
New York, New York

April 6, 1857

Samuel Markham, M.D.
Physician and Surgeon
Calle del Convento Viejo de la Parroquia Principal
Santa Fe, New Mexico Territory

Dear Dr. Markham,
Thank you for your letter dated March 1, and for the enclosures.
I have reviewed the employment contract and discussed it with my family and our solicitor. It is now my great pleasure to return your copy, signed and witnessed, to you.
It was quite thoughtful of you to send me the most recent issues of the Santa Fe Weekly Gazette, and in fact I appreciate the diplomatic way you chose to disabuse me of my fanciful imaginations of Santa Fe as a wilderness. I understand now that there is no lack of barbers, attorneys, dealers in fancy goods and household necessities, political debates or public celebrations in New Mexico Territory. I note also that half of the Gazette is published in Spanish; tomorrow I begin the search for a Spanish language tutor or, if that is not possible, a grammar I can study on my own. I had six years of Latin instruction and four of French, and trust this will ease the way.
I am pleased to relate that we have worked out our travel plans as far as Missouri's western border. We plan to leave here in early May, and will travel by rail to St. Louis. There we will book cabins on a Missouri River steamer bound for Westport Landing. Inquiries

indicate that the journey that far will require somewhere between ten days and three weeks, depending on rail connections and conditions on the Missouri River.

Now we need only instructions from you on how to best proceed once we reach Kansas. From an advertisement in the Gazette, I see that a stagecoach leaves Independence for Santa Fe on the first day of each month, at a fare of $125 per person plus a baggage charge of 35¢ per pound. From the post office I have learned that there is also mail service that travels in caravan and accepts private passengers.

My concern about the stagecoach is this: if there is any delay between here and St. Louis, we are unlikely to reach Independence by the first of the month, and would miss the connection. However we travel in the last stage of this journey, I will arrange to have the luggage brought by the mail service once we reach Westport.

Finally, if you or Mrs. Markham have any requests, either for personal items or medical supplies, please do not hesitate to send a list. My brother and I would be pleased to be of service. I will depend on the list you provided of necessary clothing and footwear, and will bring my medical equipment, including a very fine microscope which was a gift from my mother and step-father when I completed my studies. I look forward to joining your medical practice as soon as the journey allows.

Yours sincerely,
E. Carrie Ballentyne

PART TWO

Travel Diary

Monday, May 4, 1857
Baltimore, Maryland

Our first day of this journey is behind us. We are safely arrived in Baltimore, and have checked into Barnum's City Hotel. It is clean, well-furnished, and fancier than called for, but I think I will sleep very well. We had our supper in the dining room. They served a chicken fricassee that was lukewarm and too salty, but of course Nathan managed three helpings. They will provide a substantial packed lunch for tomorrow, for which we paid 25¢ each.

As predicted, Nathan spent most of this day exploring from one end of the train to the other, seeking out railroad men, engineers, and conductors to interview. There was a long conversation with a Mr. Hennessey, who has invented a shoulder and headrest that can be attached to the back of the passenger car seats (which are too low for anybody's comfort), and then there was another conversation about the construction of cots or berths that can be folded away flat against the walls. Some kind of sleeping arrangement will be necessary, Nathan argues, to make traveling through the night possible for people going great distances across country. Once the railroads reach that far, of course.

For my part, I was very ready to leave the train. I looked forward to sleeping in a proper bed. Spending twenty days in a rattling tin box is not something I care to contemplate, not even to get as far as San Francisco in relative safety. A very strange idea, but Nathan believes it will happen sooner rather than later, unless of course a war intercedes. As people here think is more likely every day. There is talk of it everywhere, even more than at home.

Ma was right about my plans to pass the time. Despite my determination, I was not able to read and certainly not to write while the train was in motion, not even with my wondrous propelling pencil. The constant noise I can deal with, but the jerking and swaying are more difficult to ignore while trying to sort through the many irregular verbs of Spanish. It is not a particularly difficult language after I have tackled both Latin and French, but it will take focused study and practice with people who actually speak it.

I might have spent the whole day thinking about Ma, but everyone in the railroad car was growing bored. Rail travel is tedious with an unexpected consequence: the other ladies began to look for ways to entertain themselves, and their attention fell on me. Nathan was off in search of engineers to talk to, so I was quite at the mercy of the Concerned Ladies of Good Family.

I wish I were better able to lie, but alas. Because I answered their questions about my destination, they conceived a project: to make me see the folly of my ways. To travel so far, to such a hostile place where I would be a nurse (I did not mention midwifery, as I know too well the reaction). No, they told me, it could not be supported. What was my mother thinking? I should be much better off in Kokomo, where Mrs. Worth has three fine, unmarried sons all gainfully employed, or in Evansville, where Mrs. Morrissey's husband is the mayor. Mrs. Conway had neither sons nor a mayoral husband to offer, but the example of her daughter, engaged to Mr. Alois Peck, a wealthy ironmonger. He is building a beautiful house for his bride, Miss Henrietta Conway, just down the street from her parents and the home where she was born and raised. A wealthy husband, a fine new house near to her mother, where she will raise her own family. What more could a young lady want? Mrs. Conway asked me that question. Rather than shock or offend any of the ladies with a truthful answer, I changed the subject.

But I ask myself what it is that Mrs. Conway really wants for her daughter. And here's the answer: she has hopes mostly for herself. She must be indispensable, needed, sought after. She will supervise and advise, and frustrate. If the daughter doesn't mind, the ironmonger will not be pleased. They will bicker, both of them discontented, for decades to come.

I am in a sour mood, it's too obvious to deny. I blame the sight of Miss Henrietta.

She sat near us but never said a word. I imagine she rarely speaks, as her mother works diligently to use up all the available air. I was tempted to test this theory by asking the bride-to-be how she managed to board the train at all. Her skirts are so big around that I think the steel cage that supports them must be wider than the door into the passenger car. Maybe she came in sideways, like a sofa.

The worst of the ladies is Mrs. Candace Newton of Gary, Indiana, who told the story of two young martyrs, the much admired Catherine and Patricia Chamberlain, who went off to preach the Good Word to the savages and were never heard from again. The lack of information did not stop Mrs. Newton from speculating—at length, in detail—about the fate these innocents faced at the hands of the Sioux. Or Navajo. Or Comanche. She really didn't know, and did it matter? She was quite put out with me for asking a question she found irrelevant.

Instead she wanted to know, hadn't I heard of the troubles in Kansas? Why, I would have to pass right through the worst of that mess, businesses and homes burned to the ground, all the fault of the useless New England abolitionists and their free-state mania, thousands of them flooding Kansas to be able to cast a vote for abolition because they could not mind their own business. What were the good people of Missouri to do but protect themselves and their property? She was only sorry that the free-staters were so quick to rebuild and had started with the newspaper office.

Fortunately Nathan returned at just this point and forestalled a debate on abolition by insisting that I come meet some people, a formulation that always makes me hesitate. Given Nathan's interests, "some people" might mean the queen of a small European country or a double-jointed blacksmith. Instead he introduced me to the extended Magleby family (two married couples, some unattached uncles and aunts, three grandparents, and ten children ranging in age from a newborn to a twenty-year-old). They had left their home in Pennsylvania and were traveling to take up farming in Utah Territory. Nathan thought I would be interested, as neither of us have ever met any Mormons before, but the men wouldn't even look in my direction, and the women were openly suspicious of me, as if I had appeared out of nowhere to claim one of their bachelors. Had I expressed any interest in joining their church, I have no doubt they would have suddenly been very friendly. But I'm not, and so I went back, reluctantly, to the ladies in my own car. It was my good luck that Mrs. Newton had gone to sleep, though her snoring is loud enough to be heard over the screeching of the wheels.

I might have tried to nap, too, but we were passing through a very pretty area where large farmhouses and barns and outbuildings are surrounded by fruit trees in blossom—I saw plum, apple, cherry, and others I couldn't identify from the distance. Men drove oxen over earth of such a deep rich color that I imagined I could smell it. The pastures were dotted with calves and foals, lambs and kids running and leaping into the air as if to snatch clouds from the sky. I was not made for farming, but I could almost imagine living here.

Then a Mr. Carl Brooks came by to see Nathan and attempted to insinuate himself. A man about my age, I would guess, with a head of blond hair slick with grease and combed so that it looked like a furrowed field. He was so very charming and full of compliments and so pointedly suave that I found it difficult to look at him, and certainly was not at all moved to be engaged in conversation. Mr. Brooks is a lawyer born and raised in St. Louis, and declared himself ready to show us around the city in his barouche. My good brother saw that my patience was nearing its end and dragged Mr. Brooks off to see Mr. Hennessey's invention.

Later Nathan said that I could at least try to be less judgmental. I asked him if Mr. Brooks was something more than a rich young man interested in self-promotion and flirting. He threw up his hands and admitted defeat. These conversations are painful for both of us, but he will not desist. He must imagine me as a lonely old woman, when I see myself very differently.

He wondered out loud why I should be out of sorts. I did not answer, but I could have. Despite Miss Henrietta and Mrs. Conway, the real source of my unease is Ma. I feel I didn't say enough to her when we parted. She seems to truly believe that we won't see each other again, but I know we will. She will look up and there I will be, the contrary, difficult daughter she raised to be a woman who must go out into the world, as she did when she was young. And of course it is difficult, I could not deny that. I will miss her every day.

Now I must write at least three letters before I can rest. I begin to comprehend that I should not have been so free with my promises of frequent correspondence. I'll have to press Nathan into service.

Tuesday, May 5, 1857
Grafton, Virginia

We departed Baltimore this morning at 7 a.m., on a much
longer train: eight passenger cars as well as cars dedicated to
luggage, mail, and livestock. The first small disaster was
averted when a porter brought the lunches we had ordered and
paid for, but which my brother forgot to retrieve when we set
out for the train station. It would have been difficult to go all
day and into the evening with no provisions at all. More
difficult for my brother than for me, so I think this is an error
he will not make again.

Now it is 9 p.m. and we are just settled into our rooms at the
Nelson Hotel, across from the Grafton train station. This is
apparently an important junction for the Baltimore & Ohio
Railroad, but otherwise it is unremarkable. The hotel is very
drab and not as clean as it should be, but we will make do.

The reason we arrived here so late is this: at about two this
afternoon, the train rounded a blind curve and hit two cows
that stood on the track. We almost derailed as a result. As

Nathan and I were in the last car but two (he insists it is the safest), we experienced the collision as a tremendous jolt that sent everything flying. The passengers in the first two cars did not fare as well as we did.

Luckily there was a Dr. Gordon on board. I volunteered my assistance as he went forward to treat the injured. The worst was Mr. Hennessey (the inventor I mentioned previously), who struck his head so severely that his skull fractured. His prognosis is dire. There were also two others, an elderly woman and her ten-year-old grandson; she broke her left hip, and the boy his left tibia. He also bit his tongue so hard that he may well lose part of it. These three were taken away by carriage, with Dr. Gordon attending.

Otherwise there were bruises, scrapes, minor cuts, a few sprains, and knocked-out teeth. The Mormon family suffered a number of injuries. They were all very stoic while they were being treated. One of their number, a Mrs. Ellen Magleby, took me aside to say that she was five months with child and had taken a hard fall. I told her what symptoms to watch for, and she knows where to find me if she should go into labor this night.

Once we came to a full stop, Nathan went off to watch as the damage was assessed and repairs were made. He returned to take his seat at the last moment, quite whey-faced and with bloody sleeves, saying only that the train was not kind to the cows. When he had recovered his equilibrium and gone off and changed his shirt in the water closet (a spot I do not care to describe), he asked whether I would look at a Mr. Ibarra, who had been injured but not seen by Dr. Gordon. So I took my bag and went with Nathan to the livestock car at the end of the train. To my surprise it was filled not with cattle but with sheep, property of the three Ibarra brothers called Eli, Jules, and Mo (these are the short versions of names that I did not

recognize and would not try to spell). They are just returned
from the Pyrenees, where they bought new breeding stock for
the family ranch in New Mexico Territory.

It was the oldest of the three brothers who needed medical
care. I found him reclining on a stack of hay bales, his back
against the wall and a slouch hat tilted down over his face. His
left wrist was bruised, but there was no sign of blood where he
had propped it against his abdomen. He roused from a half-
sleep slowly, and admitted—very reluctantly—to both nausea
and a headache. There is a bump on the back of his head, which
made the diagnosis quite obvious.

The bones of his wrist are intact, so I wrapped it, fashioned
a sling, and strongly suggested that he see a doctor when the
train next stopped.

A lively conversation went on while all this was happening,
the brothers arguing among themselves in a language that
turned out to be Basque. It is nothing like French or Spanish in
as far as I can tell, and is spoken only in the Pyrenees and
wherever else the Basque people make their homes.
Fortunately these three also speak English and, I assume,
Spanish. They all three have very dark hair and a facial bone
structure that indicates Indian blood. A mother or
grandmother from one of the many western tribes, I imagine.
Unless these features are found commonly among the Basque,
of course. Another question I kept to myself.

When we arrived here in Grafton, I again suggested Mr.
Ibarra (who prefers to be called Eli, as he reminded me twice)
see a doctor, but instead he took a room in this hotel while his
brothers stayed behind with the livestock. I was relieved, as
this way Nathan can check on him. If he is not much improved
tomorrow, I will be more forceful about a consultation.

Nathan pointed out what I had already remarked to myself:
Eli Ibarra is much like our Uncle Gabriel, despite the difference

in age. He is very strongly built but lithe, a capable individual who speaks very little and sees everything. In examining his wrist, I found his hand to be unusually large, rough, and calloused, as would be the case for any farmer or rancher, but I saw too that his nails were clipped to the quick and unexpectedly clean for someone who works with animals. I don't know if these are the habits of all Basques (or even if he considers himself to be Basque, or Indian, or New Mexican, or something else entirely). It could be a habit of the Ibarra family. Certainly Aunt Hannah's influence turned all of the Bonner-Savard-Ballentyne-Freeman family into hand-washers and nail-clippers. It is faded with the years, but the sampler that reads "The devil lives beneath the fingernails" still hangs in Aunt Hannah's kitchen.

I will check on my patient and then go to my bed. Never more will I complain about boredom during a train trip. May the rest of this journey be nothing more than tedious.

Wednesday, May 6, 1857
Columbus, Ohio

Tonight we are at the Dunne House in Columbus, a small but
very grand hotel with uniformed staff and ornate paraffin oil
lamp fixtures and fine paintings and sculptures in the lobby.
Large pots flank the front door, planted with deutzia in full
bloom. I saw a nest tucked deep into the greenery with three
bluish eggs but caught no sight of the mother. On Waverly Place
and at Seven Bells there will be new nests and hatchlings.

I felt we were too casually dressed for the dining room with
its chandeliers and pompous waiters, but there was no time to
change. They served us a beautifully done leg of lamb with
many side dishes and never gave away their opinions of our
manners or the sorry state of our footwear by even the slightest
twitch of an eye.

Sometimes I still find it hard to believe how much food my
brother can consume in a sitting, but there is never an extra
ounce on his frame. Again we were able to order a packed lunch
to be taken away in the morning, but this time at 30¢ each.

This morning before breakfast, when I went to check on Mr. Ibarra, I found that he had already left, I assume to help his brothers with the livestock. Once Nathan and I were settled in our seats (again in the car third to the last, and again with the Concerned Ladies in attendance), I sent him to find my missing patient and ask that he come to see me so that I could be sure he was improving.

We were not an hour out of the station when Mr. Magleby came to say that his wife was in distress and asked if I would attend.

The sad business took a quick end. She delivered a stillborn son, perfectly formed but very small, no more than a pound in weight. All of this happened in a baggage car, as that was the only place large enough to fashion something like a cot where the laboring mother could recline. The poor woman was very distraught, and her husband hardly less so. I am told that the family cannot afford to break off the journey even for a day so that she might rest. They assured me that her sister and her mother-in-law will provide the care she needs.

Later Nathan mentioned to me that the Magleby family was planning to join a handcart company for the journey to Salt Lake City. I hope he is mistaken. I can imagine, if I try very hard, a determined and desperate man might make up his mind to push a handcart hundreds of miles, if he has no other way of reaching his destination. But I cannot see how his wife would agree to walk behind him, children in tow. How does a woman convince herself that this is a reasonable plan? That is the question.

When we got back to our seats, Eli Ibarra was waiting, and was being studied by the Concerned Ladies. It didn't seem to bother him. He had discarded the sling I made for him, but the wrist was still wrapped. He is entirely recovered, he assured me, no trace of headache or nausea. I was not sure I could believe him, so I tried to make clear that a concussion can be a very serious matter and that he should avoid strenuous activity.

Mr. Ibarra has an expressive face but is not a conversationalist (again: like Uncle Gabriel); he listened, nodded, thanked me, and turned to go back to his brothers, but I stopped him to ask if he happened to also speak Spanish.

The question seemed to surprise him, but he let himself be drawn into conversation. He is half-Indian; specifically, his mother is from one of the pueblos. I am unclear on what a pueblo is, exactly, but I didn't think it was a good time to ask the question. I did ask what languages he spoke beyond English and Basque, and as I hoped, the family speaks Spanish as well as his mother's language, which is called Towa, if I understood correctly. Also the signing language used among Indians who do not speak each other's tongues. Now I am determined to ask if he—or one of his brothers—might be willing to act as tutor for as long as we are traveling together.

It was then that Mrs. Newton came down the aisle and in passing handed me a newspaper clipping. She looked Mr. Ibarra up and down, shook her head, and went on to her seat as if we were not worth her time. Mr. Ibarra did not take offense, and in fact I had the sense that she amused him, because he waited while I ran my eyes over the article. I realized then that he was curious, and so I told him about my earlier conversation with Mrs. Newton.

"And now she gives me this newspaper clipping because she thinks I am a babe in arms and unprepared for living in New Mexico Territory. You can see for yourself, about a massacre of whites by Muscarilla Apache on the Colorado border. Twelve men dead, women and children abducted. I suppose she thinks I will turn around and go home."

"She is right," he said, his composure intact. "These things do happen, and more often than you might think."

"Of course," I said. "Women are murdered and worse, every day, wherever they are. On the frontier or in their own kitchens in the most modern cities."

I let my temper slip, just that much, but to Mr. Ibarra's credit I did not see any shock or censure in his expression; he only inclined his head in what I think was acknowledgment. I did not shock him, but he surprised me.

He seems to be a thoughtful and sensible man, though he would not heed my advice about his injuries.

Thursday, May 7, 1857
Indianapolis, Indiana

We had a very long day today, due to not one or two but three
delays on the line, which kept us sitting in an unmoving metal
box in the hot sun. The weather was more like July than May,
and as a result tempers flared; at one point Mrs. Worth and
Mrs. Conway almost came to blows arguing over an open
window (cinders! cried one; fresh air! the other). A toddler
stripped himself out of every last bit of clothing and ran up and
down the aisle, with his blushing older sister in pursuit, until
the very stern conductor ushered them both back to their
exhausted mother. The little boy wailed for most of the
afternoon.

They told us nothing about the cause for the delays, but
rumors multiplied as the day went on. A derailment, an engine
explosion, a passenger suffering a heart attack, a band of
thieves. Nathan went off on a mission to discover more, and
came back with the disappointing news that the delays were

due to nothing more exciting than equipment failures of the most ordinary variety.

A thunder-storm closed in on us at sunset, bringing with it cooler winds and an immediate improvement in the atmosphere in our passenger car. Because the territory here is relatively flat, it was possible to watch the lightning dancing across the horizon. I do so love a thunder-storm, despite the dangers.

It was well past nine when we finally arrived here at the White Horse Inn, close enough to the train station that we could walk. Apparently Indianapolis has a large population of immigrant Germans, whose language we heard spoken at the reception desk and in the halls. Whatever language they chose to speak, it was very good of them to keep the dining room open for so many sweaty, hungry, and demanding travelers. Mrs. Newton's complaints could be heard from the other side of the room, but the waiters remained stoic.

And now I am so very tired, I must go to bed. Tomorrow should be our last day on a train. Barring disaster, we will arrive in St. Louis in the late afternoon. I hope for a cool rain that lasts the entire day.

Saturday, May 9, 1857
St. Louis, Missouri

Things were so hectic yesterday that I couldn't manage to get
down even a sentence, but now that we are at the end of the rail
journey and settled into hotel rooms where we will spend a
second night, I can make up for that lapse.

Until we arrived in St. Louis, the day was uneventful. No
delays, disasters, or medical emergencies, a light rain at
midday that soothed even the little boy who cried so miserably
the day before. I napped, off and on, for most of the afternoon.
Unfortunately none of the Ibarra brothers ever showed their
faces, and thus my hopes for a Spanish lesson were dashed.
I don't know how their livestock will be transported beyond
St. Louis, and so we have probably seen the last of the
Ibarras.

Nathan scoffed at the idea. He has spent more time with
them than I have, but I would not give him the satisfaction of
asking for information. If I find a man interesting enough to
talk to, Nathan jumps to conclusions.

At four we had our first sight of the Mississippi. The Hudson is sinewy and strong and bold, but the Mississippi is powerful, like the leg of a man in his prime strong enough to carry the whole country on his shoulders. There were so many steamboats lined up along the riverbank, so many ferries, flatboats and canoes and every other kind of vessel, as far as the eye could see, that I did not even try to count them. I thought of my Grandfather Nathaniel and Great-Uncle Runs-from-Bears traveling down this river to New Orleans in the last days of the War of 1812, and reminded myself that I must write that story down before the details fade from living memory. I will send what I write to Ma and to Aunt Hannah for corrections and additions. Uncles Daniel and Ben will get into good-natured arguments, each telling the other that old age has stirred their memories into mush. There will be much arguing and laughter. It pleases me to imagine it.

Nathan has been very careful with the baggage, especially with the trunks, leaving me with nothing more to do as the ferry crossed the river than to study St. Louis, a city of mostly brick buildings laid out on a grid, like uptown Manhattan. Beneath my feet the river pulsed like a beating heart.

We took a cab to the hotel, only to find that our reservation had been lost and no rooms were available. The clerk suggested that either Barnum's Hotel or the Planter's House Hotel would have rooms. That would turn out to be true but only, I guessed, because those are the two most expensive hotels in St. Louis. By this time it was half past six and we were both in need of baths and food, and so we checked into the Planter's House (a shocking $5.50 for each of us, but including three meals), and I sit now in a large room with a thick carpet and damask draperies, at a desk inlaid with ivory, and a drawer full of exceedingly fine writing paper.

St. Louis is a busy city. From my window I can watch the

crowds of shoppers, servants running errands, delivery boys
and business men. The endless flow of traffic is very much like
home. There are private carriages small and large, hacks for
hire, omnibuses, horse cars, delivery wagons. The difference is
that here there are also the wagons built for emigrants headed
west to California or Oregon or the New Mexico Territory, such
as I have seen in the illustrated magazines. They are more
striking in real life, with hoops that have been fixed over the
wagon bed, and then canvas stretched over the hoops like a
bonnet. Here I can say that they look uncomfortable. The idea
of spending weeks in a covered wagon moving over difficult
terrain at a snail's pace is daunting. If it turns out that such a
wagon is the only way for us to get from the Kansas border to
Santa Fe, I vow I will walk the entire distance.

As in Manhattan, St. Louis peddlers stand behind their
carts shouting out their wares in English, German, Spanish,
and in other languages I could not identify. Certainly there is
no shortage of exotic visitors in New York City, and
neighborhoods where English is not the language one is most
likely to hear, but there is something different about St. Louis.
It sits here on the river like a door to other worlds, open to
whatever the great Mississippi cares to deliver.

Now that we have arrived in Missouri, I must figure out how
to compose myself in a place where human beings are bought
and sold like cattle. I would guess that the workers on the
docks—called roustabouts, I understand—are slaves. While I
saw neither beatings nor bloody backs, I still find it very
difficult to accept the simple fact that the workers could be
shot down if they made an attempt to cross the river to freedom
in Illinois, when I am free to travel back and forth as I please.

At dinner a gentleman at our table insisted on telling us how
well slavery is regulated in Missouri. A free Black man can
even walk around unmolested, he assured us, as long as his
papers are in order. Nathan elbowed me quite sharply when he

thought I was about to challenge the man, and probably he was right to do so. I was sorely tempted. Shakespeare cautioned that discretion is the better part of valor, but I like Ma's take on it better; the night before we began this journey, she advised me to choose my battles carefully or risk losing the war. I don't like to reflect too long on what that would really mean.

Last night I was so tired that I considered sleeping in my clothes, and still once I had washed and changed I did not fall straight away to sleep. Instead I thought of all my family in the garden in the golden dusk, and I could almost smell the lilacs. In my half-sleeping state I had the idea that I could draw Ma exactly as I last saw her, from the curve of her cheek to the shape of her wrists, if only I had inherited a bit of her talent. I do miss her so.

Saturday, May 9, 1857

It has been a long and eventful day, one I would like to record,
though I am bone weary and the bed is very inviting.

Nathan and I spent the morning exploring the city, returned
to the hotel for lunch and a long nap, and went out again to
investigate some more. We walked along the Mississippi for
hours marveling at the number and variety of birds. We saw
geese, all kinds of ducks, swans, cranes, and a flock of
magnificent white pelicans that stood out like beacons against
a bank covered with bluebells. There were nests everywhere. I
expect the foxes and weasels and raccoons are well nourished.

On a hillside we got our first sight of the Missouri River. It
struck me as something of a poor cousin to the Mississippi, but
Nathan was almost insulted when I said so. He went on at
length about the dangers of the river, recounting what he had
learned from a traveling preacher who makes the journey
every month.

Apparently the river is always shifting, sometimes from one
day to the next. The pilot never knows where the channel will

be in relation to the river-bed. The bends are where most packets run into trouble, brought to a stop by snags and sandbars. The Missouri never pauses in its hunt for a meal, is the way the preacher put it. It sucks up trees and buildings and people, too, if they aren't careful.

Of course my brother has a weakness for the Police Gazette. He has always worked very hard to alarm me with stories he amplifies to that end. In this case he need not exaggerate; I have done enough reading of my own to know how tricky the Missouri can be.

We arrived back at the hotel tired and ravenous, but at supper the odious Mr. Brooks came to our table and asked Nathan's permission to join us. As if he were the elder and I just a young girl under her brother's rule. Rather than make a scene, I said nothing when he took a chair. For fifteen minutes he celebrated himself, his connections, his law practice, his home, his silver-dappled Morgan geldings, perfectly matched, that pulled his barouche. Then he suggested that I allow him to show me the Mississippi by moonlight. He looked at me as he said this, excluding Nathan.

I said I would do no such thing, but he laughed and told me that he could see through my feminine wiles. Nathan rushed to assure him that my refusal was sincere, and for once the man's smile faded away, showing more of his true nature. My lack of concern for his pride angered him, but before he could work up the courage to scold me for my regrettable manners (I could almost see the words forming) Nathan suggested that Brooks join him for a drink, if he had a tavern to recommend. They set off and I returned to my room.

I am sorry to miss those silver-dappled Morgans, I must admit.

So once again my brother has rescued me from social disaster. I expect he is listening to the lecture that Brooks intended for me. Sometimes I wonder what Nathan says in these situations. Does he placate? Did he tell Brooks that his sister is a dedicated spinster and not worth his efforts? Does he defend me? I have never asked, for fear I would not like the answer.

As I passed through the lobby, I was surprised to see Eli Ibarra. He stood against the wall, arms crossed, observing people as they came and went. He was dressed more formally than he had been on the train, and seemed to have visited a barber. My guess is that he was waiting for someone. He did not meet my eye and I did not impose.

So men in the West fall into familiar camps: some are insufferable in their attentions, and others dismissive.

I have spent an hour repacking and organizing our trunks, and now I will go to bed. Nathan is not yet returned, but I trust he will not be much longer. Tomorrow we board a Missouri River steamboat that will take us to the Kansas border.

PART THREE

Westward

1

Saturday, May 9, 1857

CARRIE HAD JUST dropped off to sleep when the tuba woke her. It took a moment to remember where she was—a very elegant hotel room in St. Louis—and to make sense of the tuba. Then other instruments began warming up. She reminded herself that if she got out of bed now, she might not get any sleep at all. To be drawn downstairs would be a decidedly irrational thing to do.

But there was a tuba and a fiddle. Then cornets began tripping over each other, a clarinet, and . . . was that a concertina?

An accordion. She almost laughed out loud at the sound of it.

Now that sleep was out of the question, her choices were simple: she could stay where she was, listening until the last polka or mazurka had ended, or she could dress and go down to the ballroom. If Nathan was within earshot of the music, he'd be knocking on her door in short order.

They shared a common passion for every kind of round dance and had mastered them all together: waltzes, polkas and mazurkas, gorlitzas, galops, schottisches. Nathan and Carrie Ballentyne were well-known at Niblo's and Lindenmüller's and a half dozen of the other reputable beer halls in Little Germany.

Carrie would never admit it out loud, but it was dancing that made her hesitate, just briefly, about accepting the position in Santa Fe. She took a whole Sunday to think it through, saddling Pearl and packing food to sustain her through the day. As soon as the ferry docked on the Brooklyn side of the river, Pearl was off, prancing with satisfaction.

In the course of that long ride, rational thought got the upper hand and reminded her that dancing was a worldwide phenomenon. There must be dancing of some kind in New Mexico Territory. Of course she could not pass up this opportunity, even if that was not the case. She would miss her people, yes. And Pearl. And dozens of other things that she hadn't thought of yet. Dancing was the least of it.

But now, here in St. Louis, was a reminder of what she was leaving behind: not just her mother; not only Amelie, the dearest and most beloved older cousin who had taught and mentored her; not all the rest of her very large family, scattered as they were from Manhattan to Montreal; but the beer halls strung along the Bowery, full of the wavering light from street lamps, pulsing with music and laughter.

After she spent a difficult day at the hospital or a challenging delivery, the thought of dancing could lift her spirits and give her the energy she needed to start again the next day. Now she was having the same reaction, to her surprise and—she could not deny—her delight.

Carrie got out of bed to turn up the lamp and retrieve the gown she had hidden away at the very bottom of the larger trunk. Periwinkle blue and scattered with small white blossoms, its gored skirt was full enough to dance even a polka.

With the dress were the ivory kidskin shoes with rosettes of the same shade of blue. After Carrie had spent days wearing sturdy boots that buttoned laboriously up the sides, the thin, supple leather and dainty heel seemed to her like something out of a fairy tale.

In the ballroom the band launched into an opening polonaise, and the familiar rush of excitement feathered its way up her spine. She gathered her chemise, pantaloons, stockings, and petticoats and began to dress with all speed. It was one of the more practical skills she had got from her training as a nurse at the New Amsterdam, but it was only possible because she wanted nothing to do with hooped skirts and never wore a corset. She had just stepped into her shoes when Nathan rapped on her door in a rat-a-tat rhythm that echoed her own impatience.

"Sister!" he called. "Don't tell me you are sleeping, not with that music in the air."

She unlatched the door and turned back to the mirror over the dresser as Nathan came in.

"Almost ready, but I still have to do something with my hair."

"Of course," he said, crossing his arms and leaning against the closed door. "And why don't we build a bridge or roof a house or two while we're at it."

Carrie spared him a grim look, but in fact he was right. Her hair was a burden, a frustration of tremendous proportions, and a drain on her time.

Every night before bed she took it down, setting aside the dozens of pins required to keep it on top of her skull, brushed it all out, and braided it into a thick plait that reached to her hips. Every morning she reversed that process, brushing it out, twisting it into a coil, and wrapping it around her head, one, two, three times, to finally pin it in place.

It was tiresome and frustrating, but Carrie never said so. Her father had loved her hair, and so she would keep it, exactly as long as it was when she was thirteen years old, the day he drowned in a logjam on the Sacandaga while she watched from the shore.

"Leave it down," Nathan suggested now. "They've seen plaited hair before, I'm sure."

This was true. And really, what did it matter if she flouted expectations and upset a few St. Louis matrons? Soon there would be no time to fuss with hair, and her plait would follow her across Kansas and into New Mexico Territory.

"All right. Let's go."

Nathan had been teasing, and now he was surprised. One eyebrow cocked, he tilted his head at her. "How bold."

"Hardly." She smoothed the bodice of her gown. "Tomorrow we'll be gone and we'll never see any of these people again. I'll never know what they think of me."

An unwelcome thought made her pause. "The dance is open to hotel guests, I trust?"

Nathan glanced down at his shoes.

"Nathan."

He shrugged. "It's a large wedding party, but there's no one at the door asking for names or invitations. Half of St. Louis seems to be there already. Doubts?"

The band struck up a mazurka.

"None." She simply could not refrain from smiling. "Let's hurry."

⁂

CARRIE CAME TO life on the dance floor, and Nathan loved to watch it happen. People who did not know his sister—and she was, undeniably, not an easy person to get to know—found Carrie Ballentyne to be too serious, without a sense of humor, quick to judge. Sharp of mind and sharper of tongue.

It was true that in the normal course of things she rarely smiled, but now Carrie was laughing, her color high, a few beads of perspiration on her brow, as he swung her around through the last measures of a schottische. He took note of a burly wedding guest who watched her openly, with unapologetic appreciation. Beside him his wife scowled, eyes narrowed as she watched Carrie, as if she had somehow willfully encouraged the man's admiration.

The matrons might cluck their tongues at Carrie's girlish plait, but they were envious of her heart-shaped face, the brilliant blue eyes she had inherited from their mother, the high color that flooded her cheeks.

Nathan thought of walking over to their table and setting the woman's mind at ease. *That's my sister*, he would tell her. *Rest easy, ma'am. She wants nothing to do with your husband.*

The corpulent St. Louis burgher who admired Carrie so openly was invisible to her, as were the other men who followed her with their eyes, young or old. Nathan had observed this dozens of times, and understood that while men appreciated the tight twist of her waist and the fullness of her bodice, it was the way she moved, graceful, strong, and still agile, that engaged their imaginations. If he were to tell her this, it would ruin some of the joy she took from dancing, and so he kept his observations to himself.

When the band stopped for a break, she took his arm and they went back to the small table they had found on the wall farthest from the wedding party. As soon as the musicians got back to work, she would be eager to return to the dance floor, but now they were both thirsty.

He signaled to a waiter and ordered ale for himself and cider for his sister, raising his voice to be heard over the singing that had started up among the guests. The bridal couple was alone on the dance floor, dancing to the melody of the serenade, and trying to ignore the comments their families and friends called out to them.

They watched all this for a good while until Carrie roused herself and half rose from her seat to look for the waiter. Nathan saw her gaze come to rest and then sharpen, one brow peaking in surprise before she turned back to him abruptly.

"What?"

She put a hand to her ear as if she had not understood him, when really it meant she had no intention of answering.

The waiter appeared out of nowhere and put down their drinks. Nathan took a good swallow before he began to scan the room. He was about to give up—whatever had unsettled Carrie, she was unwilling to talk about it—when he saw the Ibarra brothers.

They sat at a table near the door, Eli on one side, his brothers opposite him. Beside Eli was a lady who was possibly in her early thirties, but still beautiful. She was telling a story, and all three Ibarra brothers were leaning toward her, laughing. In the short time he had known the Ibarras, Nathan had seen Eli produce something akin to a smile just once or twice, but now he laughed from the belly, at ease and enjoying himself.

Carrie said, "The musicians are back. Come on."

Nathan waltzed her out onto the dance floor. A stranger would see her expression as neutral, he knew. A young woman who liked to dance, nothing else on her mind.

It was so rare for Carrie to show even the vaguest sign of interest in a man. The last time he knew of was more than a year ago. She would have denied it to her dying breath, but Nathan had seen how she brightened when Cornell Mueller was nearby. He was a friend of their Bonner and Savard cousins and came to visit with them now and then. Cornell was quiet but attentive and very bright, and his gaze fell on Carrie as often as hers fell on him. He was reading law at a firm on Broadway, and when he was finished, he would go home to Buffalo to join his father's firm.

That day came, Cornell left, and Carrie never mentioned him again. Nathan had wondered if there might be correspondence between them, but saw no evidence of that. He mentioned this to his mother, who only reminded him of what he knew already: it was not his business, and must be left to Carrie.

In her own time, she said. *And not before.*

He might have said, *And maybe never*, but Nathan could no more remind his mother of the reason they had left their home in Paradise than he could raise the subject with his sister. Thirteen years past, but the wound still seeped.

The band was very good, and the musicians had had just enough ale to liven them up. With every new dance, people drifted toward the dancing, so that by the time the last waltz was announced, his shirt was damp through with sweat.

Carrie turned her head away and stiffened ever so slightly in his arms, and in that moment he realized that Eli Ibarra was dancing with the young woman from his table. He was studying her face with interest, as if there were some secret to be found there.

When the music stopped, Eli's partner was facing Nathan and Carrie directly. He generally didn't notice such things, but the woman's left hand rested lightly on Eli's arm, and the outline of a wedding ring under her glove was unmistakable.

Carrie said, "High time we got to bed. We have to be up at five."

When they turned away, they found Jules Ibarra waiting there, head ducked, clearly waiting to ask Carrie to dance. Nathan knew that she would accept, no matter how desperate she was to be elsewhere. His sister had always been very keenly aware of shy people, and went to great lengths to make them comfortable.

Nathan went back to drink the last of his ale, and watched them dancing. Carrie did all that was expected of her: she smiled, but without looking at him directly; she spoke when it was required of her, but no more than was necessary.

At his shoulder, a familiar voice. "Ballentyne," Eli Ibarra said. "Having a good time?"

"Ibarra. Didn't expect to see you here. My sister likes to dance. We both do."

It wasn't easy talking over the music and the noise of the crowd, but Ibarra made a go of it.

"I wanted to introduce you to my friend Eva Zavala. Mrs. Zavala. We grew up together, but now she's gone off to dance with Mo."

What he wanted, Nathan was suddenly aware, was to find a way to make clear that the lady he had danced with was not his wife.

"You could tell Carrie that yourself."

Eli's gaze sharpened. He was good at getting his point across with a glance. In this case: *Tell your sister because I can't tell her myself.*

Then Eli let the subject go. He said, "Jules tells me you're sailing on the *Annabelle* tomorrow too. At least it will be more comfortable than the railcars."

In his surprise Nathan turned to face the other man. "You'll be on the *Annabelle*?"

"All the way to the Kansas border."

That was an interesting bit of information. "Your brothers?"

Eli shook his head. "Driving the sheep home overland."

This was a surprise. "Isn't that dangerous? Given the unrest."

A one-shoulder shrug. Nathan hadn't yet figured out what it meant, but Ibarra used it a lot.

"There are armed guards who ride with them," Eli said. "Ah, Eva wants to go back to her room. Pardon me. I'll see you tomorrow."

When Nathan left Carrie at her door a half hour later, he considered telling her that Eli Ibarra would be on the *Annabelle*. He could mention Ibarra's friend Eva, too, but it was a gamble. He was pretty sure he knew how she would respond. Her tone would be ordinary, and her expression slightly puzzled.

Is that so? she would say. And: *Have you finished packing yet?*

THE DREAM WAS waiting for Carrie, as she had known it would be. As she had feared. On the night before they boarded a packet to travel the Missouri, she saw herself as a little girl, standing on the bank of the Sacandaga while men struggled with a logjam. Watching as her father's feet got tangled in a snarl of roots. In that moment, before the Sacandaga took him and he knew that he would die, he sought her out where she stood on the riverbank, and their eyes met.

She had dreamed of this a hundred, a thousand times, but the dream came most often when she was especially worried or under duress. And when she woke, the eternal question remained: What had he been thinking in that last minute of his life? He had wanted her to understand something, but the river took him too quickly.

Then again, as she learned, death didn't seem to matter to Simon Ballentyne, born and raised far away in Scotland, when he had something to say to this particular daughter. He came back to her again and again when she slept, but why? What message was she meant to understand? Carrie had asked this question of the clan mothers at Good Pasture, who took such dreams very seriously. Even they had no answers, or at least, none they would share with her. It was her dream and her truth, and she must wait until the answer presented itself.

2

By the time they got to St. Louis, Eli Ibarra had had more than enough of his younger brothers. All the way across the Atlantic—in both directions—they had argued about everything and anything, pausing only as long as it took to do chores or eat. They were excellent stockmen who did their work quickly and well, but as soon as the last ewe was safely loaded for the next stage in the journey, they would pick up an old argument or start a new one.

Eli often daydreamed about taking off on his own. They wouldn't notice until an argument got to the point that they turned to him to take a stand; by then he could be miles away. It was an appealing plan with a major flaw: the responsibility for the maintenance, feeding, and health of two hundred very expensive ewes and ten immature rams was his until they got to St. Louis.

And now they were that far. The city was right there on the other side of the Mississippi, and in short order the hired wranglers would take over. As of tomorrow he'd be free to move on while his brothers drove the flock across Missouri, Kansas, and into New Mexico

Territory. It would take all summer and they'd get home filthy, reeking of lanolin, and in ferocious moods. That was how it had gone for him when he drove new stock home from the Mississippi at fifteen. It was a rite of passage, and a valuable one.

The train slowed, wheels squealing as they pulled into the rail yard. Jules, impatient as ever, slid the freight door open and leaned out to watch as the journey—the shortest part of the journey on this continent—came to its end. As soon as the all-clear whistle sounded, doors began to fly open, banging like firecrackers. Porters, conductors, and baggage men came off the train, while roustabouts, muleteers, and ferrymen swarmed on to start the process of unloading. Passengers and their luggage, the U.S. mail and the commercial freight, everything had to move. The flock would wait until the train was empty, assuming the hired wranglers had got the paddock and feed and water ready. And then they still had to muck out the car and get their own gear together.

Eli was going to remind them of all this, when Jules leapt to the ground and disappeared into a confusion of wagons and carts.

"Must have caught sight of Miss Carrie," Mo said, grinning.

Eli was careful not to show the reaction his brother was hoping for.

"You know it sticks in his craw that you'll spend a good week winding along the Missouri in her company."

Eli yawned. If he responded at all, Mo would settle in, poking at him until he had to walk off or use his fists to put an end to his brother's musings about Carrie Ballentyne. Even without Mo's interference there was going to be trouble, because Jules believed himself to be in love. He had been in that state since the first moment he saw her in the Baltimore train station. Jules fell in love easily and often, but this time his infatuation was proving to be longer lived than usual.

Mo had been indifferent when Jules pointed her out, as his tastes ran more to blondes of generous proportions. Jules was fussier; a pretty girl could get his attention, but a pretty girl with a mind of her own, that was who he wanted. Jules, as Eli saw it, was smarter than Mo by a couple of miles at least.

They hadn't yet met the Ballentynes when they first saw them in Baltimore. Carrie was just a young woman standing on the train platform and arguing with a man who would turn out to be her brother.

An angry young woman, in fact, advancing on the younger man as he retreated, step by step, arguing all the way. Their coloring and features marked them for siblings, but it would have been clear in any case. Eli had four sisters, and he recognized the kind of furious scolding that was particular to females when brothers forgot who exactly was in charge.

Suddenly she let out a frustrated squawk, dragged the bonnet from her head, and whacked him across the shoulder with it, once, twice, and three times for good measure.

Mo and Jules, enchanted, could not keep their enthusiasm to themselves. Eli didn't even try to hide his smile, and neither did anyone else on the platform. They all saw the same thing: a strong-willed, confident young woman with a dignity that outshone her temper. She had Eli's attention, in part because he rarely saw her equal in the East. Here most young women he came in contact with in social situations were too timid to voice anything but mild agreement, but there was nothing timid about this one, as she used the only weapons available to her—including her bonnet—to make her companion see the error of his ways.

Taken individually, her features were just pretty: a mass of deep mahogany hair with glints of red; eyebrows of a darker shade, slanted down just now over eyes of a strong marine blue. Her complexion was pale, but her cheeks were flushed to the color of an overripe apricot, while her wide, full mouth was a darker, deeper shade of rose. Any serious artist would have scrambled for palette and brushes.

Just in time to save the young man—and the lady's bonnet—a porter came up in a rush and handed her a box tied with string. And just that easily the anger went out of her. She thanked the porter by putting a coin in his palm and granting him a generous, undeniably beautiful smile. With that she turned and walked off, ignoring her brother. She walked with purpose, straight-backed, the box under one arm, a carpetbag in the other. The bonnet was back on her head, lopsided.

All along the platform, people pivoted to follow her with their eyes.

"She's boarding our train," Jules said, his voice gone rough.

Mo, who would have been a first-class exploring officer if he had been allowed to enlist, went off to reconnoiter. He was back in a quarter hour, climbing into the livestock car where a couple hundred ewes were voicing their dissatisfaction with this newest moving box.

His report was brief. The young lady was a Miss Ballentyne, traveling with her brother. She was on her way to take up a position as nurse and midwife in Santa Fe. He grinned at Jules as he imparted this last, quite astonishing fact. Jules looked stunned. Eli's own expression was blank, or at least he hoped it was.

Between Baltimore and St. Louis he had had a couple of conversations with Miss Ballentyne. First when she came to check on him after the train almost derailed, and then when she wanted to see how well he was healing. He had told himself that talking to her once or twice would be enough to prove that it was a waste of time, thinking about a woman who was his opposite in every way.

Except it hadn't gone that way at all. She had challenged him, asked questions and listened to answers, and voiced opinions that surprised him. And now this part of the journey was over, and there was no way to predict how she would react when they came face-to-face on the *Annabelle*.

What he needed to figure out was what he would regret more: letting her go, or digging his heels in.

3

Sunday, May 10, 1857

THE CAB ARRIVED just as the sun broke over the horizon. Carrie, far more nervous than she had expected to be, checked and rechecked the bags, counted the trunks, and tried to ignore her brother.

With a long, difficult journey before them, Nathan vibrated with enthusiasm and radiated boundless energy. Now, watching him as he helped the driver stow the baggage, she wondered whether someday circumstance and weariness would conspire to rob him of the easy joy he took in life. She could admit that when that day came, she would find the older, more circumspect brother a greater comfort, but she would miss the younger man.

The driver set off, threading his way into a ragged procession of wagons, baggage vans, private carriages, and drays, most bound for the landing on the Missouri where the steamboat packets docked. All along the way drivers shouted at and to each other and cursed their animals in a jumble of languages, in the same rude tones heard in busy ports everywhere. Horses and mules and oxen bellowed right along.

As they came in sight of the landing, Nathan turned to her. "Do you smell the pitch? They've started up the boilers. The engineers will be in a sweat already, three hours before we set out. Look, there she is, at the far end. The *Annabelle*."

Their seat in the cab was high enough to let them see over the swarms of people. Carrie took the opportunity to study the steamer on which she would spend at least a week.

There were three decks, as she had been told: the main deck, where cargo and livestock and fuel were stored along with the steerage passengers; the cabin deck, with the staterooms, grand saloon, kitchens, and laundry; and the Texas deck, where there were more cabins. On top of it all, the pilothouse sat like a topknot.

"Miss?" The driver had opened the door and was holding out an arm to steady her as she stepped down from the cab.

"Go on, sister," Nathan said. "Did you think the captain would come to collect you himself?"

She stepped out of the cab into a great crowd of passengers, crew, drivers, deliverymen, roustabouts, and peddlers hawking everything from buffalo robes to sewing needles and buttermilk.

From the ground all she could see of the *Annabelle* were the twin stacks, where flags fluttered and snapped in the breeze. If she could see nothing at all, it wouldn't matter; the stink was evidence enough that they were about to board a steamship. Coal, pitch, oil, oakum, grease, green wood, charcoal, sweat, and on top of all that, manure, old and new, from every domesticated animal known in this part of the country, all of it ground into the mud. With every step or turn of a wheel, the morass churned and belched out fresh stench. Her boots were submerged to the ankles; another four inches and the mud would spill over and coat her stockings and feet.

Her mother had insisted that she pack three pairs of sturdy boots, and once again her mother had been right.

Nathan was so delighted with the scene spread out before them that he let out a laugh. "Sister," he said. "Are we ready?"

"We are," Carrie said. "I am." But she could not match her brother's grin, and in fact the tickle of perspiration at her nape made her shiver.

"I'll go make sure that the trunks are safely loaded and stowed. See you on board." He patted a pocket to make sure of his ticket, spared her a flash of a smile with both dimples on display, and turned to wave down a man with an empty cart who would take the trunks.

Very well, Carrie told herself. She had braved the worst tenements in Manhattan; she could certainly get a couple hundred feet to the *Annabelle*. She clamped her carpetbag more securely to her side and set off, but the straight line and quick passage she hoped for did not present themselves. Instead she dodged carts, made a circle around a dead rooster, paused while a wagon bearing a coffin followed by three women in mourning passed, and tried not to study a dozen soldiers, all of them mud- and muck-caked to the knees, as they escorted a prisoner shackled hand and foot.

When she was close enough to really see the river between the steamboats, Carrie caught sight of a burned-out hulk on the opposite shore. The capsized steamer was being torn apart by laborers who scurried over it like worker ants.

Steamers wrecked for many reasons: they went aground on a sandbar and could not be shifted, they snagged on a submerged tree and got caught like a fly in a spider's web, boilers exploded, fire broke out. In just that most frightening way her mother's Cousin Ethan and his wife had died on the Hudson. Carrie had been only three at the time, but the people she loved best in the world had wept, brokenhearted, for days. It was one of her earliest memories.

"Ma'am? Do you require assistance?"

The stranger introduced himself as Lieutenant Colonel Elam Leake. He had deep fans of wrinkles at the corners of his eyes and mouth, a polite air, and an accent that sounded to her like the deepest south.

"Lieutenant Colonel, do you know what happened to that steamer?" Carrie pointed with her chin. "I was just wondering."

He was not pleased with this question. "Why worry about something like that?" He held out a crooked elbow. "I expect you need a place to rest and something refreshing to drink. May I escort you onto the *Annabelle*?"

Carrie forced what she hoped was a polite smile, shook her head, and continued on her way. If she dared to look back, she knew what she would see on his face: surprise, alarm, displeasure.

As she drew nearer, the crowd got so dense that she wondered if boarding had been delayed. Most of the people around her were simply dressed, workers or farmers, some with families, many laden with heavy packs. She heard Gaelic and German and Italian being spoken, but most of the passengers sounded like born and bred Southerners to Carrie. She was about to ask an older woman in a faded sugar-scoop bonnet what the delay might be when a man she took as a ship's officer appeared beside her.

He took her arm and shouted, full-throatedly, for the crowd to step aside, step aside, step aside, stateroom passenger boarding!

Carrie knew she was blushing, and still there was nothing to do but follow the man and remind herself that there were things in life that were unfair and, at the same time, out of her control.

Once inside the roped-off area where the gangplank met the landing, Carrie took a moment to catch her breath. She could still feel the deck passengers jostling for position, like so many ponies ready to bolt. They would have to wait until everything and everybody else was on board: wood for the boilers, cargo, baggage, livestock, all had to be properly stowed on the main deck, and only then would these people be allowed to dash for the best spots.

Carrie imagined that some protection from the weather was important to a man traveling with wife and children, but probably not as important as staying clear of the boilers. And food would be a challenge for steerage passengers. Those well-off enough to book a stateroom would dine in the saloon so enthusiastically described in the *Annabelle*'s brochure, but the deck passengers had to see to their own provisions.

Now Carrie realized that from this vantage point, waiting behind five or six other stateroom passengers, she had a clear view of the roustabouts. They were unloading wagons and passing freight down the line until it reached the men who worked the winches, chains and pulleys clanking and screeching as the cargo disappeared onto the main deck. There were no white men among the roustabouts, who wore wooden clogs on their feet and bib overalls over homespun shirts. Even so early in the morning they were all sweating visibly.

In stark contrast was the lady who stood just in front of Carrie in line. She wore a beautiful damask cape in a rich, deep blue and a high-brim spoon bonnet of velvet in exactly the same shade.

Carrie recognized the fabric only because her stepsister, a married woman who came by to see her father every day, always had to show off her newest bonnet. Margaret would expound on the structure, fabric, and embellishments: silk roses and ribbons, Chantilly lace, ostrich plumes and peacock feathers, and, on occasion, an entire bird.

This lady's bonnet was quite tame compared with the ones in Margaret's collection. There was lace, of course, but beyond that only a spray of white feathers that arched back over the crown. Her gloves had been dyed deep blue to match her cape and bonnet. While Carrie could not see the lady's footwear through the mud, she guessed the boots would be blue too.

Such a display of fashion and wealth was not something Carrie had imagined when she thought of the Missouri-Kansas border, but of course, she reasoned to herself, there would be bankers, merchants, mine owners, and every other variety of the wealthy. There were fortunes to be made in the West, and fortunes would be spent.

This particular fashionable lady held a young boy firmly by the hand, but still he tilted backward on his heels to watch the roustabouts as they worked.

"Horses," he announced. "Oxen, mules, cows, geese, chickens."

But no sheep, Carrie remarked to herself.

They were close enough to hear the workers singing as they labored, the voices braiding together in harmony and then slipping apart, deep bass and higher baritone and tenor, reverberating in tones that cut through the clamor and chaos like a drum over pipes and piccolos.

The boy had deep brown eyes, a shock of dark hair that curled out from under his cap, and a small, full mouth that he pressed hard together, in concentration or concern.

"What song are they singing?" He tugged on his mother's hand. "Ma, I don't know that song. What is it?"

"Roberto, I truly do not know." Not impatient, but resigned in tone. The boy would be an inveterate asker of questions, as Carrie had been. As she still was.

"It's sad," the boy said. "It's a sad song."

Carrie could make out a single line: "I be so glad when the sun go down."

Sad was too small a word, but she didn't share this with the little boy or his mother because there was no way to know how they might react. The lady wearing damask and velvet might well have slaves of her own.

The line moved forward with a jerk, but the boy hung back, watching the roustabouts. His mother turned to speak sharply, caught Carrie's gaze, and smiled in the way of any mother with young children hoping for patience from strangers. It was then Carrie recognized her as the woman who had been dancing with Eli Ibarra the night before. His wife, she had assumed, and that would mean the boy was his son.

The ticket clerk greeted the lady with great animation and familiarity, and with that the boy's attention finally shifted away from the slaves. Rather than step further forward so that she might hear the discussion, Carrie bit down on her lip and her curiosity both.

A steward, an older Black man called Joseph, was summoned by the clerk to show Carrie to her stateroom. He bowed to her, his gaze averted and his whole person in tight check.

And so, Carrie thought to herself, this was her first opportunity to talk to a man who lived his life as a slave.

The central staircase was filled with passengers trying to get to the cabins on the upper decks, but the process was a very slow one.

"Won't be too long," the steward said. His voice was raspy and low, as if to offer her the possibility of simply ignoring him.

She paused, considering. "Sir," she said finally. "Is this the Texas deck we're on now?" Only a little embarrassed to be asking a question she knew the answer to, in an effort to engage him in conversation.

He still did not meet her eye, but she thought she saw one corner of his mouth quirk in something like a smile.

"This here the main deck, ma'am."

And that was the end of the conversation, because the crowd began to move.

On the cabin deck he showed her to a set of double doors under a sign reading **Grand Saloon**. "This here where you find somebody to show you to your stateroom and make you comfortable. Ma'am, if I may, I wish you a good day and a pleasant journey."

She thanked him and pressed a coin into his palm. In response he looked at her directly for the first time and nodded his thanks.

The brochure about the *Annabelle* hadn't prepared Carrie for the surprise of the main saloon, draped from top to bottom and end to end in crimson red. It was enough to make a person dizzy: brocade and velvet upholstery and draperies, all of it festooned with gold braid and tassels. The woodwork was gilded, and a rug crawling with aga-panthus and blowsy cabbage roses ran the whole length of the room. She was reminded of a bordello on Thirty-Fourth Street where she had delivered a baby just months before.

Now a stout woman with an air of great importance sailed toward Carrie. Her taffeta petticoats rustled like trees in a high wind.

"I am the captain's wife, Mrs. Ashby. And might I inquire . . . ?"

Mrs. Ashby's interest waned as soon as it became clear that Carrie Ballentyne was no one of real importance. A young woman traveling with her brother, equally uninspiring.

"This is Milly." Mrs. Ashby gestured a young woman forward. "As you seem to be traveling alone and without a maid—" She cleared her throat to make clear what she thought of that fact. "Milly will see to your needs."

Now would be the time to tell the captain's wife that she could look after her own needs and would not accept the services of a slave, but she knew, too, that if Mrs. Ashby took offense, it was Milly who would suffer the consequences.

She was maybe a few years older than Carrie, trim and neat in appearance, her head wrapped in a plain yellow muslin turban. Carrie smiled at her, but nothing changed in Milly's placid expression. For all of her life this young woman dared show no other face to the world. Not anger or joy, not even boredom. She must let herself be observed by curious tourists, and could not ask for even a moment to herself. This thought was enough to make Carrie look away.

"I will stop by to check on you later today," Mrs. Ashby said quite suddenly, and sailed off to greet a couple who stood at the door.

"This way, ma'am." Milly held a hand out for Carrie's bag.

"You need not carry things for me, Milly." Carrie summoned up what she hoped would be seen as a calm, friendly smile. "But please do tell me whatever I need to know about the way things work."

From Milly she learned that the saloon itself was where the stateroom passengers spent most of their time. It was very long and somewhat narrow, with comfortable chairs and sofas arranged at intervals. At the far end, stained-glass skylights sent colors dancing across linen-covered tables that were already set for a meal.

According to Milly, the captain and one or two of his officers would dine with the stateroom passengers at noon. Supper would be served at seven, with music to follow.

Carrie was eager to see her cabin, but she dutifully followed Milly, first to an area where nursemaids would look after children, then past a barber's shop, to reach the library. This was clearly the domain of the men, as three passengers had already gathered around a table and were dealing cards. Each corner was flanked by a spittoon, and tobacco smoke had stained the ceiling a deep ochre. To Carrie it looked as though none of the books on the shelves had ever been touched. Beside the library was the bar, where, once again, only men were welcome.

"Ma'am," Milly said. "You surely have noted that the staterooms open into the main parlor? On the left are the lady cabins, and the gentlemen are on the right. There are staterooms for married couples on the Texas deck."

Carrie said, "And which is mine?"

She followed Milly down the row of rosewood doors, each topped with a fan-shaped transom window. Milly stopped at number four, and opened the door.

To her relief and pleasure both, the stateroom turned out to be as bright as the saloon had been dim, because, Carrie saw, there was another door that opened out onto a covered promenade.

On her way across the room, she took note of a cabinet bedstead with a pullout cot beneath it and shelving above, a corner wardrobe, a small table with two chairs, and a mirror in an ornate frame hanging over a washstand. All very compact and still stylish.

The door that exited onto the promenade had an inset window that could be latched closed or left open, as it was now. A welcome breeze came in, even if it did bring with it the stink of mud and river water, decaying greenery, manure, pitch, and coal. The view from the promenade was not especially inspiring; on the other side of the murky waters of the Missouri, farmhands were at work in the fields under a pale, cloudless sky.

Milly was behind her, clearing her throat again. Carrie turned to her. "I'm sorry, could you repeat that, please?"

As it turned out, there were more things to learn: about the guards stationed on the inside of the grand saloon and on the promenade. Any of them could be asked to send for Milly if Carrie required her help. Hot water would be brought at seven in the morning, at eleven, at one, at half past five, and again at nine, but of course these times could be adjusted to Carrie's preferences.

"Your trunk will be brought to you here shortly," Milly finished. "Is everything to your satisfaction?"

Carrie sat down on a chair and blew out a long breath.

"Yes. I believe I will be able to sleep well here."

At that Milly smiled. "That's good to hear, but be sure to send for me if there's anything you need. Now there's just one thing I have to have from you, Miss Ballentyne."

Carrie lifted an eyebrow. "What would that be?"

"I'll take your boots to be cleaned, and later I'll come by to sweep up."

Because of course Carrie had been trailing bits of stinky mud wherever she went.

Alone, in her stocking feet, Carrie sat at the table to sort through her carpetbag and study the stateroom that was to be her home for a week or so. She appreciated the simple decor, thankful the crimson overexuberance had been restricted to the grand saloon. In this stateroom the beadboard walls were painted ivory, while the bedding, the dressing screen, and the door curtains were celery green with a foliage pattern. The painting that hung beside the bed was another matter: a lakeside in winter, where sickly gnarled trees stood in a frozen marsh rendered in shades of gray.

She wondered if her mother—the artist—would find something to admire about the painting, and decided that she would not.

Shoeless as she was, Carrie couldn't go into the grand saloon, and neither could she explore along the promenade without risking splinters and raised brows. She wondered if other passengers were wandering around barefooted, or if they sat as she did, waiting. And more important still: she had promised Nathan not to go roaming until they had explored the decks together and they fully understood what was safe.

With a sigh Carrie closed the outer walkway door, leaving the window open. It was time to retrieve the book she carried in her carpetbag, a going-away gift from her stepfather.

The steamer lurched backward, as awkward as a three-legged mule, lurched again, and began to move slowly as the paddle wheels picked up speed. On the main deck, passengers were waving to family and friends, calling out good wishes and warnings as the steamer lurched again and came to a stop. The passengers were loud and the steamer was even louder; whistles and bells from the Texas deck, linemen and crew shouting questions and answers. The engine roared. Cheers rose up from the decks and the dock, but Carrie was not in the least tempted to join the crowd.

Instead she stared at the book in her hands for a long moment, trying to make herself open the cover. She had told herself that she would read her stepfather's gift as they headed west on the Missouri, and that time had come. That she should dread a book so much was truly nonsensical, but she had good reason.

Harrison Quinlan was an intelligent, thoughtful, kind man, but he was also a cynic of the first order. It was his firm belief that cynicism was essential to staying safe in the wider world, and thus he cultivated a rational, unsentimental frame of reference in his children and step-children. In Carrie's opinion, this had turned his daughter Margaret into a distrustful, suspicious young woman overly concerned with crime, while his only son had gone off to join the army at the first opportunity.

So it had not been a surprise that as soon as Carrie had decided to make this move, her stepfather began his research. He interviewed librarians and made a survey of publications until he found a book that provided an unflinching look at the Southwest Territories. In her hands she held the end product of his research: Mr. Gregg's *Commerce of the Prairies, or, The Journal of a Santa Fé Trader.*

The book's sole purpose was to instill in her a cautious state of mind, and she dared not hope for anything entertaining in its pages.

Many people had talked to her frankly about the dangers of this move west—she still had the clipping that sour old Mrs. Newton had pressed on her—but nothing she heard had made her doubt her decision. She wanted to believe that neither would she be swayed by what was written in this book, but the simple truth was that her stepfather had outmaneuvered her. She must read the damn thing, or admit to her own doubts and cowardice.

On the very first page, in between the title and subtitle, her mother had sketched a cat. A simple drawing in pencil, but it was Meaney and no other cat in the world. A cantankerous, crabbit old tom who had moved with them from Paradise to Manhattan. Carrie adored him, but Meaney treated praise and scolding with equal disdain. When he was in a generous mood—and the weather was cold—he would fall asleep on her lap. When Meaney died in his sleep, Carrie had been unable to talk without releasing a flood of tears for many weeks.

And here he was, a gift from her mother; Meaney went along on this journey as a reminder of the home she had lost. Her first home, and Meaney's. It had always seemed to her that his poor temper was nothing more than homesickness, something she felt but kept to herself for fear of upsetting her mother.

Under the sketch Ma had written a few words in her angular hand:

For my beloved Carrie with her wakeful, watchful, tender heart.

And how was she to read about trade on the plains while her head was full of Ma and Meaney, and tears threatened?

Procrastination presented itself as a familiar voice that came from the promenade. The little boy who had wanted to know about the song the slaves sang as they worked was again asking questions.

"Ma," she heard him say. "There are fifteen doors. That means there are fifteen staterooms for ladies, and if all of them have little boys—"

She made a sound, a clearing of the throat. "But, Beto, you already know that's not the case."

Their voices faded as they moved farther from Carrie's stateroom. She was listening very hard to try to catch more of the conversation, when a knock at the door made her jump in place.

"Ma'am?" came a man's deep voice. "I've got your boots shined up for you, and a trunk you been waiting on. Oh, and Mr. Ballentyne is in the grand saloon, and asking after you."

When she found Nathan, he was, as expected, already involved in a conversation, and paused only to introduce her to his newest acquaintance. The stranger stuck out a hand and produced a brilliant smile displaying a scattering of tiny white teeth that glistened like pearls and were not the ones issued to him by nature. "Harmon Oakley," he said. "Westport. Hardware."

Mr. Oakley was a short, stout man with a freckled pate and great bushels of carrot-red beard flecked with tobacco.

"We were just talking about some passengers who were turned away," Nathan told her. "Two couples, each with a child."

"They didn't have tickets?"

Mr. Oakley leaned toward her as if he had a secret to tell. "Had tickets, sure did. But the clerk took one look at 'em and sent for the captain."

"Why would he do that?" Carrie glanced between the two men, hoping that Nathan would give her a concise and unalarming answer, but Mr. Oakley was clearly a man who delighted in drama.

"It's the captain. Ashby." Mr. Oakley looked over his shoulder as if he feared the man might be hiding nearby. "The clerk thought those two families might be part of that New England crowd, and the captain ain't fond of Mr. Thayer and his society of busybodies, is the way he puts it."

It took some careful questioning before Carrie could make sense of it. She was familiar with the background: Congress, unwilling to shoulder the responsibility or repercussions that followed from making a decision, had chosen to let the residents of the new states of Kansas and Nebraska decide for themselves on the burning question of the day: Would slavery be allowed, or banned? In a time when politicians beat each other bloody over the issue, this was, anyone who paid attention must see, a recipe for disaster.

Eli Thayer, a Massachusetts businessman and fervent abolitionist, had responded to the Kansas-Nebraska Act by rallying like-minded groups to found the New England Emigrant Aid Society. The idea was to encourage abolitionists to go to Kansas and resettle there. The society would provide whatever help was needed to establish a man in the new territory. Then, when the time came to vote on the question of slavery, the transplanted New Englanders would see to it that Kansas entered the union as a free state.

That this did not sit well with Missourians was widely known. Southern newspapers were full of threats against the Northern Invaders and promises that Kansas would indeed be a slave state, at any cost. Then came raids back and forth across the border, free-staters and slavery supporters striking out at each other. Settlements were looted and robbed, and finally the town of Lawrence, founded by abolitionists, had been sacked. As Mrs. Newton had pointed out with such satisfaction and glee on the train.

Mr. Oakley said, "Maybe your New York papers didn't report much about what happened here a year ago. You've heard tell of John Brown?"

Carrie wondered if there was a single person in the country who hadn't heard about John Brown, but Mr. Oakley didn't wait for an answer. He launched into a recounting: Mr. Brown and his free-state volunteers had gone to Potawatomi, where they took vengeance for the sack of Lawrence.

Nathan said, "The story was in the New York papers, in great detail."

Mr. Oakley nodded and went on nonetheless, committed to the tale and not to be diverted.

"It was a bloody summer. Word is"—he lowered his voice another notch—"John Brown is still in Kansas, ready to kill anybody who gets in the way of the abolitionists."

Carrie considered countering this with what she knew from the newspapers about Brown's recent movements, but decided that it would only distract, and Mr. Oakley had yet to get to the part of the story she most wanted to hear.

Her brother, less patient, nudged. "And Captain Ashby has taken it upon himself to stop Yankees bound for Kansas?"

Mr. Oakley put a finger to his lips, eyes wide, and nodded with great solemnity. "It's more than that. Since the raid at Potawatomi Creek, his two boys are riding out with the border ruffians, is what they call themselves. Missouri boys determined to run the abolitionists off, back to Boston. Or to their graves, if nothing else works. For Ashby's part, he turns away anybody who even looks to him like a free-stater."

"But how could he be sure that those two families are part of Thayer's group?" Carrie asked.

Oakley shrugged. "He glowers at 'em and quotes the Bible on slavery—you'll know better than me what verses—until they spit out the truth. Sounds odd, I know, but I've seen him do it."

Carrie said, "And is he always right?"

The whole of his face crinkled in confusion. "I don't follow."

"Well," Carrie began, reaching carefully for the most neutral phrasing. "People often lie about themselves, don't they. They could tell the captain that they are on their way to California. Or that they've never heard of Thayer's Emigrant Aid Society. Or that they are Mormons."

Mr. Oakley rocked his head from side to side as if considering. "He don't like the Mormons, neither. So you're saying, if he straight out asks them are they abolitionists, they'd lie?"

"I don't know," Carrie said. "Traveling with children might move them to avoid the truth if it will have negative repercussions."

"Oh no." Oakley winked at Nathan and elbowed him playfully. "A lady with big words. Been to school too long, is my guess."

Nathan raised a brow in her direction, but she gave him a small shake of the head that said he should not let himself be drawn into this conversation.

Instead he asked, "What will happen to the passengers he turned away?"

"They have to find another steamer," Mr. Oakley said. "Shouldn't be too hard. Most captains ain't half so picky as Ashby."

Carrie thought of the inconvenience and cost of such a delay. "Surely he returns the money they paid for passage on the *Annabelle*?"

Mr. Oakley grimaced. "Not if his missus has anything to say about it. Tough old bird, that one. Hair on her teeth, as my Dutch mam used to say. Now if you'll pardon me, I'm off to wet my whistle."

When he had disappeared into the bar, Nathan said, "Seems there's no getting away from the slavery question."

"Especially not here," Carrie said. "Not unless you are deaf and blind. And white."

THEY SPENT THE next hour roaming over the steamer, starting with the Texas deck, where they made the acquaintance of Captain Ashby. Carrie wondered if Ashby would ask them about their political views, but he only introduced Mr. Michael Spears, the pilot.

As they were already underway, Carrie cast a sidelong glance at the pilot's house, wondering why Mr. Spears stood here with them.

"My assistant has the wheel," the pilot told her, reading her question from her face. "No cause for concern."

The pilot was younger than Carrie had imagined, and there was something both indolent and smug in his gaze. He was rumored to be the best pilot on the Missouri, and she supposed his airs were tolerated for that reason.

"Mr. Spears was born on the river," Ashby told them. "Took his first steps on a keelboat. River water runs in his veins. It's my good fortune to have him on the *Annabelle*."

Steamboat pilots earned a great deal of money, but apparently Mr. Spears also required regular servings of flattery.

"It's your fortune that keeps me here," he said to the captain. "But then we're sure to run into Steinbrenner in Westport, and he swears he ain't about to let you outbid him next time around."

The captain's face went red with surprise and something Carrie took for anger. In fact, he set his mouth so hard that his lips disappeared completely, as if he needed to seal his mouth shut for fear of saying too much.

Now that she looked at Ashby more closely, she decided that his florid complexion and the broken veins in his cheeks and nose were not the result of years in the sun. Taken together with red-rimmed, watery eyes, it seemed clear he had spent a good amount of time in the bar himself.

When they left the Texas deck, Nathan said, "There's really just one thing to know about the captain."

"Yes," Carrie said. "He's an ass."

Nathan barked a laugh that made others turn to look at him, but he was unbothered by the attention. He said, "That may be true, but he's an ass who has his whole fortune tied up in this steamer, and he has no intention of losing her. If every inch of every deck was crowded with abolitionists, he'd bring the *Annabelle* home safe."

While they made their way through crowds of people, Carrie thought about this. It was cold comfort, but it would have to be enough.

"That's the dinner bell," Nathan said. "And I'm starved. Let's go."

4

As a widow, Lily Bonner Ballentyne had taken as her second husband Dr. Harrison Quinlan, a wealthy widower well placed in New York society. The marriage was something of a scandal, primarily because it annoyed Manhattan's many hopeful widows who watched the doctor's comings and goings closely. Beyond that, the widow Ballentyne had been born and raised on what some still called the frontier, with Indians. Not just among them, but with them. And she was an artist.

She would have been cut off from all good society without debate, but Dr. Quinlan was feared almost as much as he was liked. Once the deed was done, the invitations to formal dinners and receptions in honor of the new Mrs. Quinlan began. Then they had to be reciprocated. The gatherings on Waverly Place were unavoidable for Carrie and Nathan. No amount of pleading or logic would sway Ma on this point.

We will not start out by insulting Dr. Quinlan. And there's no harm in becoming acquainted with formal events. You never know where you might end up one day, or what may be expected of you.

And so they had submitted to the tailor and dressmaker and let themselves be made worthy of fine company. When they appeared in a parlor overfilled with guests a month after they came to Waverly Place, Dr. Quinlan looked them up and down and pronounced them to be very presentable. With a truly kind smile, which wasn't enough to offset the hours spent with strangers.

Once she finished her training and took up employment, Carrie was no longer required to appear at such events, and since then she had never again suffered through six courses and endless talk of municipal politics and neighborhood romances. But here she was again, standing in the grand saloon, where people had begun to drift toward the dining tables.

"Did you have any sense of this?" She whispered the question to her brother, whose brow drew down in confusion.

"Any sense of what—that they would feed us?"

He was being purposefully dim, but he knew what she meant. The tables were lavishly laid out, from heavy damask linen to Staffordshire finger bowls. Stewards in uniform moved back and forth, very solemn, while Mrs. Ashby watched them closely from her seat at the head of the first table. No sign of the captain yet.

Carrie wore a simple skirt and a pretty shirtwaist that was technically too big for her, and therefore comfortable. Looking at the other passengers coming into the saloon, she realized just how underdressed and out of fashion she was. For a moment she wondered if she should retire to change, but that was a silly notion. First, because she didn't own any clothes to rival the ones she saw the others wearing so casually, but more important: she would not be shamed into a sudden interest in lace trim or carved ivory buttons.

"We are too early," Nathan said under his breath.

He preferred to be among the last to take a seat, but the calculations that went into timing the socially perfect arrival only annoyed Carrie. That thought was still in her head—how irritating Nathan's occasional preoccupation with social conventions could be—when she saw Eli Ibarra walking toward them with the mother of young Roberto, who had boarded the *Annabelle* just before Carrie, on his arm. She no longer wore the cape or bonnet, but her gown was just as elegantly and expensively made, of silvery dove-gray silk.

Carrie swallowed down her frustration with her brother. His expression made it clear that he was not in the least surprised to see Ibarra. He could have told her that Ibarra would be on the steamer, but had chosen not to. If she had known, she could have asked for a tray in her stateroom. Petty it might have been, but she would have done it anyway. Why she wanted to avoid him was a question that she didn't entertain for more than a split second.

The men greeted each other like old friends, getting through the business of introductions in record time. Carrie did what was expected of her and made the acquaintance of Mrs. Evangeline Zavala of St. Louis and Santa Fe, the widow of Eli Ibarra's closest friend.

And so her assumptions had been wrong. Eli Ibarra was not a married man with a child. Or at least, not married to this lady. At present.

It was Mr. Ibarra's suggestion that they sit together, a proposal he put forward with more charm than Carrie would have expected. She resigned herself to the inevitable, and they were soon seated, Carrie opposite Mrs. Zavala and Nathan opposite Eli Ibarra.

When Mrs. Zavala turned and raised her head to answer a question a waiter had asked, the elderly lady on Carrie's left turned sharply, sparse white brows lifting at the sound of a familiar voice.

"Evangeline Roberts." The frail old voice wavered. "Or I should say Mrs. Zavala—"

The younger woman blinked in surprise. "Mrs. Hamblin," she said, a little flustered and clearly surprised. "Don't be silly. You've known me all my life, of course you think of me first as Evangeline Roberts. What a surprise to run into you here. I take it you are on your way home to Leavenworth?"

Carrie considered this unexpected reunion good fortune, because

Mrs. Hamblin latched onto Evangeline Roberts Zavala, and with that, Carrie was relieved of the need to contribute to the conversation. Mrs. Hamblin, who had lived in Santa Fe for many years, was hungry for news of old friends. Questions and answers were traded back and forth as the stewards brought one course after another, from turtle soup and roasted sturgeon to a stuffed shoulder of lamb with mint sauce. There was also an endless parade of side dishes, some of which were entirely new to the Ballentynes. Carrie decided that the less said about boiled okra, the better. Nathan ate her portion, and asked for more butter beans.

The rest of the offerings were very good, but it was hard to appreciate the meal given the lively exchange of information. Thankfully Carrie didn't have to pretend not to be listening, because everyone else was plainly listening without apology.

Mrs. Hamblin asked about Mrs. Zavala's family in St. Louis, her brothers and sisters, and her business. This Carrie found interesting, but not so much that she would venture a question. Nathan didn't hesitate.

"What kind of business, if I may ask?"

"A *cacharrería*," Mrs. Zavala said. "You'll want a translation, but it's not the easiest—"

Mrs. Hamblin waved a hand as if she were ordering silence and answered Nathan's question. "It's a china and pottery shop."

Eva Zavala hid her anger well, just a slight quirk at the corner of her mouth.

Nathan said, "You trade in dishware, Mrs. Zavala?"

"Among other things," Eva said. "We have grown since my parents left Santa Fe for St. Louis. About the same time Mrs. Hamblin left."

Mrs. Hamblin fluttered her fingers, dismissing the subject, and took up something more interesting: she began in the logical place, asking about the boy.

The change in subject was a welcome one. Mrs. Zavala's tone brightened when she talked about her Roberto, who was a curious, bright, affectionate child. Yes, he was very much like his father, who'd had the same coloring and eyes, and no, he had no memory of Carlos Zavala, as he had been less than a year old when his father died.

"A terrible loss," Mrs. Hamblin murmured. "Senseless."

If the old friend of the family was hoping to talk more about Carlos Zavala's death, Carrie had the strong sense that she would be disappointed. In fact, Evangeline began to ask about the Hamblin family, the children and grandchildren, and did none of them think of returning to Santa Fe?

It was a clever feint, one that sent the conversation off in another direction because Mrs. Hamblin had six children, all still living, all with children of their own. She counted off twenty-two grandchildren and five great-grandchildren, with two more in the offing. They heard about her grandson Harry's hardware business; her daughter Jenny, who had recently come home to Leavenworth after visiting old friends in Santa Fe; and oh, had Evangeline heard of the fire that had destroyed dear Mrs. Johnson's home? What a terrible shame.

It seemed Evangeline was not quite clear on who Mrs. Johnson might be.

"But you must remember Mrs. Johnson," said the old lady. "She was your mother's seamstress for years. If I remember correctly, she made you a beautiful gown for your seventeenth birthday, with embroidered rosebuds."

The pale mouth jerked at the corner. "In any case, she certainly remembers you."

"Does she?" Something a little stiff came into Mrs. Zavala's expression. "The next visit to St. Louis I'll ask my mother about her."

"Ida Johnson is not about to forget the girl who broke her Mason's heart," Mrs. Hamblin went on, ignoring Evangeline Zavala's obvious wish to change the subject. Instead she raised a finger in mock admonition.

"Don't deny it. You did break Mason Johnson's heart, and Laurence Brown's. And Henry Osler's son Larry, who pined for you, and wait, Don Diego's oldest, what was his name—"

At this Eli leaned in closer and spoke to the old lady directly. "That would be me," he said. "Eli Ibarra. I'm Don Diego's eldest son. Mrs. Hamblin, you may not recognize me, but I remember you well enough. And pardon me for correcting you, but it was Carlos who loved Evangeline Roberts first and best."

Then he turned his head just slightly, met Carrie's gaze, and winked at her.

LATER, SITTING WITH Nathan in his stateroom, Carrie struggled to remain composed while she explained to him how he had transgressed.

"I knew you were up to something."

"My big sister, as suspicious as ever."

She held his gaze for a long moment, and he shrugged. "Yes, all right. I should have said something."

For a moment he turned back to the papers he was sorting and then told the story.

"Eli mentioned that his brothers would be driving the sheep overland, but he would go ahead. And anyway, if you had known, would it have made any difference?"

She shook her head. "You are missing the point. You should not keep information from me, for any reason at all. I am not your child to protect from—may I say—imaginary insults or bruised feelings."

He shrugged again, conceding the point. "Fair enough."

There was a long moment's silence. Carrie could go back to her stateroom now, but there was one thing she wanted to know. She could not ask directly about Eli Ibarra, but neither could she simply put out of her mind the way he had winked at her. The question was, Had Nathan taken note? And if so, could he explain to her what it meant?

"It was an instructive meal," Nathan said. "And by Eli's expression, an amusing one. More than once I thought he was going to laugh at the way the old lady was fishing for gossip."

To this there was little she could say beyond her observation that Eva Zavala's sudden appearance had put Eli Ibarra in a good mood.

But to say such a thing would be immature and spiteful, and worse still, it would draw Nathan's attention entirely in the wrong direction.

Instead she said, "I doubt Mrs. Zavala was amused. She worked hard to turn the conversation away from herself."

"And her Mrs. Hamblin turned it right back." Nathan gave a soft laugh.

"What is so amusing about the distress of a widow?"

Nathan frowned. "That's a bit of an exaggeration, sister. She was embarrassed to have her romantic history trumpeted, certainly, but wouldn't that be true of most young women?"

He cleared his throat and dropped his gaze as if something life-threatening had peeked out from under the papers spread out before him. This was her brother, always concerned about what he saw as Carrie's fast-approaching spinsterhood, but determined not to raise the subject directly for fear of offending her. Well, enough of that.

"I truly am not pining away for a husband," she said. "Why do you rush me?"

He went still for a moment. Then, straightening his shoulders: "You are afraid of men, and I wish you weren't."

Carrie drew in a sharp breath. "I'm cautious when caution is called for." Her tone, she was glad to hear, was unremarkable.

"It's more than caution." He came right back at her. "It's more than vigilance. You assume the worst—"

"No," Carrie interrupted. "What you could say is that I distrust a man who is glib-tongued and full of promises, because he is likely to be false. A man who presents himself to the world as thoughtful and caring may well care only for his own pleasure and advancement, and that at any cost—" She broke off.

"You don't want a man like Gregory Fisher," Nathan said.

It was a name she never spoke out loud and never wanted to hear. More than that, it agitated Nathan as much as it did her; even in her distress Carrie saw that all the color had drained from his face. Her own throat had gone dry, and she wound her hands together to keep them from shaking.

He said, "We all liked him, all of us."

"Da saw the truth of him." Her voice had gone hoarse. "Grandda Nathaniel would have horsewhipped him out of town."

"They were gone, and you were a little girl."

"And now I'm a woman grown," Carrie said. "And I won't make the same mistake again."

5

As NOISY AS the steamer was, Carrie had no trouble dropping off to sleep when she lay down to take a nap. She slept so deeply that when she woke at dusk, she couldn't account for her surroundings until the lineman's call reminded her that she was on a Missouri River steamer bound for Kansas.

There was someone scratching at her door, she realized. Yawning, she went to see who it was, and was glad to find Milly. She had brought hot water and towels, and was in and out in less than a minute.

Carrie roused herself, washed her face and hands, and finally went out onto the promenade, where she found Roberto Zavala standing on the first rung of the railing on tiptoe, bent over to watch the river flow by. There were other people on the promenade, but none of them were his mother.

Her first impulse was to ask him if he had permission to be out here alone, but she was fairly sure that she knew the answer to that question. She reconsidered.

"Mr. Zavala," she said, just loud enough to be heard without startling him. "Anything interesting to see down there?"

To her relief he didn't jerk. Instead he turned his head to look at her over his shoulder.

"I'm watching for snags and sandbars. You're the lady who was behind us when we boarded."

Carrie agreed that she was, and introduced herself. "Will you shake my hand, Roberto?"

He was an amiable child, and a trusting one. He climbed down from the rail and offered her a small, damp hand.

"People call me Beto. Except Mama. She calls me mostly Roberto but sometimes if she's in a good mood, Beto."

"And where is your mother?"

Now he saw through her. "I'm allowed to be out here."

She raised a brow.

The small mouth flexed into a frown. "Mama is napping. And I am allowed to be out here. Is that tall man with dark hair and dimples your brother?"

Practiced in the art of distraction too. Carrie bit back a smile. "That is my brother, yes. Would you like to meet him? We could get some tea in the saloon and all sit down together to talk."

Young Beto considered for a long moment. "Does he know about steamboats?"

"He knows quite a lot about steamers. And about trains, and everything else mechanical."

This seemed to strike the boy as promising, because he took her hand in the way of young children who have decided to be herded along. "All right," he said. "I'll see how he does with questions. And if I may say, it's too bad that he got the dimples and you did not."

With his questions and sometimes startling observations, Beto Zavala served nicely as a buffer between herself and Nathan. Putting her brother together with an intelligent, inquisitive little boy meant that their previous conversation could not be taken up again. Instead the two male creatures would entertain each other and pay no attention to her, unless it was to point out that the teapot was empty or to ask about the possibility of cake.

To her surprise, Carrie found that she was quite comfortable on a settee in the saloon, where doors and windows had been opened to let a breeze move through the room. Of course the stink of the engines and boilers at work came, too, but even that she could bear for the sake of fresh air.

She took up the first volume of Mr. Gregg's *Commerce of the Prairies*, letting it fall open to read at random. She didn't realize she was smiling until Roberto asked her about it.

"Is that a funny book?"

"Not generally, I think, but there are certain passages—"

"Will you read it to me?"

Nathan grinned at her over the boy's head. "Please, Miss Carrie, read it to us."

She ignored her brother and smiled at the little boy. "Mr. Gregg writes here about oxen on the trail to Santa Fe. He says they are 'exceedingly whimsical creatures when surrounded by unfamiliar objects. One will sometimes take a fright at the jingle of his own yoke-irons, or the cough of his mate, and, by a sudden flounce, set the whole herd in a flurry.'"

"That wouldn't be so amusing if you were caught up in the middle of it," Nathan noted drily. "But I'll grant you Mr. Gregg has a way with words."

Beto's expression was difficult to interpret, but to Carrie it looked as if he wanted to disagree, with either Nathan or the author of the book, but knew that it would be frowned upon. Then he seemed to change his mind.

"It could be Pawnee or Comanche sneaking up on the herd," he said with great seriousness. "That happens too. It happened to my father when I was a baby. It's how he died."

Carrie had to clear her throat before she could respond to this statement, and then with nothing more than the usual platitudes. Though she told herself that it was none of her business, Carrie wondered how often the boy had told the story of his father's death, and whether he knew more of the details than he shared with them.

Nathan said, "We were young, too, when our father died."

It was the right thing to say. Beto wanted to hear more about Simon Ballentyne, and his questions were far ranging: Did he have dimples, like Nathan did? Was he a Yankee? Why did he come here from Scotland? Did he like bonbons? And then, finally, whether he had ever traveled in a wagon train.

Nathan told the story of the day their father died in a few calm sentences without any embellishments. As a result it worked as neither trivial nor sensational, but neither did it resemble even slightly Carrie's memories of that day.

Toward the end of the story, Beto's gaze rose and fixed on a point behind Carrie. She knew by his expression that his mother stood there.

"Roberto," she said. "Have you been intruding where you're not welcome?"

The boy didn't seem particularly worried about his mother's question, but Nathan fairly leapt to his feet.

"We invited him to join us. Mrs. Zavala, will you have some tea?"

As the elegant woman took a seat on the settee, she turned toward Carrie. "He isn't making a nuisance of himself?"

"Not at all."

Mrs. Zavala smiled. "I fear you are being polite."

"Oh no," Nathan said. "You can believe my sister. She's never polite if she can help it."

Carrie let out a short laugh, but Beto was frowning.

He said, "But, Mr. Ballentyne, you're not being polite, either."

"Roberto," said his mother, her tone unmistakable.

"Please don't scold him." Nathan produced his widest, least resistible grin, dimples appearing in both cheeks like divots in damp turf. "He's right. I was teasing my sister, and it was rude of me. Now, let's see about getting you some tea."

If another passenger had joined their little group, Carrie knew that the conversation would have touched on the usual acceptable sub-jects: the *Annabelle*, the quality of the food they were served, the weather today and tomorrow and for the next week, the possibility of snags in the river and what that would mean. In such a setting she imagined that Beto would be quickly bored and eager to get away, but the boy seemed to like the company of adults, and his mother did not exclude him from the conversation. She only raised a brow in warning when his questions veered too close to unacceptable topics.

Once he realized that Carrie was going to be living in Santa Fe, his whole posture changed.

"We live in Santa Fe. I was born in Santa Fe," he told her. His expression shifted to something almost somber. "It was a long and difficult birth."

Nathan ducked his head. Carrie prided herself on the ability to keep reactions hidden—an important skill for a nurse—but even she could not suppress the tilt at the corner of her mouth. This wasn't lost on the little boy, who turned toward his mother, who was shaking her head at him.

"But Granny told me so. She said you were very brave and strong."

"Nevertheless," she said.

Beto flushed. "Ma, Miss Ballentyne is a midwife. She knows all about babies."

Carrie touched the boy's hand. "Your mother is trying to say that your birth was something very personal, an experience that shouldn't be shared with strangers—"

Before he could object, she held up a finger to ask for his patience. "Or even with new friends."

He slumped a little and pushed out a great sigh. "All right. Ma, I'm sorry I told about you being strong and brave. But I can tell about Pa, can't I? Because—" His expression faltered. "I already did. At least, I told them part of the story."

And that was how Evangeline Roberts Zavala came to tell them about her husband, who was killed when the Comanche attacked the wagon train he was leading, on his way home to Santa Fe.

"The trail can be very dangerous," she finished. "But recently, I understand, things have been relatively calm."

"Except in Kansas," Beto said, not quite under his breath.

His mother's gaze sharpened. "What do you know of Kansas?"

"Um," said Beto.

Nathan stepped in. "So you stayed in Santa Fe, after you lost your husband?"

"Yes," she said, looking from her son to Nathan with some reluctance. "I spent some time with my parents in St. Louis, but then I went home to Santa Fe. My father-in-law is not well, and running the hacienda is a challenge for him. Not that I can take on any part of that responsibility, but he is more at ease when his grandson is nearby. And my husband's business and property are my responsibility."

Beto stood up suddenly and pointed. "Uncle Eli!" He waved both arms overhead as if to get the attention of an unruly herd of ponies.

"You may say hello to Eli," his mother told him. "But then it's time we went back to our stateroom." She turned to Carrie. "Would you be interested in joining us? I would be happy to answer any questions you may have about Santa Fe. I gather all the information you have thus far is from men, and I have no doubt they left many things out."

EVANGELINE ZAVALA'S STATEROOM was almost identical to Carrie's own. Carrie took one of the two chairs at the small table under the window while Beto settled down with picture books on the bed, where he drifted away into a nap in just a few minutes. Carrie wanted nothing more than to follow his example. In her own cabin.

She was being unfair, she knew. Mrs. Zavala was polite, friendly, welcoming; the invitation to talk had come from her. As a child Carrie had been quiet, primarily because her sisters were talkative, but in training as a nurse and a midwife, she had learned how to talk to strangers. To women and children who needed her help. In this case she herself was being offered help, and that left Carrie in an unfamiliar place.

"First, please call me Evangeline, or Eva," she began. "In the West some things are less formal. If I may call you Carrie?"

Carrie agreed to this with what she hoped would be taken as a sincere smile.

"Then let's get off to a good start."

From the shelf she took a box wrapped in marbled paper, at least ten inches square and four inches deep, closed with clasps and secured with a leather band. Carrie, her curiosity peaking, leaned forward to watch as the mysterious box was opened and Evangeline lifted off the top to reveal something like a jewelry box. There were three layers or trays that could be pulled out, and Carrie wondered if she was going to be asked to evaluate a display of bracelets and earrings and hair clasps. Then the smells came to her to tell a different story.

She could make out butter, honey, roasted nuts, marzipan, cinnamon, anise, ginger, cardamom, cloves, vanilla, and cocoa.

"Come," Evangeline said, turning the box toward Carrie so she could see the offerings. "Please help yourself. You won't see a selection like this very often in New Mexico Territory, not until my next St. Louis visit, and that may be five years from now."

Carrie couldn't help herself; she laughed out loud. Evangeline's enthusiasm was so authentic and girlish that every hesitation Carrie had about this elegant young woman simply melted away. For the next quarter hour she paid close attention to the descriptions that Eva Zavala wanted to provide.

There were bonbons glistening with sugar crystals or dusted with cocoa in tiny, frilled paper cups, each decorated distinctively and, Carrie realized with amazement, having a name: rosolios, diavolini, noyaux, trocaderos, Cleopatras. She learned about butterscotch-glazed Brazil nuts, Italian torrone studded with pistachios, hazelnut puffs, caramelized almonds, marzipan shaped and colored to resemble strawberries, oranges, peaches, pears, and plums, and a dozen different hard candies so fragrant that the scent would hang in the air for a long while: ginger, cloves, peppermint, horehound, lemon.

"Well." Carrie laughed. "This is something out of the ordinary. You sell confectionery in your pottery shop?"

"My *cacharrería* is full of interesting things beyond pottery. You will have to explore to find all the treasures."

She gave the box a small jolt. "Do not be shy. Pick something. Really, you must."

"But there's only one of each sort," Carrie protested.

"And a dozen more boxes like this one in my trunks," Evangeline said.

"Fine." Carrie considered. "What flavor are these blue ones?"

"You should try something a little more exotic than a lozenge, but if you must—the blue is clove flavored." She pursed her mouth in mock disapproval. "Clove is what you want for a sore tooth, but I don't think it's suited to sweets. What about this marzipan peach, doesn't that appeal?"

When they had gone over all the possibilities, Carrie took what turned out to be a peppermint hard candy.

"I would have guessed that you'd pick peppermint. It suits you."

Carrie tucked the lozenge into her cheek so she could ask the obvious question. "How so?"

Her hostess gave a little shrug of one shoulder. "Unassuming, with an unexpected but pleasant bite that lasts a very long time. Why do you laugh? Have I misjudged you?"

"I don't know why it should be the case, but I think most people who know me would agree with you. Is this a talent you were born with? Matching individuals to the candy that best represents their personalities?"

"Oh, now I see," Evangeline said. "You are a cynic. Your training must be responsible, at least in part. I wonder if you can be cured?"

"Of cynicism? Others have tried," Carrie said, unable to banish her smile. "So where does this expert knowledge of candy come from, may I ask?"

"It's my father's business, confectionery and ice cream. Did you happen to visit the Grand Street Ice Cream Emporium in St. Louis?"

Carrie had not, and said so.

"Now, that's very sad. It's the best ice cream, truly." Evangeline picked up a fan of carved ivory and lace, snapped it open, and began to wave it vigorously so that they both benefited from the breeze. "He has a farm where he grows many of the plants he needs, and a laboratory to extract essences. He employs a chemist and a half dozen gardeners. There are three or four different types of mint, I believe. Are you interested in the essences? At home, doctors and healers sometimes ask for one thing or another. I've got most of them—" She began to rise from her chair, but Carrie stopped her with a raised hand. "It's good to know that you have them," she said. "But I don't need a demonstration just now. Do you make candy in Santa Fe to sell?"

With an elegant wave of her hand, Evangeline dismissed this idea. "The climate doesn't suit. This journey will last too far into the summer to risk taking these boxes further westward than Westport, so I sell it all there to a merchant who is always eager to have more. Enough of this silliness. Tell me, what do you want to know about Santa Fe?"

Caught off guard, Carrie shrugged. "What do I need to know?"

"Quite a lot. You must be wondering how you will be seen by the ladies of Santa Fe, so I'll state the obvious. They will be thrilled to welcome you. Most of them."

From this start Carrie had the sense that Evangeline would not sugarcoat the truth. "That sounds ominous."

"I can promise you this," Evangeline said. "You will find Santa Fe to be like any other small town, except it is really many different towns in one."

"Divided by?"

She seemed to weigh this question. "Any number of things. Not so much religion, as most of the territory is Roman Catholic. That number includes me and my son. My husband could not marry me unless and until I converted."

"Then I would guess color is a primary way the population is divided," Carrie said. "As it seems to be everywhere."

"Certainly, but you probably haven't considered how very complicated color can be. Among the Mexicans color and class and wealth are all jumbled together. Eli could probably explain it in detail if you ask him, but I can give you the key."

Carrie was truly interested in what Eva might have to say, and with her encouragement, the lecture went on. In Eva's understanding of things, the Spanish arrived and went about conquering Mexico not so much with bullets as with lifestyle. "The first job," she said, "was to impose Spanish culture and religion and laws on everyone here. And they did that job to perfection."

She paused, shaking her head. "The American army claimed thousands of acres, but the Spanish way of looking at things never changed. They put the Spanish first, any other white peoples next, then the Mestizos, who are just barely human. Below the Mestizos? Pueblo Indians. Below them, the rest of the tribes and Negroes."

Carrie said, "I'm not sure I get your point."

"It's simple. Before the Americans, white was white and brown was brown. White got all the privileges. Brown could get some privileges if they had enough white. Red and Black got nothing. Now the Americans have been in charge for ten years," she said. "And you know what? They still are arguing because they can't decide if Mexicans are white or brown. I've shocked you."

Carrie shook her head. "No, not in the least. I'm aware that economic theory and racism are often at odds, and when that's the case, money is all-powerful. There are so many Mexicans and Mestizos and Indians here, where would the merchant class be if not for these customers? And so what was formerly unacceptable, unworthy, unwholesome slowly improves. Mexicans wake up to find they are not brown, but white. I would love to talk to someone who has studied these issues closely, because I have had only newspapers to rely on, and newspapers can't be trusted."

Eva's smile was sad, but she got up, quite suddenly, and bent down to hug Carrie, a quick embrace as sisters often shared.

"I am so glad you'll be in Santa Fe. And there are many people for you to talk to, about anything that interests you. Starting with Eli."

"I will take your suggestion," Carrie said. "But it might be best if I wait until I've been in town for a few days at least. Then I think I'll be knocking on your door with so many questions you may regret your generosity. You belong to two of the towns-inside-the-town, after all."

"Three," Eva corrected her. "You mustn't forget that I married Carlos Zavala's heir. One day my son will be *patrón* of the Pontevedra Hacienda, in his father's place."

She stopped suddenly, as if she had recalled something that was deeply embarrassing.

"I shouldn't brag, and really, for you the simplest approach is to remember that Santa Fe has its fair share of good or bad people. We have some who are friendly and others who are as rude as the day is long. There will be some who look down on you though they have no cause, and some who will adore you—" She broke off with a smile.

"Whether or not I do anything to earn their adoration?"

"You understand me. Now, let me tell you about the Goldblums, you will like them. Or at least, most of them. Four brothers, married, with families. They are Jewish merchants, originally from Germany. Tomorrow I can tell you about the nuns, who you will not like as much."

Carrie decided to dive in. "And Mrs. Markham? Do you know her well?"

Evangeline pressed her mouth together and, at the same time, tried to smile. "Yes," she said after a pause. "I know both the Markhams quite well. You will be living with them, I know. Do you know very much about Indira?"

It seemed an unusual question, but at the same time Carrie was aware that the answer she must give was equally odd.

"I do not," she said. "Dr. Markham wrote very little about her in his letters. I will be living in her home, you're right. I should have inquired more closely."

Eva said, "I'll tell you what I can, but the truth is, nobody really knows her. Certainly no one understands her, not even the women who came west when she did."

Carrie saw that this conversation was not an easy one for Eva Zava-la, and that in itself was evidence that she could be trusted. Carrie would listen and try not to react.

Mrs. Markham, as Eva saw her, was an intelligent, gently reared woman of thirty years. She could be pleasant, her manners exacting, but was subject to swift changes of mood.

Carrie asked for clarification. "Do you mean she has a temper?"

Evangeline would not be pinned down to so simple an explanation.

"It's more than that. She will make a friend of someone—for example, Miriam Goldblum, when she first came to Santa Fe. And then one day she wanted nothing more to do with her. Miriam won't say what passed between them, but they were once close, and now Indira cuts her openly in public."

She was quiet for a moment, gathering her thoughts.

"I suppose really it comes down to a simple warning: She is by nature both suspicious and easily offended, and once offended, implacable in her resentment. She'll go so far as to seek retribution, whether the offense was real or imagined. In your shoes, I would keep some distance until you feel you can really trust her."

Carrie was unable to hide her disquiet, and Eva saw this.

"You are shocked by my indiscretion and unsure how to react. Of course. So you will observe Indira Markham and come to your own conclusions. You may decide that I am nothing more than a trouble-maker sowing discord, or—"

"I may come to the same conclusions," Carrie offered. "Has it occurred to you that I may not be trustworthy?"

Eva's smile was grim. "Yes, it did occur to me. I spent many hours thinking through all the possibilities. If you were to go to Mrs. Markham and repeat what I have said, it will make things awkward for me, that's true. But she has no real power over me, and awkward-ness will pass—" She broke off, and left the rest unspoken.

Carrie studied her for a moment, and saw that Eva was very able and willing to meet her eye. She wasn't agitated or flustered, and Car-rie's impression that the other woman was being truthful solidified.

She said, "I will share a confidence, if I may. Mrs. Markham will be in need of a midwife sometime in July. And that is why I sit here across from you."

Eva's mouth made a perfect circle of surprise. She turned to look out at the river, and then back again.

"That might be very good news, if she delivers a healthy child. Or—"

"Very bad news," Carrie offered. "If she does not."

Eva nodded.

"I worked with the poor in the city," Carrie said. "Women who are so malnourished and overworked that they lose one pregnancy after another. Some pretend nothing ever happened, some mourn the loss. Some are glad of it. In extreme cases a woman can be consumed by anger and moved to violence.

"My point," Carrie said, "is that Indira Markham will need my help, and that is the work I trained for. To help women in distress."

"So you are confident, despite her history of miscarriage?"

"Not confident," she said. "But I am experienced. Who did she have as midwife for her last confinement, do you know?"

Eva gave her a half smile. "Adelina Gray Wolf by name. From the San Juan Pueblo. She delivered Beto, and I consider her a saint. But Indira holds Adelina responsible for the last loss."

"You don't?"

"No," Eva said. "There were three other women present at the birth, and they are agreed that the child had died at least a few days before labor began."

This was a complicated and sensitive issue. Carrie would have to give it some thought before she asked more questions, or risk coming to the wrong conclusions. For now she shifted the topic.

"I'm still not entirely sure I understand how the word *pueblo* is being used. Do I understand correctly that it is just the Spanish word for village? As in, the village of San Juan?"

Evangeline was born and raised in Santa Fe and was pleased to talk about it. The Pueblos were a group of tribes, she explained. Distinct from the Apache and Navajo and other tribal families. Adelina

Gray Wolf was of the San Juan Pueblo, and so was Josefa, the Mark-hams' housekeeper.

"The nearest word I can think of to describe the relationship between the different pueblos is that they are something like clans. There are about twenty of them scattered throughout New Mexico Territory, mostly along the Rio Grande. Some farther west. Quite a few abandoned and in ruins. Each pueblo has its own history and customs and way of governing, but they will unite when they are threatened and go to war together."

"Do they all speak the same language?"

Eva shook her head. "There's some disagreement about this, but my understanding is that most of the tribes speak one of three dia-lects, all related. You know that Eli's mother belongs to the Jimenez Pueblo. He could tell you more."

Carrie wasn't ready to discuss Eli Ibarra, so she asked the more important question.

"How did the Markhams come to hire a housekeeper from the San Juan Pueblo in the first place?"

Eva's smile was open now, and no longer apologetic. "Josefa went to the convent school. She is a favorite of the nuns," she said. "I believe they recommended her when they heard Dr. Markham was looking for help. She's very smart and hardworking, and extraordinarily pretty. And—" She hesitated. "Indira Markham is more attached to Josefa than is good for either of them."

This was an unexpected turn. Carrie said, "Is she cruel or unfair with Josefa? Because she's Indian, or Roman Catholic?"

Eva lifted a shoulder and let it drop. "Indira doesn't like Indians, that is true, but there's something else off. Josefa herself has told me that she wanted to leave the Markhams almost since the day she came, but Indira won't have it."

Carrie could not hide her surprise. "They restrain her? Lock her up?"

"Oh no. It's far simpler and more effective than that. Sam Markham makes sure that Josefa's family lacks for nothing—"

"So she is as good as tied down," Carrie finished for Eva. "If she leaves the Markhams, her family is cut off."

Eva gave an almost reluctant nod.

"That was almost certainly not what you hoped to hear about the Markhams, but you will form your own opinions. As is right."

When Carrie stood to go, Eva pressed a packet into her palm.

"Peppermints," she said. "To end this visit on a sweeter note."

THE LATE AFTERNOON and early evening went by without another opportunity to talk to Nathan. He had made the acquaintance of a New Orleans lottery broker and would be busy draining the man of information until there was nothing more to learn from him, or he withdrew in self-defense.

Carrie went back to her own stateroom overflowing with questions about the Markhams that could not be answered.

It wasn't until the cold supper was laid out that Carrie saw Eva again. She and her boy were sitting with Eli Ibarra and the talkative Mrs. Hamblin, who was gesturing with both hands as if to describe something as big as a buffalo. That Eli Ibarra was sitting with them had nothing to do with Carrie's unwillingness to join the group; she had no reason to fear the man, after all. She would sit wherever she liked, and Eli and his winking eye could take themselves to the devil.

In the end she assembled a plate of fruit and cheese to eat alone. On the way to her stateroom she passed Nathan, who tilted his head at the plate and raised a brow. She waved him off toward the dining tables without explanation and closed herself up, content to be alone.

The stateroom was surprisingly pleasant as sunset drew closer. She ate, and then, with a breeze from the window dancing over her, Carrie drifted in and out of a light sleep, listening to snatches of conversation as passengers walked through the saloon or along the promenade, and trying to make sense of the various bells and whistles that the pilot used to communicate with the deck crew.

Two bells sounded and were followed by a pause—time enough to drop a weighted line into the river, she guessed—and then a man's voice called out in a deep singsong.

"Quarter twain!"

The reply came: "Half twain!"

First one leadsman and then another from opposite sides of the boat, she guessed, so that the two voices echoed back and forth.

More bells and then: "Mark three!"

Finally she got up to prepare for bed. Milly brought water and towels, and took away shoes to be cleaned and a skirt to be brushed and pressed.

Carrie climbed into the narrow bed, where she hoped to fall asleep right away, but her mind kept wandering back to Eva Zavala's stories of Santa Fe, and she reminded herself that soon she would get her own answers to the questions raised. Whether Eva's account would match her own experiences and observations must wait.

Eva was a white woman of means living in Santa Fe, and must have her own set of priorities and social expectations, after all. But Carrie's instincts told her that the situation was a difficult one that would have to be handled with caution.

Best to listen and withhold conclusions, but at the same time her mind insisted on comparing this new information with patients she had cared for at the New Amsterdam. Women undone by tragedy lost track of themselves for many different reasons and in different ways, whether rich or poor; some were consumed by anger and turned bitter and hard, and others became more religious and stricter in their observance. Some ran off. A few sought relief in death, and of those sad souls, some took their children with them.

Of course, she told herself: the women of New Mexico were just as strong and as fragile as women everywhere. She could imagine Amelie saying those exact words.

6

Monday, May 11, 1857

AT SEVEN THE next morning, Mrs. Ashby herself knocked on Carrie's door with an observation and a request. Apparently Miss Ballentyne was a trained nurse, and if that were indeed the case, would she be willing to look at some main deck passengers who were poorly?

Given what she knew of Mrs. Ashby, Carrie took a moment to consider.

"How many people? What symptoms?"

The lady's mouth pulled itself into a tight knot, but Carrie only waited.

"A family," she admitted in the end. "A married couple and three children. They may have et some bad fish, is what I was told. The usual symptoms."

"And I should treat them on the main deck?"

Another spasm of irritation crossed her face. "They didn't pay for anything else, but there were complaints, given the—" She cleared her throat. "Symptoms."

Carrie understood that the small family was suffering both vomiting and diarrhea, surrounded by the rest of the main deck passengers.

"I had them put in a junior officer's cabin," Mrs. Ashby went on. "It's very vexing, I must say. If there had been any sign of this a day ago, we wouldn't have allowed them to board. But we will fix that mistake this afternoon when we stop to take on wood."

Carrie kept her thoughts on this to herself and followed Mrs. Ashby up to the Texas deck. The captain's wife stopped outside a cabin with a door that was propped open with a bucket. The smell that wafted out had the unmistakable odor of unhealthy stool.

With her head averted, she spoke to Carrie. "I will send a boy to fetch and carry for you. How long do you think you'll need him?"

"Until they are out of danger," Carrie said. "Late tonight or more likely tomorrow forenoon. You do realize that their symptoms are not catching, unless you were to eat whatever this family ate."

Mrs. Ashby's nose twitched like a rabbit's. "It would never occur to me."

This was a woman who knew nothing of hunger, and could not imagine deprivation. Carrie said, "Please see to it that five gallons of hot and two gallons of cold water are brought here as soon as possible. The cold water must be potable, Mrs. Ashby."

The woman made a face, as if she had been called a name.

Carrie tried again. "Cold water suitable for drinking."

With that she opened the door so abruptly that the captain's wife almost stumbled in her hurry to get away.

IT WAS PAST noon before Carrie could catch her breath. In the tiny cabin where five people had finally fallen into an exhausted sleep, she leaned against the door, crossed her arms, and closed her eyes. She might have fallen asleep if not for the growling from her stomach.

"Nurse?"

As it turned out, Mrs. Finch was not sleeping. She looked at Carrie from her spot in the berth, bracketed by her two younger children.

Her husband and oldest boy slept on straw mats on the floor. All of them had been bathed—the men with the help of Thomas, the cabin boy—and wrapped in sheets, because their clothing could not be worn until it had been soaped and boiled. Two maids had come to take the laundry away an hour earlier and stayed to scrub the cabin from floor to ceiling while the whole family sat huddled together on the narrow bunk.

Carrie turned to look at Mrs. Finch more closely. "Yes? Can I get you something? Do you need the—"

"No, thank you. I'm as hollow as a drum. You have saved our lives, and we are indebted."

"I am glad to be of help." It was the usual thing to say—the only possible response—no matter how true or false it might be. In this case she might have told the truth: it hadn't been pleasant, but she had cared for people far worse off, with tragic outcomes. The Finch family would survive as long as they kept dehydration at bay, continued to sip at the winterseal and peppermint tea, and stayed away from three-day-old catfish. When she said as much, Mrs. Finch's whole face convulsed.

"No more catfish," she agreed. "Not even fresh caught."

Just then Thomas scratched at the door and brought in a great tureen, as if he knew that they had been talking about food.

"Clear broth," he said. "From Missy. The cook. She say, these folks soon be needing something with a little salt."

"And she is exactly right," Carrie agreed. "Please thank her for me."

He ducked his head. "Missy on her way up here her own self, ma'am. She say you could go, get something to eat and set awhile. They just now serving dinner in the saloon."

"Yes," Mrs. Finch said. "Please do go. If the cook is coming to help, we will be well looked after."

Carrie's stomach growled again, and Mrs. Finch smiled. "You see? You must go or faint for lack of nourishment."

Carrie considered her nursing apron, which covered her from neck to toe. It provided ample evidence of the morning's work, and so she stripped it off and went by way of the promenade to her stateroom. It was the polite and reasonable thing to do, and by chance it would also be a way to spare herself the curiosity and questions of the other passengers.

She scrubbed her hands and washed her face, adjusted a few hairpins, changed her shirtwaist, and went into the saloon to take her seat at the table. Her brother and Eli Ibarra were in the middle of a discussion of treaties and borders, but Eva was more interested in recent matters.

"Carrie," she said. "How are your patients?"

Eva might have rung a bell, so effective was this question in getting the attention of the others.

"Improving," Carrie said. She managed a quick smile. "Or I should say, not quite so miserable as they were at dawn. Thank you for inquiring."

The steward appeared with a platter of ham surrounded by fricasseed artichokes and scalloped potatoes. Luckily the saloon was quite noisy, so the growling of Carrie's stomach went unnoticed by everyone except her brother, who raised his brow but grinned.

While Carrie was occupied by the food, Eva turned to Eli and Nathan. "That poor family was fortunate that there was someone to look after them."

Carrie knew where Eva's imagination was going to take her, and so she interrupted. "It was nothing contagious," she said, raising her voice to make sure any eavesdroppers heard her. The mere hint of measles or typhoid would spread over the boat like wildfire and evoke the same panic. "They ate some bad fish."

Eva wrinkled her nose. "Unfortunate."

"Most illnesses are," Carrie said. "Nursing is not for the weak of stomach. The good news is that they will recover, unless Mrs. Ashby puts them off when we next stop for wood."

There was a short silence. Eli and Nathan exchanged glances, but Eva was less circumspect.

"Do you think she would?"

"She said she would, yes."

THE SWEET BLUE DISTANCE   101

"Well," Evangeline said, folding her napkin. "We'll just see about that. The captain's wife will listen to me. Or at least, to my pocketbook." And she stood and started for the head table, where Mrs. Ashby sat with her husband.

"Now you've done it," Eli said to Carrie. "She's always happiest when she has a dragon to slay."

Nathan said, "Mrs. Evangeline Zavala, a slayer of dragons?"

"And hardheaded about it. She married a Criollo," Eli said. "She converted because she had to, but she is always at war with Sister Agatha. That don't mean anything to you, but it will, soon enough."

"Oh, do tell," Nathan said. "Sister Agatha sounds promising."

Eli shook his head. "It's Carrie who needs to hear about Sister Agatha, and Evangeline herself who needs to tell it. I couldn't do it justice."

"Something to look forward to," Carrie said. "Eva's stories can be—"

"Exciting? Amusing?" her brother prompted.

"Alarming, is my guess." Eli picked up his knife and flourished it like a sword.

Carrie nodded. "Amusing and alarming both. Santa Fe is more mysterious with every mile."

"You and me, we should talk," Eli said.

Carrie took longer than she needed to swallow, and then managed an unremarkable tone. "When I am finished with the Finch family, we can have that conversation. Possibly tomorrow."

And she was very careful not to look at her brother.

On her way back to the Texas deck, Carrie heard her name and saw that Beto Zavala was waving at her from the corner, where a few other young children were being watched by a nursemaid.

"Will you come and say hello?" he called. "I am very bored."

Carrie knew she should not encourage his antics, but the truth was that she could not scold Beto—or any child—for his honesty when it harbored no ill will. She took a seat near the playgroup, and he came to sit beside her. "It's all right," he assured her. "As long as the nursemaid can see me, I can sit and talk to you."

"I don't have any way to entertain you, I fear."

Both dark brows lifted in surprise. "But you do. You can tell me about medicine."

The conversation that followed fit into a pattern. The boy asked questions: he wanted to know the difference between a disease and illness and sickness, why blood was sticky, why a fever scared his mother, which sicknesses Carrie had seen for herself, and how many broken bones.

Carrie answered the primary question and then attempted to provide details, where she thought it prudent. His last question gave her pause.

"Have you seen children die?"

A little boy as intelligent as this one would know she was lying if she claimed she had never seen a child die, but if she told the truth, he may well have nightmares. His mother would not thank her for putting such images in his head. She took another approach and told him about young Michael Reynolds, seven years old, who had a very sore throat and a fever that alarmed his parents. She had been assigned the case and spent a full day in the household.

"What sickness did you think Michael Reynolds might have?"

Simple truths were the best choice, Carrie told herself. "Scarlatina."

Beto nodded. "What medicines did you give him?"

Carrie had the sense that he would come back to this question repeatedly if she did not answer, and so she told him: warm salt water for gargling, tea with honey, broth, and things he could swallow without much difficulty. And then she told him the rest of it.

"But his Auntie Mabel thought he needed more to eat, so she sent out for ice cream. Because, she said, it would be soothing and nourishing."

He thought this over. "Did the ice cream cure him?"

Surprised, Carrie looked closely and saw that the question was serious. "Do you think ice cream could cure an illness?"

"No," said the boy. "Probably not. But it would make him happy."

"Exactly," Carrie agreed. "His auntie came and fed him spoonfuls of ice cream all through the day, but the next day his throat was still very sore."

Beto's agile mind jumped ahead. "And so he got more ice cream."

"He did. Until I came later that day. The swelling and redness had gone away—"

"Fever?"

She shook her head. "None at all. But he insisted that his throat was still very, very sore. It was a mystery, but only until Aunt Mabel came in with a dish of ice cream and all was made clear."

His grin fairly split his face in two. "That was naughty."

"It was, I agree."

"He didn't get any more ice cream?"

Carrie wasn't sure of this; in fact, she wouldn't have been surprised to learn that the Reynoldses' only son had insisted on more ice cream and got it once she was out the door.

"Do you think he deserved more?"

Beto pushed out a sigh. "No."

"Who doesn't deserve ice cream?"

Carrie recognized the voice and stopped herself from turning to see Eli Ibarra, who had come up to stand behind the settee she shared with Beto.

"A little boy called Michael," said Beto. "Miss Ballentyne was telling me about him. He tricked his auntie into giving him ice cream. She has lots of interesting stories about being a nurse."

Carrie cleared her throat. "I'm sure your uncle has interesting stories to tell. I don't know anything about ranching. Or sheep, for that matter."

Beto turned his face up to the uncle he so clearly adored. "But you're not a rancher, not anymore."

"Beto is right." Eli Ibarra circled around to take a seat opposite them. "I gave up ranching almost a decade ago."

"Really," Carrie said, and forged ahead with the obvious question. "I have to go soon, but first, maybe Mr. Ibarra will explain why he went to Europe to buy stock if he isn't ranching anymore."

The question didn't surprise or unsettle him.

"It was my job, once," he said. "I went every few years with my father or my uncle to see about stock, the first time when I was nine. But my brothers are taking over, and they needed the experience."

The conversation might have stuttered to a stop right then, simply because there were so many questions swirling in Carrie's head that she couldn't pin one down. She was glad that Beto was not so impaired.

"Uncle Eli's a topagafigal engineer," the boy said, with great pride. "He can measure anything, and he draws maps."

"That's almost right, Beto. I'm a topographical engineer," Ibarra said. "And it's true, I draw maps."

"Are you with the army engineering corps, then?" Carrie asked.

His head tilted, as if he didn't quite understand. "You're familiar with the corps?"

"My brother follows the progress of the surveys in the papers. It's one of his many interests. Another subject he would love to explore."

"I'll add it to the list." He gave a small shake of the head, out of amusement or resignation. Her brother had already made a reputation for himself, and while some people avoided him because they tired of his curiosity, Eli Ibarra seemed to take it in stride.

"I started my training as an assistant to Amiel Whipple, on two surveys. First when he charted the border with Mexico and then one of the possible Southern Railway routes. But I didn't go to West Point, so I had limited opportunities with the corps. Now I'm independent."

Beto put a hand on Ibarra's wrist. "But you haven't told the most important part." With great gravitas he explained to Carrie. "Uncle Eli has a telescope and a zenith sector and a transit instrument and—"

"Whoa," Eli Ibarra said, holding up one hand, palm out. "Miss Ballentyne has got no need for a full inventory, Beto. And what will you do if she asks you to explain to her what a zenith sector is?"

Carrie said, "That is not the first question that comes to mind, but I am interested. And my brother—"

"I was getting around to raising the subject with Nathan," he said. "I just have to summon up the energy."

That made her smile. "He does have an inexhaustible appetite for information about anything mechanical or scientific." She was thinking about returning to her patients when he asked his own question.

"You still looking for a Spanish tutor?"

Beto jumped up, his hands clasped together as if he were about to recite a prayer. "You want to learn Spanish, Miss Ballentyne?"

"Yes, I need to learn Spanish," Carrie said. "Would you care to tutor me?" Neatly sidestepping whatever Eli meant to suggest or offer.

"Wait, let me ask Mama." With that, he shot off, and Carrie, laughing to herself, got up to go. Eli Ibarra stopped her by simply ignoring her wish to end the conversation.

"His Spanish is fluent," he said. "Native, really. He spends a lot of time with his grandfather. The old man speaks no English. In New Mexico the *patrón* is the one who makes the rules on his rancho, and in this case, no English is allowed."

Now he leaned forward, his wrists on his knees and his hands folded together. As if he were about to teach a lesson, Carrie thought, but he had an easy way about him that was very engaging. In a few minutes he sketched out the history of Spain's occupation of the Southwest, the way trade tied Mexico to the Sangre de Cristo mountain villages, and how Spaniards adapted their architectural customs to the climate.

"You mean adobe? Mud and straw bricks, cured in the sun?"

"To start," he said. "The first haciendas, the oldest ones, are built to keep hostiles out. All the rooms open onto a *placita*—an inner courtyard, I've heard it called. Not a single window facing out, and very few doors that open to the outside."

"Like a military fort," Carrie said. "I imagine that was necessary. I'm sure the tribes were not happy about Europeans moving into their territory. Our histories, east and west, are not so different when it comes to the tribes. And now I need to check on the Finch family."

"No, wait," he said. "I'd like to know what you said just earlier. What was the first question that came to mind?"

Carrie looked at him directly and saw that he was serious.

She said, "I don't follow."

"I asked if you wanted to hear about the zenith sector, and you said, 'That is not the first question that comes to mind.' So what was the first question?"

Oddly enough his calm manner and even tone made it impossible for Carrie to deflect what was, in essence, a very forward and almost rude question. She understood that Eli Ibarra would be persistent to the point of mulishness when something interested him. As she seemed to interest him.

She hoped he would be content with a half-truth.

"I don't know," she said. "I can't remember what I was thinking."

The corner of his mouth lifted; he was not content, but he was intrigued. "So," he said, and lowering his voice, he inclined his head toward hers. "*Puede que no lo recuerde, señorita, sin embargo, puedo adivinar.*"

7

WHILE SHE WAS busy in the little cabin where the Finch family were recovering, Carrie's mind kept returning to that last exchange. The truth was she had been studying a Spanish grammar since January. More than that, Spanish was closely related to French and Latin, both of which she had studied closely. She was making good progress with Spanish in the abstract way one learned a language from a formal grammar. Certainly less stressful than studying with her Latin tutor, an exacting and cheerless taskmaster.

On Thursday, she could remember him saying in an almost acid tone, *you will be prepared to discuss the second book of* De Divinatione.

And she did recall Cicero's *On Divination* quite clearly, even now. Not that she particularly cared about its arguments against superstition, but much of the essay was stuck in her head, for better or worse. Her memory was both curse and blessing; her mind held on to things she would have gladly surrendered. Then she could not deny the advantage it was to never dread long lists of French—or Latin, or Spanish—irregular verbs. They sank into her brain and stuck there, pinned tight. The phrase *puedo adivinar*, for example, brought *On Divination* immediately to mind.

"We should have named you Mnemosyne," her mother liked to tease. "The Greek goddess of memory would claim you as a daughter, I'm sure." Then she would touch her cheek to Carrie's and say, "But I'm not about to let you go."

Ma, Carrie wanted to say. *Ma, what now?*

Here was the problem: Carrie had understood Eli Ibarra; she recognized every one of the verbs he had used. Her mind offered up a translation she could not refuse: *You may not remember, miss, but I can guess.* She understood, and he knew that she did.

She interested him, and he was thinking about her. Whether she wanted him to or not. Now she made herself a promise. When she could ask in Spanish, she would put that question to him: *What does it mean that you wink at me?*

8

DEEP IN THE fourth night on board the *Annabelle*, a fight broke out when a banker from Chicago complimented a lottery broker from New Orleans for his uncommon good luck at cards.

Carrie heard the story at breakfast from Mrs. Hamblin, who heard it from the captain's wife and was enjoying passing it along.

Eva said, "Northern sarcasm generally triggers Southern retribution. Especially these days."

Carrie was just relieved that nobody had come to ask her to tend the injured.

"They got Dr. Day out of bed," Mrs. Hamblin said. "And oh, the scowls. Mumbling under his breath the whole time he saw to their wounded pride."

"And now I have to wonder why Nathan hasn't joined us for breakfast," Eva said. "Carrie, do you think he's among the wounded?"

"Unlikely." Carrie laid her fork and knife across her plate, her appetite satisfied. "I would be surprised if he let himself get drawn into a fight. My guess is that he had too much to drink and won't show his face until midmorning."

"I note that the Ibarra heir isn't here, either," Mrs. Hamblin said to Eva. "Any idea why?" There was the hint of a sour grin at the corner of her mouth.

"None," Eva said. "And now you'll have to excuse me, I need to find my son and make sure he isn't making a nuisance of himself with the nursemaids."

Eva walked off without another word, her dignity intact, but her irritation plain to see.

"Are you going to run off too?" Now Mrs. Hamblin was angry, and her tone went harsh. "Just because I mentioned the man's name? He's not all that handsome."

To Carrie it seemed that Mrs. Hamblin was less and less able to hide her animosity. She saw now that the old woman truly disliked both Eli Ibarra and Evangeline Zavala and had been waiting for the opportunity to vent her temper. Generally, Carrie liked old women and was glad to spend time with them, but a person so sour was best avoided.

The smart thing to do would be to politely excuse herself from the table and the conversation, and still she hesitated. Curiosity was ever her downfall.

She said, "Mrs. Hamblin, my father had no patience with us as children when we showed too much curiosity about private matters. If I was too intrusive and unwilling to retreat, he'd wait until I was near a river or lake, and drop me in."

"Ha!" Mrs. Hamblin laughed. "Did that stop you?"

"Yes." And then she conceded: "For a while. Eventually."

"Do I understand that you are tempted to toss me overboard, Miss Ballentyne?"

A tickle of agitation made her swallow. "Yes," she said. "I think *tempted* would be the right word."

The thin upper lip curled to reveal a dark eyetooth, and then settled. "Then speak plainly, would you?"

Carrie considered for a moment. Mrs. Hamblin's expression was alert, her eyes bright with anticipation. Like someone who was anticipating a long-overdue dose of laudanum.

"Very well," she began. "I wonder why you find it necessary to tease Mrs. Zavala. It's clear that the subjects you raise distress her."

One sparse white eyebrow climbed high, and Mrs. Hamblin shook her head slowly. She reminded Carrie of an angry teacher disappointed with her student's inability to see an obvious truth.

"You've got the wrong end of that stick, Miss Ballentyne. She's not distressed. Indeed not. She's embarrassed. She was not the kindest young lady in Santa Fe. In fact I would say that she had a taste for cruelty and was—"

She stopped only because Eli Ibarra had appeared at the end of the table.

"She was what?" Eli spoke directly to Mrs. Hamblin, his tone calm but chilly.

"Oh, come now." She flicked her fingers at him. "You know exactly what I mean. She was haughty and conceited at seventeen. You may have forgiven her, but she led you around by the nose for a year before she accepted your best friend."

Eli's hands gripped the top rail of the chair in front of him so that his knuckles went pale, but his voice remained calm.

"What I remember," he began slowly, "is that your Gordon proposed to her at least once a month during that same year, and would not take no for an answer. No matter how politely it was put."

Mrs. Hamblin cleared her throat in a short burst, disapproval surfacing like a rash over her throat and cheeks.

"Oh, and you never made an offer?"

"I did not."

The man had a temper, but Carrie was glad that he resisted being goaded.

"But you wanted her," Mrs. Hamblin shot back. "All the young men wanted her."

What Mrs. Hamblin wanted was an argument, but Eli Ibarra was going to deny her that.

"Eva Roberts has been my friend since we were children in school," he began. "When your sons wanted nothing to do with my kind."

He gave a short bow of the shoulders to Carrie—and Carrie alone—and walked away.

"The impudence!" Mrs. Hamblin sputtered, her chin trembling. "The effrontery! Now you see why we left Santa Fe, Miss Ballentyne. The Mestizos are the roughest, rudest—" She broke off to fumble her handkerchief from her sleeve and press it to her mouth.

Carrie should have walked away, but instead she waited. She waited in part because she feared the old lady would suffer some kind of crisis, but she also waited because Mrs. Hamblin was not finished. She had more to say, and no matter how insulting or derogatory it turned out to be, it was always an advantage to know what people—especially those who were prone to striking out—were thinking. Carrie took a glass and poured water from the pitcher on the table. Passing it to Mrs. Hamblin, she watched closely as the older woman sipped and her coloring returned to normal. Finally she touched a hand to her forehead, as if to take her own temperature.

A determined look came over her as she turned on her chair to face Carrie more directly. The chin still trembled.

"I am sure no one has dared to tell you the truth about Santa Fe, but I will. You should know what you are getting yourself into, and be warned about two things. First and foremost, the stranglehold the Church of Rome has on it, and second—"

"Mrs. Hamblin—"

The old lady held up a palm. "Do not interrupt me, Miss Ballentyne. I'm going to start with Ibarra's mother, as you are so clearly friends. Doña Altagracia Ibarra. Her mother is from the Jimenez Pueblo, and her father—who knows? A *cibolero*, probably. White, almost certainly. Then she married a Basque sheep farmer, a blackamoor if I've ever seen one."

Carrie was generally good at controlling her temper; a nurse had to learn to keep her opinions to herself. Then again, Mrs. Hamblin deserved no such courtesy.

She said, "All this is irrelevant, Mrs. Hamblin, and more important, it's none of my business. Or yours."

"It is your business, if you expect to survive living among Indians.
You'll have to deal with the Pueblos, slow-witted, stubborn, lazy. Of
course even they need policing. Last time was about ten years ago,
when the army put down the revolt at Taos. That sorry business came
about because the Pueblos and the Mestizos put their heads together
and decided they could drive whites out of the territory. You think
they won't try again? Be careful or your head will end up on a pike."

Carrie could see there wasn't any way to interrupt her, and so she
composed her expression.

"And now remember Don Diego is Basque, and the Basque are
papists. Puppets of Rome. Slaves to their priests." Her whole face contorted in disgust. "It's an ungodly mess, and I'm glad to be out of it."

Her eyes narrowed. "You find me amusing, I see."

Carrie could only shake her head, but it was the wrong response.
She wondered if she could have said anything to cut off this unholy
rant.

"You think you're ready for the territories? For Indians? You have
no idea. Before you even get to Santa Fe there's a good chance you'll
see your brother scalped and tortured. Then they'll pair you with the
Comanche who cut off his privates, and you'll have him on top of you
every night. Then you'll understand."

She quivered with indignation, and more than that: a deep satisfaction.

"Mrs. Hamblin," Carrie said. "My mother's grandparents were at
the siege of Fort William Henry, almost a hundred years ago now.
They survived the massacre that followed, but many—including family members, both white and red—did not. Their son, my Grandfather Nathaniel, married three times. His second wife was Mohawk.
His daughter by that marriage, my Aunt Hannah, married into the
Seneca. She cared for wounded Iroquois at more battles than you can
comprehend. I am very familiar with the damage human beings of all
races inflict on one another," Carrie said. "At the same time, I reject

your blanket denunciation of whole nations of people, and I will listen to no more of it."

The old woman's whole frame began to shake with indignation. "You'll end up a papist!" she hissed. "Just like Eva Roberts."

"Maybe so," Carrie said. "But at least I'll never be a small-minded, pretentious, mean-spirited bigot."

She willed herself to walk away at a normal pace without looking back.

As soon as she closed her cabin door behind herself, Carrie began to shake. She folded her hands together and sat down, drew one deep breath and then another, and kept on that way until her racing heart settled.

At least Mrs. Hamblin no longer lived in Santa Fe. There would be others like her, of course, and Carrie would have to find a way to deal with them. A way that allowed her to do her work without sacrificing beliefs basic to her understanding of the world and her own role in it.

When Carrie was just eleven, her Bonner grandparents had died within a few months of each other. At the time she could not imagine anything worse than losing them, but her sorrow had been undercut, strangely enough, by the book her Grandmother Elizabeth had bequeathed to her.

What was she—at such a young age—to make of *Groundwork of the Metaphysics of Morals*? But her parents had assured her that the gift was purposeful.

"She saw something in you," her Da said. "When you're old enough to read and understand Kant, you will see the connection."

If they had ordered her to read the book, she would have balked, but instead her clever Da had suggested that it was beyond her. She had tackled the tiny print the very same day, working often sentence by sentence. She was almost twenty when she began to believe she understood, at least in part. Now the problem with the categorical imperative seemed obvious to Carrie: normal people had tempers. Keeping her own temper in check was a challenge, and she sometimes failed. Today her temper had been summoned by Mrs. Hamblin's malicious condemnation.

If she wanted to meet such an outpouring of scorn and bigotry with a calm, rational response, she would have to learn how to bypass her own anger. Now the fingers of her left hand folded in to trace a scar—a raised welt faded to pink—that bisected her palm.

She should not regret her plain speech, she told herself, but knew, too, that in the end, regret would find her. Mrs. Hamblin was not the type to keep Carrie's recounting of her family history to herself.

9

Thursday, May 14, 1857

THAT EVENING AND the next morning, there was no sign of Mrs. Hamblin in the grand saloon. Carrie had begun to imagine dire repercussions of their conversation. She even considered asking Mrs. Ashby to stop by Mrs. Hamblin's stateroom to see if she needed assistance.

By midmorning Beto had noticed her distraction and asked if she was unwell.

Eva agreed. "Your attention keeps fading away from *Commerce of the Prairies*," she said. "And I was finding Mr. Gregg's ideas about education quite ... interesting ..."

Nathan was saying, "It's especially odd that female education should put my sister to sleep. I'm sure the Grand Elizabeth will show up in her dreams to scold her. You are supposed to be following in her footsteps, sister."

Eva smiled, delighted that there was someone in the family who had earned such a title. "What is so grand about this Elizabeth, may I ask?"

"Elizabeth Middleton Bonner. Our grandmother and an extraordinary person. I forget which cousin started calling her Grand."

"Not just Grand," Nathan added. "I always think of her as Grandy."

"I think it was Cousin Robbie," Carrie said. "He was always finding new names for things and people. He called Grandda Nathaniel 'Grumpy.'"

"Still does," Nathan said.

"But what about the Grand Elizabeth?" Beto wanted to know. "Was she a princess?"

While Nathan told Beto about the grandmother who had dedicated her life to educating girls and breaking her husband out of jail, Carrie worked out for herself exactly what she should say to Mrs. Ashby about Mrs. Hamblin. She had just resolved to ask Eva for her opinion, when she looked up and saw that the older lady had come into the saloon to stand a few feet away. She focused on Carrie, her expression grim.

"Mrs. Hamblin." There was surprise and disapproval in Eva's tone, but she produced the smile that was expected of her. "*Buenos días*. Are you well?"

Mrs. Hamblin sniffed, face averted, and continued on her way just as the captain appeared at the front of the saloon and raised both hands in a request for attention.

"A few moments of your time, please," he called. "Just a few moments."

"Is all well, Captain?" called a deep voice.

And from the opposite corner: "You are causing the ladies a fright, sir."

An elderly woman who sat with her husband laughed. "Just the ladies, Mr. Hobart?"

The captain bowed in her direction. "Believe me, Mrs. Larson, there is no cause for alarm." He grasped his lapels and began to rock back and forth on his heels. "We have made excellent time on this journey. Excellent."

"Now we'll hear five minutes about what should not alarm us,"

Nathan muttered. "I hope he gets to his point soon." As if to agree, his stomach gave a loud growl.

Carrie might have made a comment about sleeping through breakfast, but first Eva leaned in close and pitched her voice low.

"He always does this. I predict a boiler needs the attention of engineers at Arrow Rock," she said. "And the first place he'll look for them will be at Wink's Saloon."

"A steamboat is a complicated vessel," the captain was saying. "And it requires constant inspection and maintenance. The engineers at Arrow Rock are the finest in the country, and they will make sure all is in perfect working order before we set out again on the last stage of our journey."

Eva raised a brow, and Nathan inclined his head in acknowledgment of her predictive powers.

"Fortunately," the captain said, rocking with more force now. "Fortunately Arrow Rock is a very pretty little town, very hospitable, and the weather is fine."

Eva whispered, "I hope you will all take the opportunity for a stroll in the fresh air."

The captain echoed her, almost word for word.

Eli was giving Eva a very stern look, or trying to. Like a teacher who knew better than to laugh at a student's antics, but was close to giving in. She shrugged in response, and in that moment it came to Carrie that these two were like brother and sister. The loss of the man who was her husband and his close friend had bound them together in a way that was more dependable and lasting than a casual romantic attachment. If things went on as they had begun with Eva, Carrie might one day hear more of the story, but she didn't know if that was something to hope for.

The captain had finished answering questions and signaled to the stewards to begin the dinner service. There was little talk until Nathan had cleared his plate for the second time. Then he sat back and smiled, his gaze shifting from Eli to Eva. "So," he said. "An afternoon in

Arrow Rock. I expect you two have suggestions on how we might entertain ourselves."

Arrow Rock existed, it seemed, only to serve the demands of travelers on the Missouri River. There were warehouses along the wharf and slaves who moved hemp and tobacco and barrels of salt back and forth from warehouses to docks to steamers. But mostly the town was there for emigrants headed west.

Originally the trail to Santa Fe had begun right here, Eva told her as they walked up the road to the town proper. Many did still set out from this point.

"Eager to get off the Missouri as soon as possible," Carrie suggested, and Eva nodded in agreement.

The town was small, but at the same time well-developed. The streets were wide and leveled and lined with stone gutters. A large and very busy tavern was the first business they encountered. From a side yard came the unmistakable smells of beef roasting over an open fire, which Nathan noted was a better advertisement than even the biggest and most colorful sign.

From what they could see, all the trades were well established in Arrow Rock. Anything a party of emigrants might need could be had here: a wagon repaired, a horse shod, new boots or aprons or martingales, dried beans and jerky, tinned sardines, hogsheads of molasses, tools and hardware, saltpeter and bullet molds.

Eva and Beto disappeared into a mercantile, but Carrie walked on with her brother and Eli Ibarra.

Beyond the shops were farms and large holding pens for cattle, mules, and oxen, bordering fields and pastures where dairy cows or pigs grazed, feasting on early grass and wildflowers. The men working in a cornfield were all dark-skinned. A white man sat on horseback in the shade of an oak tree, watching over them.

Everyone went about their day, Black and white, slave and slaveholder, as if it were the most natural thing in the world. Carrie wondered if in time she would forget to be outraged; if the roiling in her gut would subside in the end. It was a horrible thought, a betrayal of herself she could not imagine.

Nathan said, "Eli, you never did explain the name of this place." And then: "Where are you going now?"

Over his shoulder Eli Ibarra answered, "To the bluff, so you can see the answer for yourselves."

Carrie hesitated. It might be wise to go back and join Eva, but Nathan, reading her mind, scowled.

"Oh, come on." He took her by the elbow and propelled her in the opposite direction. "You aren't interested in shopping. Not with the sun shining and a winding path to follow."

She couldn't deny that she enjoyed walking in such fine weather, and so she followed along the narrow track that led up and up. It was her intention to concentrate on the landscape so that she could write something sensible in her neglected travel diary. She could describe the forest they walked through, the squirrels scolding as they passed, a waddling porcupine, the birds that clicked and sang and chattered and drummed: cardinals, grosbeaks, warblers, buntings, orioles, woodpeckers, and others that were unfamiliar to her.

She realized that Nathan and Eli were discussing the local tribes, and slowed her pace to better listen.

"Most of the Osage are well south of here now," Eli was saying. "But if you wanted to run into one, the bluffs would be the place to look. The old uncles who still knap flints for their arrows come here."

"Really?" Nathan's interest was unmistakable. "Where, exactly?"

"Straight ahead."

He took off without another word.

"Pardon my brother," Carrie said. "His enthusiasm often overrides common sense and good manners."

"He is stuffed to the gills with curiosity," Eli agreed. "But over a rock field?"

The path had narrowed, so they had to walk single file, with Eli in the rear.

"Flint knapping is something he learned to do as a boy," she said, turning her head rather than raise her voice to be heard. "He practices whenever he gets a chance."

A soft grunt of surprise. "Why would Nathan Ballentyne of New York City even know how to knap flint?"

There was nothing but simple curiosity in his tone, but Carrie heard the question he might have asked: Why would a white man of good fortune bother with the long, arduous process of making weapons?

The fact that he kept this thought to himself pleased her. She was beginning to believe that Eli was one of the rare men who didn't make assumptions. He waited, and she had the sense that he wouldn't be offended if she didn't answer his question. On that basis she decided to tell him at least some of the story. Better that he hear it from her than from Mrs. Hamblin.

"When we were young," she began, "we lived in a village in the Adirondack Mountains, not far from Canada. All the men in the family, my father and grandfather, the uncles and cousins, hunted and trapped, even the ones who learned a trade or studied. They all had a part in teaching us how to handle weapons and shoot. Uncle Daniel taught me how to throw a knife, but it was Uncle Gabriel who insisted that we learn how to use a bow and arrow."

He made a low sound in his throat, one she took to mean that she should go on with the story. She glanced at him over her shoulder.

"You see, my Grandfather Bonner's second wife was Mohawk, so my Aunt Hannah is half-Mohawk, and Uncle Gabriel's wife is Mohawk. We grew up with Mohawk cousins and uncles and aunts."

She paused to gather her thoughts, something she should have done with Mrs. Hamblin. Eli waited, no sign of impatience from him.

"Uncle Gabriel and Aunt Annie keep mostly to the old ways. We spoke Mohawk at their table, for example. The men have rifles and steel traps, but Uncle Eli and his son still use the old weapons and tools too. He likes to say that running out of gunpowder shouldn't mean that you starve to death. So we learned to hunt without guns."

"And to make your own arrowheads?"

"That was Nathan's idea. He kept asking about it, so Uncle Gabriel took him to spend a week with the Wolf clan at Good Pasture. Nathan was just eight, but he came back with a sackful of arrowheads. Really good ones too. Well made."

"I would guess there's not much bowhunting in the city." His tone was casual, but Carrie could tell that he found her story hard to believe.

She lifted her skirts and stepped over a tangle of roots. "That's true. Once we moved to Manhattan, he didn't get much opportunity, but once in a while he goes off to hunt on Bear Mountain or to Long Island with some of the cousins. He takes a rifle and a bow." She hesitated and then added, "The men in my family have always been famous for their marksmanship."

"And you?"

She bit back a smile. "Generally I hit what I aim at. Is this where we're headed?"

They had come to the edge of a clearing that stretched out to bluffs overlooking the Missouri, but Carrie stayed just where she was, at the edge of the forest. It was an extraordinarily pretty spot with blossoming redbud, dogwood, and wild plum trees interspersed among evergreens, like girls in party dresses being kept in line by sober matrons.

Nathan was the only person in sight. Now he turned toward them, holding up a good-sized rock. It had been split in two to expose the inner surface, glassy grays and dark slate colors melding.

"Of course they call this place Arrow Rock," he called out to them. "Give me an hour and see how many arrowheads I can take away. Just as soon as I find a good hammerstone."

Eli was already crossing the field, taking something from his belt and offering it to Nathan. There was a discussion she couldn't make out, but in the end the two men crouched down and got to work striking thin sheets of flint. Her brother would stay right where he was until he was forced to return to the *Annabelle*, and from the set of Eli Ibarra's shoulders, she thought he would too.

Left to her own devices, Carrie walked the edge of the field, surprising two red fox cubs that scampered away into the underbrush.

She found a large enough rock to sit on comfortably, one overhung by a few redbud trees. From that spot she studied the deep magenta blossoms and saw that they were near their end. A scattering drifted down on a breeze to land on her shoulders and lap.

It was a memory straight from her childhood, playing among the *aweriásha* trees with her cousins, before she had learned the English word. The women harvested the blossoms to make dye, but the children were more interested in eating as many as they could catch. *Aweriásha* buds were quite sweet, with just a little tang.

Now she ate a few, and for her trouble was overcome by a wave of homesickness. She stood abruptly and walked to the far side of the field, where the edge of the bluff gave her a better view of the Missouri and the streams that fed into it. A red-tailed hawk coasted overhead on warm air currents, watching for chipmunks or rabbits, and below, a steamer navigated the twists and turns of the river.

Sometimes when the *Annabelle* stopped for provisions and wood, there were as many as four steamers waiting their turns. At least twice a day they crossed paths with a steamer going in the opposite direction, but the steamboat she was watching was traveling upriver, toward the Arrow Rock docks.

It occurred to her now that there was something off.

There was smoke coming from the stacks, and more smoke that came from the bowels of the main deck. On all three decks people were moving erratically, back and forth.

As she watched, a man rushed to the railing, dragging a valise behind him. Without pausing he climbed the rail, teetered for a moment at the top to regain his balance, and leapt. In the next second he had disappeared into the muddy waters of the Missouri, and two more people followed him.

A shrill whistling rent the air, it seemed from everywhere at once.

Six, seven . . . a dozen people leapt into the river as Nathan and Eli came up behind her. She watched a woman leap, her pale blue skirts catching the wind to billow up over shoulders and head as she hit the water.

Without looking away Carrie reached for her brother's arm. "What is happening?"

"I don't know," Nathan said. "Eli?"

"She's about to . . . there she goes."

A fireball shot up, chased by a series of explosions as deep and solemn as strikes on a bass drum. Woodwork and machinery shot into the sky and then rained down on the sinking steamer, on the people in the river, on the riverbanks.

Carrie stepped back and tried to turn away at the same time, feet scrambling for purchase on the rocks. She felt herself tipping. Nathan's fingertips brushed her shoulder, but too late.

As she went down, Carrie watched cinders falling and thought of the *Annabelle*, roosting at the dock like a sleepy hen while a fox closed in.

10

She said, "Nathan Ballentyne, you are being ridiculous."

Carrie meant to sound calm and resolute, but while she was sprinting down a forest trail behind her brother, she could manage only to sound like a scold.

Nathan said, "But—"

"No," Carrie said, struggling not to raise her voice. "I don't need or want to be carried. Watch your feet!"

He came to a full stop so suddenly that she almost ran into him.

"But your head is bleeding!"

"You are being ridiculous. Nathan, it's just a scratch."

Behind them Eli said, "I'm going ahead. There's a shortcut. Follow me if you like, but it's steep and rocky and I ain't taking it slow."

They turned to face him and saw that he would not wait for even five seconds. Nathan paused as Eli started away.

"Go," she said. "You're a strong swimmer, you can help."

He threw her an exasperated scowl, and then he set off to follow Eli.

It took her another quarter hour to get to town, where it seemed every human being in a few hundred miles had come together, most of them headed for the river. While she stood there trying to get her bearings, four men trotted past with a very large, very still form on a litter. They turned toward a neat clapboard house where a doctor's shingle hung. Other still forms, small and large, had been laid out in a row and covered with a tarpaulin.

Carrie approached a man standing at the gate. He wore a badge and the studiously detached expression of a lawman.

"Sir?"

He inclined his head, one brow peaking.

"I am Carrie Ballentyne, a trained nurse. You are—"

"Sheriff." He studied her face as if he thought he should recognize her, and then shrugged. "Sheriff McNamara."

"I would like to help. May I offer my services to the doctor?"

Sheriff McNamara was not encouraging.

"There ain't much for you to do here, miss. We got three doctors in town, and all of 'em have nurses." The cheroot tucked into his beard bobbed ponderously.

In her surprise Carrie couldn't think of how to respond, but he had more to say.

"You're bleeding your own self. You need to see the doc?"

"It's a scratch," Carrie said, clamping down hard on her aggravation.

The cheroot shifted to the other side of the gap in his beard. "Am I right thinking you must have come off the *Annabelle*? You know she skedaddled?"

This brought Carrie up short. "What?"

"She just went upriver a ways to keep clear of the fire and fuss. Joe McCarthy's running the ferry, you just got to show up down there and he'll tote you straight back to your steamer."

Carrie hesitated. "I don't want to press, but I am fully trained and this seems a very bad situation. It seems wrong to just walk away, if I could be of help—"

The cheroot bobbed, dribbled ash, and settled. "That's kind of you, but this ain't unusual, not on the Missouri. So you go on ahead, get back to the *Annabelle*. And watch out for yourself, miss. Life is cheap on the Missouri, that's the truth. Keep heading west and it only gets cheaper."

There was no sign of Nathan or Eli, though Carrie took time to search for them along the riverbank, where people were still being pulled from the water, most of them beyond help. The ferry was there, and the ferryman was watching her.

"It will be an hour before I set out again," he called to her. "You can wait if you want to, or step up now. Folks, move together, would you. Make space for one more."

It seemed she didn't have many options, and so Carrie stepped onto the ferry. She had to suck in her breath to avoid the men who surrounded her, and for the whole trip she stood like that, face tipped up to catch a breeze. She was no stranger to the stench of sour clothing soaked in sweat, but the addition of tobacco with a distinctly dank aroma was almost too much.

Two men carried on a conversation directly over her head, as if she were a fence post put there for them to lean on while they talked. It was impossible not to hear them, and worse still, they had nothing more interesting to discuss beyond, first, whether Cuban cigars were worth the price, and then whether or not to buy a new mule, and finally where they'd get the best deal. They were brothers, apparently, working the family farm together.

"Maybe this young lady can give us her opinion." The taller of the two smirked at her.

His brother blew out a dark cloud of smoke and coughed so that the phlegm in his throat and chest made a noise like a child's rattle.

Carrie had nothing to add.

"So, no thoughts on mules to share, I take it."

She might have given him her thoughts about the sickness in his brother's lungs, but she knew how that would be received, and in any case, the ferryman was pulling up beside the *Annabelle*.

CAPTAIN ASHBY SAID, "I realize how distressing this is, Miss Ballentyne, but I can delay no longer. We must set out now, or add a day to this journey."

Carrie sat in the grand saloon, Eva Zavala on one side and the captain on the other. She was exhausted and, at the same time, so anxious that she folded her hands together to stop their trembling. She had found Eva and her little boy waiting for her, but there was no sign of her brother or Eli Ibarra.

"You mustn't assume the worst," Captain Ashby went on.

With all the calm she could muster, Carrie asked the obvious question.

"Captain Ashby, if we abandon them, how will they get to Westport?"

"As if Eli Ibarra needed help finding his way," Ashby said. "I guarantee you that they'll get to Westport before we do."

They sat silent for a long moment, and then Eva turned to Carrie and took both her hands in her own.

"He's right," she said. "If anybody can get from here to Westport under his own steam, it's Eli."

Carrie pushed out a long breath. "Nathan is cut from the same bolt. He is never lost."

Neither of them said, *Unless the river took them*, but the words hung there, almost visible, while the *Annabelle* jerked once and then again, setting out for Westport and the end of this stage of the journey.

11

Friday, May 15, 1857

CARRIE DECIDED TO keep to her stateroom, given Nathan's absence. She asked that her meals be brought to her, and allowed everyone to think that she had withdrawn out of worry and distress.

Actually her reasons were more complicated: she didn't want to hear strangers speculate about Nathan's fate, and she absolutely would not entertain questions about her family history. Those questions were circulating; she knew as much from Eva. The bold ones would ask ignorant questions about the Mohawk, and the shy ones would simply hint, hoping she might share a story or two about her famous grandfather, treasure to be tucked away like coin.

Better to avoid all that. Better not to hear any talk of Eli, who was missing too.

It wasn't a hardship. She read *Commerce of the Prairies*, napped, tried again to write in her travel diary. Then Beto decided that this was the right opportunity to start her Spanish lessons. He had given the whole undertaking considerable thought and had detailed plans.

By noon she had learned the words for cough, headache, pain, blood, and bleeding, and the terms for every major part of the human body, including names for fingers and the thumb. With studied calm Carrie asked the questions she had been holding back. In short order she learned how to say *Close your eyes*, and *Does your eye hurt?* and *You have pretty eyes*, landing finally, triumphantly, at the exact phrase she needed to learn.

Beto considered and finally agreed that *¿Qué significa que me guiñaste un ojo?* was the proper way to ask the question.

"But I can tell you," he said very seriously, "that if I wink at you, it means something flew into my eye."

Carrie ran a hand over his skull, smiling and, at the same time, feeling guilty to have robbed the boy of Spanish under false pretenses.

"Let's go get our tea," she told him. "Are you hungry?"

They had just stepped into the saloon when Beto grabbed her hand and squeezed it.

She looked down at him, alarmed, but he was smiling.

Carrie had to stoop to hear his whisper.

"And if I wink at you and I don't have something in my eye, that means you are my sweetheart, and I am yours."

AFTER TEA BETO set her an oral exam, and was not exactly pleased with her performance.

"You are a quick learner." His tone bordered on disappointment.

"You are a good teacher," Carrie countered.

Mollified, he went off to report on her progress to his mother. He returned in short order with a peppermint offered on an outstretched palm.

"Esta es su recompensa."

She said, "The English word *compensate* gives me a hint. Is this my reward for keeping up with your challenges? *La recompensa?*"

At supper Eva and her son joined Carrie in her stateroom. Beto took the first opportunity to challenge her: Could she conjugate the verb *ayudar* in the past tense?

"Really, Roberto," Eva said. "Remember your manners. This is neither the time nor place for lessons."

Carrie was a little disappointed, but kept that to herself.

In the evening she sat on the promenade for more than an hour watching the Missouri as it passed by: a flock of wild turkeys pecking their way through a meadow, the wreck of another steamer where a half dozen white pelicans perched to watch for prey. Men crossing a herd of cattle, swimming alongside them, coaxing and swearing by turns to keep them moving. Most or even all of the wranglers had stripped to the skin to save their clothes, but the human form was well-known to Carrie and she went back to her cabin.

Beto often joined her when she sat on the deck, and proved himself to be an excellent tour guide. He pointed out fields newly plowed, old wagons and brightly painted carriages, a truly enormous swine that walked along a path as if it were nothing out of the ordinary to take a stroll.

No sign of Nathan or Eli.

Before bed she tried to write a letter home, but the paper remained untouched in front of her. Until she knew Nathan was safe, there was nothing worth writing beyond a simple four-word sentence: *My brother is missing.* The very idea nauseated her. If her brother was lost, it was her fault and she would know, once and for all, where her own breaking point was.

12

Saturday, May 16, 1857

As SHE DRESSED the next morning, Carrie asked herself what steps she would have to take if there was no sign of Nathan or of Eli Ibarra in Westport. She could seek out a marshal or sheriff—there must be someone responsible for maintaining the peace, after all. That person should be able and willing to advise her, but she had money enough to convince them that they wanted to help, if that became necessary. If they took her seriously at all.

As a three-year-old Nathan had set out on adventures without saying a word to anyone, eventually finding his way home to show them the treasures he had gathered. No scolding, no matter how sincere, could convince him to give up his wandering ways. Ma fretted, but Da saw things differently.

"It's in the boy's heart and bones, the urge to wander," Da would say. "And it comes doon from your own Da, so he says his own self. Noo I ask, my sweet, why pretend otherwise?"

Before her mother could counter that argument, he went on. "And were no you and Daniel prone to disappearin when the weather was fine and the falls beckoned? Come to that, Lily my love, we're due for a visit to the waterfalls ourselves."

That made her mother laugh and blush, and it put an end to the discussion, which was his purpose, after all. It wasn't until she was a few years older that Carrie understood a visit to the caves under the waterfalls at the far end of the glen was a tradition for married couples. And unmarried ones, on occasion.

All these memories made her almost weak with homesickness, but Carrie forced herself to go out to breakfast, where Mrs. Hamblin was sitting with the captain's wife, their two heads bent together. Eva sat by herself staring into a mound of grits dripping butter, but Carrie's appearance across the table seemed to wake her up.

"There you are," she said. "Have you heard, we've made such good progress that we are expected to reach Westport this afternoon."

"I did hear that," Carrie said, turning to thank the steward who had appeared with her breakfast. "So now I will have to pack Nathan's things as well as my own. Will you do the same for Eli?"

It occurred to her that just days ago she would have called him Mr. Ibarra. She was glad that Eva took no note of this change.

"Of course," she said. "And won't that please the gossips."

She cast a glance in Mrs. Hamblin's direction, shook her head, and sighed. In a studied, casual tone, she said, "Mrs. Hamblin has been talking without pause since your conversation the other day."

"It was worth it if it means we don't have to sit with her at meals," Carrie said. "I find it curious, though, how sincerely she dislikes you. I don't understand it. Beyond the fact that you turned down her son's proposal."

"Don't look to me for an explanation," Eva said. "She's filled to the brim with hate for almost everyone. To imagine her as a mother-in-law . . ." She shuddered. "She has no regard for Catholics. Or Jews. Or Mexicans. Or Yankees. Will you please just ask me whatever it is sitting in your gullet? I know that look."

And Carrie knew when a battle was lost.

"All right," she said. "Was it Carlos Zavala she disapproved of, or would she have found reason to complain if you had married a St. Louis banker?"

Eva considered this for a moment. "You mean someone with no Indian blood. Criollo is the word used in the territory for someone of exclusively white ancestry, as he was. Mrs. Hamblin tolerated my husband because he was descended from the original Spaniards who invaded Mexico."

Carrie, worried that Eva would tire of her questions, hesitated again. She was relieved when Eva went on, understanding where Carrie's questions were headed.

She said, "What you need to understand is this. When the Spanish first came to the continent, the Peninsulares—those born in Spain— were ranked above everybody else. Then came Criollos, people of pure Spanish blood who were born here. Then came other Europeans, so long as they were white. Beyond those three, nobody else counted."

"And that's still the case?"

"Some people still see it that way, but not everyone. These days a Criollo is a Mexican—or New Mexican—who was born here, and whose bloodlines are purely European. Or at least, that's the claim."

"And the term Mestizo? I take it that refers to someone who is part European—"

"And part Indian," Eva finished for her. "Mrs. Hamblin probably thinks of the word as a vile curse. According to her, Mestizos are an abomination. Which explains the way she looks at Eli."

"She mentioned Eli's Pueblo grandparents," Carrie said. "She called Eli's father a blackamoor."

Eva's jaw dropped and then closed with a click. "That ignorant hen."

Carrie might have agreed, but the venom in Mrs. Hamblin's tone made it difficult to see anything amusing at all in the stories she had told with such glee.

"I shouldn't have told you that. She meant to be hurtful, and probably hoped I'd repeat her words to you. Which I have done, and I apologize."

"You are not at fault," Eva said. "Mrs. Hamblin is. She is telling anyone who will listen about your family, and as a result three people stopped me on the way here to ask questions. Intrusive questions that I couldn't answer if I had been so inclined." Her mouth tightened. "I promise you, they were sorry to have asked."

Eva brushed invisible crumbs away, her tension almost visible. She said, "Even worse, she has raised questions about Eli's interest in you."

Carrie blinked, determined not to overreact. "She is spinning tall tales. Eli has been polite and friendly, but he has no interest in me."

That might not be true, but Carrie had no evidence and was satisfied to be telling the truth, insofar as she knew it. Eva had a disconcerting habit of narrowing her eyes while she studied a person. As she did now with Carrie.

"You understand, I hope, that Eli is like a brother to me. There was never anything else between us."

Carrie should, properly, respond with polite disinterest; it was none of her business, after all. Instead a sentence was spoken before she could stop herself.

"Because he is Mestizo?"

Eva's smile disappeared before Carrie had finished saying the word.

"I apologize," Carrie said. "That was insensitive and harsh and, worse still, judgmental. I am usually not indiscreet or thoughtless, though it may take some time for you to see that."

Eva drew in a noisy breath, touched her handkerchief to her throat, and nodded. "Apology accepted. It is a painful subject, but not for the reasons you're thinking. I would like to claim that I am nothing like Mrs. Hamblin. I don't want to be like her, and as a child, I wasn't. None of us were. But—"

She broke off with a shake of the head.

"You needn't explain to me," Carrie said. "I was rude."

"Don't," Eva said, a sharper edge in her tone. "I will decide for myself what I want you to know."

That was fair, and Carrie inclined her head.

Finally, Eva said, "Eli never loved me in that way, but he did have feelings for my sister. Susan was just a year younger and we were often mistaken for twins. That's what Mrs. Hamblin remembers, Eli offering for Susan and being refused. And yes, my sister did refuse him because he is Mestizo. And no, I would not have refused him for that reason."

Now things began to make sense. "That must have been terribly difficult for you. Have you been able to stay on good terms with your sister?"

The regret and sorrow in Eva's expression were answer enough, but she was clearly determined to tell the rest of the story.

"I believe that we would have come to an understanding eventually, but Susan was traveling with the wagon train Carlos was leading home to Santa Fe. So I lost them both."

Without conscious thought Carrie reached out and put a hand on Eva's wrist. For a long moment they sat just that way while Carrie thought of Eva's son. Somehow Eva had managed to raise a bright, happy child despite disabling grief and regret, and that spoke to her character and strength.

"I have lost sisters," Carrie said when she could trust her voice. "Maybe sometime, if you would like, we could talk about Susan."

Eva smiled at her, and nodded. "And your sisters. Yes," she said. "I would like that."

THE NEXT TIME they sat down together to eat, Beto was so excited that his whole body trembled in anticipation.

"Tell her, Ma," he said. "Won't you tell her?"

"Roberto. Calm yourself."

She was trying not to smile, and failing.

"Beto would like me to tell you that we met a gentleman from New Orleans. You will have noticed him, I'm sure."

Carrie regarded the soup in front of her and realized that she did not have any appetite. Worry about her brother, she told herself. She put down her spoon and folded her napkin.

"How so?"

Eva put her own spoon aside, and Carrie saw that she was almost as excited as Beto.

"He's very tall, and he wears his hair like Bonaparte, you know, combed forward over his brow? Except snow white. And an old-fashioned coat with a full skirt and puffed sleeves."

"He's always in the library, and he smokes a pipe," Beto added.

Carrie did know who they meant, and said so. "And how exactly did he make an impression?"

"He knows your grandfather!" This burst out of Beto like a fire-cracker. Then he dropped his gaze. "Sorry, Ma."

"You are putting the cart before the horse, Roberto. Please don't interrupt." She took a sip of tea and began again.

"This Mr. Belmont is from New Orleans. He was just a young boy when President Jackson came to save the city from the British, you understand. But he did meet your grandfather and an Indian he was traveling with."

"Runs-from-Bears," Carrie supplied. "A great-uncle. Yes, they were in New Orleans in the last weeks of the war. So were some aunts and uncles and cousins."

"Was your grandfather famous?" Beto asked. "Did he know President Jackson? Did he fight in the war?"

There were so many stories to tell about her Bonner grandparents that she could keep Beto entertained for many weeks, but storytelling was a serious business, and she was too anxious to attempt it. She leaned closer to talk to the boy directly, her voice low so that he'd understand that she was sharing something important.

"You know, my brother is the very best storyteller. When he's back with us and time permits, ask him about our Grandda Nathaniel. Be sure to ask him about the Pirate Stoker, who helped steal our Ma and her brother away to Scotland when they were just a few months old."

She might have offered him gold by his expression.

"Then let's go watch for him. Can we, Ma? Can we watch for Mr. Ballentyne and Uncle Eli?"

"We had best go now," Eva agreed. "We're less than an hour from Westport Landing, and the best places on the promenade will be taken up if we don't hurry."

THE MISSOURI RIVER at Westport Landing was not quite so overwhelming as the Mississippi at St. Louis, but Carrie counted a dozen steamers and a whole fleet of smaller boats. Most of the steamers were busy taking on cargo for the journey back to St. Louis, but some would go in the opposite direction.

She could imagine her brother giving in to his curiosity. How tempting, just to step onto another steamer, one headed upriver into the Northwest Territories. Better that, she reminded herself, than at the bottom of the river.

As the steamer waited to dock, Carrie scanned the sea of faces with her hands clamped on the rail. Eva stood next to her, and Beto was tucked in between them, his face pressed against a gap in the balustrade.

"They are here," Beto said very calmly. "I know it."

A child wanting assurance, and unwilling to imagine disappointment of a particular kind. Carrie knew just how he felt. She realized she was biting her lip and forced herself to stop, breathe deeply, and summon up all the dignity and calm she could.

Tucked into her bodice was a list of steps she would have to take if she didn't find Nathan in Westport. First she would seek out the sheriff, and then she would hire trackers to go out in search of the two missing men. The newspaper office—she hoped there was one—was the place to write out a description to be posted in all the towns between Westport and Arrow Rock.

Writing out the list had seemed like the reasonable thing to do, but in the end it only gave her more to worry about. She had put together a summary of everything that might have gone wrong, or could still go wrong.

The steamer bumped against the pier, and the process of securing ropes began, but not before the captain began to wave his arms and shout at a clerk who stood on the dock. The man might have been deaf, for all the attention he paid. He stood there, scratching his jaw and looking around himself, at ease in the tumult.

"It's always like this," Eva said, almost too brightly. "It will all be sorted out in an hour, and then we can go onshore."

"A whole hour." The boy was the very picture of dejection. Carrie felt exactly the same way, but felt obliged to model calm certainty.

"Roberto," his mother said. "Do you remember what we talked about this morning?"

A frightful frown was the only answer he produced.

"Roberto?"

He crossed his arms. "Patience is a virtue. And I will need a lot of it because it will be four weeks before we reach home."

"Four weeks at a minimum," his mother said.

"A minimum," came the mournful echo.

She glanced now at Carrie. "I have assumed that you and Nathan will be traveling with Mr. Petit, too, but I never asked."

It took an effort to dislodge the idea of four weeks—at the very least—in an overheated box jouncing its way across prairie and desert, but Carrie straightened her shoulders. "I don't know, to be honest. Dr. Markham wrote that instructions would be waiting for us at the hotel. But I do agree with Beto, it's difficult to comprehend that this journey will go on for another month."

"I don't suppose the idea cheers many people," Eva said, but with an encouraging smile. "We will make the most of it, all of us."

There was still no sign of her brother or of Eli Ibarra, but Carrie was too anxious to stay in one spot and watch.

"Come," she said to Beto. "Let's sit down and read a bit of Mr. Gregg's travels while we wait."

Eva said, "What an excellent notion."

Which Carrie took to mean that she was nervous, too, and would rather be nervous alone.

As was becoming her habit, Carrie opened her book at a random page and let her eyes scan the text for something interesting—and appropriate for a young boy—to read aloud. At this moment she doubted much could distract her, but found that she was wrong.

"Beto," she said. "Mr. Gregg writes here about something called a fandango. Are you familiar with that word?"

His expression was a curious combination of surprise and concern for her cluelessness.

"Everybody knows what a fandango is," he said. "What does Mr. Gregg say?"

Carrie sat up straight and read.

Respecting *fandangos*, I will observe that this term, as it is used in New Mexico, is never applied to any particular dance, but is the usual designation for those ordinary assemblies where dancing and frolicking are carried on; *baile* (or ball) being generally applied to those of a higher grade. The former especially are very frequent; for nothing is more general, throughout the country, and with all classes than dancing. From the gravest priest to the buffoon—from the richest nabob to the beggar—from the governor to the ranchero—from the soberest matron to the flippant belle—from the grandest *señora* to the *cocinera*—all partake of this exhilarating amusement.

"Yes!" Beto jumped up to demonstrate by twirling in place. "Everybody dances and not just at the fandango. All the time there's dancing. Can you dance?"

She had to laugh at his high energy. "Yes. I like dancing."

His whole face split into a grin. "You should ask Uncle Eli, he knows all about fandangos."

There was a prickling at the nape of her neck. Carrie lifted her head and saw two familiar figures in the grand saloon's open double doors.

"Go on," Beto crowed. "Ask!"

Nathan was walking toward her, grinning, arms outstretched as if to hug her, but fully knowing that she would protest; he was covered in muck from head to toe. And beyond that, she was having a difficult time looking away from Eli Ibarra.

He stayed where he was in the doorway, leaning against the door-frame, arms folded high on his chest, one leg crossed in front of the other, his gaze fixed on her. And winked.

13

RESERVATIONS HAD BEEN made for the Ballentynes at the Gilbert Hotel, and Carrie intended to walk there, setting off as soon as she stepped onto dry land. When Nathan came back from washing and changing into less frightful clothes—once again, unpacking and repacking—she told him so. They argued the point until another passenger waiting to disembark interrupted them.

"Ma'am," he said, unable to look her in the eye. "Pardon my temerity, but did you know that it's four miles or more from Westport Landing to Westport, where the Gilbert is? That's a long walk."

Carrie managed to thank him for this information. Then she left the baggage to Nathan and asked a steward to find her a cab or carriage into Westport.

According to the last letter from Dr. Markham, two rooms had been reserved for them, with full board. *If you run into any difficulties,* he had written, *speak to Miss Herlinde and mention my name.*

Carrie took some reassurance from this last detail. Miss Herlinde would be the owner or the owner's wife, calm and competent, someone who would answer questions. Because she had many, many questions and would not be able to depend on Eva for answers, as she would be staying a few miles outside town with a friend of her mother's.

The Gilbert Hotel was in the center of Westport. Carrie paid the driver, nodded to the other passengers, and marched up the stairs and through the door. Stopping short, because the lobby was crowded by at least a dozen men with luggage, all of them scowling and muttering dissatisfaction.

Not one of them took note of her, but that was nothing out of the ordinary; the larger the group of men, the easier it seemed to ignore an inconvenient woman. Her choices were few. She could wait here surrounded by sweaty men belching smoke and aiming—poorly—at overflowing spittoons, she could raise her voice and insist that the sea divide itself, or there was a dining room to the right. She saw the sign over double doors, slightly ajar. Invitation enough. She would take a table in the dining room. Maybe there would be soup and buttered bread and milky tea and, if she were fortunate, a table near a window so that she could watch for Nathan. Sooner or later the crowd in the lobby would thin out, and she would come back then, rested and calm.

She began to thread her way through the crowd, using her carpetbag as a wedge or, in one case, as a battering ram. An elderly man, apparently asleep on his feet and unwilling to be disturbed, needed that much motivation.

Standing in the doorway to the dining room, Carrie set her sights on a table at a window.

"Miss? Pardon me, please."

She turned to see a middle-aged woman with rigid posture, her hands folded together at her waist, elbows akimbo. She wore a spotless white bib apron the size of a tent, and an expression that reminded Carrie of Mrs. O'Malley, a nursing matron who had made her life difficult when she was in training.

"Miss, do you have a room here at the Gilbert Hotel?"

Whether the woman was a servant or a clerk, Carrie could not tell. There was nothing friendly or welcoming about the round face, but the stern effect was offset by a beautiful bow-shaped, pink mouth that nature had provided with no help from cosmetics. Carrie recalled Dr. Markham's instructions and noted that this woman had a German accent.

She was saying, "You see, only guests of the hotel may take a table."

"I understand," Carrie said. "Miss Herlinde—am I right in assuming you are Miss Herlinde? Dr. Markham of Santa Fe reserved and paid for our rooms. Two rooms, one for my brother and one for myself. But the lobby is so crowded—"

The woman swung her whole body in the direction of the clerk's desk, chin jutting forward, much like a hen who had spied a fat worm. She swung back again.

"They did not let you pass? They did not give you precedence?" Her voice resonated with indignation. "This will not do. Not at all. The great selfish lumpen men, they will never learn."

Her gaze came back to set on Carrie, as if to judge her trustworthiness.

"Your name." Not so much a question as a demand.

"We are the Ballentynes. Carrie and Nathan. You are kind to intercede on my behalf. In the meantime, may I take a seat?"

Miss Herlinde's posture, already strict, became military.

"No. Only guests of the hotel may come into my dining room. You, Miss Ballentyne, are what must be called a not-yet guest. An imaginary guest. No no, that is not right. An aspiring guest? Yes. Aspiring guests must wait. It will not take me long." She sniffed, apparently anticipating a confrontation with the men in the lobby with some pleasure. "Not long at all."

In short order Carrie had two room keys, a spot by the window, and the promise of a meal.

The dining room was a pleasant place and very clean: curtains recently washed and starched, the floorboards waxed, the table linen without crease or stain. She hoped that upstairs the rooms would be as tidy and clean. Certainly they would be, if Miss Herlinde had anything to say about it.

When food was put in front of her—again by Miss Herlinde, who had yet to smile—Carrie realized how hungry she was. In the morning she had been too agitated to eat; later, once Nathan had finally shown his face, she had been too distracted. Now she considered the dishes in front of her. A slab of corn bread dripping butter, a small bowl of creamed spinach, and a dinner plate with a mound of red cabbage cooked with onion and bacon, crowded up against mashed potatoes, and topped by a thick sausage. And not just any sausage, Miss Herlinde announced, but a bratwurst made by her own brother Sefftone Ratz, master butcher. It was oven browned and bursting from its casing, and Carrie's stomach rumbled.

While she ate she watched out the window and tried to remember what she had read about Westport. A major departure point for the Santa Fe trail, with a constant stream of emigrants passing through. This was the last chance they would have to outfit themselves for the journey west, to New Mexico or Oregon or California. Westport had a liveliness, for lack of a better word. A sense of things on the move.

She started out of her thoughts when Miss Herlinde appeared at her elbow, staring at Carrie's plate.

"You do not like?"

Carrie had eaten close to half of what she had been given. "It's very good," she said.

"Never mind," Miss Herlinde said, and took the plate. "No excuses, please. Now, someone is asking for you." Her pretty mouth twitched as if she had things to say that she must hold back.

"Yes?"

"It's that Orwell Petit, the blasphemer. The bigamist." This last word came out with a low hiss.

Carrie was trying to form a question in response to such an odd and alarming announcement, but Miss Herlinde chose not to wait. "Also, he is a transporter. You are traveling in his stagecoach?"

"Well," Carrie said. "I'm not sure. I was hoping there would be a letter from Dr. Markham waiting for me here, with instructions on the next stage of this journey."

Miss Herlinde clicked her tongue, and a network of lines creased her brow. "No letter, but here you have instead the *bígamo* Petit, the transporter."

She decided she did not want a translation of *bígamo* and was sorry that Nathan wasn't here. He would have appreciated this odd conversation.

"May Mr. Petit join me here while I finish my meal?" Carrie asked. She looked pointedly at the dish Miss Herlinde was clutching.

Her jaw jerked hard one way and then the other. "It is out of order," she said. "He is no guest, and worse, I do not like to have the *bígamo* in my dining room. But I cannot allow you to be talking to him alone, without a chaperone to watch over you. This would endanger my soul and also yours. So I will bring him, but I warn you, he is not a man of God."

She thumped the plate down in front of her and marched off. Her curiosity fully aroused, Carrie watched until she came back, herding a tall, rumpled man across the dining room. She pointed at the chair opposite Carrie. "The sinner, Orwell Petit," she said. "Beware, sir. You know I have my eye on you."

"Yes, ma'am," he said, soft-voiced, ducking his head. "I am aware."

When Miss Herlinde had left them to intercept a couple at the door, Carrie took a deep breath. "Mr. Petit, is it? You wanted to talk to me?"

He was a big man, roughly dressed in damp clothes, most likely the result of a recent visit to the bathhouse. The barber had not been involved, as he wore a beard that spread out and down his chest in one direction and covered his face almost to the cheekbones in the other. A fine, thick growth of hair, with droplets of water caught in waves and curls. He held his hat in his lap, so that she could see the impression of his hatband on his brow; below that point his skin was browned from the sun, and above, fish-belly white.

"You are Miss Ballentyne?"

"I am."

"Your brother?"

"Not here at the moment, but I am the person you need to talk to. What is this about?"

He swallowed so hard that it sounded almost like a groan.

"Name's Orwell Petit. Petit's Overland Mail and Freight. Dr. Markham bought your tickets. You and your brother, more like. Where is he, did you say?"

"You can talk to me, Mr. Petit, and I'll fill my brother in."

The man had the most expressive eyebrows; one peaked while the other lowered. He cleared his throat, retrieved a handkerchief, and wiped his brow. This was a man who transported the U.S. mail, goods, and people through hostile territory, but could not talk to a woman in a public space without breaking into a sweat. She smiled, hoping to set him at ease.

"Really," she said. "I'm listening."

He glanced over his shoulder as if he expected an ambush.

"She's nowhere near. I will warn you if she heads this way, if you like. What is it you need us to know?"

It was like turning a spigot, because Mr. Petit launched into a recitation that he had obviously committed to memory.

She was to understand first that he, Orwell Petit, had been transporting mail, freight, and people between Missouri and Santa Fe for fifteen years. Second, Dr. Markham had reserved and paid for two places for them in the stagecoach that was part of a caravan leaving in two days. Their baggage would be stored in one of the three U.S. Mail wagons in the caravan, along with five cargo wagons and a company of soldiers bound for one of the forts.

There would be six guards to accompany the stagecoach, all armed with double-barreled shotguns and repeating rifles. Another group would guard the mail and the cargo. All Mr. Petit's employees were capable, experienced, and trustworthy. The driver, who went by the odd name Helmet, was considered one of the best in the territory; next to him on the stagecoach box would be Lionel Tock. Mr. Tock was responsible for the passengers' comfort, including pitching and stowing tents when more formal arrangements were not available. The cook, called Liebling, without any title or indication of gender, would travel perched on top of the stagecoach surrounded by luggage.

While Mr. Petit went on with a description of the stagecoach itself, from upholstery to oiled leather curtains that could be folded up out of sight, Carrie's mind wandered off to Eva, who had made this trip many times and could give her the kind of information Mr. Petit would not volunteer and Carrie could not ask him about.

He was winding down. "I can't pretend it will be comfortable compared to your trip by steamboat, or that it will be speedy, but I will do everything in my power to make sure you arrive safely and well-fed. If your brother has any questions, I would be happy to meet with him later today or tomorrow."

He began to rise, and then sat again when Carrie held up a palm.

"My brother isn't the only person with questions, Mr. Petit. I don't have any at the moment, but please don't assume I won't in the future."

He blinked in surprise, cleared his throat. "Yes, ma'am."

Miss Herlinde appeared as soon as he had slipped out the door. She was humming under her breath. "Watch out for him, miss. Beware."

Carrie decided that she could challenge Miss Herlinde on this matter. "He seems to me a polite man. Very shy. Perhaps lonely."

"Shy? Lonely?" She huffed in surprise. "He has eight children and two wives. One family here, one in Santa Fe. Lots of open mouths and no place to be lonely. I tell you, I wouldn't be surprised if he's got a third family hid away somewhere in between here and there. I think he started the freight business just to find new women to marry. You watch you don't fall into his trap."

When Carrie went to see her room, she found that the baggage had been delivered. Trunks, but no Nathan. Instead there was a note: he had a few things to look into and would be back soon. In fact it was early evening before he appeared at her door. She meant to ask some pointed questions about the delay, where he had been and to what end, but he begged for her patience: he couldn't appear in public until he had bathed and changed, and he was in desperate need of a meal.

Carrie went downstairs to wait for him—yet again—in the dining room, reminding herself this was Nathan. She could not change him; he would wander, and explore, and lose track of time. But he would not fail her when there was trouble afoot.

There was no sign of Miss Herlinde in the dining room, which was, she decided, a good thing. Instead a waiter showed her to a table, asked if someone would be joining her, informed her about the meal he would serve, and disappeared. Nathan came in just as the waiter reappeared with a heavily laden tray.

"So," he said, his eyes moving over the food. "This looks like home. I'm starving."

But Carrie had had enough of being ignored. As soon as the waiter left them, she rapped her knuckles on the table to get his attention.

"Nathan."

He paused, his spoon poised over a bowl of chicken and dumplings in a shimmering, deep yellow broth. "Hmmm?"

"Don't."

"Don't eat?"

"You are being purposefully dim. Don't make me wait even another minute. Where have you been all afternoon? You still haven't explained where you disappeared to after Arrow Rock, but just now I want to hear about today. And aren't you at all curious about the next stage in this journey? Because I had a visit from a Mr. Orwell Petit—"

He held up one finger while he chewed and then, endlessly, swallowed.

"Yes, I know. I ran into him at the Buckhorn, and he gave me all the details."

"The Buckhorn," Carrie said.

"The saloon on the next corner." He motioned with his head, seemed to reconsider, and sent her a sidelong glance. "Probably not a place you want to visit. That whole block is pretty rough."

She watched him eat for another minute, and then could wait no longer.

"And what were you doing at the Buckhorn?"

"Talking to Petit. Are you satisfied with the plans?"

Carrie gave her answer some thought. "It's not what I hoped for," she said finally. "But there's nothing to be done."

He looked up and flashed a dimple at her. Her clever brother was about to make an announcement. She knew the signs, and braced herself.

"Would you be happier if you could ride?"

"Of course," Carrie said. "But we can hardly set out on our own. Getting provisions together, finding a guide—it couldn't be done in a reasonable amount of time. Not safely. And finding a reputable horse dealer—that's more than I'd like to chance."

He gave a short laugh. "Mr. Lee would scold you for false modesty. You are an excellent judge of horseflesh."

"I said horse dealers, not horses. I would not be comfortable dealing with a total stranger, and neither would you."

Nathan glanced around the room and raised a hand to get a waiter's attention. After he had ordered a second bowl of chicken and dumplings, he seemed to remember that he had been in the middle of a conversation.

"Where were we?"

"Reputable horse dealers," Carrie said. "And the fact that we wouldn't know how to find one."

He lifted a shoulder, his gaze shifting to watch the traffic on the street. "I doubt we can do any better than Eli Ibarra. He knows everybody in Westport, and everybody knows him, seems like."

Carrie sat back, folded her hands in her lap, and studied her brother's expression. "Do tell."

"I mentioned to him that we might want to buy mounts before we get shut up in that stagecoach."

"When was this?"

"Today, at the Buckhorn."

She shook her head at him. "You are impossible."

"So you say, but listen. There's a man called Romero, an Argentine. One of Eli's sisters married into the family. Here, look at this."

From his shirt pocket he took a newspaper cutting and put it on the table.

ATTENTION EMIGRANTS!
CALIFORNIA FIXINS!!

Curiosities & Necessities to be Admired and Acquired at
EMIL YORK'S MANUFACTORY AND WAREHOUSE
on the Independence Road

Come and out-fit yourself with the finest dry goods,
hardware, leather goods, tinware.

FAIR PRICES.

Carrie spared him an incredulous glance. "You're in need of Mr. York's fixins?"

With a weary sigh he took the clipping, turned it over, and pushed it closer to her.

LAKELAND RANCH
MULES—CATTLE—SHEEP—HORSES

Presently Esteban Romero is the only U.S. breeder of the true
ARGENTINEAN HORSES OF THE PAMPAS. The robust, long-
lived, intelligent Argentinean is the mount of the famous South
American Gaucho, and endures where other breeds fall behind.

Very limited stock available.

ATTENTION WESTWARD BOUND EMIGRANTS

We currently have an abundance of fine MULES for sale, broken to
halter and harness. We breed for health, stamina and
disposition. Reasonable Rates.

E. Romero & Sons

10 miles SE of Westport

Nathan had a great deal to tell her about these South American
horses of the Pampas. She listened but kept her questions to herself.

"Let me ask you," Nathan said. "When she was at her best, how
many miles could Pearl manage in a day?"

Carrie thought of the long rides with Pearl. She was fairly sure she
had explored every byway and beach on Long Island, and said as
much to her brother.

Impatient, Nathan shook his head. "No. I'm asking how many
miles Pearl could give you in a day."

"If I were in a rush? Twenty-five to thirty, if the trail is good and
the weather cooperates. And if water and grazing are plentiful."

"Excellent," Nathan said. "But an Argentinean can put in sixty
miles a day, if the weather is good."

Carrie inclined her head to acknowledge the fact that—if true—
this was impressive. A horse with that kind of endurance would make
traveling from Westport to New Mexico Territory less of a gamble for
emigrants who valued speed above safety.

At Dodge City the trail split in two: the mountain route over the
Rockies, and the Cimarron route, mostly desert. According to Mr.
Gregg, the Cimarron route meant crossing the jornada, some ninety
waterless miles favored by Indian raiding parties.

The Cimarron route could only be considered if the entire party were
well armed, well mounted, sensibly outfitted and provisioned, and able

to tolerate at least two bone-dry days. Thus Petit's wagon train—and the Ballentynes—would travel the slower, safer mountain route.

"According to Eli," he went on, "Romero's got excellent stock for sale. Trail tested, five to six years old. And he is fair minded."

Carrie pushed the newspaper back across the table, pointing to the paragraph about the horses. "Here it says he has very limited stock for sale."

"I'm told he does have horses," Nathan said. "But he won't sell to just anybody. You have to have the recommendation of someone he trusts. And he has to see you ride."

"And you want to go see these horses tomorrow."

He raised a brow. "You don't?"

It would not be to her advantage to quarrel with Nathan on this point. Carrie gentled her expression and picked up her spoon. With a mouthful of dumplings, she could take a moment to consider.

Eli Ibarra was willing to vouch for them with the rancher who had valuable horses otherwise unattainable. This would put them in his debt. At home she would know what that meant, but here, in these circumstances, she had no idea. He might want nothing more than a simple thank-you, or he might expect a favor in return. Somehow she couldn't imagine him pressing an unfair advantage, but men were unpredictable and, for the most part, not especially trustworthy.

She pressed a knuckle to the spot between her brows where a head-ache threatened, and reminded herself that she would be spending weeks in a stagecoach. That was time enough to sort things out for herself, free of the distraction of random and unsolicited winks.

Nathan interrupted her train of thought.

"You know," he said, "if you'd rather stay here, I could go and decide about the horses myself. You'd trust me to pick a mount for you, wouldn't you?"

The urge to pinch him was almost irresistible.

"Fine," she said. "I take it you've already hired a rig."

"We'll set out at eight," Nathan said. "If that suits?"

14

Sunday, May 17, 1857

THE NEXT MORNING Nathan first wanted to take her on a tour of Westport, though the streets were clogged with wagons and oxcarts and livestock, and the going would be slow.

"As bad as Union Square on a Saturday," Carrie said.

"Oh, I'd say much worse." This clearly pleased her brother for reasons Carrie couldn't fathom. "But one way or the other, we have to get out of town."

"Well then," Carrie said, resigned to surrendering gracefully. "Let's have a look at Westport."

For a small town, there was a great deal of very loud activity: bawling oxen and mules, barking dogs, the bone-cracking creak and thump of wagon wheels, and an out-of-tune piano outside a saloon on which someone was pounding out "Camptown Races."

The general agitation made sense when you considered that three large wagon trains were scheduled to set out the next day. Emigrants would be nervous, unsure suddenly of this grand plan but convinced that they should have more in the way of provisions. Another few pounds of salt pork, a tin of black salve, a yard of muslin; they swarmed over Westport in search of the one thing that would guarantee a safe trip.

A gunsmith's shop was especially busy, with men gathered around the show window. Carrie, suddenly wary, glanced at her brother.

He said, "We can stop by later today."

"No," Carrie said calmly. "Not necessary."

At home there had been long discussions about weapons. Carrie had a rifled musket and a pistol, and was comfortable with both. Still her stepfather and brother believed that she should have the newest and most modern weapon available, the British Enfield rifle, which was thought to be more accurate than her weapon. Nathan had bought one for himself a few months before and was full of praise for it.

In the end Carrie only persevered because her mother took her side, but now her brother's expression told her that he still hoped to buy her an Enfield. Carrie took some comfort in the certainty that gunsmiths on the western frontier would not have such guns for sale.

She pointed out a large placard informing the public that Mr. Lime carried in his apothecary the purest laudanum, opium, Peruvian bark, imported medicinal teas, tinctures, ointments, surgical instruments, dental kits, and medical supplies.

"If there's time I'd be far more interested in Mr. Lime's offerings."

Nathan lifted both shoulders and held that pose for a long moment. Then he grinned.

"Very sensible," he said. "While you're busy with Mr. Lime, I'll visit York's Warehouse."

It was hard not to laugh at his tone, so studiously innocent and, at the same time, transparent. He might claim to want nothing more than a cake of soap when he went out to the shops, but Carrie could imagine him coming back with the soap, a slide rule, a paper of straight pins, and an oxbow.

"Not the best idea," she said to him now. "No room in the baggage. For anything."

He huffed, but didn't contradict her. Instead he developed a keen interest in a covered wagon set out for display in front of a wheel-wright's barn.

Carrie counted to herself, silently, and got as far as twenty before her brother turned to her, cleared his throat, and said, "A visit to that warehouse might be necessary, you realize. If all goes well today, the horses will need saddle blankets and bridles and—"

Carrie's laugh made him stop. He scowled and then, finally, grinned. "All right," he said, and pushed out a great sigh. "I'll leave the warehouse to you."

On the outskirts of Westport, they passed a gristmill, a dairy farm, and a tannery, but the countryside Carrie expected once those businesses were behind them didn't show itself. The closest fields were neither planted nor given over to pasture, but instead served as great arenas where wagon trains were being organized.

The sun reflected off a sea of canvas bonnets stretched over arched wagon bows; Nathan counted thirty wagons in one group, and thirty-five in the other. There was no sign of Mr. Petit's wagon train, which must be on the other side of Westport, but if she raised the subject, Nathan would want to find it, and so she kept her curiosity to herself, glad to avoid another delay.

To her it looked as if most of the wagons were the property of family groups, two or three generations setting off together. It was hard to imagine taking children on this journey, but there were a great many of them. The older ones toted supplies or water buckets while their younger brothers and sisters chased each other up and down the rows, barefooted and mud splashed, ignoring the scolding that trailed after them.

Nathan pointed his chin toward a buckboard wagon where three teenage girls sat, faces turned up to the sun so that the bonnets tied down snug would give them no protection. In no time at all they would be freckled, but that did not seem to concern them. They were very animated, talking and laughing.

He said, "For them it's a grand adventure."

A little farther on, men were trying to fit a bedstead into a wagon.

Nearby a grandmother sat in a rocking chair, knitting left untouched in her lap while she watched, and a hand on the head of the toddler who sat at her feet. His bottom was nestled into the dirt, his face hidden in her skirts.

Carrie said, "But their mothers and grandmothers know better."

He frowned at her. "How do you come to that conclusion?"

"It's obvious. Look there—" She nodded toward a woman struggling to lift a curio cabinet into a wagon bed. "No doubt she has been warned that they can't spare the space, but she's reluctant to leave the life she knows behind."

Nathan pushed out a deep sigh. "You do like to borrow trouble."

"Not at all," Carrie said. "But neither can I turn a blind eye to something so obvious."

For the next while they drove past one corral after another, many hundreds of oxen and mules but horses, too, all of them grazing, unaware of the trials ahead. Wranglers on horseback kept order, watched over the herds.

"Imagine the tack." Nathan whistled under his breath. "Wagons full of tack."

"You imagine the tack," Carrie told her brother, "while I take in the countryside."

It was very pretty farm country on this late spring morning. Patches of dappled shade spread out under chestnut and oak, maple and birch, while sunlight and shadow chased each other across pastureland. A breeze riffled through tall grasses and sent patches of wildflowers dancing: hyssop and pink fireweed, bright blue salvia, thimbleweed and marguerites as yellow as spring butter. They crossed a bridge, and Carrie looked down to see water moving fast. Spring runoff, rushing toward the Missouri and then the Mississippi and, from there, the world.

When they had been underway for more than an hour, Nathan pointed out the large flock of sheep scattered over the fields.

"I'm guessing the sheep belong to the Romero outfit. And here it is." They had come around a corner to see a sign suspended from two tall posts flanking a wide double gate. As they approached, a buck-board was turning onto the road, headed back the way they had come.

"Look," he said. "A familiar face."

Carrie recognized Mr. Petit by his beard. What had brought him here was self-evident: a string of at least two dozen mules followed along behind the buckboard, with two riders bringing up the rear.

Mules were big, rawboned, strong animals. They were generally healthier, longer lived, better in rough terrain, and far cheaper than horses. Troublesome, yes. But also smart enough to see trouble com-ing; and more important, a mule was as good as a guard dog. What-ever was happening in camp, a mule would let you know, at three in the morning or high noon.

Mr. Petit touched his hat brim as he passed, but made no move to stop and talk.

"The bigamist," Carrie remembered. "The blasphemer."

"What?" She had startled her brother, but this was not the time to recount Miss Herlinde's colorful condemnation of the hapless Mr. Petit.

"I'll tell you later. Look at the size of this place, would you? An impressive property."

Nathan turned the rig onto a lane lined with red maples and fol-lowed it around to what Carrie assumed was the main ranch house. Beyond it was a barn and stables, with paddocks and arenas close by.

A boy about fifteen years old greeted them and took charge of the horse and rig.

Nathan pressed a coin into the boy's palm. "Mr. Romero?"

"Don Esteban is waiting for you." The boy nodded toward the house, where a door opened.

Nathan held out an elbow for Carrie to take. "This will be a good day."

Carrie, all her senses on alert, kept her opinion to herself.

Don Esteban Romero was a man of some seventy years, with the posture of a general, the dignified bearing of royalty, and a quick smile that hinted at a sense of humor. Carrie reminded herself that

Eli Ibarra considered him a fair man and honest dealer. Now they would learn the truth for themselves.

It was Carrie's intention to be friendly, calm, polite, and only vaguely interested. She would admire the animals, of course, but keep what she knew to herself. Men were wary of women who showed expertise in any subject outside housekeeping and the raising of children. The best way to establish herself with these people was to demonstrate that she knew how to approach a horse, and that she could ride; that would convince them as words never could. To that end she wore split skirts and could only hope that they would not be outraged by her refusal to take a sidesaddle.

Mr. Romero—or Don Esteban, as Eli had explained to Nathan he was to be called—was gracious and welcoming, but Carrie's attention shifted toward a large paddock that could be seen from the porch through a small grove of apple trees. It seemed that yearlings were being put through their paces, but she could not make out anything about the men working with them beyond the fact that they all wore broad-brimmed hats and bright bandanas around their necks.

"Sister? Don Esteban is inviting us into his home."

She said, "Pardon me. You have such a beautiful place here, Mr.— Don Esteban. I don't know where to look first."

Nathan's grin said she had done a very poor job of pulling the wool over his eyes.

Before any discussion of the purchase of horses could start, they must take the most comfortable chairs in the parlor and be introduced to Mrs. Romero, called Doña Teresa. She came in to offer something to drink and to insist that the Ballentynes join them for Sunday dinner at noon.

Then there were all the usual questions about themselves and their journey. Most of this discussion Carrie left to Nathan. She tried to listen; she meant to listen, but her gaze kept drifting, again and again, to windows that provided a somewhat better view of the nearest paddock.

There were many people coming and going in pursuit of the usual tasks. A restful Sunday was not something anyone on a ranch or farm should expect. Most of the people she saw were men, and all of them wore hats and bandanas.

She was studying the men, she admitted to herself, because she thought Eli would be nearby. His sister lived here, after all. And he had made the suggestion that she and Nathan come look at the horses. She was being silly, she was very aware, but if she was going to encounter Eli, she wanted it to happen sooner rather than later. Like a dose of medicine, she thought, to be quickly dispatched in order to begin its work. And how odd a comparison, Eli Ibarra as a cure for—what? With some effort, she focused again on the discussion.

Don Esteban was telling the story of how they came to build this ranch. Thirty years ago they left their home in the Pampas of Argentina with a small herd of the valuable Argentinean horses. Don Esteban's purpose had been to start a breeding operation that would provide for his wife and establish his sons as experts widely admired for their knowledge, skill, good sense, and honesty, and, above all, the quality of their horses.

"And this," he said with a small smile, "we have done." With that, he turned over one hand, palm open. "You are here, as I understand from our mutual friend, to buy horses that you will take with you to Santa Fe. Let me show you what I have to offer, and you can spend the rest of the morning riding. I believe you will be pleased."

The paddock they wanted was some distance away, but Carrie insisted on walking, and so the small party set out. They passed an old couple sitting in the sun outside a cottage, who raised their voices to greet Don Esteban.

Don Esteban's workers were in general not especially tall, but there was a sense of wiry strength in the men and women both. From what she had seen thus far, they all had very dark, straight hair, almost black eyes, and skin that looked burnished to a deep caramel by the sun. Carrie could not imagine that they would all have come from Argentina, and wondered if they might be from Mexico. In any case, to her eye, South American or Mexican, many of these people were primarily Indian. The term Mestizo made more sense now.

This was, of course, nothing out of the ordinary for her own family, where Mohawk, Seminole, African and Scots, English and French lines were braided together.

A barrage of childish squeals drew her attention to the next cottage as they passed. Like the main house, it was built of red brick, the shutters and doors and woodwork painted white. White fencing surrounded the house and gardens, which struck Carrie as very odd: any rabbit worth its salt could find its way inside to the vegetable beds. Then she saw the shape of a large dog asleep in the shade on the porch. Far more effective than a fence.

The children's voices came closer, raised in a good-natured squabble.

"My grandsons," Don Esteban said. "Honking like geese." He shook his head, unable to hide either his pride or his exasperation.

The boys appeared just then from around a corner, and behind them a harried woman who must be their mother. As soon as they caught sight of Don Esteban, the argument was forgotten in the rush to get to him. They vaulted the fence, so eager to greet their grandfather that they would not waste time with gates and latches.

"Boys," Don Esteban said, lowering his chin to look at them down the slope of his nose.

And just that simply, they fell silent.

"Better," he said. "Now, Miss Ballentyne, Mr. Ballentyne, if I may introduce my daughter-in-law, Maddalen, the wife of my oldest son. These are three of my grandchildren. Jaime, Carlos, and the one scowling there is my namesake, Esteban."

Maddalen came forward to be introduced, and Carrie realized almost immediately that this had to be Eli Ibarra's sister. The resemblance was unmistakable, but more than that: Eli himself had come out of the house and was walking toward them.

The boys launched themselves back over the fence and rushed to their uncle, shouting his name.

"I believe you know my brother," Maddalen said to Carrie.

"I do," Carrie said. And stopped talking, because anything she might say could be misunderstood.

Nathan said, "Eli and I got to know each other when the steamer sailed without us."

"Yes," said Maddalen drily. "We heard about that. How many years do you think that adventure took off your life, Miss Ballentyne?"

"Too many," Carrie said.

She was aware of Eli just behind her, and did what was expected of her. She greeted him politely, asked after his health, answered his questions. All the while aware that the Romeros were watching her closely. Watching them both closely. As if they knew her, or knew of her.

The idea made her mouth go dry. It occurred to her that she could grab the first horse she saw and ride away. Surely she could find work as a nurse somewhere in Missouri.

"I know you are trying to smile," her brother said, leaning close and lowering his voice. "But it looks like a grimace." And he stepped away before she could apply her elbow to his ribs.

They continued to the paddock, the party now larger by five. Maddalen walked beside Carrie while her sons ranged back and forth, spouting questions in Spanish and English. A small lake came into view, surrounded by pastures and flanked by another barn and a covered arena. By the time they reached it, Carrie had regained her self-possession, mostly because there were horses, the best distraction of all.

In the small paddock she counted three mares, four geldings, and a donkey very close to giving birth, her belly like a great cask about to break its bands.

As Don Esteban approached the fence, the jenny let out a tremendous two-toned bray that worked like a starting bell, because they all broke into a graceful trot. A bull terrier asleep in the sun roused himself at the commotion and loped along behind, tail and hind section wagging furiously, the eyes like blue marbles set in triangles of black on an otherwise white face.

Mr. Romero was digging for something in a pocket, talking to them all in low, affectionate tones. In return they were blowing and nickering, all eyes fixed on his palm, where a pile of glittering sugar lumps had appeared out of nowhere.

Nathan said, "They are a bit on the small side."

He was right. Carrie estimated that the biggest of the horses at the fence was no more than fifteen hands—but size wasn't the most important consideration at the moment.

"Look," Carrie countered. "Strong leg conformation, big flat knees, and low-set hocks. Exactly what you want in a trail horse when you've got a long way to go."

Nathan shrugged his agreement, but Eli's head turned toward her quite sharply. She had surprised him, and she could go on surprising him. If he asked, she could talk about horses for days, but she wouldn't put herself in that position. She didn't want to see disbelief or disapproval on his face.

"That one," Nathan said, and pointed to the biggest of the horses, a gelding with a smoky-blue coat and black mane, tail, and points. There was a dark dorsal stripe as well as zebra stripes on his legs.

To Don Esteban he said, "I'd like to have a closer look at that blue roan, if he's available. What about you, sister?"

Carrie considered the horses, one by one, but her gaze kept slipping back to a sorrel mare, her coat a rich deep auburn set off by her mane and tail, as bright as corn in August, a mixture of maize and paler gold and sun-bleached white. There was a liveliness about her that Carrie found promising.

"Her name is Mimosa," Eli said. Carrie startled to find that he was standing so close, and that he had, yet again, read her mind.

Nathan turned to Eli. "What about you? Do you have an Argentinean of your own?"

Don Esteban laughed. "He has three."

Eli's gaze moved over the next pasture, a watchful father looking out for his children.

"There are other horses to see just now," his sister said.

"Yes," said her father-in-law. "Let me introduce you to Nando and Mimosa."

15

LATER, AFTER A long ride, they joined the Romero family for a meal. More than a dozen people gathered around a table under a vine-covered canopy, and it seemed they all had stories to tell or questions to ask.

Carrie listened, answered questions that came her way, but with difficulty. It was a challenge to follow so many conversations at once, and more than that, she had questions of her own to ask.

She would have liked to know Eli's thoughts on the horses, but he sat too far away, and two nieces were monopolizing him. Then again, she admitted to herself, even if he had been sitting beside her, it would have been difficult to talk with such an attentive audience.

Instead she was finally in a position to speak Spanish. Not much, and nothing complicated, but she felt as if she had got off to a good start and was pleased. The challenge came when one of the Romero grandsons asked a question that took her by surprise.

"Señorita, ¿no tenía un caballo propio en Nueva York?"

Carrie understood well enough—or hoped she did—and told him

that at home in New York she did have a horse of her own, called Pearl. In order to explain why she had left Pearl behind, she had to resort to English.

"Pearl is older, and she has earned her rest."

Suddenly all attention shifted to Carrie and the boy.

"If you had brought Pearl," he said, also in English, "Mimosa wouldn't have to go away."

"Ah," Carrie said. "Is she a special favorite of yours?"

"They are all his favorites," said one of his brothers in a dismissive tone.

"Is that so?" Carrie said. "Well, that seems to me to be right and good. To raise and train and ride a horse, you must love it. That's what I was taught."

"Then you are like me," the boy said. "But they call me *sensiblero*."

Carrie was aware of the fact that Don Esteban and Doña Teresa were watching her closely, but she kept her gaze on the young boy who was looking to her for some hint of understanding.

"I am sentimental about Pearl," she said. "I like to think of her as comfortable and thoroughly coddled, and I make no apologies for that."

Eli Ibarra made a sound deep in his throat. His expression was almost severe, but his tone was even when he spoke to Carrie directly. "And why would you need to do that?"

Carrie managed a smile. "I don't follow. Why would I need to what?"

"To apologize." He was looking at her with such intensity that she felt it like a touch.

Maddalen said, "There is a saying—"

"*Compasivo no es lo mismo que débil*," Eli supplied, and then translated, "'Tenderhearted does not mean weak.' Just the opposite."

For the rest of the day that sentence would repeat itself in Carrie's head. It was very prominent in her thoughts when she and Nathan retired with Don Esteban to his office to negotiate the sale, a process that went far more smoothly than she would have imagined. When they were finished with paperwork and bank drafts, they went to the nearest barn and came to an agreement about saddles and tack, and finished with handshakes.

Now CARRIE HAD a five-year-old Argentinean mare. Calm, grounded, sure of foot, agile, responsive, intelligent.

"Mimosa is the perfect horse for you," Maddalen had said. "She is so clever, she will know what you want before you know it yourself."

Carrie wasn't quite sure how it had come to pass, but in the mid-afternoon she found herself in a small parlor with the Romero women. She didn't know where Nathan had gone, and hadn't seen Eli Ibarra since she left the dinner table. That might mean that he had set out already, but then she hadn't had much success predicting his behavior thus far.

She could go look for her brother, but the parlor was a very comfortable place to be on a warm afternoon, with open windows on both sides that allowed a breeze to pass through. More than that, the Romero women were speaking primarily Spanish, and Carrie was paying close attention. She could follow much of what they said, as long as they did not speak too quickly. *Harina de maíz*, she was fairly sure, must be cornmeal. Someone had a *brazo roto*, a broken arm. Then she heard the word *gaucho*.

She sat up and the movement caught Maddalen Romero's eye.

"Something I can get for you, Miss Ballentyne?"

"No, thank you. I was wondering about that word you just used."

Maddalen turned to face her more directly. "Gaucho? You know the word *vaquero*?"

"A man who manages livestock on horseback," Carrie said. "Sometimes called a wrangler."

"Yes," Maddalen agreed. "That's right. *Gaucho* is an Argentine word for a vaquero of the first rank. Strong, capable, honest, and born to the saddle. The men who rode with you this morning, Manuel and Carlos and Eli, they are all gauchos. And your brother, if he spent a

few months here, I think he would also prove himself to be a gaucho.
You impressed us all when you rode out."

The morning ride across open fields was something Carrie would
always be able to recall exactly. It was not just that Mimosa was all she
could have hoped for in a horse, but the fact that the horses responded
to each other and to their riders. For the first time, something that
should have been obvious became clear to her: watching an excellent
rider on a horse he knew well was much like watching a man dance
with a woman he had come to love.

Doña Teresa was saying, "There is more to it than my good-daughter
is telling you. A gaucho knows and understands and values the horse,
mind and heart and soul. The man and the horse are in some ways the
same creature. All the men on this ranch are vaqueros, but only some
of them are gauchos."

A servant came in with a tray of teacups. Carrie took in the smell,
something unfamiliar and quite strong, but not unpleasant.

"But you must be aware there is more to a gaucho," Doña Teresa
said as she passed Carrie a cup. "A gaucho is also a trial and tribulation to the women in his life. I tell my daughters to stay away from
gauchos. Did I not tell you that, *m'hija*? And did you fail to listen, as
usual?"

The girl laughed. "Yes, Mama, the gaucho you married may be
your trial and tribulation, but you adore him. As he adores you."

"This is true," Doña Teresa said. She turned to Carrie and considered her for a moment.

"Miss Ballentyne," she said. "I see in you a woman who would not
be intimidated by a gaucho if you took one as a husband. Certainly
you would rise to the challenge."

It was time for Carrie to leave, unless she was ready to talk to these
women about potential husbands.

She said, "That is something I'll have to think about. This has been
a truly wonderful day for me, but I think we need to get back to Westport. If only I knew where my brother has disappeared to."

"Oh, that's easy," Maddalen said with a grin. "He rode off with Eli, no doubt to put some pointed questions to him, gaucho to gaucho."

NATHAN, HALF-ASLEEP IN a sunny meadow, roused when he realized that Eli had tossed a pebble that bounced off his belly.

He squinted into the sunny sky overhead. "What?"

"Getting late."

"So it is." But he stayed just as he was.

Eli whistled for his mount. Sombra was a tobiano Argentinean of a very deep brown with large splashes of white, much like cream poured over cake. Nathan's Nando followed along, as if to see what distractions Sombra might have thought up.

Nathan was very pleased with his new gelding, six years old and trail tested, with a certain gleam in his eye that promised high spirits and some measure of mischief. *Too much like you,* Carrie had said. *No telling what trouble you'll get into together.*

He yawned and got to his feet. "Carrie will be wondering where we disappeared to."

No comment from Eli, who had been very quiet since the meal. Maybe because he anticipated Nathan's questions. When they were about halfway back to the ranch house, Nathan decided that the time had come to say what needed to be said.

"Am I right to think that, without your word, Don Esteban would not have had any horses to show us?"

A soft clearing of the throat was an admission.

Eli said, "I was taking a chance, but I had a feeling it would work out. Whatever doubts he had disappeared as soon as you—the both of you—rode off."

There was more Eli had to say, but Nathan understood patience was called for. He waited.

"She is a born horsewoman, your sister. Remarkable."

"She is," Nathan agreed. "And more than that. She has a sixth sense when it comes to most animals."

Eli didn't hide his surprise.

"You'll see for yourself," Nathan explained. "Carrie knows horses. She can spot laminitis or a sore forelock or a bad tooth or colic coming on."

"And she tends to them?"

"She does. And she's had good success. The simple truth is, she likes horses better than people. You'll rarely see her smile like she smiled today when she mounted Mimosa."

Eli gave a huff of laughter.

"What?" Nathan prompted. "You plan on making her smile yourself?"

Eli wheeled around and took off at a lope. It wasn't until the ranch came into view that he pulled up. He sat looking at Nathan for a long minute, his expression grim.

"Once you turn back for home, you won't need to worry about her. I'll keep an eye out."

"That's good to know," Nathan said. "But I think you'll find that Carrie is very good at taking care of herself."

Eli looked over the countryside, his face lost in the shadow of his hat brim. Nathan wondered if he would challenge this idea that Carrie didn't need a male protector.

"You think I'm not taking the risks seriously, or that I'm overestimating her. Or both."

Eli met his eye and gave a sharp nod.

Nathan considered. Finally he said, "Carrie and me, we watched our father drown. Early spring, ice floes set up a logjam on the Sacandaga. Two dozen men—half of them our people—were trying to get things moving. It was raining hard and almost cold enough to snow when Da got pulled under.

"All the men saw it happen and went straight after Da. I went in the other direction. I tore out for home to get our Ma. I think I was imagining that she'd march down to the river, raise her voice, and shout his name, and Da would just walk right up the bank. When Ma was in need, he was always there. Nothing could stop him.

"So I ran as fast as I could, up a slope that was muddy and wet and slick, and I tripped and fell. I banged my head on a stump and passed out. It was a couple hours before they found me."

"Ah," said Eli. "That explains some things."

"It does. If you catch her in the right mood, she'll admit that she tends to overreact to head injuries, and she'd probably even admit it has to do with that day."

"The day when she almost lost both of you."

Nathan was relieved that Eli followed so readily.

"Da was dead, and it looked like I might not make it. Aunt Hannah drilled holes into my skull that night to stop the swelling, but it was almost four days later I finally came back to myself. When I did wake up, Da was already in his grave. That was the end, and it was the beginning too. Of everything."

Eli cleared his throat. "That's a hard loss."

Nando lifted his head and shifted, impatient to be off.

Nathan decided that he had said enough for the time being. "Anything else you wanted to ask me, while you've got the chance?"

Eli's mouth jerked at the corner. "Nothing you're willing to tell me. There's a story that I think I need to hear, but it looks like Carrie's the only one who can tell it."

"That's true," Nathan said. "But only because the others are all dead."

16

CARRIE WOKE TO rolling thunder and rain on the roof. She was generally a sound sleeper and most likely would have kept sleeping if not for the raindrop that hit her on the forehead. The next one hit her in the eye, and that was that: she could not command the roof to stop leaking, and so she got out of the bed and stood in the dark, wondering where her shawl might be.

The weak light from the hall was enough to make it possible to avoid stumbling over trunks. Of course, once she reached the door, her options were few and unappealing: she could go downstairs to the desk in the lobby as she was, barefooted, wearing a nightgown with no shawl or robe, and hope the night clerk was professional and competent.

Or, she reasoned, she could take the bedding off the bed and make a nest on the floor, but it would be hard to get back to sleep. Moving the massive bed was not something she could do by herself. The last and only sensible choice was to rouse Nathan, who could go downstairs and find a solution. That still meant she would have to step out into the hall and walk down the corridor to Nathan's room. Again in her nightgown, and barefooted.

The sound of rain on the roof was soothing, and for a long moment she just stood there, swaying a little, half-asleep, and listened. Eventually other noises intruded: a wagon rumbling by, a dissatisfied mule, a piano from a saloon down the street, an argument somewhere nearby. Coyotes not so far away calling on the absent moon. A couple of old men walking past the hotel, one murmuring, the other hissing in response.

She made her way to the window and peeked out between the curtain panels. As if the heavens had been waiting for her to show her face, the skies opened up.

Generally Carrie liked a good storm, as long as she was in a comfortable place with a fire in the grate and no need to venture outside. Just now, though, none of that was true. Instead she was in a hotel room with a leaky roof, a cold draft coming from an empty grate, and surrounded by trunks and bags, because in a few hours she would be in a stagecoach on her way to a new life in Santa Fe. It would be a few days at least until they could start riding their own horses. They had agreed it would be best to learn how the wagon train was managed before putting saddles on Nando and Mimosa.

Inertia kept her right where she was, watching the storm. Rain swelled and receded once, twice, and then it seemed to make up its mind to stay a while and settled in. In a warm, dry bed the sound would have put her to sleep, and she returned once again to the inevitable conclusion: she would have to wake Nathan.

Just then a man on horseback leading two more mounts came into view. Odd, at this hour of the night. Her pulse picked up as he stopped in the light of the lamps that hung to either side of the hotel's front door.

And now she recognized the horse he rode: an Argentinean he called Sombra. It was Eli Ibarra sitting there in the streaming rain for no apparent reason.

His head came up and the light touched his face as his gaze moved from one window to the next. As if he knew she would be there, waiting to be seen.

When he caught sight of her, he stilled.

Carrie's breath stuttered. She should step away from the window, but instead she studied him. His hat, broad brimmed and low crowned, was mostly hidden beneath the hood of a gutta-percha cloak spread out around him. Brass-studded leather gloves with high gauntlets. In the shadows, she could make out the shape of a rifle scabbard, a coil of rope, a canteen. Saddlebags. A bedroll. The other two horses stood in shadow, but she knew them. Both Argentineans, a mare and another gelding. And that made sense. He had left his three horses with the Romero family while he traveled to Europe.

In the few seconds it took for her to see all this, his gaze never moved from her face. A man about to set out on a long journey, eight hundred miles over plains and desert and mountains.

There was nothing between them beyond polite conversation, a few smiles, and the occasional wink of an eye, but now he sat below her window in the hammering rain and observed her without excuse or apology. The only reaction Carrie could summon up to this odd situation was the warm hum of curiosity.

He raised his right hand and pointed two fingers at her in a gesture ripe with meaning.

She said, "I see you too."

As if he could hear her, Eli Ibarra broke into a wide smile, turned Sombra's head, and moved off. Carrie watched him disappear into the night.

17

Monday, May 18, 1857

CARRIE EXPECTED CHAOS the next morning. It was always the case before they set out: baggage went missing, tea spilled, buttons detached themselves and rolled into dark corners. She resolved that this time all would be calm and orderly. She would begin the day with a visit to the stable where the horses had spent the night, speak quietly to them about what was to come, and at the same time, to herself.

They were still strangers, after all. Nando and Mimosa were familiar with each other and they had been well trained, but it took some time to earn a horse's trust.

That first part of her plan went well. She spent a half hour talking to them, stroking necks and feeding them dried apples she had bought for just this purpose. When they were relaxed, ears forward, nostrils round, tails swishing easily, she went back to the hotel, where Nathan was at breakfast, hunkered over a plate piled high with sausage, cornmeal mush, and eggs.

He pointed to her chair. "You have to eat."

Because he was excited and anxious, Carrie didn't argue. Then, as soon as Miss Herlinde brought her plate, Nathan was folding his napkin and getting to his feet.

"Saddle blankets," he said. "We need more saddle blankets."

She waved him away. The truth was, she would have found an excuse to send him on an errand if he hadn't found one for himself. He might come back with saddle blankets and Enfield rifles, barrels of molasses and lard, but she would take that chance. More than food she needed some time to collect her thoughts.

An hour later, after one of Mr. Petit's men came to collect their trunks, Carrie sat in her hotel room alone. Sunlight poured in from the window where she had stood to watch the storm, an episode so odd that she would have dismissed it as a dream if not for the damp patch on the ceiling over the bed.

But time was short, and so she considered the carpetbag at her feet, packed and repacked so many times. The urge to go through it all again was almost irresistible, but instead she took up the single sheet of paper from the desk to remind herself that she was well prepared.

The list had begun at her desk at home, on the day she sent off her acceptance of the position of nurse and midwife in Santa Fe. The paper had gone soft with use and so thin at the folds that it would soon fall into pieces. Nathan shook his head at her refusal to start over on a fresh sheet of paper, but Carrie saw this simple list as a kind of historical document. She could trace her own thinking by going over what had been added and crossed out.

The first item was the most obvious: her midwifery kit. Below that she had listed basic medicines: laudanum, black cohosh, mint, yarrow, pennyroyal, sumac, and Jesuit's bark. She could treat nausea, costive bowels, headache, and muscle strain with these. Typhoid or measles or malaria patients would be much more of a challenge, but she could provide basic aid until they reached a physician. She had scalpels and lancets, clamps and suture needles that would be useful if the wranglers (gauchos, she reminded herself; vaqueros) were as prone to injury as was indicated by the stories.

Those same instruments would be put to use if she were called on to dig out a bullet or set a broken bone. She regretted now that she had refused her stepfather's offer of a small bone saw.

Her family had always put great value on the skills everyone needed to survive, in the city or stranded in a foreign or unfriendly place. To that end Carrie had one hundred safety matches, imported from Sweden at considerable expense, a large square of waxed canvas, a good clasp knife, and a finer blade for cleaning game. Her rifle was packed in a trunk, and her pistol and ammunition in the carpet-bag.

Her personal papers, bank documents, and the likenesses of family members were wrapped in waxed linen and tucked into a side pocket along with money and an old silver coin her mother had pressed on her as a keepsake.

After considerable debate with herself, Carrie had added a lined slicker, a hairbrush, a washcloth, a bar of soap, and tooth powder. As she understood it, they would be able to get to their trunks once they stopped for the night, but baggage had a way of hiding itself, and she would not be caught out.

At the very top were the three small books Carrie had decided to take with her onto the trail: a Spanish grammar, *Commerce of the Prairies*, and her travel diary. She doubted she would have much time for any such pursuits, but decided it was worth the gamble.

These things would have to be enough, day to day. In her carpetbag there was no room for second-guessing; nor could she heft the weight of panic. A stagecoach was not a box or a trunk or a casket. It was not a pantry. A stagecoach had doors and windows. She would get through this first day, and tomorrow she would spend as much time as possible riding Mimosa.

What had she done with the dried apples she had bought from Miss Herlinde?

She found the lumpy packet tucked into the folds of the slicker, and repacked once more. Then it was time to go.

⚊∘⚊

EVA SAID, "IT's always like this. A madhouse."

They stood in the shade of an elm tree, watching teamsters and wranglers swarming over and around the stagecoach that squatted there like a dusty dead beetle. Hitching three teams of oxen to a stagecoach was a noisy business, involving a mountain of harnesses and buckles, leather straps and leads and reins.

The oxen seemed to take it all in stride, and the wranglers were cheerful. The teamsters struggling to strap trunks and boxes to the roof of the stagecoach were less sanguine. There were multiple differences of opinion, a lot of shouting, and every once in a while a long string of curses.

Luckily Beto's attention was elsewhere. He was watching for Nathan and the Argentineans, hopping up and down in his excitement.

"There." She crouched down next to him and pointed. "You see? He's talking to one of the wranglers."

"Joshua," the boy supplied. "In charge of the *remuda*. Which one is yours?"

They spent a few minutes talking about Mimosa. Even from this distance, Beto declared her to be a very fine specimen, but announced that it would be best if he had a closer look at Nando.

"Not now," his mother said. "Things are so hectic, I don't want you to get trampled."

He gave a philosophical sigh and looked to his string puppet for comfort.

"I'm wondering about the other passengers," Carrie said, but Eva had no information to share.

"Maybe there will be a boy," Beto said. "Or even a girl." The idea of another child to keep him company seemed to cheer him. Then Nathan was walking toward them, and Beto began to unbundle the many questions and stories he had collected since they had last seen each other.

Eva said, "I see Nathan is ready to ride. What is he wearing on his feet?"

Carrie lifted her skirts a few inches so that Eva could see the knee-high moccasins she wore, identical to Nathan's. "A cousin of ours cures doubled buckskin to make them," she said. "This pair is ten years old and it will last another twenty."

"Goodness," Eva said. "And are you wearing—"

"Doeskin leggings under my skirt," Carrie supplied. "In the height of summer, I'd leave the skirt off, but I wouldn't push things quite so far at this point. What a wicked grin, Eva."

"Nathan," Eva called. "If you've got Roberto, your sister and I are going for a short walk."

Carrie suspected that Eva's interest in a walk had to do with the horses. She would want to know exactly how they had got to Lake-land Ranch, and whether Eli Ibarra had been involved. It was an inevitable and not entirely unreasonable question, and so Carrie answered it without prompting.

"You could have a career as a telegram operator," Eva teased. "That was so concise I have to wonder what you're hiding."

Carrie thought of the thunderstorm the night before, and the man sitting on horseback below her window. And if she never saw him again, it was an image she would keep for herself alone, for as long as she lived.

She smiled and shook her head.

Eva would not have given up in her quest for information, but her attention had shifted to Orwell Petit, who was backing away from a woman not half his size. She advanced, he withdrew; she advanced, and he retreated until he had backed into the stagecoach. It did not sound like an argument, but it looked like one.

The lady wore a scoop bonnet that made it impossible to see anything of her face. She was small and slight, but there was a stiffness to her posture that made Carrie believe she was not young. Her gown, a brown and maroon plaid, was both conservative and ugly.

"Do you think that she's—" Carrie began.

"I'm afraid so," Eva said. And in a more hopeful tone: "Maybe it's just Orwell Petit she dislikes. Come, we need a better view."

They walked along a stand of trees until the angle revealed more of the woman who still had Mr. Petit cornered.

Framed by the dark fabric of her sunbonnet, her face was narrow, her eyes bloodshot, and her complexion almost doll-like in its pale perfection. Her eyebrows and lashes were such a very white blond that she seemed at first not to have any color at all. Odder still, there was nothing of anger or dismay in her expression. She was speaking to Mr. Petit calmly, but insistently.

"Hmmm," Eva said.

Carrie was in complete agreement.

A bit later Nathan told them what he had heard. "Mrs. Kanti Chatham by name," he said. "From Richmond. She's like a cat. When Petit was talking, she just blinked at him as if she didn't care to listen, and then repeated herself, told him what he must have, always ignoring his explanations. She just keeps at it until she gets her way."

"You are being unkind," Carrie said. "She may have very good reasons for—whatever it is she's asking about."

"Yes," Nathan said. "Her purpose is to make Petit understand that she is not to be denied."

How he came to this conclusion, Carrie didn't know, but at the same time she couldn't deny that it had the ring of truth.

Clearly Eva thought so too. She said, "Let's hope for the best."

"And plan for the worst?" Nathan laughed softly. "What would that be, exactly?"

It was not a question Carrie wanted to contemplate.

An hour later, after the four of them had taken seats in the stagecoach, they were joined by an elderly, rotund gentleman in an ancient black suit worn almost to transparency in the folds. His complexion was tinged the particular jaundice yellow that meant liver disease. Perspiration gleamed on his face. He wore spectacles that sat crooked on his nose, in competition with two very full, wildly curling white eyebrows under a brow he had clearly rubbed with inky fingers.

He introduced himself as Mr. Preston, mumbling and nodding to each of them without meeting their eyes. Then he wiggled until he was satisfied with his seat and unfolded a newspaper that he held in front of himself. A flimsy barricade, but effective.

For once Beto had nothing to say, but Eva lifted both eyebrows, asking Carrie for her opinion.

She shrugged.

"I wonder what the delay is," Eva said. "It looks to me like we should have been on our way an hour ago."

"Here's the answer to your question," Nathan said. "Our last traveling companion."

He lowered his chin to look at Carrie down the slope of his nose. It was his hope that Mrs. Chatham would be a source of distraction and, with some luck, diversion. She hoped he was right, but was fairly sure he was not.

Mrs. Chatham arrived, Mr. Petit following with her carpetbag and a sour expression. He offered her his arm so that she would have an easier time climbing into the stagecoach, but she ignored him. She climbed the two steps without assistance, lifted her skirts just high enough to reveal ankles like twigs covered in black wool, and stopped in the doorway.

There was one seat left, across from Mr. Preston and next to one of the four windows.

She stared at the empty seat, unblinking. Finally she turned to look first at Eva, and then at Carrie. The men she ignored.

"No one thought to consult me about my seating preferences?" Her tone was calm, and her voice, low pitched for a woman, was distinctly Southern in its rhythms. Beyond her accent her voice had a creaky quality that Carrie was familiar with. She heard it often from wealthy women, or not-so-wealthy women with pretensions to wealth and social status. Such women employed that kind of creaky voice like a snake used its rattle.

Mr. Petit disappeared, and who could blame him?

Beto, who did not sense the tension among the adults or simply didn't know what to do with it, sat up straight. He was an unusual child, comfortable talking to most strangers—Mr. Preston notwithstanding— and willing to step in when most his age would have retreated to let the adults carry on.

"Ma'am, look." He patted the cushioned seat beside himself. "There's a seat right here. Are you going to Santa Fe?"

"Not seated beside a child." Again her voice was modulated, cool, with that subtle creak.

Eva turned toward Mrs. Chatham, but Nathan held up a hand, head tilted, asking without words for permission to step in. He smiled at Beto.

"Let's switch seats." Nathan's tone was as calm as Mrs. Chatham's, because, Carrie understood, he didn't want to distress either Beto or his mother. "Come sit here next to my sister, and I'll sit in your place."

"Because Mrs. Chatham doesn't like children," Beto said, very matter-of-fact, and got up.

18

IT WAS NEAR noon when the wagon train started out with a jerk and rattle and a lot of noise. Wranglers shouted to each other and at their mounts and at teamsters, who shouted back. The amount of noise took Carrie by surprise, though it shouldn't have. Everything man-made seemed to crackle or rattle or jingle, while the mule teams and oxen and horses and the rest of the livestock contributed, full voiced.

"First day," Eva shouted. "It will settle down in no time."

Almost right away Beto found his way into his mother's lap, where he could watch out the window as the teamsters and wranglers guided freight, mail, and supply wagons into line.

From his seat on the box, the driver called Helmet—Carrie had still not had a chance to ask for more information about the odd name—called to his mules in a singsong, like a mother to children who needed encouragement on a long walk.

They gave him what he wanted, settling into a steady trot: twenty-four hooves striking the hard-packed trail in an easy rhythm accented by the music of jingling hardware.

The stagecoach was the fastest vehicle on the trail, so that in a short while they passed a wagon train that had set out hours before. Carrie watched as a dozen, two dozen, many dozen families began the slow, dangerous journey west.

As she had imagined, many people chose to walk beside their wagons rather than endure the torture of riding in a dark, hot wagon bed over the roughest road. The price to be paid for the freedom of movement—one of the prices—came in the form of road dust raised by wheels and hooves that hung in the air and draped itself over the quick and the dead. Soon some of these people would be coughing until their lungs rattled.

The stagecoach, with all its difficulties, was the far better option.

She felt Nathan's eyes on her, assessing. She smiled at him as broadly as she could manage, and for her trouble got narrowed eyes. His protectiveness was often unwelcome, but today she chose to overlook it.

Beto began to point out small things that Carrie would have missed: a butter churn strapped to the side of a wagon, jostled constantly. That family would have butter when they stopped in the evening to make camp. A cat stretched out over the top of the canvas bonnet, soaking in the sun. There was a wrangler riding a pure white horse, and another who was himself dark-skinned, with the broad features that originated in Africa. Wranglers from Mexico—vaqueros—she had expected, but somehow it had never occurred to her that former slaves might be interested in this life.

Little by little Beto seemed to slip away toward sleep, but now and then he roused to point out something interesting: a cage of chickens swinging from a hook fixed to a supply wagon, and then, with real excitement, a herd of antelope on a knoll not too far off.

"I haven't seen them so far east before," Eva said.

Nathan leaned past Carrie to get a closer look. "Like very big goats, with hooks on their horns. Beto, do you suppose that's where they hang their hats when they settle down for the night?"

Beto wrinkled his nose at Nathan. "Wait until you see them run. They can outrun a buffalo horse."

"Buffalo horse? Half one, half the other?"

"Silly," Beto said with a sleepy grin. "A buffalo horse is the kind of horse you have to have to hunt buffalo. Very fast and brave. A *cibolero's* horse."

Carrie thought of her travel diary. If nothing else, she would like to make a record of these conversations.

"Why do you sigh?" Eva asked her.

Carrie shook her head. "Nothing so important. Beto, you will have to remind me later about the antelope so I can tell our mother when I can write to her next. If she were here, she'd draw them down to the smallest detail. Even with hats on their prongs, if you were to ask her."

This Beto found intriguing. He wanted to hear about a mother who was an artist, and so Nathan told him how a young Lily Bonner had her first drawing lessons from her Grandfather Oak a very long time ago in the endless forests in the far north of New York State. Carrie enjoyed listening to this very familiar story, too, and thought of taking her small collection of portraits out to show Beto and Eva.

But they had weeks ahead of them, and there would be another afternoon to introduce these new friends to the Bonner-Savard-Ballentyne family. Another day when she was less likely to weep with homesickness.

"So your grandfather—" Beto paused and glanced at his mother.

"Great-grandfather," she provided.

"Gabriel Oak," said Nathan.

"He was an artist?"

"I suppose you'd call him an itinerant artist," Nathan said. "He grew up in Philadelphia but set out young to travel. The margins and blank pages in books he carried are full of drawings. A hen chasing a little girl, that's one I like especially. A bower full of roses, with rabbits sleeping in the shadowy spaces. Dandelions bursting out of a discarded boot."

"I'd like to see those drawings," Beto said, with great sincerity.

"Our Ma has some of his books," Nathan said. "Right on her bed-side table. She looks at one every night."

There was a long, rambling discussion of what Gabriel Oak's life must have been like. Most of this was born of Nathan's imagination, but the boy didn't need to know that.

Beto, still leaning against his mother, gave a yawn. "I like to draw," he said. "Though I'm not very good at it."

"Too busy talking to apply yourself, no doubt."

Mrs. Chatham's voice was just loud enough to be heard by every-one over the noise from the road.

Carrie was not easily surprised, but Eva was shocked and quite angry. She leaned forward to look at the woman at the other end of the bench seat. "Pardon me. Mrs. Chatham, is it? Were you speaking to my son?" Her tone was far colder than Carrie had ever heard it.

The Chatham woman turned toward Eva. In the frame of her bon-net, her face was as smooth as powder, with two bright spots of color high on her cheekbones. Anger spots, as Carrie thought of them.

The small mouth worked. "Very well," she said finally. "If you insist, I will speak to you directly." She rounded her eyes, pursed her mouth, and tilted her head to one side, a challenge as clear as a slap.

"It's obvious that you have some education, but you know nothing of proper child-rearing. In polite society young children are meant to be seen and not heard. You are doing the boy no favors by neglecting his training. Spare the rod, I'm sure you're familiar with the old adage. No doubt you think you know better. Or it matters not at all to you that he offends or inconveniences other people. Have you no paregoric to dose him? Asleep he would not be half so annoying."

Nathan put a calming hand on Eva's wrist and shook his head at her. Then he arched his back and yawned so deeply that he sounded something like a prowling tomcat. Finally he gave a little shake of the shoulders as if he were just waking up, and shifted his gaze to fix on Mrs. Chatham, whose expression perched midway between outrage and shock.

"Mrs. Catty—" He inclined his head. "Pardon me. Mrs. Chatty, you were talking, and I drifted off. Could we try again? If you'd like to present your callous and bigoted opinions later today, I could ignore you again, shall we say when we make camp this evening?"

In the stunned silence that followed—no more than a few seconds—Carrie saw that Mrs. Chatham was neither embarrassed nor regretful. Her eyes narrowed, she was preparing to launch a reply, only to be stopped by the rattle of Mr. Preston's newspaper.

All eyes turned toward him.

"Chatty," he wheezed from behind his paper. "Catty Chatty!" A snort of laughter followed; the paper rattled once more, and then settled.

Eva sent Carrie a wild-eyed look, fighting hard but failing to suppress a laugh. Beto looked back and forth between them, confused, but with a grin curling at the corner of his mouth. Carrie dared not look at her brother, and so, like Eva, she turned her back to Mrs. Chatham to study the landscape, where the antelope were sprinting away, gliding over the gentle swells of the prairie like skaters on a pond in the deep of winter.

19

THAT FIRST DAY on the trail, they had come no more than ten miles when they stopped to make camp. It was a disappointment, but Carrie said nothing, for fear that Mrs. Chatham might insert herself into the conversation. With that came the realization that whenever she saw the woman or even thought of her, she would find it difficult to think of her as anything but Catty Chatty.

Avoiding Mrs. Chatham was going to preoccupy them all for weeks to come, unless they could somehow make peace. She was wondering if this might be possible as they came to a full stop and the older lady flung open the door without waiting for help, left the stage-coach, and marched away, her destination a stand of trees near a stream. That was at least understandable.

The next hour was hectic, but orderly. Carrie watched and learned what it meant to make camp. Luckily Eva was there to answer questions. After four trips back and forth to St. Louis, she understood the business.

Helmet supervised the unhitching and care of the donkey teams, flicking his whip at any wrangler who showed the animals less care than they deserved; Mr. Tock oversaw the two men who drove long poles into the ground and unrolled tarpaulins for the tents, and others who fetched water and firewood. Mr. Petit went off on horseback to make sure the *remuda* was properly situated and watered and that all was as it should be with the rest of the wagons. From what Carrie could see, standing in the open doorway of the stagecoach to improve her view, some of the wranglers were changing out day mounts for night mounts.

"Mr. Petit is very cautious," Eva told her. "There are a dozen wranglers watching the *remuda* and just as many who keep watch over the wagons. And us."

Carrie might have given in to her urge to ask how likely an attack might be, but Beto stood close by.

Then she caught sight of Nathan, who had gone over to check on Nando and Mimosa. He stopped to talk to the wrangler who seemed to be in charge, a man of forty years or so, thick bodied and broad shouldered.

"Do you know that man my brother is talking to?"

Eva squinted into the sunlight. "Oh yes. That's Joshua Petit. Generally called Pate. Mr. Petit's brother. He's in charge of the *remuda*."

It took a moment for her to make sense of the man's name. Pete? Pat? She asked for clarification.

"Just Pate." Eva touched the crown of her own head, and Carrie understood.

"Bald?"

"Not a hair on his body," Eva said. "Not lashes or brows or—anything else, if rumors are to be believed. But he's a top hand. A vaquero. The other wranglers don't care whether he has hair, and nobody dares tease him."

"Then he's fortunate," Carrie said. "It's an ailment called alopecia. I've seen it twice since I began training, but both patients were women. For them it was very difficult."

"You must have some interesting stories to tell about your patients," Eva said.

"Right now it's Miss Chatham I'm curious about. I wonder where she is."

Eva leaned down to brush dust from her son's shoulders. She was full of such maternal gestures, which tended to show themselves when she was distracted.

Beto said, "Look, Mr. Preston wants to help Mr. Liebling. Or maybe he's just hungry."

Preston stood with his wrists crossed at the small of his back, rocking on his heels, much like a man fond of gambling stood at attention to watch a horse race.

"Hungry," Beto decided. "Me too."

"Always, *m'hijo*," Eva said, and ran a hand over his head.

Liebling was busy unpacking the supply wagon. Carrie was reminded of a tinker's cart as she watched him unlatch hooks and swing partitions open. In a matter of minutes a dozen cubbyholes and a long line of bins appeared below overflowing cupboards. Then Liebling pulled a large board out of a slot and fitted one end to the edge of a shelf. Out of nowhere he produced a pan the size of a wagon wheel and turned, just in time to see a wrangler coming up from the bank of the stream carrying two water buckets.

Carrie, her throat dry with trail dust, wondered if she could just walk over and ask for a drink. She was debating this with herself when Nathan bumped her shoulder to get her attention.

"Look there," he said, pointing. "The mistress headed off in the wrong direction."

Miss Chatham was walking toward a small group of buildings a quarter mile off. Over one arm was a shawl, and in the other hand she carried a carpetbag.

"Odd," Carrie said. "Is that a town?"

"Um, sort of," Eva said, turning away. "Roberto, let's go wash your face and hands. How do you manage to get so grimy?"

"Eva?" Carrie said. "What do you mean, sort of?"

There was a reluctance in her friend's posture that struck Carrie as very unusual. "Is there some trouble?"

Nathan, concerned, leaned closer.

"No trouble," Eva said then. "It's an Indian mission. A school."

"Catholic?" Nathan asked.

"Heavens no. Methodist. Roberto, do not run ahead." She glanced at Carrie over her shoulder. "You have questions, of course. Later, please."

Then she was gone without waiting for a reply.

Carrie looked more closely at the settlement: a large brick mansion surrounded by smaller, lesser buildings. An Indian mission, in Kansas Territory. Training schools, some called them.

Under his breath Nathan said, "She knows some of our family history. She's embarrassed, and I like her more for it."

Much later, after they had eaten and Beto had been settled on a pallet in the tent the women would share, Nathan brought up the subject again.

"Eva, have you ever been in that mission school?"

She answered without looking up from the handkerchief she was folding and smoothing, folding and smoothing. "Yes. Once."

"They take Indian children from their tribes. Against their will."

"That is my understanding," she agreed. She glanced around them, ill at ease.

"There's no one close enough to overhear," Nathan said. "What can you tell us about the mission?"

Eva drew in a deep breath and let it go. "It was founded by a Reverend Johnson, some ten years ago or so, and he still runs it. A man with a great deal of influence."

"And strong opinions," Nathan suggested. "Proslavery?"

Another brief nod.

"So," Nathan said. "They are here until they are obedient enough to be servants, and have forgot their own languages."

After a silence Carrie said, "The children in the school, what tribe are they from?"

"Shawnee," Eva said. "Originally from somewhere back east."

Beside her Nathan jerked in surprise, and Carrie had to clear her throat before she could speak. "Yes. From the Ohio Territory."

Eva looked more unsettled than ever. "You know of the tribe?"

Carrie put out a hand on her brother's arm and squeezed. When she was sure he would not interrupt, she started, awkwardly, to explain.

"Our Aunt Hannah and her husband lived among the Shawnee at Tippecanoe. Have you heard of Tecumseh, who launched a movement to unite all the tribes?"

It seemed Eva had not, but Carrie decided to leave that part of the story for the moment.

"Hannah and her husband joined that community and were there until the army wiped out the village while Tecumseh was away with his warriors."

After a long moment, Eva raised her head to look at Carrie and then Nathan. "You must know what is going on out here, with all the tribes. It's—"

"Inevitable." Nathan got up and walked away.

Carrie would not explain nor could she make excuses for her brother, but Eva seemed to understand what had not been said.

Sometime later Carrie looked around herself and realized that almost everyone had retired and that Mr. Petit was riding into camp. Carrie stood in the light of the fire and waved until he saw them and turned in their direction.

Carrie watched him dismount and wondered if he always looked so weary at this early stage in the journey to Santa Fe, but could not think of a way to ask after his health that wouldn't offend. Eva didn't seem to take note, and instead stepped a little closer and cupped her hand at his horse's muzzle.

"Hello, Mariah." With a light touch she ran fingers down the palomino's neck, and in return got a soft snort of welcome.

"Mariah is looking in fine shape." She glanced at Mr. Petit, and something softened in his bearing.

Carrie said, "Is all well?"

"All is well, sure." He shifted uneasily, slapped at a gnat hovering over his face, and touched the brim of his hat.

"Mr. Tock has got things ready for you," he said finally. "So I'll wish you good night."

Eva blinked in surprise at his brusque tone, but countered with something softer and kinder. "Before you go—we were wondering about Mrs. Chatham. She didn't eat with us, and I don't see her anywhere."

It was clear that he had been dreading this question, because he let out a great sigh. He jerked a thumb over his shoulder toward the Shawnee mission.

"She's had enough of us and got herself invited to stay with the Johnsons. I sent one of the men over to the mission with her trunk a while ago."

Eva glanced at Carrie. Whether it was surprise or relief in her expression was difficult to say.

"She just . . . left?" Of the many questions that came to mind, this was the only one Carrie thought he might answer.

"To wait till the next stagecoach comes through. That would be Friday."

"That is not good news for you," Eva noted. "You've lost a fare."

"Not one that I wanted to keep," he said. "And we may pick up another passenger down the road at Council Bluffs, anyway. Now, if you'll excuse me."

As they turned away, Carrie had to ask. "What do you make of that?"

Eva threw her a sidelong glance. "I don't really care why she's gone. I'm just relieved I won't have to keep watch all night for fear she'll come after Roberto with a knife."

Carrie stopped. "Not really."

"I have never seen anyone with such an unapologetic hatred of children," Eva said. "So yes. Really."

20

THE SECOND DAY on the trail was far less difficult. First, because there was no Miss Chatham, and second, because in the afternoon they saddled their horses and rode.

Mr. Petit did not forbid this, but he spent some time reminding them that if they were out of sight, he could do nothing to protect them. He eyed the weapons strapped to their saddles, brow furrowed. Carrie wondered for a moment if he would challenge them to a shooting match, and decided that it would not be unreasonable. Someone with little practical knowledge of firearms might injure a man or set off a stampede. Such accidents were easy to imagine and probably quite common.

But Petit was too busy to ride with them, and they were eager. After another spurt of dire warnings, they wheeled away from the wagon train—where Beto and Eva waved from the stagecoach window—and cantered off.

A half mile removed from the trail—here wide enough for three covered wagons to travel abreast—they settled into an easy trot overland.

Carrie glanced over her shoulder and caught sight of an animal darting off into the high grass. Low to the ground and white.

She pulled up and Nathan followed her lead.

"Did you see that?"

"See—? Oh, Chico has decided to come out of hiding. Mimosa's dog."

Carrie felt her jaw drop. "What?"

"Mimosa's dog. Called Chico. They are devoted to each other,
apparently, and have been almost since birth. He started following as
soon as we left the Romeros' ranch. Keeping out of sight."

Carrie tried to make sense of this. She scanned the ground, but
saw no sign of a dog.

"If this is a joke . . ." she said.

"No, really." Nathan was trying not to smile, and then he gave in
to it.

"How long have you known about . . . Chico?"

He sighed. "I caught sight of him yesterday. I thought he was just a
stray, hanging around the *remuda*, but Pate saw him too. He says it
happens a lot with Romero's horses. You buy a mount and get a dog
too. It's considered good luck, and really, sister, does it matter?"

Carrie liked dogs, but this was so odd.

"Does it matter if my horse has a dog?" She laughed, finally. "I
suppose not. How did Pate know the dog's name?"

"They are all called Chico. Or Chica."

After a moment Carrie stood a little in her stirrups and whistled.
She had a good, strong whistle that surprised both the horses. They
shifted, and then settled.

Carrie whistled again. "Chico!"

She was about to give up—vowing to herself that if this turned out
to be one of her brother's elaborate jokes, she would find a way to
repay him—when a dog showed himself. He stood twenty feet away,
and Carrie recognized him now. He had been in the field where the
horses were grazing, a white bull terrier with black markings and blue
eyes.

Mimosa nickered and tossed her head, but he stayed where he was.

Carrie supposed that he would approach in his own good time; for now, Mimosa had a companion and a bodyguard.

She said, "All right. Let's go on."

To the south the landscape was largely empty, an endless rolling plain, a great expanse of grasses and wildflowers. The only trees they saw followed streambeds, mostly cottonwoods.

Carrie couldn't begin to name any of the grasses, but the wildflowers she was more familiar with: flax, mallow, larkspur, and nettle.

They could still hear the noise of the wagon train from the trail, but at this distance the sound of the wind moving through the grass was a constant, punctuated by the buzz and drone of insects. The view unrestricted, the abundance of sky, all of it folded out in a way that she might have found frightening, had she been alone. But Nathan was beside her.

She welcomed the warmth of the sun on her back and the touch of the breeze on her face.

Most of all, she was pleased to have made such a good start with Mimosa. The mare was sure-footed and watchful and eager. If the weather held, there would be many more afternoons like this one. Along the way Mimosa would learn to trust her without reservation.

On the trail there was a sudden huffing and the deep, throaty roar of an angry longhorn bull who was pushing his way out of a small herd.

They stopped to watch him bellow and paw at the ground, issuing a challenge. Before it could go any further, the wranglers were right there.

"Cowhands," Nathan said. "Nerves of steel."

He pulled up closer beside her. Nando danced away, but Nathan was quick to correct this bit of playfulness.

Carrie said, "Where is it the Oregon trail splits off and turns northwest?"

"Not far now. Ten miles."

"I wonder where we'll camp."

Of course Nathan knew the answer to this question. The gathering of information was as basic to him as breathing. But he could be stingy with news, and poking at him would not take the end she wanted. Then he surprised her.

"Where the trail splits, I was told."

"And how many miles would that make for today?"

"Pate said twenty, twenty-two."

Double the distance they had traveled the first day, which was good news.

She said, "What if we wait for them there?"

It was a risky thing to do. The wagon train might be delayed for any number of reasons, and Mr. Petit would not be happy if they didn't show their faces. And still the idea of fewer hours in the stage-coach was very tempting.

She could see Nathan working through these same thoughts, one by one.

He said, "Do you have any coin with you? In case we have to take rooms before Petit shows up."

And that was reason enough to turn back. They had no money with them, and beyond that, separated from the wagon train, they could do little in the settlement except attract attention and arouse suspicion, two things to be avoided on this kind of journey.

When they got back, Beto wanted to know what animals they had seen, and was philosophical about the lack of buffalo or antelope or elk.

"We saw rabbits," Nathan told him. "And foxes, from far off. And squirrels, with black tails."

While Beto was telling Nathan about the Kansas version of the squirrel, called prairie dogs, Eva gestured to Carrie, who leaned forward to be better able to talk.

"All quiet here?"

"Quiet?" Eva held her hands over her ears in mock horror. In fact, after a few hours away, the trail struck Carrie as noisier than it had been when they first set out.

"Yes, I get your point. Let me rephrase. No difficulties?"

"None. Or I should say, nothing much. Mr. Preston—" She glanced at the gentleman who was now reading a book, still held up in front of his face like a shield.

She mouthed the next word. "Snores."

Nathan had been following their conversation. Now he glanced at Mr. Preston, brow furrowed. Carrie saw something in his expression that verged on dislike. It struck her as odd, because Nathan could sleep through a gun battle and was generally easygoing about such things.

"Most older men do snore," Carrie said. "I'm sure my brother will, when he hits fifty or so."

At least that made him smile.

At the sound of voices raised in anger, Beto went to the window. They were passing two women who walked side by side, heads turned to face one another while they argued. Each of them carried a child of a year or so on a hip, and both children looked utterly bored with the commotion.

"Sisters?" Beto asked nobody in particular, and got no answer. But the women were alike enough to be twins. They certainly fought like sisters; one would haul off with her free hand and smack the other, and then that sister took her turn.

When they had passed by, Beto turned on the spot, as neatly as a soldier on a drill. "Ma," he said. "Ma, that's none of my business. Right?"

"Exactly right," Eva said with great solemnity.

When he had gone back to sit with Nathan, Eva allowed herself a small smile. From her bag she pulled out another fan—this one painted with an abundance of blowsy roses—and began wielding it in quick, hard swipes.

Carrie said, "What a clever boy you have."

"An observant one, certainly."

"Have you seen much trouble on the trail?"

Eva sucked in her lower lip, glancing at Beto. And shook her head. But it was too late.

"Ma," Beto piped up. "What about the time the naked man got his feet all cut up?"

Eva was trying to smile and look puzzled and unconcerned all at once.

"You remember, don't you?" Beto prodded. "Mrs. Frank took his clothes away—"

"I remember," Eva interrupted gently. "That's a story for another time."

They made camp close enough to Gardner that they could watch as a wagon train turned onto the Oregon trail. Wagon by wagon, at a snail's pace.

Carrie took Beto with her to visit Mimosa and Nando.

The boy said, "I smell apples. It's too early for apples."

"That's true," Carrie said. "But it's never too early or late for dried apples, and I have two in my pocket."

They stood at the edge of the rope corral that the hands had just finished putting up, and watched as the *remuda* came in and began to graze.

"There's Mimosa," Beto said. "Why don't you call to her?"

"Let's wait to see if she comes over to see us without an invitation."

Beto looked skeptical, but soon enough Mimosa appeared, standing back about five feet or so. Her ears were forward and relaxed, her tail flicking now and then. Mimosa and Carrie considered each other for a moment, and then Carrie produced one of the dried apples, held out on a flat palm.

"Does she not like apples?" Beto whispered.

"Wait and see."

Mimosa's nostrils flared as she came forward. If Carrie didn't know better, she would say that the horse was feigning indifference. But she closed her lips around the lumpy chunk of apple and drew it into her mouth to crunch down on it.

"She does like apples," Beto said. And: "I have a pony at Pontevedra. He's called Benito, and he likes apples too."

Carrie stroked Mimosa's neck and rubbed a hand over the horse's crest, glancing down at the boy.

"Where does the name Pontevedra come from?"

The question puzzled him. "Wasn't it always Pontevedra?"

Carrie sensed a complicated and quite serious discussion hanging between them, one she wasn't sure she could do justice. Instead she said, "That's a good question. I always wonder about place-names."

Beto's gaze swung around and he smiled. "Nando. He's good at sneaking up on people."

No doubt a skill he learned from Nathan, but Carrie kept that thought to herself.

Nando bumped Mimosa's neck with his head and nickered, but his attention was on Carrie's pocket.

He made short work of the second chunk of dried apple. He was gone as soon as he had it between his teeth.

"Nando," Beto said, "Nando is a rude little brother."

Coming back into camp, Carrie was drawn to the smell of bacon and onion and meat cooking over a fire. A boy she hadn't seen before was sitting on a rock, turning a lamb shank on the spit. Mr. Preston sat nearby, watching closely. As if he feared that his dinner might be burned without his supervision.

The emigrant families all had livestock, beyond the mules and oxen that pulled their wagons. Most had a horse, some had a milch cow, but Carrie had also seen goats and sheep, cages of hens and geese, and a few hogs, too, that seemed content enough to trot along at an easy pace. She supposed that Liebling had bartered or bought the lamb from an emigrant family. That would go on only until they outpaced the wagon trains, and then Petit would send his men out to hunt. Game was, supposedly, plentiful for most of the journey.

Eventually, inevitably, there would be buffalo.

This evening Mr. Petit sat with them while they ate. He seemed in a better mood today, but no one asked him why that might be. Better not to speak of Mrs. Chatham, no matter how curious Carrie might be about the strange woman who had come and gone so quickly. That thought was in her mind when Mr. Preston cleared his throat and spoke to Petit directly. Mr. Preston never talked, so this alone made them all perk up.

"You know," he said, "I was sure I had heard of Mrs. Chatham, but I could not remember the connection and it's been gnawing at me. What can you say about her?"

Petit took his time tipping back his cup to empty it of coffee.

"Nothing, really. She's on her way to Santa Fe to stay with a relative, a lady who's—" His voice went hoarse and he paused. "A lady who's increasing, as I understand it."

"Ah, well," said Mr. Preston, wiping the perspiration from his face with a huge kerchief. "Then not the same woman."

Beto asked his mother a predictable question. "What does *increasing*—"

"She is going to have a baby," Eva said.

Beto let out a sigh. "Well bless her heart."

Eva hiccuped a laugh, but Beto wanted more of the story.

"Who is it? Who's having the baby?"

To the men, Eva said, "I know all the ladies in Santa Fe. Did you happen to hear her relative's name?"

Petit shook his head. "No, ma'am. Never heard it mentioned."

But he kept his eyes on the cup he was turning around and around in his hands. Carrie could read Eva's thoughts from her expression, and knew they were both wondering if Petit could be talking about Mrs. Markham.

A sudden, awkward silence grew up around the campfire, but the noise from Gardner swelled to fill the gap. The town was overpopulated with emigrants, and some of the emigrants had decided a celebration was in order. Gardner, as small as it was, had two taverns.

Mr. Petit was listening too. He said, "That will go on until late tonight. Do you think you'll have any trouble sleeping?"

It wasn't clear whom he was talking to, but Nathan answered him. "Not me. Not after the day we had. Sister?"

Carrie, who could barely stop herself from yawning, agreed. "I will sleep until someone shakes me awake."

"I won't shake you awake," Beto said with great earnestness.

Carrie smiled at him, but sent Nathan a pointed look. "Thank you, Beto. I trust you'd let me sleep, even if the stars start dancing around in the sky."

The little boy's sleepy expression disappeared immediately. "What—"

Eva took his hand and stood. "Not right now, Roberto. I think that must be a story from when our friends were your age."

"And tomorrow I'll tell you all about it," Nathan said. He was up on his feet, and held out a hand to Carrie.

21

Friday, May 22, 1857

AT THE END of the fifth day on the trail, they made camp at Diamond Springs, famous for the settlement that had grown up around a mail station. It was a popular stop for emigrants, Eva told her. There was a saloon, a restaurant, a general store, a blacksmith, and corrals that stretched out for many acres.

"And a spring?" Nathan asked. "Tell me there's a spring."

"More than one," Eva said. "Crystal clear water. There's even a basin to bathe in, if you can find the spot."

A bath. The idea was entrancing, but how was something like that to be arranged? And more than that, Diamond Springs might be the last chance they would have to post a letter home before they reached Santa Fe. In the few hours between their meal and sunset, Carrie would have to apply her mind to writing a letter that would reassure her mother.

Then three strangers rode into camp, looking for Carrie. With them was Eli Ibarra.

Mr. Petit walked right up to the riders as they dismounted, and it was plain to see that they were well acquainted. Men had a whole unspoken language that gave away how they felt about each other, and it all played out: hands clapped shoulders, heads bent forward, hats came off to be slapped against a thigh. A rough laugh, the lift of a chin or an eyebrow: these all had meaning not immediately obvious to a woman who happened to be watching. Even one who was watching very closely.

She saw Eli Ibarra scan the camp, and then his gaze settled on her. He nodded, lifted his chin, touched the rim of his hat, and then turned away.

Carrie liked to think of herself as calm in unusual circumstances, but she could no more hide her surprise and alarm than she could deny the color that flooded her face. She stood where she was, and could not make herself move. Not toward the newcomers, or away from them.

Wranglers and teamsters were drifting closer out of curiosity. Mr. Tock had been talking with Mr. Petit when the strangers rode up, but it wasn't long before he left the circle of men and came to stand beside Carrie. With his chin bedded on his chest and his arms crossed, he leaned to the side and toward her like a skinny pine tree in a high wind.

"They're asking for you."

She wondered if he meant to alarm her. Carrie would not give him the reaction he seemed to want, but she did wish her brother were close by. He had gone to unsaddle the horses and always took his time. Neither was there any sign of Eva or Beto, who had probably gone down to the stream where the horses watered.

In effect, Mr. Tock was correct: Carrie was alone among strangers. Or mostly strangers. Eli was a friend, and someone she had started to trust. Someone she hoped she could trust.

Beside her Mr. Tock said, "You see the man standing next to Petit? That's Titus Hardy."

This meant nothing to her, something Mr. Tock found hard to believe. "Huh. I thought everybody everwheres knew the name Titus Hardy. How about Kit Carson, that name sound familiar? Or Little

Aubry? You must have heard tell of Little Aubry. Skimmer of the Plains they called him, he was so fast."

"I am woefully underinformed," Carrie said drily.

"Never mind," Tock said, flapping both hands. "You'll hear the stories soon enough. Now, the man standing to his left, wearing a bandana around his head instead of a hat? That's Miguel Santos. Navajo. Titus took Miguel on as a partner twenty years ago or so now. Folks say there ain't any better trackers west of the Mississippi. A course those same folks ain't never been east of the Mississippi, but even so I doubt you'd find a Yankee who could track as good."

He gave a little snort of appreciation at his own wit.

"The young red-haired fella, that's Rainey Bang. A German, came over maybe ten years ago, hell-bent on turning himself into a mountain man. Done a pretty good job of it, too, but he's too sociable for that life and he gave it up. Now he picks up work where he can, mostly with Hardy and Santos this last year."

"Doing what, exactly?"

She should have held the question back, because it set him on guard. All the men she had met thus far seemed to take any question, no matter how innocent, as a challenge.

He cleared his throat. "Oh, you know, trackin one thing or another. Things . . . wander off or get lost. Or took. Trackers go out to fetch 'em back home."

"Things?" she asked. "Or people?"

"Sometimes one, sometimes t'other. That last man there, the tall one? That's Eli Ibarra. If you're going to live in Santa Fe, maybe you heard about the Rancho Catalan, or hacienda, more people call it. Biggest sheep operation in the territory, so they say. His daddy and uncle and brothers run it, but he walked away from all that to do what they call surveyin. Not really sure what that means except in the end he sets down and makes maps. He knows just about every inch of the territory."

Carrie decided that she could not stand there like a startled rabbit, no matter how interesting Tock's stories might be. She excused herself and started toward the strangers only to realize, to her great relief, that Eli had already come part of the way to her. He held out a hand.

"Surprised to see me?"

Carrie wasn't wearing gloves, something she forgot until his palm slid against hers. A workingman's hand, his skin warm to the touch.

"Yes. Very. What—who—"

"No need to panic. Where's Nathan? He needs to be here."

A prickling of unease crawled up her neck, a wariness that had to do with the familiar old battle.

"I am perfectly capable of holding a conversation without my brother."

Her tone was sharp, but he took it in stride.

"Never said otherwise."

And now they stood looking at each other. Maybe he saw that he had touched a nerve, because he stepped closer and lowered his voice.

"I should let Hardy give you the details, but I can tell you this much. Sam Markham hired these men to find you and get you to Santa Fe as quick as it can be managed."

She didn't try to hide her surprise. "And the reason for such a sudden rush?"

"His wife. I don't have any idea what's wrong, and I don't think Hardy knows, either."

Carrie wondered if all men in the West were as squeamish as their eastern brethren when it came to pregnancy and childbirth.

"It was Dr. Markham's idea for me to leave the stagecoach and ride overland?"

He inclined his head, as if to agree that there was something odd about this. Few women would be prepared or willing to do what Dr. Markham was proposing so cavalierly. But then she had been explicit about her love of horses and willingness to ride. How to explain without sounding like a braggart?

She said, "I think I understand. We exchanged letters before we agreed on my employment. The notice for the position made it clear that the doctor was looking for a horsewoman."

He grinned. "You are that."

A flush of satisfaction ran through her, but she banished it from her face. A dozen questions presented themselves, and she would ask every one of them and get answers.

"So he hired these trackers to come find me."

"That's my understanding. Nobody knows the trail better. They'll get you there in twelve, fourteen days. Depending."

She waited to see if he would list the things that might delay the journey. Weather, he might say. She doubted he would talk about the possibility of hostilities. Most people would be thinking of Indians attacking, but the list was so much longer: some good portion of the white men going west were fleeing a guilty conscience or the law, or both. Horse thieves and cattle rustlers, for example. There were many dangers, but going overland would cut the travel time in half.

"Are you exaggerating?"

"Nope." He shook his head. "Aubry could have done it quicker, but not without killing the horses. Hardy don't do things that way."

Testing him, she said, "If Mrs. Markham is in labor, two weeks is far too long. A day would be too long."

Nothing in his expression said that the news of Mrs. Markham's pregnancy was a surprise to him, or that he found her willingness to share such information inappropriate.

"Never mind," she said, speaking mostly to herself. "Dr. Markham has asked for me, and he wouldn't go to this much trouble if it weren't serious. So. I had hoped—" She cut herself off and instead gave him an apologetic smile.

"Are you anxious about the ride?" He said this with some caution. As if he had asked if she preferred a good bowl of earthworms to one of beef stew, and feared she would ask for the worms.

Carrie said, "I wasn't looking forward to the stagecoach, and I'd much prefer to ride. If you're asking if I'm frightened, I am very able to defend myself, and I'm assuming that three armed, experienced men will be able to handle any problems that come up."

"Four," Eli said. "Four men. Maybe five, if your brother wants to join us."

"Ah." Carrie glanced around herself. They might as well have been standing on a stage in a theater, because all attention was on them.

Eva had appeared again. She lifted one eyebrow and failed to suppress a grin. A scowling Beto stood in front of her, firmly held in place by her hands on his shoulders.

"This is an unexpected turn of events," Carrie said, mostly to herself.

"You must have reckoned there'd be a couple surprises along the way," Eli said. "I know your brother did. And there he is now. Maybe we can sort all this out over food. I haven't had a decent meal in more than a day."

TITUS HARDY WAS something more than fifty, and before they ever exchanged a word, Carrie knew a great deal about him. For the first ten years of her life she had lived on the edge of a wilderness where trappers and mountain men came to trade furs and buy supplies. These were men who saw nobody—wanted to see nobody—for months at a time. They were rough men, grime worked deep into every crease and wrinkle. They wore furs and deerskin they had cured themselves and moccasins they traded for, and never changed anything until it fell apart and couldn't be tied back together. When one of the trappers was in town, you could usually find him by following the scent trail.

Hardy did live most of his life out of doors, but he didn't stink. He smelled of healthy sweat and horses and sunshine and trail dust. He had blue eyes, but all his exposed skin was as dark as seasoned oak, cured by sun and wind. The scuff of white beard bristles over sharp bones and deep crevices gave his complexion the appearance of tweed. He was not especially big, but he radiated a calm authority. Sitting just across from him, Carrie realized he reminded her of Little Kettle, an elder of the Turtle clan at Good Pasture. If not for Hardy's eye color, he and Little Kettle might be mistaken for brothers.

The three trackers sat together while they ate, flanked by Eli on one side and Mr. Petit on the other. Food was a serious business for men like these. They burned what they ate like an oven burned wood. No fuel, no fire.

She wasn't sure what to make of Miguel Santos. He was tall and lean and somber, but he laughed when the others laughed, revealing strong white teeth that overlapped on the bottom. His clothes were a mixture of native and European, which was the case everywhere in the West, as far as Carrie had seen. But he was the first man she had seen in the West who didn't wear a hat, and instead wore a turban made out of a bandana. Whether his hair was long, as she would expect, or not was impossible to say.

Rainey Bang was the youngest, shortest, and hungriest of the three. He filled his plate twice and ate fast, as if somebody were standing over him set on stealing what he had claimed for himself. Carrie imagined he had grown up in a big family with insufficient food.

According to Mr. Tock, Rainey Bang was a German. That wouldn't have been Carrie's guess. He had a shock of bright red hair and a full beard that included every shade of red from clay to chestnut, all interwoven. He also had skin as thin and pale as buttermilk. Much of his face was peeling at the moment, but soon enough it would burn and blister again, and finally peel. Whatever skin he exposed to the sun would burn like that. It was the price he would have to pay as long as he chose to live and work in the West. Unless, of course, he got into the habit of coating his face with paint or clay.

Rainey got up suddenly and took his plate over to the barrel beside the supply wagon, washed it, and left it on the drying rack. Wranglers, Carrie had observed, looked after their own messes, and these men were no different. For some reason, this simple gesture made her less anxious about what was about to happen.

Nathan was sitting next to Carrie, but for once he had nothing to say. He was thinking hard; she could almost hear the wheels turning while he ate and watched the trackers. He knew exactly as much as she did about this new development, and he didn't much like being kept in the dark. When she had the opportunity, she would point out to him that he was experiencing the same frustration that she, and most other women, dealt with day by day.

Finally Hardy cleared his throat. It worked like a trumpet blast: all talk stopped, and everybody turned in his direction.

"Let me start," he said, "by apologizin. Didn't mean to unsettle anybody. Especially not you, Miss Ballentyne. Didn't mean to, but it couldn't be helped."

It took him all of a minute to introduce Miguel Santos and Rainey Bang, and then he sat back, glanced at the sun as a New York banker glanced at his pocket watch.

He said, "We're here at Sam Markham's request. Sam is a good man. A friend. He's got a problem, and he came to me to ask could I help. I went round to see Miguel and Rainey, and here we are."

There was a silence then that seemed to last a long time.

Rainey Bang leaned forward to look Hardy directly in the face. "You are not telling enough, boss."

"All right," Hardy said, lifting a hand to the younger man. "I'm getting to it."

And he did. Doc Markham's wife was expecting. This statement was followed by a lot of throat cleaning, and a long study of the ground.

"But the trouble now ain't about that."

"What is it about?" Carrie asked, to urge him along.

His brows lowered, he looked at her directly.

"Now, how would I know that? I ain't a doctor. All I can tell you is, Sam Markham wanted to get his new nurse and midwife to Santa Fe as quick as it could be managed, and we're ready, able, and willing to make that happen."

He glanced in Eli's direction. "We had one piece of luck, two days ago, or I doubt we would have found you so quick."

Eli stepped in here. "I ran into them at Green Creek spring, where I stopped to water my horses. We got to talking."

Now it made some sense to Carrie. Friends who happened to meet while out traveling would stop to visit and exchange news. In the course of conversation, they'd learn that Eli knew the young woman they were looking for and that he was on friendly terms with both Carrie and Nathan Ballentyne.

"Didn't take much convincing to get him to turn around," Rainey Bang said. His manner was all exaggerated innocence.

Titus Hardy frowned at him and then turned back to speak to Carrie directly.

"Miss Ballentyne, I understand you are born to the saddle, and I'm thinking that must be so, as Romero sold you one of his horses. But you should know that arrangements will be rough, compared to what you've got now." He paused to look over his shoulder at the stage-coach.

"If fresh air counts for something, it might suit you fine," Rainey said.

"I do have a very good mount," Carrie said. "And so does my brother. Nathan, you must have something to say to all this."

"I have something to say," came a small voice from outside the circle.

Eva crouched down to talk to him. "Roberto, come away."

"Ma, let me talk. Please let me talk."

"Let him come," Nathan called. "I'd like to hear what he has to say."

The boy marched directly to Nathan and stood in front of him, his head hanging low. One leg jiggled nervously.

"I don't think you should ride away with those men."

"You don't?"

"No. You should stay with us in the stagecoach."

"And my sister?"

He shrugged. "She can go."

Carrie had to bite back a laugh, but Eva put both hands to her cheeks in the universal gesture of a dismayed and outsmarted mother. To reassure Eva, Carrie smiled and echoed Beto's shrug.

The boy was still making his case. "It would be boring without you, and scarier too. They don't need you in Santa Fe cause you can't help bring a baby, but we need you here."

Pretty much all the men sitting in the circle were smiling openly.

Eva said, "Roberto, come now. You've told Mr. Ballentyne your thoughts. Let's leave everyone to finish their conversation in peace. Without interruptions."

"Where were we?" Rainey Bang said.

"Horses. Gear. Provisions." Miguel Santos dealt these three words like cards to be taken up and considered. He spoke English flawlessly, but there was a rhythm to it that would have its origin in his mother tongue or Spanish, or both. Just as Rainey Bang would always mark himself as a German when he spoke.

"She hasn't said if she will be coming or not," Rainey pointed out. "And the brother don't look too enthusiastic."

Carrie would have bet a large sum that Nathan would jump at this opportunity to leave the stagecoach behind and ride, but what she saw instead was doubt.

He cleared his throat and nodded in Eli's direction. "Ibarra, could we have a word, just the two of us? Won't take long."

Just like that, they walked off.

She would have liked to talk to Eva about this very odd turn of events, but she and Beto had disappeared, no doubt to discuss manners and why they were important. She imagined it was a discussion they had very often, and would continue to have well into his young adulthood. Certainly she, Carrie Ballentyne, still needed reminding now and then.

Mr. Petit went off to make sure that things were in order, and so Carrie found herself sitting across from the three trackers. Like a student waiting for an examination to start. The first and last question was a simple one: Would she go with them?

She could. Certainly she was equal to it, and she had the gear she needed. Mimosa was equal to it.

Except, it came to her, she didn't have a canteen.

"You look like you're doing long division in your head," Hardy said. "What's got you so worried? You can ask us what you want to know about the journey."

What Carrie wanted to know was where her brother was, and why he was acting so oddly. Instead she told them about her lack of a canteen and for her simple answer got a patronizing smile from Hardy.

WHEN NATHAN CAME to find her, they walked off together to talk in private.

"I don't understand your hesitation," Carrie said.

"I know you don't. And I'm not sure how to explain it, but Eli thinks I should try."

That was an intriguing start.

"Bear with me a minute," he said. "Do you remember the first summer after we moved to Manhattan?"

The subject took her by surprise. That had been a difficult period for all of them, one that they didn't often talk about. To mention it now meant that her brother had a story that he needed to tell that would make the current situation clear.

"Of course," she said. "You spent most of it with Uncle Luke and Aunt Rachel in Brooklyn."

He seemed relieved that she remembered that much.

"I don't think you ever saw Solomon, the stallion Luke bought that summer."

She shook her head, more confused than ever.

"He was a beautiful horse. One of the neighbors took a look at him and offered Uncle Luke twice what he had paid."

"I don't imagine Luke was interested."

"He turned the neighbor—George Swensen by name—down, and when other offers came in, he turned those down too. Mostly people are philosophical about this kind of thing, but not Swensen."

He broke off to look more closely at her face. "I realize this makes no sense to you, but hold on a few minutes more."

When Carrie nodded her agreement, he drew in a big breath.

"Almost right away, I noticed Swensen watching Solomon. From his second story, he could see Luke's stable, and he sat at a window for a good part of the day, watching. He watched whenever Luke took Solomon out or he was out of the stable for any reason. It was unsettling, the way he watched, and I finally told Aunt Rachel.

"At the time I didn't see any connection, and there is still no reason to suspect that Luke had something to do with it, but a couple weeks later Swensen left town on business. I was there for another month and I never saw him again."

An uneasiness came over Carrie. Uncle Luke was their mother's half brother, a quiet, thoughtful man who could be roused to violence. During the last war he had made a reputation for himself as someone who did not hesitate to kill to protect—or revenge—his family.

"Go on," she said. Her voice came rough.

"It was September before Luke was in the city again and came to see us. There was a lot of talk, like there always is. We had tea, and then he said it was time to go. I went outside with him because I wanted to see Solomon, but he wasn't there. Uncle Luke was riding a different horse, one I didn't know.

"I didn't realize it at the time, but Solomon wasn't there because Solomon was gone. He disappeared from the stable one night, about a month after Swensen took off. They never found any trace of him, and Swensen never came back to the city."

Carrie had feared this story was going in a very different direction, and now she needed a moment to organize her thoughts.

"That must have been disturbing."

"Which is why Luke didn't tell me what had happened at the time," Nathan agreed. "He admitted as much a couple years ago when I pressed him on it. Uncle Luke spent a lot of time and money trying to track Swensen down but had no luck."

The wind was up, and with the nearing of sunset Carrie was suddenly chilled. She wound her arms around herself. "Nathan, I have to confess, I'm not seeing a connection."

He cast a glance at her, and then away. "It's Preston."

"Mr. Preston?"

Nathan swiped at a patch of tall grass, looked at what he had harvested, and let the wind take it.

"He watches Beto."

Carrie wondered if she misunderstood. "Do you mean, the way Mr. Swensen watched Solomon? With that same degree of—" She could not find a word that she was willing to say aloud.

"Obsession? Desire? Covetousness?"

She nodded.

"Yes. That's what I see in his face when he doesn't realize I'm watching. You think he's reading, but he's watching Beto. When he's awake or taking a nap, at meals, just talking to Eva, Preston watches Beto, and I watch Preston. And I remember Solomon. I remember how Swensen looked at Solomon the way a drunk looks at a flask of whiskey."

Carrie put a hand on his wrist.

"You believe that Mr. Preston sees Beto as something to acquire and possess."

The tension in the line of his back eased. "That is my fear."

They walked in silence while Carrie tried to gather her thoughts.

"Is Eva aware of this?"

"I don't think so," Nathan said. "But he's sly. It took me a full day to see it. If you're set on stealing something valuable, you don't want people seeing you admire it too openly."

Children disappeared every day in the city. Some never came home because the street was the safer place. Some got in the way of a trolley or fell from a roof. In the winter a large number of outdoor children died of exposure and disease and hunger. And some found themselves in far worse circumstances.

Of course what Nathan feared for Beto was all supposition. Her brother was watching her, and he saw this thought come to her, somehow.

"I could be wrong," Nathan said. "I wish I were wrong."

They were far enough away from the camp to see it from one end to the other. Carrie watched men going about their business, the things they did day by day without fail. They cared for the animals, looked after the wagons, found water and wood, made fire and dug pits and set up camp. The wranglers and teamsters were well-trained, good men, and if there should be an attack by outlaws or one of the tribes, it was her sense that they would prevail.

But if Nathan was right, what could those men do for Beto, no matter how well-intentioned? They rarely saw the boy, and they certainly couldn't see inside the stagecoach. She thought back over the last few days, and how well Mr. Preston kept himself apart, in the background.

They couldn't ask Petit to put the man off the stagecoach. Leaving an old man on the prairie without provisions or weapons would be tantamount to executing him.

"We have no proof," she said out loud. "Petit would think us insane, after we chased Mrs. Chatham away."

"That occurred to me too."

"So what is it you want?" she asked. "You think we should both stay with the stagecoach, as a buffer between Beto and Mr. Preston?"

"Tempting," Nathan said drily. "But no. I'm going to stay, and you are going to go."

THE DECISION WAS made, and still Carrie lay awake for a very long time considering the problem at hand. She approached it from every direction and always ended up at the same conclusion: there was no way to be sure of Beto's safety without Nathan. Not unless they made their suspicions public, and that was something they would not do without some kind of evidence. She would not have the repercussions on her conscience, and there would be repercussions, even if Preston's intentions were innocent.

In one small corner of her mind, she would have liked to be able to brush off Nathan's concerns, but she could not. He had always been sensitive to the undercurrents between people, and his instincts were generally right. And so they would do this thing they had promised their mother they would not do: they would separate, and each of them would move on alone.

22

Saturday, May 23, 1857

IN THE MORNING, Eva sent Beto off with Nathan. Neither of them wanted to go, but Eva was insistent. Her purpose, she explained, was to provide any help Carrie might need while she dressed. Carrie was aware that Eva had another, more pressing purpose. There would be questions, and those questions were both unavoidable and deserving of honest answers.

She started with a cotton chemise and doeskin leggings, worn often enough to be supple and thin. When she had tied the leggings to the loops sewn into the chemise, she opened the trunk one of the teamsters had brought at her request. From it she took out a wide homespun linen tunic and dropped it over her head. It billowed up and then settled with its hem just above her knees. There were buttons at the neck and wrists that she would worry about later. If she forgot, the gnats and flies would remind her.

The last thing she took from the trunk caught Eva's eye. She got up to examine it more closely.

"A doeskin weskit," she said. "Very cleverly constructed for riding, I see."

Carrie had never heard the word *weskit* used for a long vest like this one, but she could agree that it was a practical garment.

"It belonged to my Aunt Hannah," Carrie said. "And it's been on more than one adventure in its time."

They talked for a minute about the beadwork while Carrie sat down to put on her moccasins and pull the ties tight below the knee.

"There's a long scarf," she said. "Hanging over the edge—yes, that one. Thank you."

There were things that Eva wanted to know, but she was too anxious to put those questions into words. Instead she talked about Hardy while Carrie cinched a leather belt around her middle and looped the scarf around her neck.

"He has an excellent reputation." This she had said already many times. Carrie decided that she should nudge a little.

"But?"

Eva paced the very short distance to the tent flap, and back again. "He can be hard, and generally he is considered rude."

Carrie was making sure that everything she wore was properly anchored, so that if Eva was embarrassed by what she had to say, she could pretend not to be.

"Eva," she began. "I have nursed older men who repeatedly grabbed at my breasts and buttocks. In the course of my work, I have been propositioned by married men while their wives stood by. I have been cursed in Gaelic, Italian, German, Spanish, Russian, and a dozen other languages I've forgot. Frightened children have scratched and bit and spit on me. I've seen a thirteen-year-old boy with whip scars on his back because his father objected to the way—the very normal way, in my opinion—he spoke to his grandmother. So I thank you for the warning, but I am not especially worried about rude remarks from Titus Hardy. You can take me at face value, because all of this is true, and more. Worse."

She put out her arms and did a half turn that made her plait fly. "What do you think?"

"Amazing," Eva said, with a sincere smile. "You've turned yourself into a *vaquera*. When you need a change of pace, you can take a break along the way and rope wild horses." Her voice cracked and she cleared her throat, but she tried again to strike a lighter tone.

"Would you be as pleased if a Paris modiste had dressed you?"

"If I'm smiling it's because I am never so comfortable as I am like this. Now let me think."

She looked at the two saddlebags she had packed. In one was a second pair of leggings and a chemise, two linen tunics, two of her simplest gowns, a work apron, a bar of soap, a small tin of tooth powder, a hairbrush, and a towel. In the other were some documents, and most of her medicines and medical equipment. Everything else of value she would leave to her brother's care.

"Weapons?"

"Nathan is checking and cleaning them."

Eva had contrived to be cheerful, but that time was past.

"I don't know whether to wish you a grand adventure or curse you for a fool."

Carrie picked up her riding gloves and tucked them under the belt but kept her gaze on Eva's face. "Eva, please. We've become friends in the last weeks, haven't we? So tell me what's got you so worried."

This was, of course, an insensitive thing to say to a woman who had lost family members to a Comanche war party.

"Beyond the obvious," she added quickly.

Eva drew in a deep breath. "It's embarrassing."

Carrie raised a brow, and waited.

"It's about Nathan. I don't really understand—" She paused, and then it came out in a rush. "Is your brother staying behind because of an attachment he's formed, to me?"

This was a question Carrie hadn't anticipated, but should have. They had agreed that it would be less than sensible to tell Eva about Nathan's suspicions regarding Mr. Preston. In the first place, because

Nathan could possibly be wrong. As a result, Eva's imagination had come up with a different explanation for Nathan's decision.

"Are you asking me if my brother is in love with you?"

Eva folded her arms around herself and rocked on her heels. "It sounds horrible when you say it."

Carrie chose her words carefully.

"I can't explain his decision to you, but one thing I do know for certain. He is very fond of you both, but more in the way of a younger brother. Does that help?"

Eva's color rose, an indication that she had been more concerned than she would have Carrie believe. "I would never knowingly offend either of you. It's just that I'm ten years his senior—"

"No," Carrie interrupted. "There is really no need to explain your position, because that's not an issue."

"And you can't tell me what the issue actually is," Eva added, her tone taking on a whisper of frustration.

Carrie stepped forward and hugged Eva. Out of friendship and guilt that she could say so little to calm her fears. Out of worry that she would say too much.

"It was my good fortune to make your acquaintance," Carrie said. "And I am less worried about Santa Fe, knowing I will have you there, as a friend."

23

EARLY MORNING NEAR the end of May, and the prairie stretched out around the five riders, endless greens and golds in every shade, layered together to build a landscape of rolling grasslands. And right at this moment, Carrie realized, not a single tree in sight, nor any sign of mountains or anything man-made. The world was the prairie and the bowl of the sky and the five of them, riding west. And not one thing more.

The Santa Fe trail was somewhere to the north, out of sight but close enough that they could hear something of a wagon train: the creak of wheels and hundreds and hundreds of hooves striking the earth at a pace that brought a funeral procession to mind. Carrie banished this macabre thought. Instead she summoned an image of the stagecoach where Nathan sat, a human bulwark between the silent, watchful, disturbing Mr. Preston and Beto, the boy overflowing with energy, with questions and stories. An innocent child. She would have much preferred to have her brother nearby, but they had done the right thing. The only thing.

In the first hours Hardy rode near Carrie, as she would have done in his place. It was his responsibility to make sure that she was equal to this ride, that she knew her mare and could keep pace. Some horses—Rainey Bang had a sorrel he called Ross that was a good example—didn't like the middle of the pack and would maneuver their way to a spot at the very front. Mimosa liked other horses and felt no need to improve her spot in the pack, and that was a relief.

If they ran into any kind of trouble, their mounts would mean the difference between life and death, and so Carrie spent a little time studying the other horses. Hardy and Miguel Santos each led an extra mount, while Rainey Bang had an extra mount and a packhorse. Eli had his three Argentineans.

If you valued the horse you rode, you had more than one mount on a long-distance ride where time was of the essence. There were other ways to lose horses, anything from a sudden colic to thievery. The tribes in this part of the plains were, according to the stories of other travelers, especially good at taking what they wanted or needed; whole *remudas* disappeared in the dead of night and in complete silence, despite armed guards. Carrie thought this was likely one of the tall tales wranglers told, but would not comment until she had more information.

Hardy's horses would be a temptation. They were big-boned and lean, healthy, between seven and ten years old, sure-footed and alert. They crossed water without pause or hesitation, and didn't startle when antelope ran across their path. None of them were what Carrie would call pretty, but they were the best trail horses she had ever seen. And still, to her it seemed unlikely that anyone would try to steal from Hardy. He had a reputation for rough justice, and more than that, he was on good terms with most of the tribes.

Carrie felt Eli's gaze on her and turned to see that he had come up close. When he had her attention, he pointed down to the ground. There was an outcropping of stone here that ran beside a small stream with a muddy bank. A herd had been here, and not so long ago. Elk or antelope or deer came to mind first, but then she saw a single track, and she started at its size. The animal it belonged to was bigger than the moose prints she had seen as a girl in the endless forests.

She glanced at Eli, who pressed the heel of his palm above an ear, fingers curled in. This would be the sign for horns, and that would mean—

Buffalo. Carrie rose up in the saddle to get a better view, and saw at first only the already familiar sea of grass and shrub. But the land was rising, and in a matter of minutes they had come to a stop on a low ridge. On its other side, the plain sloped away to more prairie, and a few miles farther, a lake.

The shifting green of the prairie had disappeared under a blanket of earthy colors, browns and blacks and grays, as far as the eye could see: more buffalo than she could count. Just that suddenly she understood that the buffalo herds of the plains could be described, but never imagined. No words could conjure such an image, entwined as it was with the other senses. There was a constant noise of churning hooves, calves bellowing, and bulls huffing and grunting, but more overwhelming was the smell of the herd. It rose up from the plain to hang, almost as visible as the dust that hung suspended to shimmer in the sunlight.

They waited there, five abreast, for what must have been a long time. When Carrie's vision had adjusted to the distances, she studied a herd of smaller animals watering at the lake.

"Elk," she said.

Hardy's gaze swung toward her and he blinked. He was not a man who offered praise easily, or, better said, he was not especially impressed by her sharp eyesight. He would make up his own mind about her, and could not be swayed. In some ways it was a relief, to know that she needn't try.

She asked, "They don't fight for territory, the elk and the buffalo?"

Miguel swept an arm up and out, as if to offer her the prairie's endless bounty. "For thousands of years," he said. "For thousands of miles."

Vast and verdant and nourishing, the plains welcomed all who came to feast.

Farther along the ridge and a little below it Carrie was surprised to see a small stand of oak trees. On the prairie she expected to see cottonwoods now and then; oaks were a reminder of home.

They had not arrived here by accident, Eli explained to her; it was a favorite spot for travelers, shady and cool, with a narrow stream running through it. They would water and rest the horses and in an hour's time be on their way.

She sought out a place to sit in the shade of an oak, pleased to find that even from this point she had a partial view of the grazing buffalo. Had she been alone, she might have napped; as it was she listened to the men talk, Spanish and English peppered with terms that must be one of the Indian languages.

Hardy came by to offer her a canteen.

"You'll have need of this." In the moment and to her embarrassment, Carrie could not find the words to thank him.

"Hold on to it," he said. "It's yours for as long as it takes us to get where we're going."

Hardy, Carrie decided, did not like to be acknowledged for his help or kindness, whether out of shyness or cynicism, she could not say. Rainey, on the other hand, liked to talk about what he was doing and why. It was not so much bragging as the way a teacher spoke to students, always looking for a chance to pass something along, and sure that every student would welcome his instruction.

Now she watched as he took provisions from the packhorse. He produced a bundle of jerky, a loaf of flat bread, and yams that had been baked and cut into slices, salted and peppered. It was simple food, but there was nothing plain about it. The jerky was especially spicy, and Carrie had to get up and take her canteen to the spring to fill it.

She had just finished the last bit of her bread when she caught a flash of color overhead. She leaned back and looked more closely into the branches. And then let out a startled laugh.

There were as many as a dozen birds overhead, so odd and pretty that for a long moment she could do nothing but look at them. And who could ignore such creatures? They had bright green wings and saffron-yellow heads with red markings.

She had seen parrots before—different than these, but clearly the same kind of bird—twice in her life. At a botanical garden she had come across an aged, cranky cockatoo, but more exciting was the parlor of an elderly lady on Greene Street where two macaws ruled. They talked and clicked and chirped and barked to each other and especially at their mistress, adding snatches of song and the occasional mild oath, sometimes in Russian or German. "*Keine Lust! Keine Lust!*" was the phrase Carrie remembered hearing most often, but she was an adult before she found a German speaker she could ask for a translation.

"Parrots on the prairie," she said. "That is a surprise."

"They're called *periquitos.*" Eli was nearer than she had realized, and she jumped at the sound of his voice. He said, "There's one still tending a nest, if you look."

She studied the branches overhead and caught a glimpse of a nest, very quiet just now. "I didn't know there were any parrots native to this country."

Rainey Bang barked a short laugh. "Lots of critters you never seen will come out to say hello before we get to Santa Fe."

"I am looking forward to it," she told him. "The buffalo herd today was a very good start."

Hardy took something from a pocket and slipped it into his mouth. A peppermint, from the smell. He said, "Were you hoping to hunt?"

In her surprise she turned away to look again at the herd. "Hunt buffalo? It wouldn't occur to me."

"Emigrants do," Miguel Santos said. "Most of 'em can't wait to get a buffalo, the bigger the better. You'll be seeing piles of their bones soon enough."

"I can't even imagine it," she said. "A thousand pounds of meat and bone and a pelt—"

"The bulls can weigh in at two thousand," Hardy murmured. "Sometimes more."

"That's even worse," Carrie said. "A hunter would have to leave most of it for the wolves."

"Happens every day out here," Rainey Bang told her. "Hundreds of times."

Carrie considered this. "Do the tribes hunt in that way? Taking enough for the day and leaving the rest to rot?"

She saw Eli raise a brow in Miguel Santos's direction, as if a point had been made.

"Not Indians," Rainey answered her. "The Indians are using every bit of the old buff. Every drop of blood, every bit of tendon, they are using all of it."

"That makes more sense," Carrie said. "At least, in my experience."

The men looked at one another, as if needing translation.

"What experience is that?" Hardy asked her, brow furrowed. "You been out this way before?"

Carrie wondered how much she could or should tell them of her family, if it might be interpreted as bragging. But they were all watching her, and waiting for a reply.

"My grandfather's second wife was Mohawk," she said. "One of the Iroquois tribes, if you have heard of them. I have aunts and uncles and cousins who are Mohawk. As a little girl I sometimes didn't hear English for days at a time. All our men hunt and trap, but the biggest game they ever bring home is a bear. Moose are bigger, but nobody bothers to go after them."

She had surprised them, but they didn't seem to doubt her word.

"You didn't mention any of that to us," Miguel Santos said to Eli.

"I heard some rumors," Eli said. "But I was waiting to get the story from her directly."

Hardy was put out with this turn in the conversation. He got to his feet and brushed crumbs from his clothes. "The day ain't over yet," he said to nobody in particular. "Time to get a move on."

Eli offered her a hand to pull her up from her seat, and she gave in to the impulse to ask a question.

"You've heard rumors about me?"

He held on to her hand longer than necessary as he looked down at her. "An old man on the *Annabelle* talked about your grandfather and an Indian who traveled with him. He claims the Indian was as big as a bear. They came to New Orleans just the same time as Jackson, right before the end of the war. For all I know he was just spinning tall tales."

She said, "Eva told me about the gentleman from New Orleans, but I never had the chance to talk to him. Or, more truthfully, I avoided him."

"That's too bad," Eli said. "He's a storyteller. A course, he's none too worried about the facts if they get in the way."

Carrie bit back a grin. "Do you know another kind of storyteller? They all bend the facts to suit the tale."

"So it's not true?"

He seemed almost disappointed, and Carrie found that odd and interesting. Eli Ibarra was curious about her, her family and background. As she was curious about him. The truth was, there was a spark of attraction between them, but at this moment the pull of friendship was stronger. At least, that was the only way she could explain to herself why it was so easy to talk to him.

"Oh, it's true. My grandfather and Great-Uncle Runs-from-Bears were in New Orleans at that point in time, and not just the two of them," she said. "It's really the story of how two branches of the family came together, and not considered suitable for polite company."

One of his rare grins flashed. "In that case—" He looked around as if worried about eavesdropping. "That's a story you'll really have to tell."

He squeezed her hand, let it go, and walked away.

In the midafternoon the panicked bellowing of oxen got Hardy's attention, and they turned north to follow a creek that took them back to the Santa Fe trail, where an accident had just happened.

To this point none of the crossings Carrie had seen had been very difficult even for freight wagons, but this creek was different. Its eastern bank was very steep and at least ten feet higher than the fast-moving water. Somehow half the wagon train had managed that slope, crossed the creek, and made it up the opposite—and much easier—bank, but then things went wrong.

Two wagons were down, the first on its side at the bottom of the eastern bank, half in and half out of the water. The oxen hitched to its rear axel to control speed had not just failed; they had been dragged over the edge and down until they crashed into the wagon itself. One of the oxen looked to be dead, while the other shrieked, thrashing so violently that no one could get close enough to unhitch it. The oxen pulling that wagon were just as incensed, caught up in the tangle of yoke and the hardware that kept them in step with each other.

A shot rang out, and the ox at the rear of the wagon went still.

The second wagon had turned over midstream. What became of those oxen was unclear, but it seemed to Carrie that they must have drowned and were still there on the river bottom.

Two dozen men were in chest-high water, searching for the cargo that had been ejected into the creek. The wagon itself was irretrievable, and they would not spend more time or energy on trying to shift it, but the cargo was another matter.

A truly disastrous turn of events for the family. For them this journey was at its end. What came next depended on how well they had prepared before setting out, and if they had not, the charity of strangers.

"Big storm three days ago," Rainey said. "They should have waited another day for the water level to drop. Now, would you look? They're still arguing about it."

Carrie caught a flash of red and the glint of sunlight on a blade. On the east bank of the creek, two men were circling each other, snarling like dogs. The older man was soaking wet and blood cascaded down from a rent in his scalp, but he didn't seem to notice. Barrel-shaped, muscle-strapped, he advanced on the man opposite him, half his age and size, but puffed up with anger. The old man waved a butcher's cleaver over his head as they circled each other, yelling and cursing. A crowd just stood by and watched, as if they had nothing at stake and no interest in the outcome.

"Let's move," Hardy said.

"Shouldn't—" Carrie began.

"We ain't lawmen," Hardy interrupted. "Time to get going."

THE REST OF the day fell into a rhythm. They headed southwest, sometimes at a quick trot, sometimes walking, once or twice cantering for a short period. Carrie was riding one of Eli's Argentineans for the afternoon, an all-black mare he called Luna. She was about twelve, biddable and alert, and Carrie liked her. She hoped that Luna would be available to her whenever Mimosa needed to be switched out.

Rainey rode next to her that afternoon, and it was soon evident that he had decided to teach Carrie what she didn't know about this part of the country. Many women, especially ones with good educations, would have taken offense, but Carrie did not. She would gladly take instruction from anyone who had information to share.

Soon after they'd left the scene at the crossing, Rainey began by clearing his throat and resettling his hat on his head.

"You'll have noted," he began, "that tempers run hot on the trail. Sometimes so hot that graves got to be dug. It's the trail boss what's supposed to sort disagreements out before things get that far. An outsider who sticks his nose in will make things worse all around, for everybody."

He left her for a while to consider this offering. It was a kind of rationalization for not stopping to lend a hand with the wagon train accident, and as much as it might bother her, she couldn't discount the reasoning. Many times she had come across a wealthy lady who had convinced herself that on the basis of her life experience alone she could turn things around for a poor family in trouble. If only the sad, poor people would read the pamphlets she brought them. If only they would hear the Sunday sermon at this or that church, or use a particular kind of soap. That kind of interference could take a very bad end.

She understood that Hardy had a job to do, and he wouldn't risk a delay that might turn ugly. She looked around herself for him, thinking that an apology or even a discussion might be in order. Instead she saw seven men on horseback, sitting on a rise to watch buffalo. At least, that was what they seemed to be studying.

To Carrie they looked like Indians preparing for the hunt. Watchful and alert, they did not strike her as a threat.

"Jicarilla Apache," Eli said, coming up on her other side. "Not much to worry about. If they stay put, we'll stop and have a talk."

"And if they don't?"

Rainey shrugged. "Then they'll be back tomorrow, and we'll talk then."

In time the Indians were out of sight, and Carrie was both relieved and disappointed. She watched for them until dusk crept near and Hardy decided that it was time to make camp.

After ten hours in the saddle, Carrie was as sore as she had ever been. This she had anticipated, and she knew that she would be almost as uncomfortable and stiff tomorrow, and the day after it would start to ease. Part of the cure was to keep moving, and so she took up chores where she saw them. She was aware of getting in the way of established routine, but she only had to be told once to remember how Hardy liked things to look in camp.

In short order there was a fire and coffee, the horses had been watered and staked out to graze, and Rainey was cleaning the jackrabbits he had shot earlier in the afternoon.

He cut them up and dumped them into a pot he retrieved from the packhorse. Then he added water from the stream, a third of a sack of beans, a splash of salt from a hinged box, and a big handful of wild onions from a pocket. When he had fitted the lid to the pot and set it down in the firepit, he raised his head and grinned at Carrie.

"We can eat in an hour or so. Keep an eye on this, would you please? I'll be back to see to the fire."

It was odd, to Carrie's way of thinking, that all four of the men would disappear and leave her alone to look after the camp. She had no idea where they had gone or why, except that a quick count of horses told her that the men were on foot.

To have left her here might mean they felt she was safe, or it could mean that they thought she could manage whatever trouble came her way. That thought made her take up her weapons. It was bravado, of course; if a raiding party showed up, her choices were few. She could hide, or she could fight and, most likely, die.

The steam that came from the pot in the fire smelled so good that her stomach growled. Every wolf and coyote in ten miles would be lifting their snouts to test the scent. All of them would come to investigate.

This reminded Carrie that Chico should be close by, if he had made it this far. It was silly to worry about a dog that wasn't her responsibility and was far better able to look after himself than Carrie could. And still she would have preferred to know where Chico was.

That thought was still foremost in her mind when she heard Mimosa nickering, followed by a welcoming trill. From where she sat, Carrie saw Mimosa lower her head and nudge Chico, who had appeared out of nowhere—but by way of the stream, because he was still dripping water. He put his head back and woo-wooed at Mimosa. Talkative dogs were especially good dogs, her Da had always said.

Carrie whistled, but Chico ignored her. Then she remembered the rabbit entrails. She found a stick and stirred the pile to dislodge the flies, and soon enough he was standing much closer.

"Chico," she said to him. "Any interest in these bits?"

It seemed that there was. Carrie, whose own stomach was growling, understood. She kept her distance.

Chico had stretched out halfway between Carrie and the fire, facing the horses. It was good to have him near, because the men still hadn't come back, and it would soon be full dark. She was agitated by the situation and unsettled enough to be glad of a dog who ignored her. Carrie had the idea that tomorrow or the day after he might allow her to touch him. At some point she might get a woo-woo.

From behind her, Rainey Bang said, "Look at this. You found a dog?"

Carrie's heart jumped in her chest.

"Not exactly," she said.

The others were there, too, standing in a half circle. Miguel Santos crouched down beside Carrie and made low clicking noises, but again Chico was content to stay where he was.

"He's shy," Carrie said. "He won't come to me, either, but then he doesn't belong to me."

Miguel looked at her, one brow making a peak. "So whose dog is he?"

"Mimosa's," Carrie said. She felt silly even saying it, but she hoped no one could tell. "He's Mimosa's dog."

Eli sat down beside her. "That a dog from Romero's ranch?"

In that moment Carrie realized that her only source for this information about Chico was her brother, the practical joker.

She said, "That's what I was told. I may have been . . ." She swallowed. "Misled."

Hardy let out a soft laugh, the first she had heard from him. "No, it's true," he said. "But it's rare. So he's been following Mimosa since she left Romero's ranch?"

"That's my understanding."

All four of the men seemed to find this turn of events amusing. She had imagined a different and not so welcoming reaction, but she was glad to have been wrong.

"Eli," Rainey said. "You've got three of Romero's Argentineans and not a single Chico?"

"I do now," Eli said, and winked at Carrie.

As they ate, the men told stories of dogs they had known. Carrie listened, watching colors seeping across the sky: burnished coppers and oranges, overripe peach and palest pink. She did everything in her power to hold back her yawns, and wasn't very successful.

Now she had a pallet near the fire and her bedroll. She would sleep under a canopy of stars, something she hadn't done in many years. She looked forward to it, and at the same time admitted to herself that this was only possible because the skies were clear and the ground was dry. That would not always be the case.

Sleep came quickly to draw her down, and she never stirred, until the yelping of coyotes woke her. It might have been frightening, but Miguel was on watch and stood alert, weapons at hand. The others were just feet away, three indistinct shapes in the dying light of the cook fire. She was warm and safe and sleep came again, and the dreams stayed away.

When she next woke, it was still full dark, and now Eli was on watch.

She knew him by his shape, by the set of his shoulders and the way he turned his head. Carrie wondered what he would do if she were to go sit beside him and try, yet again, to start a conversation.

Because she had questions. First and most important, she wanted to know where the four men had disappeared to just before they ate, and why they had left her behind. They had smelled of a particularly strong tobacco, similar to the kind favored by the Indians she grew up with.

They had isolated her. Out of habit, or because they worried she was too fragile to bear up under whatever threat had presented itself. And here was the problem: she wasn't content to be kept in the dark, and tomorrow she would find a way to make that clear.

It was a conversation she had had many times with other men in clinics and hospitals and sickrooms. Men who knew better, knew best. Men she had challenged, sometimes successfully. More often not.

She allowed herself to hope that Eli would be an ally, but knew that she might be expecting too much. Out of habit or superstition or fear, he might side with Hardy. It would be a disappointment, but not a surprise.

24

By the end of the second full day on the trail, Carrie had gained Mimosa's respect and trust, but winning over the trackers was proving to be more complicated. They were satisfied with her, on the whole. A woman who was not easily flustered, voiced no complaints and made no demands, was pleasant in conversation, and was as good with horses as they were. Her competence was something of an unsettling but not unwelcome surprise.

The characteristics that made her easy to travel with under such unusual circumstances had also convinced Hardy that she was not good wife material. It was during one of the stops on the second day that she heard him say as much to Miguel Santos.

Hardy was not a cruel or thoughtless sort of man; Carrie recognized this about him. He hadn't realized that she was close enough to hear this conversation, and would have been embarrassed to know she had. Thinking about the exchange over the next hour, she realized she couldn't claim to be insulted, nor could she disagree with his observation. She asked difficult questions, was unflinching in her opinions and unwilling to be the silent, observant helpmeet. Few men would want such a wife.

She was thankful, in a way, because the exchange gave her the courage she needed to make herself understood when they stopped for the midday break.

Waiting for the trout Rainey had caught and cooked over a fire to finish, Carrie looked Hardy directly in the eye, modulated her tone, and smiled. "Who was it you went to talk to last evening?"

Hardy started like a schoolboy caught cheating on an exam. The other men were looking at him expectantly.

"I did warn you," Eli said, and Hardy grimaced. Santos and Bang kept quiet, probably, Carrie thought, because in a short while they would be free of her, while Hardy was a constant in their lives.

Hardy cleared his throat and turned his head away to spit.

"A scout," he said finally. "An old friend."

"Did he come to warn you about trouble ahead?"

The man had a whole variety of grimaces, and the one she saw now was made mostly of aggravation. She thought then that he would refuse to answer her, but he must have sensed her resolve. Or it could be that he was remembering Eli's warning.

"Just shared news from the last week or so."

Eli's expression gave her no clue to his thoughts, and that was a good thing; she didn't want to be guided by him.

"I hope you understand," Carrie said. "I trust you all to make the right tactical decisions. But I also trust you to tell me when there is reason to be concerned. I won't fall into a faint, I promise you."

As the day wore on, she had to admit that no one seemed to be harboring any resentment toward her, but neither did Hardy supply any more information. She was thinking this through when it occurred to her that the men she rode with might not have anything to fear, but wagon trains were a different matter. Such as the one traveling west with her brother and friends as passengers.

The sun was high and hot, but the perspiration that dampened her neck and back would have come even in a cool rain as the possibilities played out in her mind. She glanced around herself to see where Eli Ibarra might be, and then urged Mimosa to a fast trot.

When she came up beside him, he looked surprised but pleased. He had a beautiful smile, wide and easy, his teeth very white against skin far darker than her own.

One brow lifted, as close as he would come to asking her what she wanted from him. Not a man of many words or flowery circumlocutions. Quite the opposite of Mr. Tock or Rainey.

"Did you know the scout?"

He blinked. She still didn't know what it meant when he winked at her, but blinking she understood: he was surprised.

"No, not really. Not well," he said. "Miguel and Titus know him. Was there something you wanted to know?"

"Yes. Did he come to warn you about trouble on—" She paused to steady her voice. "Trouble on the trail? Attacks on wagon trains?"

His gaze was even and calm, but it took him a long time to answer. "Not exactly."

She held back her first reaction and calmed her tone.

"Eli," she said. "I'll tell you my suspicion quite plainly. The scout came to say that a wagon train—or more than one train—has been targeted for attack. Hardy kept this from me because he thinks otherwise I'll turn around and rush back to save my brother."

His expression relaxed. "He thinks more of you than that."

It was her turn to raise a brow. "More likely he thinks I wouldn't be able to find my way."

Eli conceded the point with a shrug. "He didn't say that, but I'd guess that would be his thinking."

"Listen to me, please." She used her firmest, least accommodating voice, the one that a stubborn patient might earn after many hours of resisting treatment. "I want an answer to this question. Is Petit's wagon train in danger?"

Eli flicked a fly away from his face.

"You know the answer to that," he said. "Every wagon train on the trail to Santa Fe—on any trail—could come under attack. The scout had nothing to report about Petit's convoy, and that is the truth."

He looked away, and she saw him swallow down something he thought he should not say.

"Don't hold back," she said. "Not if you value my friendship."

"Fine," he said. "Maybe nobody made this clear before, but Petit is reliable. Somebody on the Rio Grande or in Albuquerque or wherever wants hardware or cloth or a sister who's coming west delivered whole and in a reasonable amount of time, they pay him, and he does that. He can do it because everybody—every tribe, every robber—knows how well equipped he is, weapons and men both, and how vengeful he can be. Even the bloodiest-minded tribes stay away because he pays them to let him pass."

"Then I don't understand," she said. "Does Hardy think I made up the whole story about my childhood? I am no stranger to Indians."

Something passed over his face, as if the answer to a difficult question had presented itself unexpectedly.

"Ah," he said. "I think I see the problem now."

She had to bite the inside of her cheek to stop a sharp reply, but she inclined her head. An invitation to go on.

"Nothing offends you so much as being underestimated."

The surprise of it robbed her of any possible reply. She had never thought of herself this way, and would now have to figure out why something so obvious had never come to mind. He was watching her calmly, without any hint of a smile. Waiting for her to say something. Waiting while she worked through the shock of being seen.

"Tell me I'm wrong."

Carrie looked away and saw a herd of buffalo in the distance. A very small herd, compared to what they had seen yesterday. A small, silent, unmoving herd.

She turned Mimosa's head and set out to get a better look, with Eli close behind her. The others were calling out warnings, but the wind washed it all away. At the vaguest hint from her, Mimosa broke into a canter.

Once she could see for herself what had happened, Carrie pulled up suddenly. Eli stopped beside her, and then the others were there, too, but a few feet away.

What were they expecting from her? Outrage? Sorrow? Tears? Men were uncomfortable when a woman wept, but a woman's anger was something to be avoided at all costs.

She raised her voice so that they would all hear her. "This is what you were trying to tell me. Slaughter for the love of it."

The dozen or so buffalo were all dead, each with a contingent of crows and vultures taking advantage of the unexpected gift. Foxes and wolves and coyotes would be nearby, waiting for their chance. There was enough meat spread out here to keep them all fed for a long time.

As far as she could see, the hunters—what else could they be called?—had not harvested anything from the carcasses, not hides nor horns, not meat. In a matter of weeks there would be nothing to see here but bones bleaching in the sun.

She looked at Eli with anger and resignation plain to see on her face. He said nothing, and she liked him better for it.

25

THE NEXT AFTERNOON, when they stopped to rest and water the horses, the wind came up and clouds raced across the sky, shadows skimming over tall grasses. The gusting wind set the whole prairie to dancing. Carrie stood watching for a long time. Then she remembered that she was as thirsty as the horses.

There was a stream. Or a river. Or it might be called a creek. Carrie had yet to figure out the differences, as sometimes rivers were dry channels and creeks overflowed their banks. This was probably a stream, as it fed into a small lake bordered by marshes, home to birds of what seemed like a hundred different kinds.

Once she had seen to Mimosa and her own needs, Carrie sat down by Eli on a log near the other men. She wanted to talk to him, but she saw no reason to foster gossip and would rather not encourage Rainey's very active imagination.

"You are a cartographer," she said to him. "You must have a map of where we are and where we're going."

To her relief Eli didn't hesitate or frown or ask about her motivations.

Instead he went to his saddlebags and extracted something bulky. Then he sat down beside her with a fairly large folio in his lap. It was wrapped in many layers of waxed linen.

Carrie expected a folio of the kind her mother had to keep her artwork safe, but once he had set the wrappings aside and it was open on his lap, it turned out to be more of a shallow box. There was a lid that folded back to reveal many long tubes of rolled paper wound round with strips of soft fabric. The paper itself was thick and matte in texture, with light pencil notations on what she thought must be the reverse of the map itself. As he sorted through the rolls, his head bent to scan the notations, Carrie realized that she was not the only one interested. The trackers had inched closer and now stood behind them.

Eli slipped the ties off a tube and unrolled just eight or ten inches of a map. With loops of soft leather clearly created for this purpose, he secured its corners to the box itself. He took a stick from the ground, wiped it clean, and pointed.

"You see the Arkansas River? The main wagon trail to Santa Fe runs along it for a good ways. This point here is where the trail passes over Cow Creek, a tributary. That's a major crossing, and a treacherous one at that, as you saw for yourself."

"Where the wagons capsized," she murmured, and he nodded. The stick hovered over the paper as he traced a trajectory south-southwest.

"This is where we are now. There are lakes all along this route like beads on a string, so for a while we won't have any worries about water. Now I may be wrong, but I'm guessing we're headed—"

"Jaysus Christus Herr Gott Sakrament ihr Kotzbrocken!"

Rainey leapt into the air, tearing at the sleeve of his shirt and bellowing as loud as the buffalo. Before they could get to their feet, he was already gone, galloping toward the muddy bank of the stream. Hardy, Eli, and Carrie chased after him, but could only watch as he dove into the mud, right arm extended, and thrashed until he was shoulder deep, his face and belly cradled in the muck. He was still bellowing in German, long strings of words interrupted by an occasional gasp.

Carrie glanced back at the spot where they had been sitting, and saw that Miguel Santos was still there, bent over at the waist and studying the ground. Eli saw him, too, and called out.

"What is it?"

"*Las hormigas rojas.*" Miguel walked toward them at an easy pace, but he brushed at his belly and arms and legs vigorously.

Carrie looked to Eli for a translation.

"Fire ants," he said. "Fierce little buggers."

Miguel stopped in front of them. "He must have put his hand right down on the nest when he was leaning over your shoulder to look at the map. Look, the boss is fit to be tied and he didn't even get bit."

Hardy was crouched down beside Rainey in the mud, holding out one hand. "Quit your bawling, Bang, and give over. Let me take a look."

"Hell no!" Rainey wailed. "I'm staying right here till the mud takes the sting away."

"You damn puppy," Hardy shouted. "Give over or I'll drag you back there and stick your other arm in the nest."

Eli called to him. "Rainey, you have got to get that shirt off, or they'll never stop biting."

To Carrie, Eli said, "I'll go get your medical kit."

Miguel stayed right where he was, arms crossed, chin down on his chest as he watched Hardy pull Rainey's arm out of the mud and took hold of his wrist. With the big knife in his other hand, he slipped the blade between the shirt and Rainey's skin.

His screech sent birds wheeling skyward.

"Well then, hold still," Hardy barked. "And maybe I won't have to nick you again."

He split the fabric from wrist to shoulder. With his other hand he grasped the sleeve and yanked it away. It landed with a wet thump behind him on the riverbank.

Rainey immediately stuck his arm back into the mud, turned his cheek to rest beside it, and began to shiver and shake.

Carrie saw two possible outcomes: this might be an allergic reaction, or it could just be the shock and pain. In the first case he might well die; in the second the most she could do for him was to make a paste of water and bicarbonate of soda that might soothe the bites. With luck they might come across a plant that would make a better poultice, but in any case the pain and swelling would disappear soon enough. Of course, embarrassment had already set down roots.

As if she had said this aloud, Miguel said, "Have you ever been bit by a fire ant?" His mouth contorted at one corner, and then the other.

"I've never even seen a fire ant," she said, and lowered her voice. "Are you laughing at him?"

Miguel's eyes rounded and his brows rose, an expression any girl with a brother recognized. He was aware that laughter would get him in trouble, but he couldn't help himself. He turned away, shoulders hunched and shaking.

Carrie moved closer to Rainey, who still lay prone in the mud, moaning. Hardy had walked into the stream to scrape himself down. The piece of muddy shirting was right in front of her, and she crouched down—at a cautious distance—to have a look.

Behind her Eli said, "They're real small and hard to see. There." With one finger he reached out and nudged a smear of mud. Even then she could just make out a few tiny legs like fragments of thread. One of them gave a jerk and she leapt back, almost knocking Eli over.

"Pardon." She cleared her throat. "Do we need to worry about—more?"

"Nah," Eli said. "As long as you stay away from the nest, you should be fine. You want me to drag him out of there so you can have a look at the arm?"

There was a stifled guffaw from Miguel, who still stood with his back turned.

"Yes," Carrie said, trying to ignore Miguel. "Please."

Eli walked right up to Rainey and grabbed him by the back of the shirt. The mud squelched and muttered and sucked, unwilling to give up its prize until Eli gave a huge yank and the shirt tore. Finally he got a good hold and Rainey came out of the muck, wailing like a calf.

Miguel bent over with his hands on his knees and let his laughter rip as Eli steered Rainey toward solid ground. At that moment Carrie saw her mistake and called out, "Dunk him into the stream first, and do what you can to scrape off some of the mud. Otherwise we'll all look like he does."

26

Tuesday, May 26, 1857

CARRIE LOST TRACK of the number of days they spent riding southwest. Late May, as far as she could figure out, but on the prairie it might have been August given the glaring blue skies and sunlight so intense that sometimes her eyes would tear. By late morning she had perspired through her clothes, and could only hope that when they stopped to make camp, there would be a suitable stream or lake where she could rinse out her linen and cotton.

As was to be expected, the men weren't put off by a little sweat, but they did take every opportunity to swim. While Rainey's arm kept him out of the water, the others would disappear for an hour and come back dripping. Carrie would have dearly loved to be submerged in cool water, but she could imagine the reactions if she asked to join them. Hardy might turn away to hide his embarrassment, which would answer the question she hadn't had the temerity to ask: Did they swim dressed or undressed?

She was glad of the many distractions that showed themselves every day. Herds of elk and antelope, a whole sea of buffalo, a scattering of turkeys and partridge, and her first glimpse of prairie dogs. They were small, squirrel-like creatures with round bellies, all of them busy digging in the early morning light. The expanse of field was dry and would be of little interest to any animal that grazed for fodder, but the prairie dogs put it to good use. There were dozens and dozens of mounds, at least an acre's worth.

The afternoon after the fire ant incident, they had come across a large expanse of wild plum trees, and to everyone's surprise—except her own—Carrie drew up short and dismounted. Even as she pulled her knife from its sheath, Hardy was trying to dissuade her. The fruit, she should understand, wouldn't be ripe until late summer, three months from now.

Miguel grimaced. "She knows that, Titus."

"Keep an eye out for snakes!" Hardy yelled. "What you get from those trees ain't worth a snakebite!"

"She's after something specific," Eli said.

Apparently, Titus Hardy still needed interpreters to explain her odd behaviors. To the others she called out, "What's the word for bark in Spanish?"

She repeated the answer to herself while she worked a long strip of bark from a wild plum tree, careful to get the inner layers. In the shadows beneath the trees she caught sight of a brown hare, long-eared and long-legged, frozen in place to avoid her notice. Nearby was a nest where a jill was suckling three young.

A sight she would keep to herself; it was not sensible, but she did not want this small family showing up on the cook fire later in the day. Luckily, Chico was nowhere in sight.

"And the word for wild plum?"

Rainey, always hungry, supplied that answer so that by the time she had enough bark, she had learned the wording for the bark of the wild plum tree. She already knew the word for poultice, and put it together as she remounted.

To Hardy she said, in her rudimentary Spanish, "I will make a poultice of the bark of the wild plum for Rainey's arm."

This earned her a nod, high praise from Titus Hardy for a female who dared to leave the trail without permission.

Hardy came to see Carrie in the evening after the camp had been made ready for the night. He held his hat in his hands, lower lip pooched out, and eyes downcast.

"Wanted to ask something."

Carrie wrapped her hands around the tin cup that held the remnants of the poultice she had made for Rainey.

"Yes?"

He slapped his hat against his knee. "Fire ant bites ain't nothing unusual," he said. "Ain't as good as a kiss on the cheek from your Mam. Then again, I never seen any fire ant bites that looked like that."

Carrie glanced at Rainey, who had already stretched out on his bedroll. He wore a shirt with the right arm torn off, putting most of the forty-three bites on display. The poultice was providing some relief already. His hat covered his face and muffled the constant stream of soft snores.

"He's not in danger of his life," Carrie said, "if that's what you're wondering, and he won't lose his arm." This was something she had wondered about herself at first, but she was certain now that Rainey would survive, and keep his arm. Unless a real infection set in.

Hardy's expression was both relieved and, at the same time, doubtful. She could call Miguel or Eli over to explain—in the exact words she used—so that he might actually hear her. Then she decided to forge on ahead.

She said, "You see how pale his complexion is."

"Thin-skinned."

That was nonsense, but she had neither the time nor the inclination to instruct him on the number of layers of human skin.

"I would say rather that he lacks pigment, which is why he is so prone to sunburn. His coloring—or lack of it—is very common where he comes from on the North Sea. Many people with that kind of complexion develop hives when they've been bit or stung by insects."

His whole head pulled back in surprise. "You call those hives?"

"Some of them," Carrie said. "He's got two different kinds of eruptions, bites and hives. The hives are a response to the bites, and then the bites formed pustules. As unsightly as they might be, they are scabbing over and healing. The swelling has gone down steadily, and the poultice will speed that along. He has no fever. In another day or two, he should be fully recovered."

Hardy made a deep, rumbling sound in his throat. "He don't need a doctor?"

She tried to keep her surprise to herself. "If there is a doctor available, by all means. But again, he is on the mend."

He grimaced, and she wouldn't have been surprised if he had growled, but instead he nodded and walked away.

It was then she noticed that Eli, who was cleaning his rifle on the other side of the fire, had been listening to the conversation without apology.

She called to him. "He thinks Rainey would be better served by a doctor."

Maybe he hadn't heard her, or maybe he had nothing to say to something so indisputable. She was about to turn away, when Eli put aside his rifle, stood up, wiped his hands on a rag, and started toward her. There was an unusually resolute set to his jaw, but she stifled the urge to retreat. Really, it was too silly to give in to nervousness.

She saw now that he had been swimming, because his hair was still wet. In the evening light, water droplets sparked color along his hairline and in the scruff of beard. It was something she had noticed from the start, the way his beard grew. Thick and dark, all the way down his throat to the open neck of a collarless shirt. Most Indians, in her experience, had very light beards and even less chest hair, and so she guessed this must be something from his Basque father's side of the family.

She forced herself to look away, embarrassed by the way her mind worked. It was not the time for a comparative study of male body hair patterns. As that thought came to her, a burp of laughter rose in her throat. She swallowed it back down. Her imagination was out of hand, but what to do about it?

When he reached her, he said, "He wasn't thinking of a white doctor."

She let her confusion show. "Pardon?"

"Titus isn't thinking Rainey needs a white doctor, he's got something else in mind. He's concerned and feeling bad about the whole business. He has a soft side."

Carrie bit her lip rather than say what first came to mind: Hardy was able and quick thinking, but there was nothing tender about him. He would handle a bullet wound or a stabbing in exactly the same no-nonsense, rough but efficient way. Most men were calmed by his abrupt manner, but not all.

There was a brushing against her legs, and Carrie started, only to realize that Chico had come to stand beside her. Just two days before, he had decided that she was a human being worth his time, and he showed up at odd moments. Now she ran a hand over his knobby skull.

Eli was saying, "There's a band of Kiowa pretty close to here, and they've got a healer Titus likes. That's what he was thinking about, but he didn't want you to take offense. You've done a good job with Rainey, and he knows that."

Beside Carrie, Chico settled down with a long sigh, as if he needed to express his opinion about men who could not communicate something so simple.

She said, "Did he think I would assault him because he suggested a doctor?"

There was something sheepish about Eli's shrug. His gaze fixed on the dog for a long moment before he found what he wanted to say. "Titus has never been good with women. Theories on why that might be are thick on the ground, but nobody knows for sure. What I do know is that he doesn't understand anything about you, but doesn't want to offend you. Looks like Chico has outstripped him already."

She glanced down at the dog too. "Pardon?"

"Maybe you haven't took note, but Chico pays attention to your mood, comes close when you're ill at ease. Or mad."

"I don't see that," she said, trying to be amused instead of inexplicably affronted, but not managing very well. "I'm not mad just now."

The muscles in one cheek pulled up, so that side of his mouth curled.

"No? Well, let's say you're ill at ease."

"Let me be clear. Please tell Titus Hardy that I have no objection to taking Rainey to see the Kiowa healer. It's very possible that they have a local treatment for fire ant bites, and I should like to hear about it if they do. Will you tell him that?"

He nodded, but his gaze stayed on her face. Evaluating, thoughtful. She had the urge to poke him, hard, in the chest, but she was aware of the others. Miguel Santos and Hardy were out of sight, looking at what they thought might be a problem with Ross's hoof. In other circumstances, Carrie would have moved closer to listen, but Eli still stood in front of her.

She cleared her throat. "Thank you for stepping up to clarify."

"What is it that's making you so nervous?"

He was trying to get a rise out of her, and succeeding.

She leveled her most disapproving look at him, but his slow shake of the head and that lopsided smile made it almost impossible to look at him directly.

"I'm not nervous."

"Now you're telling tales."

There was something odd about his voice, low and rough. Like the touch of a calloused finger.

She began to turn away, but his hand closed around her wrist, and she knew that she was caught out. As gentle as his grasp was, now he would know. He could feel the frantic thrumming of her pulse, and see the sheen of perspiration on her brow, just as she could, if she cared to, count his eyelashes. He was so close that she could smell gun oil on the hand that came up to cup her face. She raised her gaze to his and let him see that she was not afraid.

FOR A LONG time sleep evaded her, for the simplest and most childish reason of all: an unimportant question without any hope of an answer. But she couldn't banish her thoughts, and must chase the question back and forth across the night sky.

Had that been a kiss? Certainly his mouth had touched hers, but it had been curved in a smile for that moment in time. The result was nothing more than a quick brushing of lips. The scrape of stubble, his thumb at the corner of her mouth.

If that had been a kiss, Carrie decided, then there were two possible conclusions, neither of them very appealing.

In the first instance, it might be that kissing was simply overrated. Did young women swoon and blush when the subject was raised only because it was expected of them? It seemed to be a possibility; after all, many people resorted to embellishment as a way of dealing with disappointment. Her stepsister went off on holiday to the seaside and came home praising everything about the experience. Only much later would they learn that the weather had been cold and wet, the hotel dreary, the seaside plagued by gnats. False enthusiasm as an anecdote for—what? Embarrassment? Guilt? Disenchantment?

There was another, simpler and more objective explanation. She reminded herself of the law of parsimony: the fewer complexities required to explain something, the closer one came to the truth.

It might just be that Eli Ibarra wasn't very good at kissing.

27

ONCE THE IDEA of stopping to see the Kiowa healer was put to him, Rainey's mood improved greatly.

"Not that I am needing anything from them," he said to Hardy. His gaze shifted to Carrie and away. "Miss Ballentyne and her poultice were cure enough, and I am thankful."

It was hard to tell if this pleased Hardy or agitated him, but if Rainey was feeling better, she was satisfied.

With improved health his natural cheerful nature showed itself. Now he was in a storytelling mood, and Carrie was the audience he chose for most of his tall tales.

"Bent Bow—the medicine man at the Kiowa camp?—he likes Titus. They are friends for many years." He glanced over his shoulder as if marking how close the others might be before he went on. "We will eat well. All of us but Miguel will eat well."

It turned out that the Kiowa were closely allied with the Comanche, and that the two tribes shared many things, including a deep animosity toward the Arapaho, Osage, and Navajo. Miguel, who was a full-blooded Navajo, would stay out of sight while they were in the Kiowa camp.

After a long and complicated recitation of which tribes were allies and which enemies, very little of which Carrie would be able to keep straight, he went on. "It is good to have the Kiowa as friends because you would not like them as enemies. Not the Kiowas or the Comanches, and they are controlling most of the land between the Arkansas and the Brazos."

Carrie realized that these were both rivers, but had only a vague sense of where the Brazos might be. If she asked, he would provide a detailed and mostly useless explanation. Better to wait for an opportunity to ask Eli if he had a map she could consult. Beyond that, there were other things that interested her more. There was the risk that those questions might be misinterpreted as idle curiosity. She decided to approach from another direction.

"Do the tribes make war among themselves still?"

He gave her a sharp look, the first she had seen from him.

"Why would they not? All over the world, neighbors make war on each other."

She took a moment to consider this bit of wisdom. With a studiously calm and neutral tone, she tried a little harder.

"I wondered if the tribes here might come together to protect their homelands from emigrants. You know that there have been attempts—unsuccessful attempts—to unite the tribes in the East. The hope was that together they could drive the Europeans back."

"I did not know that."

His expression said he didn't like it, either. She had managed to anger him, and to her surprise, he told her exactly why.

"Why would you speak of this possibility as something to wish for? You're white," he said. "You'd be forced back to Europe by the Mohawk you claim as family. You'd have to give up everything you own."

Carrie decided that anything she might say would only add fuel to the fire she had started so carelessly.

"To give everything back—" He blew out a long sigh. "Is it not said that 'To the victor belong the spoils'?"

She inclined her head in acknowledgment, and was not surprised when he dropped back and left her to ride on her own.

Since the midday break, the weather had turned. Now storm clouds crowded in, banishing sunlight and raising a buffeting wind. Hardy loped past them all, and they fell in behind him. There was no reason to explain the change of pace, as storms out on the open plains could be dangerous.

Mimosa nickered in greeting as Eli passed by, and with that Carrie realized that he had taken up Chico to ride perched in front of him.

She put her face up to the sky and felt the first spattering of droplets. The urge to let out a whoop of excitement was almost irresistible.

THEY WERE IN the middle of the Kiowa camp before Carrie realized it. The curtain of driving rain hid away every detail even as they dismounted in front of a lodge dug into a bank of earth. The guards who stood watch were boys of thirteen or fourteen years, utterly calm with expressions that might have been carved from ironwood. They all wore nothing more than breechclouts and moccasins, but every one of them had a lance that they held with casual familiarity.

Most unusual in Carrie's experience was the way they wore their hair. The right side of the head had been cut very short, while the left side had been allowed to grow out. The long hair was divided into multiple segments, each wrapped with a bit of fur.

Hardy, coughing and shivering, spoke to them in their own language. Whatever he said, it worked like an incantation. Animation came back into their solemn faces, and the eldest of them spoke to Hardy at length. Then three of the young men took charge of the horses, and one disappeared into the lodge by folding back the buffalo robe that hung there as a door.

Inside the lodge there was a fire and warmth and the smell of meat cooking, women's voices, a child calling out. It was just at this moment that Carrie realized that Miguel Santos was no longer with them. She hoped he had found a dry spot somewhere safe.

The most obvious thing about this Kiowa camp, as Carrie first saw it, was the fact that the only men present were very young or very old. This might mean that the rest of the men were out hunting or raiding, but that was not a question she could ask. She was glad to see that the man they had come to see—Bent Bow—seemed healthy, though he was among the eldest.

She would have to wait until one of her own party could explain things to her, because only men sat in a circle like this one. The women would have their own council, where all the business of daily life was decided. So Carrie stayed just where she was, not so close to the women and children as to give alarm. She had arrived with a trusted ally, but still she would not be surprised if the women decided that she needed a closer examination.

Carrie knew very well how to behave in a situation like this, and so she stood straight and let herself be observed. They could turn her out if she caused offense; the only way to avoid that was to show them that she was confident, alert, and respectful. When she thought enough time had passed, she sat down where she was.

Two walls were lined with a type of container she had never come across before. Clearly made out of cured hide, they were round and had closely fitted lids. All of them, small and large, were beautifully decorated, painted with geometric designs in reds, yellows, greens, and blues.

The strong smell of Indian tobacco rose up as the men began to pass a pipe. The pipe was a tradition in every tribe she knew of, and there would be other traditions. Certain topics would have to be raised, and news would be shared before any serious discussion could begin. An impatient woman would not do well here.

A boy of no more than two years suddenly appeared in front of her. He was naked, as all the youngest children were, with a round belly and sturdy legs. He looked at Carrie's face closely, no doubt because the color of her eyes was odd to him. Before she could think of a way to engage him, he was off again.

Carrie turned her attention back to the women and noted that they were taller than she would have expected, well proportioned and quite muscular. The Kiowa were a nomadic people; they followed the buffalo and didn't plant or tend crops. This must mean that the work of skinning and curing pelts—buffalo, elk, deer—would fall to them.

She was very familiar with the amount of labor that went into skinning and curing the pelt of a single doe. Now she thought of the buffalo, as much as ten times larger, with thick, shaggy coats. It was difficult to imagine how these women could accomplish such a thing.

Carrie counted thirty-nine women of childbearing age, eleven who were beyond childbearing, and thirty-two children, four of them still young enough to be in cradleboards that hung on pegs driven into the wall.

It was likely not the usual thing to have the women and children all together in the lodge, but it could be their habit to cook and eat together while the men were gone, or it might have to do with the threat of attack, or simply with the weather.

The low rumble of thunder intruded, but none of them seemed to take note. She wondered again about the horses, and reminded herself that the Kiowa were expert horsemen and as such would know how to keep their mounts safe and fed and comfortable.

A girl of eight or nine years came closer. She glowed with good health and curiosity, but ducked her head to hide her face so that her plaits fell forward over her shoulders. No doubt her bravery had to do with Carrie's clothing; women who spent much of their time sewing were always interested in the way garments were put together. In fact, Carrie realized, she saw no evidence of European dress or fabric at all. This told her that the Kiowa—or perhaps just this particular band of Kiowa—were conservative and kept with the old ways.

The girl held one of the leather containers in her hands, this one painted blue and yellow. She met Carrie's gaze as if asking for permission, and then took off the lid and poured a small collection of beads onto the ground.

There were bright red beads made of seeds that Carrie didn't recognize, carved bone beads, and perfectly round, shiny black seed beads that were also unfamiliar. One of the men might be able to name the plants that produced the seeds she didn't recognize, but they could not be interrupted.

She wondered if the girl might understand Spanish, and thought it was worth trying.

"Las cuentas son muy bonitas."

The girl wrinkled her nose, likely, Carrie thought, to signal her confusion. Then a woman on the other side of the lodge stood and called out something in Kiowa.

There was no mistaking the wide smile that broke out on the girl's face.

Carrie, encouraged now that she had a translator, touched the small container and asked for its name.

Every pair of eyes turned toward the woman who spoke Spanish. She stood, and in a clear voice she answered Carrie's question.

"Parfleche."

Parfleche sounded to Carrie like a word borrowed from French, but she committed it to memory while juggling the stream of questions that came to her, now translated into Spanish. Their curiosity was understandable, and so she answered as carefully as she could. They wanted to know her names, where she was from, which tribes lived there, where she was going, if she had a husband, how many children she had borne, if it hurt trying to see out of blue eyes, and if the hair on her body was as curly as the hair on her head.

Then came a question she had anticipated and almost dreaded, simply because she couldn't even begin to answer it in Spanish, not yet.

"Eres blanca, pero te vistes como un indio. ¿Por qué?"

A question she had heard many times, with slight variations. *You are white, why don't you dress like other whites? You are female, why don't you marry and raise children? You are educated, you should understand the differences between the races.*

For these Kiowa, the color of her skin meant that she should fear and hate Indians. A white woman who chose to present herself as Indian was a strange creature.

"These clothes are comfortable. I like them."

It seemed to please them. The girl sitting beside her reached out, very tentatively, and touched a finger to the beading on Carrie's moccasin. Beadwork was distinctive from tribe to tribe, so the patterns used by the Mohawk would be unfamiliar to her, as the beads themselves might be something never imagined. The things she might have told the girl about Mohawk beads were too complicated, but just then one of the elderly women who tended a large pot called out something that made everyone stop and turn in her direction.

The meal was ready.

The women sat apart from the men, as Carrie had expected, but she wasn't left to eat alone. The Spanish speaker came to sit beside her, which was more than she had hoped for. Even the simplest conversation was very welcome.

After some thought she managed to ask questions about the porridge, which turned out to be corn cooked with marrow and mesquite beans. Then there was a stew of buffalo with juniper berries and, if Carrie had it right, prickly pear, called *higo chumbo*.

She knew the word *frijoles*, because she had been introduced to many different kinds of beans over the last ten days, and *búfalo* was quite obvious. There was a strong taste of juniper berries, called *bayasand*, and with that she thought she had worked out a recipe.

When the meal was over, the women went back to their work. They were busy grinding corn, braiding rope, sorting through baskets—parfleche, Carrie reminded herself—and sewing. Younger girls took up awls and sinew to piece rawhide together, while older girls cut long pieces into fringe, almost certainly to serve as decoration.

Two old women were bent over an iron kettle on a tripod. From the stains on their hands and the overflowing parfleche around them,

Carrie guessed they were making a yellow dye with lichen and cottonwood buds. Nearby two more women were filling casings with what must have been buffalo tallow, plagued by children determined to wheedle a taste.

When Rainey went out to check about the horses, Carrie was disappointed not to be able to join him. She could trust him to make sure that all was well with Mimosa, but she would have liked to see at least a little of the village by daylight, even in the rain. Instead she took a different kind of chance and offered to help with a cranky child. He was seven or eight months old, and quite put out about cutting new teeth.

In the end she had distracted him with finger games, and in time he fell asleep in her arms. It wasn't until that point that the men broke off their discussion and Eli came to hunch down beside her. He took a moment to examine the sleeping boy's face, and then dropped his voice to a low rumble.

"Bent Bow told Titus that the wild plum poultice you made was the best way to handle fire ant bites."

That was satisfying, of course, but she wondered if it would gain her any credibility with Hardy.

"So this stop was not strictly necessary," she said.

Eli glanced around the lodge, and his jaw flexed in a thoughtful way. He said, "Oh, there were other reasons."

He went on before she could remark on this odd statement.

"The storm is going to keep us here overnight, in case you were wondering."

It was not a surprise. The storm was deep and wide and in no hurry to be gone. They couldn't risk the horses—or themselves—by setting out in it, and camping would be unpleasant. Beyond that, overnighting in the Kiowa camp would give Carrie a chance to see something more of it.

"Will we sleep here, in the lodge?"

He got up. "I doubt it, but I'll find out."

Carrie would have been comfortable in the lodge, warm and dry as it was, even with the storm raging overhead, but the decisions about where they would sleep—and what they would eat, and when—would be made by the women. She imagined that sleeping in a tipi might be like spending a night in a Mohawk longhouse with a dozen families sleeping nearby. While tipis were much smaller, she hoped they would provide the same cradle of deep calm.

At the same time, she was aware that it was foolish to let her curiosity and imagination overwhelm basic common sense.

They were assigned, all four of them, to a single tipi. Whose tipi it might be they were not told, but someone had made it ready for them. A fire had been set, providing some very welcome light in the gloom of a stormy day. Four pallets had been put down around the firepit, each with a woven blanket, much like the ones Bent Bow and the other men had wrapped around themselves.

Farther back in the shadows she made out folded pelts and buffalo robes and a dozen parfleche. To distract herself from that temptation, Carrie studied the way the tipi was put together. The cured buffalo pelts were stitched together with sinew and stretched over lodgepoles made from sapling tree trunks. Just above the firepits, two smoke flaps had been cut, a bit off center.

Hardy cleared his throat. "You should be comfortable here," he said, speaking to no one in particular. "I'll go see about the horses."

"I'll come too," Rainey said, and the two of them were gone before Carrie had really understood. She turned to Eli, who sat on one of the pallets, stripping off his moccasins. Her own feet were still damp, and so she sat opposite him on the other side of the fire and followed his example.

Carrie stretched out and took stock. Her stomach was comfortably full and her feet were warm and dry. The play of firelight on the tipi walls held her attention for some time, until she realized that she was seeing something more.

A hunting scene had been painted on the stretched skins of the tipi walls in simple, powerful strokes. Kiowa on horseback raced after buffalo, shooting arrows. Then they pursued antelope and elk and finally warriors of some other tribe. Bloodied and wounded, they raced away from fearsomely painted Kiowa. There were many symbols that would tell the story, but every tribe would have different signs, and it wasn't likely that she could decipher them here. As it was, she tried to memorize some of them. If there was time enough in the morning, she could pull out the single sheet of paper she was using to make notes to herself and record a few of them.

Around and around the tipi the hunters and warriors went and never tired. Carrie could almost hear the rhythmic thud of hooves against earth. In counterpoint, rain tapped against the walls like fingers on a newly tightened drum, and Carrie slipped away into sleep.

Later—one hour or three—her bladder woke her. The tipi reminded her where she was and why, but she lay still for a few minutes, listening. Out of caution and common sense. She was a stranger among people who had every reason to suspect strangers.

The fire was low and the shadows were deep, but when she did sit up, Carrie could see that two of the pallets were empty. Eli was there, sleeping, his weapons beside him.

There was no help for it, and so Carrie pulled on her moccasins and made her way outside. She saw the vague shape of two young men standing watch nearby, and thought of them on horseback, chasing buffalo in an endless loop. She counted five more men on watch before she got back to the tipi, but didn't know what to make of that number.

Before she could lift the flap that opened into the tipi, Eli came out, yawning. He nodded but said nothing, and she assumed he was out of doors for the same reason.

Inside the tipi she was alone. Again. While she put more buffalo chips on the fire and dried her hands over it, she tried to make sense of what it might mean that all three men had disappeared. Eli would be back, she was sure of that, but she wished he would hurry. It occurred to her then that she hadn't seen Chico since midday.

From the doorway Eli said, "Did you see your saddlebags? You were asleep when Rainey brought them in. Right beside your pallet."

It felt almost like an extravagant gift, her saddlebags. She used her towel and considered brushing out her hair, but sleep tugged at her, and so she wrapped herself in the blanket and lay down.

"Do you know where Chico is?"

"Miguel took him. He knows this area well, and I don't doubt they found a cave to sleep in."

For a few minutes she studied the firelight flickering on the walls of the tipi, and wondered if the artist had realized that the effect would bring the whole scene to life. Hunters and warriors and horses, buffalo and antelope on a carousel.

She guessed what her Ma would say: *But of course the artist knew. That's what makes her an artist.*

"That was a very deep sigh."

Eli was sitting on his pallet, cross-legged. She sat up to face him. Between them the fire was collapsing into pulsing coals.

"I was thinking about my mother."

Before he could ask more questions, Carrie said, "Should I worry about Rainey and Hardy?"

She caught a flash of a smile. "No."

"You know where they are."

He inclined his head. "I don't think you'd be shocked. I doubt you'd even be surprised."

And now she understood more clearly why Titus Hardy had been in such an unusually good mood for the last day.

"Do they have Kiowa wives?"

Eli seemed to be surprised by this question. "Not wives, no. Good friends, you might say."

The question was voiced before she could stop it. "And you? No good friends among the Kiowa?"

"Miss Ballentyne." He shook his head in mock disappointment. "Such a personal question?"

She could only hope that the shadows would hide her rising color.

"Just the opposite," she said. "You were left behind to protect me, I take it. I wouldn't want to keep you from—" She paused. "Visiting with friends."

"You think I drew the short straw."

She hadn't thought of it in such detail, but she could imagine the scene now, quite clearly.

"Or lost a coin toss." Keeping her tone light.

"No. No short straw, no coin toss."

"Then I suppose it was kind of you to stay behind."

Before the conversation got completely out of hand, she changed the subject.

"Why is it that one of the women here speaks Spanish?"

"I don't follow."

"How did she learn Spanish when none of the others seemed to know it?"

"Ah." He took a moment to gather his thoughts. "She's a *genízara*."

"*Genízara*? Is that a place in Mexico?"

He glanced away, as if he lacked the words to explain and hoped to find them in the shadows.

"Back when the Spaniards claimed half the continent, they started taking children and younger people, mostly girls, from the tribes. They were brought into the households of the Peninsulares and trained to work in the gardens and households. Now, generations later, many people you see are descended from the original *genízaros*, and there's still a market for them. I'll guess that one of the Kiowa bought that woman you were talking to from a Mexican trader."

The idea took her breath away. "The tribes still traffic in slaves?"

"Not so much anymore," he said. And after a longer silence: "Didn't the Mohawk take prisoners and keep them as slaves?"

"Yes," she said. "All the Haudenosaunee took slaves. A long time ago. Not anymore."

There were stories she could tell, and she thought that even Eli Ibarra would be surprised. Her family—the Bonners, the Savards, the Ballentynes, the Freemans—had secrets and stories enough, starting with the fact that for some fifty years, the village of Paradise had been a safe place for runaway slaves on their way to freedom in Canada. They crept in by night and found food, clean clothes, and a warm bed.

When they were ready to move on, one of the men would take them as far as the border.

She could tell that story, but not tonight. Not now.

"My mother is an artist," she said instead. "I was just wondering what she would think of this hunting scene."

She gestured with her chin. "Are there more like this?"

Eli's eyes moved over the painting for a moment.

"The Kiowa are famous for their paintings. In the morning, you'll see they're everywhere."

In the silence that followed, Carrie asked herself questions. Why this urge to talk to him about her mother? What did she hope to accomplish by showing him the few samples of her work she carried in her saddlebag? It was out of character for her, and at the same time it felt almost necessary.

She retrieved the packet and untied the bindings. The pieces had been chosen for their size, none of them larger than the span and length of a hand, and all were fixed to stiff card. On the very top was a sketch of her grandparents, sitting together on the porch at Uphill House. Where Carrie had come into the world. Where all the Ballentyne children had been born.

It was done in pencil, with even the smallest details finely rendered: the scar above her grandfather's eyebrow, the widow's peak that made a heart out of her grandmother's face, the ivy that climbed over the roof of the porch, and, in the window just off center, the face of a little girl peeking out. Birdie. The youngest of the Bonner children. Recently come home to Paradise from New Orleans with a husband.

Without looking at him, she said, "Would you like to see?" Her voice was hoarse, her pulse racing. What would it mean if he did? If he did not?

She didn't glance up until he sat beside her, legs crossed. He looked at what she held in her hands, and got up to put more buffalo chips on the fire. When he sat down again, there was just enough light to see.

"I haven't looked at these since well before we left home."

"Your people, I take it. Tell me." He was very close, but all his attention was on the pile of cards in her lap. And so she did. With every new piece she told him about someone she loved but had left behind, about the places that had once been home. She talked about her Aunt Martha, who was at least five and a half feet tall but looked tiny, surrounded by Uncle Daniel and their sons. A race of giants, her Ma would say, always teasing Martha.

A sketch of her Aunt Hannah with her arms full of puppies, and another of Runs-from-Bears, who had married Hannah's Aunt Many-Doves. Her mother had drawn him standing shoulder to shoulder with Blue-Jay, his firstborn.

"That story you heard about my grandfather in New Orleans?"

He nodded.

"This is the uncle who went with him, I think the old gentleman mentioned him. He was called Runs-from-Bears. Turtle clan. He died just before I was born, but his stories are still told. Blue-Jay looks very much like him, but without the battle scars and with fewer tattoos."

Next came a watercolor that she stared at for a long moment. She thought of her father always like this, his hair tousled and on the brink of laughter. "Simon Ballentyne, my father. Born and raised in Scotland."

Eli looked closely at the portrait. "You have his coloring, and the shape of his eyes. You lost him when you were very young."

She nodded because she knew her voice would break, and counted to ten before she revealed the next piece. Her parents, very young and about to go off on their own adventures.

"This is my mother," she said. "Lily Bonner Ballentyne. She has never liked to do self-portraits, so this piece is especially precious. All these drawings and paintings are her work, but only the smallest part of it. She is rarely without paint or chalk or ink on her hands."

Carrie looked at the hunting scene again. "She would love to see this."

Eli was leaning so close that she felt his heat radiating against her.

He said, "And none of you got her talent?"

The question was a surprise, and one that unsettled her.

"Ma got her talent from Great-Grandfather Oak, but just Ma."

Of the living, she might have added. But did not.

He could press her for more of an answer, but instead he touched the hand that held the drawings.

"Show me the rest?"

There were just three left, and she knew exactly which ones they were. Not because she had picked them out or mounted them on card, but because her mother had, and she knew what her mother wanted her to remember. Ma had assembled all her children's likenesses on one sheet of thick paper. Each face was so clear and true that Carrie had to stop herself from running a finger over familiar features.

"You see that there were six of us, all together. Nathan is the youngest, then me, and four more sisters. Of the girls, only two are still living. The youngest—that would be me—and the oldest, my sister Blue. I think she was about eighteen when Ma drew this portrait of her."

"So three of her six survived childhood," Eli said.

She had to clear her throat to go on. "No. Kate died in a typhoid epidemic when she was just four. Jean was eight when she fell out of a tree and broke her neck. You see them here as children because they never grew old."

She didn't often allow herself to think of Jean, but she had begun this and would see it through. As much as she was able, she would see it through.

"I never knew Kate. And now I think I need to stop."

Carefully, quickly, she tucked the pictures under the blanket and summoned a smile. Almost daring him to ask about the sister she hadn't named. Blue, Kate, Jean, but not Martha. When she managed to find her voice, it sounded high and far away.

"It's very late."

He studied her, his eyes roaming over her face, leaned forward, and touched his forehead to her own. A brother's touch, and that was enough.

Sometime later Carrie listened: the fire murmuring to itself, the rhythm of the rain. His breathing. He had gone back to his pallet, but he hadn't yet found sleep.

When he spoke, she heard every word.

"It was my choice to stay behind with you," he said. "There's nowhere else I'd want to be."

28

THEY HAD TWO days of fine weather, a gentle breeze, enough cloud cover to spare them the worst of the sun, lively horses, and even tempers all around. It was a pleasure to wake at dawn on days like this and set out fresh.

They drank the last of the morning's coffee and began to break camp. Rainey, finally recovered from his encounter with the fire ants, sang, though the others teased him unmercifully.

"Somebody find the boy a bucket," Hardy called out. "He needs one to carry that tune before it curls up and dies."

"Sad," Rainey said, "that a man of mature years should be so envious. How old are you, boss?"

Hardy slid the big bowie knife into the sheath on his belt, narrowed one eye, and looked into the sky. "I can tell you this much, Rainey. Right now, today, I'm as old as I've ever been."

That afternoon the skies cleared and the temperature crept up and up, until perspiration soaked Carrie's hair and trickled down her back. When she had had enough, she took off her hat and loosed her plait.

There was some relief in letting the wind move through the unwinding mass of it, but at the same time she could almost feel individual strands curling with the heat.

They were moving too fast just then to hold any kind of conversation, but she saw Miguel and Rainey exchange looks. The truth was, they might be surprised or even shocked at her bold behavior, but she didn't really care. Her hair flying behind her like a flag was such a great pleasure that she would gladly endure a few scowls.

When they stopped to water the horses and switch mounts, Carrie realized that they must be close to the boundaries of the prairie. Over the last two days, the landscape had grown more parched, and green had begun to give way to shades of gold and amber. There was a stream, but soon water would be harder to find. How much more difficult was something she couldn't really estimate, and she decided that in this she would have to trust that these men would get them to Santa Fe.

That thought was still in her mind when Hardy came up from the stream leading his horses and hers, and stopped in front of her. She had the sense that he was staring very hard at her face, as if it would be wrong of him to look at any other part of her.

"Miss Ballentyne," he said, his voice hoarse. "You know this is hostile territory."

"I am aware, yes."

He gave a low growl at her refusal to be frightened. His jaw worked for a while and then he couldn't hold back.

"Don't the Indians in the East take scalps anymore?"

She had expected a different line of questioning, and it took a moment to readjust her thinking.

"The tribes in the Northeast no longer fight."

Rainey had come closer, as he usually did when any conversation was to be had, whether or not it concerned him.

"You mean, they won't fight when the next war comes?"

She looked at him for a long moment. "The tribes are not what they once were. The survivors? I don't know. I hope not. You're eager to go to war?"

Rainey gave what was meant to be a careless shrug. Carrie took this for more evidence of his youth and inexperience; but whatever his motivation, she knew that he wouldn't like the things she had to say about young men in a hurry to take up arms.

Instead she turned to Hardy. "Do I understand correctly that you think that my unbound hair is an invitation to a scalping?"

Miguel snorted a soft laugh from his perch on a rock, where he had stopped to shake a stone out of a moccasin and was cinching it up again.

She asked him directly. "Do I make a target of myself?"

He shrugged, his expression thoughtful. "Not sure," he said. And then: "Now, if your hair was yellow, I might be tempted myself."

He meant to shock her, and he had succeeded. Before she could gather her thoughts or even simply turn away, a loud, sharp whistle sounded from beyond a copse of cottonwood trees. Eli was sounding an alarm, and before the sound faded, Hardy, Rainey, and Miguel were on their feet with weapons in hand.

"Stay here," Hardy barked at her, and they ran for their horses before Carrie had even the vaguest sense of the threat. Then it came to her: a dozen or so men approaching at a gallop. She retrieved her own weapons, backed up against the trunk of a half-dead cottonwood, and made a conscious effort to slow her heartbeat so that she could hear beyond the rush of blood in her ears.

Chico appeared out of the brush and settled down beside her. Not completely abandoned, then. Maybe Mimosa had sent him. She swallowed down a nervous hiccup and forced herself to breathe deeply.

For two or three minutes there was only birdsong and water tumbling over rocks. No gunshots. Someone was talking, but the wind stole most of it away, and what words she could catch were in a language unfamiliar to her.

Silence could be more frightening than a war cry. The worst moments in her life had come in silence.

She moved deeper into the stand of cottonwoods, and Chico shifted with her. His ears stood straight up and turned one way and then the other. If she was tempted to discount the threat at hand, he was not.

The men were coming closer. She made out Hardy's voice and Miguel's. One of the riders replied at some length, and his tone was harsh. Men on the brink of confrontation. You didn't have to understand the language to hear that threat just below the surface, but now she could make out some of the language. The rhythm was different than Kiowa. The Kiowa bit off their syllables abruptly, but these men let their words play out in a lazy spool.

Then it was suddenly over. The riders set out again, moving at a slower pace. She counted to thirty and then sixty and then a hundred and sixty, and looked up to find that Eli and Rainey were ten feet away.

Rainey swung down from his mount.

"Miss Ballentyne," he called. "You can come out now."

Eli, too, was gesturing impatiently for her to come closer.

"If you want to see—" His head jerked toward the sound of the horses moving away.

In fact, Carrie did want to see who had threatened them, because there was no doubt in her mind that they had come very close to bloodshed.

Eli reached out a hand, and Carrie let herself be pulled up behind him on the saddle. In one smooth gesture he turned Sombra's head and they were moving fast toward a low ridge where Hardy and Miguel sat their mounts. Hardy had binoculars out.

To Carrie, Eli said, "Mescalero. Wanted to help themselves to a couple ponies. You see them?"

The Apache riders had slowed to a walk, and then stopped at a bend in the stream, apparently to water their horses. That wasn't anything out of the ordinary, but the men around her were clearly still tense. Maybe they wanted to go after the Apache, but they were experienced and knew what she saw for herself: four men would not prevail against this war party.

She counted fourteen horses. All but three of the riders had dismounted, while the horses lined up along the riverbank and lowered their heads to drink.

For all the days of this trip, she had told herself that Indians in the Southwest would not be too much of a surprise, but now she realized that the Mohawk she had grown up with might have been more like these Apache a hundred years ago, before they had been brought low by warfare and disease and alcohol.

She could imagine it, looking at these men. They were naked but for breechclouts, moccasins, and a great variety of weapons. They wore their hair long, and like Miguel they had tied bandanas across the brow. Their faces, shoulders, and arms were painted white and black and red. War paint.

Most of them carried spears, weapons six or nine feet long, carefully maintained and deadly. All the spears she could see were wrapped with bits of fur or leather, and trailed feathers plaited into what might be strips of buffalo pelt. Scalps taken in battle had been tied just below the blade, where they would flutter in the wind.

Carrie knew what she was seeing, and could not pretend she did not. A scalp taken in war was something to be proud of and displayed as evidence of courage and skill. She looked again and saw a flash of blond hair mixed in with shades of brown and gray.

She tried to swallow her gasp, but Eli heard it and looked over his shoulder. Carrie shook her head at him, hoping he would understand: don't draw attention to me.

He nodded.

With bile rising in her throat, Carrie forced herself to look again, and to look hard at the details her mind had simply refused to acknowledge. Fourteen Apache wearing war paint, and three prisoners, tied to saddles. Two boys, ten or twelve years old, and a woman who sat slumped, her chin on her chest.

For the rest of the afternoon, Carrie tried to recall what Rainey had told her about the Apache. There were three or four or more Apache tribes, but she recalled only Mescalero, and only because Eli had mentioned it.

A whole party of well-armed Mescalero Apache could have bested Hardy and his crew and taken all the horses, but instead they just rode away. Because they were in a hurry, or because they didn't want to lose any more men—they would win an armed confrontation with four men, but at a significant cost—or maybe they were just tired and satisfied with the day's work.

It was also possible that Hardy or one of the others had a connection to somebody in the war party. Miguel was Navajo, and for that reason he had stayed away from the Kiowa camp. Were the Navajo at odds with the Kiowa, but allied with the Mescalero Apache? Even vague connections might have been enough to break the stride of an escalating confrontation.

These possibilities occupied her not because they were important but because they were less distressing than the other, bigger issue. A problem that had no solution. It would help to talk it through, but this was not a topic she could take up with Hardy, and probably not with Miguel or Rainey, who might not even understand what troubled her.

Eli might not understand, but he would at least listen. That opportunity was hours away. In the meantime she could pretend, and so she made an effort to recall the facts. The things she had seen for herself, and those she could reasonably extrapolate from what she had been told.

The facts were devastating, but simple. The Apache raiding party had come across a caravan of emigrants or a settlement or a farm; those they had not killed outright had been taken prisoner. The woman and two boys had seen their families die. They had watched the scalpings: the sweep of the knife that made a deep, curving slash over the top of the brow, a bloody hand wound into the hair at the crown of the head, and a tremendous yank. A scalp peeled away from the skull with a ripping sound.

For now the three survivors were alive. How long they might survive she could not even guess. They would be adopted into the tribe, or kept as slaves, or sold to slavers, or killed. The woman would be raped, probably multiple times.

Just the previous day they had seen a large party of Indians in the distance. Sixty or so men and women and children moving camp, walking at a steady pace and leading mules hitched to travois piled high with lodgepoles and stacks of folded hides, provisions and tools and household goods, everything they needed to make a new home for themselves somewhere else. Near sweeter water, or rumors of buffalo, or because an elder had declared it to be time.

Carrie watched until the raiders were out of sight, and asked Miguel about the tribe they had seen the day before.

He gave her a sharp look before deciding to answer. "Ute." And then, his jaw tight: "Best stay clear." With that he turned his head to spit.

Toward evening they stopped to make camp on a rise that gave them a view of the countryside in all directions. It was not a particularly pretty view, but there was a spring and outcroppings of rock that formed a low cliff. Far to the north clouds roiled and darkened, and before the night was over, they might be glad of somewhere relatively dry to wait out the storm.

For the first time since she had joined the party, there would be no cook fire. She could only assume that there was good reason not to announce their presence, as a fire would have done. Rainey's usual easy chatter was absent as he took care of the horses and went about his chores. Miguel and Eli, watchful but just as silent as Rainey, sat down to clean their guns. Then Hardy walked off, his rifle over his arm, to sit by himself.

Carrie was very aware of the way he watched her. He was waiting for her to prove, once and for all, that he had been right to doubt her. If she wept for the woman and boys and their families, if she raged or fell on her knees to pray, if she demanded that they go back and wage battle to rescue the prisoners or insisted on going to the nearest army outpost to send troops out in pursuit, none of that would surprise him. That was what he expected.

Her silence would surprise him, and so that was all he would get from her.

Carrie went exploring on the far side of the spring and found chickweed bordered by a patch of mallow, not yet in flower. She picked as much as she could fit into a sling of muslin, rinsed it all in the spring, and brought it back to camp. With the greens they ate pemmican that was full of dried fruit, nuts, and seeds, and to this they added some of the corn bread the Kiowa women had given them for the journey.

Rainey, always hungry, regained some of his usual cheerful mood after his second helping. Hardy finished and went back to sit apart from them, and with that the tension eased a bit.

Carrie asked Miguel what edible wild plants they ate where he came from.

"My Cousin Amelie grows every kind of healing herb and edible wild green," she said. "Right in the city. I'll write to her to tell her about plants that are new to me. Once I find some."

He thought about this for a moment, and turned to Eli. "Do you know the English for *cují yaque*?"

"Mesquite," Eli said. "Honey mesquite, to be exact."

"A plant that grows in this area?" Carrie sat up a little straighter. "What parts of mesquite are edible?"

"None, at this time of year," Miguel said. "But later in the season."

The three of them talked about this thorny small tree that Carrie had yet to see, mostly because she was determined to be as normal as a woman could be in this unusual setting and company, given the events of the day. She would give Hardy no evidence he might use to tell anyone in Santa Fe that she was too fragile for this place.

Rainey's whole attention shifted across the sky, and he pointed out the storm clouds gathering to the north. Miguel turned to look for himself and shrugged off the possibility of a storm for reasons he didn't explain to her.

While the men talked about weather—something they could discuss for hours on end—Carrie laid out her bedroll, organized her clothes, and went about the laborious business of taming her hair so that it could be confined, once again, to a plait. She was aware that Hardy had come back to sit with the others, because she heard his voice coming from that direction. It was still very warm even as the sun set, and all at once a weariness overcame her.

She woke into a night so dark she was at first alarmed. The palm of the hand held in front of her face was as black as the sky overhead, where there was no moon or even a single star to provide light.

Beside her Eli said, "Cloud cover."

"So I gathered."

For a long moment she took in the night sounds, waiting to hear why Eli had roused her. She couldn't see him, but she knew he was there by the warmth he gave off, his own particular smell, and the sound of his breathing. Then something occurred to her.

"The others?" She pitched her voice very low.

"Put down their bedrolls a good ways off," he said. "We can talk."

Carrie might have objected on any number of grounds that would make sense at home in Manhattan. But she wasn't at home, and the night air was warm and soft on her face, and Eli had come to talk. To listen to her talk.

"Did you think I'd have nightmares, after today?"

She heard him turn and realized that he had put his bedroll down directly beside her. If she were in the mood to tease, she might scold him for his cheekiness.

"Did you?"

She was glad she didn't have to lie to him. "No. I was sleeping very peacefully. Did Titus Hardy send you to keep an eye on me?"

A soft, low sound came from deep in his throat, a wordless dismissal of the idea that he was obliged to follow Titus Hardy's orders.

"I think you know me better than that."

She wondered if that was true. She hoped it was.

"Titus getting on your nerves?"

She swallowed her laugh. "He acts like I'm a bomb ready to go off."

"Sure, given what we saw. He thought you might."

At least that was honest.

Carrie nodded. "I am practical, and I can see for myself when a situation is hopeless."

The study of medicine had stripped her of the comfort of self-delusion, and she knew that there was nothing they could have done for the Apache prisoners. The four men with Carrie were experienced and good with their weapons, but hardly equal to a large and well-armed raiding party. They would have done damage, but in the end the men would have died and Carrie with them. Unless the Apache decided that she had some monetary value. Then she would have joined the woman and two boys.

None of this would be new to Eli, but she must make one point clear.

"Not all women born in the East are witless. When I have to, when I am pushed so far, I hold my anger in a closed fist. That way it damages only me."

In the total dark she held up a fist and started when Eli folded his fingers around it.

"Another talent," she said, a little breathlessly. "You can see in the dark."

"I see you."

He shifted closer and brought her arm down so he could hold her clenched hand against his chest.

"Tell me," he said. "What happens if you open your fist and let all that anger fly?"

So, Carrie thought. They had been working toward this conversation, and here it was. Maybe wrapped in the dark like this she could allow herself the words. She could say what she had been holding back for so long, and deal with the consequences, whatever they might be.

"The last time I let my anger loose," Carrie started, her voice surprisingly steady, her tone unremarkable, "I was a girl, and I put a knife in my brother-in-law's throat."

29

Paradise, New York
1841

FROM HER SPOT on the porch of the trading post, Carrie Ballentyne is the first to see Gregory and Amy Fisher arrive in Paradise. An old buckboard pulls up and stops in front of the Red Dog. It is overloaded with crates and boxes and baskets, and pulled by two skinny mules.

The lady is slight and as slender as a boy, but her husband is solidly built. Carrie is considering his face and trying to decide whether he might be called handsome, when the tavern door flies open and the widow LeBlanc appears, hands on hips and a big smile on her face. Carrie can't remember the last time she saw Becca LeBlanc smile like that.

Behind Carrie the trading post door opens, too, and people pour out onto the porch. When strangers arrive in Paradise, everybody pays attention. Her sisters come out, too, to stand next to her.

Blue says, "Those must be the Yankees who bought Becca out. Fisher's the name, I think." She glances over her shoulder looking for the trading post clerk, a small, neat man who knows everything and everybody in Paradise.

"Mr. Bee, do I have that right? Fisher?"

He nods. "That's it. Gregory Fisher, and the wife's called Amy, if I remember right. Out of Boston."

Carrie considers this. "Wouldn't you have to be rich to buy the Red Dog? They don't look so rich, from what I can see."

"Yankees." Mr. Bee shrugs as if to say, What do you expect of such odd creatures?

The new owner of Paradise's only inn and tavern is helping his wife down from the buckboard.

"I can't believe they came all the way from Boston on that old buckboard," Carrie says.

Martha takes exception, always ready to do battle with her sisters.

"Maybe they didn't. You don't know. I think they must be very nice," she says. "And I am going to say hello."

At age fifteen Martha Ballentyne is simple and innocent and inordinately stubborn. This is not a battle worth fighting, and so Blue and Carrie follow Martha across the road to the Red Dog. Others decide that this is a good idea, and in no time Becca's public room is filled with people curious about the newcomers.

"Too young," George Munro says. Not caring if he's heard. "A dollar says they'll be gone before first snow," his brother agrees. Mr. Mouton adds, "Yankees . . . fie!" with a low hiss.

Yorkers are suspicious of Yankees, and especially suspicious of the Boston born, though Carrie hasn't yet figured out why this would be the case.

Becca introduces the Fishers to everybody in the broadest possible way; then she announces that the public room is closing now and any questions will have to wait until the next day or maybe even the day after that. In the years since her husband died and her children moved away, Becca LeBlanc has been running the Red Dog all on her own. A cantankerous, opinionated old lady, loved by one and all. Nobody would dare challenge her.

The neighbors, still curious, take her at her word and start to drift away, the Ballentyne sisters bringing up the rear. Martha is dragging her feet.

At the doorway she suddenly turns and darts toward the other side of the room, where the Fishers are still talking to Becca.

"Hello," Martha says, and holds out a hand. "Hello. I'm Martha Ballentyne."

The dimples she inherited from their Da carve into cheeks flushed with excitement. She looks back and forth between the Fishers, and somehow manages to capture one hand from each of them. Standing like that in a half circle, the three of them look like children about to start a rhyming game.

To Carrie's relief, the Fishers are charmed.

Amy Fisher says to her, "I am glad to meet you, Martha. I was so hoping people would be friendly. Wasn't I just saying as much, husband?"

"You were, my dear." His voice is cultured but stiff, as if he were standing on a stage reciting a poem. He smiles down at Martha in a calm and open way, glances at Blue and Carrie, and his smile widens.

"These must be your sisters," he says. "Your parents are to be congratulated on three such polite young ladies and, I will guess, the prettiest in Paradise."

Martha drops her head because she is both mystified and pleased. She loves compliments, though in cases such as this one, she doesn't really understand.

Blue says, "It is very nice to meet you, Mr. Fisher, Mrs. Fisher. Martha, come. Ma will be waiting for us."

Disappointment flickers across Martha's face, and her jaw tightens, but she has been taught that Blue is indeed the boss of her when no older relatives are nearby. Blue must be obeyed. Martha drops the Fishers' hands and crosses the room.

Outside, Martha glares at Blue. "I think you are rude. Very rude."

Blue is sensible and not easily roused, and more than that, she understands Martha, who sees so much and understands so little.

"Sister." Blue uses a particular tone, one calculated to soothe Martha's pique. "The Fishers have had a long journey and are very tired. It would be inconsiderate to take up their time just now."

Martha is not ready to be mollified.

"I don't know that word," she says. "But I know rude when I hear it. I'm telling Ma." She walks away, but pauses to call over her shoulder, "I think Ma will say that you are the Queen of Rude."

Her tone is not strident, but her feelings have been bruised, and it will be a while before she and Blue are on good terms again. The conversation on the walk home will be difficult, and Carrie would rather not be a part of it. She watches as they turn off the Johnstown Road, and when no one calls for her, she's relieved.

To herself she must admit why she is hanging back: standing underneath the public room windows, she can hear Becca and the Fishers talking. The conversation is about practical details: the size of the cabinets and the pretty curtains at the windows and how well maintained the furniture is.

Carrie is thinking about going to Lake in the Clouds to visit her cousins, when she hears the name she didn't want to hear.

"The Ballentyne girls seem very sweet," Amy Fisher says. "Maybe one or two of them will be interested in working here with us."

Mr. Fisher says, "The middle one is extraordinarily beautiful, but quite slow, I think. Sad."

There is a pause, and then Becca answers the question hiding in his observation.

"It was a difficult birth," she tells them. "Twins, you understand. Kate and Martha. But Martha came second, and she was too long without air. She's a sweet thing, but yes, quite slow."

"And her twin?" Amy Fisher asks. "Is she also afflicted?"

"Do you mean slow? No, Kate was as bright as a light. Typhoid took her away. They've had some terrible losses, the Ballentynes, but then Nathan came along and that boy—" She laughs. "That boy."

Becca makes them laugh with stories about the youngest, cleverest, and cheekiest of all the Ballentynes.

DESPITE THE GENERAL *lack of confidence in Yankee tavern keepers, the Fishers win over the citizens of Paradise within a month.*

Carrie is on her way to school when the first snow of the season begins to fall. She passes Sadie Blackhouse, who carries a bale of hay on her bent back, but this doesn't prevent her from stopping to talk to Wiese Metzler, who is standing outside the bakery with a loaf tucked under each arm.

"Those two." She points with her chin at the Red Dog. "Keep a clean taproom, don't overcharge, ain't full of themselves like most Yankees. And the mister? My seventy-third birthday might be coming at me, but I still got eyes in my head, and he's about as handsome a man as I've seen."

"And a generous pour too," says Mr. Metzler, smacking his lips.

The Fishers work hard to attract custom and make people feel welcome. Even Jane McGarrity will admit that Amy Fisher knows her puddings and pies and how to get the most out of a pork shoulder. Greg Fisher's stories and rhymes and riddles have won over people not so taken in by his good looks.

Best of all, all the people Becca had to let go when she cut back on her hours over the previous year are welcomed back and treated fairly. Two more men are hired to look after the garden and livestock, and within a week the skinny mules have begun to fill in, and they have company. From local people Amy buys hens and a rooster, a milch cow, and a sow. Finally, Carrie's Uncle Ben sells Amy the two best riding horses he can spare.

It isn't until Carrie sees for herself that Barnaby and Petunia are well treated and looked after in the stable behind the Red Dog that her worries about the Fishers settle down.

And then Amy hires Martha to help in the kitchen.

It is impossible not to be pleased for Martha. Having work frees her, somehow, and her moods even out. At the supper table they hear about Amy's custard recipe, the way Amy likes sheets to be folded, and Amy's family back in Boston. Martha tells these stories to every Bonner, Savard, Ballentyne, and Freeman in Paradise; she wants every one of them to come to the Red Dog so she can introduce them to Greg and Amy Fisher.

People who never set foot in a tavern—Quakers most notably—are suddenly regular customers at the Red Dog, if only to stand along the wall and watch. Martha is sure that this has mostly to do with the music.

"In the evening there's singing," she tells Uncle Daniel and Aunt Martha. "They know every song ever sung, everywhere in the world, and everybody sings along, with such pretty harmonies. I can't be there for the music." She casts a sad look her father's way. If only she didn't have to be home for supper.

Da says, "Martha, my love, you belong here with us evenings. And here you will be, so long as I live."

"And years beyond that," says Nathan, and thumps his spoon on the table to make his point clear.

It is bitterly cold at Christmas, but in the room Martha and Carrie share, the windows are left open a crack so long as music drifts up the hill from the Red Dog. "Angels from the Realm of Glory" and "The First Noel" and "God Rest You Merry Gentlemen" in two- and three-part harmony. Martha sings along, softly, softly, until the very end of the last song.

In the New Year, Blue and John Young make it known that they will marry in June. Ma is pleased because John owns the mill and Blue will not have to leave Paradise to set up housekeeping; Da is satisfied because John is hardworking, has a wicked sense of humor, and is dedicated to the oldest Ballentyne daughter's happiness. Nobody else can tease Blue into high dudgeon as quick. Grandda Nathaniel declares John to be a likely young man, and Grand Elizabeth looks Blue directly in the eyes and asks her if she wouldn't rather go to college. She could read law, or study literature or philosophy or history. Whatever she wants to learn, wherever she wants to pursue an education, that opportunity is available to her.

"You know how fond she is of your John," Ma says later. "She's happy for you, Blue."

But Carrie isn't so sure. Grand Elizabeth wants as much education for her granddaughters as she can talk them into.

Martha tries to be happy for Blue, but it's almost impossible. The idea that Blue would not be sleeping in the next room, that is something she cannot take in stride; Martha simply can't imagine her life or her family without Blue. It does no good to remind her that Blue will be just across the Sacandaga at the millhouse.

In the night she whispers to Carrie, "What if my hair gets tangled? Blue is the only one who can untangle without hurting. What if I have a nightmare? What if I need her?" There are no answers that will satisfy her, and so she comes up with a solution of her own.

"John should live here with us," she announces the next day at breakfast. "Blue has a room to herself, and he could share it."

Later, her face swollen with tears, she tells Carrie that it's not fair. Martha is a sensible and logical young lady, surely Carrie must agree, while their parents are being unreasonable and mean-spirited. On the verge of sleep she says, "We shouldn't have to lose another sister."

Toward spring Ma and Blue begin talking about the wedding, but only when Martha is not nearby. Carrie is anxious and sad for all of them—Blue, Martha, and Ma—until the day Nathan asks the question that at first seems to put everything right.

"Sister," he says to Blue. "Why don't you have the wedding party at the Red Dog? That would make Martha happy, wouldn't it?"

In fact, it did.

On a mild afternoon in June, Blue and John Young marry in a simple ceremony in the garden at Uphill House, and then they all walk together down to the village to the Red Dog for the wedding party. Martha goes straight into the kitchen because, she tells them, Amy cannot manage without her.

She hardly looks at Blue, and her eyes are damp with tears.

"Let her come to a quiet place with it," Aunt Susanna says to Carrie. "In time she'll see that she hasn't lost her sister."

Aunt Hannah and Aunt Martha are not so mild.

"This is Blue's day," Hannah says. "And she deserves all the happiness we can gather around her."

Aunt Martha looks grim when she tells Carrie what she's thinking. "Martha can't have all the attention all the time."

Aunt Martha and Uncle Daniel have a house full of boys who are always cooking up schemes. She ran out of patience long ago, is how Aunt Martha puts it when she knows she has been too curt. But not this time. She has had enough of Martha's tantrums; she says that plain so that she can be heard.

Despite the worry about Martha, the party takes off. There are speeches and toasts and a lot of teasing, and all the cousins are together and looking for ways to make mischief. The aunts are all watching, looking to forestall the next disaster. Carrie dances with her Grandda Nathaniel, with cousins and uncles, eats until she can eat no more, and joins in the singing.

In the twilight Blue and John walk home to the millhouse, trailing good wishes behind them. They are holding hands, Blue's head touching her new husband's shoulder. The golden light of the evening washes over them all, and Carrie is very close to tears until Michael, the incorrigible, the youngest of Martha's wild boys, smears a bit of buttercream on her cheek and darts away, giggling.

Sometime later Nathan falls asleep with his face in a plate of wedding cake, and the Ballentynes set out for home. First, Ma stops in the kitchen to talk to Martha, and when she joins them again, there is a deep worry line between her brows.

In the morning Carrie wakes to the news that both Martha and Amy Fisher have disappeared and are nowhere to be found.

30

For a moment Carrie wondered if Eli had drifted off to sleep, but then he turned toward her. She felt the touch of his breath on her cheek and heard him swallow, once and then again.

"Martha?"

"She was safe. Hiding." Carrie told him about the caves behind the waterfall at Lake in the Clouds, where her Da had found Martha. Uninjured, unaware of the tumult she had caused, sound asleep on an old bear pelt.

Her voice failed her for a moment, but Carrie was determined to tell this story properly and completely, now that she had started. She would tell it once, and never again.

"Da got her home, and the shouting went on for hours. She didn't know, she didn't remember, she had no idea where Amy might be. In all the time after, she never told what she knew. If she knew anything at all."

"Amy didn't come home, I take it."

"No. A search party found her the next day, at the bottom of a cliff on the north side of the mountain. It looked like an accident."

"But wasn't." Not so much a question as a prediction.

Carrie's memories of those first weeks after the wedding party were a jumble of raggedy images. Her Da's fury, barely kept in check. Martha's pale face flushing with anger as sudden and bright as a match. The Red Dog shuttered. The way Blue came home every day to sit with Martha, as if she didn't have a household of her own and a husband to look after. And then, finally, the arrival of the circuit judge.

Lionel Bell was well-known in Paradise. In public he was a generous, cheerful sort, well liked despite—or because of—his terrible puns. In the courtroom all that fell away. As a judge he was respected for his resolute dedication to the law, and for the way he ran his sessions. Judge Bell had small eyes that seemed to disappear when he frowned, which he always did when he barked questions at a witness, even somebody he was friendly with otherwise.

With Martha he was gentle, and still she shook so much on the witness stand that her voice wobbled with it.

"There was an inquiry," Carrie told Eli. "The circuit judge came and took testimony. But without witnesses or evidence, he gave up and called it an accident."

"Greg Fisher was questioned?"

"Oh yes. For hours, but he was like a statue, sitting there. He answered questions, but mostly he didn't remember, didn't know, couldn't say. People thought he would sell out and move away," she went on, her voice growing hoarse. "And that would be the end of it. But he didn't, and it wasn't."

Paradise, New York
1842

IN PARADISE PEOPLE call the house on the hillside where the Ballentynes live Seven Bells. It is halfway between Downhill House, where the Savards make their home, and Uphill House, where Nathaniel and Elizabeth Bonner have lived for many years. Carrie likes everything about Seven Bells, from the chimes that hang on the porch and gave the house its name, to the creaky third step on the stair in the hall, and even the smell of her mother's paints. She plans to live here for all of her life, but just now she leaves at first light, slipping away.

She takes one of the many footpaths that crisscross the wooded hillside, on her way to Uphill House.

For days she has been arguing with herself about where to take her worries. No one else seems to be aware of the coming storm, and she finds that too heavy a burden to bear. Her grandparents are the only choice. They will try to find a way out from under the trouble that hangs over all their heads.

Grand Elizabeth is sitting in the garden, studying the sunflowers with their drooping heads. From the barn comes the sound of Grandda Nathaniel scolding Knuckles. She is the most stubborn mule he has ever had the misfortune to hitch to a wagon, he croons to her. Never, he says, has there been a more rock-headed beast.

Knuckles brays in delight.

"There's my Carrie girl."

Gran's smile is so bright and welcoming that Carrie feels better just walking toward her. She leans down to hug her gran, and draws in the familiar smells: scalded milk, linen dried in the sun, lavender water, mint, cloves, and gum arabic.

"Did you make a new batch of ink?"

Grandy holds out her hands with their swollen knuckles and crooked fingers, stained with fresh color, a deep brown-black. "Your Uncle Gabriel brought me some gallnuts, but don't worry your head about me. Daniel's two oldest boys were here and did all the work while they told tall tales. My, those two—I start laughing the minute they come in the door. Now pull that stool over next to me. Sit yourself down and tell me what's wrong. Don't deny it, I can see the trouble in your sweet face."

There's nothing Carrie wants more, but finding a place to start is the problem. Grandy is patient; she knows how to bide her time.

"It's Martha," Carrie says finally.

From her grandmother's thoughtful expression, Carrie sees that she already knows, when Carrie's mother had not.

"Nathaniel was right," she says, sighing. "You would think I'd be used to it by now."

This is almost a relief and, at the same time, a disappointment. If her grandfather suspected what Carrie fears has come to pass, then the trouble is real and unavoidable. She can't remember another time when being right felt so wrong.

Carrie could get home in less than ten minutes by way of the shortcut that brought her here, but Gran's running days are long past. They walk along, the three of them, at a pace that doesn't tax anybody but drives Carrie to a distraction she struggles to overcome.

Grandda is talking about a letter from Uncle Luke, and she's glad of it. If they were to ask her questions about Martha, she would have to tell them about the morning sickness, and that would feel like even more of a betrayal.

They pass the stunted hawthorn tree that every child in Paradise knows and fears. Some claim it's haunted, but what nobody can deny are the three-inch-long, dagger-sharp thorns. Martha especially dislikes the tree, and as a little girl once dragged an ax out of the barn announcing that if nobody else in the family cared, she would cut it down herself. For the birds. For the little birds.

She knows very well that their people never cut down a tree unless there is good reason, but she still argues and pleads and predicts dire events if the tree isn't cut up and burned. In the end there was no changing stubborn Bonner minds, and Martha had to concede defeat. As a result the hawthorn stands there like a mean old hag waiting for the opportunity to pinch and poke and draw blood.

Martha wasn't afraid of the tree for herself, but she hated the shrikes, the birds that favored hawthorns. Shrikes were just average-size, but they subdued their prey—smaller birds, mice, salamanders—by impaling them on the hawthorn's spines, much as a hunter will hoist his kill into a tree to protect it from scavengers.

Carrie dislikes the shrikes too. They look innocent but have the bloody disposition of hawks and vultures.

Now, so close to home, Grandda says, "Boots, our Carrie looks at that hawthorn like it's going to jump out and grab her."

And just that simply, tears spill over. She turns her face away to not be found out. This is a ruse that would never fool either of her grandparents on a normal day, but just now they are preoccupied because they have come in sight of the house, and the conversation before them will not be easy.

Grandy Elizabeth says, "We're going in, but you stay out here in the sun and fresh air, and I'll send Nathan out for you to keep an eye on."

Carrie will remember this moment as the last peaceful one for a very long time to come.

FOR THE NEXT month, most of the talk in the village is about Greg Fisher's chances of living long enough to get married for a second time. In low voices men debate whether it will be Simon Ballentyne or Nathaniel Bonner who takes care of Fisher. Carrie hears this talk, and so does Nathan. Later, when they are alone, they will compare what they've heard.

Nathan tells her, "Mr. Small says that Uncle Gabriel is the hottest head, and Mr. Blackwell says on top of that, he's the best shot. So they think he'll be the one to go after Mr. Fisher. Mr. Bee thinks Da will get there first. Mr. Campbell says he won't be surprised if they find Fisher with a knife in his throat, compliments of Uncle Daniel or maybe one of his boys."

All the cousins have been dragged into the business with Martha and Greg Fisher. They do love gossip, but in the end they want details because Martha is family, and family sticks together. To protect her they have to understand the threat.

"When I come into the village, I feel like I have a target on my back," Cousin Jennet says.

"Don't be silly," Nathan tells her. "Nobody would dare touch you."

"But they shoot questionssss," Jennet hisses. She leans hard to one side, back hunched in imitation of the worst gossips, and goes on. "The plan is to catch one of us and subject us to merciless torture until we confess everything we know about Martha's baby."

Jennet loves playacting, but she's also good at reading the mood in the village, and she sees, just as Carrie does, that there is one question that is foremost on everyone's mind. She thinks of that question like a cask of black powder, and the answer a flame held to the fuse.

This morning Aunt Annie and Birdie are walking through the village when Margene Peabody—new to Paradise, hired to keep house for the Johnson family after Nora died—stops them and asks straight out when Martha's baby is due.

"I don't believe my ears," Birdie says. "Annie, have you ever heard anything so rude?"

"Not that I recall," says Annie, giving Margene her most severe stare. Then she says, Nosy old woman, *in Mohawk, and Birdie agrees in the same language, but she never takes her eyes off the woman, who has gone very pale. At this point she realizes that escape would be a good idea, but Birdie is not about to let her off so easily.*

"Mrs. Peabody," she says. "Let's be honest for once, here with an audience all around us." She raises her voice, to be sure that people peeking from around corners can hear her. "You don't want to know when my niece's baby is due, do you? You want to know if she fell pregnant before or after Amy Fisher died, isn't that so?"

Margene Peabody is bold, but she isn't foolish enough to answer the question. When she has scurried away, Aunt Annie and Birdie set off again. Birdie's face has gone red with anger and frustration. Annie's expression is unreadable.

The biggest problem, the one that seems to have no solution, is the fact that Martha wants to marry Greg Fisher, but Ma and Da won't hear of it. Sometimes together, sometimes separately, they sit down with Martha to talk. Again and again they explain to her: she can bear and raise her child in her own home, and they will love it as she is loved. Martha doesn't pull faces or disagree or react at all; she stares out of the window or at her hands, folded in her lap.

In time Carrie realizes that Martha is so calm because she has figured out how to get her way. A week ago she stopped eating, and today she has refused water.

And so the summer that began with a wedding ends with one too. Greg

Fisher, pale, a tic fluttering in his cheek, won't look at her father or grandfather, but he is polite to the women and reaches out to put a hand on Carrie's shoulder as he passes. She steps away, the very idea of his touch filling her mouth with spit.

They marry at four in the afternoon at Uphill House. Martha is the prettiest bride Carrie has ever seen, though she has lost her waist; she is already big with child, and Carrie hears the aunts whispering about twins. There is no wedding party because, everyone explains to Martha again and again, they are still in mourning for Amy.

By evening she is the new mistress of the Red Dog, and will sleep in the marriage bed where Amy had slept just a few months previous. For the first time in weeks, Carrie has a few minutes alone with Martha. While she helps unpack and put away her sister's clothes, she considers how to ask the question that bothers her most.

Earlier in the day, Martha had been shivering with excitement, but now a melancholy has settled over her. She looks at Carrie, and there is no joy in her, no satisfaction in getting what she so desperately wanted.

She says, "I can't stop thinking about Ma. About the things she said to me. Ma is never mean. Why would she say such hurtful things?"

Before Carrie can think of an answer, Martha goes on.

"She says she's worried about me, but that's just silly. I have a husband now, and a house of my own. Bigger than Uphill House." She throws out both arms, laying claim.

What Carrie wants is to slap her face with all the strength she can muster, and then to run away. Instead she says, "That's not what Ma meant. She was thinking about Amy."

If Martha suspects that Greg Fisher played some role in his first wife's death, she has never said so. Every person in Paradise has an opinion on this matter, but it seems as if the idea has never occurred to Martha.

Now she dashes frustrated tears away with angry swipes of her hands.

"Just this morning I tried again to explain, but she wouldn't listen. Why can't she understand?"

Carrie isn't sure she wants to hear this, but she can't step away, not now.

She says, "There's a difference between understanding your reasons and approving of them."

Martha's frustration and fury erupt as tears begin to pour down her cheeks.

"I know that Ma and Da want me to feel guilty about how I got a husband, but I thought you would understand. It isn't my fault that Greg liked me better. I didn't ask him to, but he liked me better. How is that my fault?"

31

CARRIE WOKE, DISORIENTED, groggy, beneath a gauzy blue sky and noticed two things: first, Eli had been asleep beside her, but now there was no sign of him, and it was oddly quiet. She heard no voices, none of Rainey's usual off-key humming, nothing of the horses or the familiar sounds of breaking camp.

The things she did hear were ordinary enough to be calming: a fitful wind riffling through the grass, the slow belch of frogs, the flap of huge wings passing overhead—an eagle or a vulture would be her guess—birdsong, water moving over rocks. She was very thirsty, she realized. And beyond that she had a headache, an empty stomach, and a growing certainty that she had told Eli Ibarra more than was wise.

Still no sound of horses or men. Maybe Titus Hardy had decided she was more trouble than she was worth.

With a hand that was, she saw, in need of scrubbing, she fished a handkerchief out of her tunic and wiped her face, already slightly damp with perspiration though the sun was barely up.

She righted herself to look around and saw that the men were a hundred feet away, near the rope corral and the campfire Rainey must have got started before the sunrise. The four of them were studying the vapid, pale sky as if some great secret had been written there for them to interpret. And in fact, Carrie realized, it felt like thunderstorm weather. An uneasiness in the air, a low buzzing, as though a mosquito had got caught in her hair. A particular kind of heat. If the temperature kept climbing and the air stayed so damp, they would all melt into smelly puddles by midmorning. A thunderstorm would not be the worst thing. It would come in like a headmaster determined to impose order, and after his lecture, the weather would settle. If the lightning wasn't severe, the horses wouldn't mind, and neither would she.

Carrie got to her feet and walked in the other direction, toward the spring that came up from a clutch of boulders, ducking through clumps of juniper and vetch. Before she crouched down, she checked for anthills and was relieved to see nothing alarming. The water was clear and cool. She filled her canteen and drank and drank again, and her headache retreated.

By the time she had washed—insofar as washing was possible— and seen to her needs, the men had settled down around the cook fire and were pouring coffee.

At home Carrie drank coffee in the morning and assumed she would go on the same way, if indeed coffee was available in Santa Fe. Then she discovered that wranglers made a coffee that was so strong and bitter that it soured her stomach. If there was tea in Santa Fe, she would drink tea; otherwise she resolved to drink water—which might need to be boiled first—and nothing else.

It was too hot for coffee, anyway; the wind made short work of her damp clothing as she walked toward the fire, where all four men sat staring at each other. There was some trouble, but they were not going to talk about it in front of her.

Hardy said, "Come eat something, right quick. We got to be on our way."

Carrie considered asking what they were worried about, but decided that Titus Hardy would turn the question into a tug-of-war. She would pull; he would push. It would have to wait until they first stopped to water the horses, because she didn't have the energy. Because she had slept too little, and talked too long.

Rainey had made a big stack of griddle cakes. She took two and sat down—not next to Eli, but directly across from him. She met his eye and nodded, and he did the same. There was nothing she could say that wouldn't sound wrong, and in such cases it was better to say nothing at all.

Really, she told herself, she had said too much in the dark. Far too much about things that were best forgotten. She asked herself if she had been wrong to trust him, and decided that she had not. And still she wished she hadn't told so much, but at the same time she knew she should have told the rest. The whole story.

For once Mimosa's calm whinny of greeting didn't distract Carrie or lift her spirits. She decided she could not be sociable, and that the best course of action was to be as alone as she possibly could be under the circumstances.

They started out under a milky-blue sky, riding into a buffeting wind. As soon as it was practical, she set herself apart from the men; not out of sight, but not close enough to talk. Mimosa and Chico were more than enough company, and watching Chico was a fine distraction.

He hunted in the tall grass and dispatched a skinny rabbit almost without breaking stride. Satisfied with the meal, he dashed off to run in circles—a celebration of sorts, it seemed to Carrie—before he took up the hunt again. Three rabbits seemed to satisfy his hunger, and after that he stayed close. He kept pace without any trouble, even at a fast trot. A gallop would be more than he could match, Carrie was sure, and that was worrisome.

As time passed and the day grew hotter, she started to consider the weather. It was overcast, with a wind coming from the south that was so warm that it might have been radiating off a hearth. She had grown up hearing stories of people who had not paid the weather the attention and respect it was owed, and forfeited their lives. Where this very warm, inconstant wind originated was the question, and she summoned up the memory of the globe in her mother's library. From where they were now, she believed that Texas was to the southeast and beyond that was the Gulf of Mexico.

When the sun had finally burned through the haze, there was no relief, just the opposite: the air grew denser and wetter.

She couldn't be sure how much longer they had been riding when they climbed a low ridge through a plantation of cottonwood trees and came to a streambed that was close to dry. Without being told, Rainey grabbed the shovel from his packhorse and walked down to the bed, where he started to dig. Soon enough there was a shallow pond of water that the horses were willing to drink. It would be gritty, Carrie was well aware, but they would fill their canteens nonetheless.

Then she turned away and caught sight of the sky to the north, and she forgot about water. Where a few hours ago the sky had been murky, now a living wall had grown up, something out of a dark fairy tale: bulbous, churning clouds in shades from dirty white to gray to charcoal, and from within, flashes of lightning.

There was endless sky on the prairie, so much sky that it still took her by surprise in the morning when she first woke. Carrie had spent the first part of her life in the mountains and the second in a crowded city, and now she was learning what it meant to live in the open, in a world that seemed, at this moment, to be far less constrained. It made sense: more sky meant more storm clouds.

That was a fine bit of reasoning and might have quieted her concerns, if not for the men who generally took the weather in stride as something to be tolerated in bad conditions and otherwise ignored. That was what she hoped to see.

Instead Miguel, who generally refused to be alarmed by—or interested in—anything, was paying attention. There was an alertness about him, as if he had come face-to-face with an angry bull and was weighing his options. Eli's posture was just as tense, his gaze shifting across the sky as he scanned for something Carrie could only guess at. Rainey was rubbing a hand over his face and shifting nervously from foot to foot, but Titus Hardy was the very picture of grim resolve.

He said, "We'll have to ride for the Cimarron."

Carrie had to clear her throat. "Cimarron?"

"A river, mostly dry," Eli said, moving toward her. "With high banks and some caves."

"Where we could wait out the weather," Rainey added.

"I take it there's more to fear here than a string of thunderstorms."

"If you want to call a *derecho* a thunderstorm," Miguel muttered.

"True," Rainey said. "There's thunderstorms and then there's *derechos*."

Hardy didn't waste time with translations or definitions. "We can give the mounts another quarter hour, and I suggest you use that time to get yourself ready for a hard ride, Miss Ballentyne. There'll be no stopping along the way to piss."

Agitated, anxious, Carrie marched off to see to her needs and came back to find that Eli had just finished shifting her saddle from Mimosa to his Luna. His own saddle was now on Nobo, the youngest of his three horses.

As she passed him, she said, "Tell me what it is we're running from. What is a *derecho*?"

He had been ready for the question and didn't mince words. "A string of thunderstorms, but that's not what Hardy is worried about. The Kiowa call it *mánkayía*."

He translated: The great horse. The whirlwind. A tornado.

At first she could not imagine what a *derecho* might be, but now she had a word that made sense. Whirlwind.

Eli said, "You must have read about tornadoes in the papers back east."

Of course she had. The newspapers devoted many columns to stories of the tremendously destructive storms that came out of the plains. Stories that were hardly to be believed, and now she might actually see one.

"Tornado," she echoed. Her voice caught. "Can we outrun a tornado?"

He glanced over his shoulder toward the sky. "There's no way to know if one will actually show up."

"That isn't an answer to the question I asked." She swung up onto the saddle and took up the reins. Eli edged in closer so that Nobo gave a low nicker of surprise.

He said, "Are you equal to this?"

The question stuck like a slap. It surprised and confused her, but before she could think how to respond, he winked.

His slow smile and that damn wink.

She put her heels to Luna and took off.

The ride itself demanded all her attention, moving fast over terrain that was unfamiliar. The gentle rolling plains she had come to like began to look like a rumpled blanket after an uneasy sleep. With Eli behind her, she followed Miguel over swells and ridges, around wallows and through patches of timber; they jumped one, two, three streambeds, passed a burned-out cabin and a small herd of buffalo milling with their faces pointed directly into the wind. In the far distance Carrie saw some of the wild horses she had heard about, and was sorry that there was no time for a closer look. Not with the wind up to tricks and the wall of clouds behind them.

For all her life it had seemed obvious to her that the wind could take on a personality. Today it came roaring from the southeast, fitful, unpredictable, almost malevolent in this moment, blowing so fiercely that the horses swayed. Then it fell back to dance in the grass before roaring back, full-throated. Trees buckled and bent in half, branches broke free with a crack as loud as a gunshot, and saplings were wrenched out of the ground.

Luna seemed unconcerned and pushed on, sure-footed and eager to please. Even the buffeting wind failed to faze her, but Carrie could not claim as much. The urge to look over her shoulder to the northern sky was hard to resist, but it would gain her nothing and might cost her focus and resolve.

A fat raindrop struck her hand, and it occurred to her that she should have taken two minutes to put on her gloves and retrieve her slicker from her saddlebag. This thought was still in her head when they came over a ridge and started down a slope, only to come to a sudden and dangerous stop when Hardy's horse shied and reared up. He had control of the mare in a matter of seconds, but in that brief pause, Carrie saw what had spooked her.

Not forty feet in front of them a black bear stood erect, its muzzle and chest and paws bright red with fresh blood. At its feet was a half-eaten deer carcass, and all around was a pack of wolves determined to help themselves to venison. They were darting in and out, nipping hard at the bear's lower leg. The roar of the angry bear was ear-shattering, but the wolf pack seemed unconcerned.

As they rode off at an angle to bypass the confrontation, a big gray wolf leapt onto the bear's back and sank teeth into its nape.

And then they were out of sight, riding hard as the wind suddenly turned cool enough to send gooseflesh up Carrie's back. Now she could not help but look behind her at the sky and wished she had not: the bank of storm clouds had taken on colors she had never seen before in the sky. A jaundiced yellow blossomed under broad swatches of a deep, venomous green.

Suddenly the shearing wind began to pelt them with waves of hail that swelled and retreated. At first the bits of ice were as insubstantial as rice, but soon they were the size of peas, and then walnuts. Carrie curled forward over the saddle to make herself as small as possible while the sky spit, first lazily and then with a vengeance. Despite her firm resolve, she could not hold back a yelp when she was struck and struck and struck again, hail hammering her back and arms and legs. That none of the horses broke and ran was something Carrie would marvel at long after her own bruises had faded.

She was as good as blind in the downpour, but Luna knew to follow the horse in front of her, down an embankment, through a channel of fast-running water strewn with rocks and boulders and foliage stripped by the wind.

Then the triple flare of light, and a lightning strike that broke the world in two.

32

CARRIE ROUSED FROM sleep and found that she was curled on her side on the earthen floor of a cavern. It was a relief to be on solid ground and out of the storm, but she had no memory of this place. Had she fainted? Been knocked unconscious?

Out loud she said, "I have never once in my life fainted. Never."

At the same time she could not deny the ache in her head. Something had happened that she wasn't able to recall. With some hesitation she raised her hand to her forehead, and jerked at the sting. For a moment she stared at the drying blood on her hand and then the scrapes on the hand itself.

"Why am I bleeding?"

Eli was there, she realized now. He crouched just across from her, his wrists on his knees, watching so closely he might have been expecting her to begin convulsing. Then he got a better look at her, and she saw him relax.

"There was a lightning strike real close," he said. "Luna reared, you lost your seat and landed hard. We got you this far." He paused to look around himself in the dim cavern. "And put you down there, where you are now. Rainey and me, we carried you. Maybe twenty minutes ago."

"So I didn't faint."

"I never said you did. You got knocked out. There's a good-sized lump coming up at your hairline."

Carrie was not in the habit of weeping in front of anyone at all, but now there were tears on her cheeks, and so she wiped her face with her sleeve.

"Luna?"

"She'll be fine by morning. And so will you."

She sent him a sharp look, but he only raised a brow as if to dare her to contradict him. Carrie folded her knees to her chest, wrapped her arms around her legs, and rocked a little. A concussion was not in her plans. Probably the men had overreacted.

When she felt more certain of her voice, she said, "The others are safe? The horses?"

"For the moment."

"What is this place?"

"Caverns. An old *pistolero* found them what, thirty years ago. That is, the tribes have always known about them, but he was the first outsider to come across them."

There was a very slight hesitation, while he decided if he should comment on the habits of colonials. Then he gave a shake, as if talking himself out of it.

"His gang holed up here when there was somebody after them. Now everybody knows about this place. We're lucky the caves were empty."

He looked over his shoulder into the shadows. "This is the smallest of them. The horses are in the bigger ones, half with Titus, half with Miguel."

"I need to see Mimosa."

Eli stood up. "Thought you would. We can go have a look now while things are calm."

Calm struck her as an odd word to use, but she put that thought aside and concentrated instead on getting to her feet without keeling over. She walked toward the opening, with Eli right behind her, because, she realized, he saw that she was unsteady on her feet.

Out in the open, she leaned against the rock face and breathed in cool air that was, in a word, delicious. Air that made the whole world gleam and tasted of juniper. It must be late afternoon, from the angle of the light, and the world seemed born again, verdant and fresh.

Just below them a narrow, twisting streambed was carved into the earth, its banks crowded with shrubs and grasses scrubbed free of dust. There were mesquite thickets bristling with thorns that made her think of bloody German fairy tales. There was a plant that was new to her, great clumps of swordlike leaves with long stems that shot up six feet or more. Called yucca, Eli told her when she asked.

She studied what she could see of the sky. It seemed that the thunderstorm had run its course. It was entirely possible that Titus Hardy would want to push on until sunset, but Carrie could not imagine finding the energy.

To Eli she said, "Will he let us rest here until morning?"

The question surprised him. "We're not moving until the weather has cleared."

Carrie pointed upward. "Blue sky."

He shook his head. "I'll guarantee you there's no blue to be seen to the north. And feel, the wind is coming up again, hotter than before. There could be a whole line of storms getting ready to march right in here."

She had no reason to doubt him, but she was confused. "What about the tornado? It passed over?"

Eli blinked. "No tornadoes. Not yet."

This was a subject that could wait until she had had some water and her head didn't ache so much, and still she couldn't let it go. Hours of keeping up a frantic pace, for apparently no reason.

"How do you know?" she asked him. "If you were in the back of this cavern with me, maybe you just missed it."

He didn't often laugh, but Carrie saw now that he was having trouble keeping a straight face. Then he held up both palms as if to ask for patience, drew in a deep breath, and cleared his throat.

"You remember the noise when the train hit those cows on the track and almost derailed?"

The change in subject confused her at first, but it was not something she would forget. "Of course."

"Good," Eli said. "Now multiply that by a thousand. That's what a tornado sounds like. No mistaking it. No missing it."

She considered. "So there is still the possibility."

"Oh yeah. So let's go see the horses and get some provisions to tide us over." He reached for her arm, but she pulled it away.

"I can walk."

"I see that," he said. "But the way is narrow and wet and gritty. And you're not steady on your feet."

"You go first and I'll match your footing."

"By God, woman, you are contrary."

She had managed to unsettle him, for once, but she kept her gaze steady and fixed on him, and in the end he went ahead.

The fair thing to do, Carrie knew, was to tell him he was right and ask for his arm, because she wasn't sure of her feet. The fall would not kill her, but it might mean a broken bone, or something worse than a concussion.

Instead she shook her head to clear it—and was immediately sorry, given the bolt of pain that rewarded her—and narrowed her focus. Ten minutes later she was trembling and sweat soaked, but she looked up to see that they were on a small spread of stony ground, with a path that led onto a wider, flatter outcropping of rock. At the far end, horses stood at the mouth of a cavern, where Rainey was rubbing down Nobo with some sacking. Just behind him was Mimosa, and between her front hooves Chico, who had found himself a surprisingly big bone and was gnawing bits of meat and marrow from it.

"How—" she began, and Rainey looked up and grinned at her. "Chico? Miguel is always taking him up on his saddle. Softhearted when it comes to dogs, that's Miguel. Nobo's got a graze on his hock. Want to have a look?"

Carrie was glad to have something to do. She checked the graze and was looking over other horses—five of the ten were here—when Hardy came out into the open. His wet hair stood up in spikes all over his head, and to Carrie he looked like a half-drowned cat. This thought she kept to herself; no doubt she looked just as bad.

"Best get back under cover," he said. "There's more weather coming our way." With his head tilted back so he could study the sky, he pulled on an earlobe, in the way of a child with an earache.

"My ears have been popping," he said, mostly to himself.

Rainey, moving on to rub down Sombra, nodded sagely. "It is true, the boss's ears are always hearing things nobody else can hear. Like a saint."

The wind had begun to gust, and Carrie decided she would have to save her curiosity about St. Titus Hardy for another day. It did make her smile, but then a crack of thunder jolted through them all—she saw it happen—and the urge to laugh left her just as suddenly as it had come.

Eli managed to gather the provisions they would need but not before the next storm came up. They had full canteens, jerky and corn cake, and what wood he could find to feed the small fire. He made a last trip for their saddlebags and this time came back wearing his hooded gutta-percha cloak. Beneath it he was still wet, but at least he was not any wetter.

Carrie, eyes closed in an attempt to calm her aching head, was no help at all. From her spot near the fire, propped up against the saddlebags, she listened to him moving. In good conscience she couldn't be petty and order him to sit down and stop making noise. She was glad of the fire, not only for the heat but because without it they would be stuck here in the dark.

Finally he sat beside her and she realized he had changed into dry clothes, as she had done while he was out gathering wood.

"Warm now?"

The damp in her hair was enough to make her shiver, but there was nothing to be done about that, and so she kept it to herself.

"Storm's coming closer," she observed.

As if summoned, lightning lit up the bit of the sky they could see, with thunder crowding in on its heels. Carrie leaned forward to press her forehead against her knees, then felt Eli's arm around her, drawing her in close. As her brother would have done in such a situation. A kind and caring gesture, and one she would not overthink. She made herself relax against his side. He was very solid and warm, something she might have told him if she could think of a way that wouldn't sound like flirting.

"Is this the great horse the Kiowa talk about?"

He barked a short laugh. "No. Not even close."

For a few minutes they listened to the storm.

Eli said, "I'm guessing you don't want to talk about the things you told me last night. Hold on, no need to pull away. It's just that you should know that when the time's right and you feel the need, I'd like to hear the rest."

She thought, *You're not alone in that*. It was only Nathan who knew. Who probably knew more than she did. It was her younger brother who had found her, empty-eyed and bloody.

She cleared her throat and still could not find words, but then surprised herself.

"Martha wasn't such a spoiled, heartless wretch as I made out."

It seemed he had nothing to say to this, but when Carrie raised her head to look at him, she saw that he was annoyed.

He said, "We should save this talk for another time, but you have to understand something first. It's you I'm interested in, and the things that are important to you. Nobody and nothing else."

And that was the right thing to say. Carrie realized that if he used the opportunity she had given him to ask more about her sister, she would have been more than disappointed.

Eli said, "Do you want to try to sleep?"

"I don't know if I can. A tornado is still possible, isn't it? I don't want to miss it."

Now she was close enough to lean her head against him so that she felt his voice coming up from deep in his chest. Shocking behavior, she told herself. But she was not a strong enough person to turn away from such warmth and comfort.

Eli didn't seem to notice her self-doubt. He was saying, "There's no predicting this kind of weather. When things get to this point, pretty much anything is possible."

"So just our bad luck."

"I don't know about that," he said, a rougher tone coming into his voice. "I'm pretty comfortable just now."

And how was she to interpret that?

"Are you flirting with me, Eli Ibarra?"

That made him laugh. "If you have to ask, I'm doing a poor job of it."

The thing to do, Carrie told herself, was simple. If she didn't want to know anything more of this man, she could move away and sit alone on the other side of the fire, wrapped in her bedroll. Or she could throw caution to the wind.

"Men don't generally flirt with me," she said. "They find me intimidating."

She could feel him studying her. "Who told you that?"

"My stepfather, for one. Also, some of the doctors I work with. They don't hesitate to say what they think, especially to a nurse who doesn't worship them. My Cousin Adam tells me I'm intimidating, though he means it as a compliment. And Titus Hardy, as you have seen for yourself."

"Old men and boys," Eli said, sounding amused.

A little irritated now, she tried to pull away and found he was not willing to let her go.

"Hey. I'm not laughing at you."

"Why are you laughing at all?"

"Because some men are blind and some are stupid and too many are both at once."

She drew in a sharp breath. "I see." Though she did not. Uneasy now, she said, "I should at least try to sleep for a while."

If he was put out by the change in subject, he didn't show it, but he did surprise her.

"Didn't you tell me just a couple weeks ago that I shouldn't sleep with a concussion?"

"I wasn't actually completely sure you had a concussion."

"Ah," he said.

"Ah?"

"I just realized that you draw in a sharp breath right before you lie. Because that was a lie."

She stiffened a little, but gave it up as a bad job.

"Fine. It's true that a doctor would say that it isn't wise to sleep with a concussion."

"I take it you disagree."

"I have doubts. So long as you can rouse the patient every few hours, sleep shouldn't be prohibited."

"So good. I know what my job is."

She laughed, a short, bright bark of surprise. Carrie thought, *Where did that come from? I never laugh like that. Is that his doing?* And then she gave a great yawn.

When she woke, an hour or a day later, the storm had passed. Outside it was full dark, not a star to be seen. She was still tucked up against Eli, who was not asleep, but seemed to be making a study of her face in the dim light of the fire.

He said, "I was just about to wake you. Here."

Carrie sat up and took the canteen he offered. She drank, and then turned her head aside to spit out the sand it left in her mouth.

"Headache?"

"Quite a bit better," she told him. "What are you doing?"

He had pulled a saddlebag closer and was digging into it. With a yank he extracted a great pile of bound papers. Carrie recognized the cover art immediately.

"Why do you have so many copies of *Frank Leslie's Illustrated*?"

"They were meant for my father, but they'll keep the fire limping along, maybe until dawn." He was taking handfuls up to twist into paper logs.

"You think the temperature will drop?"

He looked at her from under the shelf of his brow. "It's more the light I'm interested in. Unless you're still cold?"

"No," she said. "Not at all."

There was a longer, comfortable silence filled with the sound of paper being fed into the fire and the wind whistling through cracks in the walls. She might have fallen back to sleep, sitting up exactly as she was, but she remembered the conversation that they had begun and never finished.

Carrie curled on her side, her head bedded on a bent arm, and studied Eli Ibarra for a while. He was aware of her gaze but seemed unbothered by it.

The question was spoken before she even realized it was sitting on her tongue. "Why is it that you flirt with me? Is it just something you do with younger women, as a matter of course?"

She saw the muscles in his jaw flex, as if he was trying to hold back a smile. His gaze fixed on her, curious and almost pleased. Maybe he had been waiting for her to raise this subject. She found it hard to swallow, suddenly.

"Is it about sex?" she said, her voice catching. "Is that what you're hoping for?"

He blinked at her, held his breath for a long moment, and let it go with a soft sound. "Is that what you imagine?"

She meant her tone to be calm, but feared there was a defensive note to it. "I don't imagine anything." And heard, too late, the indrawn breath that preceded that statement.

One corner of his mouth curved up and somehow took away the sting.

In her head she cursed half-heartedly at his compulsion to tease. To come close and step back, to test her at every turn. She wasn't equal to this game, it was that simple. She would step back, and hope it would be possible to count him as a friend.

It wasn't what she wanted, but it was what she knew how to do. Step away, turn her back.

⟿

ELI CONSIDERED CARRIE, and realized that what he had before him was a woman overwhelmed by frustration and anxiety, and just now it was his doing. She had trusted him enough to put a difficult question into words, hoping for—what, exactly? A discussion? A seduction? But she had surprised him, and in response he had put his foot in it.

Most likely she had decided that her behavior had shocked him. As it probably would have shocked any of the men she knew from New York, if she had ever dared to raise the subject of sex.

Now she lay on her side, facing away from him. If he left things as they stood, that would put an end to it. And maybe that would be the best thing. In Santa Fe she would need friends, and he could be that to her.

But if his instincts were right, together they might be capable of joy. Friendship alone would be safer, but friendship would never be enough. To make that case, he only had to think of the unmarried men of Santa Fe, the ones with some property or a business but without a wife. Mike Henry was single, well enough off, and looking for a wife. Jake Saracen, José Luis Bilbao, Rob Ramsey. All single men of property, all of them would see Carrie Ballentyne as a prize to be won. All of them white, or close enough to white to pretend.

Rob Ramsey had come west from Michigan not five years ago and was probably just now realizing that he'd never find the kind of wife he wanted in the territory. Maybe he'd write home and ask his sister or mother to find him a girl to marry. Ramsey would see in Carrie only what he wanted and expected to see. A young woman of good family, educated, refined, pretty. A family history that might make a grandmother blanch, but wouldn't worry a man who moved across the continent and survived everything in his way.

As Mrs. Ramsey she would be obliged to give him children. To run the household and present herself as a good wife, content with what fate and her husband handed her. But that wasn't Carrie, and none of the men who would see her as a prize would suspect the truth.

He understood something, after hearing the story about her sister, that most men wouldn't see or credit: not so far beneath the surface there was a deep well of anger Carrie kept locked down tight. That was the real reason she kept herself separate. She wasn't inclined to trust any man, but even less trustworthy was her own nature, and the fury that kept her going. She remembered too well what she was capable of when the subject of her sister came up.

In Santa Fe she would turn every suitor away and carry on as she had at home in New York: polite, cordial, but unapproachable. He could imagine this. Carrie was dedicated to her work, her patients, to a few friends, her horse. She would keep Chico, that was certain. She had decided that those things were all she needed. All she deserved.

Looking at it that way, he decided it would be best to be direct. He was gambling his pride and his heart both, but to walk away from her would be cowardly and plain stupid.

Eli moved, quietly, to sit beside her. Then he leaned over and lifted her onto his lap, wrapped as she was in her bedroll. She was warm and soft and smelled of the pine needles caught in her hair, of juniper and leather, of honest sweat and of herself.

One eye cracked open and closed again. "It's you."

"You were expecting someone else? Rainey? Miguel?"

Both eyes opened and she considered him. "No," she said. "Not either of them. Titus Hardy, maybe."

He didn't try to hide his smile, but his voice faltered and wavered. "Titus Hardy can't have you."

Their faces were just inches apart when he held her like this, her head against his shoulder.

"On that point we can agree."

"Good," he said. And: "I should have answered your question."

He felt the tension rising up to run through her, a wild creature aware of danger and casting sleep off, ready to bolt. He watched her swallow.

She said, "It would be the polite thing to do."

Carrie Ballentyne was frightened, but she wasn't a coward.

"You asked if I was interested in you for sex."

Another convulsive swallow. "That was the question. I take it you aren't interested. How very awkward. Are you married? Is that it?"

Surprised, he drew in a sharp breath. "No. Are you?"

She shook her head. "Most decidedly not."

"Then that's a place to start. Do you want to be married?"

With a push she sat up a little straighter, and now they were almost nose to nose.

"Eli, I asked you about sex, and you've changed the subject."

"I don't think I have."

She began to worry her lip. "Fair is fair. You have to answer my question before you ask any of your own."

It was an odd conversation, but that was nothing unusual. It was one of the things he liked about her, the way her mind worked. Suddenly his own nervousness subsided, and he smiled at her. A full smile.

"Yes."

She looked at him askance. "Yes, what? Yes, you'll answer—"

"Yes, to sex."

With a small sound that might have been dismay, she collapsed backward, clearly trusting that he would catch her.

"Were you hoping I'd say no to sex?"

She shook her head, eyes tightly shut. "I really don't know what I was hoping." And before he could respond, she held up a hand. "That's not entirely true, but I can tell you in all honesty I wasn't expecting a counteroffer."

Carrie sat up again and began to wiggle away from him. Tangled as she was in her bedroll, she let out something close to a growl.

"All right," he said. "It took you by surprise. But you can still answer me."

As he studied her, it occurred to Eli that when she was older, the crease between her brows, the one that gave away her mood, would settle in. The line of her jaw would soften, and her mouth would lose some of its fullness and color. They would both get old, but he hoped they held on to the spark that came to life when they were at odds. Right at this moment, he was watching her think. She would be wondering if she might have been wrong about the course her life would take, and if that were the case, how mad she should be, and whom she should blame, beyond herself.

So he waited. He could be patient.

She said, "You do realize that I wasn't asking for a proposal, don't you? I was asking for—"

With her hands cupping her face she got the rest of the sentence out.

"Sex."

"You want to have sex." The words felt foreign in his mouth, like pebbles. "You are asking me to have sex."

A flicker of doubt crossed her face, as if he were denying her.

He reached for her hand and insisted on having it. "Of course. Of course I want to."

In that moment it seemed that she hadn't heard him, or understood him, or, it occurred to him finally, that she simply believed he was lying.

He said, "I don't think about much else these days."

Carrie felt her heart lodge in her throat. The first thing that came to mind was the obvious question as an answer: If you think about me that way, and I am agreeable, why not?

But she couldn't. As forward and unlike herself as she was being, she couldn't go that far and risk truly shocking him. Worse still, she knew she was scowling but couldn't help herself. She had started this conversation and must carry on. And that was her own fault.

She meant to hide her frustration but did a poor job of it. "Why must you up the ante, can I ask you that?"

He was inordinately amused. "'Up the ante'? You're a cardplayer. I should have guessed. I bet you're good."

She might have said, *Well, yes. I am very good.* But she dropped her face and shook her head, more confused than ever.

"This isn't a game I'm playing with you," Eli said. "It was an honest question."

She thought of walking out into the night. If she had the time and solitude, she might be able to make sense of all this, and find a reasonable next step. Because the question he had asked, the question he insisted she answer, was not reasonable. Carrie was about to announce her intention to go outside, when he reached over and took both her hands.

"Listen," he said. "I can see two reasons you asked me your question. The first is that you're human. Nothing wrong with that, but if it's that simple, I'm not the only choice or even a logical choice. The other possibility is that it's me you want."

He drew a deep breath and held it for a count of one, two, three heartbeats. When she nodded, he went on.

"If you want me, then I have to ask you if you're thinking this will happen only once. Because if it's me you want, once won't be enough, for either of us. You'll have to take my word on that. So are you thinking that this will stop when we get to Santa Fe? Or that we'll go on in secret, for weeks or months or years? Because to that I would say no. I won't hide from anybody, even for you."

There was the taste of blood in her mouth, and Carrie realized that she had bit her lip hard enough to break the skin.

He was waiting for an answer, his head tilted to one side.

Her voice stronger than she had imagined, she said, "I can imagine marrying."

"Me."

"Yes," she said. "You. If we—suit."

His smile was a beautiful thing, but she had more to say.

"I don't know if we will suit."

He considered. "We have got along pretty well in what I'd call difficult circumstances."

"Oh yes," she said. "Or we wouldn't be sitting here like this. We are suited in terms of temperament and intellect. But there are other matters. I have some concerns."

Eli looked both surprised and intrigued. "About . . . ?"

"Kissing. Do you consider yourself good at kissing? Because that one time . . ." Her voice trailed away and would not return.

"You were disappointed," he suggested, his expression unreadable.

"Um," Carrie said, and would have drawn her hands away, if he would only let them go. "Um, I don't know if *disappointed* is the right word. But if we don't suit that way, and wait until after . . . a ceremony—" She broke off, unable to put into words the worst she could imagine.

"You worry I'll look elsewhere. Would you do the same?"

Eli felt sweat trickle down his throat. She was looking at him as if he were speaking a language she had never studied, and he supposed that was a good way to think of where she stood.

He said, "I can't imagine a situation where I'd want anybody else. Before you give me a history of the way you've seen people betray each other, I can promise you this: if I can't be the kind of husband to you that you expect for me to be, I'll tell you so and we'll decide how to move on from that point. And you will do the same, if that day comes."

The frown line between her brows smoothed out, but not for long.

"Carrie, there's another part to it, one you ain't comfortable talking about. You're worried about sex. You think you won't like it, but once we're married you'll be stuck with it."

The frown line deepened. "Must you be so—"

"Plainspoken?"

"I can't criticize you for that, can I?"

"I have a way around the problem. It's really not complicated. We won't go ahead with any kind of wedding—that's something we'll need to talk about, too, another time—until you're sure you're comfortable with that part of things. You tell me when you're sure enough about sex that you want to make it legal."

He had a hard time holding back a grin, because Carrie was flustered, and at the same time it was clear that she was pleased with what she was hearing. But it turned out she could still surprise him.

"There's still the first part of it—"

"And that would be?"

She smacked his shoulder. "You just want me to say it again."

Eli raised a brow and smiled. "Say what again?"

"Never mind."

She began to turn away, and yelped when his arm wrapped around her waist to stop her. Eli put his mouth to the nape of her neck and breathed in her scent. Then he nipped her ear.

Carrie shivered.

Into her ear he said, "Now, don't rush off before we figure out about the kissing."

So, Carrie thought. This is the start.

Eli turned her to face him, cupped her head in his hands, and drew her close. Carrie wrapped her own hands around his wrists. Her breath came in a short gasp, and then he was kissing her. A light kiss. The corner of her mouth, her lower lip, her chin, her nose. His kisses were gentle and sweet, and yet a fluttering began in the very center of her body, something odd and new but somehow still familiar.

It occurred to her that she could go her whole life and never be so aware of her own body as she was in this moment. She might live to be an old woman remembering the taste of him, the smell of his skin, until even that much faded away. She could sacrifice this and all the rest of what was to come, the things she understood in a superficial way, and tell herself it was the most rational, safest choice.

Against her mouth he whispered. "Should I stop?"

A breathy sound was all she could produce. She met his eyes and saw a vulnerability she hadn't imagined.

"No," she said. "Not quite yet."

33

IN THE MORNING Carrie found Eli to be exactly the same man he had been the day before. That was right and good, she told herself. For her part, she only looked in his direction when she couldn't stop herself. While they ate beans and biscuits from the cast-iron skillet, the men talked. Eli took part in whatever subject came up. He talked no more or less than usual, wiped his plate, and went on to take care of chores, and she did the same.

While he saw to his weapons, she pulled ticks out of Chico's ears with the tweezers from her kit, mended a tear in her leggings, dug mud out of her moccasins, and listened to Rainey's stories about storms on the North Sea.

Eli spoke to her in passing, as easy and friendly as ever, and she wondered if the others noticed that her voice was raspy and her color high. Carrie told herself that as unappetizing as the idea might be, the others could already be talking when she was out of hearing. *Do you think* . . . and *Did he say* . . . and *I didn't take her for* . . .

When in truth, nothing had happened. Nothing beyond kissing. A particular kind of kissing she had never imagined.

Midmorning, Hardy studied the sky and decided it was safe to ride. In fact there was no sign of storm clouds, but otherwise the day was just exactly the way she remembered the one before: a hazy sky, a warm, gusting wind out of the southeast. Still, with the horses rested and grazed, it made sense to move on. She looked forward to the solitude of the ride as she would have anticipated a soapy bath and clean towels.

Time in the saddle was her chance to figure out just what had happened, and why. She wasn't entirely sure that she wouldn't panic, or laugh, or tear up. Possibly all three at once when she remembered that she had promised to marry a man she had met just weeks before.

There was one, really only one, question. It had been re-forming itself in her mind since she first woke, but she believed now that she had the right formulation: Had she really bound herself to a man who was, in most ways, a stranger?

She could blame it all on the excitement of the day, the race to find shelter and escape the violence of the storm. If she thought long enough, she might even be able to convince herself that it was the bump on her head that had robbed her of her usual cautions. At the same time she recognized both these options as untenable; her conscience wouldn't allow her such simplistic rationalizations.

The truth was, she had been drawn to Eli Ibarra from the first time she saw him, surrounded by bleating sheep in an overheated railcar.

Nothing would have come of that under normal circumstances, this she knew with certainty. It wasn't the first time she had felt the stirring of attraction, but rarely had she sensed any interest in the other party.

Eli Ibarra had changed all that. She didn't understand it, and wondered if she ever would.

Dissatisfied with herself, she turned her attention to the world around her and found that the landscape provided some distraction. They had left the high grasses behind and rode through a sparser, drier terrain. It wasn't yet desert, at least if she understood what that word meant. There was still grass enough to attract not just buffalo, antelope, and turkeys, but emigrants.

They passed a smallholding, nothing more than a cabin, a barn, and a paddock, where a few sleepy mules slept in the shade, and then another. Wash drying on a line, a woman at a well who looked up and waved. Carrie waved back, heartened by the small gesture.

And then everything changed, quite suddenly, and they were riding through a town. A very small town, certainly. No more than a trading post, a saloon, a livery, a feedstore, a church, and an inn. Farther out there were ranches, but not many that Carrie could see, and modest in size.

A woman standing outside the feedstore stared at Carrie openly. The rest of the day she would be busy telling everyone about a white woman dressed like an Indian, riding with men. Carrie couldn't begrudge the woman that bit of excitement. There would be little enough of it here.

The inn was not the biggest building on the street, but the sign that hung over the door was impressive. Someone had worked hard to get the lettering exactly right, and had done an admirable job.

THE SPRINGFIELD HOTEL
GEORGE SPRINGFIELD, PROPRIETOR
NEW SPRINGFIELD, TEXAS

That they were now in Texas was a surprise, but before Carrie could ask about this, she realized that Hardy was signaling for them to stop. The plan, he said, glaring at each of them as if he expected dissent, was that they would eat a proper meal in the inn's dining room. The horses could spend that much time in the paddock behind the livery.

Carrie liked the idea but doubted they would be welcome—as filthy as they were—in an inn. In this she turned out to be wrong, and was glad she had kept her reservations to herself. They were welcomed quite warmly, and in a matter of minutes she found herself in a private room where two young maids were already filling a hip bath with hot water. While she soaped and scraped accumulated dirt from her skin, she reminded herself that Texans were not New Yorkers. If she insisted on anticipating their behavior based on past experience, she would forever be the outsider, ill at ease, awkward.

Later, waiting to be served with the men in the dining room, she turned to Titus Hardy.

"It was very thoughtful of you to go to such trouble. Thank you."

"No trouble," Hardy said gruffly. "Can't deliver you to Sam's door looking like you was drug ten miles on a bad road. You'll get grimy again before we ride into Santa Fe, but not as bad as you could be."

Rainey laughed. "You think they'd send her back east cause of some grime, boss?"

"No idea, but I'll tell you what. It ain't a theory I want to test. Now here's the food. Say your blessings if you got 'em, and dig in."

They ate brisket in a spicy sauce, potatoes, black-eyed peas, pickles, new turnips, and fried parsley. There was little talk during the meal; the food was good, and they were hungry. Rainey ate as if he hadn't seen food in a week, but Eli wasn't far behind.

He sat directly across from Carrie and rarely looked up from his food, but soon after they sat down he slid one foot forward and bumped hers. She tucked both feet back underneath her chair, but he had long legs and, apparently, a plan. He wanted her to react. If she blushed or dropped her fork or began to choke, any of that would satisfy him.

Carrie did drop her fork into her lap, and the next time his foot came searching, she poked it, hard. He tilted his head to one side, as if he were listening to a question whispered in his ear, and turned to look toward the front of the dining room.

"Rain." His tone even, unconcerned.

The others turned to look for themselves.

"Not enough to slow us down," Titus Hardy said, and began to push back his chair.

"But I'm still eating." Rainey glanced toward the door that led to the kitchen. "Or I would be."

"Gluttony," Miguel said. "Isn't that one of the sins your priests are always scolding you about?"

Carrie didn't know what was more surprising: Miguel's biting criticism or the fact that both Eli and Hardy showed no reaction at all. This was apparently between Rainey and Miguel alone, a conflict of long standing.

Rainey sent Miguel a thoroughly reproachful look.

"I am hoping there will be pie. Tell me you won't eat pie if they bring it to the table."

Miguel's mouth twitched.

"Ja," Rainey said, satisfied. "I know you and your sweet toot."

The burst of laughter that Carrie could not hold back made her the center of attention. Miguel raised an eyebrow in her direction, which only made her laugh harder.

"What?" Hardy was looking at her. They were all looking at her.

She managed to stop long enough to explain. "It strikes me as funny," she said, looking at each of them in turn. "That Miguel would have a nickname like Sweet Toot."

It seemed that the others were so accustomed to Rainey's German accent that they screened most of his mispronunciations out, but soon enough three of four men were struggling not to smile. To Miguel's credit he just shook his head and left the table, and soon enough they got up to follow him.

Carrie asked Hardy if she could pay her portion of the bill at the desk in the lobby, but he flapped a hand to dismiss this idea.

"Take it up with Doc Sam," he said. "It ain't my money."

She was considering this, that Dr. Markham had thought so carefully about the journey and anticipated what she might need. His thoughtfulness gave her reason to hope that things might be different in Santa Fe than they were in New York's clinics and hospitals.

After she sought out the necessary, she realized that the others would be waiting in the rain, and she hurried toward the front door, where she saw Eli. He had her rain slicker over his arm and a half grin on his face.

Her impulse was to reach for the slicker, but after a moment's hesitation she let him help her into it. As he straightened the hood and pulled it into place, he studied her face.

"Very helpful," she said. "Thank you."

"You are in high spirits." His voice was pitched low and a bit rough. "It's good to see you laugh."

"I don't know if Miguel would agree with you."

"Miguel doesn't interest me," he said, and kissed her. A short, hard stamp of the mouth that made every nerve in her body spark. And he was going to kiss her again if she didn't stop him.

She whispered, "They'll come back to see what's keeping us."

One brow climbed up his forehead. "Do you think so?"

With exaggerated caution he peered out the window and up and down the street even as he cupped her elbows and pulled her closer. "The least we can do is make it worth their while."

By midafternoon there was nothing left of Carrie's high spirits. Behind them in the northern sky, clouds were gathering, building another great fortress, pewter and steel and gun smoke colors and now traces of sulfuric yellow.

More disturbing, Titus Hardy seemed unconcerned. They rode along at an easy trot, and if he ever looked back at the ominous skies, she did not see him do it. Now she wished Eli were closer, but he kept his distance, as she had hoped he would just hours before.

She tried to be distracted by the terrain, but it was not especially inspiring. There was the occasional small farm, and in the distance men driving sheep, but she saw not a single buffalo or elk. That didn't mean they weren't nearby, of course. As a girl she had been taught how to see in the forest, but things worked differently here. It would be a while before she learned how to read the signs.

Carrie had begun to look forward to the next river crossing, some of which were very exciting, when she realized that they had left the rain behind, and the sun was out. To the west there was blue sky, and the promise of better weather tomorrow. Titus Hardy had led them through, yet again. She didn't have to like the man, but she must acknowledge that he was an excellent guide.

The next time they stopped to rest and water the horses, the stream was more substantial. Now the banks were lined with willows; small, wind-twisted elms; and the cottonwoods that seemed to thrive in every landscape, no matter how harsh. She planned to go down to the water to wash the dust from her neck and face, but then she realized that Eli was walking away, taking long strides to catch up with Titus Hardy. Hardy had started to climb a butte, and was moving fast toward a plateau just beneath the crest.

Eli stopped suddenly, as if he had remembered something crucial. Then his gaze found hers and he gestured. She was to follow him, and quickly. Carrie would be glad of a walk after so long in the saddle, but Eli's manner struck her as odd. She started after him, and Rainey and Miguel stepped in just behind her.

She said, "It's good to be out of the wet, don't you think?"

This was meant for Rainey, but Miguel gave a gruff laugh. "You try to remember that feeling when we're crossing the jornada."

The dry days were coming now, she knew that. But she wasn't in the mood to entertain Miguel's dire predictions.

"I'm sure you're right," Carrie said to him. "But I've made it this far. With help, of course. What are those two looking at?"

Titus Hardy and Eli stood on the rocky plateau, their heads canted at the same angle and fixed on the northern sky. It was then that she realized that they hadn't escaped the weather after all. She picked up her speed and reached Eli, short of breath.

The storm front was maybe five miles away moving east, away from them. The great mass of clouds, muscular and hulking, seemed to stride across the prairie like bad-tempered giants, lightning sparking in their long beards. The worst of the storm seemed to be moving off, but still she shivered, and gooseflesh ran down her arms.

This was a kind of violence she hadn't imagined; it made her understand just how small she was, as every human being was who walked on the face of the earth.

Just then an odd shape dipped down from the low belly of the cloud bank. Something like an umbilical cord or a tail, coiled and whipping back and forth as it reached for the earth. Then another one just like it began to form, not as much as a mile away, and in the distance, a third. Dancing over the landscape like wild horses, raising huge clouds of dust and dirt and foliage and even trees. She had her grandfather's excellent eyesight, and still could hardly credit what her eyes told her. A tornado—because of course those were tornadoes dropping out of the clouds—plucked a tree out of the ground, as easily as she might take a splinter from her finger. One, two, a half dozen trees disappeared into the funnel, the noise of it loud enough to make the ears ache for days.

She thought of the small farmsteads they had passed, and of New Springfield, where she had bathed and eaten so well and laughed. What was a house but a box made of wooden sticks or chunks of pottery, and what was such a box to a tornado? What could a herd of buffalo be? She imagined a game of bowls played by those giants in the clouds, two-thousand-pound buffalo bulls being tossed across the prairie with a casual touch of the whirlwind.

In the distance the tornadoes rode across the prairie, as untamed, unpredictable, and destructive as any force in nature. Beside her was Eli, a solid presence, warm and pulsing with life. He made her feel safe, and how odd that feeling safe could be so very frightening.

34

CARRIE STOOD UP in her stirrups to get a better look at the wagon train that inched along in a cloud of sand and dust. She had begun to wonder if they would ever see the Santa Fe trail again, but this must be where the route over the mountains and the desert route reunited. Of course, it wasn't Orwell Petit's wagon train; it would be weeks before her brother and friends got this far.

"Where are we, exactly?"

Hardy shifted in his saddle, tugged on the brim of his hat, cleared his throat once, twice, three times. It still amazed her, how hard it was for the man to answer a simple question.

He said, "Just out of sight is the Pecos River, and a good-sized town called San Miguel."

Eli and Miguel had nothing to add, but Rainey was never without a comment.

"We're headed up into the Sangre de Cristo Mountains now," he said. "That's what the Spanish call them. Blood of Christ mountains. That's the Catholic way, they like things bloody."

Carrie wondered about San Miguel, but they were so close to Santa Fe that her impatience and nervousness outweighed her curiosity. She was glad when they set off at a trot, angling away from the trail and its cloud of dust.

Heading up into the mountains meant leaving the stretches of desert behind, and while she wouldn't admit as much to the others, it was a relief. Carrie had been prepared for the heat and the lack of water, but she hadn't imagined the monotony or the way a relentless sun leached color out of the world. A spare scattering of yucca and mesquite against stretches of sand and rock face reminded her of pale complexions plagued by rashes and boils. More difficult still was the simple fact that each mile was like the one before it: endless, blinding bright, monochromatic, with a wind that muttered endlessly and never tired of playing with the sand.

It wasn't until dawn on the fourth day that she began to see that there was color. Sand was a misery she could not rationalize. It gathered in the folds of her clothes and the scarf she wore tied across her face; it crept into ears and moccasins and grew damp with sweat between toes. But it had colors. She passed the time working out how she would describe what she saw in a letter home.

Here the sand was off-white, or buff, or sometimes a silvery taupe color deepening to caramel, colors that shifted with the sun throughout the day, layered with blue and purple and pink shadows. More difficult to describe was the plant life, because while there wasn't a great variety, yucca and mesquite and sage all bristled with shades of green.

But she would put some effort into describing the stone that built this world. At home they would find it hard to imagine cliffs in layers of color that brought fruit and spices to mind: peach, pear, kumquat, orange, melon. At dusk some cliffs flickered the flaming orange of saffron threads, the color set off by a calmer gamboge.

She was learning to appreciate the particular beauty of the desert, but she would be glad to have this part of the journey behind her. The advantage of riding was that the trip was shortened by weeks. Nathan

would be spending far longer in this intriguing but inhospitable landscape. She hoped he would be better able to tolerate it than she would
have been.

SHE WOKE TO a wider spectrum of color, all around. Mesquite seemed
to be everywhere, but now for the first time she saw yucca in bloom.
She might have tried to sketch the way the long asparagus-like stalks
swayed in the breeze, clusters of large creamy white flowers nodding
lazily. Smaller cactus, new to her, put out deep purple cup-shaped
blossoms. She would try to remember the plants so she could record
them in her journal: oleander, juniper and aspen, barberry and pinyon
pine. There were dozens more she would ask about.

She decided that people like herself who came from the East Coast
were spoiled by green.

Eli, already awake and busy with the horses, glanced over and
called to her. "Almost home."

Home. The word struck a chord, just slightly out of tune. She
might spend the rest of her life here, but in her mind home was where
her mother was and always would be.

That morning they rode past a trade caravan of some fifty wagons.
Rainey paused now and then to exchange news with drovers, but
all Carrie's focus was on getting past the wagon train as quickly and
safely as possible, now that the trail was winding its way uphill and
had narrowed. Then again, Mimosa was sure-footed and smart, and so
Carrie let her have her head. In the end they managed just fine and
put the wagon train behind themselves.

Clear, clean air made Carrie realize how hungry she was, long
before they next stopped to water the horses and let them graze.
Mimosa had proved her value many times over and without complaint, and she deserved a reward. Carrie would dig out the remainder
of her dried apple supply for her. Titus Hardy would laugh and call
her sentimental, but she would not have to deal with him for very
much longer.

On the edge of a town named for the Pecos River, Miguel and Rainey put up a rope corral alongside the stream. Then they all walked toward the four adobe buildings that seemed to be the entire town. Pecos was unassuming, but the setting was fairy-tale-like. To the west was a broad, undulating mesa, and to the north the hills climbed to meet more cliffs in layers of color. Carrie breathed in deeply, amazed at air so clear and crisp it had a taste of its own.

There was time to study the adobe buildings more closely as they walked to the cantina. They were all the same faded, uneven peach color, with rounded corners and flat roofs. All the doors and windows stood open; she saw no window glass at all, but shutters painted in strong blues and yellows and reds. A black dog slept in the shade, a litter of puppies pressed into her side. Laundry flapped on a line here, as it did everywhere.

Even before she stepped into the cantina, Carrie could sense how the thick adobe walls kept the room cool and dim despite the heat of the day. In June the cantina was comfortable, but she wondered if the walls—even five feet thick—would be as effective in August.

Inside, the room was very simple. A large crucifix hung on white-washed walls as the only decorative touch, and the furnishings were minimal. A very old cat who had lost a tail and an ear sat on a table, washing a paw. The tom paid them little notice, but the man who came through a doorway at the rear made up for the lack of enthusiasm.

"*¡A redo vaya!*" He threw out his arms and shouted it again: "*¡A redo vaya!*" He was surprised, clearly, and pleased to see the men.

Things began to happen very quickly: a woman joined them, and then another, who was likely her mother. These were people who could not limit themselves to a simple hello and a handshake; they talked and hugged and talked more, questions spilling over each other. And their questions were not just tolerated but met with answers more than one or two words in length. For once Miguel was just as talkative as Rainey.

Carrie smiled when she was introduced, spoke very little, and was glad that much of the conversation was beyond her comprehension. She was aware that the women were asking questions about the young woman with such good manners who was dressed like a gaucho. Somehow or other they sensed a connection, because there were glances darting toward Eli. His face gave nothing away; Carrie hoped the same was true of her own.

Because she was thirsty and also in the hope that the subject would change, Carrie asked if she might have water.

There was water enough, she was told, and food, if she would please take a seat—just then a gang of children rushed in and surrounded Rainey. They meant to drag him outside, but when the older of the women raised her voice, they paid attention. Her cries of *Let him eat, he's so hungry!* won Rainey his freedom.

In short order Carrie was seated at a round table, with Eli on one side and Rainey on the other, and a great rushing back and forth began. First to appear was the promised water jug and clay cups, and then the food began to arrive: a great bowl of beans speckled with herbs, a covered serving platter, a dish of salt, another dish of finely chopped chilies, and finally a tureen.

Rainey took the lid off the tureen as Eli pressed a ladle into her hand. "It's called *pozole*. Something like stew."

Carrie's eyes and nose told her that *pozole* was made of mutton and onions and vegetables she didn't recognize. Pillowy kernels of hominy bobbed among chunks of peppers and chilies, and with the rising steam came the smells of coriander, garlic, and something that might have been cumin. Her stomach growled in response. It was then she realized that everyone was watching her, exactly as they would watch a person about to dive from a cliff into an unruly sea. Concern and fascination warred for the upper hand.

For weeks now Miguel and Rainey had been telling her stories about the food in New Mexico. Every account ended with a warning, so that she was reminded of ghost stories told on summer nights at Lake in the Clouds.

"Emigrants can't handle chilies," Rainey would announce with the unapologetic condescension of someone who has conquered a difficult skill.

"Lily-livered," Miguel added, more matter-of-fact. "All the *tejanos.*"

Tejanos, Carrie had learned, wasn't a reference to Texans but to any white-skinned emigrant from the East. And it was not complimentary, according to Eva.

"I doubt many will refer to you as a *tejana*, at least not in your hearing," she had said. "You might hear yourself called a *gabacha*, that's quite commonly used and fairly unassuming." There were more terms she might hear, and Eva had been happy to explain. Carrie wondered to what degree the men might be cleaning up their stories for her ears. As it turned out, Rainey had saved his best story—as he saw it—for the previous night, and the question was partially answered.

"Once I am sitting in the La Faena—Red Rosita's place—this was maybe three years ago." Rainey wiggled a bit, settling into his story. "When a Swiss farmer comes stumbling in. A big fellow, built like a bull, and pure *bolillo*, on his way to the goldfields—"

It was rude to interrupt a story, but as Rainey himself often did just that, Carrie stopped him.

"*Bolillo?*"

Miguel pointed to Rainey, whose sparse blond hair hung in his face. "There's a *bolillo* for you. Pale and gold, like white bread. Talks funny."

Hardy grunted, whether at the interruption or to emphasize this commentary on the meaning of *bolillo*—and Rainey picked up his story again.

"So this Swiss, he lost all his gear trying to stay ahead of a band of Ute who liked the look of his hair. Then he crashes in here and asks for water, and he is telling Rosita he hasn't had food in two days. And she gives him a plate—"

Rainey paused to shake a hand and blow out an imaginary flame.

"She tried to warn him, but he didn't have Spanish or maybe he did but he was too hungry to listen. And there I am sitting, watching him take a big spoonful of Rosita's *chilate de pollo*—hot enough to make even a Yaqui break into a sweat—and thinking to myself I should get out of the way."

Here he paused and glanced at Carrie as if to judge her reaction. She turned a hand palm up and inclined her head, unwilling to look impressed or even very interested.

A determined look came over Rainey's face.

"And now everybody is watching the Swiss. He chews and swallows and then he stops. Just stops. He looks one way and the other way—" Rainey demonstrated. "And his whole head turns red. Fire red. He jumps up, grabs the water jug, and tries to pour it straight down his throat, and then he runs outside, headed I'm thinking for the horse trough, but before he gets there—"

"He drops down dead," Miguel finished for him.

"The last time I heard that story it was a French trapper," Eli added.

"Name of Moreau," Hardy confirmed.

Rainey shrugged philosophically. "It's still true," he said to Carrie. "Serrano, guajillo, ancho, de árbol, habanero—Miss Ballentyne, beware."

Sometime in the future she would look into these stories he told of sudden death by chili peppers, but now, ladling *pozole* into her bowl, she examined what might be a very small, very green tomato. Chilies were, she thought, red, but she couldn't be sure of that. Then she saw that just to her right was a platter of warm tortillas, the thin, round, foldable cornmeal cakes she had first tasted a few days before and liked.

Rainey saw her examining the food and waggled his eyebrows at her.

So she took a tortilla, folded it into something resembling a spade, and dipped it into her bowl, where she let it soak for a count of five.

Looking first Miguel and then Rainey directly in the eye, she bit into the tortilla. She chewed, trying to describe for herself the tastes and textures, both familiar and new. Then she swallowed, picked up a spoon, and began to eat.

She could do nothing about the color that flooded her face, but she would make it obvious that she was enjoying the *pozole*. Which was, in fact, very spicy. And good.

Of the many people who came in to greet them while they ate, a few—mostly younger women—took a pointed interest in Carrie. They asked questions, waited patiently while she pieced together an answer, asked questions of their own that Eli helped her answer, and invited her to their homes.

In Manhattan visits tended to be formal events, conforming to social conventions that many considered sacrosanct. You sat in a parlor with a lot of women who might be strangers or someone you had known all your life. The talk was of nothing important. You watched the clock until the twenty minutes required by such visits were up, and went on your way.

Almost always it was a waste of time, but Carrie had the idea that visiting the women who invited her to their homes in Pecos would be more rewarding. A young man about her own age asked if she would like to see the ruins of the Pecos Pueblo. He would be honored to escort her, and tell her something of the history.

Eli lifted his head and looked the young man in the eye. Just that much was enough to convince him that there were other, less difficult ways to spend his time. He excused himself politely and disappeared.

Carrie wasn't sure how she felt about this blatant possessiveness, but it wasn't something to debate with him at this moment. On the other hand, she really did want to see the ruins, and made that clear. As soon as it was polite, they thanked the women—who still watched closely—and walked off together. Titus Hardy, Rainey, and Miguel, caught up in a noisy conversation with the local men, waved them off.

Carrie only caught a few words, but that was enough to make her curious.

She said, "It sounds as though Padre Martinez is in trouble with someone called Lamy. Or Lamby?"

"Lamy." Eli shook his head, amused. "The Catholic bishop. There's a feud going on for a couple years now, since Lamy came in. A French priest, so you can guess how that went over. Sounds like the Mexican priests have dug in their heels."

"It sounds complicated," Carrie said. "But church disputes are generally about one thing. Money."

"Mostly it's about tithing," Eli said. "When Lamy came in, he doubled and tripled the cost of basic church services. If you want to bury somebody Catholic out of Santa Fe, you have to have deep pockets. I've heard of final accountings as high as one hundred and forty piastres. That's about the same amount in American dollars."

Carrie felt her mouth drop open in surprise. "But common workers couldn't afford that, could they?"

"Few people can," Eli said. "And that's what Martinez and the other Mexican padres are up in arms about. That, and the way Lamy is interfering in the way they have always done things."

"I will do my best to avoid getting involved."

"Good plan." He glanced at her more closely. "Did the food not agree with you?"

She shrugged. "It will take some time to adjust, but I think I'll manage. I quite like the flavors. Of course Rainey won't believe me."

Two boys went by, leading a string of donkeys laden with bundles of hay.

Burros, Carrie reminded herself. Here donkeys were called burros, and they were apparently the most popular beast of burden. Everywhere you looked you saw them, pulling carts, loaded down with huge bundles of merchandise, or with people on their way to church. There were no saddles or bridles, and oddest of all, riders didn't sit on the burro's back but astride the hips. They carried sticks or slender branches and used them to tell the animal where it was meant to go.

"New Mexicans love their burros the way Englishmen love their dogs," Rainey told her. "They work hard but there is much affection for them too. I have seen a grown man cry when his burro died."

She asked Eli about this characterization. "Are the people here so tenderhearted about animals?"

It seemed not, because his mouth turned down at one corner and he shook his head. "About burros, sometimes. Also dogs, for the most part. But cockfighting is very popular, as you'll see."

This was disappointing but not unexpected news. Cockfighting was popular everywhere, country and city. As was dogfighting. As were bear- and boar-baiting.

She said, "There's nothing I want to see less than bloodletting for the sport of it. I'll stay clear."

Eli stopped and pointed with his chin. "You see the broken walls up ahead? That used to be the Walatowa Pueblo. Now their pueblo is at Jemez, another day's ride past Santa Fe."

Carrie considered. "But why would they abandon their pueblo? Drought? Crop failure?"

"Apache raids, mostly."

A dozen questions came to mind, but all Carrie's attention was taken up by the simple fact of what had once been a village where hundreds of people had made their homes. Where adobe walls still stood, they glowed in the afternoon sun.

"How do you get to the upper stories? I don't see any staircases."

"Ladders and handholds, mostly. And ropes, so you could climb up through a hole in the floor. Then they could pull the ropes up to keep raiders from following."

"It's like a . . ." She paused, rethinking. "Not like a beehive at all, but I'm still reminded of one."

At her feet and all around, there was a scattering of pottery shards, some as big as her hand. She thought of sending one home to her mother, but the idea of taking anything away from this place struck her as rude, for want of a better word. Like sifting through the ashes after a neighbor's house burned to carry away small, precious things they assumed forever lost.

She wondered if Eli would understand what she meant, but instead of asking, she followed him closer to the ruins and listened as he pointed out details she would have missed.

"Are all the pueblos built in the same way?"

"For the most part. We'll go to the Jemez Pueblo so you can meet my mother's people."

That was an alarming idea, but she managed a small smile. "I'll look forward to that."

He took her wrist and pulled her closer. "First there's something else we need to talk about."

She laughed. "You can't be serious."

"Not that." And his grin gave him away. "All right, not just that. You need to decide how much you want to tell Doc Markham. You'll be standing at his door before sunset."

That was a sobering idea. "You mean, what to say about us."

Carrie still found it hard to use the word *marriage*. In fact, she was fairly sure she hadn't said it at all, not even to Eli. No doubt he had noticed, but he hadn't commented, and she appreciated his reserve. Now she took a deep breath and shared all the things she had been fretting over for days.

"I am a terrible liar," she told him. "Even if I wanted to mislead the Markhams, I couldn't do it for very long. And there's the legal obligation I can't walk away from. That I don't want to walk away from. You know I signed a two-year contract."

Eli studied her face for a long moment. "You signed a contract to work as a nurse and midwife, but nothing beyond those responsibilities. There was nothing about being a servant or a companion or a nanny."

This was true, she had to agree.

"Then I see no problem. You have your work and I have mine. I'm gone a few days at a time, never more than a week, and you'd get bored with nothing to occupy you. The issue ain't the work, Carrie. It's where you'll sleep."

She would not blush, though this was the other subject she found almost impossible to talk about. They had come very close, that night of the *derecho*, but since then their sleeping arrangements had never provided any privacy. Beyond a kiss now and then, they had not had the opportunity to explore any further. In her mind she had not been able to leave the subject alone, but they hadn't spoken of it.

Carrie was determined not to be embarrassed, but she had to clear her throat before she could speak.

"Try as I might, I cannot imagine how I would tell the Markhams that I won't be joining their household. That I'll be spending my nights across town in Eli Ibarra's bed."

That made him laugh. "You're skipping the step that will make all the difference."

"Yes, all right. It's just as hard to imagine coming into the household and saying, first thing, 'Oh, by the way, I'm going to marry Eli Ibarra, but I am looking forward to my work with you as a nurse and midwife.'"

His chin dipped to his chest, and his gaze sharpened.

"Because they'll think you've taken leave of your good senses?"

This was what Carrie had worried about, that he might interpret her concern as having to do with whom she was going to marry rather than the fact that she planned to marry someone she had known for such a short time. On its own, that idea could still take her breath away. Considered in isolation from all else, it was ridiculous to even think of such a thing.

Many times every day she went over this in her mind, setting herself hard questions. It was her intention to make a thoughtful, careful list of reasons she should not, could not marry, but every time, her mind went blank. It was an unusual courtship, that couldn't be denied, but there was nothing of coercion or frenzy about it. Eli was someone she truly liked and admired and wanted to be near, in ways that were new and unsettling. She liked his touch and the way he looked at her. He wanted her as a man wanted a woman, but he was interested and wanted to hear what she had to say.

Not so long ago she had believed that she could live a solitary life and be satisfied, but it was harder to hold on to that idea now that she knew herself as half of a whole, how good and right it felt.

Others would not see things this way, she was aware. Eva's sister had refused Eli because he was Mestizo, and it was possible that the Markhams would expect and demand that Carrie do the same. But she was equal to disapproval when it was founded solely in bigotry. More than equal.

"No," she said firmly. "I am very sure of my decision, and I do not want or need their blessing or approval. But it will still be a shock, especially as Mrs. Markham is—traditional, from what I've been told." She hadn't related any of the things about Indira Markham she had learned from Eva, and wouldn't do that now. It would be too much like breaking a confidence.

She took his hand and held it tightly.

"I think generally I'm good at approaching difficult subjects with all kinds of people, but in this situation—" She broke off.

"Yes," he said. "I see your point. What do you need to smooth the way?"

"A month," she said. "Or maybe six weeks, depending on her situation. In that much time, I'll know how to approach both of them about our plans in a way that will cause the least—upheaval."

She couldn't quite read his face, and it occurred to her that he knew the Markhams and could anticipate their reactions better than she could.

With his free hand, he cupped her cheek and leaned close.

"A month or six weeks of what? Acting like strangers?"

She shook her head at him. "No, that would make both of us unhappy, and it would be dishonest. But we could be two people who are attracted to one another, wanting to spend time together."

"Falling in love."

It was a challenge, but she met it.

"Yes." Her voice wobbled, and so she repeated herself, more firmly. "Yes."

He turned away to think—as he always did when the matter at hand was complicated, something she had noticed early on—and his eyes moved along the trail that they would be following to Santa Fe, and very soon. The familiar noises—wagon wheels, jangling harnesses, drovers calling out to each other, the lowing of cattle and oxen— drifted down to them.

There was a familiar whistle from the cantina. Titus Hardy, wanting to get back on the trail. They set off in that direction, but slowly. Titus Hardy did not like to be kept waiting, and Eli did not like to be rushed.

He said, "So let's try this. Tomorrow I'll go see my parents, but the day after I'll call for you in the evening, to go walking. We'll see how Mrs. Markham likes that much." His tone was matter-of-fact, but she could hear the reservations simmering just beneath.

"We can try that," he went on. "But you need to be thinking about how you'll handle things if it turns out Mrs. Markham don't like the idea much at all."

PART FOUR

Santa Fe

35

THEY HAD TRAVELED so far so quickly because Titus Hardy brought word: Carrie's help was needed in Santa Fe, and urgently.

He had had no details to offer, but Carrie was assuming that this change in plans had to do with Mrs. Markham. If she had gone into labor as much as six weeks prematurely, both mother and child might well be in their graves. It was a grim thought, but not one that could be dismissed.

On that basis alone she decided to send the men away. She would enter the Markham household alone.

Once she worked this out for herself, some of the nervous energy she had been hoarding disappeared, and that gave her room to realize that they were headed downhill. To the north was what she thought must be old Fort Marcy—a great bulk perched on a ridge that looked down over the town called Santa Fe.

As hot as it was, a shiver raced down her spine.

On the way into Santa Fe, she told the others what she had decided, and was unsurprised to see relief on Hardy's face. Titus Hardy, Carrie was convinced, would absent himself from anything having to do with childbirth. As would most men.

Eli took Mimosa with him to stable with his horses; Rainey sorted out her saddlebags; Miguel stayed in his saddle, nodded, and touched a finger to his brow; and Hardy wished her well but made sure she understood: it would be a long time before he came this way again.

Rainey called warnings and suggestions over his shoulder until he was out of earshot.

Then Carrie stood alone in a narrow lane on a summer evening, watching the sun slip away from the world so slowly, casting shadows as it went. Colors shifted across adobe walls in shades of indigo and hyacinth, gamboge and terre verte. She wondered whether the town was always so quiet at this hour. No matter; Santa Fe would have its rhythms, and she would learn them.

In front of her were double doors of carved wood. A sign had been painted on the wall, one that appealed to her for its simplicity:

SAMUEL MARKHAM, M.D.

PHYSICIAN & SURGEON

MÉDICO Y CIRUJANO

Now was the time to remember who she was, and who had trained her. If there had been tragedy here, she knew how to meet it. She could provide some measure of physical comfort and relief from pain, but what she could do for a grieving mother was limited. She hoped that Mrs. Markham would have a priest or a minister whom she was seeing for that kind of support. In Carrie's experience of doctors, they not only made the worst patients themselves, but were equally unable to make objective decisions about treatment when family members were ill.

She found her handkerchief and wiped her damp hands, her face and neck. Finally, she struck at her clothes in a vain attempt to dislodge more of the trail dust. When she had done as much as could be managed without soap and water, she pulled the rope.

Somewhere in the depths of the house, a bell jingled. Before the sound faded away, she heard movement. A woman, by the lightness of her step. Coming swiftly.

The door opened. Based on what Eva had told her about the household, Carrie thought that the young woman who stood there must be Josefa, and so Carrie smiled. In return she got just a quirk at the corner of the girl's mouth, a raised eyebrow, and a nod.

"How do you do. I am Carrie Ballentyne, and I believe Dr. and Mrs. Markham must be expecting me."

An older servant took the saddlebags and disappeared before she could ask his name. As Carrie walked with Josefa down a corridor toward another set of doors, she asked the most important question.

"Is everyone in tolerable good health?"

Josefa was surprised by this question, but it was too late to sort through the confusion, because they were already walking into the *placita*, as Eli had described it to her, completely surrounded on all four sides by doors that would open into rooms of all kinds. She would describe it as an open-air courtyard when she wrote home. The fact that there was no overhead covering was odd, in her experience, but in good weather—and weather was generally good in New Mexico, if she understood correctly—the family would spend most of the day here. This was the heart of the house, dense with potted plants, full of color and birdsong and slanting evening light.

A table sat in the very middle, and at the table was a young girl. A pretty girl despite an irritated expression. Dressed expensively, with her hair tied into a complicated cascade of ringlets. Apparently the primer she held in her fisted hands did not meet with her approval.

From deeper in the *placita* came a man's voice, in a familiar accent. "Lulu," she heard. "Try once more, please, and then you may go."

Carrie realized that Josefa had slipped away, and so she must handle the formalities on her own.

"Dr. Markham?"

The girl started at the sound of Carrie's voice and jumped up from the table. Her whole face opened in a smile that showed off a gap where her front teeth had been and would reappear, soon enough.

"Hello!"

"Hello," Carrie said. "You are Miss Lulu, I gather. I can't quite see your father, but I hear him."

Lulu hopped across the tiled floor, took Carrie by the hand, and without a word of explanation pulled her through a wealth of greenery to another open area that had been furnished like a small parlor. A scattering of small tables surrounded walnut furniture with velour upholstery, so out of place in New Mexico Territory that at first Carrie didn't trust her own eyes. Three of the largest paraffin oil lamps she had ever seen sat on end tables, two with etched-glass chimneys and one—the base painted with a hunting scene—with an opalescent glass chimney that would be beautiful when the lamp was lit.

"Mama." The girl was excited, but she kept her voice at a noisy whisper. "Look, Mama, she's here. She's here, finally. The nursemaid. Here she is, finally come to take care of me and my sister. Mama!"

Carrie was gestured forward and made her way carefully through a plantation of small maple, magnolia, and olive trees in elaborate ceramic pots. Dr. and Mrs. Markham had been resting on chaise longues and the doctor shot up, embarrassed to be caught in such a position, but Mrs. Markham stayed just as she was, turned on her side with her whole body curved around a swaddled infant. A household not in mourning, but dedicated to the quiet that would soothe a newborn. All Carrie's worries slipped away, just that easily.

So for the time being she would be a nurse. How soon it would be before someone called on her as a midwife she couldn't guess, but she would be glad of some time to get to know the household and medical practice. And to learn more about Lulu, who thought of her as a nursemaid for some reason. Some unsettling reason.

Dr. Markham was making introductions, but all Carrie's attention was fixed on his wife, who was awake now. She righted herself to a sitting position, the sleeping infant tucked into the curve of her arm as her husband talked.

"You see Mrs. Markham is recently delivered of a daughter, just ten days ago."

"My sister," Lulu offered, in case there was any confusion. "She has a name, but not the one I wanted. She's called Imelda. You have to be quiet because if she wakes, she will cry."

She glanced over her shoulder and saw by her mother's expression that she had overstepped her bounds.

"I'll go see if Josefa needs me," she said, and was gone.

Once Lulu was out of the room, her mother squinted in Carrie's direction, rubbing her eyes with her free hand, as if something quite inexplicable stood before her.

"Miss Ballentyne," she said. "I am glad you are here and safe. But what are you wearing?"

There was a small, awkward silence.

Dr. Markham said, "My dear, remember that Miss Ballentyne has come on horseback. Not a half hour ago she was still on the trail with Titus Hardy and his men."

"And for no good purpose," Mrs. Markham said. She cupped the baby's swaddled bottom lightly.

A change of subject was called for, and Carrie knew exactly what would distract the new parents. A mother with an infant wants to be congratulated and praised and admired, and these were things Carrie could do, and did, striving for the right tone. Aware still that Mrs. Markham was both fascinated and horrified at the sight of a young woman dressed like a wrangler, and that Carrie would have to retire and wash before she dared approach to look more closely at the baby.

She turned to the doctor to say as much, and was able to see him now more clearly, as he had come forward.

Sam Markham was quite tall, but rail thin. When the clothes he wore had been made for him, he had been a good thirty pounds heavier; now he was haggard, with deep lines bracketing his mouth and cutting down his cheeks. The perspiration on his brow didn't have to do with heat, but pain.

And so here was the surprise. She was a midwife, but her patient, at least in this case, was not the newly delivered mother but the father. Dr. Markham himself. She wondered if they had been aware of this all along, and chose not to tell her. She would find out soon enough.

Mrs. Markham rang a small silver bell that brought Josefa to the door to hear Mrs. Markham's instructions: Bathwater was to be heated for Miss Ballentyne, without delay. She expected fresh towels to be laid out, luggage unpacked and clothing tended to, and the chamber aired. For Carrie she had more specific instructions: There was good strong soap that she should use liberally when she bathed and—she emphasized this point clearly—washed her hair. In an hour's time, when she was properly refreshed, there would be a light meal waiting for her in the dining room, where the Markhams would join her once Lulu had been settled down for the night.

Everyone was polite and well-mannered, every word was carefully chosen, and everything was wrong, somehow. Her sense of unease receded a bit when Josefa took her to one of the doors that opened off the *placita*.

They had given her a large bedchamber, with two windows and a fireplace that seemed to be plastered directly into the wall with smooth, almost maternal curves and dips. The bed was generous, with a bundle of netting that could be let down to create a barrier that would keep mosquitoes at bay. There was an armchair, a desk or work-table with two pretty oil lamps, a highboy, and a washstand tucked behind a screen painted with a garden scene.

She resisted the sudden urge to scratch her head and the dusty, dirty hair that had so alarmed Mrs. Markham. She would use all the soap available to her and gladly, but there was little she could do about her clothing. Everything in her saddlebags was much the worse for wear after weeks riding overland. Even the single day dress she had packed and never worn would be wrinkled and saturated with dust and sand.

This problem still occupied her when Josefa came to tell her that the bath was ready. She was a quiet, observant young woman, not unfriendly but reserved. Her thoughtful expression gave Carrie pause.

"Is something wrong?"

The younger woman gestured to the day dress draped over Carrie's arm. "Let me see what I can do with that while you bathe."

"Ah," Carrie said. "Might Mrs. Markham turn me away from the table, do you think?"

This made one corner of Josefa's mouth curl with something between amusement and regret. "She might."

Carrie found this oddly reassuring, not because it confirmed her impression of Mrs. Markham but because of what it told her about Josefa. Her English sentences were perfectly formed, but her accent made it clear that Spanish and the language of her pueblo were her mother tongues. Most crucially she understood and interpreted subtle clues.

"Then please, if you can improve it at all—" She handed over the dress. "Josefa, may I ask you about Dr. Markham's health?"

This direct approach turned out to be just what was called for. It seemed to Carrie that Josefa might have been waiting for this question.

"As you saw, he is not well."

"How long has he been ill?"

Carrie would not have been surprised if Josefa simply chose not to answer, out of loyalty or fear or custom. On the other hand, if she did answer the question, that could be an indication of how worried she was. But Josefa was not surprised by any of Carrie's questions and was very willing to relate what she had observed, in exacting and troubling terms. She explained briefly, but in a way that made Carrie think she paid attention when the talk turned to medicine.

She spent some time organizing her things—the few things she had been able to take away from the stagecoach—and used that time to consider what she had heard. From what Josefa said, the signs pointed to some problem with Dr. Markham's digestion. Surely he must have consulted a physician; there were four in Santa Fe, after all. Three of them were army surgeons at the garrison, while the fourth was retired, a man who lived still in Santa Fe. She had read his name in the newspaper, and it came to her now. She could only hope that Dr. Benenati had been consulted, and at the same time she knew how reluctant physicians could be when it came to seeing to their own health. In fact, it seemed likely that Dr. Markham's condition might remain a mystery until a crisis presented. She doubted that he would allow her to question him, but at some point medical necessity would outweigh social convention.

The dining room was a surprisingly large room to find in a house made of adobe. The wooden floor was waxed and polished, the furniture—all originating from the East—gleamed, and spotless damask linen covered the sideboard and table. The oil lamps in their wall sconces behind cut glass shades lit every corner of the room and reflected off wine goblets, window glass, china figurines arranged on a shelf, and a silver bell set beside Mrs. Markham's place. A porcelain teapot and matching cups and saucers sat waiting on a silver tray. And a place had been set for Carrie.

Dr. Markham rose to greet her, held her chair for her, called for Josefa, and then sat, perched on the edge of his own chair. He was anxious, but his wife was utterly calm.

Carrie realized now that Mrs. Markham would not be predictable. Her home, her way of speaking, her habits all showed her to be a daughter of wealth and breeding, with very specific ideas of proper behavior. And yet, surprisingly, Mrs. Markham had her baby at the breast, hidden behind the blanket draped over her shoulder. In Carrie's experience, women of high social rank rarely nursed their own children. Perceived wisdom held that unless a new mother cared to ruin her figure entirely, she engaged a wet nurse. More truthfully Carrie suspected that the unwillingness to nurse was at least sometimes a matter of what could only be called distaste or revulsion. For many of that class, putting an infant to the breast was a messy, unnecessary, and unbearable duty. Where and how this idea had started she couldn't know, but it struck her as unfortunate. A lost opportunity for both mother and child.

If Mrs. Markham was nursing, it might be that she understood the benefits and was not so concerned about the social conventions. She hoped that was the case.

While Indira Markham nursed, she talked, to everyone and no one. Had Josefa simply failed to note smudges on the chimney of one of the oil lamps? Did Dr. Markham mean to intimidate Miss Ballentyne by leaning forward as he did? How unfortunate that her trunks would be so delayed; they would have to do something about her clothing, or she'd be stuck in the house for weeks. And Carrie must eat everything on her plate; she was far too thin, and it made her freckles stand out. Of course, a lady who traveled without sufficient protection from the sun had only herself to blame.

Carrie did the polite thing and pretended not to have overheard the criticism. Instead she lifted the cover on her plate and found cold roast beef, buttered wheaten bread, pickled cucumber, and preserved tomatoes. The food was very good, but she was aware that Mrs. Markham watched her closely as she ate. This she would have to bear until the lady of the house had decided she was trustworthy.

"You must tell us about the journey," Dr. Markham said. "Titus Hardy is an excellent guide, but rough at times. Clearly you managed."

Mrs. Markham shot her husband a frown but spoke to Carrie. "Yes, we must hear about your journey, but right now I assume you'll be wondering why we sent Mr. Hardy to bring you here at such a pace."

She didn't wait for Carrie to comment, and in fact never even looked in her direction.

"You will have guessed that I was in labor," she went on. "I had so hoped that you might get here in time, but as you see, everything worked out for the best."

She paused to shift the infant in her arms, cooing softly under her breath.

Indira Markham had a wide, sincere smile; a long, slender neck; and beautiful eyes. She was well-spoken and courteous and could have been any of the young women Carrie had known in Manhattan: the daughter of a physician or judge, the wife of a banker or manufacturer. Like those women of good family, Indira Markham was perfectly groomed and carefully dressed. The only outward sign of discomfort was the way her fine blond hair had gone limp in the heat, even so early in June.

But it was her tone that gave Carrie pause. It was congenial, and still reserved. A woman allowing another woman into her home, and unable to hide her doubts. That was fair, Carrie told herself. Any sensible person would be cautious.

With a softer voice, Mrs. Markham said, "We are relieved that you survived what must have been a difficult journey. Aren't we, Dr. Markham?"

"Yes," he said. "Of course."

"So you see." She paused to smile in what Carrie took for encouragement. "You needn't worry about me. Your first and primary responsibility is Lulu. I know she will benefit greatly from your attentions. And of course learning about the household will take up much of your energy. Let me assure you, you can depend on Josefa to show you everything."

Carrie glanced at Dr. Markham, who was studying something on the far wall, his brow furrowed. She understood that he was not going to intercede, and thus she had no other option than to be direct.

"I look forward to spending time with Lulu," she said. "When my work in the dispensary allows it."

Mrs. Markham's head came up quite sharply, tilted to one side, her mouth pressed into a severe line. A look of disapproval that any servant—any housekeeper or nursemaid—would recognize.

"Miss Ballentyne," she said slowly. "As you can see, I no longer need a midwife, and accordingly, your responsibilities must adjust to this new situation. And now I must retire. I wish you a good night's rest."

She rose from her chair and turned in such a way that the baby shifted on her arm, almost clumsily. Imelda, they were calling her. The small face peeked out from the swaddling clothes for no more than a few seconds, but that was long enough for Carrie to see, and understand.

Dr. Markham sat quietly after his wife left the room, gaze still fixed on the far wall. Carrie had a dozen questions, but to put any of them into words in a sensible, reasonable way struck her as almost impossible. He would have to speak first.

Santa Fe was a quiet place, far quieter than Waverly Place. She could hear Josefa moving around the kitchen. Someone walked past the house; a burro brayed. Finally church bells counted out the hour: ten in the evening.

Somewhere in Santa Fe was the house that Eli Ibarra called home. He would be busy still, brushing, feeding, and watering the horses. His gear and instruments had to be unpacked, and there were dozens of other small chores that would occupy him. After such a long absence, there would be no food in the larder, and so he would go out, she imagined, to find something to eat and say hello to friends.

Maybe he was sitting in a cantina right now, drinking beer and telling stories about his brothers' quarrels. He would say nothing of her, not yet. That was the agreement.

Titus Hardy and his men were gone; Nathan was still weeks away, and so was Eva. That meant that Eli was the only person she knew in Santa Fe. The idea of him would be a comfort, if she only knew how to find him if the need arose. She wished that she had thought to have him draw her a map of the town.

Tomorrow, she told herself, tomorrow there would be time to explore Santa Fe and find things for herself. Tomorrow, after she had learned about the adjustments to her responsibilities, because Mrs. Markham no longer needed a midwife. She had given birth.

The doctor cleared his throat.

"You saw, I think, the nature of Mrs. Markham's . . . problem."

Not a question, really, but she must acknowledge the facts. "Yes. I take it the child was stillborn?"

She spoke very quietly, but he jerked as if she had spit in his direction. His eyes flew to the door, and he sat frozen for a long moment before the tension in his shoulders left him.

"You must never say that word in her hearing. Believe me, Miss Ballentyne, the repercussions would be dire. She can be—" He shook his head.

"Do you have a treatment plan?" Carrie asked.

His expression shifted from surprise to disbelief. "I know of no treatment for extreme grief or delusions born of such grief. Do you?"

It was a rhetorical question, but she approached the subject from a different angle. "Would you say this is a case of puerperal insanity?"

He spread a hand over his face. Shook his head and shrugged.

"Where did the doll come from, Doctor? Was it your daughter's? I take it she had a different name for it."

Now when he looked at her, his face was flushed. "Does that matter?"

"I would say so," Carrie said. She was overcome with sadness for them all, but knew that emotion would be of no help. In a tone she used to talk to patients about things they did not want to hear, she went on.

"It's important because Lulu must be terribly confused and upset."

He grimaced, his face drawn down in the most disapproving frown Carrie had yet seen from him.

"Did she look upset to you?"

Carrie let her silence do its work. Finally, his shoulders bent forward in surrender. Not to Carrie, but to the truth she was asking him to acknowledge.

His voice came thick with tears. "There's no cure for puerperal insanity."

"Some women will come back to themselves, given time and patience. And close observation."

His laugh startled her. "I can't put her in an asylum. If there were family members who might be willing to step in . . . I wrote a letter after her last miscarriage, but there's no one."

He was a physician; he knew full well that his wife's condition could worsen, but to know this and to face it fully were very different things. It had been about two weeks since the stillbirth—Carrie shifted a little at this word, though she had not spoken it out loud—and he was in a desperate place. His wife's sanity, his own poor health, a young daughter caught in the middle. Carrie asked herself what she could do for them, if she could make a difference somehow.

He made an effort to look at her directly. "Breakfast is at seven, and after that, you and I will go to the dispensary and get started. You must be very tired. I will say good night."

His intent was clear, and Carrie saw that nothing she could say would be of any use. And still she stood, and held up a hand to stop him as he turned away.

"Please pardon the personal nature of my observation, but I believe you are having gastrointestinal troubles."

He stopped but didn't turn back to face her. "All my life. Especially when I am under duress. Good night, Miss Ballentyne."

Carrie walked back through the courtyard to the room that was hers, for as long as she was part of this household. For as long as this family remained intact.

She paused to feel the cool night breeze on her face and saw a pair of bats dancing overhead. A mockingbird's song, lyrical and familiar, made her remember that there would be nests to watch come spring.

Somewhere nearby an owl called, another familiar and comforting sound. Like a messenger from home, wishing her a peaceful night's rest.

36

ELI SAW TO the horses first. Hauling water, spreading straw, and shoveling feed, he ignored the growling of his own stomach. Another hour with currycombs and brushes saw all four Argentineans groomed and settled, and then Eli considered his choices: his supply of jerky, the dusty dried peppers that hung overhead, or a hot meal.

Chico trotted along beside him as he walked down the lane to Red Rosita's. Eli was glad to have the dog along; he was curious, alert, and by nature cautious. It remained to be seen if Chico was smart enough to stay clear of rattlers, something his last, far too curious dog had never learned. Now he'd take Chico into Red Rosita's and see how he did in a crowd of people.

As he walked toward the cantina, his stomach growled again. He was looking forward to the food. Rosita was a friend, one who liked the challenge of feeding him. Her habit was to put down one plate and then another and watch, arms crossed, while he showed her food the attention it deserved. Sometimes he wondered what she'd do if he complained—too salty, gristly, not enough peppers—but he knew where the boundaries were and would never insult her.

Eventually she would decide he had had enough and she'd pour him a measure of *tesgüín*. If she could spare the time, she'd give him what gossip she considered worth passing along, and he'd put coins down to pay for his meal and head home.

Eli knew going in that this time he'd be stuck in the cantina for a couple of hours, no matter how fast he ate. He had been gone for close to a year, after all. A local who went all the way to Europe and came back again was somebody everybody wanted to talk to. Eli would have better stories than any newspaper, and he would answer questions about things newspapers never thought to explain.

Quincho Diaz was the first to pull out a chair across from Eli. He fell into it with a groan and bared his jumble of teeth in a grin.

"So," he barked. "I hope this trip you got the chance to visit a butcher or two. Tell me, do those stuck-up *peninsulares carniceros* know what they're doing?"

Then the undertaker Llabrés wanted to know if a man could make a living raising sheep in the old country, in a climate that was rumored to be harsher than they had right here in New Mexico Territory. Farmworkers and *ciboleros* nursing their beers found this a particularly funny question from somebody who wouldn't know which end of the horse to feed and which to stand clear of.

More questions, one from a drover so young he hadn't yet sprouted a beard. He asked about the sea monsters men called whales, and what they ate. Others asked about pirates, freebooters, and the British Navy.

Soon enough the questions took a turn toward subjects closer to home. Memín Perez, a shepherd who worked for the Zavalas, wanted to know what it was like to ride halfway across the continent on a train, and how soon railroads would come so far as Santa Fe. Then José Bilbao, the most nervous man in five hundred miles, all his fingernails bitten to the quick, took that opportunity to change the subject to politics.

He wanted to know about the territorial government, and seemed to think Eli had answers. Specifically, now that Meriwether had resigned as governor of the territory and they had to make do with Bill Davis as acting governor, how long would it take for President Buchanan to appoint a replacement? And would he send them an abolitionist or a slave-stater?

After a quick look around the cantina to be sure that neither the sheriff nor his deputies were present, Eli said, "Bilbao, are you still locking horns with the law?"

Bilbao frowned, his whole face crumpling like a ball of wet paper. "That's not why I'm wondering."

The others in the room studied their beers, as if nothing unusual were happening. Bilbao had a temper that was respected, if not feared.

"Never mind that," Manuel said. "What I want to know is, what will get here first, the railroad or the war? Any idea on that, Eli?"

This was not the time for a debate on slavery and states' rights.

Eli looked around the room, one brow raised, and wondered out loud if nobody had any news to share.

The stories came at him in waves: who had died since he left, when and why and how; which boundary disputes had been settled and where new ones had popped up; that drunk soldiers had torn up the Casino Arrabal and brought misery on their own heads; how many emigrants had gone west to look for gold or back east, tuck-tailed; how the Navajo were dealing with the army, and what resistance cost them, cost all the tribes.

Rosita said, "Let the war chief take care of the army on his own, Manuelito's got warriors enough. No more talk of war."

The barber, half-asleep, sputtered to full attention when she yelled his name.

"Chema Tejeda! Tell Eli about how your Eduardo managed to get married."

Sudden silence and all eyes turned to the man who sat, most of his face hidden behind a sleek waterfall of hair. Chema was one of two barbers in town, and on that basis he was the best source of information—and gossip—in Santa Fe.

Now he sat up straight, only too happy to tell the story.

"Eli. You know how long our Eduardo has been waiting to marry his Paloma?"

Eli nodded. "A good while."

"More than just good," Chema said. "You probably don't recall that the trouble started with the nuns."

He waited for the low muttering of disapproval to fade away.

"The sisters convinced Paloma that a big church wedding and a mass with the bishop was the only sure way to hang on to a husband. And avoid hellfire."

Rosita, hands on hips, spoke up, as she always did on this subject.

"And how much did the church want in fees to make that happen?"

At the top of the list of all the things that made Rosita mad was the way Bishop Lamy filled his coffers. She wasn't the only one who was resentful about this, but she was more rebellious than most and willing to say so. The women of Santa Fe, astonished by Rosita's temerity, were always remarking to each other how odd it was that Red Rosa didn't seem worried about going to hell.

Tejeda said, "Forty piastres. Can you imagine? They appealed, but the bishop, he wouldn't budge. So now you got Eduardo, who's impatient, and Paloma, who's stubborn, and it looks like there's no solution. Until Eduardo came up with a little wager, a way to raise the money. About Padre Olivier."

Hoots of appreciative laughter all around.

Tejeda asked Eli, "You ever meet Olivier? The French priest Lamy sent to Nambé, maybe four years ago now."

"He knows that," Rosita said, scowling. "Everybody knows that."

Quincho said, "But Eli's been gone near a year. He probably doesn't know the details." He turned to Eli, and held out his hands. "See, the bishop booted poor old Padre Rubio back to Torreón so he could put Olivier in the Nambé Pueblo church. Olivier was young. Slender, pale as cheese, big blue eyes." He put both hands over his heart and sighed dramatically. "Adonis."

Rosita huffed. "Lamy should have known, a pretty young priest is always trouble."

"It was a bad move on the bishop's part," somebody muttered from the far end of the cantina.

"It was a stupid move," Rosita said, and didn't whisper it.

Tejeda picked up the story again. "It started toward the end of March, my Eduardo stood up right here"—he pointed to a spot near the bar—"and announced that the French priest Olivier would be gone by the end of April, and he'd put good money on that."

Eli looked over all the men in the room. "And you took him up on that bet?"

"It made sense!" Llabrés had gone red in the face. "Olivier was one of Lamy's favorites, so it looked like easy money. If Eduardo Tejeda was so much in love he wanted to spread his coin around on foolish bets, who am I to deny him?"

Quincho threw up both arms, fingers wiggling in frustration. "You have eyes in your head, but damn, Llabrés, you don't see much. Don't you remember Lamy booting six priests out of his territory less than a week after he got here?"

"I don't see the connection," Llabrés said, arms folded over his chest.

"Men," Rosita spit. "Llabrés, think about why Lamy got rid of those priests. Those priests in particular. It's how Eduardo got the idea."

Now Hartmann, who went to mass every day and confessed nearly as often, got to his feet. "I'll tell you why. Because those priests had—had—"

Every man in the room watched, enjoying the dentist's discomfort.

"Wives." His voice cracked.

"Well," Rosita said. "I wouldn't go that far. You know a priest who can afford to pay the marriage tithe?"

"Wait," Hartmann said, truly affronted now. "Priests don't *get* married. They can't be married. A priest who wants a wife can only *pretend to be married.*"

Rosita put back her head and laughed. "Priests fucking like rabbits anywhere you care to look. You call that pretending?"

Eli estimated it would take another hour of arguing before the crowd in the cantina would agree how Eduardo had pulled off his trick, but the important part was already clear. Padre Olivier had put aside his vow of celibacy in favor of a young woman in his bed, and somehow Eduardo made sure the bishop found out about it. Olivier was gone the next day; Eduardo won his bet, collected his winnings, and paid the wedding tithe. Now he was married.

Eli got up to go, and Chico stretched and yawned and got up too. Then Rosita followed him out the door, and gestured him closer to say something she didn't want anybody else to hear.

She said, "Titus Hardy and his men stopped in here on their way out of town."

Eli should have anticipated as much.

He cleared his throat. "Rainey had some stories to tell, is what you mean to say. About the new midwife. Miss Ballentyne."

She patted him on the shoulder. "He did, but hold up, that's nothing much to worry about. Wasn't anybody in here just then except Ray Ingalls, and you know he's pure deaf."

It wasn't often he saw Red Rosita unsure of herself, but she was hesitating now.

He asked her, "*¿Qué pasa?*" What's up?

That was when she told him about what was going on with the Markhams.

Outside, Eli paused to listen to the commotion just across the way at El Taquito. Chico had been quiet the whole time he sat at Eli's feet in the cantina, but now he gave a low growl. He disapproved of the whistling and shouting and stamping that came from the gambling den. Most likely they were throwing dice, with most of the players drunk.

He clicked his tongue, and Chico settled without an argument.

The trouble at El Taquito might settle, too, eventually, but it was just as likely that there would be bloodshed. When you mixed men and liquor together with gambling and whores, tempers tended to flare. It occurred to him that one of his cousins or brothers might be over there raising hell, but he put the thought away. Tomorrow he would go out to the ranch to see his people, and that was soon enough. Right at this moment he was worried about Carrie.

He had thought of her on the other side of town, sleeping peacefully. Sam Markham was rich, and rich men with families were careful. Markham had armed guards, experienced and well paid, who kept watch through the night. An attack or raid or burglary was unlikely, but Eli realized now that he hadn't thought much about other kinds of trouble that might be waiting for her.

A half hour ago he thought he would fall asleep right where he sat, but he was awake now.

It was the kind of summer night he liked best, with a breeze that felt like a gentle touch on the cheek, and a sky full of stars. He could take a walk, make sure everything was peaceful over there. Of course Carrie wouldn't like it. He imagined her, frowning, her head tilted back so she could look him directly in the eye while she advanced on him, a hand planted firmly on his chest.

Let me remind you, she would say, *that I am more than capable of taking care of myself. I have weapons. I know how to use them. And what kind of trouble exactly are you imagining, that would make you walk across town in the middle of the night?*

Just at that point he realized that Carrie didn't know where he lived or how to find him. She was as good as stranded in a household with a man who was dying, a woman who had lost her mind, and Lulu. A clever child, but a child, still.

He reminded himself that there were more people in the house: Josefa, Manuela, and Carlos. All of them more than just capable. That might be enough to let him get to sleep.

Chico was sampling the air, his head swinging back and forth as he took in Santa Fe. Looking for something. A good time. A fight. A meal. A female.

If Chico was so inclined, they would take a walk. Just a short one, across town and back again.

37

In the morning Carrie woke to light pouring in through two deep-set, arched windows to shine on Lulu, who sat on the floor, legs crossed and hands folded primly in her lap.

"Good morning," Carrie said, wiping sleep from her eyes.

The girl hopped up. "Good morning!" And then, in a great rush: "I'm supposed to say that Josefa will be bringing your clothes in just a few minutes. And I wondered if you might need some help. As you don't know your way around."

The girl wanted her attention—or, Carrie corrected herself, Lulu needed her mother's attention. Because she could not have that one thing she never imagined she might lose, she was hoping for someone who was willing to pretend with her that nothing had changed and her mother was readily available to her.

How much Lulu had been told about the stillbirth, how much she had reasoned out for herself, those were questions that Carrie needed to ask, but not just yet. First, she had to earn Lulu's trust, and that would require that they spend time together.

She was about to suggest that Lulu join her for breakfast, when the girl's attention shifted to the window that looked out over the narrow street. Children were passing, girls just a little older than Lulu, agitated and breathless and urging each other to hurry, hurry, hurry. Lulu pulled a stool over to the window and climbed up on it to look out. Carrie came closer too.

The little girls had crossed the street and were running alongside a high adobe wall.

"Lulu, what is behind that wall, do you know?"

Without taking her eyes away from the girls, she said, "The old convent. And the bishop's house and a rectory. Then the parish church, and then the boys' school. All the way at the other side is the Academy of our Lady of Light, where the nuns teach girls. Look, that's Sister Agatha. Oh, they are in trouble, those three. It's a very bad thing to be tardy."

A nun had appeared from around the far end of the wall. Her face, already narrow, was pressed tightly on all sides by a stark white wimple that set off the black linen of veil and habit. She stood, arms crossed and hands tucked into the wide sleeves, motionless, and said nothing. Her gaze fixed on the girls who stood in front of her, heads bowed. For as much as thirty seconds, they were all silent. Even watching, so far removed, was painful.

In a whisper Lulu said, "At least she's not yelling."

In fact, Sister Agatha continued to say nothing at all, and then without warning she straightened her right arm and pointed away from herself to a spot that was out of Carrie's line of sight. The girls broke and ran.

Lulu pushed out a whistling breath between her missing front teeth. "That was exciting."

"I would call it more awkward," Carrie said. "But I don't know very much about the way Catholic schools are run."

Lulu squared her shoulders and stepped down from the stool, where she sat and once again folded her hands in her lap.

"I'll explain."

And she did just that, launching into a brief lecture on the fine points of Catholic education by the Sisters of Loretto here in Santa Fe. She had been paying attention, this little girl, and she was observant. When she finished explaining the complexities of the Catholic schools, she went on to describe the Baptist academy, founded by a Reverend Read.

"People like Reverend Read," Lulu summed up. Then she amended her evaluation. "People like him better than Sister Agatha."

According to Lulu, there were three nuns who taught in the school, and another who stayed in the convent and was never seen. The housekeeping nun, Lulu called her. There were rumors children weren't supposed to hear about, if Carrie might be interested.

Discretion was the only real choice here, and so Carrie changed the subject.

"Will you be going to the convent school?"

"No," Lulu said sadly. "It's not what my mother wants."

This gave Carrie pause and made her wonder in that moment if Mrs. Markham had envisioned Carrie as her daughter's governess. Not a topic to raise with Lulu.

"Then to Reverend Read's academy?"

Lulu blinked at her, surprised. "Only boys in his school."

So the only choice for a young girl interested in learning about the world was to attend a Catholic school—which might involve converting, as far as Carrie knew.

"The nuns ain't all cranky," Lulu said quite easily. "Just mostly Agatha. Do you know any nuns?"

"I know quite a few nuns who are nurses, some I've met through work and some through friends. I don't know any sisters from the order of St. Loretto, or any who teach, but I expect they are like people everywhere. Some can be—"

"Cranky," Lulu supplied.

It was as good a word as any, and as much as Carrie was comfortable saying. It would not be a good idea to share any more of her thoughts on the subject, because someday Lulu might indeed end up in a Catholic school classroom. In the course of her education, she would learn that some nuns were well-meaning but ineffective, while others liked children and teaching both, and then of course there were the ones who shouldn't have been teachers to start with. If Lulu was fortunate, there would be few Sister Agathas in her future.

Carrie knew a lot about teachers and teaching; it was a family calling that began with her Grandmother Bonner more than fifty years before. For a moment she wondered if her Cousin Jennet, who taught the youngest students in the Paradise village school, might be willing to come to Santa Fe. She could start a school of her own, one independent of both the Baptist and Catholic churches. Girls welcome.

The idea made her smile: she hadn't been here for a full day, and her mind already turned to rebellion.

Carrie had begun the long process of brushing out her hair and pinning it up while she listened to Lulu's recitation. For weeks she had worn a plait, but here in Santa Fe there was no excuse; she was an adult, a mature woman, and could not present herself like a fourteen-year-old. She had just finished when Josefa knocked and came in with a stack of towels and linen in her arms. Lulu ducked behind her and was out the door, almost colliding with an older woman carrying more laundry. The second woman resembled Josefa so strongly that Carrie was sure they must be related.

"Your clothes," Josefa said. "Everything from your saddlebags has been brushed and pressed. I've kept back one of the skirts to soak."

"You are very efficient," Carrie said. "And thoughtful." Then she spoke to the other woman directly and asked her name, in her careful Spanish.

The older woman glanced up at her and dropped her gaze again. "Manuela, señora."

Manuela, Josefa explained, was her father's sister, also of the San Juan Pueblo, and she was here every day to help with the cleaning and laundry.

"You will rarely see my aunt. She stays out of sight."

Because, Carrie understood without being told, Mrs. Markham

wanted the servants who cared for her family to be invisible. Manuela left, murmuring a few words to her niece as she went, in a language that Carrie took as Pueblo.

She would have asked about this, but Josefa, busy with sorting through the laundry, had more to say.

"The doctor is waiting for you in the dining room, did you know?"

"He said last night what time I should join him. And Mrs. Markham?"

"Sleeping, for another hour at least."

Carrie considered for a moment. She said, "Lulu spends a lot of time with you in the kitchen?"

Josefa hung a skirt on a hook, and then turned to look at Carrie directly. A challenge was coming. Carrie didn't know this younger woman at all, but she could see that she would not simply accept Carrie because she had been told to.

She said, "Yes. You don't approve of her spending time in the kitchen, or with us, or both?"

"I'm glad she has a place to spend her time," Carrie said. "A safe place."

That was as close as she could come, at this moment, to raising the topic of the doll Mrs. Markham insisted was a living infant.

Josefa was studying Carrie closely. Finally, she said, "We watch over Lulu, all of us who work for the Markhams. We watch closely."

"I'm glad to hear it," Carrie said. "And what can you do for Mrs. Markham? Can you think of anything that we should be doing for her?"

After a moment Josefa shook her head. "I can tell you that Lulu is safe and well looked after." About her mistress she would say nothing more.

DR. MARKHAM HAD already finished his breakfast when Carrie joined him. There were just a few crumbs on his plate, which might mean he had had a big appetite, or no appetite at all, but Josefa served Carrie a meal that would have fed two hungry men: eggs, beans and ham, cornmeal mush, and biscuits with butter and honey. She thought of Eli and what he would eat for breakfast. She knew nothing of how he lived, whether there was a housekeeper or if he cooked for himself.

"So I'll start," Dr. Markham said, "with a summary of the kind of cases I see here, and the therapies and medicines I most often use."

While she ate, she listened to the doctor talking about the dispensary, the scope of his practice, and how he liked things to be organized. Not a word was said about Mrs. Markham, and Carrie was fairly sure that he would stop her if she tried to pick up last evening's conversation where it had ended. Sooner rather than later she would have to raise the subject, no matter how little he liked it.

When she had finished, Dr. Markham called to Josefa that they were leaving for the dispensary. To Carrie's surprise, this did not require that they leave the house. Instead they walked through the *placita* and down a short corridor to another door. The doctor used a key that was clipped to his suspender by a chain to open the door, and then paused to glance down the hall.

He said, "This kind of hallway is called a zaguan." His tone was almost peevish, as if he had just realized that she didn't speak Spanish, and must take that into account. With the door open, familiar smells were there to greet Carrie, sharp and caustic, sweet and herbal. She would concentrate on things besides Dr. Markham's irritation. It was something nurses learned to do quite early in their training.

Beyond the reception area, there were two rooms for exams, another that must serve as a surgery, and one large room outfitted with six hospital cots, all neatly made up and empty.

"Feast or famine," Carrie said, mostly to herself.

"Yes," said Dr. Markham. "Big cities or small towns, that is our lot."

"When were the beds last all occupied at once?"

"Six months ago," he said. "Typhoid. I saved six, lost nine. It hit the pueblos much harder, as is almost always the case."

They sat in his office, roughly the size of a storage cabinet. His desk took up most of the space, and as thin as he was, he had to turn sideways to get to the chair behind it. Carrie sat in the single chair opposite him and listened as he went on talking about the practice. There was nothing particularly alarming or off-putting in what he had to say, and certainly nothing surprising. Dr. Markham had trained in New York and held tight to the methods he had learned there. Carrie had her own basic rules, but he did not ask, and she did not volunteer that information. Generally, physicians were not interested in either a nurse's or a midwife's opinions.

At the same time, most physicians considered themselves perfectly capable of delivering an infant. In fact, they often complicated a birth that was already difficult. If a child presented so awkwardly that the birth could not advance, a midwife with narrow, strong, flexible hands was far more likely to coax that new life into the world than any doctor with tobacco-stained fingernails and filthy shirtsleeves.

Amelie had warned her about such things many times. "In a crisis, do not volunteer information," she had cautioned. "The physician will not thank you for it, but he will remember your attempt to interfere, as he will call it. Or worse still, decide to teach you a lesson."

Carrie already missed Amelie, who had a dry sense of humor and little patience with physicians who were unaware of their ineptitude. She said as much, on occasion. Any other midwife who was so blunt with a doctor would face repercussions, but there was something about Amelie that made men pause.

"My face," she would say, when Carrie raised the subject. "My Mohawk-Seminole-African-Scots face."

"Your frowning face," Carrie would counter. "The intelligence that cannot be overlooked or denied." And then the subject would be put aside.

She wished with all her heart for Amelie, who would almost certainly know what to make of Mrs. Markham's condition.

"Later this morning, if we aren't busy, we'll go see about a horse for you."

The shift in subject took her by surprise. The doctor mistook her expression for reluctance. "Would you rather wait until your brother is here to advise you?"

"That's not it," she told him. "It's just that Nathan and I bought horses from a rancher near Westport, the day before we set out with Mr. Petit. Then later we crossed paths with Mr. Hardy, and I rode my own horse all the way here."

He lowered his chin to look at her over the top of his spectacles. "That will save some trouble, but I have to ask, where have you hidden it?"

Of course he would ask this very obvious question. She would have to talk about Eli Ibarra now, before she had had a chance to work out the best approach.

"There was a fourth man riding with Titus Hardy," she said. "Eli Ibarra, a surveyor. I think you must know him. As we arrived so late in the day yesterday, he took my horse to stable with his own."

Sometimes calm confidence could smooth over a clumsy answer, but as it turned out, Eli's name had been enough.

"Eli's come home? That's good to hear. You know, we should just walk over there. I'd like to see this horse of yours, and we'll bring her back here and get her settled across the way at Guevara's."

For a moment Carrie was so taken aback that she couldn't respond. Then she remembered that Eli was leaving town today to see his family. Odd that she should be disappointed and relieved by a single fact.

She said, "It would be nice to take a walk." It was the truth, if not the whole truth. Eli wouldn't be there, and almost certainly he had taken all the horses with him. She could only hope that Dr. Markham wouldn't press for details. He would expect her to be surprised and even unsettled by the idea that Eli Ibarra had left town with her horse, but she could not be either of those things. Between here and there, she would have to think of something. In the meantime Dr. Markham would introduce her to people he thought she should know. She would make the most of that opportunity.

Leaving the house, they turned left and then left again. Ahead Carrie could see and hear something of the plaza, but first they walked past Santa Fe's only hotel, quite large and well maintained. The sign hanging over the main entrance read simply:

U.S. HOTEL

FONDA

PRIMO GUZMAN

The first line, in strong black lettering, looked freshly painted. Below it, *fonda*—the Spanish word for hotel or inn—was very faded. Was it meant to be symbolic of the U.S. Army's victory over Mexico? She asked the doctor, and got a surprised look from him.

"Nothing so sophisticated or thoughtful," he said. "They changed the name to suit the territorial government, but only on that sign. Everyone still calls the place fonda." Once he had started talking about the hotel, he paused long enough to tell her that the owner often suffered with gout, that his wife was losing her hearing at a relatively young age, and his youngest son was a troublemaker with a weakness for gambling, in particular when it came to horse races and dogfights.

Then the plaza opened up before them. On the right was a long, low building. All the buildings were built of adobe, but this dominant one looked to be the oldest and most careworn. Dr. Markham frowned at it, in a way that reminded Carrie of someone who was ashamed of something of value but no beauty.

"It doesn't look like much," he said. "But that's the seat of the territorial government. Officially it is El Palacio Real. The Palace of the Governors. Another time we'll stop in there so you can meet the governor. Today the market is enough of a distraction."

And that was certainly true. Outdoor markets were always interesting. People came to buy or sell or trade—salt or spoons, goats or piglets, brooms or buckets, meal or seed corn. At the same time, the Santa Fe market was undeniably different from the markets at home. In Manhattan, markets were full of people who were always moving and making noise. Merchants called out to customers, bragging about their wares, exaggerating outrageously to keep the customer's attention and draw her in. Butchers bellowed creative insults at each other in a half dozen languages, and some of them sang impromptu songs about the quality of their wares.

Santa Fe was a more serious place. Somber, Carrie might have said, despite what seemed to be an abundant harvest so early in the summer and beautiful weather. The smell of fresh earth and herbs was familiar and comforting in a way she hadn't anticipated. Baskets of squash and melons, blackberries and tomatoes and herbs were watched over— mostly by women. They were the ones who handled sales, as well, negotiating prices in many cases in an almost silent pantomime, inso- far as she could tell.

In several places she saw baskets overflowing with what looked like clumps of sugared nuts. Carrie got up her courage far enough to ask what they were called, and was surprised to learn that these were pine nuts—piñones—that had been roasted and sugared. The young woman who was selling them assured Carrie of their quality.

"*Las nueces más deliciosas.*" A great treat, the most delicious.

Dr. Markham raised a doubtful eyebrow. "*Muy caras.*"

She didn't argue with his criticism of the price but explained, her eyes fixed on her hands, that the harvest had been poor. It seemed she would have gone on, but Dr. Markham held up a palm to stop her, and walked on.

Now Carrie had evidence that the doctor's patience was near its end, so she followed him at a brisker pace, looking around herself to get a sense of what was being offered: long braids of onions and dried peppers, sacks of corn and beans, new peas, honey in casks, rock salt. In the section of the market where trappers and tanners sold their wares, Carrie saw every variety of leather, tanned and raw. There was a toddler napping atop a great pile of buffalo hides while an older brother watched over other, more valuable leathers and pelts and furs.

When Nathan arrived it would fall to her to educate him on a new place and new customs, though that was usually his role to play. In that moment she realized that she saw no sign of Sam Markham any- where nearby. It wasn't anything to worry about, she told herself. He would find her when he was ready to move on, and in the meantime she would look her fill.

The marketplace was awash with color, so bright that her eyes began to tear. Color began with the people themselves. She saw few faces that looked like her own; for the most part the people around her were Mexican or Mestizo, Pueblo or Navajo, or something else entirely. In Manhattan she had had Italian patients, who would not have looked out of place in Santa Fe. Only their hair—unruly masses— would differentiate them from these people, whose hair fell sleek and straight from their scalps.

She realized, too, that she saw no one whom she recognized as clearly African. Of course it was guesswork; she hadn't been here long enough to recognize the ways individuals signaled their allegiances and kinships. A particular way of cutting or parting hair might be associated with one tribe or another, just as jewelry or beading could signal family or clan or tribe allegiances. Accent—which languages an individual spoke, and how—was the clearest way people announced their place in the world, and it was the first thing two strangers evaluated when they met. *You are one of my people,* or *You are like my people,* or *You may be like some of my people but I don't recognize you as a friend.* And then: *You do not belong. You are a threat that must be turned away.* She had seen instant dislike and open hostility rise up among immigrants in New York. One group of Germans turning their backs on another on the basis of a single word. A Bible story that repeated itself again and again, everywhere and always.

Carrie would not know how to interpret what she heard until she learned not just Spanish but at least some of the other languages being spoken all around the plaza. That would take time and effort, and the cooperation of the people who spoke those languages. Assuming they would be willing to share something so precious with her. To them she must look like just another one of the great flood of emigrants who never stopped coming, unfamiliar and unaware, and still they assumed so much, consumed too much, like a plague of locusts.

The Indians tended to gather in specific areas in the plaza, and they were somewhat easier to pick out, as they dressed much like the Kiowa they had sheltered with on the trail. Men and women both wore traditional clothes made of cured skins and wool and homespun.

Practical clothes with little ornamentation. The finer embroidered and beaded tunics and leggings and dresses, the ceremonial costumes and headpieces, would be stored carefully away, and rarely seen by whites.

In contrast, the Mexican and Mestizo women wore gauzy, loose-cut white blouses under sleeveless tunics with long scarves looped around their shoulders. Their layered skirts reminded Carrie of tulips: tightly wrapped at the waist but flaring out so that the hems swung around ankles to allow easy movement. Their bright colors—scarlets and purples, oranges and blues, and a hundred different shades of green—put her in mind of the hummingbirds she had begun to keep track of in her letters home.

In Spanish she asked a young woman what the tunics she was selling were called, and in reply got a shy smile as well as a brief lesson in the names of the clothing that was unfamiliar to her. The tunics were called huipil and the long woven scarves were rebozos. The woman held out a scarf for Carrie to examine, this one of beautiful deep blue with intersecting white stripes. She wondered about the dyes that were used, but that was a conversation that would have to wait for another day, and most likely a translator as well.

It occurred to her just then that the love of color she saw all around her might have something to do with the landscape. Santa Fe was an island in a sea of sand, a world cast in shades of ochre and umber, rusty greens and sepias. Of course strong blues and deep greens and bright reds would appeal.

Finally she caught sight of Dr. Markham standing in the shade under the awning of a shop on the edge of the market. A general store, with the name Goldblum in arching letters across a plate glass window. He jumped a little when she came up, starting out of his thoughts, but before she could apologize for causing a delay, he half turned toward the shop door.

"As we are here, I'd like to introduce you to a lady who will be in need of your services later in the summer. If you have no objection."

Just the opposite, she might have said. It was a relief to know that the doctor had not forgotten what she had come to Santa Fe to do.

The general store was good-sized, with a long counter and a wall of shelving filled with bolts of fabric and boxes neatly labeled. On one side of the room were household items, from barrels of crackers to cook pots and brooms, and on the other, tools that a carpenter or rancher or farmer would need. Two women and a young girl stood at a table examining a bolt of dimity and arguing about the color. In one corner an old man slept in a rocking chair, a ginger-colored dog at his feet, both snoring and muttering back and forth like an old married couple. A man in a handsome suit studied a catalog, leaning over the counter and squinting at the page, while he asked the clerk who hovered just at his elbow for information.

There were customers enough to keep four clerks moving quickly, something that worked to Carrie's advantage, as being the center of attention never sat well with her. Any stranger—in particular any white female who dressed well and presented herself as well raised—would be of great interest in a town this size. For the moment Carrie looked like all the travel-weary emigrants, but that would change. At that point she would lose her ability to disappear into corners.

"Dr. Markham." A middle-aged man came out from behind the counter, wiping his hands on a bit of towel. He was polite, welcoming but dignified, with a yarmulke pinned to a full head of graying hair. Eva had told her about the Goldblum family of merchants, four brothers who had come to the States from Germany and stayed on the East Coast only long enough to meet young women of good families, most often at Shabbat dinners or religious ceremonies. All four married within a year and moved west, family by family, to settle in Santa Fe.

It had struck Eva as a very unusual story, which it certainly would seem to be to someone who lived west of the Mississippi. Sometime Carrie would have to tell stories about the emigrant neighborhoods in Manhattan—German, Irish, English, French, Italian, Polish—each with its own customs and habits.

Now Mr. Goldblum—this one called Zalman—inclined his head and shoulders toward Carrie in the way of fastidious clerks unsure of a person's status but unwilling to chance offense. To Sam Markham he said, "How may I help you today?"

Dr. Markham made short work of introductions. Some would judge him to be abrupt and awkward, but Carrie appreciated his efficiency. He finished by asking if Mrs. Goldblum was available for a short consultation.

"Better than that," said Mr. Goldblum. "All three of them are here, busy sewing for the—what is the word—layettes. Please, go back to the apartment. You will be very welcome, Miss Ballentyne."

Three of the four Goldblum wives were expecting. This was important information that Carrie hoped Dr. Markham would have shared with her even without prompting. But he might not have known. Or worse, remembered.

In Zalman Goldblum's comfortable parlor, Dr. Markham repeated the introductions, telling Rivka, Miriam, and Chava Goldblum something of Carrie's training and experience. Then he stepped back to let the women talk—maybe, Carrie thought, because he really couldn't rely on his memory.

As expected, each of them wanted her to understand that they were far from homes and families that they missed terribly. At the same time they were proud that the Goldblum brothers were so successful in establishing businesses here, and considered themselves fortunate in their husbands. Two of them were from Boston, and the youngest, Rivka, from New York. She mentioned her father's haberdashery, and brightened when Carrie could say that yes, she knew of it.

Chava wanted Carrie to hear about her own mother, a midwife. "She came west with us in '46, and delivered my first two."

"And also my daughters," volunteered Miriam. "Rivka is new at the business, though. It's her first."

That was an interesting fact. Carrie wondered if she had been trying to conceive for more than ten years, a question she would ask when she saw the young woman privately.

"To be honest," Chava said, not willing yet to give up the floor, "I wanted Mama to stay, and I think she didn't want to leave. But my father couldn't do without her for even one day more."

Her sisters-in-law exchanged knowing glances, but kept their opinions to themselves.

"We are so glad to have a new midwife," Rivka said, for the third time.

"I hope to be of service," Carrie said. "I realize that Dr. Markham has been looking after you, but if I could ask some basic questions—"

"Excellent idea," Sam Markham said. "I'll leave you to it, then."

Carrie wondered if this visit had been calculated to afford him the chance to slip away, but in the end it didn't really matter. It wasn't a big town, and they would find each other soon enough.

As the door closed behind the doctor, another on the other end of the room opened, and a very pretty, very quiet girl brought in a cart holding a tea service. A white woman who worked as a servant struck Carrie as odd, given what she knew about Santa Fe, but then Chava introduced her as a family member.

"Danya has been with us since she was six months old," she told Carrie. "She is a tremendous help with the children." There seemed to be nothing else of value to tell about the girl, but Carrie didn't like the curt dismissal.

"Hello," she said, addressing the young woman directly. "You must have been very young when you emigrated. Do you have any memories of home?"

"Santa Fe is my home," Danya Goldblum said. "I want no other."

There was a defiant edge to her voice that earned her a sharp look from Chava, and she inclined her head in acknowledgment.

"Miss Ballentyne," she went on in a softer tone. "Welcome to Santa Fe. I am glad to see you arrived safely. Your help is needed in the dispensary."

All heads turned in Danya's direction. It was a challenge, of sorts, but she held up her head and kept her gaze on Carrie.

"I wanted to ask," Danya said, "if I may. I heard today that Eli

Ibarra rode into town with Mr. Hardy and his men. And you, of course. Is that so?"

Chava's brow drew down so that a deep V appeared. "And if it is? The surveyor is none of your concern. Don't you have a letter to finish writing?"

Carrie answered the question, not even looking in Chava's direction. "Yes, we all rode in together. Is Mr. Ibarra a friend?"

"Yes," Danya said. "A good friend."

She turned to the tea service and made short work of pouring and passing cups, putting an end to the discussion that continued to occupy Carrie. The Goldblums objected to what, exactly? That the girl had friends? Male friends? Dark-skinned friends? But this was not a subject she wanted to discuss with the Goldblum wives; it never ended well when a midwife let herself get caught up in family dynamics, and so she concentrated on them as expectant mothers.

Her first and most important duty as a midwife was to listen closely, and she did that now.

Male doctors would never replace midwives, in Amelie's opinion, because they didn't care to listen to women talk about personal matters. The few who understood the importance didn't know how to listen without interrupting, always sure that their comments and suggestions would be welcome.

In the end, a woman did need to talk about her pregnancy, and to be heard.

From Rivka, Carrie heard about severe morning sickness that lasted all day long, until just recently when she felt the first flutter that allayed all her fears. She believed her baby would come near the end of the year, and her sisters-in-law nodded in agreement. Chava, who thought that her time would come in the last of the summer, spoke of heartburn and leg cramps, and asked whether Carrie had any teas to recommend that might be a help.

"Something other than laudanum," she said. "I truly cannot tolerate the taste."

Carrie blinked her surprise, but held back the questions that came to mind. Instead she'd ask Dr. Markham about medications the dispensary gave to expectant mothers. If in fact they dispensed laudanum so easily, there might be complications ahead.

Then Miriam, who had two girls and was by her own reckoning very close to delivery, announced that she had no complaints. No heartburn, no cramps, she slept well and was able to eat. And more than that, in case the midwife Ballentyne was wondering, she, Miriam Goldblum née Dobkin, would be thankful to bring a healthy child into the world. She was not hoping in particular for a son.

Chava's left eyebrow peaked.

Carrie kept her expression blank, but she was amused. Sisters and sisters-in-law knew how to tweak each other in ways that men overlooked or didn't understand. Whether the purpose was gentle teasing or the intent was cruel, every woman knew when barbs were being lodged.

Of course Miriam was hoping for a boy, as was her husband. But she didn't want to say so, out of superstition or tradition or simple fear.

Carrie was about to thank them for the opportunity to visit and to assure them that they could send for her at any time about heartburn or any other issue, no matter how small. Tea for Mrs. Chava Goldblum—Carrie wondered briefly if she would always have to use full names to avoid confusion—would be ready later in the day, and would be delivered.

At that Chava stopped her. She leaned forward, lowered her embroidery to her lap, and spoke more softly.

"You just arrived, of course, but may I ask—" She paused, Carrie thought, to gather her courage.

"Are you comfortable with the Markhams?"

She had hoped that this subject wouldn't be raised so soon, but it was too much to expect. There would be rumors about Indira Markham, that was inevitable. Whether out of real concern or something less admirable, everyone must want to know what had happened and why Mrs. Markham had not shown herself—or her newborn—for so long. Of course it was also possible that the Goldblum wives could provide information that would be helpful, but Carrie simply could not indulge in gossip.

This was, in fact, a test. They wanted her to tell them about Indira Markham, but if she did, they would never really trust her. And they would let everyone else know that she wasn't to be trusted.

She said, "I am very comfortable. I lack for nothing."

"And Josefa?" asked Miriam. "Do you think you'll get on with her?"

Carrie didn't hesitate. "She has been very helpful, and from what I've seen, she is an excellent housekeeper."

"Unusual," Miriam said. "For her kind."

"You must be referring to her youth," Carrie said, her tone cooler now. "I will assume you are referring to her youth."

There was a short, tense silence. In that moment it seemed that Miriam would take up the challenge and talk of her dislike and distrust of Indians. But Carrie never wavered or looked away, and Miriam Goldblum dropped her gaze.

Carrie summoned up a friendly smile and asked one last question. "Can you tell me where I'd find Mrs. Zavala's shop?"

She had surprised them, of course, and she went on to explain.

"We traveled from St. Louis to Council Bluffs together," she told them. "And I heard quite a bit about her business."

Rivka's face broke into a smile. "What good luck for you. For both of you," she said. "Of course you want to see her shop. I'll take you."

"Oh, please." Chava, exasperated, held up a hand. "You can't run around in the sun, Rivka. Not in your condition. Danya can show her."

Carrie might have protested, but then again this was an opportunity to talk to the girl who declared herself a good friend of Eli's. Danya seemed self-possessed and confident, unswayed by the disapproval of her elders, and willing to take a position. This was someone she wanted to know.

38

ALL THE PLANS for the day came to a sudden end as Carrie opened the door to the general store to find that Mr. Goldblum was right there, just about to enter.

"Miss Ballentyne." He took a step back, and then another. "The doctor has gone back to his dispensary. There's been an accident, and he will need your help."

He told her what he knew: A wagon had tipped over and crushed a man's leg. Leon Cuevas by name, he worked the hide and tallow concern on the other side of town.

"Dr. Markham said I was to wait to tell you until you finished talking to the sisters."

Carrie picked up her skirts and ran.

She avoided the market, circling around on the far side of the plaza, and slowed only once when she realized that she was looking directly at the parish church Lulu had been telling her about just this morning. The little girl had described the whole setting perfectly; the church was a plump adobe-pink hen, surrounded by smaller buildings, her chicks. No sign, Carrie was glad to see, of the Sisters of Loretto. One challenge at a time.

Friends and family of the injured man had gathered outside the dispensary. She could almost identify them, though she had never seen Leon Cuevas. She took a man in his seventies for a grandfather. He held a little boy who had fallen asleep with his face pressed into the man's chest and his fingers twisted into a hank of snow-white beard.

Carrie saw all this in the few seconds it took her to slip through the crowd and into the dispensary, where still more people stood watch, all silent except for the click of rosary beads. All eyes turned toward her, and without a word the crowd parted to make a path so that she could pass.

There was a slick of blood just outside the surgery. She stepped around it, opened the door, and found that once again she was too late to be of help. Dr. Markham had already finished the amputation. A man of perhaps twenty was assisting him as he dressed the stump. They both looked up at Carrie as she came in.

"Nurse Ballentyne," he said. "This is John Edmonds. He'll assist you here. I assume you know how to proceed."

He didn't explain, but Carrie saw for herself that he would not be able to stand for another five minutes. His color, so pallid at breakfast, had taken on a greenish tinge, and there was a tremor in his hands.

While he stood, leaning against a wall to gather his strength, she pretended that he was not in need of medical assistance himself. There was no reason to embarrass him in front of his patients.

She said, "Prognosis?"

"What do you think?"

Carrie took Leon Cuevas's pulse and lifted his eyelids to check the size of his pupils. Sometimes secondary injuries were overlooked in the rush to save a life, but she saw no evidence of a blow to the head, at least not yet.

He was no more than twenty-five, heavily muscled in the way of men who worked with large animals. His hands were calloused and gritty, dirt worked into the nail beds and creases in the skin. He smelled of oxen, of rendering tallow and sweat, and of the blood that soaked his clothes.

That he had survived the surgery was a testament to an excellent constitution, but that would not be enough to save him. He had lost most of his left leg and far too much blood; infection was almost unavoidable with this kind of injury.

"He'll be gone by morning. Maybe later tomorrow, if he fights. I will get as much fluid into him as I can, of course, but there's little else to be done."

Sam Markham nodded. "I'll talk to the family. They'll want to see him right away, but let's wait until he's cleaned up at least a little. John is a very good assistant." He was looking at the boy but didn't take the time to introduce them to each other properly.

When the doctor closed the door behind himself, Carrie caught sight of two women, one quite young. Leon's wife or sister, his mother. Holding each other up in the face of disaster.

"They should be in here with him." Carrie spoke mostly to herself, but caught John's expression: relief, first and foremost.

She said, "Do you know the family well?"

He nodded. "I do."

"That will be a great help. But first I will need a number of things: my medical bag, which is next to the table in my room, as much hot water as you can bring me, strong soap, rubbing alcohol, washcloths, and clean sheets. Can you ask Carlos for help with the hot water?"

"Yes," he said. "I'll ask him right away."

Alone with the young man whose life could be counted in hours, Carrie sat.

She said, "This is a terrible, tragic thing that has happened to you. If you can summon your strength and fight, we will do everything we can to save your life."

A reaction would have been a surprise, but she still watched for a full minute. A flicker of an eyelid, a click in the throat, these would be evidence, to Carrie's mind, that the man was still aware of the world. It seemed that Leon Cuevas was not.

Carrie had not yet had a chance to speak to the older man she had seen on her arrival, but she knew his name was Carlos. He was quick and quiet, very alert, and she was glad of another set of hands. He brought a large basin of very hot water just as John returned. Carrie washed her hands with the soap provided, wishing she had thought to ask for her nail brush. John washed his hands, too, without questions or hesitation, which eased some of Carrie's concerns. When she uncorked the bottle of slippery elm from her bag, he asked the first question.

"May I ask—"

While Carrie cut away the dressings so recently applied to the stump, she gave him a short and insufficient answer that amounted to a challenge. The next day, when they both were rested and not busy, she would show him.

Then she examined the surgical incision closely. The stitches were well placed and regular, and there was very little seepage. Dr. Markham might not be strong enough to last long in an emergency, but his work was careful.

Working with John, she cleared away the bloody linen and replaced it. Under the stump she folded a towel, stopped to wash her hands again, and poured the distillation of winterbloom and slippery elm over the surgical incision, waited a minute, and poured once more.

In a quarter hour she had wrapped the stump carefully, first with a layer of gauze she saturated with more slippery elm, and then again, taking care to wrap with the right amount of tension.

By this time Carrie understood some things about John. He was a skilled, exacting, observant nurse. As young as he was, John made it possible for Dr. Markham to continue to practice medicine. When he was too ill to see patients, John would provide basic care.

It was time to bring the family members in, but Carrie found she couldn't hold back the questions that were stacking up in her mind.

"I don't know how much Dr. Markham told you about me," she began. "Or even if you knew another nurse had been hired."

John was sorting through the soiled linen, but he glanced up at her and smiled, a little awkwardly. "He gave me your letters to read."

"Ah, well. Good. But I don't know anything about you. How did you come to work with Dr. Markham?"

"My father wanted to try his luck in the California goldfields. We left Florida in a wagon train. The men thought we were well prepared and armed."

He spoke only briefly about the attack by an Apache war party. The wagons burned, animals and provisions laid waste or stolen, young women and children abducted, and men killed. One survivor. John had been knocked unconscious early in the attack and woke, gasping for breath in the smoke from the burning wagons, underneath the bodies of his father and older brothers.

"They thought I was dead, so I survived," John said. "I expected to die. But an army scout came by later that day, and he brought me here to Santa Fe, to the Catholic church."

This part of his history was familiar; in Manhattan orphaned children roamed the streets every day of the year, and the ones who were too slow to avoid coppers got caught up to be handed over to one of the churches, Catholic or Protestant. Nuns made sure that every child was baptized (and thus claimed for their creed), fed, and clothed. If they couldn't reach any family members, the orphan would remain in the care of the church.

"If Doc Markham hadn't talked Mrs. Markham into taking me in, I might still be there, pulling weeds in the bishop's garden or headed off to seminary. But Dr. Markham said he needed an assistant, and as I could read and write, he wanted to train me himself. That started the next day, and I've been working here ever since."

Most important, he told her, was the fact that he liked the work and had been accepted at Bellevue to train as a doctor.

Carrie supposed that this was the reason Dr. Markham had started looking for a nurse; John would be gone, and Markham could not continue practicing medicine without him, or someone like him.

"Your skills are impressive," she told him. "I think you will do well in medical school. In the meantime, as you know the practice and the town so well, I will depend on you. I hope you won't mind answering questions."

The compliment surprised and pleased him, and Carrie really was glad that John was here. He would be someone, she thought, she might be able to talk to.

Sitting watch over a patient who was unconscious and unlikely to survive was—on the surface at least—an uncomplicated business, especially when family members were able and willing to help. Carrie was glad to have Leon's mother and wife there, and glad, too, for Josefa and Manuela, who brought them fresh water and what seemed like an endless supply of clean linen and dressings.

John went to see to other patients as they arrived, and so the three women took turns feeding water and broth into Leon's mouth, slowly, carefully, watching to make sure he didn't choke. The first time he really swallowed—a good sign—his mother broke into a beatific smile.

"*Puede tragar.*"

"*Sí,*" Carrie confirmed.

She sat on one side of the table, and the two Mrs. Cuevases sat on the other, talking softly, praying, using a damp handkerchief to wipe the sweat from Leon's face. They did not ignore Carrie, but they were either unsure of her language skills or intimidated. There was no way to know how much they had heard about her. Rumors, certainly, which might be accurate but could also be as fanciful as a fairy tale.

In the late afternoon, Carrie's stomach reminded her that she had had nothing to eat since breakfast. The rumble was so loud that it couldn't be ignored, and Anita—Leon's wife—got up and left the room. It seemed unlikely that she could have taken offense, but Carrie was suddenly too weary to worry very much, if that was the case.

Then Anita was back, carrying a basket. Behind her was a younger man with two corked jugs. He put down his burden, paused to look at Leon, his face still and unreadable. He made the sign of the cross, and left again.

In short order Mrs. Cuevas was offering Carrie something wrapped in a piece of fabric.

She said, "*Por favor, come con nosotros. Sería un honor.*"

Even if Carrie had wanted to refuse the kind offer of food, her growling stomach would contradict any excuse she might offer. She thanked them for their thoughtfulness and unwrapped what turned out to be spicy lamb and black beans wrapped in a tortilla.

In Carrie's mind sharing a meal required that they speak to each other, though they were strangers. She began by asking about Leon, and as was usually the case, his mother especially felt the need to praise her boy. From what Carrie could follow, he worked hard, was helpful at home, went to church, was generous and fair-minded, and had once thought of being a priest. He had married just months ago, and was a loving husband to Anita.

Anita wanted to hear about her husband's injury and how she should care for the wound when he was home again.

Carrie told her what she wanted to know, keeping to herself the fear that the information would likely never be put to use. Just above the dressings on his left leg the skin was too warm, the first sign of infection setting in. She told them what they would need to know, though it was not easy, with her limited Spanish. With a combination of language, facial expressions, and pantomime, the most important points were made, including the fact that Carrie would come to their home twice a day until Leon had recovered completely.

Anita and Luisa Cuevas learned nothing that they would be able to put to use, but Carrie took away a dozen new words: *el muñón* for the surgical stump, and *crudo* for its raw, weeping state. The injury was due to *plastamiento*, the tremendous weight that had shattered his bones. Amputation was the only choice.

She said nothing—not yet—of fever or infection, but Luisa's expression was resigned and somber. Anita was not entertaining any thoughts of death. This man who had been her husband for such a short time would live. Of course he must live.

The difference between the two women was obvious: the elder Señora Cuevas had seen too much over the years; she understood what Carrie wasn't saying.

Through the rest of the day and late into the night, they worked together. They fed and washed him, changed his bedding when it was fouled, bathed his face and neck with water laced with vinegar. Just as the church bells tolled eleven o'clock, Anita fell asleep in the chair where she sat. It seemed Luisa had been waiting for this, because she moved closer to Carrie and asked the question that had been hanging in the air between them.

"*Tiene mucha fiebre, ¿no?*"

Carrie didn't know where she would find a thermometer in the dispensary, but that didn't matter. She knew, as his mother knew, that Leon had a fever. Changing the dressings and cleaning the incision site and sutures, she had seen plentiful evidence of an infection that had set down roots and begun to move.

"*Sí,*" she told his mother. She took a moment to find the right words, and put it as clearly and plainly as she was able: the infection was moving fast, and there was no way to stop it. "*No tenemos nada para detener la infección.*"

She said this just as Dr. Markham came into the room.

When he had finished examining his patient, he spoke for a while with the women, in the hushed tones of the sickroom. Carrie caught somewhere between a third and a half of what he told them: Leon was a strong young man, and he had a chance of surviving this. A chance.

To Carrie he said, "John will take over for three hours, and you should use that time to sleep."

In fact, John stood just behind the doctor in the shadows, where beads still clicked and women murmured their way through the rosary.

Just before the hall opened into the *placita*, Dr. Markham paused, and Carrie did too. The night air was cool and sweet, and Carrie turned her face up to the breeze and listened while the doctor murmured to himself. In the dim light of a single lantern, she could not make out much of his expression. She wondered if he was about to mention his inability to finish with the patient, and what that meant about her role here.

He cleared his throat. "You are a skilled and compassionate nurse," he said, studying his shoes as he spoke. Then he lifted his gaze and met her own.

"I understand that you have medications you have brought from New York, but you must agree to never use anything that is foreign or Indian or otherwise unfamiliar to me unless we have discussed it first, and I grant permission."

She blinked in surprise and then, hesitantly, nodded.

Dr. Markham turned and left her there, without another word.

39

June 10, 1857

Dear Amelie,
Just a few minutes ago I finished a letter to Ma, with a long
accounting of the journey. Nathan would call me lazy, but to my
mind it is simply common sense not to write out the story again. If
you read that account first, what I relate about my first days in
Santa Fe may be less confusing.

I'll begin with this very rough drawing of Dr. Markham's
property. You see the central open placita, which is where people
spend most of their time—for a good part of the year, as winter is a
relative term, I am told. Around the placita the house is divided
roughly into four parts. My chamber is in the lower right hand of
the residence, with windows on two sides. There are two more
chambers in this part of the house. From my chamber through the
placita and the passageway, I can reach the dispensary in two
minutes or less.

You know that when I arrived here late on Sunday evening
there was some reason to worry that Mrs. Markham was not well. I

feared she had lost the child and might herself have died. In fact, she did indeed miscarry about two weeks previous. I have no details about the delivery. The subject is forbidden, even when I am alone with Dr. Markham in the dispensary, but what I observed is troubling enough. To be exact: Mrs. Markham insists that she gave birth to a healthy daughter. She carries a doll wrapped in swaddling clothes with her at all times, talks to it and sings to it. She can and does speak to her husband and to Josefa, who keeps house for the Markhams, as if there were nothing unusual about a child who makes no sound and never moves.

I am, as she sees it, here to supervise Josefa and to be a nursemaid to Lulu, the first-born—a bright little girl her mother ignores, for the most part.

At the first opportunity, I reminded her, politely, that I am here as a nurse and midwife. Mrs. Markham's reaction was cold and dismissive. She gave birth to a healthy child and is recovered, and so, she told me, she had no use for me as a midwife. I would have to take up other chores in the household.

That conversation happened just a few hours after I arrived.

Yesterday I was in the dispensary for all the afternoon and much of the night with a laborer whose leg had to be amputated after an accident with a fully loaded wagon. You know well how cases like this end. The infection spread so rapidly that I suspect there was some other internal injury. His fever drove him into convulsions toward sunrise, and he was gone not an hour later.

This morning after his family had taken the unfortunate Mr. Cuevas off to arrange a mass and burial, I slept for a few hours. At midday Lulu came to ask me if I was coming to the table.

Neither Dr. nor Mrs. Markham joined us. We ate, just the two of us, a very good meal, and Lulu took that time to tell me all about the neighbors. She is shockingly well informed, but I'm not sure where she has learned what she knows. She does speak Spanish like a native, but she is rarely allowed outside the house and never without supervision. That is the official stance, but clearly, she has her ways around it. An example of the information she shared with me: The postmaster, originally of Minnesota, wrote home and asked his mother to find a proper wife for him and send her west. When she arrived Mr. Whiting didn't like the look of her hooked nose and sent her off again on the next wagon train. Lulu saw this as a practical response, because, she said, they had very little chance of learning to like each other.

We haven't talked directly about Lulu's own family or her mother's health. If we had been sitting together someplace more private, I think she might have raised the subject. This situation with her mother is a terrible strain on her, of course.

After the meal Josefa brought word that Mrs. Markham wanted to see me, and that I was needed in the dispensary as soon as I could manage. As soon as I stepped into the <u>placita</u> Mrs. Markham raised her voice and called my name. Lulu turned around and went back to the dining room. Later I learned that she spent the rest of the day in the kitchen with Josefa and Manuela. They are devoted to her, and protect her when they can from family troubles.

Mrs. Markham sat in the shade with her doll held to her breast. She did not ask me to be seated, and so I stood while she told me what a disappointment I was already, and how poorly I was fulfilling my duties. I never interrupted, even when the accusations became ludicrous. I can't think of a more appropriate word, because she insisted that I had mishandled her delivery and that I was spreading rumors in the town, lies about her newborn. She grew more and more agitated so that I had trouble composing my expression. She took every blink of the eye or twitch of a muscle as proof that I was contradicting what she knew to be true.

Finally Dr. Markham came in, and she collapsed as if she had just run a long distance. He apologized for the delay in bringing her medicine and dismissed me, saying that I should take his place in the dispensary. Then he sat beside his wife to give her a very large dose of laudanum.

I spent the afternoon in the clinic with John Edmonds, Dr. Markham's assistant. A very capable young man who knows everyone and makes it possible for me to talk to the patients who come in. While I cleaned and bound a gash the barber (Mr. Buzz Kelly) had given himself in a careless moment, I thought of the scene in the <u>placita</u> and asked myself the obvious question as I was trained to do by you and Aunt Hannah: <u>Ubi est morbus.</u> Where is the illness?

The illness is in Mrs. Markham's mind. While I was training I saw mild cases of puerperal insanity (Mrs. Gidney comes to mind, and Miss Bridge, I know you remember these cases because we talked about them at length). This seems a much more serious case. I fear Mrs. Markham may be now or might soon be a danger to herself and to others. There are no alienists or institutions for the insane within a thousand miles. And even if there were, Dr. Markham would not allow her to be admitted to such a place. He has decided that laudanum is what she needs. Opiates and rest will cure what ails her.

My effort to talk to him about what I observed achieved nothing, and so for the moment all I can do is continue watching closely. If her behavior worsens, I will take steps to keep Lulu and the household staff out of harm's way. I feel as though I were tied, hand and foot, in front of a woman who desperately needs help. I cannot provide it, and if I could, she could not accept it.

It is early evening now, and my hand aches for having written—close to twenty pages. Small miseries are all I have to claim for myself. It will be many weeks before I can hope for a letter from you, and in the meantime I will do what I can for the Markhams and the residents of Santa Fe. I miss you and Ma and all my people very much.

Your loving cousin and appreciative student
Carrie

Postscript. I debated with myself about including this story, and find that I must. When I dressed Leon Cuevas's amputation site I used the winterbloom and slippery elm distillation in the hope that it would slow the onset of infection. I knew of course that there was very little chance it would be effective on such an injury, but I thought it would be best to try.

Dr. Markham learned of this a few hours later and was displeased. I am to understand that I misstepped. He will not tolerate the use of any 'foreign or Indian medicines' in his dispensary.

I hear you asking, 'What did you expect?'

Too much, is the obvious and disappointing answer.

40

In the very early evening of Carrie's second full day in Santa Fe, Josefa brought her supper on a tray. Lulu had already eaten and the Markhams were retired for the evening, though the sun had not yet set.

Josefa's gaze traveled over the table, strewn with closely written pages. For the first time Carrie saw something of real interest in the younger woman's expression.

"You write letters?"

"Yes. To my mother, and cousins, and an aunt. They will be waiting to hear that we—that I arrived safely."

Letter writing, to Carrie's mind, was almost like having a conversation, if you thought intensely enough about the person you were writing to. Beyond that, she knew of no better way to distract herself, something she needed just now because it was almost seven o'clock.

They spoke for a few minutes about nothing very personal or important. The timing was unfortunate because Carrie had been hoping for the opportunity to talk to Josefa. But not now, for a very good reason.

Eli would be coming, quite soon, to take her walking. She was unsettled when she thought of seeing him again but could not stop smiling. Such a lack of self-control was embarrassing even if no one here knew her well enough to take note.

Josefa had just turned toward the door to go back to her work when the church bells began to ring the hour. On the seventh chime, Josefa left to see who had knocked at the front door.

If she went to the window, she would see him, but Carrie sat frozen where she was. Forcing herself to breathe evenly, slowly.

Then Josefa was back, calling softly from outside her door. "Miss Ballentyne? *Tienes un visitante.*"

Silly hen, she scolded herself as she smoothed her skirt and her hair. *Silly hen, silly hen, silly, silly hen.* She opened her door into the *placita*, her face composed, she hoped, in a friendly but neutral expression.

The man who stood there was certainly more than sixty years old. He was talking to Carlos, in the relaxed way of old friends. Then Carlos caught sight of her, and they turned in her direction.

"*Buenas noches*," said the visitor. "*Les traigo una carta de mi pariente Eli.*"

Carrie took the letter he held out to her. A letter from Eli. She somehow managed to say the necessary polite things, though her throat had gone dry and her hands began to tingle. She excused herself far too quickly and then, alone in her room, did nothing but stare at the letter for a long moment.

She had seen enough of Eli's handwriting on his maps to recognize it here. He had written her name with ease, the ink very dark against the paper. His handwriting was uniform, but there was an angularity where his teachers would have expected curves. Concise, consistent, but distinctive.

The seal broke with a crack like a bone splintering.

Dear Carrie—
I write to say that I will be delayed getting back to Santa Fe by a
few days. I am well and you are not to worry about me. The reason

for the delay is this: some of my mother's people are here from her pueblo to settle an old disagreement. You will understand that this will take time. The Elders will not be rushed, and until they have had their say nobody goes anywhere.

I had planned to wait to tell my parents about you—and to have you here with me when I do that—but things have gotten complicated. Now I will have to tell them before I start back. When I come to take you walking in the evening the day I get home, I will give you as many details as you can tolerate.

The man who brings you this note is a first cousin of my father's, a Basque. His name is Iñigo. He has no English and will put your Spanish to the test. He was here visiting when I arrived and has agreed to bring you this note. Also, he brought your Mimosa back to town to make her comfortable in his stables, just at the end of your street. Doc Markham keeps his horses and rig there as well.

Iñigo is a good and trustworthy man, and his wife is his equal. I think you will have a friend in Violante.

I have given them some idea of our plans for a specific reason: I am concerned about where you find yourself. Before I left Santa Fe I learned from a friend (I will introduce you as soon as the opportunity presents itself) that all is not well with the Markhams. In the normal course of things Violante would be able to tell me what is wrong there, but she has been here visiting for two months and has not had word.

The point is that if you find yourself in need of help you can call on Iñigo or Violante at any time. You could walk over to their casita just beyond the main stable in less than five minutes.

You are more than capable of handling trouble should it come, but I don't like the idea of you in an unfamiliar place with no one at your back. Do not hesitate to call on Iñigo if the need arises, please.

I cannot say how disappointed I am not to see you today. You are constantly in my thoughts, querida. Mi amor.

Eli

When she was upset and at odds, Carrie wrote notes to herself. Stern notes, unflinching and direct. She was very good at scolding herself in writing. It was at least five years since she had begun recording what she thought of as her admonitions, and she still had every slip of paper, all tucked away in an otherwise pristine copy of Reverend Peter Bullions's *Principles of Latin Grammar*. It struck her as a safe place, in a volume that no one was likely to pick up.

At this moment the Bullions volume with its burden of admonitions was on its way west and would arrive with Nathan and her trunks. Carrie could not wait.

In her smallest, neatest hand she wrote slowly, reaching for the right words. She wrote out the questions that needed answers only she herself could provide, and that should be enough to ease her mind. For the moment. In the end, she limited herself to three:

On what grounds do you trust this man?

Are you capable of seeing him clearly?

What does he mean—what do you want him to mean—when he puts the words mi amor down on paper, for you to read?

41

DAYS COULD PASS quickly, Carrie reminded herself the next morning. The trick was to stay busy.

She started by walking to the post office to mail her letters. It was so early that the shopkeepers were still getting ready for the day, but there was a good deal of activity in the plaza. Men were gathered in front of the long, low adobe building that Dr. Markham had pointed out to her.

The seat of the territorial government, he had told her. *Officially it is El Palacio Real. The Palace of the Governors.*

He said this without any hint of a smile, but it struck Carrie as almost comical that such a plain, unadorned building should be called a palace. She would get used to it, she told herself, but it would always make her smile. At one end of the palace was the U.S. Post Office, which might be mistaken for a jail given its barred windows and heavy door.

Two dozen men or more stood waiting. There was one group in front of the courthouse, and smaller groups near the palace. They were like men everywhere, insofar as Carrie could see. In every city in every state, in every country, men like these were responsible for local governments. These were the men who ran Santa Fe and governed the territory. Their conversations would be about land, and whom it belonged to, or should belong to, and how it would best be put to use. And that would mean what minerals or ores or rocks could be dug up and taken away, how water could be diverted to or away from it, how much labor would cost and whether the locals could provide what was needed. And of course they would be talking about what they would think of as the Indian problem.

By their clothes it was easy enough to sort the men into groups. Clerks, attorneys, messengers, business owners, some very distinguished men who might be the *patrónes* Eli had told her about, men who owned huge tracts of land and employed many dozens of people to look after their property and animals. All of them had been here before the United States stepped in. They regarded themselves as sons of Mexico or Spain or both. There were not many Indians nearby.

Carrie supposed the conversations would be in Spanish or English or some mixture of the two. The few Indians she saw nearby would speak their own languages. She would have liked to listen, but that possibility disappeared as soon as she came into view, for a simple reason: they all stopped talking.

It was to be expected, she told herself. Eva had warned her that there would be a great deal of interest in a female newcomer, a single young lady of good family—a phrase Carrie had come to detest— with resources of her own.

They probably knew as much about her as John, who had read her correspondence with Dr. Markham. That idea made her wonder where John spent his free time, and how talkative he might be.

These men interrupted their discussions to watch her walk by, alert, even eager. Despite her limited and hard-used wardrobe, they failed to assume she was a domestic of some kind, and thus not worth their time.

Eva had prepared her for all this, and it still came as a surprise.

"Miss? Miss Ballentyne?"

Startled, she stopped as two men stepped out of the shade and moved toward her.

"Miss, pardon me. Rob Ramsey is the name, and this here is Jake Saracen. I know it's rude, approaching you like this out in public, but things work different here than they do in the East." He glanced at his friend, who jerked his chin to indicate that he agreed.

They were both fairly young, well-groomed and well-dressed. *Friendly* was not the right word, but *intrusive* would be going too far. Carrie just wasn't sure what to do with such enthusiasm.

"Didn't mean to startle you," Rob Ramsey was saying. "Just a friendly hello and welcome to the territory."

"And an invitation," added Jake Saracen in a rich bass voice.

"That's right," Rob Ramsey said, frowning at his friend. "There's a fandango coming up end of the week. It would be a good way for you to meet folks, and lots of fun."

"I'd be honored to escort you," Saracen said. His gaze was direct and—only one word came to Carrie's mind—*challenging*. It was time to steer the conversation into calmer waters.

"Mr. Ramsey, Mr. Saracen, I am very pleased to make your acquaintance. Now if you'll pardon me—"

Jake Saracen ducked his head and ran a thumb down the line of his jaw, his mouth curling into a one-sided grin.

"So that's you saying no to the fandango?"

Ramsey snorted a laugh. "Saracen, maybe it's you she's saying no to."

"Gentlemen," Carrie said. "I am still finding my feet here. Eventually I'll go to a fandango. Eventually."

"Fair enough," Saracen said. "But I'll wager you gotta eat, pretty much every day. Would you be willing to sit down to a cup of coffee?"

"You are persistent, but I am truly busy—"

She caught sight of a few men who had begun to edge closer, and something like panic made her jump. It wouldn't do to run away, she reminded herself, but a brisk pace, surely that wouldn't offend anyone.

She stepped into the post office thinking of Lulu's stories about the postmaster. All she really knew was that he was in want of a wife, and that was the case for many men who had emigrated west. Carrie would make no assumptions.

In fact, Mr. Whiting greeted her professionally, with a friendly smile that wasn't overly familiar. Later she realized he never met her gaze. A shy man, with a beautiful complexion and shiny blond hair that had been oiled, perfumed, and molded to his skull like a second scalp. In Manhattan this was nothing unusual, but here she would have expected something simpler. Pomade, or tallow. Or bear grease.

It wasn't until she was ready to leave that he cleared his throat and spoke a full sentence.

"Miss Ballentyne, if I may ask a question?"

"Certainly."

He cleared his throat again, and sweat appeared on his brow.

"Did you know there is going to be a fandango at the old fort on Friday evening?"

THE REST OF the day was far less socially challenging. First, because Dr. Markham had gone out to make home visits. This left Carrie in charge of the dispensary, something she would not have dared without John Edmonds. She said as much, and was honest with him about her expectations.

"I am a good nurse," she told him. "But until I have a better command of Spanish, it will be hard to convince anyone that I can be trusted. Spanish is the key to my success here."

John understood this statement in the way she hoped he would. He spoke Spanish with her whenever possible, stood aside, and let her talk without correcting her errors, interceding only when he saw that she was losing track—which happened often. He offered a few words in English, and when she had found her footing again, he retreated.

As she had anticipated, there were patients who wanted nothing to do with her. She was a *tejana*, a white woman from the East. She listened as John treated an old man complaining of a cough, and understood some of what he muttered under his breath. But still, she was encouraged. By midday she had begun to believe that eventually she would be able to talk to the patients without a translator.

A *cibolero* called Tom Samson, who did speak English, was Carrie's first real challenge, not so much for the broken wrist that brought him to the dispensary as for the way he stank.

She would have expected buffalo hunters to be much like the fur trappers she had known as a young girl in Paradise. Men who lived rough, coming into a town to trade furs and get supplies once a year. Bear-men, her Cousin Jennet had called them, shouting out their arrival with great glee. When Mr. Samson stepped into the foyer, Carrie thought of Jennet, who could have written paragraphs to describe the odor that filled the dispensary. Carrie would try to do it justice.

She had delivered babies in some of the poorest areas of Manhattan. As bad as the tenements were, Tom Samson was worse, a combination of buffalo, dried blood, dung, tobacco, rancid clothing, and rotting meat.

"Mr. Samson." She addressed him formally and with all the authority she could call her own. "You need to bathe before we can treat your injury."

In reply he held up his swollen wrist as he would raise a club, and glared at her.

"When did that happen?" John asked from the far corner of the small room.

"Day before yesterday."

"Right," Carrie said. "Then another hour or two won't make any difference."

A young Mexican woman had to step out of Samson's way as he stomped off. Her expression was a perfect combination of outrage and horror, and her whole body curved around the infant she had tied to her chest with a rebozo. By the sound, a newborn in significant distress.

Carrie knew the look of a first-time, inexperienced mother. Any midwife would recognize her trouble. Deprived of sleep, her body still mending, she was being driven to desperation by an infant she could not comfort.

In Spanish so rapid that John was obliged to translate, she introduced herself as Yatzil Morales, and explained that her son would not settle. Carrie asked for his name, and the boy's mother frowned at her.

"Tiene solo diez días, aún no tiene nombre."

A child of ten days did not need a name, it seemed. Maybe this had something to do with religious rites or superstition. Those things were unimportant at this moment, and so she kept her silence while the young mother told John about the boy's symptoms.

John's discomfort with the translation he was obliged to provide was puzzling. It might have to do with infants, or new mothers, or this particular new mother's undisguised anger and frustration, but it was the first sign Carrie had seen of his youth and inexperience.

She caught some of what Yatzil said. *Ruido* meant "noise." Carrie's guess was that the infant cried constantly, and others in the household had no patience. When the new mother paused to take a breath, Carrie held up a hand and then posed a question that wasn't exactly right, but she didn't yet know the Spanish word for colic. *Pain* was a word she did know.

"¿Crees que tiene dolor en el estómago?"

Yatzil's eyes were suddenly damp. She stepped toward Carrie and held out her child. This was an overwhelmed newer mother so relieved to find understanding and compassion in others that she flooded with tears.

Carrie smiled, as she always found herself smiling at new creatures like this one, whether angelic and peaceful or in poor health and angry. The urge to welcome and care for a newborn was always there. This particular button-like face topped with a hank of feathery dark hair was contorted with outrage. He did not like this world where he found himself, and he was going to voice his dissatisfaction.

Carrie examined the boy, asking questions that John translated.

She wanted to know what Yatzil was eating, how often she put her son to the breast and how well he nursed, the nature of his bowel movements. While Carrie showed her how to massage the boy's abdomen very gently, John watched with keen interest.

"A newborn's digestion needs some help," she said. "Letting go of gas doesn't come easily."

Now when John translated, Yatzil's expression shifted. All the anxiety slipped away; it was the mystery that had caused such distress. Now that Yatzil had been given a clear and reasonable explanation for the symptoms—and a way to comfort her son—she could breathe again.

She said, "*A veces arroja leche, pero nunca se tira pedos.*"

John was fighting back a smile, but he translated.

"He brings up milk, but never farts. She didn't realize that babies have to be taught how to fart."

Carrie had heard far odder things, and was able to nod and assure Yatzil. Telling a young woman that she was a good mother was sometimes the most effective medicine.

When the boy not yet named had fallen into sleep and Yatzil had a recipe for gripe water, she left, far calmer. For her part Carrie had learned the Spanish for colic, chamomile, fennel, ginger, and lemon balm, as well as the phrase *Massage will help him pass gas.* She thought of Eva's Beto, and how he would react to the idea that she had learned the word for fart without his help.

While they got ready for the next patient, Carrie asked John the obvious question, one she would have put to Yatzil directly had there been time and privacy. And a better command of the language.

"John, does she have no mother or sister to help her?"

He cleared his throat. "No. She's one of Leona's. From El Taquito." And seeing that he would have to be more specific, he provided another hint. "It is a *prostíbulo.*"

The word was unfamiliar to Carrie, but John's embarrassment was translation enough. Yatzil was a prostitute, and there would be many others like her living so close to an army base. Carrie would have to ask—possibly Josefa, but preferably Eli—about prostitution in Santa Fe. How it was organized, where prostitutes lived, and whether they worked out of households established for that purpose. They would need a great deal of her attention. Most of the patients Carrie cared for at home had been poor, and poor women often had little choice but to support themselves and their families by taking money for sex. She could not feign surprise or discomfort to find that the same was true here. She was the same person in Santa Fe as she had been in Manhattan; she would look after these women as she did the others. She would deliver their babies, treat those infants and their mothers for bellyaches and rashes and worse, sit with them when death could not be put off.

For the women who came to her as a midwife, she would provide information and medicinal teas. She would do the same for women who did not care to bear children.

In training with Amelie, she had spent a good amount of time in the garden and forest, learning how to harvest and prepare those plants that could be put to use. They did not always work for any number of reasons, but they were often helpful, and worth the effort that went into gathering and preparing them.

It was possible, of course, that Dr. Markham would forbid her to use medicines she compounded herself, no matter how simple or well-known. What she would do if that should happen was a question she put aside for the moment.

They saw a fifty-year-old sergeant from the garrison who needed a tonic for his headache. He had the red flush of a man too fond of liquor, a surplus of ruptured veins on his nose and cheeks, and a curled lower lip that revealed two yellow teeth where there should have been four.

He was suffering not so much from a headache as a hangover.

"Sergeant Reynolds," Carrie said, her tone neutral. "The military hospital would also have what you need for a sore head. Is there a particular reason you came to the dispensary?"

She saw him weighing the cost of lying to her face. It was that, or admit that he was here to avoid being reported for drunkenness. In the end he shrugged and dropped his gaze.

On the way out, he pulled John aside. He didn't bother to lower his voice.

"Is Doc Markham ever coming back to treat folks here? I don't much care for females in a dispensary. Damn useless creatures. Over-educated bitches."

He seemed almost to relax after that, as if his preferences had been too heavy to keep to himself and he was glad to be free of the burden of discretion.

When he had gone, Carrie said, "Sergeant Reynolds's insults are surprisingly weak for a soldier. I've heard far worse, and many times."

She meant to settle John's discomfort, but instead she had shocked him. Carrie considered some of the stories she might tell when she knew him better, and decided that the day might never come.

There were new voices in the waiting area, and Carrie turned to see who had come for treatment.

"One of the nuns is here with a little girl. A student, is my guess."

John glanced up. "Sister Isabel. That's Carlotta López with her."

Carlotta, eight years old, had a very ugly infected spider bite on her left wrist.

"I sent a note home with her two days ago," the sister told them in her soft Southern accent. "And I did my best to make clear that she needs medical attention. It's possible they couldn't decipher my Spanish, I suppose." She hesitated. "Or it might be that the note never made it home."

She put a hand on the little girl's head as Carlotta's shoulders curled forward, a silent confession.

"In any case," she said, her tone still gentle, "I brought Carlotta to you myself. I will wait in the other room while you treat her."

But the girl reached out and grabbed Sister Isabel's hand so suddenly and with such fervor that they all jumped in surprise.

"Por favor, Sor Isabel, no vaya."

Carrie said, "Please do stay, Sister. Carlotta would like that, and we don't mind. Do we, John?"

His nod was a little reluctant, but he didn't explain his doubts until later, while they were getting ready for the next patient.

He said, "I was sure she would cry."

"Really?" Carrie looked up from cleaning the examination table. "In my experience children who grow up on farms are very stoic. They take pride in denying pain."

"Sure," John said. "But she's not growing up on a farm. She's one of the López kids. Her father runs the saddlery down past the warehouse. Anyway, I was talking about Sister Isabel."

He drew in a breath, as if he regretted opening the subject but felt obliged to finish.

"Sister Isabel can't stand it when one of the children is in pain. It has got her into trouble more than once. Sister Tenderheart, the Pueblo people call her."

In between the patients, there were visitors. Women, sometimes alone, sometimes in small groups, appeared in the dispensary with a single goal in mind: they wanted to see Carrie. The idea of a midwife trained in a proper hospital in the East was intriguing, but they had a concern.

They agreed that Dr. Markham was intelligent, polite, and proper; it would be wrong to challenge his choice of a nurse and midwife. Certainly, they could not ask about her education or references. And still, a few braver women decided that they must take it upon themselves to get answers to these questions. And so they came.

Most of the visitors were of childbearing age, and all of them were white. A few had been in Santa Fe for fifteen years or more, but most were more recent emigrants, and uneasy in this strange place. Carrie wondered if they would come to her with their homesickness, expecting to find a kindred and unhappy spirit in her.

A few were the wives and daughters of army officers, of men who worked for the territorial government, of importers, exporters, merchants, land agents, and livestock traders. There were women, just as proper but more modestly dressed, who worked alongside the husbands who had learned a trade. Some of the visitors were quite friendly but too bound by manners to ask the questions that most concerned them. Others didn't hesitate.

They asked in roundabout ways about her training, where exactly and how many years and with whom she had studied, and when she had first delivered an infant on her own, and whether there had been any tragedies she could recount. The last question was the most pressing one, because for a reason that Carrie had never been able to figure out, women could be much like children who enjoy being frightened by stories of ghosts and monsters. They wanted to hear the worst, as if by acknowledging what could go wrong, they were insulating themselves from harm.

John kept busy during these short interviews, but he was listening as he came and went. Usually his face gave nothing away, but now and then she saw him fighting the urge to smile. Less often he had trouble banishing a scowl. They would have to talk about all this, but it had been a long day. Tomorrow would be soon enough.

For all of her working life, Carrie had looked forward to the walk home at the end of the day. No matter how tired or overwhelmed, how crowded the streets or disagreeable the weather, walking soothed frazzled nerves. An hour on horseback would have been equally effective, but it was a dangerous business at home, riding crowded city streets. She liked the walks, but then if the weather was particularly extreme or the hour very late, she would leave work—wherever she was that day—to find Mr. Lee, her stepfather's valet, waiting for her.

Her work in Santa Fe was not very different from what it had been at home, but the trip from the dispensary into the house was another matter. She walked out one door, through the short, dim corridor into the enclosed *placita* with its profusion of potted trees and flowering plants in terra-cotta.

Eva had told her about the way households were usually run here. The main meal of the day, usually at noon, was dedicated to family.

"And then, after the table is cleared, there's something called *sobremesa*. It's a lovely custom, sitting together to talk after a big meal."

Carrie said, "So, a paradise where everyone is content?"

"Well, no," Eva admitted. "Of course not. I have to admit that squabbles and arguments are not uncommon. Latin temperaments can be volatile, and emigrant families are no better. They drag their disagreements and troubles with them. And still I think that the *sobremesa* is one of the customs that hold families together, especially in difficult times."

It hadn't occurred to Eva that the Markham household could be so out of order.

Now Carrie stepped into the *placita* and found Lulu waiting for her. The little girl's welcome was exuberant, full of dramatic gestures and questions that tumbled over each other too quickly to be answered.

"I'm starving, are you starving? It won't be long now." She flung out her arms and whirled in place.

"Will your parents join us, do you think?"

Lulu's whirling came to a slow stop, and her gaze shifted away.

"Don't know. Maybe."

Carrie walked through to the kitchen, where Josefa was arranging serving dishes. Every day she seemed a little more at ease with Carrie, and now she smiled.

"You had a busy day. You must be hungry."

"I did. I am. Josefa, are Lulu and I eating alone this evening?"

"Dr. Markham is still out," Josefa told her. "An old friend of his is dying, and he'll stay until the end. I would expect him sometime tomorrow in the afternoon, depending."

"And Mrs. Markham?"

Josefa's shrug was almost exactly like Lulu's.

"She ate a bowl of soup an hour ago, had her medicine, and has gone back to sleep."

"If she's not well, I should check on her."

Josefa paused to look at Carrie. "If you must. But let me warn you, she will not thank you for waking her."

Carrie sat down at the long worktable. "You know, as strange as it might seem, I am very capable both as a nurse and midwife."

Josefa went on with her work, and for a moment Carrie thought that she was going to overlook the attempt she was making to start a difficult but important conversation. Because Josefa didn't want to be drawn in, or she was afraid of the repercussions, or it might be that she didn't trust Carrie and was keeping her at a distance.

But then she did sit down, and for a bit they only regarded each other and listened: Lulu was singing to herself while Carlos swept in the *placita*. A wagon rumbled past, headed toward the parish church.

Carrie would wait. She had spent enough time in the longhouses at Good Pasture to understand that such matters could not, would not, be rushed.

Finally, Josefa spread her hands flat on the table, as if to study them.

"I can tell you what I think is wrong with Mrs. Markham. I can tell you what my aunt thinks is wrong. I can even tell you what Mrs. Markham believes about her own health. But first, you must have an opinion."

So a test, of sorts. To find out what kind of healer Carrie might be. Josefa was cautious, and that was more than reasonable.

"She has lost three and maybe more children," Carrie began. "I don't know how or why; the doctor hasn't given me any details. Worse, I have no way of knowing what Mrs. Markham is like under normal circumstances. She may be the most composed, reasonable person, or she could be prone to extremes of mood. On the face of it, without more information, it looks as though she has forfeited her sanity in her attempt to have another child, out of—" She paused, considering carefully how to phrase her thoughts.

"Anger, grief, disappointment all play a role, but my instincts tell me there's more going on here."

There was new animation in Josefa's expression. "Go on," she said.

"It would go very badly if Dr. Markham should hear any of this, you know that."

"Not from me," Josefa said.

Carrie inclined her head in acknowledgment, and went on.

"The question, in as far as I can see, is if Mrs. Markham has lost her capacity for reason, or if her behavior is a—*mask* is the word that comes to mind—if it is a mask she wears. If that's the case, if her behavior is calculated, then the question would be, to what end? What is it she is working toward? It could be something as uncomplicated as a wish to go back home to Richmond, to force her husband to take her back. Or she could have a different purpose. One that could take a very dark turn."

Josefa was not surprised by this possibility, and that in itself was telling.

Just then Lulu came tearing into the kitchen to announce that she was starving and to ask what they were talking about with such serious faces, it wasn't nice to keep secrets. Josefa was more than equal to Lulu, and diverted her by wondering where the new candles for the dining table had got to, she couldn't find them anywhere, unless Lulu happened to know where they might be?

When the door had closed behind the little girl, Josefa said, "Thank you for your openness. These are all important questions, but to me it seems very simple. Mrs. Markham doesn't know what to do with her anger. It is poisoning her, and it will poison everyone in her reach."

Carrie exhaled and realized she had feared what Josefa might have to say.

"Then, essentially, you and I agree. What does your Aunt Manuela think?"

There was something both sad and bitter about Josefa's smile. "That's even more simple," she said. "My aunt thinks Mrs. Markham is a witch."

THAT SINGLE WORD kept Carrie awake for a very long time. She knew very little about the subject beyond the vague stories of witches being tried and executed long ago in New England. Puritans and

Pueblos would have very different beliefs, but in both cases the under-lying issue would have to do with fear.

Long ago her Da had told her how it worked, in his rational, unadorned Scots way. According to Simon Ballentyne, people built laws and customs to serve like brick walls around ideas that fright-ened them. For the most part, people felt threatened by what they didn't understand.

It had made sense to her as a young girl, and it still made sense. More than that, as an adult she had seen for herself how fear could build upon itself and erupt into mania and violence. From this per-spective it was possible to imagine that Indira Markham might be a danger to her own people, and at the same time be in danger. Did the Pueblos shun women they believed to be witches, or expel them, or worse?

In the normal course of things, she would go directly to the patient's doctor with her observations and questions. But Dr. Markham was still absent, and even if that weren't the case, Carrie had come to believe that it would not be wise.

LA CABALLERIZA GUEVARA was just a minute's walk away, but it took Carrie another day to make her way to Iñigo's stables. She wanted to see Mimosa; more pressing was the need to introduce herself more properly to Eli's cousins. How the Ibarra and Guevara families were related was another mystery yet to be resolved. *Cousin* was a word that people used when the actual relationship was too complicated or pri-vate to share, but it was not used lightly, and Carrie wanted this intro-duction to the Guevara branch of the family to go well.

But first there was Mimosa, and so Carrie walked toward the fenced pasture where horses were grazing. Mimosa turned her head immediately when Carrie called, and let out a huffing, elongated nicker. At the same moment Chico rose out of the shade beside a fence post, and they both started toward her. Carrie was so pleased at this welcome that her throat swelled with tears.

A stable hand passing by called to her, his smile broad and sincere. "*Una hermosa yegua.*"

"That is true," Carrie assured Mimosa. "You are a beautiful mare. So, have you been keeping Chico out of trouble?"

At the sound of his name, the dog collapsed at her feet with a contented sigh.

When she knew she could put off the visit no longer, she turned toward what Eli had called Iñigo's casita, his little house. Even as she turned onto the path that led to the front door, Iñigo appeared in the doorway. He was a tall man, strongly built, and he filled the doorframe in a way that made the house seem child-sized.

His whole face transformed when he smiled, his cheeks folding into pleats and his eyes disappearing into wrinkles. He came toward her, both hands extended and speaking so quickly that she caught about half of his welcome: How good of her to visit, how glad he was to see her, how pretty she was, and what a beautiful horse she had brought to his stables, Mimosa was a pleasure to work with, oh, and was Carrie hungry? Thirsty? Could he offer her tea, or there was some fermented mare's milk, if that would suit.

Without waiting for answers, he put his head back and shouted, "Violante!"

But she was already there, a woman half his size who stepped up behind him and gave him a playful shove. Where her husband was lean, she was round, her cheeks as smooth and glossy as buns just out of the oven.

She sent him an expression that could only be interpreted as mock dismay.

"Where are your manners, old man? What do you mean, letting Eli's bride stand at the door? Carrie—I can call you Carrie? Eli described you to me. I was wondering when you'd find your way over here. Come in, please. Come in and sit down."

It took a moment to overcome the surprise of being referred to as a bride—*la novia de Eli*—but Carrie did her best to respond to the outpouring of good wishes amplified by curiosity.

The conversation did not move as slowly as she had feared, as Violante had kept house for more than a few of the emigrant families and for army officers over the years. Her English was very good, and there was something acrobatic in the way she jumped from Basque when she spoke to her husband, to Spanish when she was addressing them both, and then to English when Carrie wasn't equal to the Spanish.

Carrie accepted the invitation to join them for supper, which triggered a whole cascade of new questions. Was she not expected to join the Markhams for the meal? Would they worry? Should they send word?

It seemed to Carrie that Violante was providing an opening, one Carrie could use if she cared to tell her story. To make herself clearer, Violante sat down across from her. Her eyes, a faded blue in a deeply tanned face, reminded Carrie of Dr. Blackwell, who had a way of looking at a patient she was trying to diagnose.

"There is trouble."

It was not a question, but Carrie nodded.

"Iñigo," she called over her shoulder. *"Arazoak daude. Arazoak!"*

Carrie's Basque was still nonexistent, but it was clear that Violante was declaring an emergency and needed her husband's opinion.

Now they were both sitting across from her, watching her for some sign of what she might want. An elderly couple, but healthy and vigorous and eager to help. They wanted to stand up for her, and she was glad of their support. Or would be glad, if only she knew how to start.

Iñigo leveled his gaze at her, and his expression—sincerity, interest—was encouragement enough.

"Por favor," he said. *"Cuéntanos todo. Todo."*

Tell us everything.

She was here to do just that. These were two trustworthy people who had lived here for more than thirty years, who knew the history and the families, and the Markhams. More than that, they had drawn her into the circle of the family, and with that thought, the last of her hesitation slipped away.

She started with the day she arrived, and when she had finished—it felt like hours later—Iñigo and Violante sat quietly for a long moment. Iñigo's mouth was pursed, as if he had tasted something tainted, while Violante simply looked thoughtful. Then she turned to her husband, one brow raised.

"I'll start out tomorrow, first light," he said.

"Do you know where to find the doctor?" Carrie felt an unexpected flash of hope.

"*Eso creo.* I have some ideas."

"So you don't think I am worried for no good reason?"

Violante shook her head. "If not for Josefa and Carlos, I would insist that you come stay with us. You and Lulu both."

Of all the questions that came to mind, one forced itself to the forefront. It was so important that she asked it in English. "Do I understand correctly, you believe that the house is not safe?"

Violante let out a long sigh. "While Carlos and Josefa are there, you have nothing to fear. Iñigo will find the doctor, and then there will be a reckoning."

That was ominous. "I don't understand what you mean."

Here Iñigo cleared his throat. "There is no excuse for the doctor's absence when his wife is so unwell. It's not like him to be irresponsible."

"It wasn't like him, but he has changed," Violante said.

Carrie said, "He may be very sick himself."

Violante shrugged, clearly unwilling to give the doctor the benefit of the doubt. Carrie wondered why Violante should distrust Dr. Markham, but a different question came to mind. She struggled with a way to say it that would not cast doubt on her own sanity.

"Manuela thinks Mrs. Markham is a witch."

Nothing changed in their expressions, and so she went on.

"My first reaction is that this is superstition, but if the belief is widespread—"

Violante's smile was grimmer now. "Let me see what I can learn."

"Will you talk to Manuela?"

"That depends," Violante said. She stood abruptly. "But right now it is time to eat."

Over the meal the conversation turned toward more traditional subjects. Carrie answered questions about her family and home, and with some gentle prompting talked a little about Eli. There came a point when she couldn't hold the most pressing question back even a minute longer.

"Do you have any idea when Eli will be able to come back here?"

Iñigo brushed off her worries with a smile. "Believe me, he will be back soon. He is not happy about the delay. He knows that you will have more suitors than you can count."

To Violante he said, "Look, she's flushing. Have they been knocking on your door already?"

"Let me guess," Violante said. "Jake Saracen."

Carrie could not deny the truth of this. She told them about her trip to the post office. "I try to be friendly but not too friendly," Carrie finished. "The way I talk to my brother's friends. But they were—"

"*Terco*," Violante supplied in Spanish. "Bullheaded."

"Never mind." Iñigo's tone was meant to soothe his wife. He wasn't so concerned about Carrie, which might be a compliment.

"That will all end when Eli is back."

The idea that a man was coming to claim her as his property was not one that appealed especially, but Carrie's Spanish was not equal to this subject, and the idea of discussing it at all, even in English, was disconcerting. She would talk to Eli about it, that was a certainty. As soon as she saw him again.

"It is getting late," Iñigo said. "I'll walk you back to the Markhams' place. Tomorrow sometime toward evening, I'll be back with word of Dr. Markham."

At the door, Violante drew Carrie aside. "I want to tell you how happy I am that you and Eli have found each other. He was doubtful it would ever happen, but now you're here. We are all so pleased."

Carrie would have liked to hear more about Eli's doubts, whether he had voiced them or if this was Violante's interpretation. Another subject to take up with him directly.

42

A NOTE FROM Miriam Goldblum came at dawn: she was in labor, and hoped Midwife Ballentyne would come, without delay.

Carrie had last attended a stillbirth when the train to St. Louis came close to derailing; before that, she had delivered a patient's fourth child and second daughter on the last day of April.

A busy household in French Town, with children and cousins, an aunt, and two grandmothers underfoot. Both the grandmothers had far more experience than Carrie when it came to catching babies, but the mother had wanted a midwife. People indulged women in labor, for better and, sometimes, for worse.

That had been a quick labor and uncomplicated delivery. Six hours from start to finish, and there she was, a healthy little girl with dimpled cheeks and rounded knees and elbows. She took to the breast without hesitation or fuss, and was to be baptized Marie-Louise.

Today Carrie focused on that particular delivery as she dressed and checked over her supplies. There was always an undercurrent of excitement at this stage, offset by the long list of things that might go wrong. She had lost mothers and infants and, on two occasions, both mother and infant. What made those experiences bearable was knowing that later she would write down the details in her daybook and then go over them with Amelie. If she could identify where and what and why things had gone wrong—something that was not always possible—it made her a better midwife.

Here she had no Amelie, and she would have to learn to mentor herself.

She listed the important points to remember: the mother was healthy and well nourished, and had two successful births behind her. The household was scrupulously well looked after. There would be no lack of clean water, the means to heat it, or hands to do that work. Carrie assumed that the Goldblum wives kept their larders and storage cabinets filled to the brim.

Beyond that, the timing worked to her advantage; rather than watch for Iñigo's return all day long, Carrie had something else to occupy her, possibly through the night and into tomorrow.

The young boy who had come to fetch her was almost dancing in place, he was so anxious. Carrie decided she would have to skip breakfast.

"Reizl will feed you," Josefa said, and then from the door as Carrie set out she called to her in Spanish, "I'll tell John he'll be alone in the dispensary today."

Carrie was deeply pleased to realize that she had understood every word.

As she followed the boy—one of the Goldblums, she assumed, but too shy to introduce himself—Carrie tried to recall what she knew of Reizl, the only one of the wives she had not met during her first visit days before. Reizl, who would feed her, according to Josefa. It was so odd a comment that she would wonder about it until she could ask for more information, but there was no predicting when she would have that chance.

The boy led her to a recessed entrance at the rear of the general store and bounded off. Then the door swung open before she could raise her hand to knock.

The woman who stood there was someone she had never seen before, but simple logic told her that this had to be Reizl Goldblum.

Not a young woman—Carrie would guess that she had already seen her fiftieth birthday—but she held herself like someone closer to Carrie's own age. Her posture was perfect, her bone structure defined. Reizl Goldblum reminded Carrie of ballet dancers she had seen perform onstage, but someone who came from one of the Mediterranean or North African countries, with her high coloring and strong features. It was the way she dressed that really set her apart.

This Mrs. Goldblum wore an unusual loose-cut day dress of light, flowing fabric, block printed with birds on flowering branches. Even in the shadowy hall, the colors were vibrant: greens and golds and splashes of scarlet and ultramarine.

She had a good smile, and used it to advantage while she stepped aside and inclined her head, inviting Carrie to come forward.

"Welcome, Miss Ballentyne. I am Reizl. Levi's wife. Come in, please. I'll take you to Miriam, but first you and I will talk."

In less than a minute Carrie found herself seated at a table set for breakfast. There was tea and coffee, bread still warm from the oven, and, most surprising of all, a smooth brown egg in a cup. An unexpected but very welcome egg.

"You are surprised," Reizl Goldblum said. "Someone told you there were no hens in New Mexico Territory?"

"They did," Carrie said. "But I am glad to have been misinformed."

Reizl said, "There were once hens, but some years ago now a pestilence wiped out every flock."

"Do you know what the disease was?"

She pressed her lips together, as if it caused her pain to speak of such things.

"If it had a name, we were never told. Hens keeled over, dead. No warning. But my Levi knows how much I love eggs. Go on, eat. I've already had mine."

Carrie picked up a spoon and broke the shell. The firm egg white gave way, and the liquid yolk, a glossy deep saffron yellow, showed itself. She paused long enough to sprinkle salt and then began, determined not to rush, while Reizl told the story of how her hens came to Santa Fe.

"I was missing eggs," she said. "Nothing tasted right to me. One day Levi said, 'Reizl, your clothes are loose on you. Soon the wind will blow you away.'

"So." She shrugged. "I tried to eat more, and while I was trying, my Levi, he was writing letters home to his people and mine. Six months later a ship rounded the horn and then stopped at the first port in California. My brother was on the boat, with two dozen hens and four roosters."

Carrie couldn't hide her surprise. "And how did he get from the Pacific Ocean to Santa Fe? It is a difficult journey, people say."

"My Levi met his ship," Reizl said with great satisfaction. "He hired ten men to guard them on the trail home. Ten men, all armed, to look after the hens. The roosters could fend for themselves, that's what he said. Joking."

"And that was the beginning of your flock?"

"Yes. Now I have about forty hens and always more roosters than I need. We sell the eggs we don't use, but still everybody wants to know where the hens are. This is the question you will hear. And you will not be able to answer, because I won't tell you, either."

Carrie had to smile at this playful bit of storytelling.

"Don't people offer to buy birds? I would think that some emigrants would want to start their own flocks."

Reizl's mouth curled downward on one side while the opposite brow climbed high. "Not everybody is good with chickens, you know. Especially in this climate. It takes a certain—" She paused, and then shrugged. "Kindred feeling. But you're right. Three times I have sold birds to someone—not just anyone, but someone trustworthy—who wanted to start a flock. And three times they failed."

And she smiled, as if she had described the most amusing game, one at which she was the all-time champion.

Carrie said, "When I finish here today, could I take payment in eggs?"

Reizl rocked her head from side to side, and answered with a shrug. For Carrie to interpret without words.

It was then that she realized that she needed Reizl as a friend. For her eggs, yes, but also because she reminded Carrie of the women she had studied with at the New Amsterdam. Quick-witted, observant, plainspoken. And unusual. It was a word she disliked when it was used to describe a woman, but sometimes it was the only choice.

"That was very good," she said, putting her spoon aside. "And now I have to ask, is there anything you wanted to tell me about Miriam? No problems thus far?"

Reizl shook her head. "No problems. Except I must warn you. You will never come across a woman so anxious, so nervous, as Miriam. Her husband, that one has nerves of steel. She could have waited another four or five hours to call you, but no. The only possible trouble, I took care of."

She pointed with her chin toward the door that led to the adjoining apartment. From her first visit, Carrie knew that each of the brothers had their own living quarters, two here and two elsewhere on Goldblum property.

"I don't understand."

Reizl pressed her lips together and then let a puff of air go. "It's simple. I got rid of them."

Carrie felt herself start. "Pardon?"

"I sent Chava and Rivka away. Gave them a chore that will keep them out of town until late in the day. You think I'm interfering? That's because I am. I am interfering."

Her expression was grimmer now, but unrepentant.

"If you knew the trouble I'm saving you, you would thank me. And one more thing, you should be prepared. Miriam is stubborn. To say she is stubborn like a mule is an insult to the animal. You can deal with this?"

Carrie had to smile. "I can," she said. "I haven't come across a woman in labor yet who can out-stubborn me."

"Good," said Reizl.

They had come to the open door of a bedchamber where servants were busy getting things in order. Linen and dressings were being stacked, trays of food and tea laid out on small side tables, jugs of fresh water were lined up against the far wall, and a servant was busy arranging beeswax candles everywhere, though it would be twelve hours before the sun set. There was so much activity in the room that at first the only sign of the laboring mother Carrie could make out was the very top of a high, rounded headboard.

Reizl said a few words, and the servants shuffled out, revealing Miriam. She lay in her bed, head tilted back. A compress covered her eyes, and her hands rested on the great swell of her belly. The day was already very warm, and there was a sheen of perspiration on her throat.

Standing beside the bed, her hands tucked into her sleeves, Reizl made a tsking noise.

"Such drama," she said. "And so far to go yet. So tell me, what's wrong?"

"Chava and Rivka have abandoned me."

"Oh, those two." Reizl gave an exaggerated sigh. "You don't need them here, telling you what you're doing wrong and what you did wrong yesterday and even still, what you'll do wrong tomorrow. You've got the midwife Ballentyne and me. What more could you want?"

Miriam had pulled the compress off her eyes to show her scowl.

"Never mind," Reizl said. "I'll answer the question myself. You want a healthy child with as little fuss and pain as possible. So, no Chava, always knowing best and telling you so. No Rivka, with the tears and the caterwauling. And where have your manners gone? You don't say hello to the midwife Ballentyne? Tell me, have you seen her hands? Look."

Carrie had no idea of where this was going, but could see no way to forestall it. She held out a hand. Reizl held out her own hand beside Carrie's, and Carrie heard herself draw in a sharp breath.

She had seen mangled hands before, but the patients had always been men who worked with heavy machinery or large animals. In the worst cases, amputation was the only choice, but Reizl was missing only the small finger on the left hand. Every other finger—every bone and joint—had been broken, and none had been properly set. Her hands resembled claws, and would make any kind of fine work—such as sewing—impossible.

"You see?" Reizl was saying. "You see. Beautiful strong hands. Long fingers, narrow palms, perfect midwife hands. And my hands, you know about them." She pulled away, and her hands disappeared back into her sleeves.

"You be glad of the midwife Ballentyne, my girl. Things could be much worse for you."

It took some time for Carrie to collect her wits and sort out her supplies, simply because Reizl and Miriam were such a distraction. In between labor pains—which were still far apart and mild—they talked. About their husbands and children, about sisters-in-law and their families, about neighbors and army officers and the wives of the army officers. And about chickens.

No information was divulged, and this struck Carrie as funny. As if she might have a plan to rob the Goldblums of their flock if they said too much.

Carrie wondered if she should suggest that Miriam try to sleep while it was still possible, and then realized that Reizl had somehow robbed the laboring mother of her tension and anxiety. Her good mood would not last very long, and so Carrie let them carry on.

Women in labor were unpredictable. The timid housewife whose whole life revolved around church and charity and caring for her family might curse her husband, her other children, and the midwife to eternal damnation in the fires of hell. The next day Carrie would attend the wife of a city commissioner, generally known as demanding and intolerant, and learn that a difficult woman could make her way through labor and delivery with grace and good manners.

Some wanted to be left alone as they labored, while others wanted every female relative and friend nearby. In this case Reizl knew Miriam well, and made sure she had as much talk as she needed, and no more.

At noon Reizl excused herself to make sure that the men and children were being properly fed.

"Your tray will be coming in too," she told Carrie. "I won't be gone more than a quarter hour." And then she paused at the door.

"Maybe two."

Deprived of Reizl, Miriam's attention shifted to Carrie. She wanted to know about her training. She wanted to see what was in the carpetbag where Carrie kept her supplies. The medicines interested her especially, and she studied each bottle and box closely, and declared herself dissatisfied.

That medicine labels should be written in Latin struck her as absurd and, more than that, duplicitous. English would be simpler, after all. Latin was another way to hide the truth from patients.

A particularly strong contraction put a stop to this line of inquiry, and then Carrie asked Miriam to get out of bed.

She widened her eyes and smiled as if Carrie had make a joke.

"I am serious," Carrie assured her. "On your feet, please. Walking will do you good."

"But that's ridiculous." She yanked the coverlet up to her neck. "Nonsense. Did you come up with this idea? I can't imagine a real doctor asking such a thing of a woman so near to delivering."

"Hmmm." Carrie hummed under her breath while she gathered her thoughts and decided how to handle the mulish version of Miriam.

She said, "I can assure you that my position on this is nothing out of the ordinary. Any doctor or midwife would encourage you to walk. The idea is to let gravity do some of the work."

"Gravity?" Miriam's voice took on a rasp, and she yanked the sheet up another few inches in a dramatic gesture that most actresses wouldn't dare try.

"Gravity," Carrie confirmed.

"What is this gravity? I knew you would try to bring some Indian potions into the room. Well, I won't have it. I won't have any of your gravity. Where is Reizl? She will put an end to your absurd ideas."

Carrie realized that her choices were limited. She could try to explain Newton's law of universal gravitation, or she could change the subject.

"Walking will speed up labor," Carrie said, approaching from a different angle.

"Ridiculous. Where did you hear such a thing? I want Reizl, she will tell you what's what."

"Reizl is not your midwife," Carrie said. "I am your midwife. You sent for me and asked if I would attend you."

Miriam frowned, but Carrie didn't give her a chance to interrupt.

"Because I am your midwife, you will have to trust my decisions. If you can't, then it would be best if someone else attended you."

This shocked her out of her outrage.

"You would leave?"

"If you do not walk, I will. Yes. Walking will help labor progress, and so you will walk. Let's start with a turn around the room."

In the end Miriam climbed down from the bed, but she had walked no more than ten steps, leaning on Carrie's arm, when she stopped.

"Do you treat all your patients this way? Because if you do, I'll have to listen at the door when Chava goes into labor. You two will be at each other's throats."

At the door Reizl said, "Miriam, what's all this nonsense? I do you the favor of sending Chava away, and you start sounding like her at the first opportunity. Keep walking, and stop badgering the midwife."

As the day wore on and her labor progressed, Miriam worsened, and Reizl's power to distract waned. At the end of a long and difficult contraction when it was almost time to push, Carrie decided to try something that often worked to focus the mother's mind.

She said, "I delivered a baby on a horse trolley last year. Middle of January, full dark at five in the afternoon. The snow was knee-deep and the wind was merciless. Just awful weather. The trolley was full, but more people kept pushing their way in until we were packed together."

Carrie was growing concerned about how little movement she was seeing, but she kept that to herself even as she got up and went to the table where food had been laid out. She picked up a large silver spoon and an elegant tray, walked back to the bed, and hit the tray three times, with as much strength as she could muster.

Both Reizl and Miriam jumped, but Carrie's attention was on the swell of Miriam's belly, where she was relieved to see that the newest Goldblum was jumping too. Small knees and elbows poked out in a flutter, and settled again.

"Was that really necessary? Did you need to scare me half to death? Is it too much to ask for—"

"It is too much," Carrie assured her. "But with any luck I won't have to do that again."

"Good," Reizl said. "But what I want to know is about the woman in labor on the horse trolley."

Grumpy still, Miriam agreed. "It's bad manners to start a story and not—"

A contraction carried her away, and it was a few minutes before it had finished with her.

Without further urging, Carrie went on. "You can imagine," she said. "The aisle crowded with people, everyone tired after a day of work, everyone out of sorts. Broken-down wagons and carriages blocking the way, so we were inching along while the weather got worse and worse. There were sharp little exchanges between strangers. 'Sir! You are standing on my foot.' 'Madam! Your package is poking me in the ribs,' and so on.

"There were two ladies who kept complaining about the breath of the man who stood beside them. 'Like the hottest day in August,' one of them said. 'Worse,' said the other."

Miriam's next contraction was particularly hard and long, but when it had ebbed, she didn't hesitate to make demands.

"So? And? Will you drag this story out until dawn?"

"That's not my intention," Carrie said. "If you listen, I'll tell you what happened. I had a seat on the aisle. In the row before me was an old man, sound asleep with his head against the window, and a lady. She kept leaning forward as if she was looking for something on the floor. She was moaning, I'm sure now, but with the noise of the trolley and the traffic and people griping and complaining, I really didn't hear her. Then she let out a shriek."

"A shriek?" Reizl's eyes were perfectly round.

"A shriek that any midwife would recognize."

Carrie glanced up at Miriam from the station between her upraised legs. "Are you ready to push, Mrs. Goldblum?"

She roared, "When you finish the damn story, I'll push!"

The contraction ebbed, finally, and Reizl was ready.

"So tell us," she said while Miriam panted. "Was she alone, this woman? A stranger, alone in New York City?"

"I don't really know. She didn't speak English, and I don't speak Russian."

"But what did you do?"

"I asked the other riders to clear the end of the car so that I could tend to her. It took some convincing."

A year ago on that trolley, Carrie had been truly angry, but enough time had passed that she could almost smile at the memory.

Over the next hour, while Miriam worked on delivering quite a large child, Carrie told the story in bits and pieces. She described the banker who insisted Carrie was wrong, he had six children and knew what women sounded like when they were about to deliver, and how could a young lady such as herself claim to be a midwife?

"Men," huffed Reizl.

"In the end it was the mother herself who convinced him. She bent forward and vomited. Splattered her lunch all over him. People moved out of the way then. Some thoughtful person dropped a newspaper on the mess on the floor. I got down beside her and delivered her baby."

"Well," Reizl said. "Well. That is what I call a fortunate woman. How did she thank you?"

Carrie glanced up. "She didn't. In fact, she punched me in the face. Mrs. Goldblum, we are almost there. I see a head of dark hair."

Reizl's brows drew down in undisguised disappointment. "Miriam," she said. "You couldn't hold off a couple minutes? We'll never hear the end of the story at this rate."

Carrie laughed, Miriam pushed, and her third child and first son slid into the world just as the parish church bells began to ring seven o'clock.

While Carrie tended to Miriam, Reizl washed and swaddled the boy. It was good to see that there were things Reizl could do even with mangled hands, a thought Carrie kept to herself.

"*Mazel tov*, Miriam. A fine son, a strong boy. David will bust his buttons, he'll be so proud. Is that not so, *yingl*? And your sisters, just wait. They will adore you."

Miriam, exhausted but jubilant, grinned. "I knew it was a boy. I told them, I said it was, but they laughed."

When Reizl put the baby in her arms, Miriam began to weep, tears running down her face that would have wet the newborn's head if Reizl hadn't been ready with a handkerchief.

At the same time, Miriam's hands fluttered over him and then settled gently, gently.

"Hello," she whispered. "Hello, little boy. Someday you'll have to explain to me what took you so long. Such a strong boy. Reizl, do you see?"

"I see," Reizl said. "What a happy day. Your David is in the parlor, all the men are with him. I'll go and tell them the good news. A fine healthy boy. Well done, Miriam. Well done."

Carrie, still occupied with the business of birth, glanced up and grinned at Reizl, who paused to touch her shoulder.

"And you, you are a sly one. Are you going to tell the rest of that story?"

"Certainly," Carrie said, taking a moment to wipe her brow. "And all it will cost you is a few eggs."

IT WAS JUST eight when Carrie left the Goldblums' apartment. After a birth—even one as unremarkable and satisfying as the one she had just attended—she usually wanted nothing more than a sound sleep. Without much thought, she started across the plaza, on the way to her comfortable bed, in a room that she called her own, in a house where she was a stranger and did not feel welcome.

Since midday, she had been resolutely refusing to dwell on Iñigo, who was out looking for Dr. Markham. By now he would be back, with some kind of news. Good or bad. A happier thought came to her: Eli would be on his way; in fact, he might be here. While she was attending Miriam Goldblum, he might have passed by, on his way home. Maybe he was there now, wondering if he could call on her or if the complications would be more than either of them could handle.

He might be at home, and Carrie knew where he lived.

John had drawn her a simple but carefully composed map, marking places he thought she might want to go: bakery, post office, apothecary, seamstress. This small, thoughtful gift took Carrie by surprise to such a degree that her voice cracked when she thanked him. Her interest in the map didn't strike him as suspicious, she was glad to see, and he happily sat down to add more detail. When she asked, he added Fort Marcy—the garrison and the old, abandoned fort—the bank, the grocery store, the newspaper office.

In some cases John knew the Spanish but had forgotten the English names for things. He had been in Santa Fe for so long, and rarely had reason to speak English, he explained. He hoped his lapses in memory wouldn't slow him down in medical school.

Abacería, they worked out quickly, was Spanish for grocer.

With his help Carrie learned where all three of the cantinas were, where the Petit brothers lived and had their transport business, and finally, that *agrimensor* was the Spanish word for surveyor.

"Eli Ibarra was riding with Titus Hardy, wasn't he? So you know him." John had pointed to a spot kitty-corner to Gustavo Aguilar, the grocer. "I learned basic mapmaking from Eli. This is where he lives."

It would be a matter of minutes to walk to the point John had drawn on the map, and still she hesitated, she had to admit to herself, because she was a stranger here. She understood too little of the customs, and even less of what was expected of her.

But she would not be timid. She had not seen very much of Santa Fe, and there was no reason to deny herself a short walk in the last light of day. Instead of crossing the plaza, she turned right and right again, onto a lane that—like most lanes here—had no name.

She was not the only one out in the fresh air. People went about their business, pausing when they noticed her to murmur greetings. An old woman ambled along, trailing three young children, each carrying a basket. A man came out of the printer's shop, owned, as a sign told her, by a Mr. Morris.

In the next building was Mr. Davis, the legal representative of the Glengarry Mining Company. Then came the *ferretería*, a hardware dealership owned by Mr. Carson, whose wife was near her delivery date. She had stopped by twice this week, out of anxiety about the birth or curiosity about Carrie. Or both.

Most shop owners lived in apartments attached to their places of business, and now Carrie caught sight of Mrs. Carson reaching up to take something from a shelf. No drapes or curtains on the windows— most likely, Carrie told herself, because of the climate.

Directly across from the Carsons was an adobe building like many of the others, but this one had a small enameled plaque fixed to the wall beside the front door.

ELISEO IBARRA

INGENIERO AGRIMENSOR Y TOPOGRÁFICO

CARTOGRAPHER, SURVEYOR

She touched the words lightly, surprised at how relieved she was by something so simple, and found she could still laugh at herself. Had she started to believe that Eli was a product of her imagination? The challenges of the first week in Santa Fe had been more trying than she realized.

Tomorrow or the day after, Eli would bring her here to show her the home they were meant to share. That idea was still too large to absorb; it filled her with anxiety and a stunningly simple satisfaction. More important, it reminded her that it would not be wise to stand here staring at the door. That was the kind of behavior someone was sure to notice and remark on, so she turned around and headed back toward the dispensary, and let herself think about Iñigo and the task he had undertaken.

He could be waiting now to tell her that Dr. Markham had died and would never return. What would happen then—to the doctor's family, to his medical practice, to her place here—those questions buzzed around her head like gnats.

It occurred to her that she could go directly to Iñigo's casita to put an end to the mystery, but found she had neither the energy nor the courage. Instead she went through the door that connected the dispensary to the house. There was, as always, a guard standing nearby. He nodded and touched the brim of his hat without saying a word.

She let herself into the short, dim hallway, moving quietly for fear of disturbing Mrs. Markham, who might be sleeping or could be in the *placita*, cocooned in a shawl and watching from the shadowy corners she favored.

Except not. This evening the *placita*—directly in front of her—was filled with light and the low murmur of voices. Men's voices, talking together as friends or family talked. She couldn't make out more than the rhythms she recognized as Spanish rather than English, but there was nothing of conflict or competition to be heard.

She thought of going back to ask the guard who the visitors might be. Going to her room would mean intruding on a gathering of strangers, and that idea was not at all to her liking. In her mind she went over her options, and had to acknowledge to herself that her only choice was to climb through a window or to face the strangers and summon up her patience and courtesy.

A snatch of conversation came to her, one she recognized. Dr. Markham's voice.

The relief she felt was a muted, stunted thing, followed immediately by a flush of anger. She wondered first if there had been a sick friend on his deathbed; the doctor was back, in good spirits, at ease. He disappeared for days, leaving her to deal with all his patients, people she didn't know and who would have no reason to trust her. There were whispers in the town, apparently, that the doctor was forgetting his duties. She doubted he would even be aware of that. Certainly, he wouldn't expect any criticism from her. She could tell him what she thought of his behavior, and no doubt he would fire her on the spot. She walked into the *placita*.

Dr. Markham sat at a table where an elaborate meal had been laid out and thoroughly enjoyed. His color was good, and on the basis of the way he spoke and held himself, Carrie had to conclude that his health was much improved. Even more surprising was the fact that Mrs. Markham sat beside him. Iñigo was there too. He noticed her in the shadows before the others, gave her a half smile and a nod. Of course. The Markhams didn't know about Carrie's connections to the Guevara family, and this was not the time to make them aware. Iñigo's unexpected appearance spared her questions she was not yet ready to answer. Especially not just now, with Dr. Markham finally returned.

Markham's time away hadn't done anything for his wife's health; she was still pale, glassy-eyed, and even thinner and more drawn. Still, she sat close by her husband, a hand on his arm. Whether she was following the conversation—Dr. Markham and Iñigo were arguing, amiably, in Spanish—she couldn't tell. Across the table from her sat Jake Saracen, a cigar in one hand and a goblet of wine in the other.

Dr. Markham called to her.

"Miss Ballentyne," he said, animated and cheerful. "No need to hide in the shadows. Come in. How did it go at the Goldblums'?"

As if they had seen each other earlier in the day. As if he had been here keeping track all along.

"A healthy boy," Carrie said. "Mother and child both doing well."

There was no reaction from Mrs. Markham—not pleasure at the good news, not jealousy, not the slightest hint of curiosity. She might have been deaf. Then she raised her head and looked at Carrie directly, and there was some spark there. Dissatisfaction tinged with suspicion.

"You have a suitor," she said. "He was about to give up on you."

"Now, Mrs. Markham," Jake Saracen said. "I'm not so easily discouraged. Miss Ballentyne knows me that well, I'm sure."

Mrs. Markham looked at Carrie, her jaw rigid as she forced out three light, utterly sarcastic words. "Does she really?"

Before Carrie could compose any kind of answer, Iñigo stood, excusing himself and speaking of the wife who waited for him at home. This was a disappointment that far outweighed Mrs. Markham's suspicion and sour disapproval, but there were no options open to her. Carrie must wish Eli's cousin a good evening and watch as the only person here she truly needed and wanted to talk to went away.

"Come join us, Miss Ballentyne," Dr. Markham said.

His manner was friendly, but Carrie could not risk sitting down at the table and joining in the discussion. Mrs. Markham's cold expression might be tolerated, but Carrie was angry. Truly angry, and she could not trust herself to keep her anger in hand.

She said, "Dr. Markham, I am glad to see you safely at home. Mr. Saracen, thank you for stopping by, but I have to retire or risk falling asleep in front of all of you."

Without waiting for a reaction or permission, she left them, closed herself in her darkened room, and pressed her back against the door.

Dr. Markham had come home, looking well rested and at ease. It was the best possible resolution, but with it came the awareness that a living Dr. Markham might be as big a challenge as a dead one.

43

AT THREE IN the morning, Mr. Carson came to fetch the midwife. The night guard woke Josefa, who came to Carrie's door with the news.

Even at that early hour, Carrie roused quickly, a basic skill for any midwife, but still not pleasant. Just now she didn't mind. In the morning she would not have to sit across the breakfast table from her employers and raise difficult topics.

Mr. Carson was waiting in front of the house. When she appeared in the doorway, he dragged his hat from his head with hands that shook a little. He was rawboned and unkempt, but there was a dignity about him.

"Miss Ballentyne."

"Mr. Carson."

He took her bag and they set off. They had not gone more than a few feet when he began to talk, his voice low and intense and vaguely alarming.

"I've been thinking about something. A question I'd like to put to you, as you are a midwife and know the business."

This could be almost anything: an inquiry about how long labor would last, or how soon it would be before he might resume marital relations. But he surprised her.

"I cain't help thinking that God should have come up with a better way to put human beings on the planet," he said. "The idea that a tiny thing like my Tess—you seen her, you know—should push something the size of a melon out her nether parts, that strikes me as irresponsible planning. I hope you won't mind me saying such things to you?"

He didn't wait for an answer, but continued to voice his concern about God's wisdom, which must have to do, he reasoned, with the fact that he just didn't like females.

She couldn't disagree, but really, providing a sympathetic ear was what was called for, so she listened. It wasn't until they arrived at his home that he finished.

A young man was waiting to let them into the shop. He took the lantern from Mr. Carson and gave him a brace of candles in its place. Not a word was exchanged, and Mr. Carson didn't think to make an introduction. Most probably because the younger man was Indian. Carrie couldn't know what tribe he belonged to, and that made her want to stop and talk to him. In fact, she had resolved to introduce herself in such situations.

Right now, in the dead of night with a woman in labor in the next room, she let that resolution go, with regrets.

She followed Mr. Carson as he wound his way around shelving and tables piled high with goods. Familiar smells came to her: sawdust, oil, tar, iron, coal, sulfur, tobacco. She noted, once again, how smells could rouse memories of home at the oddest times.

At the door into the family apartment, Mr. Carson stopped and dropped his head to study his own feet.

"You'll look after her?"

"Of course. You aren't coming in?"

In the reflected light of the candles, all she could see on his face was misery.

"Cain't," he said, his voice pitched low. "She won't have me in the house. Says I'll make a fuss and ruin her concentration. So I'll just go sit in the stable. The burros are good company when a man's troubled."

As he turned away, she said, "When you hear the baby cry, come on back. At that point she will want you again."

The Carsons had a Mexican housekeeper called Magdalena Luna, whippet thin and leather hard, with seven children of her own. She spoke English, and Carrie was glad of that, because Tess Carson spoke no Spanish.

Señora Luna told Carrie what she needed to know quickly and without embellishment, looking her in the eye without accusation and still, quite clearly, with reservations. Carrie liked her for it. She preferred this kind of honest reception to false cheer.

"You could handle this without me," Carrie told her, and saw some of the reserve slip from the older woman's expression. It was proper and reasonable to show respect, if Carrie hoped to be respected.

Tess Carson, who listened to the whole exchange with interest, finally asked about her husband.

"I'll bet he wailed in your ear like a lost calf."

"He is agitated," Carrie agreed.

That made one woman laugh and got a smile from the other.

"The man can face down horse thieves and card cheats without breaking a sweat," Mrs. Carson said. "But he goes wobbly kneed at the idea of a woman giving birth."

"You aren't feeling anxious?" Carrie asked her. "Women in labor for the first time almost always are."

"This is not her first time," Señora Luna said. "It is her third."

Which, Carrie realized, explained Mr. Carson's anxiety. It also meant that she did not have a full patient history, though she had asked the usual questions when Mrs. Carson came to the dispensary to introduce herself. Now she could only hope that there would be no complications she hadn't considered or prepared for.

"I am sorry for your loss," she said. "Were your first two born sleeping?" An old-fashioned phrase for stillbirth, but one that most women found comforting.

In between contractions Carrie heard the story of how Suzanne and Julia Carson—two and three years old—had been lost to the putrid sore throat just six months earlier. The little girls had been nursed by their mother and Señora Luna in this very room, and here they had died.

It was a common story and a devastating one, a tragedy that had drawn the two women together in a way that went beyond the usual relationship of housekeeper and matron.

"But you should understand," Mrs. Carson told Carrie. "My mother gave birth eleven times without a problem. And every time she was up the next day, cooking and cleaning and busy in the dairy. Last letter I had from my sister Eliza she had seven—all girls—and not a moment's trouble, either. Ma said us girls all had good hips. I guess I can manage a third time. Ain't nothing to it."

Señora Luna, her expression solemn, wiped Mrs. Carson's forehead with a cloth dipped in cool water, but she didn't offer an opinion of any kind. She didn't say, as many women would, that there was nothing to worry about, that God would provide, or that all would be well. No false bravado, but cool water and a gentle touch.

By midday Tess Carson's prediction had come true, and Carrie put a good-sized, very loud little girl into her mother's arms.

Mrs. Carson held the child to her chest, and began to shake.

Carrie first thought was that she might be convulsing, but then she saw the truth of it. The woman was terrified to start over again with a child who could be taken from her without reason or warning. Just six months ago she had learned that lesson. Carrie imagined that she hadn't allowed herself to think beyond this birth, but now she could no longer keep her fears at bay. Her whole heart in one small creature, utterly vulnerable. Her sobs came up from the deepest part of her being.

Later Carrie would wonder what she would have done without

Mrs. Luna, who was not shocked or frightened by any of this. Who seemed to have prepared herself for exactly this.

"Tess. Tess. Of course you can. Of course you can. Look how strong this little girl is."

Her voice was low and steady and firm, and the rhythm of her speech was melodious.

"Look at her face. Look at her, the way she's looking at you. This little girl is a new light in the world. She is your new light. Now it's time to introduce her to her father, don't you think?"

IT WAS NOT the first time Carrie had delivered two healthy infants in less than twenty-four hours, but it was still—and she thought, would always be—greatly satisfying. Now, at midday, she was free for a while. This would not have been the case at home; at the New Amsterdam, it was expected that she would fill the rest of the day with her usual duties, no matter how tired she might be.

Life was different in New Mexico, where people were more sensible about things that could not be changed. Because no one could demand cooler temperatures, they gave in gracefully by means of a custom they called siesta. John had explained to her that shops and offices and even cafés would be shut now that the summer had settled in. Siesta meant simply that from noon until half past three or four, everyone got out from under the sun, retiring to doze in rooms made a little cooler by thick adobe walls.

When the sun had loosed its grip, the town woke up. Businesses opened and people ventured back into the light of day to take up wherever they had left off.

The dispensary closed, too, unless there was an emergency. Carrie hoped that there would not be one today. She would limit herself to two hours of sleep and use the rest of the siesta to catch up on paperwork. She had to record both births in her daybook, as she had recorded each patient she had seen, day by day, this first week in Santa Fe. At the bottom of each day's entries, she asked herself the question:

Was she meeting her responsibilities to the best of her ability? And the more important question that as yet had no answer: What if her best was not good enough?

When siesta was over, she would seek out Dr. Markham, and they would talk. She was determined to speak plainly, and if he was unwilling, to compel him to listen. For Lulu's sake this conversation would have to take place in the dispensary, in the spare, clean rooms where she had spent so much time over the last week. Where she might no longer work, after she spoke to Dr. Markham.

It would have happened just that way, if not for Lulu, who had slipped away sometime during the siesta. When Josefa went to rouse her at half past three, she found her bed rumpled, but unoccupied.

Josefa, competent and calm as always, began by knocking on Carrie's door, as Lulu stopped by to visit at least twice a day. Carrie looked up from her daybook and then around the room, as if Lulu might be hiding in plain sight. Then she got up to help Josefa look for the girl.

The doctor and his wife were still napping in the *placita*, and so Carrie and Josefa checked cabinets and blanket chests and shadowy corners. Then they went to search the dispensary and found John, who was getting ready to open the doors. He volunteered to check in the convent garden, and went off to do that while Josefa headed toward the plaza.

"What can I do?" Carrie asked. "Where should I search?"

Josefa, distracted, took a moment to answer.

"Violante," she said. "Go see Violante and Iñigo. Lulu sometimes wanders over there to see the horses."

CARRIE CALLED A hello into the open door of Iñigo and Violante's casita, waited, and called again. The wind came up and brought her snatches of talk from the nearest stable. She turned to walk in that direction, trying not to imagine what would happen if Lulu stayed hidden. Because, she told herself, of course she was hiding. Dr. Markham had come home, and Lulu had snuck out to teach him a lesson.

Growing up bracketed by strong-willed sisters, Carrie understood what Lulu was about. Little girls forbidden the outlet of anger found other ways to assert themselves. Martha had cut all the hair from her own head over what she saw as an unjust distribution of cake. Jean, according to family lore, had once barricaded herself in the necessary when Blue refused to lend her a particular hair ribbon. She had been about Lulu's age at the time, and never budged until it was Da pounding on the door.

The quest was possibly universal; all over the world, girls puzzled over how to teach their fathers a lesson. That was what was happening now, and nothing more. Lulu was too clever to be enticed into a stranger's carriage, certainly. The idea was almost ludicrous; Carrie wanted to laugh at this idea—carriages were seldom seen on the Calle del Convento Viejo.

At the stable door she stopped long enough to listen for familiar voices, and was rewarded. Violante crooning, as women did for small, fragile things. Murmuring from Iñigo and a male voice she couldn't identify, all in tones that a midwife recognized. While she tried to decide whether to knock or simply walk in, Chico appeared at her side, nudging her hand with his nose.

It might be silly, and she would have a hard time explaining her feelings to anyone, but Chico's coming to greet her gave Carrie courage. If something was really wrong, he wouldn't be leaning against her leg, and so she walked into the shade of the stable, where Iñigo, Violante, some of their workers, and a disheveled Lulu were gathered in a stall in a half circle.

She called out, but they were all concentrating so intently that it wasn't until she stood beside Violante that they took note.

"Carrie." Violante put a hand to her breast. "What a surprise. Now look, do you see? Our Bricia has foaled. *¡Qué potrillo más precioso!*"

The new colt was in fact beautiful. For the next few minutes they all admired him as he wobbled around the stall trying to make sense of his legs. The mare ran her nose over him, as if she wasn't quite sure about this creature, but when he began nosing for the teat, she encouraged him.

"*Sí*," Carrie agreed. "*Muy bonita.*"

To Lulu she said, "You've put a great fright into Josefa. She's out searching for you. John too."

Lulu's face went slack and then flooded with color.

"My mother?"

"A quarter hour ago both your parents were still sleeping in the *placita*—"

She didn't wait to hear more. Lulu ran for home, her hair streaming behind her. Carrie could only hope that Mrs. Markham was still sleeping.

"Is the little girl in trouble now?" Iñigo asked, looking concerned.

Violante pressed her mouth shut as if to stop herself from answering the question.

"I don't think she's in trouble," Carrie offered, though she had no grounds for such a prediction. "I'll just go see if I can be of any help."

"Good," Violante said. "But first, quick, we will come by to fetch you at eight."

This brought Carrie up short. "Fetch me? For what?"

Violante's good humor came back, just that easily.

"The fandango, of course," she said. "Don't even dream of saying no."

"But I can't—I couldn't—not without . . ."

The workers were all watching her with great interest.

"You can. You will have us as chaperones, and anyway, you think he would want you to sit alone while everyone else is enjoying themselves?"

Carrie was glad that Violante said that much in English, but she raised a hand over her head and left rather than be drawn into a discussion that would quickly rob her of her composure. She would stop and spend a few minutes with Mimosa instead, and settle her nerves that way.

All was quiet at the Markhams' when Carrie slipped in through the side entrance. From the sounds in the kitchen, Josefa and Manuela were cooking, but they both stuck their heads out and gestured for her to join them.

John was alone in the dispensary, but Carrie needed to know Lulu's fate.

"What happened?" Carrie asked. "Did they not notice that she was gone?"

Neither of them had been truly worried about Lulu. She was a clever girl and could look after herself. Manuela went out into the kitchen garden with a knife and a basket while Josefa explained. This had not been Lulu's first unapproved venture into town. The girl had come up with a number of ways to get in and out unseen.

"And if her mother did notice?"

Both Josefa's brows went up. Then she changed the subject.

She said, "You look very agitated. Did the birth not go well?"

They talked for a few minutes about the Carsons' new daughter, but Carrie's mind kept wandering away to Violante, who would come by at eight with her husband, unless Carrie could find a way to divert her.

Josefa knocked on the table and she started out of her thoughts.

"I asked why you're so agitated," Josefa said.

It took a minute to organize her thoughts, but in the end she said it as simply as she could manage: Iñigo and Violante Guevara intended to take her with them to the fandango. Nothing she said to dissuade Violante had any effect. They would be here at eight.

"You will like the fandango," Josefa said, turning back to the dishes she was wiping.

"I don't doubt it," Carrie agreed. "But I have so many things to do here—"

"Nothing that can't wait until tomorrow."

In her surprise Carrie could think of no way to counter this point.

"That may be so," she said finally. "But there are other problems. You know exactly what clothes I have with me. I would look a fright showing up in my blue cambric. And also, I don't know that the Markhams would approve."

Josefa tilted her head to one side as she wiped a pot, apparently debating with herself. Then she looked at Carrie directly.

"If Iñigo and Violante invite you, the Markhams will approve."

At Carrie's sharp look, she stepped back from so bold a prediction. "Dr. Markham would approve, and that would be enough."

This was not going as Carrie had hoped; she began to search through her pocket for a kerchief to wipe her brow.

Josefa was watching her quite closely. She said, "If you had something to wear, would you be happy to go?"

And there was the question. At the end of a very challenging week, it had always been her habit to find some kind of entertainment—usually dancing—to shake off the mood. She and Nathan had danced sometimes until one or two in the morning, and it never failed to lift her spirits.

If only Eli were here, she would go gladly.

She said, "Josefa, the fact is I don't have anything to wear. I told Violante so, but she didn't believe me. So I will just have to send them on without me."

"We'll see," Josefa said.

To pursue this conversation any further struck Carrie as a waste of time and energy. She was needed in the dispensary, and after supper she would have to seek out Dr. Markham. The conversation she had been thinking about for days could wait no longer.

The very idea made her stomach go sour. Her frustration and anger swelled into her throat, and in that moment she decided to act on her own behalf for once.

"I would like to go to the fandango," she said to Josefa. "If there's a solution to the problem about my clothes. You seem to have some ideas on that subject."

44

IT WASN'T UNTIL Violante and Iñigo called for Carrie that she realized how much they were looking forward to the dance. They almost shivered with excitement, this older couple in their best clothes. Traditional costume, Carrie guessed, brought with them from Basque country.

Iñigo wore a blue-and-red-striped waistcoat under a dark blue sack jacket. A broad red sash wrapped around his trim waist added a hint of elegance, underscored by the slouch cap tilted over one eye. Violante was even more colorful. She wore voluminous blue skirts and a beautiful heavily embroidered shawl in bold colors that she had tucked into a red bodice. The flush on her cheeks and her smile gave Carrie a sense of what she had been like as a young woman. Now in their old age, they still made a handsome couple.

As they left, quietly, Carrie glanced back toward the *placita*, empty now that the Markhams had retired. She had not yet managed a private discussion with the doctor, and wondered if she would have any more success tomorrow or the day after or ever.

Once on their way in an evening still bright with sunshine, she smoothed over the skirts Violante had loaned her. The fabric swung like a bell around her ankles with every step.

"You are very sly," she said to Violante. "I made excuses on the basis of my lack of party clothes, and all the while you had already solved the problem. It is very kind of you to lend me your things."

The clothes had been waiting for her when she finished in the dispensary, carefully laid out on her bed. Carrie had hesitated before dressing, pausing to admire the fabric and needlework. No doubt Violante had worn this as a younger woman; over the years the red of the skirts had faded, but it was still very pretty.

"You don't like surprises?" Iñigo was asking. "Violante don't like them, either, for herself, but for others—"

He jumped aside before his wife could pinch him, but they were both laughing.

"I am so glad it fits you," Violante said. "We could not let you miss the fandango."

The stream of people making their way up the winding road to the old fort were in high spirits. Most of them were young, but there were far more middle-aged and older people than Carrie would have anticipated. All dressed in their best clothing.

Iñigo said, "I built it, you know."

Carrie glanced up at him. "You built—"

"Well, mostly I dug. Kearny wanted a moat, all the way around and eight feet deep. Of course, I didn't do all the digging. About half the crew were regular army, and the other half they hired."

Violante stepped in to translate what Carrie had missed, and just then tall adobe walls came into sight. Iñigo's gaze moved over the fort with something like nostalgia.

"Oh yes," he said. "General Kearny and his Army of the West swooped right in once the war with Mexico was done. Americans in, Mexicans out, and a huge worthless fort nobody wanted."

"Old man, don't be silly," Violante said. "It wasn't just the Americans who wanted a fort. *We* wanted a fort. We thought we needed it, but it didn't turn out that way. And since then we've had a proper place for a party. Could not have planned it better, is the way I see it."

Carrie knew something of the history, which was not particularly complicated or unusual. In 1821 Mexico had finally won independence from Spanish rule, but it wasn't long before the U.S. made its move under the banner of Manifest Destiny. The war that began with the U.S. annexation of Texas ended in 1848 with a treaty that halved the size of Mexico and doubled the territory of the United States. This very land, Carrie reminded herself. Ten years ago this had been Mexico, and before that, Spain. The historians and politicians would argue about treaties and borders for centuries, but rarely would they consider how the people came to grips with such monumental changes. Violante spoke of the fort and the war in neutral terms, but kept her real thoughts to herself.

This was certainly not the place for such a discussion. The gates stood open while people poured in, and out, and in again, the excitement building. It was too noisy to talk, so Carrie followed her hosts to a small table just off what must have once been the parade ground, looking around herself with great interest.

Inside the walls the only evidence that this was once meant as a military fortification was the odd star shape of the structure as a whole, and a blockhouse that sat half underground halfway down the parade grounds. The fort was large enough to house as many as three hundred soldiers, as Iñigo had told her, but there were no barracks or stables or anything else left. Instead the space had been transformed into something like a beer garden: rough tables and benches, a long raised bar where food was being set out, another where ale and beer and the liquors that had been made in this area for what might be a thousand years were closely guarded by an older woman with a forbidding frown.

Most of the conversations were in Spanish, girls laughing together, children shouting challenges, men gesturing with arms and hands and exaggerated expressions as they told tall tales. Along the periphery a whole army of matrons—*las abuelas*, or grandmothers, Carrie had heard them called—sat on stools that must have been brought in especially for them.

The matrons talked among themselves, but their eyes were fixed on the crowd, roaming back and forth to seek out daughters and nieces and any unmarried girl who might forget what was expected of her. A bodice that revealed too much, a flirtatious giggle, the girl who allowed young men to stand too close.

Carrie saw all this in a matter of seconds and then turned her attention to the raised platform in front of the blockhouse where a group of men, elaborately dressed, were unpacking instruments. She counted seven guitars, no two alike. They differed in size and number of strings and shape, and even in color. Beyond the guitars there was only a box drum, where one of the musicians already sat with a toddler in his lap.

"The Chávez family," Iñigo told her. "That's Ernesto, with his youngest grandson. They start out young in the family business."

"Is it just men who play?"

The question surprised Iñigo. "*Claro. ¿Qué más da?* The men play and sing, the women sing. See there, the *abuela*? As a young woman, Carmen Chávez had a golden voice. Now she is just *la alburera*."

Violante turned to Carrie.

"Do you know this word? The *alburera* is a woman of quick wits and a sharp tongue, one who always outwits the men. Men, they say *alburera* like it has a bad smell, but from a woman? It is a compliment. I would be pleased if people thought of me as *alburera*."

Iñigo seemed ready to argue this point, but Violante sent him off on an errand that Carrie didn't quite catch. And no matter; whatever Iñigo had gone to do was beside the point. Violante wanted no men nearby for what she was planning to say.

She put a hand on Carrie's wrist.

"I have to admit, at your age, I loved this." She gestured around herself. "Music and dancing and boys on a summer night."

She shook her head as if to stop herself from saying too much, but she could not help almost wiggling in pleasure at such memories. Then she made an effort to be serious.

"But you have to be careful. If Eli were here—he really should be here—you would have his protection, and the men would mind their manners. Now they will be as forward as you allow them to be, and that would have consequences. So I have a suggestion."

Carrie leaned forward. "Yes?"

"When the music starts—you see they are picking up their guitars now—Iñigo will dance with you. Then he brings you back to me, and when the next man approaches, I will touch your wrist like I am now if you should dance with him. But. If there is reason to refuse him, I'll keep my hands folded like this. Then you refuse politely. You will do this?"

Carrie wasn't sure what to make of Violante's suggestion, and still, the decision was very simple. These two people had taken her under their protection, and were looking after her as they looked after every other younger woman in the family. It would be the height of foolishness to dismiss the advice of someone who knew the way Santa Fe worked. And if Violante was overly cautious, Carrie didn't mind. She was a stranger here, and caution was called for. Beyond those very prim thoughts, Carrie had to admit to herself at least that it was a great relief to know she wasn't obligated to dance with one stranger after another.

Then the music started and Iñigo appeared beside her, executing a bow that any courtier could be proud of. Carrie stood up to dance with him, her heart thundering with the novelty of it all. The music, the crowd, the dances themselves, all of it was deeply, utterly stirring.

Iñigo was almost seventy, but he swept her away as if he hadn't yet seen his thirtieth birthday. The whirlwind of dancers separated for the briefest moment, and they were drawn into the heart of the dance.

Somewhere nearby a man put back his head and let out a high yipping sound of pleasure, one that others took up so that the voices, braided together, lifted into a sky threaded with dusk in shades of copper and gold, azure and pearl. The music went on and on, the rhythm of the guitars and the box drum amplified by the way men stamped their feet. The earth itself shivered.

ELI RODE INTO Santa Fe just as the music began.

Hours before, he had resigned himself to the fact that it would be too late to call on Carrie by the time he got home. Beyond that he was bone-tired and needed nothing so much as sleep.

But there was music, and a fandango. Where there was music and dancing, Iñigo and Violante would be. Iñigo and Violante, who had promised him that they would look after Carrie. And that would mean taking her with them to Fort Marcy.

In fact, he could see Carrie tonight. Once he had looked to the horses and scrubbed the dirt from his head and hands and put on clean clothes, he could head up to old Fort Marcy. Where a dozen men would be watching her, determined to get her on the dance floor.

Carrie would hesitate to dance with strangers, but that wouldn't work to her advantage. If she refused to dance, people would wonder out loud about the new midwife. Was she *una fresa*? Too prideful a person, too fine to dance at a fandango. A real strawberry. Maybe, it was suggested, she'd be more comfortable at a ball, the far fancier and more formal events put on by the rich at the Guzman fonda.

He trusted Violante to explain what Carrie should do, might do under circumstances, dare not do. He trusted Carrie to be practical and to listen. Rather than cause offense, she would dance.

Eli picked up the pace.

At home he went through the chores that could not be ignored or put off. Water, oats, hay, straw. He brushed all three horses down, talking to them in tones they knew: they had done well on the trail today, and earned their rest. With his pulse throbbing in his ears, it was difficult to sound calm, but he was not a boy and he could master himself. Something he would have many occasions to demonstrate over the next days and weeks.

Eli was aware that he was smiling like a besotted seventeen-year-old as he set out, walking fast, for the fort. In the clear night air, the music drifted down like mist to get caught up in a wind that carried it away into the night.

There was always a crowd of men outside the fort, passing around a jug, telling jokes and tall stories. Eli slid by without being seen and was glad.

In front of him, half the old parade ground was filled with dancers. People in their finest clothes, colors almost glowing in the last of the light, moving as the music required of them, but alive with the joy of it. They could not be silent, and the noise—the guitars, the voices raised in song, the laughter—filled the world.

He had missed this kind of dancing and looked forward to it now. At the same time it struck him, in this moment, as a foreign and strange enterprise, and the reason was obvious. He had spent the previous day at his mother's pueblo, dancing with his grandfather and uncles, his hands coated in white clay, dressed as they were dressed, in the colors of the land around them.

It had been too long since he had last spent time at the pueblo, but it was all immediately familiar. He took comfort in the dance, a solemn, demanding undertaking that required careful attention to each meaningful step in the prescribed path, and not just from the dancers. From the *kiva* to the plaza they danced, and the dance drew everything together.

He watched for a minute more until he knew where to find Violante and Iñigo, and watched still for Carrie among the dancers. They shifted and parted and came together to the rhythm of the box drum, until finally he caught sight of her. Her head tilted up, she was listening to Jake Saracen, who was dividing his attention between dancing and, as was forever the case, talking. She wouldn't be able to make out anything in the noise, but as long as Jake could hear himself, he wouldn't much mind.

In St. Louis he had seen her dance for the first time. The Carrie he had just begun to know, the young lady from the train, serious and sincere, had transformed on the dance floor into a different creature. Dancing, Carrie Ballentyne came alive. The sight had robbed him of breath, and with that, it was clear to him that it didn't matter how little they had in common; he was on the brink of falling in love, and for once the idea didn't frighten him.

Now he walked into the fort to claim Carrie for himself.

As THE MUSIC came to a stop, Carrie turned toward the table where the Guevaras sat, but Jake Saracen caught her wrist and shook his head.

"Hold up now, Miss Ballentyne. Where you running off to? Lots more dancing to do."

She considered how best to respond to this very good-looking, very confident man. He flirted, but there was no malice in him. And still she needed to draw a line.

"I wish you many excellent dance partners," she said. "But I will return to my friends." She used a tone that the men she grew up with would recognize.

In the first moment, she thought he might ignore both manners and common sense, but then he let go of her wrist and instead offered her an arm.

He said, "Thank you, Miss Ballentyne. May I call on you again?"

She answered in the only way she could, with a small, unconvincing smile. It would be a mistake to offer him any encouragement, but neither did she want to offend him, if it could be avoided. She needed friends in Santa Fe, and Jake Saracen could be one of them. He was a very good dancer; he told interesting stories and answered questions without challenging her right to ask them.

"*Ven rápido*," Violante called to them. "Girl, you are flushed. Come sit and drink something."

She did not include Jake in this invitation, and that left him with no options. He bowed, and left them.

"That was great fun," she told Violante. "I hope he's not the only one who can dance."

The musicians were picking up their guitars again, just as two men began to approach Carrie from opposite directions. A glance at Violante told her that she should refuse both of them, and that was what she did, once in English and more slowly the next time, in Spanish. She meant to be kind, but of course it might not be taken that way.

"You don't want me to dance with the postmaster?" Raising her voice to be heard.

"Forget the postmaster," Violante shouted back. "This one coming up now, this one you should dance with."

Carrie turned and saw a man approaching, walking through the dancers as if they didn't exist. A very unladylike sound came up from her throat, and then Eli was in front of her.

"*Ahí estás*," Violante shouted. "*Lento como el burro.*"

Eli didn't even look in Violante's direction. Instead he took Carrie's hand and drew her to her feet. He lowered his head to speak into her ear, his voice steady and clear and low enough to drown out the noise.

"Is she right? Tell me, *querida*. Did I stay away too long?"

The warmth of his breath made every nerve jump.

She said, "You're here now. That's enough. Are we going to dance?"

"Yes." He gave her a slow smile. "*Vamos a bailar.* Dancing is the right place to start."

At first she was preoccupied with the simple fact of him, and barely took note of the music. This only worked, she would realize later, because he was such a good dancer that she could follow his lead without much thought or effort.

It was common knowledge that many religions discouraged and even forbade dancing of any kind, but she had never thought very closely about the rules and conventions that played no role in her own life. Now, for the first time, she realized how dancing mimicked the things that men and women did when they were alone, behind closed doors. Color and heat flooded through her, something she could not hide or deny, not from Eli.

And so she concentrated on the small things: the texture of his shirtsleeve under her fingers, the solid circumference of his forearm, the warmth of the hand that rested at her waist. There was nothing soft about him anywhere, but his touch was gentle.

He smelled of soap. Not of the everyday lye soap, but the milled soap sold in drugstores and fancy goods shops. From this she knew that he had stopped at home to wash and change and see to the chores that couldn't be ignored. He was a practical man. Sensible. Her people would approve, a thought that had come to her before.

Glancing up—very quickly, because she was suddenly too embarrassed to meet his gaze—she was surprised to find she had forgotten how very tall he was. Tall and lean and muscled in the way of men who worked hard for a living. Powerful in the purest sense of the word.

She was dizzy with elation, unrecognizable to herself, and glad of it.

The music stopped. Carrie might have lost her balance, but his hands cupped her elbows and kept her upright. Just then she saw him make a decision. He pressed his mouth to her temple. A brief, warm kiss that anyone might have seen, and still she couldn't do anything but smile. For that moment they smiled at each other like idiots, and she was so caught up in what she saw on his face that she thought of pulling his head down so that she could kiss him properly, damn the repercussions.

In another place and time, with another man, she would have seen a smile as something as simple as the flexing of the zygomaticus muscles in response to social cues. Automatic, and usually without any deep meaning. But Eli's smile worked like the drawing back of curtains on a stage.

He was still the strong, capable, thoughtful man who had befriended her during a difficult journey, but she hadn't seen what was now in front of her: a man who could laugh. Who liked to laugh. Not so long ago, she had doubted she would ever marry. She imagined a quiet life for herself, but somewhere between Manhattan and this small town on the western frontier, she had realized that a solemn, quiet life would eventually bore her to death.

The dance ended, and he pulled her closer rather than shout. "Let's sit with Violante and Iñigo for a while," he said. "Then we'll go home."

He said those words: *we'll go home*; she had heard him clearly. What he meant, that was the question. Before she could figure it out or ask, she saw that Rob Ramsey had taken a seat next to Iñigo, and was waiting for her. Because she had agreed to dance with him.

Eli figured it out before Carrie could explain.

"You promised Ramsey a dance?"

She gave a small, mute nod.

"How many others?"

Her voice cracked. "Two."

"All right," Eli said. "You dance. I'll watch. And then we'll go."

"But—"

"Iñigo and Violante will follow us—at a distance. That will check the gossip. Most of it, anyway."

He faced her, and with a very formal bow from the shoulders, thanked her for the dance, using a lot of flowery prose that brought her to the brink of an unladylike bark of laughter. Whether his purpose was to annoy Rob Ramsey or to make a point with her wasn't clear until he straightened, and winked at her.

How strange that something as simple as a wink could set every nerve to vibrating.

Mr. Ramsey was a gentleman, utterly correct and polite, but he was not quite equal to the triple step that the dance required. Carrie had no wish to hurt his feelings, and so she showed him an unremarkable expression, pleasant but not exactly inviting.

Toward the end of the dance, she saw that her next partner was waiting for her. Joe Landry was a clerk in the courthouse, very formal but for his ink-stained fingers. Tonight there was a swipe of ink on his cheek as well, but nobody had bothered to tell him. He had asked her to dance soon after she arrived, had seemed pleased when she agreed, but now she saw little interest in his expression as they began to dance.

He held himself apart, and made no effort to talk. This was the Joe Landry who had approached her with such eagerness outside the post office, she was sure of it. All she saw now was a mild distaste. She understood then that he had seen her dancing with Eli and come to some conclusions that angered him. A white woman who spent time with a Mestizo was foolish, or a whore.

What he would say when he learned she was going to marry Eli, that she could imagine too.

Her gaze drifted toward the gates. Eli was there, leaning against the wall with his arms crossed, watching her dance with the dull Mr. Landry under a clear night sky and a moon so bright that it cast shadows. Moonshadow, her Da had liked to say, meant that mischief-makers would be out in full force.

The last man she had agreed to dance with was Albert Henry, an assistant land manager. Not that she understood very much about his work, but then she didn't need to. He volunteered that information and much more, without pause.

To his credit, Al Henry was a very good dancer. He was so accomplished that he could do a half dozen other things at the same time. He bellowed greetings to friends and compliments to young women, passed along messages in a thunderous bass that cut through the music, and in a spotty but enthusiastic Spanish he asked about a horse he hoped to buy.

Suddenly he seemed to remember the woman he was dancing with.

"So," he said. "I bet nobody has told you about Sol Taylor. Standing over there, blond hair shaved close to the scalp?"

Carrie agreed that she saw the man in question.

"Sol Taylor," he repeated. "A first-class wrangler, but don't ever call him a gaucho, he don't take kindly to it. In general he ain't fond of anything or anybody even a little bit Mexican. Now here's the thing. The rumor is, Sol has six toes. That is, twelve toes, six right, six left."

He waited for a reaction, and so she dutifully raised an eyebrow. This seemed to be praise enough.

"You see the man he's talking to? That's Pete Terney, a barkeep at the Pepperharrow."

Mr. Terney, he wanted her to know, had one bright blue eye and one mud-brown eye. Both real.

"When I first met him, I thought to myself, 'Why, that's the most realistic fake eye I have ever seen.' Then the joke was on me, because it ain't fake."

When his contemplation of Mr. Terney's eyes had come to an end, he was launching into a story of the fort's quartermaster, who had a fancy stick he liked to beat lazy recruits with. When the music stopped, Carrie's ears were ringing, and she was glad of a break.

Mr. Henry bowed politely, and asked if he might walk her home.

It was an outrageous thing to suggest, and he knew it—his cheeky grin gave away the game.

"And if I said yes, the gossips would talk about nothing else for days. You may not have to worry about your reputation, but I—"

He held up a hand, palm out, to stop her.

"There's a way around that." A dimple appeared in his right cheek, and he ducked his head a little but kept her gaze. "Here's what we'll do. I'll propose, you accept, and all the *abuelas* will be satisfied. They'll still gossip, a course, but that knife'll be too dull to draw blood. So what do you say, why don't we get hitched?"

"Now I have to laugh at you," Carrie said. "But it's your own doing."

He inclined his head as if a response required some deep thought. "You could laugh at me on the walk home."

"Oh, I will. But you won't be there to appreciate it."

He clasped a hand to his heart in melodramatic dismay. "All right," he said, his tone congenial. "But you know I ain't about to give up so easy."

Carrie would have ordered him gone, if it had been in her power, because Eli was walking toward them. There were just a few seconds to come up with a plan to defuse what might turn out to be an awkward interception.

She said, "Mr. Henry, do you know Mr. Ibarra? May I introduce you?"

The fact that they were both vaguely insulted by this was oddly gratifying.

"Oh, we've met," Eli said wryly. "Long time, Al."

Henry sighed and touched a knuckle to his brow. Squinted and looked at Eli sideways. "That's true enough. But it could have been a little longer, if it was up to me."

Carrie swallowed a laugh, but could not hide her smile.

"I'll just sit with Mrs. Guevara," Al Henry said. "And wait till Miss Ballentyne finds another spot on her dance card for me. Won't be a hardship, a course."

Violante, unusually quiet through all this, rolled her eyes.

"It's true," he insisted. "If I thought I could get you on the dance floor—"

She flicked her fingers at him, unimpressed. "*No trates de engrasarme, joven. Descarado tejano.*"

At his blank look she frowned, but Eli provided a translation.

"She says you shouldn't waste her time trying to butter her up. I'm guessing that goes for Miss Ballentyne too."

"Well, hell," Al Henry said, his hands on his hips as he twisted one way and then the other to look each of them in the eye. "If you're going to be like that."

When he had walked away, Carrie said, "That was unfortunate. His feelings are hurt."

All three of them—Violante, Iñigo, and Eli—laughed at this openly.

"First he would have to have feelings," Violante said.

Iñigo looked like a judge about to pass down a verdict he regretted. "Al Henry," he said. "*Es un timador.*"

On the walk from the fort down to Santa Fe, Eli and Iñigo kept up a lively discussion about the new foal while Violante and Carrie walked ahead.

She asked the obvious question. "*Timador?*"

"A trickster."

"I see. I'll be on my guard. Now tell me, did you know Eli would be back today?"

Violante shook her head. "Not me, no. But Iñigo, probably. *Es un maestro guardián secreto, mi esposo.*"

Carrie couldn't imagine this. First, that Iñigo was a keeper of secrets, and second, that his wife would take pride in that fact.

Violante glanced at her. "Really, this is what concerns you just now? The trickster Al Henry is on your mind. Nothing else?"

They were both very aware of the men behind them. Eli's voice was impossible to ignore, even when he was speaking Basque, as he did now. Iñigo said something, and Eli drew in a short, sharp breath in agreement. A habit she had noticed early on. Before she had any idea that they were headed toward each other.

Now that he was here and things would start to move forward, she had to face a question she had been avoiding: hardly two weeks before, she had explained to Eli that they must wait to make their attachment public. Out of caution and self-preservation, out of a sense of responsibility to her employer, out of fear for her reputation, as an individual and a midwife.

The urge to tell him she had been wrong was almost irresistible. She would gladly go with him this very night, to turn away and never spend another night under the Markhams' roof.

And of course it was impossible. A responsible midwife could not leave a patient in such obvious, serious trouble. It didn't matter that Mrs. Markham had never allowed Carrie to examine her or provide any kind of care. It didn't matter that she was abusive and mean and seemed to enjoy causing embarrassment and discomfort. But it did matter that she was in pain, and unable to recover from her loss because she could not face it.

The simple truth was that Carrie had left her home in New York and traveled across the country to care for Indira Markham, and she had failed. She had been misled, yes. Dr. Markham should have provided a full history, but then again, she should have asked more questions. Asking the right questions, that was the trick. Amelie had a natural talent for finding the questions that would open doors that had seemed to be nailed shut.

She imagined Amelie here, and just that simply, she knew where she had gone wrong. Amelie Savard would not talk to Mrs. Markham; she would listen.

All of this she would have to tell Eli, but not just now. Not tonight. Tonight she would have a short time alone with him, ten minutes or a half hour at most, in a quiet corner. Somewhere. She hoped he had a plan.

ELI's PLAN WAS simple. Instead of delivering Carrie to the Markhams' door, he took her hand and kept walking, as if it were the logical thing to do. He had told Iñigo about this plan, so there was no discussion in the street where the Markhams' house guards would hear.

Carrie seemed content to follow along. She was not, in the first line, a patient woman, but in this she was willing to be led. It wouldn't last long, he was aware of that.

Just minutes later Iñigo and Violante wished them a good night and slipped away to their casita.

"Are we going to see Mimosa?"

This was something Eli liked about Carrie. When unsure, she often simply sorted through the evidence available to her and came to a conclusion. She was seldom wrong, in his experience of her. She wasn't wrong now.

"I want to see how she's faring."

"Of course. At ten o'clock at night, that's what you want."

He grinned. All day he had wondered how strict she would be about the time they could spend together. Her willingness to walk alone with him into the shadows was a good sign. Her hand was cool in his, the fingers long and straight. Eli lifted it to his mouth and kissed her knuckles as they came to the first stable. Inside, the horses shifted, and then settled.

In the moonlight Carrie looked very pale, her eyes enormous, and there was a very small tremble at the corner of her mouth. For the first time he hesitated.

"You aren't afraid of me."

That made her smile. "Of course not. But there is so much to tell you, I don't know where to start."

With one finger Eli caught a wayward strand of hair and tucked it behind her ear.

"That's just fine," he said. "Because I do. I know where to start."

He took her face in his hands and tilted it up.

"You're smiling, *querida*."

One brow rose in surprise. "So are you. Can you kiss me while you smile?"

"I think I'm equal to the challenge."

He let his breath touch her brow, her cheek, the line of her jaw. First just that whisper of breath and then the lightest brush of lips against skin. Drawing in her scent to hold it tight.

Then, all at once, he had had enough of waiting. He caught up her mouth with his own and let the kiss take over.

CARRIE WAS STARTING to understand that there was something mysterious about a lover's kiss. Something that could not be explained by an accounting of the act itself. This thought was in her mind while his lips brushed over her cheek, and then he was kissing her, and it all disappeared. Everything inside her shifted and liquefied and began to flow from that point where they were joined. Eli's kiss, the soft suckling of his mouth, the brush of his tongue against hers, it was like discovering a hidden path that might lead anywhere, and must be followed.

The only reasonable thing to do was to surrender. To allow herself to disappear into the mystery, to set out on that path with him. The promise of it filled her with terror and joy.

45

DR. MARKHAM WAS at the breakfast table in the morning, without his wife or daughter. When Carrie came in, he spared her a gruff few words of greeting, but did not meet her gaze. Instead he turned his attention back to his newspaper, ignoring both the food in front of him and Carrie. She talked instead with Josefa as she came back and forth with platters and dishes. Through all that, Dr. Markham never raised his head or acknowledged them.

And so it was time—past time—to say what must be said.

"Dr. Markham," she began, hoping he couldn't hear the very slight wobble in her voice. "Do you realize what difficulties arose here during your extended absence?"

Now he did look at her. She knew what it was to be in a physician's disfavor, but this was more than anger with a nurse who failed to follow orders. He had looked much improved on the first day after his return, but his complexion had gone off again. There were beads of sweat on his brow, and though he tried to hide it, a tremor in his hands.

"Not just in the dispensary," she went on, because she realized she might not have another chance. "But here in the house, with your family."

Color rose unevenly on his unshaved cheeks, and the muscles of his jaw tensed. He moved the plate in front of him an inch to the right, and then to the left.

"An odd observation," he said. "As you all look to be in good health. You especially, Nurse Ballentyne."

The mocking tone was quite subtle, and still unmistakable. He hoped to rouse her temper; she would not allow it.

"My health is not the issue. Tell me, Dr. Markham, is that really what you see when you look at Mrs. Markham? Good health?"

He pressed his mouth together into a bloodless line, but silence was a weapon Carrie had learned to counter long ago. She presented a question, calm, factual in nature, with no hint of her true feelings.

"How much laudanum is she getting, day by day? Are you aware?"

"That isn't your concern, Nurse Ballentyne."

He meant it as a correction, of course. Reminding her of her place.

"But it is my concern, Dr. Markham. You offered me a position as a midwife in connection with your wife's expectations."

This was a formulation Carrie disliked, but she was on thin ground here and must judge each and every step before her.

He inclined his head. "As you are aware, that situation was resolved before you arrived."

"As we are both aware, it was not. Not really." With as much firm resolve as she could muster, Carrie said, "I would like to examine Mrs. Markham."

She had surprised him, she saw it in his eyes.

"Why?"

After a moment's consideration, she decided that honesty was the only policy.

"Because if she should not recover, if things go very badly for her, I want it to be clear that I provided the best care possible, given the restrictions placed on me."

He put both hands on top of his head, fingers intertwined, and leaned back in his chair. There was nothing pleasant about his smile.

"The only restrictions placed on you are the product of an inferior intellect, Nurse. But if you insist, go on and try to examine my wife. A word of warning, she keeps a very sharp filleting knife near her right hand. I look forward to your report. I'll be in the dispensary, waiting to hear it."

After Carrie finished her breakfast, she went in search of Josefa and found her in the small kitchen garden, a favorite spot for all the household staff. At one end three old juniper trees provided both a screen from the street and the deep shade that was so prized in the hottest part of the day. She opened the door to the sound of Josefa's voice, for once speaking the language of her pueblo. Her tone was soft with a note of gentle chiding.

At the door Carrie paused in surprise.

Josefa sat on a low stool with a basket of herbs at her feet and magpies perched on shoulder, wrist, and knee. A juvenile had made itself comfortable on her head, a bit of fabric in its beak.

Carrie didn't know very much about magpies beyond the fact that they were related to crows, but she did know many crows. A few she knew very well. Crows were smart, and it seemed that magpies were both smart and inclined toward making friends with humans. This small flock was entertaining Josefa as if they had nothing more to do with their time, jabbering and calling back and forth while they explored a sack of fabric scraps.

Fabric in pieces too small to be put to use, some knotted together, others frayed, provided the magpies with distraction. Crows could not resist anything shiny, but it seemed magpies had broader interests.

They were striking birds, boldly marked in deep black and bright white against the dark green of the junipers. Josefa called these juniper trees *táscate*, another bit of Pueblo Carrie would have to write on her vocabulary list.

One of the largest of the magpies flew to the top of the tallest juniper and preened, spreading wings in a geometric display, much like the gesture a gambler made, flicking a wrist to produce a perfect fan of cards. In direct sunlight the black tail feathers threw a rainbow of iridescent greens and blues.

She was wondering about the Spanish word for magpies when Josefa glanced over her shoulder and read the question from her face.

"*Urracas*," she supplied. "Do you have these where you come from? Or just crows?"

They talked for a minute about the birds, and then Carrie told her that she was going to knock on Mrs. Markham's door and raise the subject of an examination.

For once the younger woman was unable to hide her reaction. Had Carrie discussed this idea with anyone?

"I just discussed it with Dr. Markham. He was quite happy to tell me that it wouldn't go well."

Josefa rocked her head from side to side while she thought.

Carrie wanted to project calm confidence, but it would be foolish to disregard what Josefa had to say.

"You look like you have an objection."

"No, just the opposite." She stood, causing birds to flutter and squawk. "I can smooth the way for you, I think. Come into the kitchen and I'll give you what you need."

In the kitchen Carrie waited while Josefa put together a tray for Mrs. Markham's breakfast. They talked of nothing more serious than plans for the day and how Lulu had managed to cut off one of her plaits when she was three, out of anger, Josefa claimed, at everyone and everything.

Thus far Josefa had never asked Carrie even the most basic personal questions. Not about her family in New York, her training, or her work. It was hard to know if this was simply good manners or habit among the Pueblos, or maybe, she reminded herself, it was possible that Josefa wasn't very interested. She had a large family and circle of friends of her own and might not see Carrie as a potential friend.

This morning she had thought that Josefa would ask about the fandango, but she never touched on the subject. Of course, it was likely that Josefa already knew exactly how often Carrie had danced, and who her partners had been.

Not a pleasant idea, but it would be best to know.

She said, "I have to return Violante's things to her later today, but they should be hung out to air first."

Josefa hummed her agreement and added a small dish of butter to the tray.

"Would you be so kind—" She began well enough, but then her voice wobbled and she let the rest of the sentence disappear.

"I'll hang them out." Josefa glanced at her. "Violante's things suited you. You looked very pretty. Everybody says so."

Carrie must have looked startled.

Josefa held out the tray for Carrie to take. She said, "You mustn't forget how small Santa Fe is. News moves fast. It's the medicine she'll want, as she is due for her next dose. If you bring her that, she's not going to chase you away, at least not immediately."

Carrie glanced over the tray lined with damask linen. A covered dish of porridge, a roll, butter, a cup of tea, a carafe of water, and a plain prescription flask. Tincture of opium, according to the label. A product of a U.S. Army medical laboratory in Philadelphia. She wondered if Dr. Markham bartered or bought all his supplies from the army hospital.

No matter where the laudanum originated, there should be a written script with dosage instructions.

"I don't see any directions," she said. "How many drops does Mrs. Markham get?"

"She will tell you," Josefa said. "Quite forcefully, she'll make clear what she needs. Now I have to see Manuela, and help with the laundry."

She turned to leave the kitchen and then stopped.

"You should know that Eli is well-liked," she said. "By my people. By the whites and Mestizos and the Criollos too. He is respected for his work and mind and loyalties. And he stands where other men like him often walk away."

This time Carrie had no choice but to smile.

THE MARKHAMS HAD a suite of three rooms that Carrie had never seen. Now she knocked on the sitting room door and went in without waiting for permission.

With shutters closed and curtains drawn, the room was very dark and the air dense and stale. In any other sickroom she would have stopped to open windows and air the room, but she had the strong sense that her time here would be short, and so she could waste not a minute.

Carrie rapped on the door to the next room—the Markhams' chamber—and entered.

The room was a surprise, and not an unpleasant one. The window shutters were open to let in a breeze and sunlight, and there was the smell of fresh linen and heliotrope in the air. Mrs. Markham sat beside the window in an armchair overpopulated with cushions and pillows. Tucked against her left side was Lulu's doll, swaddled like a newborn.

So, no improvement.

Without looking to see who had come into the room, Mrs. Markham said, "Bring it to me here."

Carrie hesitated. "Mrs. Markham—"

The thin shoulders straightened, but she didn't turn.

"I have your breakfast and your medicine," Carrie went on. "And I'd like to talk to you."

The silence lasted for more than a minute, but Carrie had expected as much. She used the time to regulate her breathing and gather her wits.

"Leave the medicine," her employer said finally. "And go. This child is very sensitive, and I won't expose her to your ill humors."

Carrie waited. Another few minutes passed, and a far more agitated Mrs. Markham cast a look toward her for the first time.

"I want my medicine," she said. "Now."

"I understand that," Carrie said. "And I will bring it to you there. But first I have some questions."

A short exhale of breath, and then another.

"Go on, then, if you must."

"I'd like to hear from you about the day your daughter was born. Details about your labor and the delivery in particular interest me. I'll make a written record."

Her head came up with a jerk.

"A written record for me?"

"Yes, of course. I will make a copy for you."

"No!" She had turned in her chair so that she faced Carrie fully. "There will be only one copy, and it will be mine. Mine alone."

"All right," Carrie said. "Would you be willing to start now? After you've had your breakfast and your medicine?"

This was the real test, and Mrs. Markham took some time to consider the options before her. Laudanum would send her to sleep and cut short any story she wanted to tell, but her dependence on the drug was powerful. Carrie was gambling that her need to be heard would move her to compromise.

"A half hour," Mrs. Markham said. "I'll start and talk for a half hour, and then I'll take my medicine."

Carrie said, "Do you think that will be enough time—"

"No," Mrs. Markham interrupted her. "But it will do for a start."

WHEN CARRIE JOINED John in the dispensary an hour later, there was no sign of Dr. Markham.

"Out on a call," John said, not meeting her gaze.

It was unfair of the doctor to require John to lie, and neither could she challenge it without running the risk of compromising John's education.

"So who is waiting to be seen?"

The question restored his calm, and the work restored Carrie's.

About half the patients she saw that morning were strangers to her, though every one of them knew her and seemed eager to learn more. An elderly man whose joints were terribly swollen with arthritis told her that the best she could do for him was to hold his hands for a few minutes. She was sure she had misunderstood, but went along with the request. Later, John told her that Hugo Ramirez made a habit out of asking young women to hold his hands to relieve the pain from arthritic joints.

"He really believes it," John said. "Or at least, he's convinced most people that he believes it."

"Does he impose in other ways?"

John was quick to put this question to rest. "No, no, nothing like that. His daughter would—let's just say she wouldn't have it."

"Have I met his daughter?"

John looked up from the daybook page. "I don't think so. She owns the cantina just beyond Eli Ibarra's place, and you haven't been there yet, have you?"

Voices came to them, women speaking English as they stepped into the waiting room.

"Miriam Goldblum," Carrie said. "I would have gone to check on her later today, but I expect she wanted to get out of the house."

She glanced at John, who had gone very red in the face and seemed to have lost the power of speech.

"What is it? Are you unwell?"

He shook his head. "No. I just remembered something I need to get. I'll be back. As soon as I can."

Carrie reminded herself that John was often awkward with young women who came into the dispensary. He was naive and still relatively inexperienced, but he seemed to understand this was an area for improvement. At the same time, she was surprised that Miriam Goldblum would make him blush and retreat.

She went out to greet her patient, who had brought her newborn, both her daughters, and Danya with her.

The first thing that Carrie noticed was not the new mother, who looked to be in excellent health, or even the infant, who was working his way from a grumble to a full-throated cry. She noticed Danya, because the girl was blushing. She was pretty under any circumstances, with regular features, a fine complexion, and great masses of shiny dark hair. Now, her color high, she looked less like a girl and more like a young woman. And of course she was just that. At seventeen most girls here would be married and starting families.

Carrie turned her attention to Mrs. Goldblum's health and recovery, and examined the newborn, who regarded her with great suspicion. Carrie saw this as a good sign; better a strong-minded newborn than a placid one. Surviving the first year of life would be easier on children who could summon up the energy to be doubtful.

There were many questions, which all came from the boy's young sisters. They wanted to know whether the umbilicus would disappear into the little brother's belly, about the suck blister on his upper lip, the patch of flaky skin on his scalp, when he would grow a beard, and why his chin trembled when he was nursing.

To Carrie's surprise, the questions delighted their mother. Everything seemed to delight her; she had none of the usual complaints or problems, and no sign of the melancholy that often made a new mother's life more difficult. Of course she also had a household full of sisters-in-law and servants to spare her the drudgery of caring for three younger children. No doubt the help she had at home contributed to her quick recovery. Miriam Goldblum had ventured out into town, earlier than was advisable, because she was eager to show off her beautiful family.

Apparently Danya's only purpose on this outing was to carry baskets, pick up dropped handkerchiefs, and run after little girls who wandered away.

Danya stood near the door, her hands clasped together and her gaze fixed on her shoes. Ready, it seemed, to slip out as soon as she could be sure she could do that without drawing attention to herself. Carrie wondered what had happened to the confident young woman she had met in Chava Goldblum's parlor. This Danya was tentative, unsure, and on the verge of giving up her plan, whatever it might have been.

It wasn't until the family had left that John came back. He was empty-handed, and when Carrie asked him about the errand that had sent him running out the door, he mumbled and flushed and made excuses.

She was about to ask him if he wasn't on good terms with the Goldblum family, when the answer—the obvious answer—presented itself. He was on very good terms with one member of the family.

John Edmonds and Danya Goldblum were of an age, both attractive and healthy, both gentle spirits. And in love. How far this attachment had gone, if they had ever had the chance even to talk, wasn't clear. And it was none of Carrie's business; she would not intrude. There would be enough interference from Danya's own family, once they saw what was happening right beneath their noses.

Most religions were strict about mixed marriages. One of her friends in Manhattan had disappeared at sixteen, rushed away to live with an aunt in Virginia when her parents realized she was far too well acquainted with the son of a Lutheran pastor. Catholics who dared to marry outside the church were excommunicated, and Quakers were cut off from family. Jews were especially vigilant, and Danya Goldblum was the daughter of a large, close-knit Jewish family.

Danya knew this, of course. Carrie remembered something she had said that day in Chava Goldblum's parlor: *Santa Fe is my home. I want no other.*

Heartache enough for everybody.

For the rest of the day she was so busy that she had no time to think about John and Danya, or this morning's remarkable session with Mrs. Markham, or even Eli. Who would be coming by to take her out walking in just a matter of hours.

Then all her plans to stay occupied and productive had to be put aside, because she was called to a birthing, this time at the Casino Taquito brothel, where a prostitute was in labor. She could have done without a delivery in the hottest part of the afternoon, but then it was her first visit to the part of Santa Fe that directly abutted the garrison and was, predictably, home to saloons and gambling dens and a brothel. She considered the timing her good fortune, because even drinkers and gamblers and prostitutes slept through the heat of the afternoon, and she would attract little attention.

The madam met her at the front door, her expression polite but her gaze very sharp indeed. Señora Leona Justo, as she introduced herself, showed her to a small chamber where they found a hugely pregnant woman—possibly as old as forty—sound asleep on her bed.

Señora Justo was not pleased, but Carrie persuaded her to let the woman be.

"If she can sleep, she should sleep. When labor starts in earnest, just send for me. I'll come straightaway."

She kept to herself the hope that she wouldn't hear from Madam Leona until after her walk with Eli.

The sun reflecting off adobe walls was so bright that Carrie had to hold up a hand to shield her eyes from the glare, but her ears were in working order. The finch's familiar call was there when she stepped out of the brothel, but she couldn't remember seeing any finches here at all. Then she realized she wasn't hearing one now.

Her heart rose into her throat as she scanned the street. And there he was, Eli Ibarra, his smile flashing white against the rich coppery color of his skin. Then he was gone, backing away into shadows. This was the right thing to do, of course, and it made her want to run after him.

AT FIRST LIGHT Eli was out of bed and moving. He took the horses to Iñigo to let them graze, and watched for a few minutes while they greeted Mimosa. His Sombra was more interested in Chico, and the dog could not contain himself, he was that satisfied to have his whole pack together again. Eli whistled to the dog, but could not entice him along. Chico wasn't about to leave his charges without protection.

Walking home, that picture kept coming back to him until he realized that people on the street were watching him, a man laughing at nothing in particular. Walking through the plaza, Angela Cuevas smiled at him as if he had just handed her a gift, and called to him. *"¡Bailar se adapta a ti, Eliseo!"*

So it started and so it went on. He told himself that there was no good reason to take exception. Angela was right; he was a very good dancer.

He stopped to see Inez Aguilar, who cleaned for him. He could see that she was consumed by curiosity, but still she kept her questions about the *gabacha* midwife to herself. She didn't ask because she knew he wouldn't answer, but not everybody was so easily put off.

When he first moved back to Santa Fe, people paid attention. He was a single man, an educated surveyor with a business of his own and connections that stretched a couple hundred miles in all directions. He was on good terms with the territorial government, the army officers, merchants and transporters, ranchers and vaqueros and sheepherders. Of course young women paid attention. Young women with skin the bluish white of new milk, others with the deep coppery color of his mother and her people, and everything in between. White women looked but never expressed anything that might be taken as interest, while the parents of Mestizo girls showed their admiration openly.

Impeccable manners, the mothers said of him, while fathers took note of the home he built with the help of his brothers and cousins, the beautiful horses, and his family connections.

When it was clear he wasn't looking to get married, some people had decided he already had a wife at his mother's pueblo. Others thought it was more likely that he kept house with a Mestizo somewhere along the Rio Grande.

Soon enough people would hear that he was going to marry the midwife, a white woman. A *gabacha*. What the reactions would look like did not interest him especially, but he couldn't pretend it wasn't important. For Carrie's sake he had to pay attention. Before they got to that point, though, he had to get this place ready for her.

He liked his house. He liked everything about it, but he understood Carrie would be more comfortable if she could arrange things in a way that suited her. He paced the rooms, trying to imagine her reaction.

The building was divided roughly in half: his business on one side, and his home on the other. Far less space, far plainer than she was used to, but well-built, with a *placita* and four good-sized rooms opening off it: his chamber; a second, empty chamber; a parlor used mostly when it was too cold to sit in the *placita*; and the workroom, where everything else happened—cooking, first and foremost, when he had time to cook. He couldn't call it a kitchen as it was right now.

Details like this they hadn't talked about. Would she want to cook? Did she know how to cook? She worked for a living, and the family had help, people she liked and told stories about. The question of cooking was something they would work out between them, but one thing was already clear: if she wanted to cook, then she would need more than a rusty fry pan, a couple of chipped clay bowls, and spoons he had carved himself when he was a boy.

He wondered if Carrie would be pleased to see that the floors were tiled and there were murals on many of the walls. His sister Ilaria's work, but he wouldn't say so unless she asked.

He took some ribbing in town whenever he did something to improve the property, but he let that slide. To have glass in his windows said all anybody needed to know about his success, but he doubted Carrie would realize this. For a Mestizo it was an extraordinarily fine house and sufficient evidence—for anybody who needed evidence—that Carrie was not settling for a wastrel.

While Inez cleaned, Eli went out to spend money. At the trading post and Carson's hardware and finally at Padilla's mill, he got most of what was missing in the kitchen: pots, pans, metal spoons, knives, a saltcellar, a hand mill for grain and a grinder for coffee beans, a basin and pitcher, bowls, plates, toweling, a bucket, candles, a new oil lamp with a large clear glass chimney, a big can of paraffin. He bought lumber—damned expensive as it was—because unless he put up shelves, there was no place to put all the new things.

By the time he got the tools and hardware organized, the church bells were ringing noon. His stomach was telling him the same thing. Inez, finished with the cleaning, went home to cook for her family with a handful of hard-earned coins.

Eli realized then he had spent half the day collecting things for the kitchen but had not once thought about food. There was nothing at all to eat, and so he did the logical thing: he walked over to Rosita's and sat down at the table he liked best. She had already set a place for him.

There was nothing much to see but a covered dish of warm tortillas and a jug of water, until Rosita came in from the kitchen with plates fanned out along her arm like scales. His gut growled at the smells: onion, sweet corn, the dark red beans he loved best, pork, chilies, cilantro.

"Eat first," Rosita said. "Then talk."

He was hungrier than he had realized. In fact, he ate with such appetite that Rosita beamed at him.

Twice the door opened, and twice she rose from her chair to show the unwanted customers an expression so dour and forbidding that they retreated without question or argument. In fact, there was nobody in the cantina, and that was so odd that it gave him pause. She didn't want an audience for whatever news she was going to pass along.

When his plate was empty, she leaned toward him across the table. "I like her."

Eli nodded. "Me too. When did you meet?"

"I haven't met her. Not yet."

"Then how do you know you like her?"

She had a way of shrugging her shoulders that said she would not entertain such questions.

"Fine," Eli said. "Then tell me why she's likable."

She nodded, and for a moment stroked the tabletop, something he had seen her do many times when she was working through a problem.

"While you were gone," she started, "the whole town was watching her. Already on the second day the old women were telling stories about her."

Rosita did not consider herself an old lady, and probably never would.

Eli listened while she talked about Carrie's first week in Santa Fe: how she had dealt with the tragedy with the oldest Cuevas son, whom she had seen in the dispensary, the short work she made of a rude *tejano cibolero*, and how much she knew about herbals. Best of all, Rosita told him, was her willingness to be taught by old women who had no formal schooling.

"She's learning the language quick," Rosita said. "And it's getting better every day. All in all people are impressed. And listen now to something truly astounding: Mimi Torres says she will go see the midwife Ballentyne at the dispensary, maybe even tomorrow."

Mimi Torres was considered the meanest of the mean old ladies, but that was not something he was going to tell Carrie. He was confident she was equal to that half-sized harridan, though he would not say that out loud.

"And the bad news?"

Rosita didn't often hesitate to express an opinion, but she was hesitating now. Eli looked at her closely and saw a combination of aggravation and worry in her face.

"There's a problem, you should tell me about it."

She raised both hands and dropped them to her lap. "If there's a problem, the boy says. You want a hint? I'll give you three. Rosita Padilla, Verena Tejeda, and Ximena Chávez."

Eli sat back and crossed his arms. "I can only have one wife, according to the church."

"Yes," Rosita said. "For years now you could have had any of the most marriageable from here to Juarez, but you kept your distance. Then last night in front of half the town you made your choice. A *gabacha*. Did you think nobody would notice?"

Eli heard himself sigh. "So you think she's not equal to the challenge of a few girls looking at her cross-eyed?"

Rosita shook her head at him. "I hope that's all she has to deal with, and in that case, yes, I'm sure she is. But tell me this, how will you deal with the white men looking at you cross-eyed?"

This question had been on his mind every day for weeks, but he respected Rosita and took a minute to consider what she was trying to tell him.

"I'm aware of the stakes," he said. "I'm ready."

She leaned back. "Glad to hear it. If you get shot by a jealous *tejano*, I won't have anybody worth feeding."

He grinned at that. "I'm glad you like her."

One black brow arched. "I wouldn't go that far, not yet. But time will tell."

If he pointed out she had just contradicted herself, she would be mad at him for days. And in fact, she was serious, and he knew it.

He got up, ready to get back to work, but Rosita pointed at his chair. He sat.

"What else?" he said.

"You need to get her away from the Markhams. Sooner rather than later. There's trouble, and it's only going to get worse."

"I know about this," he said.

"You don't know everything," Rosita said. "It's not so much Mrs. Markham. I think it's fair to say she's unhinged—don't wince, my boy, *unhinged* is the right word—but I don't think she's dangerous. It's the doctor you need to keep an eye on."

"Because he went off for a couple days?"

"*Insolente como siempre.*" She muttered under her breath at a volume he had no trouble hearing: "I should send you home and wait for you to figure it out for yourself."

Eli inclined his head. "Pardon. I'm listening."

She took a cup from a shelf, poured water, and drank it. When she spoke again, her tone was quieter.

"Since he came back from that unexplained trip, there's something wrong. Talk to John, he can tell you in detail."

Eli liked John and considered him a friend, so this suggestion was one he could agree to without hesitation.

"I'll do that," Eli said. "But what kind of trouble are you talking about?"

She shrugged. "You know the doctor has always been a reasonable man for a *tejano*. On the slow side sometimes. Blind the way men are—no blinder than most of you, but never mean. At first I wondered if the trouble with his wife could be turning him into a drunk, but there's something more going on. He's out wandering at all hours, stumbling and talking to himself. Night before last he fell asleep in the plaza. On the ground. Quincho had to hoist him up on his burro to get him home. Yesterday he was walking through the plaza as unsteady on his feet as any drunk I've ever thrown out on his ear."

She pushed herself away from the table, stood, and lowered her head at an angle he recognized: do not disrespect me.

"Listen to what I'm telling you. You had best get your Carrie out of there and not waste any time."

The idea almost made him smile. "Now I know you haven't spent any time with her. If you knew her at all, you'd know I can't just order her out of the Markhams' place."

"No?" Rosita's brow lowered. "She won't obey you?"

He shook his head. "Not when it comes to her work. Or anything else, for that matter."

Rosita considered him for a long moment, her mouth pursed as if she had bitten into something unexpectedly sweet.

"Good," she said finally. "Maybe she has a chance of surviving here after all."

There was a lot of work he wanted to get done, but Eli took a few minutes to stretch his legs and raise his face to the sun, which was how he saw Carrie coming out of the brothel. His surprise lasted only as long as it took him to remember that any woman could have a baby, and then he just stood and watched.

She was wearing a sunbonnet that shaded her face, and was about to walk by without even seeing him. He didn't like that idea, so he called to her in a way that wouldn't draw anybody else's attention. On the trail they had compared birdcalls, and had some fun competing. With Rainey they had talked about birds she was seeing for the first time.

Eli watched her face, and as soon as she realized what the birdcall was—and was not—he slipped away home.

⊸⧇⊶

CARRIE HAD BARELY got back to the dispensary when a young girl called Marieta Ocampo brought a message from her father's ranch on the far northwest border of Santa Fe. Gertrude had been laboring since early morning but wasn't making any progress, and could the midwife please attend?

Marieta had come on a burro, so Carrie walked over to Iñigo's stable to saddle Mimosa. To her satisfaction Mimosa took an interest in the burro, which inspired Chico to rouse himself from a sleeping spot in the stable. He inspected the newcomer, much like a quartermaster could cast a critical eye on stock offered for sale to the military. But the jennet was a pretty frosted-white burro with near-perfect confirmation. She was larger than most jennies, in Carrie's experience, with a spritely step. Beyond her good looks, the burro was clearly unintimidated, and that was enough for Chico. In another five minutes they were off, and he took up his usual spot trotting alongside Mimosa.

It was Carrie's first time riding out to see a patient, and just as she expected, it was far more pleasant than hailing a Hansom cab or finding a seat in a crowded horse car.

Riding along at enough distance to avoid the dust cloud raised by the burro, Carrie suddenly remembered where she had heard the name Ocampo. At the Ocampo ranch they bred, trained, and sold burros. Day by day Carrie saw more burros than horses or mules or dogs; they were used to transport huge bales of straw, stacks of firewood, baskets of fleshy maguey leaves. The same animals were gentle enough to carry lame grandfathers to church and tired children home from the field. Nearly everyone had a burro, so a man with a talent for breeding them would make a good living.

The ranch was very large, many buildings and paddocks and stables spread out on a mesa like a rumpled blanket. Burros grazed peaceably, watched over by large dogs who took immediate note of Chico. They followed him with their eyes, and most likely would do that until he was off the property.

Later Carrie would laugh at herself that it took so long to realize that the patient they wanted her to see was not human. It seemed Marieta had assumed that Carrie would know that she was being called to birth a burro.

Pío Ocampo was a short, barrel-shaped man in his sixties, quite bald. In fact, Carrie saw no trace of hair on his exposed skin, which was the color of lightly toasted bread, tinted pink along the cheekbones. He looked, she realized, much like the gingerbread men she had liked so much as a little girl, but there was nothing childish about him. She saw in his face the same concern and worry she saw in men who never seemed to think much about what it means to give birth until they heard wives and daughters screaming.

A boy stepped up to whisk her horse away. Chico hesitated until Carrie waved him off, and then she walked with Pío Ocampo to the stables. The whole time he talked, glancing at her with every sentence to see if she understood his combination of Spanish and English, which was surprisingly easy to follow.

Gertrude, she learned, was his favorite burro. In forty years of breeding and training burros, he had never had a more intelligent animal. He talked about his burro like a man who is inordinately proud of a daughter, knows that he talks too much about her and may be inviting mockery, but simply can't keep his delight to himself.

"Gertrude," he told her, "understands when people talk. Spanish, English, don't matter, she knows. You are thinking this is no more than a good sheepdog can do, but if you saw for yourself—" He broke off with a shrug of his shoulders, as if he knew what objections she would raise.

"Another time you'll see. Right now we've got a nose and one hoof."

That gave her a better sense of the problem. In the normal course of things, the head and front hooves showed themselves at the same time; if one or both hooves failed to show up with the nose, the presentation had to be corrected. Dystocia was often a fairly simple problem to solve, but sometimes it became a problem with no solution.

She told him what he needed to know. "Señor Ocampo, I can't promise you a good outcome, but I can usually get a loop on a foal's pastern and set it right. With help. Has this never happened before in all your years—"

"It happens," he said. "Usually my wife comes in and there's a conversation. She talks to the jenny, the jenny talks to her. Eventually they work things out. She has a midwife's hands, like yours. But she's away."

Carrie liked this small man, who was so concerned about his burros, but more than that, she liked working with animals. They required no stories about distraught mothers punching midwives, no long explanations about the medicines she dispensed. As long as there was a living creature to nuzzle when all was done, they were satisfied. More than satisfied.

She said, "I will do what I can for her, so please, show me the way."

46

ELI STOPPED WORK midafternoon, decided he was satisfied with the new shelves in the kitchen, and walked down to Chema Tejeda's barbershop. Most of Chema's customers were successful men, merchants and ranchers, men whose opinions were valued by other men like themselves. There was another barber in Santa Fe, an emigrant from Arkansas called Buzz Kelly, a name Eli was sure the man had made up out of whole cloth. The thing about Kelly was, he wouldn't have anybody in his barber's chair with skin darker than his own, and the man was as white as chalk.

So Tejeda's barbershop was where successful, respected men who couldn't call themselves white met to run a kind of shadow government, though nobody would dare put that into words. They talked here about serious matters and went out into the town to get things done behind the territorial government's back. And they gossiped. Unless one of their own family members was in a mess of some kind, they loved rumors and debated them with relish.

Whenever Eli heard somebody complaining about women's gossip, he thought of Tejeda's place and smiled to himself.

He wanted to show up at Markham's door cleanly barbered, but there was another reason for this stop. He didn't doubt Rosita's word about Sam Markham, but there had to be more to the story, and he wanted details going in. Maybe he'd hear something at Tejeda's that would give him an idea for how to open up the discussion with Markham.

I'm calling on Miss Ballentyne was the simplest way to get things started, but it wouldn't be enough. Markham would blink at him, and pretend not to understand; of course Eli couldn't mean to declare an interest in a white woman. *I'm calling on Miss Ballentyne to take her walking.* That wouldn't work, either. The idea of Eli Ibarra "taking her" anywhere would raise hackles.

He needed to open the conversation on good terms, because he wanted to win them over. Right now they thought of him as an educated, polite Mestizo, one who knew his place. Whether or not they could accept him as someone who knew his own worth was the question.

Last night had been the first test. People watched him on the dance floor with Carrie; they took note of the smile she gave him and the way they moved together. It was as good as putting an announcement in the *Gazette,* and still it was possible Carrie hadn't noticed that people—mostly white people—were looking at her from a different and less-than-flattering angle.

Tejeda's *barbería* was the one place Eli was likely to hear more details about Markham without asking first, and so he went in, nodded to the six or seven men who lounged there as if this place were a private club, and sat down in the cracked leather barber's chair.

"I was wondering when you'd show up," Tejeda said.

"Too busy dancing," called Quincho Diaz. A low chuckle echoed through the shop.

From a corner Porfirio Muñoz called out, "You ready to be interviewed? Got a spot in the next edition of the *Gazette.*"

Muñoz was always on the lookout for things to put in the paper. It was hard going, he would tell anybody who asked, keeping a paper above water in a place this remote. Soon he'd give up and go home to San Diego. He had been threatening this since his first day, years ago.

Eli ignored Muñoz and spoke to Tejeda directly.

"Chema, if you nip my ear this time, I'm going to use that scissors on you. And not on your hair, either."

Another low ripple of appreciative laughter, and then Chema, good-natured, wrapped Eli's face in a hot towel, exactly as he had hoped. Hidden like this, he could listen to the talk and keep his reactions to himself.

The conversations—sometimes one, sometimes as many as three braided together—touched on the usual subjects. Crops and rainfall, wagon trains coming and going, what the priests were up to, and did anybody know the details about the fight between two *ciboleros* outside the Casino Taquito? Apparently one of them was in his grave and the other on the run, with the *alguacil*'s deputies close behind.

"Of course deputies," said Chema. "Our illustrious *alguacil* isn't about to risk breaking into a sweat over a lowly *cibolero*."

"I still haven't heard how it is that Chucho managed to get himself named sheriff," Eli said.

"Nobody has," Miguel Álvarez said. "And we were here when it happened."

Muñoz cleared his throat to call attention back to himself.

"I made up my mind, I'm going to see the governor tomorrow about Markham."

"The acting governor, you mean," said someone from the back. "Meriwether is on his way back to Kentucky, so until Buchanan appoints somebody—"

"Bill Davis is what we've got."

There was a pause, and then the floodgates opened. From every corner came commentary, most of it critical. Had Porfirio Muñoz lost his mind? He published the *Gazette*, he should know that Davis and Markham played chess at least once a week. How did he imagine it would go over with the rest of the *tejanos* if the Mexican Muñoz managed to get lily-white Markham booted out of Santa Fe?

Muñoz stood firm. He didn't list his grievances with the doctor, but Eli was sure that it had to do with something more than drink. He waited, impatiently, for somebody to say something specific, but the discussion went in a different direction.

"If Markham goes, it will take six months to replace him." This from Miguel, who had three boys who would not stop beating on each other; every week at least one of them ended up at the dispensary.

"Miguel is right, it will take too long."

Tejeda flinched, and Eli realized it was Diego Martinez talking. Martinez owned the smaller of Santa Fe's two import-export businesses and made a lot of money trading with Mexican merchants. He was also a Criollo, a son of a son of Spain, pure-blooded and, as he saw things, superior in every way to the men around him.

It was a temptation to point out to Martinez that he sat here with the Mestizos and *genízaros* and other full-blooded Mexicans and Indians because Buzz Kelly—the white barber—would not have him, Criollo or not, as a customer.

Martinez was saying, "Where do we go in the meantime? The army surgeons want nothing to do with us, so it's the Mexican bloodletter in Albuquerque or rattles and chants."

The deep silence he got in response to the casual insult to the tribal healers should not have surprised him, as most of the men here were some part Indian. A full three minutes passed, and then Eli heard him getting up and making his way out of the building.

"So long, Martinez," Tejeda said.

"*Pinche cabrón*," muttered Quincho, who had a Navajo grandmother.

After a long moment, Muñoz said, "There's Benenati."

Tejeda whipped the towel from Eli's face and turned to face the room, holding his scissors up high as he made his opinion known. "Enzo Benenati is ten times the doctor Markham ever was. And he still is."

Nobody could deny the truth spoken plain. The rest of the truth—that Benenati would most likely refuse to come out of retirement—didn't need to be said, either.

"I am going to talk to Bill Davis about it," Muñoz said. "Maybe he can persuade Benenati to step in until we can get another doctor."

Somebody came in, and the way the mood shifted and discussion came to an abrupt end made it clear that the newcomer wasn't much liked.

It was Pato Estrada standing in the doorway, studying the room as if there were treasure hidden somewhere. As *alguacil*, Chucho was bad enough, but Estrada, one of his deputies, was worse: a blowhard, one who kissed *tejano* ass if it did him any good, or maybe, the rumor went, because he liked the taste.

"Ibarra," the deputy said, pointing at him with a jerk of the chin. "I hear you're courting the *tejana* midwife."

Eli let his face go blank, nodded his thanks to Chema, and walked out into the plaza. Estrada hated to be ignored, and he would look for opportunities to pay the insult back, but at the moment, Eli couldn't make himself care.

Before the deputy came in, nobody had wanted to offend Eli by mentioning Carrie, but now they were talking about it. He reminded himself that none of what they had to say mattered. He didn't know yet how his conversation with Markham would go, and saw no value in anticipating trouble.

His pocket watch told him he had a quarter hour and really only one thing to do with it. On summer evenings like this one—warm but breezy—it seemed like all of Santa Fe turned out to enjoy the weather. Whole families wandered through the plaza, children chasing each other while mothers shouted warnings and fathers laughed at their antics. A month ago Eli would have found friends to sit with, but now he just raised a hand in greeting and moved on. They would be drinking and playing monte, telling stories, asking each other for advice about women or the cost of gunpowder. A good way to spend an evening, but not so pleasant as the one he had before him.

This thought was in his mind when Iñigo came around the corner, head pivoting left and right as he scanned the plaza. He stopped when he saw Eli no more than six feet away from him.

"What? What's wrong now?" Eli cleared his throat, a sort of apology for his tone.

Iñigo held up both hands. "Nothing. Well, something, but nothing terrible. You on your way to the doctor's place?"

Eli nodded.

"She's not there," Iñigo said. "Pío Ocampo sent for her, and she's not back yet."

"Huh." Eli thought about this. "How long ago?"

"Couple hours. I doubt she'll be much longer."

"I take it Carmen is away."

"In Nambé, visiting her sister. And it's Gertrude who's in trouble."

Now it made more sense. Any reasonable man took care of livestock, but Ocampo was sentimental about his burros and would not hesitate to call on doctors or nurses or midwives to treat them. Because he paid without complaint whatever he was charged, even the army surgeons came when they were needed at the Ocampo ranch. Eli wondered if Carrie had realized what a midwife might be called on to do in New Mexico Territory. He guessed she wouldn't mind. Few women were so attuned to horses, and she had a gentle touch.

Iñigo put a hand on his arm and jolted Eli out of his thoughts.

"Violante says to bring you home to supper."

It would never occur to Iñigo that somebody might turn down a summons to his wife's table, and that left few options. Eli went with him.

VIOLANTE BROUGHT A tureen to the table, braised oxtail in a thick sauce crowded with spring vegetables and hominy.

She handed him a bowl. "Why the long face?"

Eli shrugged. "Maybe I'm just hungry."

"Ha! That I can help you with."

Iñigo pushed back from the table. "And I can help you with the rest of it. I'll get one of the men to saddle your Sombra."

"Eat," Violante said. "And then you head out to Pío. Enough with the long face."

An hour after Carrie arrived at the Ocampo ranch, Gertrude gave birth to a good-sized jack. Pío Ocampo was ecstatic, his sons were ecstatic; all the men on the ranch seemed to be. Jennies in the other stalls called out what Carrie had to interpret as shouts of congratulations. The stall was crowded with men who wanted to get a look at Gertrude's newest, and that was how Carrie slipped away. They didn't seem to notice.

It was just then that she realized that Pío Ocampo's wife was the only woman on the ranch, and she was away. There was Marieta, but she was a young girl, and where she might be was anybody's guess. A wife or a sister or a grown daughter would have hot water and soap ready for her. Usually there would be a cup of tea as well. Sometimes something to eat.

It would be awkward to go back into the crowded stable to ask Ocampo for this kind of help. Of course, he had not blinked at the sight of the arm she bared to reach into his beloved Gertrude in order to get a rope around her foal's pastern. He had not blinked when a secondary, unexpected gush of blood and amniotic fluid had drenched her, either.

She couldn't ride back to Santa Fe as she was, so she went to the nearest horse trough, sat down beside it, and thrust her arm in, right up to the shoulder. The water was cold and the cold was welcome, but she couldn't sit here half-immersed in a horse trough much longer, so she took up a scrap of wood from the ground and began scraping blood, amniotic fluid, and the glycerin she used as a lubricant off her skin. There was nothing she could do about her clothes unless she were to strip down completely and declare herself the Lady Godiva of

New Mexico Territory. Still, the idea was appealing, because she would stink to the heavens before she got back to town. Midwifery was not for the squeamish.

It took another quarter hour to find her horse, and it might have taken longer if not for Chico. He must have caught her scent, because he came trotting over a low ridge with Mimosa right behind him.

At last she mounted, adjusted her split skirts, and took off for Santa Fe. She had a good memory for directions, but a glance at the sky told her she wouldn't be there when Eli came to take her out walking. She wondered if he would sit down to pass the time with the doctor and his wife, or if they would tell Carlos to send him away. And if that happened, she could imagine Eli insisting. Polite but unbending. Eli had handled Titus Hardy easily enough, and she didn't doubt he could handle the sour, miserable *tejano* doctor that was now Dr. Markham.

The road was well traveled and dry, and so she urged Mimosa to a trot and then an easy gallop. Chico kept up, his mouth wide open in what could only be described as a delighted smile. At that very moment three Indians came around the next bend, all of them on horseback, all of them startled at the sight of a white woman galloping down this back road in clothing that was stained with blood and gore.

She stopped. It was the logical thing to do: she would greet them and introduce herself, if they spoke any English. If they didn't, then what? This question was in her mind when one of the three—the youngest, it seemed—let out a shout, put his heels to his pony, and broke into a gallop. It happened so fast that Carrie had no time to be afraid or even startled. The three men tore past her, looking straight ahead. As if she were a ghost. Or a witch. A creature best avoided.

"Well," she said to herself. "What to make of that?"

She started off again, rounding the bend where she had first seen the Indians. Another rider, a quarter mile off, but one she recognized. She knew him by the way he sat in the saddle, by the tilt of his hat, by the way her heart began to race. It wouldn't do, she told herself, to gallop toward him. That would be childish, and unladylike. The proper thing to do would be to continue on at a normal pace; she could wait five minutes more.

Without further thought, she gave Mimosa a short, sharp kick, and galloped toward Eli, pregnant burros and fleeing Indians and unreliable, untrustworthy doctors forgotten.

She said, "Do you think I scared them off? I don't even know what tribe they were."

Eli bit back a smile, tilted his head to one side, and tried to look serious. "Navajo. Not easy to scare. More likely they're off to get a war party together."

BEFORE SHE COULD come back with a smart reply—he could see it forming—and without thinking much about it, he leaned over, slipped an arm around her waist, and hauled her over to sit sideways on his lap. The horses, both well trained, didn't even sidestep, but Carrie sputtered in outrage.

So he kissed her. She had both hands fisted against his chest—still holding Mimosa's reins, he noted—for the split second it took her to remember that she liked him and liked kissing him.

It was a rough kiss, warm and deep and tasting of Carrie. He kept kissing her until her hands crept up and her arms closed over his shoulders, and then he broke it off.

"So," he said. "You're looking after burros now?"

He didn't often see her flustered, but the kiss had thrown her off balance.

"Who told you where I was? John? Iñigo? Or . . . tell me it wasn't Dr. Markham."

"Not Markham."

He didn't recognize what she was wearing, but assumed it was what she wore when she was attending a birth. The bodice was cut loose, and had sleeves that attached with buttons and ties at the shoulders. All of it streaked and dirty. She saw him taking her condition in.

"I look like I just slaughtered a hog." She tried to draw away—worried now that he would be offended—and he held her where she was.

"Let me go, please. I stink. I stink, and I'm rubbing it into—"

The only way to stop what promised to be a long and unnecessary explanation was to kiss her again, and that was what he did.

This time she scowled when he stopped, a line appearing between her brows. He had seen that line before, most usually when she was arguing with Titus Hardy or scolding Rainey.

"Wait," he said. "Let me guess. Too much kissing?"

Just that quickly her expression shifted from aggravation to embarrassment.

"I wouldn't go that far."

She looked away, one tooth sunk into her lower lip. "We are out here in full view, though."

This time he couldn't hold back the laugh. "You think we're shocking the birds? Or maybe the herd is offended."

She jerked, turning to follow his line of sight.

"Oh," she said, already entranced, the state of her clothing forgotten. A perfect end to this day: wild horses grazing and at ease.

"Look at them. Look how beautiful."

He had to swallow before he could make his voice work. "Do you want to get a closer look?"

"Really? We could—"

"Really," he said. "Mount up."

A few minutes later, they were moving toward the mustang herd at an easy walk. The ponies grazed almost lazily, but the stallion was alert and watching them closely. He was well-known for his quick wits and quicker feet; at the Te Tsu Geh Pueblo they had given him the name Biter. Once he decided you were a threat—and most people were—he was gone, and his herd with him.

Carrie watched, her eyes moving from pony to pony and back again.

"They aren't afraid of us?"

The stallion raised his head to sample the air, giving the impression that he had heard Carrie's question and wanted to answer it himself, in the simplest way: he whirled, and in a great cloud of dust, the herd disappeared over the next rise.

Without pausing or discussion, Carrie turned to follow them, and Eli went along too. Carrie was good at hiding her reactions, but just now she couldn't contain her excitement.

When the herd stopped to graze—the stallion still watching the riders—she let out a happy sigh. "I suppose we need to start back."

"Another half hour. There's a stream just there, and I'm thirsty."

They sat about a half mile away from the herd, on the bank of a slender, winding stream. Carrie's skirts were wet to the knees and her sleeves to the shoulders, and still she wielded the small brush she had got out of her saddlebag like an instrument of torture. Now she had started again on her nails, but to Eli's eye she had already banished every trace of blood and muck from the crevices.

Her head came up sharply. "Will Dr. Markham send somebody to look for me, do you think?"

An interesting question. Was she worried about alarming the Markhams, or the coming dark, or was she nervous because she sat beside him, wet, bedraggled, and half-undressed? He took the most diplomatic route.

"Spread out your skirts so what's left of the sun can get to the wet parts. We'll be on our way right soon."

"Too soon."

"We have an hour or so. And we can use that time to talk. Tell me about your unnatural relationship with that brush first."

She smiled, studying it. "You know I grew up surrounded by doctors and healers. Every one of them is very strict about cleanliness. Dirt and muck in a wound, no matter how little, can mean infection and complications."

"And that's your experience, too, or just what you were taught?"

Carrie blinked at him, frowning. "That is my experience. Do you doubt it?"

"Oh no," he said. "It's your work and not mine."

⤙⤚

SHE KNEW SHE must look vaguely offended, as was her usual reaction when someone tried to mollify her with diplomacy. They still had a lot to learn about each other.

He said, "Maybe you haven't realized this about me yet, but I'm not big on talking—"

That made her smile. "I had noticed, yes."

"So if I go to the trouble to say something, I mean it. I don't doubt your skill or your decisions as a nurse or healer or whatever you want to be called."

"That's good," she said, and leaned forward to press her mouth to the line of his jaw.

⤙⤚

ELI WAS VERY aware of the challenges they would have to get through. The trip across country had proved to him that they were well suited in most ways. The exception, the thing that wasn't clear to him yet, was whether she would come to him as a woman and a wife. He thought about what she had survived as a girl, and knew that he couldn't assume she would be able to leave all that behind.

But the way she kissed him.

At first she had been shy and uncertain; then, at some point along the way, she had decided that she liked all of him. She wasn't afraid to show him affection, and with time, he was increasingly sure, they would suit each other very well.

He was thinking about this as the evening came down, thinking of all the subjects that still had to be raised.

She said, "There's something bothering you."

He drew in a deep breath. "Yeah. Today I heard men talking about Markham. None of it good. Is he violent behind closed doors?"

It was a question with sharp edges, but she didn't withdraw.

"At first I thought the problem was grief and self-recrimination about his wife's condition," she said. "Some men turn to drink in situations like this. Men who can't bear to think of themselves as powerless are prone to it, I think. I would guess he's never had to admit defeat, at least not in this way. Not that there's any excuse for his behavior."

Eli had to clear his throat. "Is he striking out?"

"Not that I've seen, not physically. But his demeanor has changed, and that makes me wonder about his health. He has lost so much weight. The thing is, I expected him to be reserved. He was reserved given his upbringing and class. But now there's a streak of bitterness, even cruelty there. Something close to malice. He makes me think—"

She couldn't go on, but Eli had followed her thoughts anyway.

"He reminds you of Greg Fisher."

Carrie folded the piece of linen she had used to dry her hands. "Yes," she said. "But to answer your question, he's not violent. At least, not in my presence. Lulu is safe because Josefa and Carlos watch over her closely and would take her away, if necessary. Iñigo and Violante are watching too."

"He's an employee of the territorial government," Eli said, his tone sharper than he meant it to be. "There's talk of asking the governor to fire him for drunkenness."

She wasn't surprised at this turn of events, and he reminded himself that she would not forgive him for underestimating her. Now she was just glad to hear that other people were aware of the problem.

He told her, "The governor might ignore the complaints. In fact, I think that's the most likely reaction. He's just a temporary appointment and he won't want to meddle."

He stood without warning and held a hand out. When he had pulled her to her feet, he paused, weighing words.

"You'll walk out the door if you're in danger."

She nodded. "I'd go to Iñigo."

He shrugged his agreement. It was a plan, but not the plan he wanted. But it wasn't the battle that needed to be fought at this moment.

Her sleeves were still soaking wet, but she reached up anyway and pulled his head down to hers.

"Still not enough kissing," she said against his mouth.

He grinned, and started working on the problem. No hesitation at all.

47

THE CHURCH BELLS were tolling nine when Carrie and Eli rode into town.

Not yet full dark, and Santa Fe was alive with movement and sound on this warm summer night. From the parish church there was muted singing, and on the other side of town, near the garrison, men shouted in a way that needed no translation. There was a fight of some kind. No doubt bets had been laid.

Carrie could have asked Eli if there was likely to be a knock at the doctor's door anytime soon, but they had been walking the horses side by side in a comfortable silence that she hesitated to disturb. Tomorrow they would talk to Dr. Markham and his wife, together, and then there would be little silence and less peace.

At Iñigo's they dismounted and handed the horses over to the most senior of the wranglers, a Pueblo, she guessed, but she hadn't yet learned his name. She wasn't even sure if it would be rude to ask his name; some tribes were that protective. Eli spoke to him for a while in a quiet way, and here was something else she did not know: what the language was called. She was about to ask, and then saw how Eli's gaze had focused on the Markhams' place on the other side of the road.

The guard stationed at the front doors was leaning against the wall in the light of the house lanterns, arms crossed and chin bedded on his chest. They could hear his wet snoring where they stood. Nearby a cat howled, in protest or admiration. Farther off, coyotes echoed the song.

There was no light from the house that Carrie could see, and this disturbed Eli.

"Is that what you'd expect at nine?" Eli asked her. "Do they go to bed so early?"

"They do, quite often. Neither of them are well. But usually Josefa has the lamps lit at this hour."

Eli studied the house for another minute and finally asked her a question she had anticipated.

"Will you wait here?"

Was this the time to make a point? It seemed she couldn't help herself. She scanned the street and the front of the house again, listened closely, heard nothing.

"Are you seeing something I don't see?"

"I'm going to check on the other two guards. If they're sleeping, it's tricky. A man with a loaded weapon, asleep on the job, he won't wake up feeling peaceful."

She considered. "And you are bulletproof?"

"No, but I know how to approach them."

He was right, of course. His steady, calm competence was one of the things she had first admired about him, after all. If he was being overly protective, she would assume he had a good reason for that. So she agreed and waved him off.

Eli slipped into the shadows, utterly silent.

Carrie might have followed the guard's example and fallen asleep leaning against the high adobe wall around the old convent, but it was a matter of minutes before the front doors opened, startling the sleeping guard so that he slid down the wall and woke with a thump.

She expected to see Dr. Markham standing there, but instead the two house guards—who had not been sleeping, it seemed—came out, with Eli just behind them. Rather than raise her voice, she crossed the street to talk to Eli, who told her exactly what would happen next.

"The guards will rouse Carlos and have him check that everything is in order."

"I could do that too."

"Oh no," he said. "Not until we know what's going on."

"Is this just caution on your part, or do you have reason to suspect trouble?"

"I'm not sure myself," Eli said. "But I'm standing right here until I know it's safe."

They didn't have long to wait. The front doors opened again, and so abruptly that Carrie jumped. The guards stood there looking confused, but not alarmed.

"Carlos?" Eli asked, his voice low.

He got a shrug.

"What I want just now is answers. Really the most important issue is what will happen with Lulu."

Carlos was always here. She had never known him to leave the property.

According to the guards, there was no sign of Josefa, either.

Eli turned to face Carrie. "Your decision on how to proceed."

She drew in a deep breath, trying not to imagine the worst. Where were Josefa and Carlos? What would make them leave? Was Lulu with them? She knew Josefa and Carlos wouldn't have voluntarily left Lulu alone in the house without them.

"If nothing else, I want to check on Lulu. Right away."

The next challenge was whether Carrie should wake the Markhams.

"There's no other way to check on Lulu," Carrie explained. "You have to go through her parents' chamber to get to hers."

The guards had gone back to their posts, but Eli and Carrie sat at the table in the *placita* in the light of a paraffin lamp and went over what they knew, which was very little.

Overhead the moon slipped in and out of cloud cover. Carrie was very much awake and aware, her pulse racing. There could be a perfectly reasonable explanation about Josefa and Carlos, or it might mean disaster.

Eli said, "An owl."

The sound made her smile.

"That's an old friend," she told him. "He's come by pretty much every evening since I got here."

She couldn't make sense of his expression, and wished in that moment that she hadn't told him about her nightly visitor.

"Does the owl have special significance for you?"

"In the pueblos, yes. A harbinger of death."

Carrie shook off the shiver that ran down her arms, and got to her feet. "I don't want to put off finding Lulu any longer."

It was fortunate that Carrie knew the layout of the Markhams' suite of rooms, because the candle's flame was weak. She let her memory guide her through the sitting room to the door of the chamber itself and stopped there.

How many hours had she spent walking through the wards at the New Amsterdam in the deep of the night? She had a candle. She had Eli waiting just feet away. She had a terrible sense of dread that throbbed like a bad tooth.

She listened and got nothing more than the sound of her own breathing.

Enough, she told herself. *Enough*. She knocked, not as firmly as she intended but still loud enough that anyone sleeping in the room would wake.

"Dr. Markham? Mrs. Markham?"

Nothing. She knocked again and waited.

She had spent a lot of time like this when she was in training. They went out in pairs to see patients too sick to come to the clinic. At least half the time the biggest challenge was getting through the door, especially when the very old needed medical attention. They locked their doors and were too deaf to hear the visiting nurses knocking, or their grasp on the here and now slipped, and they thought themselves elsewhere. Many times they had died, quietly, and it was the visiting nurses who found them.

Dr. Markham was far too young for her to be thinking this way, and so she knocked again, and settled into a particular mindset. In nursing, the more tense or serious a situation, the more calm was called for. At least, the face she presented to the patient and the patient's family was calm, while one part of her mind wondered why the doctor was so long in coming and another ran over lists of complaints, comparing one disease to another and looking for answers.

Since the day she arrived, she had been observing and categorizing Dr. Markham's symptoms, but there was little to work with, as he would neither answer questions nor allow even the most rudimentary exam. Sam Markham might have been sold a bad bottle of whiskey, or there might be a bleeding ulcer that had finally got the upper hand. There were a dozen other illnesses that could and did kill off a fifty-year-old male, regardless of class, income, or education.

Behind her Eli waited, so quiet that she might have believed herself alone in the house.

She cleared her throat and pushed through her uncertainty.

"I'm going to open the door, Dr. Markham."

Then finally, a small, hushed sound that could be almost anything. A breeze in the shutters, a mouse in the kitchen. She imagined a sheet being thrown back but instead heard the same sound again, a small sliding of one object against another and then the clattering of tin against tile. Someone had reached for a cup or a dish, and knocked it to the floor.

She opened the door.

ELI STEPPED INTO the chamber right behind Carrie. In the frail light of their candles, he saw two people in the bed: Mrs. Markham was on the far side under a great mountain of bed linen. On the near side of the bed, fully dressed from boots to the hat that sat on his chest, was Sam Markham. Beard stubble—more white now than dark—stood out against patchy skin. His eyes, bloodshot and leaking tears, were fixed on Carrie. His mouth was open, too, the jaw creaking like a rusty hinge as he tried to talk.

"Dr. Markham," Carrie said. "You are very unwell. Can you tell me what's wrong?"

Eli wondered if she really didn't know, or if she was trying to get the doctor to talk. He wanted to talk, that was clear.

"He's drunk."

"No, he isn't. Or at least, that's not the only thing wrong. Do you recognize the smell?"

Eli considered for a moment, and realized that the strongest smell in the room wasn't whiskey, but piss. The doctor had pissed himself, and more than once, given the look of his clothes and the bedding underneath him. He hadn't recognized it at first because the smell was unusually, profoundly sickly sweet.

Without turning, Carrie said, "Please check on Lulu, through that curtain. Try not to wake her."

Eli pushed the doorway curtain aside and stepped into the room just as an oil lamp came to life. In front of him were Carlos, Josefa, and, asleep in her bed, Lulu. It wasn't until that moment that Eli began to breathe again.

They had stayed to watch over Lulu.

They spoke only for a minute, and very softly. Then Eli went back to the main chamber, Carlos beside him.

Carrie had been busy.

In a matter of minutes she had stripped Sam Markham out of his clothes and covered him with a sheet. The soiled bedding was rolled up along the middle of the bed. This struck Eli as odd, but odder still was the fact that Mrs. Markham had not yet stirred.

He reminded himself that opium eaters could sleep like that, when the habit got the upper hand. Now he saw that he had assumed too much. Mrs. Markham was dead, and wrapped, clumsily, in bedsheets. A makeshift shroud.

The doctor was still trying to talk. His mouth formed a word without sound, once, twice, three times, and then his whole body stiffened. In frustration or anger or pain, it was hard to tell.

He asked Carrie, "Is there a wound?"

She shook her head. "No wound. He's asking for water. We need a doctor, as soon as one can be got here."

It was a short discussion: tracking down an army doctor would take time, and it was unlikely that one would agree to come, if Eli or Carlos were to do the asking.

"Dr. Benenati," Carlos said. *"El médico italiano vendrá."*

When both Carrie and Eli looked at him, he explained that he had visited Dr. Benenati a few days previously to ask what to do about Sam Markham's condition. This was a surprise—house servants were not encouraged to engage with the family on personal matters—but it was also very useful.

Carlos was sweating and anxious, sincere in his wish to help.

"He said we could call on him?" Carrie asked, unsure she had followed the exchange.

Carlos nodded, looking between them. *"Sí,"* he said. *"Ya me puedo ir."* And for emphasis: "I go."

In a heartbeat he had left them to study the Markhams.

Eli said, "What is it, do you think?"

She glanced at him. "I don't know. A disease of the kidneys is my first guess, but it could also be a hemorrhagic infarction. Bleeding in the brain. I hope Dr. Benenati will know how to treat him. Now I'm going to check on Josefa and Lulu."

THE MARKHAMS RENTED a small room for John's use at the fonda. Eli was there in two minutes, and the boy was at his door almost immediately. He blinked, confused, and so Eli put it plain.

"Sam Markham is in bad shape, maybe dying. Benenati is coming to tend to him. Don't ask me what's wrong, you can talk to Carrie about that. Mrs. Markham is dead. Probably too much laudanum, but we don't have any details. You're needed at the house, quick as you can get there."

Now John was awake, his color leaching away. "But—"

"You've got questions I can't answer. Will you come to the house?"

When he nodded, Eli turned and trotted back the way he had come. Just as he got there, Benenati was dismounting from his old burro, with Carlos trailing some ways behind. He was glad to see the older man. Benenati had come to this part of the territory as a young man, when it was still Mexico. He had been the personal physician to various Spanish officials, and his Spanish was fairly formal. He also spoke Towa, the language of his wife's pueblo, and English came easily to him. *Don't be too impressed*, he told people who were interested in his history. *I've forgot just about everything I once knew of my mother tongue.*

That was Dr. Benenati, self-deprecating in a way that most people didn't understand.

"Eli Ibarra," he said now, coming forward to shake his hand. "What can you tell me about the trouble here?"

"Mrs. Markham is dead, don't know what killed her. Carrie says Dr. Markham is in a very bad way."

"Carrie?"

"Ballentyne, the new nurse, the midwife."

He touched his brow as if to thank Eli for this reminder, and together they walked into the house.

"Tell me," Benenati said. "How did you get mixed up in this?"

"Carrie," Eli said. Before he could give it much thought, he said, "I'm going to marry her."

Behind his spectacles Benenati's eyes were very bright in the light of the lantern, but there was nothing of surprise or shock there.

"Ah," he said. "So it goes."

⚭

CARRIE'S ANXIETY BEGAN to wane when Dr. Benenati and John arrived, one after the other.

The doctor was stooped with age, flecked with liver spots, and a martyr to arthritis, but his gaze was clear and he was as sharp as any physician Carrie had ever worked with. He saw what needed to be done and issued a short list of tasks in a firm but calm way. Carrie was so relieved to know that she could surrender the Markhams to someone with experience that she came close to tears.

Violante and Iñigo appeared out of nowhere—more of Eli's work, Carrie was sure—and they took Josefa and Lulu away to sleep in their casita. A priest came in to ask if extreme unction was needed, and whether he could perform that service or if he should rouse Bishop Lamy. He stood by praying as Mrs. Markham's remains were taken to one of the rooms in the dispensary where Dr. Benenati would examine them later.

The nuns would be by within the hour, he told Carrie. She didn't understand but was loath to ask for details.

"To care for the remains," Eli explained. "They will keep watch overnight."

Now the word had spread, and neighbors, most of whom Carrie barely knew, began to appear, as seemed to happen everywhere when someone died. She accepted the tea someone pressed into her hands, smelled cooking coming from the kitchen. Two women she didn't recognize came out of the Markhams' room with baskets of bed linen, and two others went in with more. She wondered where they put Dr. Markham while they set his bed to rights, but could no more get up to ask than she could fly away.

Through all this Eli came and went on one errand or another, always stopping to catch her eye to see if she might need him. In fact, Carrie would have liked him to sit beside her, but there were responsibilities that took precedence.

Together with John she sat down with Dr. Benenati to answer his questions.

His manner was calm and his demeanor businesslike, but he had a friendly smile and congenial way about him.

He said, "I only spoke to Dr. Markham once when he first came to

Santa Fe, and after that once during a typhoid epidemic. What I know I've heard from Carlos. Carlito worked for me when he was a boy, and still visits every week. So from the two of you I need as much medical history as you can provide."

Because Carrie was more familiar with Mrs. Markham's condition, she started there and tried to be both thorough and concise. The doctor listened without interruption and then turned to John.

"Anything to add?"

"I didn't know about the doll," John said. "I didn't realize that her mania was so serious. But I can tell you what I observed about Dr. Markham over the last year or so. His health began to fail last summer, I believe."

There came a point when Carrie could not hold back her own questions any longer.

"May I ask if you have a diagnosis?"

The doctor lifted a shoulder, a shrug that said she would not get what she asked for.

"I will do a postmortem tomorrow, but I would guess that Mrs. Markham took an excess of opium, in one form or another. In such an extreme case of puerperal insanity, suicide is not uncommon. If it was suicide. It is unlikely but possible that Dr. Markham helped her along, given his own condition. But that is a question that will never be answered unless he feels the need to confess."

John cleared his throat. "What condition is it Dr. Markham has?"

The doctor took off his spectacles, rubbed his eyes, and felt in his pockets for a handkerchief to wipe the lenses. When he had put himself back together, he looked at Carrie quite closely.

"What do you think, Nurse Ballentyne?"

She thought of all the times this question had been directed to her while she was a student, and what she had learned about doctors. The way they asked a question could be read as easily as the question itself. Some were looking for praise of their teaching excellence, some were curious about how much a nurse could understand, some took pleasure in embarrassing students, and some were truly interested in teaching. What did Dr. Benenati want from her? She was surprised to realize that she didn't really care.

"He has been very thirsty," she started. "I noticed from the day I arrived how often he called for water. Over the last ten days, he often couldn't walk without swaying or knocking into walls. He's very disoriented much of the time. I understand that the men in town think he has been drinking. I thought he was drinking, too, based on the evidence. But this evening when I came in—he is in and out of consciousness, as you saw—the bed linen was so completely soaked in urine—"

"And that changed your opinion?"

"Yes." She drew in a deep breath and pushed on, determined for once not to censor herself. "It occurs to me that this may be what the Mohawk healers I grew up with call honey urine. At the New Amsterdam they call it diabetes mellitus. Based on his symptoms now and my limited experience, I think this case is quite advanced."

John, frowning, looked from her to the doctor and back again. "Honey urine?"

"An excess of glucose in the urine," Dr. Benenati said. "Diagnosed by taste. Primary symptoms are tremendous thirst and the constant need to urinate. I had a professor who called it the Pissing Evil."

He blinked, and cleared his throat as if he remembered that his audience needed more coddling than he was providing, but then went on.

"There are differing theories on the origin of the disease, but most medical men think it follows from an injury to the kidneys, or a disease specific to the kidneys. Whether that is actually the case is still to be proven."

Carrie realized now how much Dr. Benenati reminded her of her stepfather. Like Harrison Quinlan, Dr. Benenati had a talent for explaining things with confidence that stopped well short of lecturing or self-promotion.

"The condition is a fatal one?" John's question went to the heart of the matter.

"It is," Dr. Benenati's smile was grim. "Very rarely I come across reports of patients who respond to a change in diet. No bread or alcohol or sweets of any kind. A diet of nothing other than fatty meats, cabbage, and similar vegetables."

"So the prognosis—" His voice cracked.

"Very poor. He will slip into a coma, and never recover from it. I would say a week, at the very most. Three days, is my guess."

Carrie had expected this, but to hear it said aloud and in such plain terms struck John as a heavy blow.

"It's hard to comprehend," Carrie said. "The repercussions will be—"

"Overwhelming," John supplied. He was trying very hard to master his reaction, but of course he realized that his plan to study medicine had suddenly collapsed. Carrie wondered if Dr. Markham might have made provisions for John in his will, but she hesitated to say as much for fear of causing more disappointment if that were not the case. It certainly did not seem likely.

John said to her, "Will you go home to New York?"

That question, so far from her mind, took her by surprise. "No," she said. "At least, I don't plan to. At the moment."

And now Dr. Benenati was looking at her with both concern and curiosity. "If it's not too personal a question, won't you stay, Miss Ballentyne, and continue your work here once you marry?"

John drew in a squeaky breath, but Carrie didn't look at him. Eli must have told the doctor their plans. She could not imagine why, just at this moment.

Dr. Benenati asked, "Is it not yet public knowledge?"

In the same moment, John said, "Who are you marrying?"

"Me," Eli said. He had been sitting quite close, out of sight. He came to the table and took the chair beside Carrie.

"Yes," Carrie echoed. "I am going to marry Eli. Though we haven't decided when, exactly. John, your eyes are going to pop out of your head."

She hoped that he would credit the sharpness of her tone to the terrible events of the evening, and more, that he would keep his questions to himself for now.

To Dr. Benenati she said, "I would like to keep working, but everything will be uncertain until Dr. Markham improves enough to make decisions—"

"Unlikely," Dr. Benenati supplied, the word bringing Carrie up short.

At the far end of the *placita*, a door opened, and a woman's voice called for the doctor in a low but insistent tone.

"Enzo!"

"Carrie, you haven't met Maduhenía," John said. "Dr. Benenati's nurse. And wife, of course. She's been with him since he first came to Santa Fe, it must be—"

"Forty-five years." Dr. Benenati smiled at them both, used his cane to rise from the chair, and paused while he was summoned once more. He spoke a few words of Pueblo—Carrie was beginning to at least recognize what language she was hearing—and his wife, grumbling, retreated. Carrie hadn't caught even a glimpse of her, but she had a clear image in mind of an old woman with a face like thunder when she was annoyed.

Dr. Benenati hesitated still, gathering his thoughts before he spoke.

"It's fair to say that you will both be needed for at least the summer. I hope you will come talk to me about your plans so I can share my thoughts." He nodded to them all, and walked toward the room where Dr. Markham lay dying.

John left quickly, but Eli stayed where he was, close enough that Carrie leaned into him, glad of his warmth in the cooling night air. It was close to midnight, but she could not imagine going to bed to sleep. She couldn't imagine sleeping ever again, though she would have welcomed the escape from the jumble of questions that filled her head. In all of the turmoil, there were things to be thankful for. Lulu was alive and well, and surrounded by responsible people who cared for her. Carrie was thankful, too, that she wouldn't have to assume responsibility for Mrs. Markham. Two sisters had come from the convent to care for the remains and keep watch until the burial could be arranged.

"You look close to tears," Eli said, beside her. "Sleep would be reasonable."

"What I want just now is answers. Really the most important issue is what will happen with Lulu."

"It depends to some degree on what actually happened here," Eli said. "I don't really know what happened. Do you? Who made decisions. Who acted on the decisions."

"I can imagine," Carrie said. "But there is no way to know unless Josefa or Carlos were nearby and are willing to explain. I would not, in their place."

One eyebrow peaked. "And why is that?"

Surprised, she turned toward him. "In New York, in the city, there are not many Indians, but there are many people descended from the slaves brought to this continent in ships. I have seen how these things work. If the authorities can point to someone dark-skinned, they just stop looking any further for a suspect. If the son of manumitted slaves volunteers information about a crime, he is almost certainly going to be seen as the sole suspect. My guess is that the Indians here in the West are treated the same way."

His face was almost blank, free of surprise or satisfaction or anger.

"It is that way," he said. "Exactly."

"The opposite will be true for Dr. Markham," she said, lowering her voice. "No matter the evidence, the authorities will insist on believing that he played no role in his wife's death. And that would be true even if he weren't on the brink of death."

He didn't ask the obvious question, and Carrie thought he probably saw what he wanted to know on her face. Dr. Markham did play a role in his wife's death, whether he had given her an overdose of opium or let her do as she wished.

If he were to recover, Dr. Markham would start all over again. He'd go to San Diego or Austin and open a new practice; he'd find a suitable lady of good family who would be willing to raise his daughter, and remarry. For Lulu's sake, she wished him dead.

"In stories, people with fatal illness tend to be wise and kind and concerned with the people around them," Carrie said. This was something she often thought about but had never put into words.

"Go on," Eli said.

"I think it's more true to say that when a person faces an illness like this one, with no real hope of a cure, they stop pretending. Whatever is darkest is let loose."

"And if there's nothing dark?"

She smiled at him. "I suppose then a quiet death is the reward. Eli, I don't want you to go, but we both need to sleep."

Eli left and Carrie retired to her room. She took a lamp, an extravagance she allowed herself given the day behind her and the ones before her. Without it she wouldn't have seen the shallow basket sitting on her worktable.

For a long moment she stood and studied what waited for her in the basket. Without stepping any closer, Carrie could make out at least four envelopes, with her own name written across the first in a strong but uneven hand. She had never seen Mrs. Markham's handwriting, and still, she recognized it.

There were letters addressed to Carrie, to Lulu, to the general secretary of New Mexico Territory, and finally to Mrs. Michael Colby of Manhattan (Dr. Colby's wife and, if Carrie remembered correctly, Dr. Markham's sister). She knew the Colbys from her work, and had a good impression of the doctor's wife. This letter would answer many pressing questions, but in her current state, she could not imagine reading it. She took all of them with her and sat down on her bed.

When she woke in the morning, the letters were beside her still, unopened.

THE DAY CAME on hot and merciless, which meant that Mrs. Markham—laid out in the dispensary by the Sisters of Loretto—must be buried without delay. In the normal course of things, Dr. Markham and the priest would work out the details between them, but in this case the parish priest presented himself at seven in the morning.

He brought word from the bishop: if, as rumors indicated, Mrs. Markham had committed the mortal and unpardonable sin of self-destruction, no funeral mass could be said for her, and she would be denied burial in the graveyard behind the church. For that reason Padre Jalbert had come to ask for an official cause of death.

He addressed this crucial question to Dr. Benenati. Carrie stood nearby and listened, but it was all familiar. Roman Catholics made up a large part of Manhattan's population, and she had witnessed such conflicts before. What she couldn't have predicted was Dr. Benenati's reaction.

As the priest talked, a muscle in Dr. Benenati's jaw jumped, something she took as a warning.

"Surely you understand," the priest repeated for the third or tenth or twentieth time, "His Excellency, Bishop Lamy, must be sure that she died in a state of grace. Otherwise—" He shrugged.

"That would be a shame," Dr. Benenati said, his voice cool and his Spanish razor sharp, each word cut off cleanly.

Padre Jalbert nodded eagerly. "Yes, it would be a terrible burden to place on the family."

"You misunderstand me," Dr. Benenati said. "The family will survive the tragedy, but you will have to explain to the bishop that you failed in the errand he gave you. This family will pay you no bribes to secure Mrs. Markham a spot in your graveyard. Even more galling for the bishop, there will be none of the hefty fees he charges to say the funeral mass and pray at the graveside."

An hour later Eli came by, and Carrie told him about this confrontation, reconstructing the Spanish to the best of her ability.

"They are old enemies, Enzo Benenati and the Catholic church," Eli said. "What did you decide about the burial once he chased the priest off?"

"Today just after sunset. Dr. Benenati is in the dispensary now—"

Eli said, "I know what work he has in the dispensary."

They were talking in the *placita*, which was as busy, it seemed to Carrie, as a train station. She was speaking English with Eli, because she thought it best not to chance eavesdroppers.

Someone unfamiliar to Carrie came in, flanked by men of lesser standing. They wore no military insignia, but held themselves like men who knew how to use weapons. And did so gladly.

"Who is that?"

Eli blew out a long breath. "It was inevitable," he said. "But I was hoping he'd wait until after the burial. That's the sheriff of Santa Fe County and two of his deputies."

Carrie gathered together her energy. "Should I quake in fear?"

Eli's mouth turned down at one corner. "He'll underestimate you. It will be amusing to watch."

Carrie bit back a laugh.

In fact, Sheriff Jesus Maria Sena y Baca had come with questions similar to the ones the priest had asked. His English was very good, if self-conscious and stilted.

First and most important, he told them that he wanted to know whether Mrs. Markham had died by her own hand.

"Can this wait until tomorrow?" Carrie asked. "Dr. Benenati will have finished his examination and written out a death certificate. Anything I tell you now is just guesswork."

Sheriff Sena went on as if she hadn't spoken, addressing Eli. "If it's not suicide, it's murder. She was young and healthy, after all. If it's murder, somebody will hang for it."

Determined to be heard, Carrie forced her way back into the conversation. She said, "Who says she was healthy, may I ask? Do you happen to be a doctor? And beyond that, who would your primary suspect be?"

He raised a brow, surprised and displeased by her forward manner. "The husband is always the primary suspect in such cases. I want to talk to Dr. Markham before I leave."

Carrie was wondering how to respond to this extraordinary statement while Eli scanned the far side of the room.

"Chucho," he said, slinging an arm around the man's stiff shoulders. "*Vamanos.*"

They all marched off so quickly that Carrie wasn't sure exactly
what had happened, but she was glad to see the sheriff leave.

She crouched down to a boy who had taken hold of her hand. His
expression was very solemn, but she hoped he would respond to her.

"*¿Puedo ayudarte?*"

Her offer of help was met with a half smile and a solemn nod. The
boy turned and pointed to the far end of the *placita*, where John had
set up a temporary dispensary. Patients stood three and four deep
waiting to speak to him; Carrie wondered what proportion of them
were here not because they were ill but out of curiosity.

She sent Carlos back to John with the message that she would be
there to help just as soon as possible, and then she went outside. In
that moment it seemed that she could not take another breath in this
fine house where disaster had set down and meant to stay.

A few minutes later, Eli came looking and found her in the magpie
garden.

"How did you get rid of the sheriff and his men?"

With his eyes closed and his head tilted back, he looked utterly
relaxed, and that was just a little too much for Carrie, who had to stop
herself from pinching him.

"Explain."

"I took them to Madu, so she could answer their questions."

"Madu? Do you mean Maduhenía, Señora Benenati? I still haven't
heard her Towa name—"

He waved the question away. "Let's leave Towa names for another
day." The corner of his mouth jerked, and Carrie was reminded of the
fire ants and Rainey's howls of pain. Sometimes it was just not possible to anticipate the things men would find amusing.

She was glad to hear that Maduhenía—Madu—would answer the
sheriff's questions. She hadn't spent any time with the older woman,

but knew somehow she was not to be trifled with. She was Violante's polar opposite: Violante was quick to draw people in and make friends of them; Madu held people at a distance, even, it seemed, people she must have known for many years. The acquaintance could not be forced, and so Carrie would have to wait.

She said, "Will they survive the interview?"

"Sure," Eli said. "Madu barks and bites, too, but not in a case like this. She'll strip them of insulting questions, tell them what she thinks they need to know, and show them the door."

"A useful woman," Carrie said.

He hummed his agreement.

"Well," Carrie said. "I need to get back to work."

Eli reached out and took her wrist before she could get to her feet.

"Wait. Are you ready to tell me yet what's gnawing at you?"

In fact she did want to tell him, and couldn't explain to herself why she had hesitated. She settled herself again, and gathered her thoughts.

"Mrs. Markham wrote me a letter early on the day she died."

His expression gave nothing away of his thoughts, a fact she would have to learn to accept.

"She wrote other letters, too, and left them with me to post. And I haven't read the letter she wrote to me. I can't make myself read it."

Her tone was edgy, but Eli wasn't put off. It was a comforting thing, knowing she could be out of sorts and not have that get in the way.

He said, "Does it matter if you read it or not?"

The question caught her by surprise. "It might," she said finally.

"All right, then. Is there some hurry?"

"Maybe," she said, and now she was smiling despite her worries because he was so good at cutting through nonsense. Maybe someday she would find it annoying, but at this moment she was very glad of the way he looked at the world.

"One consideration," he said. "There might be something about Lulu. What she wants for Lulu."

"Yes, fine. I'll read it," Carrie said, feeling stubborn. "Maybe tomorrow."

"Maybe tomorrow is a good plan," Eli said. And: "I'm going over to Violante's to see how Josefa and Lulu are doing. Can you come, or are you needed in the dispensary?"

"The dispensary," she said. "I'll stop by to see Lulu after siesta. I suppose I'll see you next at the burial?"

"If not before."

He gave her a quick, almost brotherly kiss on the cheek, and left.

Late that afternoon, when Carrie was thinking that she had to get ready for the burial, a messenger came from the Casino Taquito: Bonita Ruiz—the prostitute she had been called to attend—was now really in labor, and there was more blood than Señora Justo had anticipated.

Babies had no respect for social engagements. There were times, at home, that Carrie had regretted missing a concert or a friend's visit to attend a birth, but it was a small inconvenience. Today she was almost relieved to be called. Better a birth than a burial.

She asked Carlos to pass word along to Eli, and set out. Santa Fe was still under the spell of the siesta and the streets were mostly empty. She saw only a cat sleeping in the sun, a pig sleeping in the shade, and a hummingbird, a tiny burst of color, feeding from a clump of sage. It had taken weeks for her to finally see a hummingbird, and now they were everywhere. She wrote a description of each one she saw, and would send what she had learned to Amelie, who would be delighted by the little birds.

At the casino the situation was dire. Bonita had been in labor for many hours, and was faltering. Some births went wrong from the start, and this was one of them.

At one point Carrie wondered if she would lose both mother and child, but in the end Bonita lived and her daughter, very small, was stillborn. Bonita just shook her head when she was offered the small, quiet form. Instead she managed a narrow, grim smile, and one comment: *"Menos mal."* Just as well.

Señora Justo, who came to the door to see what progress had been made, shot accusatory looks at Carrie and Bonita both.

When the patient was stable enough, Carrie looked out into the hall, just as Señora Justo was coming down it, arms crossed, her expression aggrieved. Carrie felt a little sad for this woman, who was so deeply dissatisfied with everything in her life, but sorrier still for the young women who had to deal with her, day by day. It was possible that she assumed Carrie would disapprove of her business establishment. Ten years earlier she would have been right, but working in the poorest neighborhoods of Manhattan had made Carrie see things in a different light.

Now, she did not mince words or resort to euphemisms, because she understood that those strategies would not be appreciated. Her directions were straightforward: Bonita must have at least ten days of bed rest, free of all work; she needed foods that would build up her blood, and a great deal of water.

"Most important," Carrie said, "is that someone check on her several times a day. If she starts to bleed heavily, you must send for me right away."

"Oh," Señora Justo said, some amusement in her tone. "You are a doctor now?"

"I am not a doctor," Carrie said. "But I may be able to help her. Of course, if you prefer someone else, that is your right, but please don't delay, or she may slip away before you realize how serious the situation is."

The older woman made a sour face. "I have been looking after these girls for more than twenty years. I know what they need and how to care for them, without *tejana* directions."

Carrie nodded, careful not to show the reaction the woman was looking for. She had learned, early in her training, that being calm and resolute was the only way to respond to the relentlessly negative.

"Then I leave you and wish Bonita a quick recovery. I will call to check on her tomorrow."

With that she had finally surprised Señora Justo, who had expected a different end to the conversation. A demand for payment that she would not get from Carrie.

She gathered her supplies, washed with the water and sandy soap provided, and went out into the night.

It was not really a surprise that Eli was waiting for her. He took her bag and they walked, quietly, through the sleeping town. The night sounds, different from the ones she had grown up with, were still familiar enough to be comforting.

He was waiting for her to ask, and so she did. "How did the service go?"

"Just about what you'd expect," Eli said. "There was an argument beforehand. Violante wanted to keep Lulu at home, and Dr. Benenati said it was never a good idea to shield a child from inescapable truths."

"And?"

"Lulu stood between Josefa and Violante during the service. I wasn't there, but later Josefa told me that Lulu was very composed. Too composed, almost, for a girl her age."

"It's the uncertainty about what comes next," Carrie said. "She knows her father is dying, but what then? That's a very frightening thing for any child, so she's ignoring it."

Eli said, "You know the authorities won't let her stay here with you. Not if you're married to a Mestizo."

A flush rose up from Carrie's chest. In the dark she could make out very little of his face, but she knew he was studying her closely. This was a test, she understood that.

"I will do whatever I can for Lulu." Her voice cracked, and she cleared her throat. "But I won't give up my life—or your life, or our life together—for hers. That would be a disservice to all of us."

She might have pointed out that they didn't even know what arrangements had been made for Lulu in her father's will, but that wasn't the real subject at hand. Eli had been asking her for a declaration. He was still unsure of her commitment to him; for the moment, at least, he was reassured.

"Listen, Ibarra," she said in a more playful tone. "You'll have to try harder if you want to be rid of me."

He pulled her up against him and kissed the top of her head.

She said more solemnly, "You don't know me very well. Not yet."

"I know you," he said. "It's just sometimes I have trouble believing my luck."

IN HER ROOM Carrie held the letter in her lap for a long minute, looking at her own name written in Mrs. Markham's hand. She thought of Eli, who refused to make complex things out of simple ones, and wondered if she could learn that trick from him.

She set all four letters on top of her cupboard, sat down on the edge of her bed to take off her shoes, and fell asleep before she'd even removed the second one.

48

As a STUDENT Carrie had been unsettled not so much by death as by the vagaries of dying. Patients slipped away without warning in the middle of telling a funny story, or they held on, in terrible pain, choosing agony out of fear of the unknown. Now, with his wife in her grave, Dr. Markham was in his final sleep, the coma so deep that nothing could rouse him.

He was dying, but life would not wait, and for the most part things had returned to normal. John worked in the dispensary; Carrie saw patients who were recently delivered or about to give birth; Dr. Benenati made home visits and Madu attended Dr. Markham, day and night; Josefa cooked while Manuela cleaned and Carlos swept the tile floors.

They all watched Lulu, who had forgotten her habit of asking questions, and never mentioned her mother or asked to see her father. Neither did she ask what would become of her when her father was gone. She spent her nights with Violante and Iñigo, but returned home at first light to spend the morning with Josefa. She sought out Carlos and Dr. Benenati and John at times, but only, it seemed, to assure herself that they were still nearby. When the opportunity came, she sat beside Madu, and seemed to take some solace in her company. She was polite. Attentive. Silent.

"She will set the pace," Madu said, and no one disagreed. No one said what they were all thinking: Lulu would lead the way for as long as she needed, or until law and the government intruded.

The doctor died at dawn the next day, and once again the house was filled with neighbors and friends, well meaning and curious. The nuns took over the task of preparing Dr. Markham for burial, and the first lawyers showed up at the door along with Padre Jalbert, who brought word from the bishop: the funeral and burial would take place the next day.

In the early afternoon, a message came for Carrie, asking if she would attend a first-time mother in labor.

Eli showed Carrie the way to the small adobe house on the edge of a vast cornfield where Umberto and Dolores Delgado farmed. Carrie sent Eli away with the usual warning: A first child was generally in no hurry to leave the warm, dark sea where it swam so contentedly. It could be many hours before she could start back home.

Later she realized that Eli had ignored this advice. Instead he sat in the shade with the young husband and his brother talking and playing *tejas*, a game that reminded Carrie of pitching pennies, one of Nathan's favorite pastimes as a boy. She might have been annoyed, but she realized that Eli wasn't staying to keep watch over her; he had stayed because there was no father or uncle nearby to keep Umberto and his brother calm. More proof that Eli was, in his heart and bones, a kind man.

Dolores Delgado surprised Carrie, too, by delivering her son just six hours after the first labor pains. He was a fine boy with a great deal of dark hair, bright brown eyes, and the toasty brown color of all the Mestizos Carrie had seen thus far.

Soon after the boy went—with great enthusiasm—to the breast, three generations of Delgado women came in and took over care of mother and child.

"That was a happy delivery," she told Eli as she closed her carpetbag. "They should all be just like that."

But high spirits didn't last long, and on the walk back to town, they talked about the funeral and what was to come.

Carrie said to Eli what she could say to no one else.

"I am thinking I should burn the letter. Unread."

He took his time to think this through. Eli was unwilling to be rushed about anything, it seemed. She liked this about him, usually, but not today.

"If not for Lulu—and you—I would be happy to ride out of town and never look back."

This wasn't true, not really, and telling untruths had a side effect for her she had never been able to escape: tears began to roll down her face.

She hated weeping in public, and dashed the traitorous tears from her cheeks as she and Eli crossed into the town proper. Eli put a hand on her shoulder and steered her down a lane she was unfamiliar with. It was very narrow and dim but not in the least cool. Before she could ask for an explanation, they came out near Red Rosa's cantina, and then they were at his house.

She hadn't been inside yet, for what had seemed like good reasons.

Eli stepped back and gestured to the door he had opened.

"Come on, Ballentyne," he said. "Don't be a coward."

She fell asleep immediately, every detail of the house and the chamber slipping away unnoticed. When she woke she was confused for a long moment, but comfortable. The bed was firm and smelled of fresh hay, and best of all, a breeze came through the windows on two walls and washed over her. One wall had been painted with a complex scene of people and sheep and pastures, but otherwise the room was very simple in its furnishings.

Outside, children were playing, throwing a ball for an excited dog who yipped enthusiastically. Rosa was scolding a girl called Nena who apparently didn't know how to *fregar una sartén* properly, but she would learn, *por Dios*, if it meant scouring out every pan in the kitchen.

"*¡El burro sabe más que tú!*" Rosa shouted, and then a door slammed.

Listening to the cantina owner scold with such vigor, Carrie had to wonder if Nena might actually be dumber than a burro.

"She can be loud," Eli said from the door.

"I don't mind," Carrie said, and sat up. "Eli, you took my shoes off and I didn't even notice."

He sat down beside her, not touching, but close.

"You were tired."

As if to agree, she yawned as she looked around the room. Eli's clothes hung from pegs on one wall, and there was another line of pegs—the wood still bright—on the other. It was possibly the sweetest thing anyone had ever done for her.

"Show me," she said, and went with him, room by room, to see what he had made ready.

Carrie knew that he was nervous, because for once he couldn't hide his disquiet. It was there in the way he ran a thumb along the line of his jaw. Did he imagine she would find fault? Yes, she decided, that was what worried him. That she would turn into the rich young lady from New York, shocked to learn that there was no indoor toilet, no running water in the kitchen, and tile instead of fine carpet underfoot.

He might worry about this for a very long time, she knew that. Raising the subject to reassure him would not really help. Instead she observed out loud things she liked and found interesting and surprising. The murals his sister had done, which were beautifully complex and would require a lot of study and, of course, a conversation with his sister. The overhead fan with thin leather blades framed in wood, as big as palmetto leaves, set in motion by pulling a braided string.

His instruments truly interested her. She wanted to know where they had been invented and manufactured, whether he had learned to use them when he was an apprentice, if he had any surveying work planned for the next weeks.

"Because," she said, coming to the point, finally. "Because we will have to get married before I can come to you here."

They were in the small *placita*, sitting across from each other at the table where they would take their meals.

His smile was slow and sweet. "We'll be better able to make plans tomorrow, once the will is read."

She hoped he was right. She said, "If a woman could write a will—one recognized by the courts—I would be less worried about Lulu. I'll be surprised if Dr. Markham even thought to mention her."

Eli considered for a long moment, his fingertips striking a rhythm on the table. "But there's the letter she left for you."

She lifted her face to look at him, knowing what he was going to say next.

"It seems odd, to me, that you could leave the letter unopened for so long. Do you have them with you?"

She said, "I was afraid to leave them in my room. There are so many people coming and going."

He left it right there, waiting for her to decide what she wanted to do. Of course he thought she should read the letter; of course he wouldn't tell her so.

She marched off to retrieve her bag, took out the letter addressed to her, and sat on the edge of the bed, staring at it for a long moment. Eli stood in the doorway, watching her.

"You're right," she said, her voice creaking. "This may be the equivalent of a testament. It might be considered a legal document. Would they take it away from me, if they knew about it? The sheriff or the governor or the bishop? Or I imagine that Dr. Markham's attorney might claim it. Really, I'd rather burn it."

He let her think, silent and easy.

"Fine," she said, and abruptly opened the envelope and read aloud.

Mrs. I. E. Markham
Calle del Convento Viejo de la Parroquia Principal
Santa Fe, New Mexico Territory

June 14, 1857

Miss Ballentyne,
I have neither the strength nor the presence of mind to maintain decorum, and so I must be blunt. This letter is addressed to you because you are a citizen of the United States and have reached your majority; thus the courts will not be able to turn you away without cause. Also, I believe that you are judicious and fair-minded and will do what is right.

Today Dr. Markham handed me a book written by a Dr. Joseph Ralph and published in the year 1840: A Private Treatise on Venereal Disease. He used a slip of paper to mark a chapter titled "On Gonorrhoea"—vulgarly called Clap. In this way I have learned that all the pain and sorrow of the last five years, the small graves that haunt my dreams, are to be laid at my husband's doorstep, and not mine. I don't know where or when or from whom he caught the infection; neither do I care, especially. Iacta alea est. Of course, the river I am about to cross is the Styx rather than the Rubicon, but the die is indeed cast.

Dr. Markham chose to make his confession this morning because he believes he has at very most three more days to live. His kidneys, he reports, are failing him. Please note that I am not asking you to attend to his needs while he dies. No doubt others will step in to do that. The nuns, I imagine, hoping for a donation. My sole concern now is what is to become of my daughters.

Imelda will go with me to my grave, but I am deeply worried about Lulu and what will become of her. All four grandparents are deceased. Dr. Markham has a sister called Aurelia, who has raised three children to be responsible, personable adults. She is also my

*friend. You will know her husband, Dr. Michael Colby. Dr. Markham
agrees with me that our daughter should be placed in their care. You
will have noted that there is an envelope for them, which I ask you
to post immediately by express, if at all possible. We believe this is
the best chance Lulu has to grow up in a loving environment.*

At the end of this letter you will find:

*First, in an envelope addressed to the general secretary, is a
statement granting you authority in matters relating to Lulu. In it I
speak for both myself and Dr. Markham, but his signature is
missing, due to his condition. This will be a matter of concern, but I
trust Mr. Bixby to resolve it easily enough.*

*Second, the letter to my friend and sister-in-law, Mrs. Michael
Colby in Manhattan.*

Third, a letter addressed to Lulu.

*Finally: I was not a gracious or kind employer; in
fact, as I intimated above, I have often been deranged over the last
few months. Severely deranged. Whether my behavior is due
to an excessive use of opium, a sin for which I will shortly be called
to account, or to the postpartum disruption of humors,
I cannot say. In the end I regret the way I spoke to you,
though my criticism of your clothing on arrival was
reasonable.*

*You can see by the way my handwriting is devolving that I have
exhausted my resources.*

*Dr. Markham begs me to forgive him his many sins
so that he may die at peace. It seems his conversion to Catholicism is
forgotten. I might have reminded him that his priest could
forgive him, but I am both angry and petty. I will wait
until I see him in hell to laugh in his face at his plea for
forgiveness.*

*Yours most sincerely,
Indira Markham, née Ewell*

Written by her own hand this 14th day of June, 1857
Witnessed by Josefa Gray Wolf of San Juan Pueblo
Witnessed by Sister Marie Louise

STATEMENT REGARDING THE MINOR CHILD
LUCINDA ARABELLA MARKHAM
BORN SEPTEMBER 16TH, 1850
SANTA FE, NEW MEXICO TERRITORY

We, INDIRA ANNABELLE EWELL MARKHAM and DR. SAMUEL ANTHONY MARKHAM, a married couple, being of sound mind but rapidly failing health, do hereby inform all individuals, related to us by blood or not, as well as legal, religious and government authorities of the following:

On this day, June 14th, 1857, we assign full legal and physical custody of our minor daughter, LUCINDA ARABELLA MARKHAM, to the nurse ELIZABETH CAROLINE BALLENTYNE, to take effect immediately even before our deaths, which will be a few days at most in coming. We take this unusual step out of concern for our daughter's personal and emotional well-being.

As our daughter's guardian, Miss Ballentyne shall have full legal responsibility for Lucinda's health and well-being, and authority in all matters.

It is our hope that this arrangement will come to an end when Dr. Markham's sister and her husband, Dr. Michael Colby of Manhattan, assume guardianship of Lucinda. We estimate that six months will be necessary, given distances and legal matters to be resolved, before they will be able to take her into the family in New York.

If Dr. and Mrs. Colby cannot take our daughter in to raise, for whatever reason, Miss Ballentyne will continue in that role. No one else, no matter the degree of kinship, will have any authority over our daughter.

To make it possible for Miss Ballentyne to provide appropriate care for Lucinda, we hereby direct all our lawyers and bankers to release $50 (U.S.) every week to Miss Ballentyne to pay for any and all expenses incurred. These funds will be issued until Dr. and Mrs. Colby become her legal guardians, and should that not happen for any reason, until Lucinda has reached her majority and can claim her inheritance. No limitations shall be put on Miss Ballentyne by any person or institution in regard to her choice of where or in what manner she will take up housekeeping.

Signed: Indira Ewell Markham
For herself and her husband, Dr. Samuel Markham, who is incapacitated.

Written by her own hand this 14th day of June, 1857
Witness: John Edmonds, physician's assistant, Santa Fe
Witness: Sister María Isabel, Santa Fe Parish Convent

49

DR. MARKHAM WAS buried at sunset. An unusually mild wind came up as Carrie came to stand at the grave with Lulu and Josefa. Her gaze kept drifting to the gaudy sky, an eruption of oranges and reds and egg-yolk yellow.

The sermon wasn't loud enough to be heard beyond the first and second rows of people gathered to see the burial service. For that reason, it seemed, people began to retreat, slipping away from the graveside and out of the cemetery. Carrie was about to turn away herself and take Lulu with her, when the praying came to an end and someone touched her elbow to gain her attention.

Thomas Bixby, Dr. Markham's attorney, was a short man with a potbelly and a great shock of prematurely white hair. He wore a monocle on his right eye and a patch over his left, so that you couldn't be sure where he was looking. But he had a kindly expression and a reserved, polite way, and Carrie had no reason to dislike him.

Violante and Josefa took Lulu between them and started home, leaving Carrie to talk to the lawyer.

"A sad occasion," he said, as if speaking only to himself. "Sad indeed. But the eternal clock ticks. It ticks without pause or mercy, and it continues on its monotonous path whether we are here to take note or not. Dr. Markham has left us, to his surprise and ours. If he had known how short his time would be, I don't doubt he would have given more thought to his will, but young men seldom do."

This short speech felt like something that had been lovingly crafted and rehearsed, but Carrie had no idea how to respond. Before she could think of a single word to say, Mr. Bixby went on.

"The reading of the doctor's last will and testimony will start in a quarter hour in my office, I think you must be aware?"

"Yes," Carrie said. "I hoped to attend."

"I guessed as much," said Mr. Bixby. "But I'd like to spare you the trouble, if I may. I can tell you now that Dr. Markham's will was written almost ten years ago, right after he brought Mrs. Markham here as a bride. And it says nothing at all, really. Not about anything of importance."

Carrie bent her head a little closer to Mr. Bixby's. "I'm confused, sir, about your purpose."

He nodded, almost cheerfully. "Of course, of course. Let me get to the point. I am the executor of Dr. Markham's will and so I can say with certainty that he left all his property and assets to his wife. As is usually the case, he directed that if his wife should die first, his entire estate should be divided among his children."

Carrie looked at him, wondering if she could speak bluntly.

"I can see you have questions," said Mr. Bixby.

Carrie had more than questions; she had a directive written by Dr. Markham's wife. But she was loath to hand it over to this man. Kind men could also be unscrupulous, and Lulu's well-being and future were hanging in the balance.

"Are you saying that there are no directions in the will about his daughter? He names no guardians, makes no provisions?"

"That is exactly what I am saying. My sense is that you have the girl's best interests at heart, so I wanted you to know. I reminded Sam many, many times that he needed to update his will, but he never came to me to do that. It is unfortunate."

"I would say irresponsible," said Carrie.

Mr. Bixby's color rose, but he nodded his head in agreement.

"And what will happen now, according to the law?"

"I will have to locate her next of kin. We can only hope there is a responsible aunt or cousin who is willing to take the little girl in. The Markhams' relatives are all in New York and Virginia, I believe. It may take six months or more to make arrangements. Which leads me to the next, very pressing question."

These topics should be discussed more formally, and not out of doors. Mr. Bixby was very aware of that, and so, Carrie concluded, there was something that worried him enough to approach her in the open.

"I'm listening."

"It has to do with the house and the dispensary," he began. "Dr. Markham was renting the property, you see. It did not belong to him."

What followed was a short but convoluted accounting of investments, expenses, bookkeeping, and the laws of the territory. In short, Mr. Bixby told her, there were two unavoidable but regrettable conclusions to be drawn. First, everyone would have to vacate the property within three days. Everyone, including Lulu.

"Wait," Carrie said. "This is what the law says, but what of the owner? Who does the property belong to?"

"Dr. Benenati," said Mr. Bixby.

"And Dr. Benenati is requiring us to leave the house—and the dispensary—within three days?"

"No, no, no. I didn't say that."

Carrie took a deep breath. "Then what are you saying?"

"That is the second conclusion I mentioned. Once the will is read and all is made public, it will be clear that Dr. Markham died in debt. Penniless, to put it plainly. He has delinquent liabilities, including the annual rent on the property."

"And no funds for Lulu's upkeep," Carrie finished for him.

"That is so." His distress was sincere, but he went on, determined, it seemed, to make her aware of the details.

"It may be six months or more before relatives can be found who will take Lulu in, but as things stand at this moment, she is without a residence, and without the resources required to see to her needs. The law . . ." His voice trailed off, and he took a moment to wipe the sweat from his brow with a handkerchief.

"I'll just tell you what I believe will happen, according to the law and custom here in Santa Fe. The bishop will assume responsibility for Lulu, and the church will take her in as an orphan."

Carrie said, "No, that won't happen. No. Lulu is my responsibility."

Mr. Bixby was shaking his head. "You are very kind to offer, Miss Ballentyne, but you have no standing under the law. The church will claim her, and they will get her."

Carrie managed a grim smile. "But I do have standing, Mr. Bixby. Mrs. Markham wrote a document in which she named me her daughter's guardian. It was witnessed and signed. I have the original document in a secure place, but I have made a copy. If you will return to the house with me, you can see the original and take the copy with you."

His whole face went blank for a moment. "But—"

"Also," Carrie said, "I will speak to Dr. Benenati about vacating the house. I have a proposition for him which I think will meet with his approval. If I am right, Lulu will be able to stay in the only home she has ever known."

50

E. C. Ballentyne
Santa Fe, New Mexico Territory

June 30, 1857

Dearest Ma,
When I left Manhattan you told me that I would need to be patient,
coming to a new place so different from my own. That it would take
time to know if I could truly be at home here.

The weeks since I arrived in Santa Fe have been challenging, for
me as a nurse and midwife and as a woman. I want to tell you every
detail of the weeks since I last wrote, but that would require twenty or
thirty pages, so I will leave the details to Nathan, who is still on the
Santa Fe trail, making his way here. There has been no hint of bad
news from the trail and we expect him within the next week.

Now, as simply as I can put into words, the news I must share:
First. Both Mrs. Markham and Dr. Markham are very recently
deceased. Dr. Markham suffered from diabetes mellitus (Uncle
Quinlan can, of course, provide details); Mrs. Markham delivered a

still-child some weeks before I arrived here, and never recovered fully. Hers was the worst case of puerperal insanity I have ever observed, but in her last days she was more herself. I wrote about her case to Amelie, and she could now share that information with you. Mrs. Markham's immediate cause of death was an overdose of laudanum.

Second. With the reading of Dr. Markham's will it was revealed that he had been in financial difficulties for some time. As is right and lawful, the executor will pay the Markhams' many outstanding debts. To that end, many of their possessions may have to be sold, so that very little—if anything at all—will remain in the estate as Lulu's inheritance.

Third. Dr. Markham included no directions about his daughter in his will, but Mrs. Markham left a directive, signed and witnessed. She has named me her daughter's guardian until other arrangements can be made.

In a separate letter addressed to me, Mrs. Markham provided more detail. She wanted Dr. and Mrs. Colby to take responsibility for Lulu and to raise her. Mrs. Colby and Mrs. Markham have been friends since they were children. Mrs. Colby is also her sister-in-law, as you will be aware. The nature of the relationship was unclear to me before I read this document. Mrs. Markham trusted the Colby family and believed they will take on responsibility for Lulu. A letter to Dr. Colby from Mr. Bixby will go out with the post along with this letter to you. Given distances and unforeseen delays, it may take six months or more before Lulu can be safely delivered to her Aunt and Uncle Colby. In the meantime I am responsible for her welfare here in Santa Fe.

Mr. Bixby, the family attorney, is not sure that the provisions outlined would stand up to a challenge in court, but given the circumstances, he believes it is best if we proceed according to Mrs. Markham's wishes.

Lulu is a bright little girl, funny and clever and deeply

*thoughtful. I hope that I can provide a peaceful place for her to begin
to recover from the sudden loss of both parents.*

*Fourth. Dr. Enzo Benenati is a retired physician here. It was
Dr. Benenati who sold Dr. Markham the medical practice, and
leased the house and dispensary to him. Dr. Benenati has agreed to
take up his practice again, temporarily, until another physician can
be found. He has asked me to stay as nurse and midwife, and I have
agreed. He and his wife (she is from a nearby pueblo, and has been
a midwife for some fifty years) have moved back into this house,
which they own, and are very happy to have Lulu remain here as
well until further plans can be made for her.*

*I will return to this point, but at this moment I have to
interrupt with news of a personal nature.*

*Elias Ibarra, called Eli, is 32 years old, a surveyor and
cartographer trained by the army engineering corps. His father is
Basque, and came from Spain some thirty-five years ago to see if
sheep farming could be successful here. His mother is a daughter of
the Jemez (also called Walatowa) Pueblo.*

*I am going to marry Eli, and in all probability will be married
by the time this letter reaches you. We will wait for Nathan to
arrive before we take that step. You must wonder how this happened
so quickly, and I will try to explain.*

*I have written to you about Eva Zavala, a native of Santa Fe I
met on the Missouri River packet. She quickly became a close friend.
Eli was on the packet, too, and Eva introduced us. They were
playmates as children, and as adults Eva married Eli's closest
friend. Given all these connections, Nathan and I were much
thrown together with Eli on the packet. Then, when I had to
leave the stagecoach to journey overland because Mrs. Markham
was thought to be in dire need of my help, Eli joined the three men
who had been hired to guide me.*

*This journey overland was, as I have written before, challenging
and invigorating to an extreme I had not imagined. It was during*

*that time—close to three weeks—that our friendship grew into
something more and I developed a real admiration and then
affection for Eli.*

*I dislike having to tell you this in such an impersonal and
detached way. I don't have Grandy's talent for making words dance
on the page, and I so much want to make you understand that my
decision to marry is not a hasty one. It is the end result of many
hours of contemplation and discussion. I was tempted to write
'debate' rather than 'discussion,' and that will give you a sense of
how well he suits me.*

*Our plan is to have our photograph taken as soon as it can be
arranged, but here are things that you can't read from an image. Eli
is thoughtful, intelligent, industrious, kind, and the very soul of
patience. In that way he is so much like Da that sometimes I have to
blink back tears. He is also very stubborn. The angrier he is, the
softer his voice. I have seen this, but his anger has never been
directed toward me.*

*Most surprising to me is that he is playful in a spontaneous, open
way that draws me in. I haven't laughed like this in many years.*

*It will not be easy for us as a couple. Eli is half Pueblo Indian,
and there will be outrage in some quarters. It is possible that my
services as a midwife or nurse will be rejected by some. But I am not
so easily put off, as you know, and I will stand my ground.*

*And so we will marry. The where and when and how I leave to
Eli, with Nathan to witness it all. When he returns home to you, he
will be able to answer your questions honestly. Maybe you will be
able to get him to tell the story of where he and Eli disappeared to
after a steamer (not ours) blew up at Arrow Rock.*

*You will have seen a complication, I am sure. Once I am married
I will leave the Benenatis' residence and be at home with Eli in the
adobe house he built for himself some ten years ago, where he also has
his business offices. Santa Fe is not very big, and the house is just a
short walk away, but the question of what to do with Lulu has no
easy answer. I cannot in good conscience take her away from the only*

home she has ever known, even as her legal guardian. This is a matter for more discussion. Or debate. Fortunately, all parties are concerned first and foremost with what is best for Lulu.

My working relationship with Dr. Markham was troubled, but I believe that I will work more effectively with Dr. Benenati, and I will continue to work for him as long as I am needed. Eli is away for at least a few days every month when he is surveying. I believe we will fare well together, both of us content to see the other at work which is challenging and fulfilling.

I know this letter will alarm you, but I hope you will also understand that I have truly found my place here. As a nurse and midwife, as a friend and wife, and as myself, the daughter you raised, who loves you and misses you and thinks of you every morning when she wakes and at night before she falls asleep.

Ma, you know how I struggled to regain my balance after Paradise. You were struggling too. Once we got to Manhattan we never spoke of Martha or her girls, did we? We avoided those memories at all costs, and we each struggled on, alone. On the overland journey, Eli and I often spoke late into the night, and little by little the story seeped out of me. He knows the worst of it now. No, that is not exactly right. He knows most of the worst of it, and waits patiently for me to find the words to tell the rest. It was the way he listened, his quiet acceptance while I told of those losses, that made it possible for me to open the door I had held shut for so long.

I would like to write about my memories of Martha and her sweet girls. Such good memories, I don't want to keep them all to myself.

Sending you all my affection and love,
Carrie

PS Please share this letter with Amelie and my sister Blue, and, if you find it useful and appropriate, my step-father and his daughter Margaret. If she is interested.

51

ELI SPENT THE first part of July watching Carrie run. She started her day in the dispensary but was soon off to visit patients, to check on women who had given birth a day, a week, a month before; she saw women who were about to give birth, or should have already given birth. Wherever she might be, she ran home to spend time with Lulu, to talk to Dr. Benenati, to sit a few minutes with Josefa or Violante in the magpie garden. Then out she went again, unless she was needed in the dispensary.

She ran all day long, but tried her best to be there for three meals every day. For Lulu's sake, she said. But she sat next to him, and held his hand beneath the table. This was possible only because Dr. Benenati had gone out of his way to tell Eli that he was welcome to take his meals at their table.

It was a kindness Eli wouldn't soon forget. It did him good to feel Carrie shiver at his touch.

Over breakfast and dinner and supper, they usually managed to talk to each other for a few minutes—depending on the company—but there were subjects she didn't want to hear about. Getting married being the most obvious.

"I like Nathan, you realize that. I don't mind waiting for him," he told her. "But there's the question about—"

She would put a hand on his wrist—or, more often these days, his knee—to stop him.

"You decide. Really, Eli, I want you to make the decisions. I'll be happy with whatever you choose. Isn't that a good thing, that I don't make a fuss?"

It should have been easy to agree with her; there were legions of stories about weddings gone wrong. Men warned each other: a wedding turned daughters into demons and wives into harpies. Feuds flared up that could last for years. Of course, exaggeration was an art form in Santa Fe, and the stories were living, growing things, so he felt mostly safe ignoring them. Then Rosita reminded him about her sister, and before she could tell—yet again—the long and complicated story about poor Angela, he had extricated himself.

His office was the place he went to think things through. Surrounded by pencil stubs, quills, his collection of slide rules, gauges, grade rods, reams of paper of a half dozen kinds, and books, he found it possible to focus. Sometimes he needed to read a chapter of Gummere or Davies, Flint or Day, to get settled.

Turning his mind to his work did help, and there was plenty of it. Letters to answer, others to write, a report he had promised as soon as he got home. And still he sat there for long stretches, trying to put a finger on what was off about Carrie.

He kept track of the things that occupied her. She was watching for her brother, she was worried about Lulu, she was troubled by a patient with a stubborn infection, another whose infant wasn't thriving, by Manuela's sour stomach. She lived her life like this, at a run, looking after everyone. Or it might be that she was starting to realize she didn't want to be married. To him. Maybe to anybody.

Their plans were public knowledge, and of course, people were talking. He had been stopped by a half dozen men, none of them white, all of them wondering if he knew what he was getting himself into. Because they were polite and never talked about Carrie, not directly, he listened calmly to concerns that were mostly founded in fact and observation. He nodded, acknowledging the issues, and left things right there, no hard feelings.

Then Al Henry, wobble-kneed with *tisgüín*, plopped himself down across from Eli at Rosita's and wagged a finger in his face. His blue eyes bloodshot, he talked about how a clever man moved fast when he saw something worth snatching up that maybe was more than he had a right to. And ain't that pretty girl from New York a rare sight out here in the desert.

Eli leveled his gaze at Henry, his expression as blank and forbidding as a night sky in the dead of winter.

"That's how you figure, is it." He began low and easy. "See, if you was to ask me, I'd say a clever man's one who knows how to mind his own business and especially one who don't talk so loose about another man's wife. Unless he's looking for trouble with a keen edge."

The whole room went quiet while Al Henry turned red in the face, got up sputtering, grasping for sharp words to fling back in Eli's face, words that would remind Eli who he was and was not, so that the big half-breed would slink away and never come back. Then he tripped over his own feet and hit his chin on a table edge, and he was the one slinking away with blood dribbling down his face.

The story made its way around town before morning, and that suited Eli. He had a reputation as somebody good with his fists and just as good with a knife, when the situation called for it. Al Henry just needed reminding. After that, nobody white tried to talk to Eli about the woman he was going to marry.

Carrie was hearing things, too, he was more aware every day. Women pulled her aside or went looking for her at the dispensary, wearing their concern like halos, sure that their advice and wisdom were righteous, and, by the Virgin, the overeducated, prideful young lady would listen and be glad that a God-fearing Christian woman was there to show her where she was going wrong. There were only two or three who would venture so far, all of them white. Women who looked like Eli himself rather than Carrie—some of them—were mad, but they were mad at Eli, and he could live with that.

He wondered if Carrie would think it was asking too much to want to hear about Miriam Goldblum stopping her in the middle of the plaza to warn about the mixing of races. Josefa and Violante had let hints drop about this kind of thing, but it was Rosita who told him about Miriam Goldblum putting a hand on Carrie's arm to turn her around.

Rosita scowled when she saw his surprise.

"You think your woman will change her mind because some *ramera* frowns at her?" She gave a sharp shake of her head. "She's made of stronger stuff than that."

That day before dinner, he came in to find Josefa putting bowls out on the table. She took one look at him and started talking. She had been waiting for the chance to tell him what he should have figured out for himself. She talked fast, determined to have her say before anybody else came in.

"You," she said, "are just as dumb as every other man out there. Let me tell you what you're missing. Her father is dead, yes. But what if he wasn't? What if you knew her parents would be showing up on the next stagecoach? That wouldn't worry you?"

It was dumb. No other word for it. "She's worried about what my mother will think?"

"Among other things," Josefa said. "When are you taking her home to meet your people? Have you talked about that?"

All through dinner he went over that simple question. The table was crowded, and it seemed everyone had things to say. The Markhams had never invited anybody to join them for a meal, but the Benenatis wanted everybody at the big table in the *placita*. It was noisy and confusing—sometimes three or four languages crisscrossing—but never boring. Today none of it suited him, not the least little bit.

He lowered his head to talk into Carrie's ear. "Something to talk to you about during siesta."

She glanced at him as if she expected to see a rash on his face. "Something wrong?"

And right then Manuela came in from the front hall to say a boy had brought a message: Chava Goldblum was in labor and could the midwife come; Reizl said there would be eggs.

CARRIE TOOK A minute to finish the beans and broth in her bowl, squeezed Eli's shoulder as she got up, and apologized. Over the noise she whispered to him, "I'll come to you when I'm done at the Goldblums'. It may be really late, but we can talk for a little while at least."

She told herself that he seemed satisfied with that, but she herself was not. It suited Carrie when she was busy and work was plentiful, but Eli deserved more of her time and attention than he was getting, and she needed more of those same things from him. More concerning was the fact that she would be called to the Goldblums' today. Yesterday Miriam Goldblum had stopped her in the plaza to make sure that she, Carrie Ballentyne, knew that she was throwing her life away by pledging herself to a man who was mixed blood. She would be shunned, Miriam promised her, by every white family in Santa Fe. And so would her children.

Carrie had listened to this and more, growing cold and colder with every word. She waited, and when her accuser had come to a breathless conclusion, both brows raised as if in anticipation of an act of contrition, Carrie had looked at her calmly.

She said, "Two of your good sisters are near their time. Will you ask Dr. Benenati to attend? Of course, he'll want to know why you haven't sent for Madu, the most experienced midwife in this part of the territory. She is his wife, in case you've forgotten, so he'll know that you've rejected her. Or will you manage without a midwife or doctor, all by yourselves?"

Miriam's jaw had dropped. When she managed to find the words she wanted, her tone was less accusation and more outrage.

"But Madu is—Madu—"

"An Indian, yes. As my help is unacceptable, your choice is to call on Madu or do without a midwife. I wonder what the rest of the family will say when you tell them how you've arranged things."

She had walked away quite proud of herself, but fate had caught up with her, because now Chava was in labor. Carrie wondered if Miriam had bothered to relate the episode on the plaza to her family. It might be that all the Goldblum women were of the same opinion, and had called on Carrie despite her choice of a husband. The distrust of Indians, even Indians who had proved themselves many times over as allies, ran deep. Dr. Benenati's wife had been delivering babies for some fifty years in every pueblo and village within a day's ride. Women relied on Madu's skill and gentle touch. This thought was in her mind when she came around the corner and saw that Reizl Goldblum stood waiting for her in the open doorway. Her smile was wide and heartfelt, and she held out both arms, as women sometimes did to greet an old friend who had been gone too long. Wishful thinking, Carrie told herself, but she returned Reizl's smile and allowed herself to be embraced, drawing in good smells: baking bread, coffee beans, fresh milk. Reizl's small, mangled fists thumped her on the shoulders with great enthusiasm. Then she pulled Carrie inside.

They stopped right there as a spiraling howl came to them from deep in the house.

"Chava?"

Reizl's head tipped to one side, and her shoulder came up to meet it. "Who else? She screeches like a mad goose. But no need to rush, really. Come, I have cake."

Carrie asked herself what she had been expecting. A general condemnation before she was admitted to the house? While she ate a piece of plum cake, Reizl talked about her chickens, and then asked if the story was true about Pío Ocampo, that he called her to deliver a burro, and she went.

This was a more welcome topic for conversation than yesterday's scene with Miriam, and so while Chava screeched every now and then, Carrie told Reizl about Gertrude.

"Usually his wife helps with difficult deliveries," Carrie finished. "But she was away, and I didn't mind."

Reizl's head rocked from side to side for a moment, but then Chava shouted so urgently that Carrie jumped up from the table.

"Tell me," Reizl called to her back as she left the room, "how you feel about cats."

ALL WAS SAID and done just after two in the morning. Chava had been a good patient, if a particularly loud one. Easy to persuade, quick to take direction, uninterested in any discussion of Carrie's personal life. Or at least it seemed that way until just before Carrie made ready to leave.

She thought that Chava was asleep, but Reizl came in to have another peek at the child, and she roused.

The girl was small, but perfectly formed, with a head of feathery dark hair.

"You can never have too many daughters," Reizl said. In the light of the lamps her face seemed to glow.

"I'm happy with my girls." Chava's voice was hoarse from all the yelling, but she smiled down at the little button of a face. "This one will follow in the footsteps of her mother's mother and grow up to make us all proud."

Carrie was always touched when a new mother called on the memory of her grandmothers. It was a custom among her Mohawk family, and she herself could recite her Aunt Hannah's lineage all the way back to the years before the Revolution. *I am the daughter of Sings-from-Books of the Kahnyen'kehàka people*, Hannah would say. *I am the granddaughter of Falling-Day, great-granddaughter of Made-of-Bones, great-great-granddaughter of Hawk-Woman, who killed an O'seronni chief with her own hands and fed his heart to her sons.*

That was what she should have told Miriam the day before. Miriam would not understand, but still it felt like what she should have done. Carrie would claim her Mohawk aunts and mothers and grandmothers, and then start again with her mother. *I am the daughter of Lily Bonner Ballentyne, the granddaughter of Elizabeth Middleton Bonner, the great-granddaughter of Cora Munro Bonner and Maddie Clarke Middleton, who lived extraordinary lives, stories without end.*

"What are you thinking about?" Chava asked. "You are a thousand miles away."

"More than that," Carrie said. "I was thinking about my family. My Mohawk mothers and grandmothers. None of my blood, but still rooted in the very heart of me."

Reizl cleared her throat. "Now that you bring up the subject—"

Carrie started, realizing that yes, she had provided an opening. She could imagine no conversation that she could want less just now, but she fumbled.

"What subject do you mean?"

Chava was frowning. "She means Miriam, of course. Our Miriam who doesn't mind her own business."

"You note she's nowhere to be seen," Reizl said. "After yesterday's commotion, I thought you shouldn't have to deal with her. Whatever she told you, you put it out of your mind. She doesn't speak for me."

"Or me," Chava said.

Carrie was very tired, but she left the house in far better spirits. Then she saw that Reizl's husband was waiting for her.

"Your Eli came by at midnight," he said. "I sent him home to sleep and promised I would walk with you."

This brought Carrie up short. In the light of the lantern, her expression must have been alarming, because he held up both hands, as if to stop a bolting horse.

"It's no trouble," he said. "Two minutes there, two minutes back, and then to bed for me."

It was hard to make sense of what arrangements Eli had made with Levi Goldblum, but she walked beside him and kept her eyes averted, unsure of how to address him. He set off, but not in the direction she had expected. They did not cross the plaza to walk to the Benenati house, but in the opposite direction. To Eli. He was taking her to Eli.

At the door he said to her, "Thank you for the way you care for my family. You are not just skilled and professional, but kind, even when you are not shown kindness. Good night."

He had been carrying her carpetbag, and he put it down beside her along with a basket she didn't recognize. Before she could think of a single thing to say, he had disappeared around the corner.

She opened the door without a sound, and carried the bag and basket inside.

Santa Fe was asleep at this hour. The saloons and gambling parlors and the brothel were quiet. The military reserve might have been a ghost town. She listened and heard nothing more than the wind, the cry of an owl, and, far off, coyotes singing to the setting moon.

The odd thing was, she had planned this. She meant to be here. As scandalous as it was, she had resolved to come to Eli tonight, knowing that word would reach every corner by morning. Josefa would find her bed unslept in, and she would smile her satisfaction. And *satisfaction* was a word best left unconsidered just now.

Carrie left her things in the hall. The kerosene lamp that stood on the table in the *placita* had been moved to a shelf in the hall with the flame turned low. Just enough light to find her way. He had planned this. He had taken precautions, for her. The thought made her heart race.

On the trail Eli had been a sound sleeper. Quick to rouse if there was any hint of trouble, but able to drop off as soon as he laid his head. Carrie knew she couldn't surprise him, not in his own house. He would be awake now. One possibility that occurred to her and was tempting for a minute at least: she imagined sitting down where she stood and sleeping right here.

Really, she said to herself. *What silliness. Why? For what reason? To what end?*

She could have growled in frustration at her own nervousness.

Fine, she thought. She was here because she wanted to be here, and to pretend anything else was an injustice to herself and to Eli. Carrie walked down the hall to Eli's chamber door, opened it, and slipped inside. There was another kerosene lamp here, a smaller one she hadn't seen before. By its meager light she could make out the shape of the bed, and the shape of the man in the bed. He lay on his side, turned away, a light blanket draped across his hips. In the lamplight the skin of his back gleamed like amber.

Carrie walked to the bed, her heart thundering in her ears, and looked at Eli. Eli, who seemed to be sound asleep. He could not be asleep, she had been sure, but now she was paralyzed by the possibility. What could she possibly say if she woke him?

Move over?

An uninvited laugh came up. She bit it in half, swallowed it back down. If he woke to find her laughing at him, he was likely to take offense. Or not. She knew so little of the way men thought of this whole business.

What business would that be?

She batted the question away. *You have done many hard things in your life,* she reminded herself. *This is, by comparison, not difficult. Here is the man you mean to marry.* Because she did mean to marry him, and soon. Very soon. But not tonight.

Carrie began to turn away, planning each step: through this door, down the hall, through another door, a right turn, and left turn, a half mile's walk would take her past the plaza, past the parish church, and then—

His hand closed around her wrist, and Carrie let out a peep like a mouse caught up in claws.

Half turned toward her so the light touched his face, he smiled. His voice was sleep roughened, a deep rumble.

"Miss Ballentyne," he said on a half yawn. "What are you doing here in the middle of the night?" Imitating the Catholic priest's stilted language, one eyebrow arching. And then the wink.

That wink. It worked like a flame to dry paper; as she flushed with surprise and outrage, irate beyond all experience, there was only one possible response to such cheek. She raised her hand to slap him, but he had both her wrists now and he was pulling her, lifting her over him, and then she was on the bed. Fully dressed, looking up into the face of the laughing, naked man who held her. She took stock: the curve of his jaw, the shape of his nose, his cheekbones like wings thrusting up under the skin. Oh, he was beautiful, but somehow the urge to slap him was still with her. Then he leaned down and used his teeth to work loose her first button.

"What?" Her voice caught. "What?"

Eli stopped and leaned back. "Did you want to sleep in your clothes?"

On the trail they had wrestled once or twice, playfully, in the evening when they were far enough removed from the others. She could not match this man's strength, but she had some tricks learned over long years of wrestling with Ballentynes, Bonners, and Savards, rough and always ready. Eli thought she would be easy to bring down, but that was, very simply, out of the question. Carrie let out a low, rough scream that came up from her belly, and with that, she managed to surprise him. Just that simply she was on top of him. He still held her wrists, but she, too, had teeth. She nipped his jaw, or meant to, but he ducked to one side, and her teeth clicked shut on nothing at all.

Eli's laugh was almost breathless. "It's like that, is it?"

He flipped her over.

"You faker! You cheat!"

"Faker? Me? Darlin, everything here—" He lowered his hips so that she could not mistake his meaning. His lips at her ear, he whispered, "Everything here is real."

SHE WOULDN'T GIVE up easily. Lying here waiting for her, Eli had hatched this plan, knowing that she disliked surprises. In a day or a week, she would find a way to pay him back. Tonight she would end up laughing, but soon enough she would come for him.

He loved her laugh. Carrie laughing was worth any tussle. Twice she managed to slip away, only to leap back, fists flying.

As he looked at her now, she reminded him of the fairies in the stories Violante had told the Ibarra youngsters years before. Carrie's hair, shaken loose from its pins, rioted around her. Flushed, her eyes shining, she might have been such a fairy creature.

Eli took control, and when she was on her back once again and looking up at him, he told her what he remembered.

"Reina Mab."

She stilled quite suddenly, intrigued, confused, wanting to hear more. "Queen Mab?"

He nodded. "Ah, you know about Queen Mab. Violante told us her favorite story about the lovers, but really it was the fairy that made an impression on me. *Reina Mab, la partera de las hadas.* A midwife to all the fairies, she brings men what they want most, but only in their dreams."

Carrie giggled, and at the unexpected sound from her own throat, laughed outright. "Violante told you the story of Romeo and Juliet?"

Eli ran a hand over her hair, smoothing it away from her face. "If there's a midwife called Mab in that story, then yes, my fairy queen."

Her smile softened, but her breath came quick. "Oh dear," she said, her eyes rounded in mock distress. "You've found me out. What's a fairy to do?"

She caught his hand, the fingers still wound in her hair, and brought it to her face. When she kissed his palm, every nerve in his body came alive.

He said, "Oh, come on. Is that the best you can do?"

CARRIE LOVED KISSING Eli, but this time, in the dark, lying together, she needed more. She wanted more, and she wanted it from him. This awareness had come to her weeks ago, but she had resisted the idea, and rarely allowed herself to think about it. She had simply forbidden her imagination to consider the mechanics. Now it was time, and so she raised her hands and began to learn the feel of him.

Beneath her palms she measured the heavy beat of his heart. She took note of textures: smooth skin, a peppering of small scars, a healed welt, a light mat of feathery straight hair that narrowed as it ran down his torso. His navel was a shallow dip in a flat belly, and all of him was ridged and roped and defined by muscle. In the light of day, she would make a map of him and commit it to memory.

He was on his side, curled around her, his breath on her brow and in her hair.

She said, "Let me up." She did not say *Undress me* or even *Let me undress*; those words were beyond her just now. Eli understood, or seemed to. He pulled away and sat on the edge of the bed, content to watch as she made herself ready for him.

Later, she thought, much later, days or weeks or years from now, she would thank him for this kindness. For his calm certainty. She stood and began to work buttons and ties and hooks, dropping her things to the floor until there was only the chemise. Worn so thin, mended so often, in the lamplight it concealed nothing. The thinnest milk poured over pale skin.

As she turned to Eli, the chemise sliding down and down to pool at her feet, the flame in the paraffin lamp flickered once, twice, and went out.

After a moment she said, "Where is Queen Mab with her fairy dust when you need her?"

He reached for her hand and drew her down to sit beside him. Hip to hip. He was so big and so perfectly made, she felt like a thief. Claiming a man she had no right to.

He said, "I'm out of paraffin, but tell me, did you want to see me, or do you want me to see you?"

"Well, both." Carrie heard the wobble in her voice. "You know I'm not good with surprises."

"Then it's my job to distract you till the sun comes up."

Somewhat later, her voice cracking, all calm a distant memory, Carrie spoke to him in the dark.

"Maybe I should reconsider my position on surprises." Her fingers traced over his most sensitive skin, taking his measure. Eli rubbed his face against her shoulder. "We can take all the time you need. When you're ready—"

She lifted her face to him. "Don't I feel ready to you? You're the one with the experience. You must know how to read—" She drew in a breath. "Read the way my body responds."

"Oh yeah," he said, his voice rougher. "Your mouth—"

"Oh no. No." She half turned away. "I don't want a report."

ELI STIFLED A surprised laugh and drew her back to him. He made his voice as serious as he could with a naked Carrie in his bed. His fingertip circling a taut nipple, he said, "You don't want to hear about your breasts? They are beautiful, did you realize? And here—"

With one hand he covered her mound, fingers delving, seeking, and then finding.

"Your scent. The feel of you, so slick but very tight."

"Eli," she moaned. "Please don't talk to me about—"

So he kissed her. To make her forget the words, to drag her back down with him into the place where language was useless. When she was free of all that, he moved over her, drew her up against him, belly to belly, and would have wept for the pure joy of it. Then she opened to him, and he claimed her for himself.

MUCH LATER, JUST coming out of sleep, Carrie realized that Eli was studying her. His head bedded on his upper arm, his gaze clear and focused.

The light made her eyes water, so she closed them. Then she said aloud what she had imagined saying.

"According to my Aunt Hannah's people, we are married now."

Here she was, playful when he had expected serious. Eli wondered if she'd surprise him like this forever.

"My mother's people would agree."

Abruptly he launched himself out of bed and went to a trunk in the corner. He crouched down and opened the lid, but only for a brief moment. When he came back to bed—striding naked across the room—he was carrying a folded blanket.

"My mother wove this blanket. It's a tradition in some pueblos, a man's mother does this for his bride. She finished it years ago, and when I was setting out to come back to Santa Fe, she sent it along for you."

Carrie blinked at him, at the blanket, at him again. Cautiously she took it from him and spread it out over the bed.

Eli said, "The name of the pattern is Vallero Star."

All her attention was on the blanket, her fingers tracing the complex pattern of eight-pointed stars.

"That blue is my mother's favorite color. There's a specific kind of larkspur she needs for the dye. The flowers grow near the Walatowa Pueblo, and so she spends a good part of May there, harvesting it with her sisters."

Carrie lifted a corner and studied the weaving on both sides. Then, finally, she raised her head, not trying to hide the tears in her eyes.

"It's the most beautiful thing," she said. "She really is giving it to me, as a gift?"

Eli sat beside her. "For you, yes. Because I told them about you, and that I was going to marry you. Did you think they wouldn't approve?"

Her shrug said that she had been worried about just that. About his family, and whether they would accept her. That was why she was reluctant to talk about the wedding.

"It means a lot," she said, her voice thick.

He said, "I'm an idiot. I should have realized."

Carrie shook her head. Her eyes still swam with tears, but she was smiling.

Eli cleared his throat. He wanted to ask her not to cry, but knew somehow that this would strike the wrong note. She cried because she was happy.

Then she folded the blanket and held it in her lap while she kissed him. A new kind of kiss, sincere and trembling, as much as a vow. For some reason his mother's gift of a blanket made it possible for her to put aside the last of her reservations.

"I have to get to the dispensary," she said. "Walk with me, and you can tell me what plans you've made. Nathan will be here soon, after all. Maybe today. I assume we have to have a ceremony of some kind, but I hope we can avoid the bishop."

52

WORK, CARRIE DECIDED, was the only way to keep her mind off Eli. Until Nathan was here and they could go ahead with their plans, the less thinking about Eli, the less remembering Eli, the better.

Explaining this decision to him might be awkward, but she believed he would see the logic. She was prepared for that discussion the next day and the day after, but he simply failed to raise the subject. There was nothing different or unusual about him; he was attentive, teasing, subtly affectionate, but apparently Eli Ibarra had got all he needed from her and wasn't thinking about more.

Confusing, and yes, a little off-putting. Was it a courtesy of some kind to step away after a first . . . she didn't even know what word to use. Was it up to her to raise the subject? Did he think she needed time to recover? To heal? Did men think of women as creatures who could not survive the breaking of a hymen without drama?

She would have told him, if he had asked, that yes, she was a little sore, but she couldn't say she was in pain. Riding might be difficult, but that wouldn't last long. What she wouldn't tell Eli or anyone, what really consumed her thoughts, was the way the sensations themselves echoed.

Words came to mind, repeatedly, unbidden, and seemed to echo: *tumid, turgid, tumescent.* She would have banned them, if such a thing were possible, but they would not be cast off. Her traitorous, endlessly curious mind insisted on revisiting the experience: the heavy fullness of an invasion that was so strange and then, suddenly, so right.

Her teachers had always praised her ability to focus on the assignment or subject at hand, but that skill seemed to be gone, at least for now. Until she reckoned out for herself about sex in general and sex with Eli in particular, she was at the mercy of her memory. The memory that others so envied, that made it possible for her to absorb a new language so quickly. Just now her remarkable memory had the upper hand.

Thole what ye cannae change, that was what her father would tell her. Bear up. In this situation she had no alternatives.

At home she could have talked to Amelie, to her mother, to the nurses she trained with. She could have asked blunt questions, and for the most part, they would have provided answers.

This was on her mind again, as she went into Carson's hardware store and straight back to the door that opened into the family apartment. Mrs. Carson answered the door herself, her four-week-old infant on her shoulder. A little girl called Alice.

It didn't take very long to determine that Mrs. Carson continued to heal at a good pace, and that her daughter was thriving. There were sleep disturbances, as ever and always, and a heat rash on Alice's scalp and cheeks and bottom. There was little to be done, beyond keeping her clean and dry, as Mrs. Carson already knew, and a simple ointment that Carrie had brought with her.

"I wonder if you've met Reverend Read yet. The Fort Marcy chaplain. Next Sunday we will be dedicating Alice to the church. Would it be rude of me to invite you? The congregation is very small, but his sermons are always interesting."

Carrie had rarely seen Reverend Read. Looking after the Protestants in Santa Fe kept him very busy, it seemed. This was also not the time to explain that she was not Protestant or Roman Catholic. Such discussions tended to be drawn out, and sometimes less than friendly. The only way to handle the invitation was to accept politely.

"Unless there's somebody in labor, certainly. You'll have to tell me more about the congregation."

While they talked, Carrie tried not to let her gaze wander to the window that looked out directly on Eli's front door.

"Won't you please call me Tess?"

Carrie realized she had missed something, and smiled and ducked her head.

"I would like that. Of course."

In fact very few people had made this offer thus far. It was a complicated thing to negotiate, depending on the language they were speaking, local customs, the nature of the conversation, and the degree to which formality was called for. French and German and all the other European languages had a similar set of requirements, but learning a language in a classroom was very different from being immersed in a churning sea of voices.

She was on a first-name basis with Eli, of course, Eva and her son, Josefa, Iñigo and Violante, Reizl and Danya Goldblum, John, Madu, and Rosita, but it was still a matter of some confusion. For Spanish the issue had to do with pronouns and verb conjugation: If you were talking to somebody, anybody, you had to choose between *usted*, the formal pronoun, or *tú*, the informal. Speaking to a stranger or a recent acquaintance, the one who was older or richer or had more status could raise the subject: *¿Podemos tutearnos?* Can we be informal? Of course, the more senior or respected person was the one to ask this question. Or not to ask it.

Carrie doubted she would ever reach this degree of familiarity with anyone outside her own family.

"Carrie?"

Tess was smiling, and Carrie was mortified. She had drifted away again, looking out the window.

"I apologize for my rude behavior," she said. "And I won't attempt to make excuses."

Really what she meant to say was *Please do not ask*. So she tried to go on with her questions about Tess's health, but her patient had other ideas and, in fact, was determined to ask.

"Did I hear right, you're going to be our neighbor soon?"

Really, she should just accept the fact that these conversations could not be avoided. Since Mrs. Markham's death, people she had never met or hardly knew wanted to talk to her. About half their questions had to do with Mrs. Markham's cause of death. (Was it true that, and did Carrie know if, and poor little lamb, orphaned and all the money gone and what was the plan?) The other questions were about Carrie and Eli. Some people didn't limit themselves, and asked both about the Markhams and about Eli Ibarra.

Of course Tess Carson had heard the stories, and of course she saw Carrie's preoccupation with the view out her window. But the question had been asked politely, and there was nothing fraught in the way Tess looked at her.

"Yes," she said, or tried to. She had to clear her throat. "Yes, that's true."

The baby had begun to fuss. Tess loosened her bodice to free a breast. "It'll be good to have you as a neighbor," she said, guiding the trembling mouth to her nipple. "My Spanish ain't what it should be. It's good to talk American with an educated lady."

Later, Carrie thought, she would have to come to terms with this statement, but not right at this moment. Instead she said, "I miss talking to my mother and family. I still talk to them in my head, I have to admit."

The baby nursed, a fist buried in her mother's breast, swallowing rhythmically. Tess touched the sparse hair on Alice's scalp and glanced at Carrie, almost shyly.

"Will you come by to call once you get settled in? You know, just to have coffee and talk?"

Settled in, she had said. Carrie liked this turn of phrase. There was nothing judgmental in it, no disapproval in her tone. She managed a true smile.

"Of course," she said. "I hope you will also call on me."

Tess's smile shifted, just a little. Just slightly, and became less than it was. Brittle, almost. She was unable to mask her discomfort, just as Carrie was unable to overlook it.

Tess Carson liked the idea of Carrie as a neighbor and a friend, but there was a line, and while Carrie had crossed it, Tess never would.

53

THAT AFTERNOON CARRIE drifted in and out of a light sleep, her linen damp with sweat, and waited for the siesta to be over. Eli would be asleep. The heat didn't affect him very much; he would shut out the sun, leave shutters tilted open to encourage breezes, and nod off. He slept on his back, and she imagined that in this weather he would be sleeping naked.

As a nurse, a midwife, the stepdaughter and niece and cousin of doctors, she knew that there was nothing unusual about her interest in his body. It might be excessive, but with time—and familiarity—calm would be restored. With that thought came a way to settle the issue, at least until they could get married: if she could not banish the memory, she should at least enjoy it. This unsettling idea was still in her head when she heard footsteps outside her door. A quick, light knock, every nerve kicking up sparks, and then Josefa was there, a smile on her face.

Carrie sat up. "What?"

"A rider," Josefa said. "A beautiful rider on a beautiful Argentinean horse."

As her troublesome, nosy, noisy, much-loved little brother swung down from the saddle, Carrie could not contain her smile. Tough as a pine knot, Ma liked to say about her youngest. But the journey had left a mark, and Carrie took note. He was very tanned and seemed broader in the shoulders; he had a scar high on his right cheek. None of that surprised her, but then he stepped into a puddle of sunlight, and the color of his beard flared like a flame. A true Ballentyne red, the exact color of Martha's hair.

She moved closer, expecting a hug. Needing one, too, but he stepped away.

"Hold on," he said, his teeth flashing white against his tanned skin. "I stink."

She laughed. "That's a lovely greeting." She grabbed him by the shoulders for the hug she must have, getting a nose full of trail dust and sweat and horse, and underneath it all, Nathan.

"The wagon train—" she started, and he cut her off.

"A day or two behind me. Rode ahead because I couldn't wait to see your pretty face." He glanced at the house with its smooth adobe walls; the tall, carved wooden doors; and the cool dark hallway beyond. Josefa and Carlos stood there, waiting to see if they would be needed. She introduced them, thinking the whole time how best to juggle things.

She needed time alone with Nathan so she could give him all the news before someone else—Lulu, or Violante, who would rouse from the siesta to meet Carrie's brother, or even Dr. Benenati—said something that her brother should hear from her. She might be able to manage it, with some luck.

Violante did arrive, but took charge of Nathan's horse and turned back right away. She spoke to him like a boy about to be reunited with lost family. In fact there were four Argentineans in Iñigo's pasture, Eli's three, and Carrie's Mimosa. And Chico. She told her brother that Nando would be so well looked after it would take some work to get him back on the trail.

Carlos put Nathan's saddlebags in the empty chamber beside Carrie's. There was a lot of rushing back and forth, dirty clothes taken away, slightly less dirty clothes dug out of the saddlebags to be brushed down, and water to fill the hip bath. Nathan slid right in behind a closed door, and Carrie was glad of the few minutes she'd have to herself.

She paced back and forth, listening to her brother trying to talk to Carlos with the help of his limited Spanish, and laughing at nothing in particular. Nathan, as ever. He would never change, and she found that inordinately fine and comforting, in this moment, at least.

Josefa put a great variety of food out, and they sat in the *placita* around the table. Nathan ate, and Carrie watched him and thought about the questions she should ask and the things he needed to know.

"And?" she said. "Were we right to suspect Mr. Preston?"

Nathan glanced at her. "I'm not sure."

"He didn't make any . . . interest known? Or you warned him."

He took a moment to swallow. "Nothing that obvious. A few days after you left us, Preston went with some of the wranglers to a trading post in the evening. One of the wranglers and Preston himself didn't come back."

Carrie had to swallow before she could speak. "Because?"

"The Petit brothers had the same question. The two men who did come back were so drunk they couldn't remember their own names, even a day later. So the Petits went off to look for Preston and the wrangler."

"They were—"

"Dead," he interrupted. "Got some bad liquor, according to the barkeep. Four men dropped before he realized it was the drink that finished them off. He was white-faced and shaking, but why, I don't know. Maybe he had a shot of the bad whiskey and was waiting to drop down dead. Maybe he had poisoned the bottle to get even with one man, and it got out of hand. The Petits weren't willing to wait for the sheriff to show up, so that's where they left it."

Carrie studied her hands for a long moment. "No guilty parties to condemn, it seems."

"Plenty of guilt," her brother said. "But no way to put a name to it. Now we've been sitting here close to an hour. Are the Markhams at home? Will I meet them after the siesta?"

Carrie thought of the time she had spent writing and rewriting the letter home to explain it all. And just like that she remembered she had made a copy to tuck away so she would recall, years from now, exactly what she had been thinking at this turning point in her life.

"I'll be right back!"

Nathan frowned at her. "Where are you running off to?"

"Right back!"

By the time she sat down across from him again, she was damp with perspiration.

"You asked about the Markhams. It's complicated, but I wrote it all down in my last letter home. And I made a copy."

She put the closely written sheets of paper down on the table.

"Please read it, and then I'll be better able to answer your questions."

"You can't just tell me?"

"You'll interrupt me a dozen times and I'll lose my temper, so no, I can't just tell you. Read the letter."

"What are you going to do while I'm reading?"

"I'm going to sit here and watch you."

Nathan didn't try to argue with that.

Twice he glanced up at her, blinking his surprise, and twice she nodded.

Then his back straightened and his brows peaked. He held out the pages and shook them at her. "Where's the rest? It cuts off in the middle."

At the last moment Carrie had decided that she didn't want Nathan to read what she had written about Eli. Out of a kind of loyalty, she supposed. It would be cowardly not to speak the words herself.

"Let me explain," she started.

Footsteps in the hall. They both turned in that direction and there was Eli, walking toward them. Eli, tall and strong and confident, his smile welcoming.

"I heard a rumor," he said. "And here you are."

Carrie was very glad that they had the *placita* to themselves. They could talk to Nathan calmly, and that was a relief. But then she hadn't reckoned with Eli, who still had surprises up his sleeve.

Eli leaned over to clap a hand on Nathan's shoulder.

"You survived that stagecoach," he said. "Well done. Did Carrie tell you we're getting married?"

ELI KNEW BEFORE he said it that Carrie hadn't told her brother about their plans. He also knew she was fretting, and gambled that she'd be relieved to have it out in the open. Eventually. Just in that moment she was mostly peeved, but her brother took it in stride.

He put an arm around his sister's shoulder and pulled her close. "I knew you had it in you. Now tell me—"

But then Josefa came in with a tray of sugary little cakes, and at the same time the Benenatis were coming into the *placita*, Lulu skipping ahead. Carrie's discomfort could almost be seen hovering over her like a rain cloud.

Eli touched her shoulder, and she came up out of her thoughts, a little reluctantly, to listen to her brother introduce himself.

Nathan was never at a loss for words, even with strangers. He wiggled his way past social conventions and, on occasion, taboos; found the topic that would open the door; and off he went. In the next hour he talked to Josefa, to Manuela (with Josefa translating), to Iñigo— who had shown up at some point—again with Josefa translating. With Madu his demeanor changed and he held himself more carefully, as if he were standing in front of the clan mothers at Good Pasture. Then the subject turned to the Ballentyne family in New York, and Eli decided to act.

To Carrie he said, "Let's take your brother to my place. Show him some of the town."

She gave him a smile he had come to recognize: she was both

embarrassed and thankful. Just now she needed quiet and a place to sit with her brother, but insisting on that was beyond her in this company. He wondered if in time she would be better able to assert herself in a setting like this. From the stories Nathan told, she had been more than capable of that before she came west. He had to hope she would find her way back to her confidence.

It took another half hour to extract Nathan from his new admirers, and then they ran directly into John as he was leaving the dispensary for the day. He looked preoccupied, but he seemed glad to meet Nathan and shake his hand. In less than a minute they had made plans to meet. John Edmonds was a serious young man, at times almost somber, but Eli liked him and imagined it would be interesting to see how he got on with Nathan. Something to look forward to.

It was pure luck that they got to Eli's place without being stopped again. Nathan slowed down constantly to examine something; then the questions would start. However long he stayed in Santa Fe, he would be seeking answers, and for every answer, there would be two new questions. He was, in a word, exhausting. Eli was glad to have him here.

Eli took his time showing Nathan the house, forcing a slower pace for everybody's sake. Carrie insisted she had work in the kitchen, a claim that skirted a bald-faced lie by an inch. When he rounded his eyes at her—over her brother's shoulder—she grimaced and shooed him away.

"Go see the office and workroom," she told Nathan. "It will be one of your favorite places anywhere."

"I'm here to see you," Nathan said. And without a pause: "So, if I remember right, Eli, you have a zenith sector."

They spent the rest of the afternoon examining Eli's instruments and tools. During the journey west, Eli had spent a significant amount of time with Carrie's brother, but this opportunity to study him was not to be wasted.

Eli generally wasn't good at anticipating how women would judge a man's looks, but in Nathan's case he had heard him called handsome first by Eva Zavala, and then today by Rosita when she brought him word of a *tejano* who rode into town on an Argentinean.

Nathan was intelligent and personable, and Eli liked him for the way he pursued the things that interested him; most men—most white men, in his experience—were blind to everything but profit. And sex, in some cases.

There was no denying that Nathan's interest in surveying was sincere; more than that, he was a natural talent when it came to geometry and measurement. It was his first acquaintance with the upward-facing telescope known as a zenith sector, but in a matter of minutes Nathan had taken in all the details and was itching to try his hand. Something they could do, Eli promised him. But not today. And not tomorrow, either.

"Why not tomorrow?" Nathan asked, his gaze fixed on a clamp that held the telescope steady. And: "Look here, is this screw sitting right?"

Over a light supper at Rosita's, they talked of things that none of the neighbors sitting all around them would find interesting even if they spoke enough English to follow the conversation. That they listened anyway was not a surprise, because the Ballentyne siblings were bright and animated and full of good spirits.

Carrie told her brother about the one letter she had had from home thus far. She could recite it word for word, which might be a product of continual rereading, or more likely, this was one of the memory tricks she had to her name.

"Lizzie has a daughter, born early in the spring. After Jay's four boys, Uncle Gabriel finally has a granddaughter."

Nathan grinned. "Annie will teach her how to keep all the cousins in line. What's her girl-name?"

"Ska'neróhkwa." And to Eli: "The Mohawk word for turtle."

"Because she was so slow getting herself born," Nathan suggested.

It went on like this for a while, though she paused now and then to fill Eli in on what was clearly a complicated family tree. At one point

Nathan cocked his head and, glancing from Eli to Carrie and back again, asked the question that was overdue.

"Eli, what do your folks think of our Carrie?"

Carrie answered in his place. "I haven't met them yet."

"But tomorrow, with any luck," Eli said.

Carrie jolted. There was no other word for it. He had meant to surprise her, but had miscalculated. What he saw on her face was shock. So he put a hand on hers and ducked his head to look her directly in the eye. "As soon as I heard Nathan was here, I sent word home. My parents will be waiting for us tomorrow at the Te Tsu Geh Oweenge Pueblo."

Her expression didn't change much, but she had lost all her color.

"Carrie," Nathan said. "Stop being so hissy and listen. He's not done explaining."

That made her bristle, but before she could get into an argument with her brother, Eli leaned in closer.

"There's an older priest there. He'll marry us in the pueblo chapel as a favor to Madu."

"And you want your parents there, with us." She took a deep, calming breath, raised her head, and smiled at Eli. "Good. What time do we need to leave?"

THERE WAS A lot to be done before morning. The most important thing would be talking to Dr. Benenati and Madu about women who were close to birthing. They wouldn't be gone even overnight, but you could be sure that someone somewhere would go into labor.

Then she would sit down with Lulu. It was unclear to Carrie how she would react. The little girl knew that Carrie was going to marry Eli, and approved. Whether she understood what that meant about where Carrie would live—and sleep—was another question.

Carrie left Nathan with Eli to explore the rest of the town, and went to the dispensary, stopping first in the kitchen to talk to Josefa to explain what was planned for the next day. Josefa was not in the least surprised, of course, and once again Carrie was thankful for the younger woman's calm good sense. And then Lulu came in, covered in dust and muck after spending a satisfying hour tending to the horses with Iñigo's wranglers. She was flushed and her hair was damp with sweat, but she smiled. Just at this moment Carrie could see that Lulu was still capable of joy, something that could not have been predicted.

Carrie patted the *banco* between herself and Josefa, and Lulu sat down. Yawning, she leaned her head against Josefa's shoulder.

"It's past your bedtime," Carrie said. "But I wanted to tell you about tomorrow."

When she had finished—it took just a few minutes—she had to wonder if Lulu had heard her at all. There was no reaction to be seen on her face, no pleasure, no surprise or disquiet of any kind. But she was thinking.

She said, "Can I visit you at Eli's casita?"

"Of course," Carrie said. "At any time. But you realize I'll still be here in the dispensary for some part of the day. Sometimes most of the day."

The girl's nod was almost dismissive, as if this were self-evident and didn't need to be said. Then she asked a question Carrie had been avoiding. "But what are you going to wear?"

To her own surprise, Carrie did have something new to wear.

Soon after Carrie arrived in Santa Fe, she had called on the town's only seamstress to order a workday dress, as quickly as could be managed. Mrs. Gillette was an awkward little woman, but an expert with a needle and, to Carrie's great surprise, the owner of a Wheeler & Wilson sewing machine.

First, Carrie had appealed to Reizl Goldblum for help in finding suitable fabric.

"You know Eva will have trunks and trunks of the stuff. If that stagecoach would ever get here. *Nu.*" Reizl shrugged philosophically.

"If the stagecoach came in tomorrow, then I wouldn't need to have anything made," Carrie reminded her.

Reizl waved away her logic. "You couldn't pass up something new and pretty, I don't care how rational a being you may be."

Carrie let that discussion go, and instead followed Reizl into one of the storage rooms behind the store. By nature she was careful with money, but for once she did not count pennies. She came away from the shop with a medium-weight block-printed India cotton, a lighter tabbinet, muslin, and a very fine batiste. With those fabrics the seamstress would make her two sets of clothes, each with a chemise, pantaloons, a skirt, a bodice, and a blouse.

Mrs. Gillette had looked over the fabric and then more carefully studied the sewing pattern and sketches Carrie supplied. Bit by bit her eyebrows arched up her forehead.

"Turkish dress?"

That she was familiar with this more recent fashion was a very good sign.

"Yes," Carrie said. "You're familiar with the style?"

The seamstress gave her a half shrug, and then put down the pattern with a sigh.

"I did read about this Turkish dress business, a few years back. At the time I thought the fascination would die out. But the customer is always right, as my husband never tires of reminding me. So yes, I can sew this for you—you've got good fabrics to work with—but I'll need payment in advance."

Carrie agreed this was reasonable, and further agreed that there would be no refunds if she came to regret her decision. She could only hope that once the seamstress began working with the fabric, her disapproval would soften.

While Mrs. Gillette took measurements, she continued her study of Carrie, as her craft required. Looking for challenges, calculating inches, and considering the location of seams.

"You're wearing doeskin leggings," she said, quite suddenly.

Carrie glanced down at herself. "I am. I often do."

Mrs. Gillette gave a tight shake of the head. "Well then, this Turkish outfit will be an improvement. I don't imagine I'll ever sew such an odd thing again, unless of course you come back to me for another?"

"Very probably," Carrie told her, but thinking to herself that she would wait to see how good a seamstress Mrs. Gillette really was.

Carrie had not yet looked at the clothing Mrs. Gilette had made for her, and decided now that she would do that in the morning. She meant to get a good night's sleep, but her mind was too busy.

It seemed Eli was also awake, because he came to whisper at her door, and she went to sit with him in the *placita*. It was a shocking thing to do, but if someone had seen him, their complaints wouldn't be heard until it was too late and they were well and truly married.

They were quiet for a good while, sitting side by side.

He said, "I've been wondering about something."

This was unusual for Eli, who rarely hesitated to ask a question.

"Go on." Carrie rubbed her cheek against his arm.

"You'll find it odd. But have you been to any family weddings since Martha's?" And: "You're surprised."

It took a long moment to organize her thoughts. "To be asked about Martha's wedding? Yes. I am surprised." She tried to smile, but could not manage it.

"And you're mad," Eli said casually.

She could hardly deny that. "To answer your question, I haven't been to a family wedding since Martha's. Why is this important? Are you rethinking—"

"Absolutely not." There was a firmness in his tone that put her doubts to rest.

"Then please explain."

He took a moment. "Martha is on your mind a lot lately. I think she visits you in your dreams, because you talk in your sleep."

"We've spent one night in the same bed," Carrie pointed out.

His head canted to one side, and his tone dropped. An apology of sorts. "You did a lot of talking, and I think it was mostly Martha you were talking to."

"That's not unusual in our family," Carrie told him. "Aunt Hannah's first husband still calls on her now and then to talk, and Aunt Martha gets visits from her mother, the infamous Jemima. I'll tell you some of the stories about her. She was a reliable source of horror stories when I was little, and she was long gone at that point. Aunt Martha resented visits from her mother, but her protests did no good. Dead Jemima was as stubborn as living Jemima had been. There are more stories about the ones who come back to visit, but pardon me, I have to say that you sensed Martha was nearby. Because she is. I feel her like a mosquito bite."

He was quiet, keeping questions and observations to himself, something, Carrie told herself, he might have done earlier. For some reason his willingness to let the subject go so suddenly irked her, and she spoke before she thought.

"She may show herself, she may not. In any case, I can handle my sister. And now I need to sleep—"

Carrie startled when Eli pulled her onto his lap without warning. With his mouth against her ear, he said, "I've ruined your mood, and right before we get married. Let me cheer you up, will you?"

"But of course," she said, already laughing. "You won't have to work very hard to do that."

54

CARRIE WOKE AT first light on her wedding day. In her mind she had a list of tasks to be done, each logical and necessary and none of it odd or challenging. And still there was a slight tremble in her hands when she took up soap to wash.

She brushed out her hair and plaited it, this time with Josefa's help. It was good to have Josefa with her, if she couldn't have Ma or Amelie, Jennet or Blue. Eva was still out on the Santa Fe trail, and so she had Josefa, the very soul of calm goodwill.

When she left to see to her duties in the kitchen, Carrie closed the door behind her and turned to see Martha sitting in the very middle of her bed, studying the box of clothes Mrs. Gillette had made. Martha picked up a chemise to examine the stitching, and Carrie watched.

And that, Carrie realized, was what came of thinking so hard of home and the people she most missed. Martha had heard her, somehow, and had come all this way from where she had lived and died to keep Carrie company on her wedding day.

For what seemed like a long time, Martha sat there absorbed in her study of the clothes Carrie would wear. Finally, she looked up. Her smile was sad but calm. "Beautifully done buttonholes."

And then she was gone, her examination of Carrie's wedding clothes completed.

Carrie dressed. She saw for herself what Martha had seen: every stitch was perfectly placed, all facings and hems exact. The Turkish trousers—cut wide, but cinched tight at the ankle by ties—were in the same fabric as the overskirt, which fell just to her knees. Outrageous, but here on the western frontier, Carrie had seen far more revealing clothes.

All in all, the outfit was simple but well made, and had a certain elegance to it. Mrs. Gillette had found the time to tend to the details: piping at the shoulders and a touch of beading. She had gone even further with the chemise, finishing the neckline and cuffs with embroidery that any Parisian modiste would have been happy to claim as her own work.

She took a moment to stand in front of the mirror, turning back and forth to watch the overskirt swing out. The fabric was prettier than she had thought, almost bronze with a dotted pattern overprinted. An oddity, but she had been odd now for so long, she took some pleasure in staying true to herself.

THEY LEFT AT dawn, just the three of them, riding west along a river that would feed into the Rio Grande. This was a trip Carrie had wanted to take since she first arrived in Santa Fe, but there had never been the opportunity. Nathan was clearly shocked by this admission from his sister who had always been eager to go exploring.

Her brother asked directly if they could stop to see the river, but Eli gave a reluctant shake of the head.

"The turnoff to the Te Tsu Geh Pueblo is right around the next bend. The Rio Grande is due west."

Carrie thought about this. "We could take the time to see the river on the way home, couldn't we, Eli?"

"It will probably be too late in the day," he told her. "The dancing and food and talk go on for a while."

Carrie hadn't realized this. "I thought it would be the ceremony and signing papers. I didn't realize—is this so we can spend the day with your parents?"

"Of course," her brother said. "And you wouldn't want it any other way."

Eli's mother. Her mother-in-law. More than once she had tried to draw him out about this woman who would be so important in her life. Her questions confused Eli, who believed that the gift of the blanket his mother wove with her own hands was evidence enough that Carrie was welcome. They thought of her already as the wife of the eldest son, and wasn't that the issue?

They had had this discussion many times, but Eli felt the matter was still unresolved for Carrie. He raised the subject again. This earned him a deep sigh and a twitch of her shoulders.

"Why do I feel like I'm about to hear a lecture?"

That took him by surprise.

"No lecture," he said, so calmly that her anxiety subsided.

"What, then?"

One corner of his mouth turned down. "Will you wait till I'm finished before you comment?"

"Yes," Carrie said, impatient now. "I will wait."

"Good. Maybe we haven't been together long if you tell time by the calendar, but some things won't be measured that way. I think I know you pretty well, and you know me. So I can say that I see you as a rational, practical, sensible woman. Starting from there, I've got some questions."

Her color began to rise. "Go on."

Eli said, "Do you think that you might be worried about something other than getting married? I'm thinking that maybe it's not my Ma who has you so tied up in knots."

Her brows drew together, but she answered honestly.

"It's not unusual for someone in my position to be concerned about being introduced to a new family."

He inclined his head in agreement, and when it was clear she had
nothing more to add, he didn't push.

THEY HAD BEEN riding for some time when Nathan decided they
had been silent too long.

"You are far away in your thoughts, sister."

She managed a half-hearted smile. "Thinking of home. Ma and
Amelie especially."

Chico came bursting out of a ditch just then, dust caked in every
wrinkle and his muzzle red with the blood of the hare that had been
unlucky enough to cross his path. He was looking very satisfied with
himself and glad to be on the road.

Carrie thought this would be a good time to raise a subject that Eli
seemed to be avoiding. He had never really explained how it was that
Madu got involved in sorting out the arrangements with the church.
Bishop Lamy was notoriously slow to sanction a wedding, and insisted
on reading banns many weeks before the wedding date. The fees charged
for reading banns, use of the church, and the services of priests and
attendants were considerable. And none of that had happened. Somehow a priest from a small pueblo had got permission to marry them,
without first jumping through a single hoop.

She meant to put this delicately, but Nathan saw through, as she
should have known he would. "You're on the bad side of a bishop?
That was fast work, even for you, sister."

She batted at him, and he danced his horse away.

"I am not on his bad side, but he's on mine. All the worst things
you see in Catholic clergy and none of the good ones."

"All right," Eli said, giving in. "I'll tell the story before you make
up one of your own. It starts with Francisco Chavez, the sharpest
thorn in the bishop's side."

Eli was a good mimic, and they got a sense of two old men growling at each other. Both demanding respect and tribute, and neither
willing to bend so far. The bishop had all the power of the church, but

Chavez had the Pueblos, and a long history in the Sangre de Cristo Mountains. Lamy was new to the territory.

"So the priest won't obey the bishop's orders, I take it," Nathan prompted.

"That's the mildest way to put it," Eli agreed. "Chavez lives off the charity of the Pueblo. They feed him and clothe him. They nurse him when he's sick and look after his burro and fix whatever breaks. But he doesn't pass the plate after he says mass because nobody has any money to put in it. He won't accept any kind of tithes."

Carrie saw the problem. The priest had nothing to give his bishop, and worse, he didn't care.

"Lamy didn't put up with it for long," Eli went on. "A few months after he got here, he sent a French priest to the pueblo to replace the padre."

Eli squinted into the sun and readjusted his hat, and Carrie had the idea he was debating with himself about how much to say.

"So here's the thing," he went on. "Maybe half the pueblo is baptized. Of course for most of them that don't mean much; they get baptized to please the padre, but they'd never call themselves Catholics. The other half, the ones who won't be baptized, wants nothing to do with the church, but they consider the padre to be one of their own."

"So what did they do?" Nathan asked. "Just kick the French usurper out?"

Eli smiled. "That's not the way things work in a pueblo. No kicking, no bloodshed, not even a raised voice. The French priest shows up, and Padre Chavez vacates his casita so the younger priest can move in. And right then, everything stops. Suddenly nobody in the pueblo knows a word of Spanish. No Spanish, no French, no English."

"Of course, he couldn't know any Towa," Carrie said. "And had no time to learn it."

Eli's grin was grim. "True. So you can imagine how it went from there. He couldn't beg, buy, or borrow as much as a pepper."

"I'm guessing he left right quick," Nathan said.

"He wanted to," Eli said. "But his burro disappeared. In the end he walked to Santa Fe to confess to the bishop that he wasn't equal to the challenge."

"And how many times did this episode repeat itself?" Carrie asked.

Eli's smile was easier now. "Lamy sends another French priest every couple years thinking he'll be able to unseat Chavez."

"Interesting," Carrie said, and in response to Eli's raised brow, she tried to put her thoughts into words.

"Lamy can't comprehend the fact that anyone would disobey him. Certainly not Indians. He doesn't see them as thinking human beings."

"He's not alone in that," Eli said.

"It won't be pretty if he ever figures out he's being outwitted by Indians," Nathan said.

"His pride will never allow him to see that," Carrie said. "More's the pity."

⚜

WITH THOSE FEW words, Eli was reminded of the early days with Carrie. He had seen her first in Baltimore, where she had caught his attention because she was striking, yes, but her confidence was just as appealing. He still smiled when he thought of her taking off her bonnet to beat her brother with it.

She was able to stand up for herself in a way he didn't associate with white women or, at least, not white women who came from the East Coast, leaving a finer and easier life behind. At first he assumed that it was Carrie's training and work as a midwife that accounted for the unusual aspects of her character. That simple explanation was one that made it easier to keep his attraction to a white woman in hand. But it hadn't lasted long.

Little by little, she had shown him what she was made of. She told her stories in a detached way, nothing of self-pity to be found. She spoke of her Indian friends and family with perfect ease. But when she was pushed, she could push back, and hard.

On the trip overland, she had proved herself competent and quick and brave. It was the night in the Kiowa camp that had shown him the one thing he had believed to be impossible.

Eli had never met a white woman who understood what it meant to belong to a tribe. To be one of the people. He knew of a few white women who made a place for themselves with one of the tribes—the Diné, the Numunu, Nuu-ciu, and In'deh—but unless they came as children, they never quite fit.

But Carrie did fit. She wanted to belong, and understood what it meant. With that he had realized that she could be happy as his wife. Riding into the Te Tsu Geh Pueblo, he didn't need to worry that she would judge or criticize, or try to teach because she knew better. There would be no loud commentary, no veiled insults or knowing smiles. She might dislike some things about this place, but she would take the people at face value.

The very fact of her existence was a revelation. A woman made for him exactly.

Carrie had seen the ruins of the abandoned Walatowa Pueblo at Pecos, but Nathan had not, and Te Tsu Geh was something very new for him. He went very still because he was focused on drawing in every detail. When she wrote home about today, he would be able to fill in the details that she had overlooked or forgotten.

She wondered if she would have had the courage to do this thing if he hadn't been beside her.

They rode by fields where people of all ages, men and women, were busy tending corn, squash, beans of more than one kind, peppers, and greens. The plots were spread out in a circle around the pueblo itself, like a necklace of dusty green against adobe walls as rich in color as ripe peaches.

Adobe, Carrie understood, needed to be maintained like any other building material, and she pointed this out to Nathan as they passed a small group of younger men repairing a wall.

The workers took note of Eli first, then Carrie, and again, with broad smiles, looked back to Eli. They called out greetings and comments that were—apparently—funny. Carrie was beginning to suspect that you could go anywhere in the world and hear the same kind of banter. Men sometimes treated each other like bear cubs, rough and rougher still, learning how to use their claws.

Nathan didn't have any Towa, but the conversation wouldn't have interested him anyway. He was too busy taking in every detail about the pueblo, which was very lively on this summer morning. Everywhere you looked there were people at work. The smallest children played games while girls and women tended the *hornos*, the ovens shaped like beehives that stood in the open. Others were sewing or scraping hides or sorting through baskets. Boys just old enough to be seen as men carried supplies or jugs or baskets.

Then someone called out a word, and all faces turned toward the riders.

The children came running to surround the visitors as soon as they dismounted. All of them had hair and eyes of a true, deep black, and none of them wore much in the way of clothing. Whip-thin, muscular, flexible, they seemed to glow in the sun.

Some of the older, more dignified children took the horses away to the troughs, while still others went from one doorway to another, climbing ladders to the upper levels, calling out. Carrie thought it was probably a good thing that she hadn't learned very much Towa yet; adults were coming out into the open square, and Carrie didn't need to know what they were saying about her.

Then Eli put a hand on her shoulder, and her tumbling thoughts began to quiet.

"Look," he said to her. "You see the man there with the white blanket? That's the *cacique*, the chief. And those are my parents, just to his right. Come." He took her hand and she followed, nervous and struggling not to show the truth of that.

Altagracia Ibarra wasn't smiling, but Carrie hadn't expected a smile; she expected to be closely studied by this woman whose son she was claiming. Altagracia stood straight and firm, but still four decades of child-rearing, housekeeping, and laboring beside her husband had left a mark. Some joints too loose, many others stiff and reluctant. A network of lines that whispered over her face like the finest cracks in porcelain.

All her pelt rubbed off.

That sentence came to Carrie out of her childhood, unbidden, in the voice of Martha, whose beloved doll had lost every thread on her boiled-wool head until she was bald. Martha, who valued loyalty above all, took this as evidence of goodness and a kind disposition.

Again Martha was close by as Carrie came face-to-face with her new mother-in-law.

Altagracia wore a rebozo folded over her head, covering hair that was showing white at the temples. And then she smiled, and the years fell away. Now she could be any one of the Mohawk women Carrie had known all her life. Strong, hardworking, serious, maternal to the last fiber, judgmental, but capable of kindness too.

Don Diego Ibarra was a big man, broad, well muscled, and very well padded. He smelled of lanolin, and that explained how hands that had done so much hard labor could still be pleasant to the touch.

"Miss Carrie, it is a great pleasure to meet you." His voice was low and rough, and reminded her for that moment of her Grandfather Nathaniel. Something about the way he chose his words, a thoughtfulness that others might see as hesitation. His English was fluent and colloquial, but struggled up through a deep sea of Spanish. Carrie was pleased that she didn't have to strain to understand him, not after many weeks in Santa Fe.

He was smiling when he said, "It may anger my good wife, but I want to be the first to welcome you to the family."

Doña Altagracia huffed a breath in a way that made Eli give a low laugh. Carrie had the idea that the raised brow he got from his mother was identical to her own, but the Ibarra men did not seem worried at all.

Don Diego looked at Carrie, and winked. The winking was a family habit, then, and a way to focus a woman's attention where a man wanted it. She had it figured out now, but doubted her insight would help very much when Eli next winked at her.

In Spanish he said, "Elias took his time finding a bride, but he doesn't rush important decisions. Clever."

Another soft snort from his wife, and then, in clear Spanish: *Men. Always congratulating themselves.*

That this was said in jest was clear, as there were smiles all around. To Carrie it was also clear that Eli's mother was kindly disposed toward her and ready to be pleased. Carrie gathered her courage, but she had barely opened her mouth when all attention shifted toward the high, wavering voice of a very old man.

Everyone parted to make a path, and the priest came into view, braced by young men on either side. Old age had settled his spine to such a degree that Carrie thought he would have once been considerably taller. Now he was very thin, with skin like the finest gauze draped over the bones of his face. In the shadows he would seem to be carrying a skull on his shoulders.

She shivered that such a dark idea should come to her, and focused on the way the priest spoke to those who were close by. Some he spoke to in Spanish, but for the most part he spoke Towa.

Just behind her, Eli leaned forward to speak into her ear.

"Not so bad as you feared?"

"Not so bad at all," she agreed. Then she remembered Nathan, and began to scan the plaza for some sign of him.

"He got someone to show him around," Eli said, and jerked his chin at a spot on the roof where her brother sat, legs dangling over the side while he studied the landscape.

"Easier for both of us," Carrie said, and got a smile for her trouble.

Then Altagracia was beside her. She took Carrie's elbow and led her to the spot where the priest sat.

Padre Chavez held out both hands to her as she came forward. He had a broad, friendly smile and apparently just four teeth, which could be mistaken for wooden laundry pegs. His eyes were a warm brown, though cataracts had closed over the right one and begun to invade the left.

There was nothing of the riches of the Catholic church to see here.

He wore a tunic woven from rough wool that would not be pleasant against the skin, and on his chest was a crucifix that looked like he had carved it from stone. Around his waist was a belt with what looked like a simple rope knotted and looped to resemble a rosary. Small stones had been drilled through to serve as prayer beads.

Carrie, who was familiar with the preferences of the very old, lowered her head and waited to be addressed. She was aware of the fact that the priest had lowered his head to look at her, his eyes peeking out from overgrown eyebrows the color and texture of straw.

"Good day, miss. Why are you here? Is it true that you want to marry this man?"

He gestured, and Eli came forward without hesitation to take the hand offered. He seemed very calm, without doubt. Carrie realized that she had been holding her breath, and let it go.

Carrie had come to the Te Tsu Geh Pueblo to marry the man standing beside her, yes. She nodded and managed to summon up the right words. First in English and then, more hesitantly, in Spanish.

"Yes, Father. I am here to marry this man. To marry Elias Ibarra."

The priest's good eye was fixed on her with an intensity that belied his age. There was reserve there, too, and she imagined he was wondering about her motivations. In Spanish he said, "And why do you want to marry him?"

Color flooded her cheeks, but Carrie knew what she needed to say, openly, in front of these people who were his blood. What Eli deserved to hear.

"I love him. I love Eli, and I want to marry him."

And so she did.

The chapel was in disrepair, Padre Chavez told her, but the *kiva* would serve very well. Carrie had never seen a *kiva* before, but she had heard them described. This one was fairly large, round as a penny, and sunken into the earth, so that only the roof and a few feet of the walls could be seen from ground level.

On the plaza a half dozen men took up drums and rattles. It was such a comfort to Carrie, this echo from her earliest memories. She realized Nathan was beside her, and that his expression was somber. Later she would talk to him about the days they had been at home in the longhouses at Good Pasture. Those were happy memories.

There was a door set at an angle in the ground, one made of slender tree trunks lashed together. Just now it was propped open to reveal the top of a ladder.

"Nothing to be afraid of," Eli said.

As if she might be scared off by a ladder. She wrinkled her nose at him and he ducked his head, a kind of apology.

"Then you had better go first," Carrie told him. "That way you can catch Nathan if he falls."

Inside, standing at the bottom of the ladder, Carrie admired how well designed the space was. Sunlight streamed down from the open port and filtered through the space. More slender tree trunks and branches had been woven together into a support for the roof, and otherwise the only structure to be seen was a firepit, now cold, and a dozen more tree trunks cut into short chunks to serve as stools.

There was nothing here that would normally be found in a chapel or church. No altar, no statues, not even a crucifix, which confirmed Carrie's thought that the priest had divorced himself from the trappings of the Roman church and was content to meet with the Pueblos where they were most comfortable. No wonder he was at odds with the bishop. No wonder the bishop couldn't get the upper hand.

Beside her, Eli was talking to his mother, his tone low and easy. They were smiling at each other, and that was good. A grown son who still liked his mother and wanted to talk to her, that was the best of signs.

It was a small group that gathered close around: Eli's parents, Carrie's brother, a few women who might have been cousins, and the cacique, who she guessed must be the sachem, and who had been introduced to her by his Towa name, Póyo-taa.

Without fanfare or explanation, the priest bowed his head and began. The wedding ceremony was unfamiliar to Carrie, but Padre Chavez spoke a clear, slow Spanish, and she was able to follow. His speaking voice had the creak of old age, but still there was a resonance and warmth to it. Good priests and preachers and politicians had this talent and used it to advantage. Padre Chavez used his voice like a ribbon to bind them together.

The crucial question came, directed first to Eli.

Novio Elias Ibarra, ¿tomas tu a novia Elizabeth Carrie Ballentyne, como tu esposa, prometes amarla, respetarla, protejerla abandonando a todo y dedicandote solo a ella?

He answered in a clear, unwavering voice, and when her turn came, Carrie did the same. She had no idea what would come next, but the trembling in her hands had stopped.

When they had had a good meal, the family sat together, out of the sun. With Eli to one side and Nathan on the other, Carrie felt overwhelmed by good fortune. The conversation was free-flowing, hopping from language to language. Eli translated Nathan's English for his family, and his parents' Spanish for Nathan. Carrie could have done this, too, but she was too comfortable and too amused to rouse herself even that far. Then the subject turned to names.

Don Diego asked if they had Mohawk names, a subject Nathan could warm to.

"We all had Mohawk child-names," he said. "Mine was Echo Talker because even very young I'd argue with anybody, even the echos in a cave."

Carrie laughed. "As is still the case today."

Eli cupped the curve of her skull in one hand, and a great shiver ran down her spine. She wondered if he wanted to get away, to be alone, but the storytelling was important on a day like this, and she turned her mind back to Altagracia, who was asking about Carrie's Mohawk girl-name.

Nathan ran a hand over his jaw, attempting to look thoughtful but unable to hide the mischievous quirk to his mouth.

"She was very little, just a few months old, when Ma realized that when she was outdoors, birds would come to sit near her."

Carrie said, "There were always dozens of nests nearby. Song sparrows and thrushes and larks. And wrens. And orioles. They stayed close by because Ma fed them in the hardest weather." Her voice was a little hoarse.

Nathan gave an indulgent shake of the head. "And crows. And ravens. And grackles. And the least favorite of all, in our family at least, shrikes. Carrie could name them all at two, so the story goes. It was Aunt Annie who gave her the Mohawk girl-name Little Bird."

Eli's father was charmed, it seemed, and Altagracia had questions. "Are they still called to you, the birds?"

Carrie was uncomfortable discussing this business—though she couldn't say exactly why. She hoped the simplest answer would be enough to satisfy them. "Yes. The smaller birds seem to be drawn to me still."

Eli translated and Nathan held up his hands in mock surrender. "Smaller birds. I wasn't in the house a half hour when I saw a whole flock of magpies waiting for you to come outside."

"Those are Josefa's magpies," Carrie said.

"Really? Have you told them that?" he went on, warming to the subject.

"At home crows are very fond of Carrie," Nathan pointed out to the Ibarras. "Ma is sure that some of them followed us when we moved to Manhattan."

And now she couldn't hold back her scowl, but he was not worried. He would have gone on, but Eli's father stepped in.

"I don't think you have hummingbirds where you were born," he said. "What do you make of them?"

Now she could smile. "They are small works of art," she said. "Small works of art."

Somehow she had managed to strike the right tone, because, as she learned, Altagracia had great respect for the hummingbird. There were stories, she told Carrie, of hummingbirds coming to the aid of hungry children, and interceding with the gods when the rains stayed away and the corn withered.

"And fire," her husband said. "The hummingbird saved a whole pueblo by calling in the rain to put out the flames."

"These are important stories," Altagracia said. "And when we next meet, I will tell them to you."

55

THE SUN WAS just setting when they rode into Santa Fe and left Nathan behind at the doctor's place. All his high spirits had finally been dampened by the heat and the long day, and he seemed content to kiss his sister's cheek and wish them a good night. He handed Eli his reins and saluted him. "Well done," he said. "Skillfully managed, brother."

It made Carrie smile, and Eli was glad of it. She had been in a thoughtful mood since they left the pueblo, and not inclined to talk. They were still quiet for the short trip across town and for the time it took to unsaddle the horses and see to their needs.

Chico made a bed for himself in a corner of the stable and collapsed into a jittery dream-filled sleep.

"Chasing prairie dogs?" Carrie wondered out loud.

"Or bitches in heat," Eli suggested. "He kept busy at the pueblo, from the couple times I saw him. Blue-eyed puppies coming later this summer."

Carrie hiccuped her surprise. "I didn't catch any of that."

"You had other things on your mind."

Her smile told him she had something to say, so he picked up a curry-comb and went back to work. Giving her room to gather her words.

"I like your mother."

"That's good," Eli said. "She liked you too."

She smiled like someone who had just crossed a difficult bridge, and could not quite believe that fate could be kind.

It wasn't until they sat down with the food they had brought back from the pueblo that she raised the subject most on her mind.

"He'll be going home soon."

Eli had wondered when she would want to talk about this, and had spent some time thinking about it.

"I'll be sad to see Nathan go."

She glanced up as if to make sure he meant what he said. Then she dropped her gaze again. "I wouldn't be surprised if he's back within a year or less. He has always been something of a rolling stone."

"You won't have time to be lonely," Eli said. "Eva will be here, I'm guessing tomorrow."

"It will be good to have Eva and Beto nearby," Carrie said. "Though I am at a loss on how to tell her all the news."

Eli leaned back in his chair and crossed his arms. "Well, sure. There's been trouble, but there's some good news too."

Her face came up, half-lost in shadow, half-aglow in the lamplight. A flicker of a smile, banished before it could settle in.

"Already fishing for compliments," she said solemnly. "And married less than a day."

She was up and away before he could get hold of her, darting around the table in one direction and then the other. Carrie laughing, her color high, her eyes shining, was the most beautiful thing he had ever seen.

MUCH LATER, AFTER the moon had set but before the first light of the new day, Carrie woke.

She knew where she was. In the dark she couldn't see the man who slept beside her, but she knew Eli by his shape and the sound of his breathing, by his smells and the texture of his skin. She knew the feel of him, his deepest touch, and that knowing was what had pulled her out of sleep.

If she were to wake him, what then? He might startle, forgetting in that first moment that he had a wife. He might just wrap an arm around her and fall back into sleep. Or he might pull her underneath him and start the whole business from the beginning. For the third time this night.

Did she want that?

Eli said, "I can hear you thinking."

It was too dark to see his face, but she knew he was smiling. A soft smile, almost hesitant. She shifted a bit closer, to feel the touch of his breath on her face.

"Really? So what am I thinking about?"

"The same thing I'm thinking about."

She drew in a startled breath, but he hadn't finished.

"Mostly I'm wondering how to make you comfortable. It's all new for you and you're unsettled about it. Or am I wrong?"

She said, "*Unsettled* is a good word. I'm unsure of—everything."

Eli was surprised, but the only other thing she sensed from him was a new curiosity.

"Now you better tell me more," he said. "Or I'll never get back to sleep."

"Fine," she said. "But I have to start at the beginning. In the Baltimore train station."

"You took note of me in the train station?"

Carrie's voice came a little rougher than she liked. "I had no idea who you were, of course. But yes, I noticed you standing in the open door of the livestock car. It didn't go any further than that, not until the accident when I came to look at your head."

"You were very serious, almost disapproving," Eli said. "As if I had hurt myself like a kid playing rough with my brothers."

Carrie hummed low in her throat. "Nurses learn to hide their reactions, but I can promise you I wasn't being critical. Then you came to talk to me in the passenger car, and I recognized something unusual about you. Men—very few men—would have talked so freely with a female they hardly knew. I was drawn to you just for that reason, at first."

There was some light now, enough to make out shapes and lines. Carrie put her hands on his cheeks and touched her brow to his. She felt every breath he took.

Carrie said, "And then it grew into something more, and more, and now here we are. You ask how you can make me comfortable, and so let me tell you what was going through my head when I woke. I was thinking about you, about this bed, about last night and the sex. I have been thinking about the sex since that night of the tornadoes on the trail. I think about it constantly."

She swallowed. "Now this is the hard part."

"I'm listening," he said. "Whatever you've got to say, I want to hear it."

"Eli, if I tell you that your throat, the sight of your throat, makes me a little weak, that sometimes the sound of your voice makes my whole body clench, would that shock you? And there's more. I want to know what it feels like when you're—"

Her voice broke, but she pushed on. "Inside me. Because that's what I was thinking about when I woke up, here in this bed. Our bed. My boundless and incorrigible curiosity about you. About your body, and the things we do. I studied anatomy and physiology, you realize that. But how is it that this subject was never mentioned? Such a monumental force, but women are left in the dark. Women who train as nurses generally know nothing at all of sex except that it could be the end of all their aspirations. In time I realized that most young women had been taught to believe such things. To see themselves in that way.

"When we moved to Manhattan, I saw how most people live. Men want a certain kind of life. What they want is what a woman should want, they believe that. It doesn't occur to them that a wife or sister or daughter might be miserable, and if they are made to see that, then it's the woman's fault. Most men think like that. Almost all men. But not you."

⟚

CARRIE MADE AN effort to keep her breathing steady while she waited for him to say something more. Anything.

"Have I bored you to sleep?"

"I don't think I've ever been less bored, but then again, I'm not sure what I can say to any of that. Except I'm sorry for white women who spend their lives doubting themselves, and I'm glad you didn't get caught in that trap."

He studied her face as he spoke, and saw that her forehead was damp with perspiration and her face flushed from throat to hairline. Still she met his gaze. She had taken a chance, and was not about to back down. Eli felt a rush of affection, a caving in of the last of his resistance to this woman.

He said, "There are a couple things I can tell you that might ease your mind."

She blinked at him and gave a hint of a nod.

"You like my throat, and I watch the way your breasts move under your clothes, the fullness of them, the curve. Here, I'll show you—"

Carrie, suddenly fully awake and wide-eyed, struck his hand away and barked a laugh.

"Not ready to give up the chemise? Then let me talk about the crease at the top of your thigh where it meets the curve of your buttock—"

"Eli."

"Or we could talk about my—"

She leaned forward and covered his mouth with her hand. "Stop. Stop. Stop." After a moment she took her hand away, watching him warily.

"I admit I'm relieved that you're not put out by my . . ." Her voice wobbled a little.

"Enthusiasm? Delight? Eagerness?"

The muscles of her jaw fluttered, and that made Eli want to grab her up and do all the things he had been thinking about the two of them doing for weeks and weeks. But he composed himself. Mostly.

"Carrie, don't you realize how happy you make me? Out of my head happy." And more softly: "Everything about you suits me. And I'm just as curious as you are."

Her smile was a little shy, but something more was lurking there.

"Good," she said. "You make me happy, too, you know. You're curious, and I'm curious. Could we start with one of my questions about you?"

He grinned, and Carrie had the sense he would enjoy the conversation just as much as she would. She could count on Eli to make her laugh.

56

JUST A WEEK after Eva Zavala and her son returned to Santa Fe, Nathan set out for home. He was not going to buy a ticket on any of the stagecoach lines; instead, he planned to ride Nando and lead the horse he had bought from Iñigo. In Eli's opinion it was a reasonable approach, but Carrie saw nothing sensible about her brother's plan at all.

Nathan had a simple goal: he wanted to see something of the country on his way east. Of the war looming closer every day he said nothing. Carrie didn't raise the subject, either, because she didn't trust her temper. The evening before he was to leave, she spent a half hour writing a new admonition to tuck away in Bullions's *Latin Grammar*. She wondered sometimes if Catholics who confessed their sins to a priest felt the way she did when she had finished: hollow, echoing.

This time a single note was enough to give her the perspective she sought: *My brother is foolhardy and I am a coward.*

Both statements were true. At the same time, Nathan was an adult. He was capable and clever and good with weapons; if he wanted to ride cross-country on his own, there was nothing to do but wish him well.

My brother is foolhardy and I am a coward.

The sentence went around and around in her head, distracting her so that she dropped things and forgot what she was doing. During siesta she fell into an uneasy sleep and startled awake, expecting to see Martha beside her. Martha would say, *Not Nathan. Don't let the littlest one get lost too.*

Nathan finished with his errands and came in for supper just as Eva and Beto arrived to spend the evening with them. It was meant to be a farewell dinner, but Eva took over, and instead of solemn toasts or good wishes, she and Beto entertained them all with stories from the Santa Fe trail.

"I have a story about a game," Beto informed them. "It started when I told Nathan about whistle-pigs. He didn't believe me. He told me I was a born inventor to come up with the idea of a whistle-pig, and wanted to know if they preferred Bach or something more recent."

Carrie could imagine this discussion exactly, especially as she was unfamiliar with the animal called a whistle-pig.

"He said that I must be thinking of the quill pig, and then *I* didn't believe *him*. I thought he made that animal up."

Eva was smiling at the memory. "It started with whistle-pigs and quill pigs. Then Beto brought up *moldwarp* and Nathan countered with *quickhatch*. But the real duel began with Nathan's *bandiscoot*."

Nathan, all smiles, stood to take a bow.

Beto wrinkled his nose. "I was sure he made *bandiscoot* up, so I asked Mr. Petit, and then I asked Mr. Liebling, and then I asked some of the wranglers—but it wasn't until I got to Big Bull that anybody had an answer. He said yes, he was familiar with the bandiscoot."

"A clever man," Nathan said. "Widely traveled."

Beto blinked. "Who has the telling of this story?"

Eva drew in a sharp breath. "Roberto."

Nathan raised both hands. "Don't scold him, he's right. I beg the storyteller's pardon. Please carry on."

"So," Beto said, purposefully not looking at Nathan. "Big Bull was telling me about the bandiscoot, when Sam Wright came up, and he said, 'Don't believe Big Bull, he earned that name fair and square.'"

Beto waited for the laughter to ebb—he had a good sense of the rhythm so important to storytelling—and then leaned forward. He looked at each of them in turn as if to be sure they were paying attention.

"Sam says to me, 'Tell you what, you ask Ballentyne what he knows about the Texas toe-toe.'"

"*¡Maldición!*" Eli shook his head. "If the wranglers got started—"

"It was fun!" Beto was eager to assure them. "I made a list of all the animals Nathan and the wranglers told me about, and now it's my job to figure out which ones are real. Mostly it ain't hard. But I have to do it myself because once the game got going, there was no way to know who was making things up and who wasn't. Well, mostly anyway. There was Bluey Brown, he always goes too far and gives away the game."

"For example?" Carrie asked.

"Well," Beto started slowly. "Where Bluey grew up, he says there's an otter that has a bill like a duck and a tail like a beaver and it lays eggs like a chicken. But he didn't know how eggs hatched in water and, more suspiciously"—he pronounced the word very carefully—"he couldn't remember its name."

"You'll have to come up with a name on your own," Carrie suggested, and to this Beto nodded enthusiastically.

"Oh, I did," he said. "Bluey's beaver."

Nathan said, "You must keep a record of your research. I imagine you could publish it one day."

A great yawn escaped Beto in lieu of an answer, and within a quarter hour things came to an end. Nathan volunteered to walk the Zavalas home. He would be back at first light, to take his leave.

ELI SAID, "If you can't sleep, you might as well talk to me."

"I didn't mean to wake you."

He sat up and crossed his legs. "You haven't asked, but I could talk to your brother."

Carrie was glad of the dark, because there were tears that she might not be able to hold back.

"You mean, try to change his mind? You know that won't work. But maybe we could steal his horse. Or tie him up like a calf and force him into a stagecoach."

Eli had nothing to say to this, but his hand moved down her back in a gentle motion, the simplest kind of comfort.

"No," she said. "There's only one thing to do."

He waited, quietly, patiently, for what she needed to say.

Carrie listened to him breathing. The heart of a strong, healthy man in his prime would beat somewhere between sixty and ninety times in a minute. Eli's resting heart rate was always between forty and forty-five, a fact she kept to herself out of superstition. Strong hearts could stop without warning, a lesson she learned on the banks of the Sacandaga on the day her father died.

She said, "I have to have faith in him."

Eli hummed his agreement. "Is there anything harder for you than letting go?"

The question took her by surprise and triggered a waterfall of images and flashes of memory. Things she had hidden away from herself so thoroughly that she sometimes believed that they had never been real. Now she wondered if it would even be possible to shut them all away again, or if the door would refuse to be closed.

But they were talking about Nathan. Her brother, who had survived the worst with her, and who was about to go out into a bloody world again. Alone.

She would have to have faith in him.

"I'll survive," she said, hating the tremble in her voice.

Eli ran a thumb down her cheek. "I don't doubt you," he said. "You doubt yourself, but I don't doubt you for a minute."

———

THE NEXT DAY Nathan was gone, and it seemed as if all of Santa Fe had decided that the best way to cheer Carrie up was to keep her busy. Over three days she attended two difficult births and one very easy one. Then, finally home and wanting nothing more than her bed, she found a soldier waiting for her with a message. W. H. Davis, the acting governor, had a daughter-in-law who was here on a visit. She had gone into labor weeks earlier than expected. Would the midwife Ballentyne attend?

Carrie had yet to figure out whether some people called her by her maiden name because they disapproved of her marriage, if they forgot, or if there was some more complicated reason. Just now she was too worn out to correct the soldier, so instead she asked for a half hour to wash and change.

In the governor's mansion, Mrs. Josie Davis was not happy to see the midwife Ballentyne, and wanted her to understand, first and foremost, that she would not give birth in such a raw and uncivilized place as Santa Fe.

She interrupted herself with a gasp as a new labor pain clamped down.

Breathing hard, she came to her point. "The very idea is—insupportable."

Mrs. Davis showed common sense in one way, at least: she allowed Carrie to examine her. Her face and hair were wet with sweat but her voice was firm, even commandeering as she continued with her argument.

"You've examined me. Now I beg you, give me something to stop labor so I can wait for my physician. He should be here early tomorrow."

A moment came for every new mother when she realized she was no longer captain of her ship. The creature she had nurtured in her belly for so many months was now in control. Some women took this philosophically, but that was not Josie Davis's mindset.

"There is no such medicine," Carrie told her, very careful to keep her tone neutral. "You are six centimeters dilated, Mrs. Davis. Your child is on its way, and will not be stopped."

Mrs. Davis considered her, narrow eyed. "I am sure you're a fine midwife." She said this with all the sincerity of a con man hawking stolen merchandise on a street corner. "But this child must wait for Dr. Young."

Carrie spoke bluntly. "There is no need to condescend, Mrs. Davis. I am not denying you out of hurt pride. I am telling you that no herb or tea or medicine that will do what you are asking exists."

Because she saw more fear than condescension in the woman's face, she stopped there. It was, after all, the woman's first child, and none of the things she had arranged or been promised had come true. Her husband was off with his troops, her doctor was a day away, there were no aunts or cousins, sisters or sisters-in-law to support her. For the sake of a safe delivery, Carrie reminded herself, keeping the patient calm was crucially important.

She sat down beside the bed, composed her face, and explained.

"Your body is ready to give birth," Carrie told her. "It won't respond to orders, no matter how forcefully worded. This child is coming, in a matter of hours."

Before the laboring woman could summon up words to match her thunderous expression, Carrie went on.

She said, "If you don't want me to attend you, there are doctors at the army outpost. We could send for one of them. Or all of them, if you like."

An army surgeon was possibly the worst choice, and every woman of childbearing age knew this. Any sensible woman would prefer a midwife, but Mrs. Davis was not easily deterred.

"I know about the army surgeons." She swiped at the sweat rolling down her face. "Two were here before you, just an hour ago. One reeked of whiskey, and the other stank of manure and whiskey both."

Carrie inclined her head. "Dr. Benenati would attend, if you like." She gaped. "The old Italian?"

"Yes, I suppose that is one way to describe him."

"Would you want him attending you?"

It was a challenge, but one easily countered.

"In your situation I would want an experienced midwife," Carrie told her. "I've seen surgeons delivering babies, and it's rarely pretty. If there were no midwife available, I would welcome Dr. Benenati's help. He is very skilled, unusually perceptive. And gentle."

Mrs. Davis, carried away on a crashing wave of pain, still managed to scowl at Carrie. When it passed, she fell back against the pillows. With tears streaming down her face, she nodded.

"Bring me the Italian," she said, her voice cracking. "Make him wash with carbolic before he steps into this room."

OVER THE NEXT week, Carrie delivered five more infants, and by the time the last one was safely swaddled and set to nursing, her knees were wobbling. Eli was waiting, as he usually did, with the husband of the laboring mother.

She wished he had not come to see her home, and thought it best to say this clearly.

"I am in a very sour mood," she told him. "And the only cure is a walk. I like to walk, even after a long day. Especially after a long day. So now I will walk home."

He walked along a few steps behind and to her right.

"You are wobbling, did you realize?"

"Walking will sort me out."

"Here's what I see," Eli went on, his tone conversational. "I see you sweating in the heat. Your lips are cracked. I'm guessing you need water, and a lot of it."

To this reasonable observation she said nothing at all.

"More to the point, I see you inching along, watching your step so you don't fall. My last point—"

Carrie snorted softly, but he was not deterred.

"My last point is that we are still more than a mile from home.

You're thirsty. I'm thirsty. If we continue along at this pace, we'll die of thirst before we get there."

Without further discussion he swept her up in his arms and began to trot toward town.

"You are high-handed," she mumbled against his shoulder. "You are imperious. You are even bossy, and it doesn't bode well."

But Eli kept up his pace, humming agreement to every criticism and dire prediction she voiced. Oh yes, he was listening. He heard every word, and solemnly agreed that she was correct about his short-comings.

At the front door, yawning so fiercely that it made her dizzy, she raised a different subject.

"All I need is fresh air and a few hours' sleep. Really. Then I have to be at the dispensary."

"Good plan," said her husband, hauling her up higher in his arms to kiss her forehead. "Excellent. Can you get to bed under your own power, do you think?"

He was about to put her down to stand on her own two feet, but Carrie held on tighter.

"You've got me this far," she said. "Don't stop now."

In the normal way of things, a week of rushing from delivery to delivery was followed by a day or two or even four of quiet. There was still work at the dispensary, but no one came to call her to a woman in labor. Eva had noticed this and asked about it, to Carrie's horror.

"Oh no," Carrie said. "Don't talk about it or the quiet spell will end." She snapped her fingers. "Just that quickly."

Eva was unimpressed by this bit of midwife superstition.

"The suspense would do me in," she went on. "Always waiting for a knock on the door, at three in the afternoon or the morning. So let's hope for at least a few days of peace."

Carrie had stopped by the Cacharrería Zavala, as she often did on her way to the dispensary. First, to explore the shelves, which were full of the surprises Carrie had been promised, but more importantly there was always some news to share, particularly about small things happening in Santa Fe that Carrie missed. Often amusing, sometimes confusing.

Today Eva and her three clerks were unpacking the last of the stock that had come with her from St. Louis. From what Carrie could see, fabrics. Eva held up a bolt of an unusually fine calico with a pattern of stylized stars and moons.

"You are wrinkling your nose," Carrie observed. "Is something wrong with the bolt? Water damage?"

"Nothing so simple. I fear I may have overestimated my customers' willingness to expand their fashion horizons. But I suppose we will see. If nobody else likes it, Reizl will."

AT THE DISPENSARY Carrie started her mornings with Lulu, unless there were emergencies to deal with or she was called away to a birth. They read and talked, and Lulu asked questions. Sometimes her questions were nothing out of the ordinary for a girl her age, but at times she didn't hesitate to raise dark subjects. About death and dying and the idea of dust to dust. These were things Carrie had given a lot of thought to at an early age, and she didn't discourage Lulu's interest.

From Lulu she went to work with John, looking after patients. He was distracted and even despondent at times, at least in part, Carrie assumed, because he mourned the Markhams, who had shown him kindness when he was most vulnerable. And of course he was wondering if he'd ever be able to get to medical school. Carrie had already written to her stepfather about John, but until she got some word from him, she would not mention this possibility to the young man who had become, against all expectations, a friend.

In general her morning's work was busy and satisfying. There were the universal problems that she would see if she were working in Africa or China or the North Sea, many routine. She saw children with sore ears and adults with sprained joints or bowel problems.

At midday Eli came in, and they sat down together at the Benenatis' crowded table. She should have been hungry, and in fact she wanted to be hungry, but for three weeks now Carrie found it difficult to eat at midday, though the food was plentiful and good. Her lack of appetite drew some attention, but she blamed the heat—early August was the worst, they told her; almost as bad as late August—and that was an excuse everybody accepted. In fact, people clucked sympathetically and assured her that in time—a year or two or three—she would be more comfortable. Good-natured teasing, Carrie decided, and left it at that.

Carrie liked ending her morning with the Benenatis, where there was always something interesting being discussed or debated or argued about. The tone rarely ventured beyond the congenial, though on occasion someone would leave the table abruptly.

In fact, Carrie's lack of appetite was a simple matter of anticipation. After the midday meal came the siesta. People went home to wait out the worst heat of the day in rooms made almost bearable by thick adobe walls and windows that funneled the breeze—if there was a breeze—deep into shady rooms. The siesta was for sleep, and always on the way home, Carrie's body would remind her that sleep was a good and necessary thing.

But it was not the thing she wanted. It seemed such a waste of an opportunity, these hours alone with Eli without anybody watching or listening or interrupting. Today on the short walk home, Carrie listened to Eli's story about a letter from a *patrón* who wanted to hire him to survey property he was thinking of buying.

"That's a good thing, isn't it?"

Eli turned a hand over, empty palm up. "It would be, if he had paid me for the last work I did for him."

Talking with Eli was far more appealing than sleeping next to him in the heat. They talked about projects he might accept or reject; about her work, and if it meant what she thought it meant when a very proper old Mexican lady openly studied Carrie and told her she was a woman with *buenas caderas*.

Sometimes the discussions on the way home carried right into the house, into their room, and finally into bed. As was the case when the subject of hips—good or not so good—evolved into a more general discussion of female anatomy.

On the third day without Carrie being called to a woman in labor, Eli left to do some work at a ranch thirty miles south. He would be gone two or maybe three days, and Carrie found herself hoping that the quiet spell would come to an end. Attending a woman in labor— or two, or three—would keep her so busy that there would be little time to worry about Eli while he was gone.

Not ten minutes after he rode off, Eva walked in, all smiles.

"Carrie, come. Right away, come. You'll like what I've got up my sleeve."

It was the fourth or fifth time since Eva was back in Santa Fe that she had whisked Carrie off without warning. Most often they ended up at Eva's comfortable home on the banks of the dry basin of the Rio Chiquito. There was a little garden and a *placita* where they sat and talked until work called Carrie away.

Other times she took Carrie to see things she hadn't yet noticed. She suspected these outings had something to do with the fact that Beto was away, spending a month with his grandfather at Pontevedra, the rancho the older man hadn't left in years. Eva understood his grief, and was glad that her son still had a grandfather to teach him.

"I keep thinking Beto should be coming home, but it will be another week. And maybe more. My father-in-law would hide him away from me if he could, to raise on his own."

"Señora!"

They both turned to see Inez Aguilar hurrying to catch up with them. She was someone Carrie liked, and just recently she had been more able to talk to her and learn something about her life. Carrie smiled at Inez, hoping to put her at ease.

"Chabela?" she asked.

Inez gave a sharp nod of the head. "*Rompió aguas.*"

Inez was anxious not for herself—she would have no more children— but for her only daughter, whose water had broken. Carrie summoned her calmest tone as she asked for more detail, and she listened closely to Inez's careful accounting. Eva stepped in closer, too, as women did when a friend came face-to-face with the excitement—and anxiety—of childbirth.

Now Eva asked the usual questions: How long had Inez been in labor with Pedro, her first? It was the right subject to raise; women needed to recount their birth stories. The ritual provided comfort and perspective and, probably most important, a reminder that women did this every day, all over the world, and would continue in the same way until the end of time.

Carrie promised to stop by in an hour, and Inez hurried away home, breaking into a trot almost immediately.

"Tell me again where we're going," Carrie said.

"I didn't tell you to start," Eva said. "But look, we're here. You see, Reizl is waiting for us."

In Carrie's experience the two Goldblum apartments above and behind the general goods store were always full of people, but today was different. There was no sign of any Goldblum except Reizl, and not even the sound of voices.

She ushered them into her parlor with a sweep of the arm and a truly triumphant smile. A table had been set for an elaborate meal with china, silver serving dishes, crystal glassware. And three chairs.

Reizl went off to talk to servants in the kitchen, and Carrie turned to Eva. "I'm confused. Intrigued, but confused. Where is everyone?"

She explained that twice a year, the Jewish families in New Mexico Territory gathered together to trade, and share news, and plan. "Somebody has to stay behind, and Levi and Reizl claim that privilege. He looks after all the businesses, and Reizl—"

"I do nothing!" Reizl came in, arms wrapped around herself, she was so pleased. "I have time to myself. No fussing, no arguments, no negotiating every little thing."

From the other end of the apartment came a high, light giggle. A young child's giggle.

Reizl sighed. "And always, there's a fly in the soup."

Carrie's impression was that Reizl's discontent was all show, because she couldn't hide her delight when the door flew open and a very sturdy little girl, about three, came stomping in.

"Pearl," said Reizl. "You are pretending to be a buffalo? Well, be a little girl for a while and come say hello to our guests."

The little girl gave a mighty shake of the head, much as a buffalo would before charging.

"How sad." Eva cast her eyes down. "I would have liked to visit with Pearl. Well, all the more for us."

The child's eyes went wide at the sight of the table, lost under a multitude of platters and serving dishes.

"Off you go, buffalo girl," Reizl said. "When you are done grazing outside, you can come back in and watch us eat people food."

Just that simply, the little girl turned and stomped out of the room.

Carrie raised a brow at Reizl. "You didn't say there would be entertainment."

"My granddaughter," Reizl said, with great pride.

As if Pearl had heard this—and did not like it—the door opened again and a little face showed itself.

"Is that buffalo back again?" Reizl asked no one in particular.

Pearl crossed the room in a few hops and ended up on her knees beside her grandmother, head tilted to one side so she could bat her eyelashes with great effect.

"Pearl! Very nice of you to join us. Now will you show Mrs. Ibarra how polite you can be?"

It turned out that the girl could, but she was far better at being entertaining. A fourth chair was added to the table and Pearl sat with them, her head swiveling back and forth as she considered the offerings. Between brisket and noodles, chicken and dumplings, pickles and sauerkraut, she fished in her pockets and produced treasures for everyone to admire. A rock shaped like a heart, a tiny doll whose porcelain face had been scrubbed clean of paint and expression, a bone polished so that it gleamed, and with each precious small thing came some part of a story.

A servant came in and leaned close to say something to Reizl, but

Pearl's young ears took in every syllable and she shot away from the table.

"Manners!" her grandmother yelled. To her guests she explained that a playmate had come, someone Pearl especially liked. This raised the more general subject of children, and Eva was answering a question about Beto when there was another interruption.

This time the knock was from the door that led into the shop. Levi Goldblum, tall and slight and white-haired, leaned in, gesturing to his wife. There was another man standing just behind him.

"I recognize that man," Carrie said to Eva. "But I don't remember his name."

"I know him." Eva's easy humor was suddenly gone. "That is the sheriff. And he's looking at you."

Jesus Maria Sena y Baca, employed by the territorial government as sheriff, wanted someplace to talk to Carrie. His manner was formal.

Mr. Goldblum seemed to be vaguely amused by the sheriff, but he offered the use of his little study off the shop. "It's not much, but it's private."

Without discussion, Eva came, too, and Carrie was glad of it. She could and would speak for herself, whatever the sheriff wanted, but if her Spanish failed her, she would be glad of Eva's help.

She greeted the sheriff as custom required and then wasted no time.

"Are you here about a medical matter? Does someone need a midwife?"

He gave a small shake of the head and answered her in very stilted English. His English was no better, Carrie remarked to herself, than her own Spanish.

"No babies. I'm here because someone has sworn a complaint about you."

Eva made a deep sound in her throat. The sheriff raised a brow in her direction. "You have something to say, Eva?"

She answered him, her derision on full display. "I am here as a witness, Chucho."

Muscles jumped in his jaw when she used his nickname, but he didn't complain. He had called Eva by her first name too. Carrie kept her gaze fixed on the sheriff.

"What complaint? Who has filed a complaint?"

For a moment it looked as though he was going to ignore the question, but he glanced at Eva and reconsidered.

"A lady who arrived in Santa Fe two days ago with Moreno's post run. She's staying at the fonda."

It made no sense. "I don't know anyone who came to town two days ago. And I certainly didn't treat a new patient since then."

He inclined his head. "If you are telling the truth—"

At Eva's indrawn breath, he shifted his gaze to her and blinked, slowly.

She said, "*Fanfarrón, bravucón y presumido.*"

This was not the time to ask for a translation, but the sheriff flushed a bright red, which told Carrie that Eva had struck a blow.

"Señora Zavala." His tone was cold. "You have no part in my business with Señora Ibarra." And to Carrie: "May I assume you will cooperate with the investigation, and come now to answer questions?"

Carrie considered. She had no sense of her rights in this situation, but she realized that there was a chance the sheriff could make real trouble for her. Why he would want to do that was the first question to be answered, and to that end she would need to talk to many different people. And to find out something about the woman staying at the fonda.

She said, "I will answer questions, yes. But I have a patient in labor who is waiting for me. I'll come to you when she is safely delivered."

He hesitated, his jaw clenching and releasing. Then he bowed from the shoulders and turned to the door.

"Wait," Carrie said. "Who exactly filed a complaint about me? And what is the claim?"

"A Mrs. Chatham," he said. "From Richmond. As you are so busy today, the details must wait until you have time to answer my questions."

"GOOD LORD," EVA said as soon as the sheriff closed the office door behind himself. "I can't believe she's actually here in Santa Fe." Her mouth turned down at the corners, as if the very idea had a foul taste.

Such a strong reaction took Carrie by surprise. "You know this Mrs. Chatham?"

Eva blinked. "Yes," she said, frowning. "I know her. And so do you. Catty Chatty?"

The name Chatham had struck Carrie as familiar, and now she remembered why. Mrs. Chatham, stick-bug thin and spare and sour, had spent that first day on the trail with them. Nathan had called her Catty Chatty; as usual he was both rude and accurate. But the woman had called it down upon herself: she had insulted Eva openly and, worse, had been cruel to Beto.

"I put her out of my mind," Carrie said. "But of course you would remember. Do we know anything about her?"

"Oh yes." Eva drew in a deep breath and let it go, more slowly. "She told the Petits that she was on her way to Santa Fe to nurse a sick relative. A relative expecting a child."

The memory solidified for Carrie and, with it, a dawning dread. She had never imagined coming across Mrs. Chatham again, and even less had she thought of her in connection with Mrs. Markham. Now that the possibility was before her, she felt slightly nauseated.

"It may be a misunderstanding," she said, determined to sound reasonable even if her thoughts were not. "In any case, I have no time for Mrs. Chatham just now. I have to see to Chabela."

"I have time," Eva said, a familiar grim set to her mouth.

What had Eli said about Eva on the packet? *She's always happiest when she has a dragon to slay.* Carrie was both encouraged and alarmed by the idea.

A few hours later, in the worst of the afternoon heat, Chabela's labor slowed enough for her to sleep. Inez set out a simple meal, and Carrie found she was truly hungry for once. They had just finished when Inez's Marco came tumbling through the door into the casita, ten years old and made of rubber, yelping his news at such a pace that Carrie caught only a word or two.

Inez turned toward the window. "Look," she said. "Eva, bareheaded in the full sun. How her Mama used to scold her. How I would scold her, if I thought she might listen."

She was pleased to see Eva, but Carrie had the idea that Inez took some pleasure in Eva's lack of a bonnet. As if Inez counted on the younger woman to flout expectations where she herself could not.

Eva came in with an overfilled basket and began to unpack small gifts for Chabela and Inez and the new baby. Useful, thoughtful things that would not draw attention or envy.

"I've got something for you too," she told Carrie. "Not quite so pleasant. But let me catch my breath." And: "Oh yes, Inez, please. Water. How is Chabela coming along?"

When Inez went to check on her daughter, Eva changed the subject abruptly. She spread her hands on the table as if to pin down her thoughts.

"Let me say where I have been so far," she began. "First I went to warn Josefa about Mrs. Chatham. She has not shown her face there. Not yet."

Eva held up a palm to ward off Carrie's questions.

"Wait. I'll forget some of the details if I'm interrupted. After Josefa I went on to the fonda. Chucho said she took a room there, and she did."

One of Eva's husband's cousins worked at the hotel, and she had thought she'd be able to get some questions answered. Instead it seemed that Edmundo had been away from the fonda running errands and had nothing to tell her about Mrs. Chatham.

"I had more luck with Primo and Alma. But not much more."

The Guzmans had a reputation for keeping to themselves, and rarely interacted even with the hotel guests. Nevertheless, Mrs. Chatham had insisted on an audience with them both.

"So it is the same woman?"

"Oh yes. But even without the physical description, I could recognize her. Mrs. Kanti Chatham is demanding and impatient, but that's as much as Alma would say."

She paused to finish her water and then moved straight on.

"Next I went looking for Tom Bixby. Actually I heard him before I saw him. The man sounds like a growling bear when he snores, and there he was at Buzz Kelly's, waiting to be shaved, and half-asleep." She couldn't help grinning at the memory.

"And then?" Carrie's voice came a little strained now, and Eva took note. She gave the rest of her report in plain terms: She had gone outside with Mr. Bixby to talk in private, and that was when she learned that yes, he had met the new arrival. Mrs. Chatham had sought him out because he was the Markhams' attorney.

Carrie tapped the tabletop, trying to get a hold on her impatience. "And what exactly did she want from Mr. Bixby? Did she say?"

"She did indeed." There was something very lawyerlike about Eva when she had a problem to sort through. Many people were capable of taking in a lot of information and making sense of it, but Eva had a skill that others lacked: out of a jumble of facts, suppositions, misconceptions, and bald-faced lies, she constructed an objective, rational story. She told the lawyer about their day with Mrs. Chatham on the Santa Fe trail, and instilled a sense of dread in him, just as she meant to.

"So we went together to talk to Jesus Sena."

At Carrie's blank look, she explained. "The sheriff? Lord, I still cannot get used to the idea of Chucho as sheriff. *Incompetente, bueno para nada, perezoso* . . ."

Carrie wasn't sure if this was a curse or just a harsh judgment on the sheriff's character, but now was not the time to ask for a translation. Eva had already moved on, and Carrie readjusted her thinking.

"Did Indira Markham ever tell you about her family back east?"

The question took Carrie by surprise, but it was not difficult to answer.

"We spent so little time in the same room," she said. "There was never any sharing of stories. There's no word of brothers or sisters in the last testament she wrote out. In that document, at least."

"I knew her for ten years," Eva said. "In all that time she never mentioned siblings. But here's the crux of the problem. Mrs. Chatham claims that Indira Markham was her younger half sister."

Carrie closed her eyes. "Does she have any proof of that claim?"

Eva had asked that very question at the fonda, when she talked to Mr. Bixby, and in the sheriff's office. And nobody had an answer.

"Fine," Carrie said. "Let's assume for a moment she can prove that Indira Markham was her half sister. What is it she wants?"

Eva was unhappy, but she was not a coward; she would tell the worst.

"Everything," she said. "She wants whatever inheritance there might be, she wants Indira's clothes and jewels and books. To get the things she wants, she has to get Lulu first. Of course she doesn't talk about it that way."

Carrie, taken aback, could only watch as Eva stood and made ready to go.

"I take heart in the fact that Mrs. Chatham doesn't know that there is no inheritance, or that Indira's jewelry was sold to settle the grocer's bill. We'll see if those details make her change her mind about where Lulu should be raised."

LATE IN THE night Carrie's vague concerns about Chabela's labor took shape. During difficult deliveries this sometimes happened, but she had learned to keep such insights to herself; to raise an alarm so early would be more than cruel. At that moment Chabela's labor was long and hard, but the difficult part was still to come. If it happened at all, Carrie reasoned to herself.

All the small stories she relied on to amuse and distract a woman in labor were just as effective with Chabela as they had ever been, despite Carrie's sometimes awkward—and apparently funny—attempts to tell them in Spanish. Through all that, she was able to keep her tone light and positive, while another part of her mind juggled other concerns.

At the New Amsterdam, Carrie could have a nurse or another midwife step in almost immediately, but in Santa Fe she had thus far managed on her own. Until this birth. For Chabela she would have to call in Madu, or risk disaster.

Carrie had witnessed many deaths—as a student, as an apprentice, and finally in her own practice. She had lost patients to blood poisoning following sloppily done abortions; others had died due to a drastic failure of the placenta. There were a dozen kinds of deaths she had documented that could be blamed only on poverty: women too young, too old, overworked, undernourished, dependent on gin or burney. Women who gave up.

And then there was childbed fever.

Carrie had never lost a mother or child to puerperal fever. It was the thing she feared most, an unforgivable failure, and there would be no one to blame but herself. Childbed fever could be avoided, and by something as simple as handwashing.

She had come to Santa Fe not knowing if Dr. Markham would even be familiar with the concept of contagion, or if, like so many physicians, he simply rejected the germ theory of disease. More than that, she was almost afraid to raise the subject with him, and so she had raised it with John Edmonds.

"Are you familiar with the work of a Dr. Oliver Wendell Holmes, of Boston?" She added, "His work on labor and delivery, more exactly."

John's interest was immediate. "I'm not, but it sounds as though you think I should be."

Carrie lent him her 1847 edition of *The Contagiousness of Puerperal Fever*, as well as notes on the research done in Austria by a Dr. Semmelweis. Then she waited. He would come with questions, or he would pretend the exchange had never happened, the simplest way to put an end to a discussion.

It was just the next day toward evening when they were getting the dispensary ready to shut down that he began.

"I'm not sure I understand," he said, in his usual cautious manner. "There's a hospital in Vienna with two childbirth wards. One where the doctors deliver their patients, and the other where the midwives deliver everybody else. Is it right that a woman who delivers in the doctors' ward is three times more likely to die of puerperal fever?"

Carrie confirmed that it was. And not just in Vienna.

"And the difference, according to this Dr. Semmel—Semmel—"

"Semmelweis. And also Dr. Holmes."

He acknowledged this with a nod. "They believe that puerperal fever is contagious, passed from person to person. That doctors carry infection to patients from ward to ward, unaware. It's on their hands and clothes and instruments, and they pass the germs—if that's what they're called—to women in labor."

Carrie nodded. "Yes, you've got the basics down."

He was so caught up in thought that she wondered if he even heard her answer.

John went on, "And Holmes and Semmelweis both claim that handwashing is the solution. That dirty hands account for thousands of deaths."

"Many thousands of deaths," Carrie said. "And not just hands. Hands and forearms and shirtsleeves, sheets and towels, anything that comes in contact with a wound may start an infection that can't be stopped. Washing with chlorinated lime solution or something similar is the first step to preventing childbed fever."

The next question was not easy to answer; John wanted to know if this new work on contagion and germ theory and puerperal fever was widely accepted by doctors. It was the turning point in the conversation that Carrie had worried about. She could tell him about the poor reception both Holmes's and Semmelweis's work had received and how slowly this was changing, or she could approach it from a different angle. She told him instead about Matron Rosenmeyer.

"Midwives—most of us, anyway—have been promoting sanitation for a long time," she said. "Anybody who trained at the New Amsterdam—and not just nurses—learned all about it from Matron Rosenmeyer.

She's famous for her methods. When a student neglects proper sanitation, her temper . . . well, it's something you would not forget. The angrier she is, the heavier her accent gets, until she sometimes mixes German into her English. She always ends with the same words."

Carrie cleared her throat and arched her shoulders, reaching for the memory of a fastidious, uncompromising German nurse. "Dis jung voman," she began in a low, harsh whisper. "Dis jung voman is comink to us for help. To the New Ahmsterdam she is comink. She is dinking she will go home wid her child, but no. No. Instead you are goink to send dem bot to a bauper's grave."

Matron Rosenmeyer had meant to put the fear of God into students, and now Carrie had done the same for John. Or, she had to consider the possibility that he was trying not to laugh at her performance. But he was a serious-minded young man, and she had managed to sway him. John began to wash his hands more often and more carefully, and often used the carbolic Carrie stored out of sight. Out of Dr. Markham's sight.

But it wasn't John who was coming to help with this birth. It was Madu, who had certainly never heard of Dr. Holmes or Semmelweis, but who had been delivering infants for more years than Carrie had been alive.

Carrie could not, would not order Madu to wash her hands. Lecturing her about germ theory and contagion was unthinkable. And really, she reminded herself, there was no practical need; no healer she knew had ever seen or heard of a single case of puerperal fever in any of the Haudenosaunee longhouses. Childbed fever was a creature of places where sewage ran in the streets. Where the poor lived crowded together in a maze of dark rooms, filthy because hot water and soap were beyond their means. Where men who studied disease and how to cure it thought very little about the patient before them. The same doctors who spent an hour in the morgue prying diseased organs out of the dead and then went on to attend a woman in labor, stopping not to wash, but to light an expensive cigar. Some of the older doctors wore the same suit coat for every hospital visit, unconcerned with crusts of blood or the stains left by bodily fluids. In fact, some seemed to be proud to wear such coats as proof of their experience and skill.

No, Carrie would send for Madu, and be thankful for her experience and help. She had been thinking of Madu as someone she would talk to about other matters as well. She wondered what a wise older woman who knew the bones of this place would make of Kanti Chatham.

Chabela's transition was much like others in Carrie's experience. An hour of the worst contractions before she came to that quiet place, the short, restful few minutes between labor and the urge to push. Not everyone achieved that short respite; often panic overwhelmed a laboring mother, and her moment of peace was lost. But Chabela was strong and smart, and she listened to what her mother and her midwife told her.

Carrie watched closely as Chabela's body recentered itself. Before she even left New York, she had learned the Spanish words and phrases a midwife must know, and she used them now.

Is it time to welcome your child? Are you ready to push?

Chabela looked distracted, dazed, turned inward. And still she nodded.

Inez and the elder cousin held her crouching form half-suspended between them, their heads bent close. They were crooning to her, singing and praying and using their voices and hands and a cloth dipped in cool water to comfort and encourage her. They were in high spirits, this close to a much-anticipated arrival, and still Chabela wasn't hearing them, Carrie could see. At this stage some women retreated. Nothing existed except the child she was working so hard to push out into the world.

In this case, it would not happen as easily or quickly as anyone would wish.

"Geometry won't be ignored," Amelie would have said. Which meant that even an extraordinarily strong and resolute laboring woman would have trouble pushing a large child through a narrow pelvis.

Carrie singled out the younger cousin.

"Chelo, can you please go fetch Madu? Tell her I've got a—" Carrie wished just then that Eva hadn't gone home to sleep. She didn't know how to say *difficult presentation*, and had no time to try to work it out. She started again.

"Please ask Madu to come. Tell her I need another pair of hands, and quickly."

An experienced midwife would understand the nature of the problem. And of course, Carrie reminded herself again, she could be wrong. Madu would not appreciate being called away from her bed and her husband at this hour, only to find Chabela with a healthy newborn beside her. But she must take that chance; it was more important to have the help she might need.

Just a few minutes later, Carrie was in her spot in front of Chabela, bent low to watch the baby's head as it began to crown. This was always a moment that took her by surprise, no matter how often she saw it happen. Chabela was dripping sweat, her breath hoarse and her voice ragged, but she freed an arm from her mother's grasp to trace her own skin, stretched paper thin and taut, and then touched her child's head. The first touch.

Almost in response the baby began to turn and inch forward.

Carrie made a cup of her hands, still wet with soap and carbolic, and was rewarded with a tremendous gush of amniotic fluid that soaked her from neck to waist. Something she hardly noticed because Chabela was screaming, a high spiral of sound to match a huge push.

With that she birthed her child's head, but almost instantly it was gone, retreated back into the birth canal like a turtle into its shell. Exactly what Carrie had suspected. One shoulder—or, if the fates were cruel, both shoulders—had come up against the pelvic bone, and with that, everything stopped.

Her choices as midwife were few, and so Carrie made ready to flip Chabela over onto all fours. She had never done this maneuver alone, but she could do it, and would. She would do it if she must, but she still hoped for Madu.

At the door the younger cousin gasped and then jumped out of the way to let Madu pass.

Without looking at her, Carrie said, "A shoulder—"

"So I see," Madu said. "I'm no good on the floor at my age. Let's get her up on the kitchen table."

57

CARRIE SLEPT UNTIL almost noon the next day, and then Eva came to see her, full of questions. Was it true that, and did Chabela really, and had Carrie heard the rumor that . . .

Carrie let the questions roll over her until one came along she felt compelled to answer.

"What exactly happened with the shoulder? Did you have to break it, or did Madu take over and do that?"

Yawning, Carrie shook her head. "No shoulders were broken. Bruised, yes. And Madu did not take over, but she gave me directions that made all the difference."

That surprised Eva. "You needed directions? You never had a case like this before?"

Carrie knew that she would be answering these questions for weeks to come, and decided that she would tell Eva everything so that she could handle some of the inquiries herself, as she seemed to get some satisfaction from setting people straight. She had to smile at this idea.

"I've delivered in situations like this before, but I had a nurse or another midwife nearby. There are only minutes to act when a shoulder gets lodged in the pelvis because the cord is almost certainly compressed. The physical shifting of the mother to all fours usually changes the way the child is positioned, and things will start to happen."

"But not this time," Eva prompted. And at Carrie's look of surprise, she shrugged. "You know women talk."

This was another truth about childbirth; the story would be passed from hand to hand, changing as it moved in ways that couldn't be predicted. Even in her own mind this happened. From every delivery she retained not the most important or significant memories, but random and often odd flashes; just now if she closed her eyes, it was Inez she saw first, standing on the other side of the kitchen table with a hand on her daughter's shoulder, eyes closed and praying in a hoarse whisper, while outside, male voices rose and fell under the night sky. Chabela's aunts were all in the house, waiting to be called on, but she also had a father, a husband, brothers, uncles, and they had gathered together to wish the newest of their kin safely into the world.

Carrie shook herself free of the image and took up the story again.

"Things didn't really get going until Madu came in."

Eva frowned. "You said—"

"She watched. She directed, you could say. She pointed things out. Things I would have seen, but maybe just a little too late."

"Like?"

Carrie gave some thought to how to describe what had happened.

"At a crucial point, Madu said, 'That stubborn boy child is turning purple, so get a move on.'"

A no-nonsense midwife, Carrie told Eva, was the best kind of help to have at a difficult birth.

"So you had to reach in—" Eva stopped. "What is that like?"

Carrie considered, and then decided that her friend didn't need to be coddled.

"Have you ever reached into an oven where the fire has just recently gone out? It's like that, that hot. The pressure is more difficult to describe. If a man wearing a wet glove were to squeeze your hand with all his force, that would be similar. But there's no time to think about any of that while it's happening. You've got minutes to shift the baby and find that sliver of space that will make the difference. You have to get the pressure off the cord, otherwise—"

Otherwise, she continued to herself alone, *otherwise you get a child like my sister. Like our Martha. Whose spirit hadn't been nearby in the last days.*

She cleared her throat. "Even a minute, two minutes too long, and you end up with a still child, or a live child with a dimmed mind. So I spent maybe two minutes trying to turn him, and I was about to try the next thing—"

Eva's raised eyebrow stopped her from skipping ahead. "And what was Chabela doing at this point?"

"Screaming. So I was about to try to deliver an arm, but Madu said, 'Wait, he's thinking about it.'"

Surprised, Eva drew back her head like an affronted hen. Carrie forged ahead with the story anyway.

"So I took a deep breath and gave another nudge and everything just . . . slid into place. Chabela pushed with everything she had left, and the boy shot out into my hands."

Carrie thought of Eli, who wouldn't be home for another day at least. He would have appreciated the rest of this story.

"I almost dropped him," she confessed to Eva. "But if you tell anybody I said so, I'll curse you for a tattletale."

MR. BIXBY KNOCKED on Carrie's door late that day, just as Santa Fe was stirring out of siesta. He gave a stiff little bow as he greeted her, but his gaze skittered away.

Many times in her life, people she trusted had told her that men found her intimidating. Others used the word *annoying,* which Carrie suspected was nearer the truth. She hadn't spent enough time with Mr. Bixby to gauge whether she annoyed or intimidated him; in any case, she didn't have the patience to coax him through polite conversation that might inch him toward a more comfortable place. Right now there were topics that needed clarification that could not wait.

"Mr. Bixby," she greeted him, stepped outside, and pulled the door shut behind herself. "Time for Sheriff Sena's inquisition?"

The lawyer started off at a pace suitable to a stroll in a park, but seemed willing enough to talk.

"About the inquisition, as you call it. First, I should explain that it's not the sheriff we're going to see. In fact, it's the governor, the interim governor, you understand, who will be handling the inqui—the inquiry. So we'll be meeting at his home, which is—"

"I know where the governor's residence is," Carrie said. "I was there a week ago when his daughter-in-law was in labor."

He blinked, confused. "They called you to attend the birth?"

To take offense would be a waste of time, and in any event, Bixby seemed to realize that he had misstepped, because more throat clearing was necessary. They had been walking for a few minutes before he found a way to start again.

"Do I understand correctly that your husband isn't going to join us?"

"He's away on business. Is that an issue?"

"No no, no issue at all." He touched a handkerchief to his damp brow, looking relieved.

Carrie wondered what she was missing. She doubted there was anyone in a hundred miles who hadn't heard that she had married Eli Ibarra, but then again, they weren't often seen together in public places. Would there be someone at this meeting who took exception? And what bearing would that have?

She asked, "Who else will be at this meeting with the governor, beyond Mrs. Chatham and the sheriff?"

He stopped in the shade of an olive tree and seemed to be gathering his thoughts.

"As far as I know, the interim governor and one or two of his aides. The sheriff, and Mrs. Chatham's lawyer, I assume. But first if I may raise a question—"

"Please," Carrie said. "Go on."

"You told me the story of how you first met Mrs. Chatham when the wagon train started out. I've heard the same story from Mrs. Zavala. But when Mrs. Chatham came to see me yesterday, she never said a word about you. Either of you. I mentioned your name, but there was no sign from her that she had ever met you. Now it looks as though she was hiding the connection. Why would she pretend you were a stranger?"

Carrie considered for a moment. "Good question. Another question— one that is before us just now—is how she'll react when she sees me, and how I should react if she pretends we're strangers. Now I wish Eva were here with me. It would be very difficult for Mrs. Chatham to deny both of us."

Mr. Bixby again touched his sweaty brow with a handkerchief, considered for a moment, and turned toward her quite suddenly.

"We could send for Mrs. Zavala."

Carrie shook her head. "Now I'm wondering if I should meet with Mrs. Chatham at all. You did tell her that the guardianship arrangements had been approved by the courts?"

"I did."

"She's not one to accept a no, it seems. When will Judge Ford be here next?"

"Ah," he said. "You think we should let her approach Hank Ford directly with her complaint? Interesting strategy, but tricky. He will be here fairly soon."

In fact, Carrie knew too little of local politics to guess how a judge might react in such a situation. Eli, of course, would know. But just now it was up to her to settle on a strategy. It felt something like playing chess for the first time, or opposite someone whose skill level was a complete mystery.

The governor's residence was another five minutes away. She might ask Mr. Bixby to go ahead and announce that the meeting must wait for Judge Ford. She liked the idea for more than one reason. First, Mrs. Chatham would be outraged, which would be somewhat awkward, but potentially entertaining. More to the point, Carrie had liked the judge when they appeared in his courtroom with Mrs. Markham's irregular declarations about her daughter's future. Ford was a dour, severe older man, irascible, and sharp-tongued, but also perceptive, quick-witted, and fair. She doubted he would take kindly to Mrs. Chatham's sarcasm and superior attitude.

She said, "It's tempting to just turn around, but I don't think it would be wise. I agreed to answer questions. If I go back on my word, Mrs. Chatham will find a way to make the most of that."

Mr. Bixby rocked his head from side to side, weighing the choices before them. "I see your point. But I can hardly imagine how you will approach this."

She gave him a tight smile. "I will step very carefully. And remind myself that Judge Ford is on the horizon if things should go very wrong."

THEY FOUND THE front door of the governor's residence standing open, an invitation, as Carrie interpreted it, to come in out of the sun. Then they waited there in the portal, listening to the normal sounds of a busy household: water being swept off tile, an older man humming to himself as he worked. Far off a newborn was wailing, and in another part of the house two women were debating something, one with a Boston accent and the other whose English had its origins in the poorest London neighborhoods. This conversation was interrupted by the shriek of a parrot, cackling, ¡NO MENTIRA! ¡NO MENTIRA!

She would have to ask for a translation later; parrots often swore like sailors, and she wouldn't like to embarrass Mr. Bixby. She looked forward to writing about it in her next letter home. At least, she told herself, the parrot with his ¡NO MENTIRA! had lightened her mood.

All Mr. Bixby's attention was focused on a set of double doors that stood partially open. The governor's office or parlor or library, Carrie assumed, given the low murmur of voices. Three or four men talking, their tones amiable. To those came another voice, feminine, distinctly

Southern in origin. Carrie stepped forward just far enough to see into the room from an angle, and stopped.

The lady who sat in the governor's library was Mrs. Chatham, and at the same time, she was someone entirely different.

The Mrs. Chatham they met on the trail had looked much like any other middle-aged woman of moderate means; her clothing was well made, neat, and modest, but simple. No frills or embroidery, tucks or pleats. If pressed, Carrie might have guessed her to be the wife of a clerk or a pastor.

In contrast, the narrow, frowning, plainly dressed harridan from the stagecoach had transformed into a wealthy, stylish woman. She was utterly feminine, flirtatious, and fashionable. An actress about to step onto the stage at Wallack's Theater as Lady Macbeth was no less prepared than Mrs. Chatham was for this meeting.

She understood her craft. She had ignored the strong, saturated colors and patterns of recent fashion and made the most of what mourning demanded of her. Her gown, figured silk, was a deep, dark blue accented with carved jet buttons, black velvet piping, and lapels. The yards and yards of silk had been folded and cinched, scalloped, and molded by petticoats, hoops, and corsets. With the right manners and a suitable accent—those things she had at the start—a woman with a skilled modiste and a lax moral compass could go far.

She was, everyone was meant to understand, a lady in mourning for her half sister. The only thing missing was an adversary. That role, Carrie realized now, was meant for herself.

58

Mrs. Chatham sat on a divan with some of the wealthiest and most prominent of Santa Fe's men gathered around her. Captain Brooks of the 3rd Infantry Regiment; Mr. Botka, the president of the bank; Mr. Muñoz, the newspaper editor; and Mr. Ogden, who owned a half dozen mines. The sheriff stood aside, his hands at the small of his back.

The one person Carrie did know, at least a little, was Jake Saracen. She had last seen him at the fandango, the night Eli came home. The night they had first danced together. She missed Eli and would have been thankful to have him beside her, but she could deal with both Jake Saracen and Mrs. Chatham on her own. That she promised herself.

She stepped into the room with Mr. Bixby at her side.

Kanti Chatham was saying, "Of course you see the nature of my concerns."

Her head turned as she met each man's eye. Oddly enough, her Southern accent was more pronounced, but the creak in her voice, the one that Carrie so disliked, was dampened. Her tone, once sarcastic and rude, now skimmed the boundaries of flirtation. Men of a certain age seemed drawn to this kind of woman. Carrie had never understood why that should be, but she saw it happening now.

"My niece is here without the comfort or protection of family," she was saying. "It would be a dereliction of my duties not to take responsibility for her. Richmond is where her dear mother was born and raised. What could be more fitting?"

Fitting. An interesting word to use because, it occurred to Carrie, nothing fit. The timing of the story she was telling would not stand close examination.

Mr. Ogden was leaning toward Mrs. Chatham. Carrie had heard a good deal of talk about him, a corpulent fifty-year-old with a great ruffle of chin beard, usually bored and still easily charmed by a shapely figure. And yet it seemed Mrs. Chatham hadn't yet quite won him over.

All polite smiles and deference, he asked her a direct question. "Tell us, what plans do you have for your niece?"

She closed her eyes as if to imagine this wondrous life her niece would have.

"Lucinda will have every advantage. Her playmates will be the children of the old Richmond families, many of whom are her cousins, once or twice removed. She will have servants of her own, and excellent tutors."

Carrie meant to hold back her reactions, but something must have flickered across her face at the mention of servants. Because, of course, Virginia was a slaveholding state. The idea of Lulu with a slave of her own made Carrie recoil. This reaction was enough to draw Mrs. Chatham's attention.

It was Carrie's good fortune that Mr. Bixby chose that moment to step forward.

"I see we are late. Apologies. Mrs. Chatham, allow me to introduce Miss Ballentyne—"

"No need, Mr. Bixby," Carrie said, her tone neutral. "Mrs. Chatham and I have already met. For a day we shared a stagecoach on the

Santa Fe trail. Unless she's forgot me. And my brother, and Mrs. Zavala. And of course Beto."

Mrs. Chatham smiled, one brow raised in an elegant arch. "Miss Ballentyne! What a lovely surprise. Forget you? Hardly possible, though I will confess, I didn't recognize you at first glance—"

"And I would say the same of you."

The smile stiffened just slightly.

"You've been out in the sun without a bonnet," she went on. "You are as brown as an Indian!"

Jake Saracen did not trouble to hide his grin, but Carrie spent not one moment of her attention on him. She was sorting through strategies and trying to make sense of where this was going. As she took the seat Mr. Bixby held out for her, directly across from the divan, Mrs. Chatham made her next move.

"Mr. Bixby, I must confess that I'm confused. What is the delightful Miss Ballentyne's connection to my poor sister and her family?"

Now Carrie knew that she must assert herself, calmly and with confidence. She said, "I am Lulu's guardian and responsible for her welfare until Dr. and Mrs. Colby arrive for her."

Mrs. Chatham's expression cracked like a sugar glaze.

"There's some mistake," she said, first to the governor and then to the other men. "Mr. Bixby did tell me about the guardianship agreement—and I have some concerns about that document that must be resolved—but he gave me a different name." She glanced at the lawyer, who looked vaguely confused himself.

Mrs. Chatham's frown made the skin of her chin and cheeks fold into something less than youthful. Carrie wondered if she was aware of that fact, but unable to control her expression.

"I'm not—" Mr. Bixby began, and she cut him off.

"Mr. Bixby, you told me that a Mrs. Ibarra had been given custody of my niece." She had one hand spread on her chest, the other reaching out to latch onto the arm of the divan.

Carrie answered again on her own behalf. "I recently married," she said. "When I am seeing patients, I still go by my maiden name, but otherwise I am Mrs. Ibarra."

"Ibarra?"

"Yes," Carrie said, quite easily. "Elias Ibarra is my husband. You're wondering about the name? My father-in-law is Basque. My mother-in-law is a daughter of the Walatowa Pueblo."

Mrs. Chatham's head jerked as she turned to the governor.

"Do I understand correctly that my niece has been given into the care of a mixed-race couple? And the court approved this?"

"Judge Ford did approve it," the governor said. He was frowning, as if the lady's criticism were aimed at him in particular.

"Well, I am very sorry to hear of it," Mrs. Chatham said. "This is what comes of greedy shortsighted politicians. They wanted as much land as they could get from the Mexicans and gave no thought to the brown tide that would follow. I see I have offended you, Miss Ballentyne."

"Mrs. Chatham, I am Mrs. Ibarra, as you have been told. And you offend me in every way possible."

"Then this meeting was a waste of my time. I will see you in the judge's chamber."

CARRIE WENT FROM the governor's residence straight to the dispensary, where John was just finishing up with one of the Álvarez boys. The latest battle with his brothers had left this one with a sprained ankle and a broken toe, but he sat still while John bound the joint, and let no hint of pain show on his face. Probably because his mother stood there, watching.

There were no messages from patients waiting for Carrie, so she went into the house—blessedly shady and cool—to find it almost deserted. She was glad of the time to herself and went to sit in the magpie garden to think.

The birds were pleased with her company and put on a show to distract her.

Juvenile magpies were as lively and awkward as pups, and like all little creatures, they loved wrestling and wrangling, arguing and teasing. One of the smaller birds rolled over to wave its legs in the air, sending out an invitation that was quickly answered. Oddly enough, magpies clearly liked to be tickled, and that made her laugh out loud.

Almost in response a small magpie—she thought it must be the one Josefa called Guapo—landed on her knee.

It was quite a while later when she heard familiar voices in the kitchen and Lulu came out the side door in a rush. She stopped suddenly at the sight of Carrie surrounded by magpies.

She said, "Guapo doesn't like anybody but Josefa." Her tone was vaguely accusatory. Whether it was Guapo or Carrie who had disappointed her, she couldn't tell.

"He's testing me," Carrie said. "To see if I'm worthy. Come sit next to me, I think he was waiting for you."

For the next little while they did nothing but watch the magpies and listen as people came and went in the house, their conversations drifting out, Towa and English and Spanish.

Carrie bumped Lulu with a shoulder. "Do you want to come stay at our place tonight? I'd be glad of the company."

Lulu regarded her, her gaze suspicious. "But why? Are you afraid?"

That was a very good question, but she wasn't sure of the answer. Was she afraid of Kanti Chatham? Should she be?

"It's my nature to be cautious," she said finally. "No interest?"

The little girl gave a noncommittal shrug. "Chico would be glad to see me."

"Chico's across the road at Iñigo's," Carrie said. "You probably see more of him than I do."

A disgruntled Lulu stood up so abruptly that Guapo squawked and flew off.

"You haven't been paying attention," she said, her chin tilted up. "An hour ago Chico trotted right past here on his way home, following Eli. Does that mean I'm not invited to stay anymore?"

"Of course you're invited," Carrie said. "And now we're in a hurry."

59

IN THE SHORT walk home, Carrie tried to order her thoughts about the afternoon's meeting at the governor's residence. She wanted to give Eli a full picture of what had happened and what was coming, and at the moment she wasn't sure she could do that. But there was one thing she could do and would not put off any longer.

"Lulu," she said. "This may sound strange, but I need you to be cautious. If someone you don't know comes to the door or stops you in the plaza—or anywhere else—turn away, and come as quick as you can to me or Eli, or Eva, or any of the adults you know well."

There was suspicion and doubt in Lulu's expression, but nothing of fear. And Carrie was glad of it.

"You're not going to tell me why."

"Not yet. I need to talk to Eli first."

Just then they came around the curve in the lane, and there he was, standing in the open stable door of the home they shared. Covered with road dust, he put out clouds of sand as he walked toward her, his teeth flashing white against skin the color of old honey.

His kiss was quick and certain, a stamp of approval.

"I see you've brought Lulu home," he said. "Has she seen her room?"

It was like setting flame to tinder; Lulu dashed into the house and disappeared. Carrie put her forehead against Eli's shoulder and inhaled dust and the smells of the desert.

She said, "You need to change out of those clothes and take a bath. And I'll find something for you to eat."

He laughed. "I'm happy to see you, too, wife."

When she looked up at him, he started, as if there were a gaping wound on her cheek, one he hadn't known about or imagined. Carrie was generally quite good at hiding her emotions, but he saw right through her.

"Come fill the bath," she said, pulling away. "I'll scrub your back and tell you the whole story."

It was past sunset by the time they had a chance to really talk. There was a meal to get ready, and chores for both of them. Lulu went to the stable with Eli to help with the horses, and for the whole time she had an animated discussion with not Eli, but Chico.

Finally, when they had eaten and washed and finished with the chores, Lulu announced that she was tired and going to bed.

Eli had worried that the small room where he had built a bed and put up shelves would be too simple for Lulu, raised with her mother's insistence on excess.

"She likes her room," Carrie said. "She's a little girl. Of course she is delighted."

He shrugged, a shifting of a shoulder. "She likes the door, mostly."

With that, Carrie realized that she had been thinking like a *gabacha*. Like the foreign white woman she still was.

In Santa Fe—in the entire territory—the houses of all but the wealthiest were divided into rooms that were kept separate by hanging a piece of fabric or weaving, if at all. But not here. Eli had built this house with doors to close off certain rooms, and she hadn't recognized the significance.

"Ah," she said. "It's the privacy. It must feel magical to her. A place to keep secrets, to sit and watch the moonrise—"

She stiffened.

"What?"

"Where is Chico?"

Confused, Eli sat up to study her face in the light of the lantern.

"I don't mean to startle you," Carrie said. "But Chico should sleep in her room. I'll go—"

He was already out the door before she could finish the sentence, and back in less than a minute.

"All right. She's got Chico on the floor beside her bed. Now you want to tell me why she needs protecting?"

It didn't take quite so long as Carrie feared to recount the whole story, from that first day on the trail until today's confrontation in the governor's parlor. Eli listened, all his attention focused on her face, and never interrupted.

When she had almost finished, she realized a headache had settled between her brows, but she would be thorough.

"The last thing she said to me when I was leaving the governor's house has been echoing in my mind ever since."

"Get it out now," he said. "Or she'll be showing up in your dreams."

"There's no room in my dreams for Kanti Chatham," Carrie said. "Martha would make short work of her."

"Is there some reason you don't want to tell me what she said?"

She shook her head so that her plait fell over her shoulder.

"I was almost out the door when she called after me, 'Have Lucinda ready at eleven tomorrow morning for my first visit.' As if it were already decided, and there was no way to stop her from taking Lulu."

Eli lay back, one wrist under his head, and made a deeply contemplative noise.

With that, Carrie realized that she should have known how he would react. He was constant and rational, and almost more important, he was secure within himself and trusted his own instincts. In this case his instincts told him that caution was called for. She considered herself constant and rational but lacked his certainty. Beyond that, Eli knew this place, and she did not. It was very good to have him at home.

He took in everything she had to tell him and arrived at a simple conclusion: Mrs. Chatham's appearance in Santa Fe was no more complicated than a greedy relative determined to lay claim to as much as possible. If she hadn't set her sights on Lulu as a way to achieve that goal, it would be easy enough to ignore her until she ran out of steam.

"Yes," Carrie agreed. "But Mr. Bixby told her that there was nothing in the estate beyond unpaid bills. Doesn't she believe him?"

Eli held out both arms and shrugged. "Dishonest people assume everyone is dishonest. Or maybe there's something else going on we haven't figured out yet. Best we get everybody together to talk it through."

He took a moment to put out the lantern, and she watched the play of light on his face, the way shadow cast a mask that made him into someone she hardly knew.

60

WHEN CARRIE HAD explained the situation in the simplest terms to
the group gathered in the Benenati *placita*, Iñigo stood up abruptly.

"Hay una solución fácil."

The older man's easy solution was simple in at least one way. Mrs.
Chatham would disappear into the desert and never be seen again.
He assured them that it would not be much of a challenge.

This casual suggestion that Mrs. Chatham be disposed of would
have shocked any of the women Carrie had known in New York City;
here, it shocked nobody at all. Carrie saw that Eva was angry, but not
about the idea that Mrs. Chatham should die. Her concern was for
Lulu alone. Violante was put out by her husband's suggestion.

"Don't be foolish," she told him. "The idea is to keep our girl safe,
not to put you in front of a firing squad."

"We can agree on that," said Dr. Benenati in a soothing voice. "No
firing squads."

Violante raised one sparse white eyebrow and tilted her head to the
side. "I can imagine the *tejana* in front of a firing squad."

Carrie wasn't quite sure how serious this debate was, but her growing disquiet ebbed when the subject changed. They were all aware of Lulu, who sat nearby and was following the discussion closely.

Eva said, "Lulu could stay with me. The Chatham woman wouldn't dare look for her there."

"If we try to hide Lulu away, people will think we're up to no good," Josefa pointed out.

Lulu put her book aside and spoke to them all. "I can hide myself away, you know."

The serious mood in the *placita* slipped, just for that moment, while each of them remembered the times they had searched for a little girl who didn't care to be found.

"In fact," Lulu went on, "hide-and-seek is my favorite game. But who am I hiding from? Who is the *tejana*?"

All eyes turned to Carrie.

"She's a relative of your mother's. A half sister coming here from Richmond."

There was nothing of surprise in Lulu's expression. Nothing of happiness or fear, either. In an oddly patient tone that might have originated in a classroom, Lulu set about correcting Carrie's mistake.

"That's not right. My Aunt Aurelia lives in New York. She's married to Uncle Dr. Michael, and they are coming to get me. So I can live with them where there's no adobe and no mountains or desert, not even burros. Just a flat place with tall buildings and trains and a lot of white people."

This was not the best time to try to give the girl a better understanding of New York, but more to the point, it would be best to avoid any detailed discussion of her future there. In fact, they hadn't yet had word from Dr. and Mrs. Colby.

Eva went to sit beside Lulu. "I think this aunt must be a good deal older than your mother, so they didn't grow up together. That might explain why you haven't heard of her. In any case, she's here and she wants to meet you, because you are her family."

Lulu's frown deepened, but she listened as Carrie and Eva outlined the little they knew, supplemented with what could only be surmised. They believed that Lulu's Grandfather Ewell had married twice. With his first wife, he had a daughter called Kanti. Later he married again, and Indira was born to his second wife. Finally, Indira Ewell married Samuel Markham, and came with him here to Santa Fe.

"Then they had me," Lulu finished. "So Aunt Tejana wants to see me, now that Mama is dead?"

There was a fraught silence while some of them tried not to laugh in surprise. Carrie cast a fierce look around the *placita*, and silence fell.

"Aunt Kanti, or Aunt Chatham." Carrie said this with no trace of humor.

Distracted for the moment, Eva said, "He named his daughters Kanti and Indira. Unusual."

"Indira is Sanskrit for 'beautiful one,'" Lulu announced. And in response to the surprise she saw around her: "My mother told me so."

Dr. Benenati inclined his head. "Your Grandfather Ewell was a Sanskrit scholar, if I remember correctly. The names Kanti and Indira are probably well-known in India."

Lulu turned to Eli to ask a question, her jaw set in a resolute line. She wanted answers, and thought he would provide them.

"How does Aunt Coyote even know about me?"

Carrie didn't for one minute believe that the substitution of *coyote* for Kanti was accidental, but at this point there was a bigger issue to handle.

Eli said, "My guess? Someone wrote a letter when you were born."

She was doubtful. "You think my father wrote to Aunt Coyote? Or to the Sanskrit man?"

At that moment Carrie remembered her discussion with Dr. Markham about his wife's condition, her first morning in Santa Fe. He hadn't denied the symptoms or what they meant: his wife was suffering from puerperal madness, and so he had written home to see if there might be someone who could dedicate herself to caring for her in her extremity. Maybe he had written to his wife's half sister, or to her father.

This made her wonder about Dr. Markham's correspondence. Someone had gone through his office, almost certainly Mr. Bixby. But what had happened to the doctor's papers?

Lulu had more questions and was quite unhappy that no one had answers for her.

Eli said, "We aren't sure what she wants, except that it has to do with you."

"Well, I'm not afraid of this trickster aunt." Lulu brushed off her skirt in a dismissive way. "Let her come so I can ask her questions."

THE BENENATI HOUSEHOLD went on high alert, the women determined to show the *tejana* that Lulu was brought up in a bright, cheerful, and, above all, clean household. Every floor was swept, every surface polished; rugs and cushions were taken out to be beaten free of dust; glass, silver, and pewter were buffed.

Just before eleven, Madu, Violante, and Manuela went off, only to come back more formally dressed.

Lulu liked having *las abuelitas*—her little grandmothers—gathered like this, on chairs that Carlos set out specially for them. The three sat shoulder to shoulder like a trio of judges waiting to hear testimony.

Carrie took a moment to consider how Kanti Chatham would react—not to Lulu but to the people gathered here. Half of them white, half Indian or Mexican or Mestizo. In the governor's parlor there had been only white men. Mrs. Chatham had been determined to impress them and win them over to her cause, but this crowd she might not even acknowledge.

⧉

ELI DECIDED SOME heavy-handed praise was called for. He leaned down to whisper to Carrie.

"Have some faith, Ballentyne. Lulu and her *abuelitas* will make short work of Aunt Tejana."

Someday soon he would tell Carrie some of the old stories about the trickster coyote, whose schemes to get the better of everyone—anyone—always went awry. He schemed and maneuvered but never came out where he wanted to be. Though Eli had yet to see this Mrs. Chatham, he had the sense of her as a trickster and thus someone who would bring herself down.

But this fancy woman who had them all worried surprised him. She stood at the door alone. No bodyguard, no sheriff, not even an attorney. No officers from Fort Marcy, nobody from the governor's office.

She stood in the *placita*, very much at ease. Her eyes moved from face to face, pausing to consider Eva, and then settling on Lulu.

Beside Eli, Carrie shifted uneasily. Her impulse would be to greet the woman and offer her common courtesy: a seat, something to drink, introductions all around, empty talk of the weather. He was not surprised that she resisted the impulse. Eva, of course, did not resist at all.

"Mrs. Chatham," she said. "We meet again."

This took Lulu by surprise, and she slanted a sharp look in Carrie's direction, as if she had been found out in a lie.

"We forgot to mention that to you," Carrie said. "Mrs. Chatham spent a day on the trail with us."

Lulu was truly irritated, and her whole face transformed to tell Carrie that she had misstepped. It was then that shouting in the street put a quick end to the already awkward visit.

61

CARRIE WOULD WONDER, later the same day, if it wasn't a good thing that the visit had been interrupted just then. John shouted for help from the dispensary, and Carrie paused for the briefest moment, looking first at Mrs. Chatham and then Eli.

He put a hand on her shoulder and urged her forward.

"I'll be here to look after Lulu."

"And see Mrs. Chatham out?"

"First thing."

Carrie followed Dr. Benenati into a dispensary crowded with agitated men, not a white face among them. It took just a few words from the doctor to clear the room, but the crowd didn't go far. They lingered outside the dispensary to wait for news.

The man on the examination table was known to Carrie. Emilio Garcia owned the largest apothecary in town, a popular gathering spot on the plaza, at least for Spanish speakers. He was a careful, polite man and, insofar as Carrie had observed, an excellent apothecary with a wide understanding of medicines and herbals favored by everyone from the German dentist to *ciboleros* to *tejanos*.

Now he sat on the table, every muscle twitching in a face awash in blood from a gash on the brow.

Dr. Benenati was peeling away the towel that Mr. Garcia held to his head, making soft clucking sounds. *"Milo, mi amigo,"* he said, utterly calm. *"Ha surgido una fuga."*

In fact, Mr. Garcia had sprung a leak, but that was not hugely alarming; even minor scalp wounds were notoriously bloody. Dr. Benenati got to work, Carrie supplied materials, and in a short time the wound had been cleaned and dressed. The row of six neat stitches looked something like a third eyebrow in the middle of Mr. Garcia's forehead, but more unsettling was the bruise on his throat that was blooming in dark blues and angry greens.

Carrie had questions she could not ask, given the man's age and social standing. Dr. Benenati had no such limitations.

"You've got lumps and bruises coming up, big ones. Who did this to you?"

The patient coughed, and held up a palm to indicate his larynx was not cooperating.

"I will tell you," Mr. Garcia said finally, his voice so raw and rough that Carrie thought there must be significant damage to his throat.

"Purdy did this," he said. *"Con su bastón."*

Carrie had never met Jack Purdy, the quartermaster at the military garrison, but she had heard the stories. The man had a trigger temper, and he also had a fighting cane, a *bastón*. Custom made back east, people said, of hickory with a brass handle. Soldiers who crossed Purdy were introduced to the cane, and spent weeks in the military hospital recovering. How Purdy evaded repercussions was a subject of wide speculation.

"Rest," Dr. Benenati said to his old friend. "You'll have a bitch of a headache in short order."

Emilio Garcia looked up at them with a sorrow so clear on his face that Carrie felt the force of it like a shove.

"You know I can't," he said. "I have to turn myself in before Chucho comes looking for me."

Dr. Benenati frowned. "And why would he do that?"

One thin shoulder jerked up. "Because I shot Captain Purdy. I was aiming to kill him, but I only got him in the shoulder. Too bad, eh?"

MRS. CHATHAM WAS nowhere to be seen when Carrie went back to the *placita* to take her place beside Eli, but everyone else was there listening to Mimi Torres, who had just arrived. She came especially to share the news—a job she enjoyed and considered her right, as one of the oldest women in Santa Fe. Her job, she would tell anyone, was to educate those who were too busy or lazy to go investigate for themselves. The story of the fight in the apothecary she told with the vigor and excitement of a young man who had just come back from his first battle. It might have been something to smile about if the subject weren't so dark.

It all began, she told them, when Captain Purdy came to the apothecary looking for Garcia, and instead found Paco, Milo's twelve-year-old grandson, talking politely with three older women who were arguing with each other about the cost of beeswax.

"And what does he do, this *malvado hombre*?"

She turned her head to spit. "He pushes the old women out of the way and starts to yell at Paco. He pulls out a pouch and scatters what's inside all over everywhere, shouting, '*Punche! Punche!* You sold me disgusting *punche* tabac. I paid for white tabac, and you give me fuckin red tabac.'

"He is screaming like a panther now, and Paco is backing up, arms over his head, shaking and shivering he's so scared. He can't answer questions, but Purdy keeps shouting. And then he goes quiet for just a second and his eyes open wide and he decides that Paco isn't answering him because he don't speak English."

Mimi stuck out her chest and thumped it with a fist like a commander about to dispatch troops. "'This is the United States of America.'" She belts this out in a deep bass. "'You speak English here, or you can get your sunny brown ass back over the border where you belong! English! Do you hear me, *chinchudo?*'

"So Paco puts the big heavy canister of tabac on the table, but his hands are shaking so hard he can't pry the lid up. Purdy is leaning down to shout at him, sputtering, when the lid comes unstuck and goes flying. And that was the moment—"

Mimi paused, finger raised, as if she didn't already have their attention.

"At that moment Purdy turns as red as chili peppers in September and slams his cane down so hard that the counter—the very counter!—splits, right down the middle, and everything shoots off. Canisters crashing like artillery fire, I tell you. And now Paco is trying to get away. But Purdy—" She groped for the image she wanted.

"Like a wolf after a lamb. Like a wolf, I tell you."

She took a deep breath and assured them that someone—Mimi thought probably Tudesque, the silversmith, but maybe it was Samba, the baker—went running to get Garcia.

"Now, Milo rushes in and sees Purdy holding that *maldito bastón* over Paco, screaming curses. The boy is crouched in a corner, hands raised to protect himself. And what does Garcia do?" Mimi looked around, waiting for somebody to answer her so she could scold them.

"I'll tell you what Garcia does. He bellows like a bull and puts himself between Purdy and his grandson. But it doesn't help. Purdy wants Milo now. He wants to *pisarlo como una rata*. Like a rat! He starts to bring the *bastón* down on Milo's head, but you remember how quick Garcia is, like a *saltamontes*, a whippersnapper—is that the right word? No, it's grasshopper! He moves like a grasshopper! He grabs the captain's ankle and the big man falls flat on his ass. Right into the mess from the counter, including all the broken glass."

She paused to smile at the memory. Eva was smiling, too, as were Josefa and Carlos. For her part, Lulu just looked weary and confused, ready to fall asleep on the first comfortable lap she could find. But Mimi was telling her story, and common courtesy kept the little girl where she was.

"Now Purdy is really mad. Still on the floor, he swipes at Milo with the *bastón* and catches him and *oh qué bofetazo!* Right across the throat. Milo starts honking like a goose, trying to get his breath, and Purdy is screeching about glass shards stuck you know where, and you know what happens then? You think maybe Purdy threw up his hands and gave in?"

Her mouth puckered, once again on the verge of spitting. "No," she answered her own question. "Not that one. Instead he goes staggering across the floor, still looking to break Milo's head. Except Milo's gone. We're all looking around for him and he's right there, down on the floor, searching through the mess for something. He sees Purdy coming and gets up, just a second too late. Purdy brings the damn *bastón* down on his brow."

Mimi clapped her hands twice, folded her arms, and sat down.

Madu jumped to her feet. "And then? What then? Spit it out, old woman."

Mimi shrugged. "So much talking. My throat is dry, and I could use—"

Eli put himself between the two old women, hands raised. "I heard the rest from Samba when he passed by a half hour ago. Purdy hit Garcia with the *bastón*—twice—and Garcia shot him before he could take another swing."

"Shot him?" Josefa stood, a hand pressed to her throat. Everyone was on their feet as if a fire alarm had started sounding from the church steeple.

"Shot him," Eli repeated. "That's what he was looking for, down on the floor. His pistol."

Iñigo shook his head sadly. "Milo was never any good with a gun."

"The bullet went through Purdy's shoulder," Eli confirmed. "Didn't hit anything vital."

What Carrie saw around her in the faces of the people she had come to like and care about was unmistakable: anger, shock, and fear.

It didn't matter what Purdy had done, how horrible his crime or well deserved the repercussions, if an army officer died at the hands of a Mestizo or Indian or Mexican, there would be revenge of the bloodiest sort.

"Tell the rest," Madu said.

"You know the rest," Eli told them. "They took Purdy to the army hospital, and Garcia came here to get fixed up. Then he went to turn himself in. He's probably sitting in the jail already, telling his rosary beads while he waits for the mob to come after him."

Carrie often took no note of the church bells tolling, but today she started at the sound.

"Is it really just noon? It feels like a week has passed since sunrise."

"It feels like a week since I last ate," Eli countered. His humor had turned dry and dark, but she understood why.

They had settled in at the table when Carrie noticed that Lulu was standing on the bench, arms at her sides, as if to make a speech. Most likely, Carrie was sure, about her aunt's visit.

Lulu said, "Aunt Tejana doesn't know any Spanish."

There was a grin lurking at the corner of the girl's mouth, as if her aunt's lack of Spanish were a good joke. The adults glanced at each other, shrugged their agreement, and went back to passing bowls and plates.

Dissatisfied, Lulu's voice rose to a higher pitch. "And that's good. I'm glad Aunt Coyote doesn't know any Spanish."

What Lulu wanted was attention, and to that end she was mocking her aunt. A stranger might well miss the sly tone, but Lulu was known to everyone at the table. Just now she wanted to make clear that she had an advantage over her aunt.

Lulu said, "If somebody doesn't speak your language, they can't really know you. You can sound polite and friendly when really—"

She broke off because Carrie stood up, letting her anger show.

"So you amused yourself, insulting your Aunt Chatham in Spanish."

Lulu lifted one shoulder and let it drop, a mulish look on her face. "Didn't hurt anybody."

"Except yourself. You were unkind, and worse, you took pleasure in being unkind."

The girl's expression flashed from surprise to embarrassment and to a white-hot, heartbroken anger.

"You don't know so much." Her chin tilted up.

Eli and Dr. Benenati both made deep sounds in their throats, and Lulu whirled in that direction to glare at them, her blush deepening.

"You, either! None of you know anything about Aunt Coyote. But I do. I know about her."

Josefa had been standing in the doorway and heard the whole exchange. Now she spoke to Lulu directly, and at the sound of her voice, the girl jerked. Josefa's few words in Towa were not so soft as they sounded, because Lulu deflated. Carrie was relieved to see it. The tears that ran down Lulu's cheeks were not about anger or frustration; somehow Josefa had managed to tap into the grief that Lulu had been holding back for so long.

The girl ran off, and Josefa followed her.

The group finished their meal in relative silence, talking for a brief minute about where Lulu should spend the rest of the day, which guards were on duty tonight, and what precautions needed to be taken. Josefa and Lulu never came back to the table.

62

THEY GOT ONLY as far as the grocer Aguilar before Carrie came up out of her thoughts and remembered Eli was beside her. She said, "I have to look in on Chabela. I might as well do that now. You could go ahead home, it won't be very long."

Eli wondered if she was ignoring the trouble coming at them, or truly unaware of it. Before he could think how to say this, she poked him gently. "Don't whine. I really won't be long."

"Carrie," he said. "I'll be waiting for you right here."

She was confused, and that suited Eli in this moment. He was confused himself.

"Is this about Mr. Garcia?"

Before he let his temper get the better of him, Eli took a close look at her face. What he saw there was concern that had nothing to do with her own well-being or safety. Her concern was for Garcia, whose fate was already sealed. Eli calmed his voice and laid it out as plain as he could.

"It's about Garcia, yes. But more than that, it's about a Mexican who shot a white army officer. In self-defense, sure, but that doesn't matter. Not to the army. They took this land away from Mexico—who took it away from my mother's people first—and conquerors can be depended upon to do one thing: remind everybody else that the whip hand is theirs. Before morning, soldiers will break into the jail to grab Milo. They might hang him, but more likely they'll be in a hurry, and they've all got guns. Never underestimate an army's blood-lust."

He forced himself to stop. She knew about the rebellion at Taos, but she didn't know what part he had played in it. When word came to them about the siege, he was the only son allowed to ride out with their father, but it was all for nothing. They could not get near the pueblo, and so they watched the army flex its muscle. The colonel in charge of putting down the rebels showed no mercy, and so Eli learned what an artillery barrage did to adobe and wood and human flesh. Colonel Price's men had enjoyed their work, chasing down survivors to execute them on the spot.

He had meant to shock her with the simpler truth of what the Fort Marcy garrison was capable of, but somehow he had given more away. There was an alertness, a compassion, in the way she looked at women in pain. He saw something of that on her face now.

"You needn't worry," she said. "I'm not so naive as you seem to believe." She went up on tiptoe to kiss him, right in the middle of Santa Fe. "I shouldn't be more than a half hour with Chabela."

Then she was gone, leaving him there awash in memories he would do almost anything to be free of.

CARRIE SPENT TIME with a new mother not just to make sure she was healing but also to see how she was coping. Chabela looked, as most women do so soon after giving birth, exhausted.

Her son was unhappy too. When the newborn was minutes old, Madu had looked at him and grinned, telling Inez that her first grandchild would keep them all hopping. That might well be true; certainly he was testing his mother's goodwill right from the start. The longest he had slept peacefully, according to Inez, was two hours.

Chabela started when she heard her mother say this, and would have protested, but Carrie interrupted. She waited until Inez had left the room with the baby, and turned to Chabela to tell her what she needed to hear.

"Time has no meaning when you've got a newborn. In time—it might be days, but probably weeks and maybe even months—he'll settle and find a rhythm. Until that happens, you have to take advantage of the help you're offered. And if it's not offered, you must ask for help. Hand the boy over to your mother or an aunt or a cousin so you can sleep without interruption for a few hours at a time. Stop up your ears so you don't hear him yelling, and sleep."

Chabela, red-eyed, could only nod.

"Sleep now. You don't need to worry about him until it's time for his next feeding."

In the kitchen Inez held the boy, swaddled in homespun linen, not against her shoulder or in the crook of her arm. Instead she had one hand against his chest and one on his bottom. She held him at an angle that kept his head from falling back, and to Carrie, in that minute, it looked as though Inez was about to send him off like a rocket.

Then Inez began jiggling his bottom while she sang to him, and he took all this with nothing more than a wide-eyed stare. He looked as though he was falling asleep.

When he was calm, Inez passed him over to Carrie, who took a seat on the kitchen bench. She stretched his seven pounds out along the seam of her legs, his head at her knees, and paused to let him take in her smells. When she began the exam, he grumbled, and so she talked to him and told him about himself.

"Your color is very good," she began. "What an alert little boy you are. Your fontanelle looks to be pulsing just exactly as it should be. You've done a fine job keeping your lymph nodes in order and your liver too. No sign of jaundice. Just right. I always wonder how you do it, keep a tummy full of organs packed in the right order when you're so new to the business."

Her tone lulled him until she unwrapped the linen strip that covered his umbilical stump. Then he roused himself to protest. "I realize it's uncomfortable," she told him. "Don't make a face. Do you want to be the only little boy in the world without a belly button? No? Then you'll bear up for a good week or so while it's cooking. That's better. Just a minute more. Shall we have a look at your hips?"

Inez was watching closely. Her serious demeanor had relaxed while she listened to Carrie's patter, and now she shook her head in surprise.

"You are so good with him," she said. "He's a fine, strong boy, but not an easy boy."

Inez knew that few babies were easy at this stage, but she was nervous and overwrought, still dealing with what had been a difficult and traumatic birth.

Handing the baby back to Inez, Carrie said, "It's good Chabela has you and the rest of the family to help her."

Eli was waiting, but Carrie hesitated, wondering how much Inez knew about the violence at the apothecary and what was to come. Inez was Mexican, married to a Mestizo, so they would be vulnerable if things went badly.

In the end she took the simplest approach. "Will you be safe here tonight?"

Inez ran a hand down the baby's back, her gaze fixed on something far away that Carrie couldn't imagine.

"We will be safe enough," she said. "My Tavo and Chabela's Martin are making arrangements now. It's not the first time."

Carrie had questions she hesitated to ask for fear they would be too personal and intrusive, but there was one matter she hoped Inez would be willing to talk about.

"Explain to me, if you would, why the army officers don't close off the fort to make sure the troops can't—" She considered for a moment. "So they can't indulge their need for revenge."

"Oh, they will forbid the men to go into town," Inez said. "And then they'll look the other way when all hell breaks loose. Let me explain, because if you are going to spend your life here as the wife of a Mestizo, you need to understand."

She paced the room with the sleeping infant on her shoulder as she spoke.

"Most of the soldiers—maybe all of the soldiers, privates or sergeants or officers of any kind—to all of them, we are less than human. Anybody whose skin is darker than yours. So if one of us gives them even a flimsy excuse—" Her head averted, she was likely remembering other confrontations.

She cleared her throat. "We know how this goes, and we are prepared. I promise you."

Carrie liked Inez for her common sense and practical nature, and ventured one step further on that basis.

"It will sound childish, but I have to ask. Eli says there's no hope for Mr. Garcia. I take it you agree?"

Inez, mouth pressed into a hard line, nodded.

AT HOME CARRIE'S first impulse was to drop into bed and sleep for as long as the heat let her, but Eli had things to say. Serious things, things he meant her to take as gospel. The Gospel according to Eli.

As a girl she had listened to other gospels. Her father, her uncles, her grandfather, every one of them had rules for their wives and children that were not to be challenged. Most of those rules were reasonable and necessary. Most, but not all. Even at a young age Carrie had understood how serious the men were and at the same time she knew that her kinswomen had never learned the habit of blind obedience. None of them.

These were stories Carrie hadn't yet told Eli, and so she resolved to listen and save her reactions for much later.

Eli came to the end of his short lecture and, finally, smiled at her.

"I know you're not naive," he said, more softly now. "But you are still new here, and I can't bear the idea of something happening to you."

Carrie said, "Can we sleep for a while, do you think? I'd like to nap."

His smile was more open, almost as if she had pleased him with her lack of reaction. "Good," he said. "Let's sleep."

She woke toward evening to find Eli sitting beside the bed. He handed her a cup of water, and she drank it so quickly that she was rewarded with a throbbing pain between her eyebrows.

Eli's smile was easy now. Familiar. And there was a quirk to his mouth that she liked. He leaned close and whispered, as if there might be somebody listening.

"I'm gone for days, and remind me, did you ever welcome me home?"

Eli in a playful mood was a joy and a relief after such a day. There were things to talk about, but not now. Not this minute or hour or many hours. Here in their room she could quiet her mind. She could leave Santa Fe to its own designs and forget about vicious quartermasters and angry mobs.

She ran a finger from his knee upward until he grabbed her wrist and flipped her over. Their noses touched, and Carrie let herself feast on the sight and smell of him while he ran his nose over her skin, breathing her in. Impatient, she wiggled and he gave in with an exaggerated sigh, kissing her until her head began to spin. One hand had just closed over her thigh, his touch so gentle, almost tentative, when he lifted himself up and looked over his shoulder toward the front of the house.

"What?"

"Somebody at the door."

She grabbed his ear to keep him where he was. "Let's pretend we're not here."

"Too late."

"¡Hola!"

The voice was familiar and, under most circumstances, very welcome.

Andy Leroux was an old friend. Like Eli, he was a surveyor, but one who worked for the territorial government.

Eli swung his legs off the bed and sat up. "Do you think—"

"Yes." Carrie began to put her clothing to rights. "He's here because Helen has gone into labor."

63

ANDY LEROUX WAS the deputy surveyor for the territory, a position that the surveyor general would have given to Eli, if he had wanted it. The surveyor general had had a hand in Eli's training and held him in high regard, as Andy told the story.

"Eli knew better," Andy said. "He knew he'd hate it stuck in the middle of the territorial bigwigs with all their hemming and hawing and never being able to get a straight answer. He could do the work, eyes closed, but he told Pelham no thanks."

Carrie was glad to hear all of Andy's stories about Eli before she knew him. She liked this squarely built, ginger-haired, pale-as-milk Minnesotan for his sunny disposition, sincerity, willingness to tell stories, and insatiable curiosity.

He and Eli talked about everything, usually starting with work but then about things that seemed to interest most men: the weather, horses, arguments brewing between old rivals, wagon trains, the advancement of the railroad westward, and what the newspapers had to say about slavery, the compromise, and John Brown, and if this wasn't war, with towns being burned down and men setting up ambushes, then by God they should just get started. There was no peace to be made anymore, not in the Capitol, not anywhere. When they had come to that conclusion—as they always did—they started with the ongoing machinations of bishops and rebellious Mexican priests.

Once in a while, they would tell stories from their apprenticeship days, to great whoops of laughter. And when they had both had just a little too much to drink, they'd pay a visit to Rosita, and she would put them through their paces.

Carrie thought about this competition of theirs quite often, because it made her smile. People came from all over town to watch two grown men sitting side by side in front of a frowning Rosa. She held an old notebook close to her face and began to write with the stub of a surveyor's pencil, calling out numbers as she wrote them.

"*Dieciséis*," she began. "*Cuarenta y seis más treinta y nueve. Doscientos setenta-ocho veces doce.*"

Then a dramatic pause. "*Menos veintisiete. Más ochenta y ocho.*"

Eli and Andy added and subtracted and multiplied and divided at an astounding rate of speed. Other men in the cantina scrambled for paper and pen, in an attempt to join the competition. In her first experience of this odd game, Carrie had almost gasped when Rosa came to the end.

"*¡Divididos por doce!*"

Eli had closed his eyes and might have been asleep while he calculated, but Andy was a more entertaining contestant. He shivered and jerked and screwed up his face, crossed his arms and uncrossed them, jiggled one foot, and hummed. And then he exploded.

"One hundred thirty-two!"

His answer came in English, but nobody seemed to care or even wonder at this jump from Spanish to English. As it turned out, Eli had a slightly different total to offer, with memorable results.

For an hour the whole cantina debated. Rosa's list of numbers was appropriated and read aloud again, more slowly, and with a lot of critical commentary about her handwriting.

"What if you can't come to an agreement?" Carrie had asked, once they were home again.

"Never happens," Eli told her. "Everybody pretends to give in. 'Well damn, I see now. Should have . . . ' 'Of course not, I just forgot to . . . ' 'Don't be an ass, I can see for myself when I make an—'"

"That works?"

"Usually," Eli said.

It was at the first calculation competition that Carrie met Andy's wife, a cheerful, unflappable woman called Helen. Helen knew Eva and liked her, and she was the first to suggest that as soon as Eva was back in Santa Fe the three families should socialize.

Shortly after that first meeting in the cantina, Andy and Helen came to call in the evening. While the men talked about a piece of equipment that needed repair, Helen had gestured for Carrie to follow her out of the room. Almost certainly to raise the subject of her pregnancy and a birth that could be no more than weeks away. Helen was strongly built and looked to Carrie like the Scandinavians she knew at home. Ruddy cheeked, with thick blond hair, work-worn hands, and a belly close to popping.

"You're getting close," Carrie had said. "How are you feeling?"

"Oh, the usual complaints. My back, mostly. But I managed to birth our first two, I'll handle this one. Only one, I hope."

Carrie understood that Helen was worried, as every woman must, about surviving the birth. Both of them, mother and child, were at risk. But in this case Carrie could see there was something else on Helen's mind.

"Another set of twins has you worried," she said. "But it's not very likely."

Helen looked up at the ceiling and blinked hard, trying to hold back tears. "Ya? Well, my grandmother had three sets of twins. My mother had two."

There was little Carrie could offer her in the way of comfort. At least, nothing beyond goodwill and intentions to do everything in her power to help.

When Helen had composed herself, she looked at Carrie directly and managed a one-sided smile.

"I'm hoping you will come look after me, when things start to happen."

"Of course. But we should sit down so I can get a history first, if you can manage it. Come by the dispensary some morning when you're able."

Helen Leroux had come to see her at the dispensary the next day with her two little boys. Redheaded twins, three years old and as wild as fox cubs. Another set like these two was an idea that would have kept Carrie awake at night too.

"I tell myself that my boys haven't got the best of me, and if I'm lucky, this one will be a girl. A gentle, sweet girl."

Carrie wondered how much experience Helen had with little girls, and decided not to ask. More to the point, she wouldn't tell tales of the many little girls—family, friends, and patients—in her own past. Many of them capable of leaving Markus and Lars Leroux in the dust.

And now it had come so far; Andy was here to fetch Carrie.

"She says that she's right on the verge and she'd be glad of your help. I dropped the boys off with János and Magda Botka so you'll be able to hear yourself think. And to hear Helen holler, because she's good at that."

"She's on her own?" Carrie pitched the question so that there was no trace of disapproval, but she did find the idea unsettling.

"We have help now," Andy told her. "The Cabrera sisters are there with her. When I left, Helen had just set them to hauling and heating water, so probably we should get a move on."

Carrie was careful not to look at Eli, who had just recently explained that she should not, could not be out in the town until things had run their course with Milo Garcia. So now he had only two choices: he could refuse his good friend the help he had been promised, or he could walk his wife through Santa Fe and what was likely to be the scene of a bloody abduction. She hoped he would not try to forbid her to go. To publicly defy him would be a difficult breach to heal.

Andy was looking back and forth between Eli and Carrie, and it struck her then that it was odd that he didn't seem to be worried about the day's violence or the trouble ahead. Eli was having the same thought, because he raised the subject and told Andy what he had missed.

The color drained from his face quite suddenly, so that his freckles seemed to jump to attention.

Carrie gave Eli a pointed look. "No more discussion," she said. "I'll get my bag and we'll leave."

To her own surprise, this simplistic approach worked. In five minutes they were on their way to the Leroux house, situated just across from the newer Fort Marcy in one direction, and the territorial jail in the other.

They walked across town at a good pace, but not so fast that anyone would pay attention to them. In the plaza, groups of men, most of them Mexicano or Mestizo, stood together talking, heads bowed. They spoke to each other, but all eyes were fixed on the narrow lane that ran between the Palace of the Governors and the courthouse. The jail was just there, out of sight, and in it sat the apothecary Garcia and other unfortunate prisoners waiting for the next visit of the circuit judge and their trials.

With Eli on her right and Andy on her left, they turned down the lane. They passed the jail and the courthouse stables and then, on their left, the southeast corner of the garrison. New Fort Marcy, as some called it.

Carrie hadn't yet toured the encampment and hadn't really been aware of how big it was, though people talked about it almost constantly. Many locals argued that they needed more troops. It might be true that this year, so far, there had been only some minor trouble with the Navajo, but you never knew. You just never knew with Indians. She had heard these phrases so many times that it made her want to scream.

Her opinion—had she dared to voice it—would be ignored. As a *tejana* she was, as they saw it, deeply and fatally misinformed.

They had discussed the matter just the day before. There was nothing Carrie could tell Eli that he didn't already know, but sometimes her temper got the best of her. "Eli," she had started. "Do the governors and landowners and the military really think the tribes will just give up and hand everything over? Don't they understand that the tribes will fight to the death for their way of life?"

His gaze was steady, and his tone solemn. "I remember you saying something like that to Rainey on the trip overland. I can't disagree."

Carrie was torn between letting this subject go and pushing onward. Plain speech.

She said, "To me, this is the hardest part. Because the governor and his people do know. They see the truth of what's happening to the tribes. They see but they pretend not to see. If you confront them, there will be outrage or—worse, in my view—amusement. Later, out of my hearing, they will tell each other that *tejanas* were just not made for the climate. Or the politics."

She drew in a shaky breath, ready to give up this useless diatribe, but Eli waited and she carried on.

"I haven't even touched on the Mexicans. In Washington the Congress congratulated themselves on taking so much land from the Mexican government, but they can't decide what to do with the Mexicans themselves. Make them U.S. citizens? Please. The argument about color will go on for years, believe me."

She had confused him. "Um, color?"

"Color," she repeated. "If the politicians decide that Mexicans are white, then they have to be given the full rights of citizenship. If they lump them in with the tribes, then that is not so much a problem, but there would be more reason to fear rebellion. Who could deny any of that, and who can talk about it with any degree of calm?"

"You mean Eva," he said.

"Eva, yes, who lost her sister and husband to the Comanche. The Apache took everything from John Edmonds. Mrs. Carson's parents were killed in a raid on their wagon train, and there are others. A lot of them. So it's not a subject that can be discussed objectively. Certainly, the emigrants don't care to talk about the effects they have on the tribes. *Filthy animals.* I've heard Pueblos called that."

Her voice cracked. Eli pulled her close and tucked her head beneath his chin.

"You are always at the mercy of your anger," he said softly. "It leaves you no room to breathe."

THE WHOLE CONVERSATION came back to Carrie as they passed Fort Marcy, and with that she realized that her hands were trembling not in fear, but anger. Eli knew her well. Anger drove her, she could admit that to herself and even to him, but recognizing the truth of a thing didn't mean you knew how to change it, or even whether it needed changing.

Andy, unaware of the battle being fought in her head as they walked along the cordillera, was pointing out things he thought might interest her. The home of the bank president got a longer description. It was as big as the governor's residence and built of brick rather than adobe. There was no sign of life, and that was by design. They would all be in the *placita*, sealed off from the town but not from the sky overhead. Helen's two boys would be there too. She hoped Mrs. Botka was equal to the challenge.

The next house was Andy's. It was much smaller than the banker's residence and made of adobe, but not small when seen in comparison to most of the houses in Santa Fe. There was a recessed porch that would be in the shade for much of the day, and she was fairly sure that Andy had added it in an effort to make the mud house—as easterners referred to adobe—more comfortable and appealing. There were also windows on the outer walls, another indication that this was recently built for a *tejano*.

The property was bordered by large boulders, and on every one of them sat two or three *correcaminos*, the odd, long-legged birds that ran everywhere, as if they had no wings to fly with. The birds scattered suddenly, but not because people approached. They scattered because a spiraling wail was coming from the house.

"You see how it is," Andy said, picking up his pace. "When Helen gets to hollerin, everybody pays attention."

It did happen, now and then, that a birth was over before Carrie came through the door. Today Carrie was greeted by the sight of a crowning skull covered with wet red hair.

Things moved very quickly. Carrie shooed the dumbstruck Cabrera sisters away; she closed the door in Andy's face and settled in front of Helen, who was crouched with her back against the wall, the tile floor slick with sweat and amniotic fluid.

"Just in time," she said to Helen. "This child is rotating to show us the face under all that hair. And here we are . . . the brow and . . . goodness."

Helen jerked, spraying Carrie with perspiration. "What?"

"All is well."

"Is there something wrong with the eyes?"

"Nothing at all. Just wide open, scowling at me. In just a minute more—"

Before her head was entirely free, Helen's first daughter opened her mouth to squeak, and then launched into a wobbling, distinctly displeased wail. Carrie swaddled the girl hastily and handed her to Helen. A compact nugget of a child, blazing with life, covered in waxy white vernix.

"She's beautifully rounded, elbows, knees, and belly," Carrie said, loud enough to be heard in the next room and over the wailing. "A perfect human being, but already at odds with the world."

"Ah," Helen said, her hands closing over the baby. "Well then, we'll have to call her Annie. After my mother. And it's starting again. Didn't I tell you so?"

From the next room, Andy called, "I'm happy with girls, Helen. You were hoping for girls, too, and now we've got 'em."

"Hold on . . ." Carrie called. "This next one could be a boy."

"Poor Annie, if that's the case," said the new father. "Three big ginger-headed brothers, that's nothing I'd wish on anybody."

It was some time before things were calmer. The second twin, just as wide-eyed as her sister but without the grumbling, brought a little breathing room with her.

"Daisy," Helen announced. "For Andy's mother."

"She's the more composed of the two," Carrie said. "She'll be the voice of reason."

There were tears running down Helen's cheeks, but she managed to laugh at the same time.

"Have you not met our Lars? The quieter twin always hatches the wildest schemes."

Carrie thought of the twins in her own family and couldn't disagree.

Helen drew in a shaky breath. "Four redheads. I told Andy that two were enough, but did he listen?"

"You can't blame Andy," Carrie said, trying to strike a playful tone. Always difficult with a newly delivered mother.

"I can blame Andy," Helen insisted. "I do blame Andy. Ginger-headed sweet talker. Oh, he gets his way, he does, the Great Seducer."

"Can I come in now?" Andy stood at the door, blushing a particularly deep shade of pink at odds with his red hair. Carrie concluded that he was embarrassed to have heard himself described as a seducer. She got up to step out for a few minutes, pausing to look closely at Helen, who had put both girls to the breast while Andy looked on, blinking away tears.

"I'm in the next room," she said. "Call if you need me."

Carrie needed water and something to eat, but first of all she wanted Eli and news of what was happening in town. She thought she'd find him waiting for her in the *placita*, but the space was only dimly lit by a lantern on a side table, and empty.

The sounds of the house were all familiar: the thin wailing of newborns, the murmur of adult voices, water being poured from one vessel to another. Nothing of Eli. Another minute and she realized that

Lupe and Consuela were in the workroom off the kitchen. Eli liked to listen to stories told by younger people, and she expected to find him there.

The Cabrera girls—young women, really, almost old enough to marry—were still busy with buckets of water and piles of linen to be washed. There would be a great deal of laundry in this house for at least a year, but they looked capable and unfazed by the work. Lupe was the smaller of the two, pleasantly rounded with a dimple in her chin, and teeth, very white, that were just a little too big for her mouth. She glanced up at Carrie and hissed at her sister to get her attention.

"*¡La partera!*"

It suited Carrie to be seen first as a midwife, rather than a *gabacha* or the white woman who had married a Mestizo. She smiled and they took that as encouragement, glancing at each other to be sure they were not imposing before starting with their questions. They had many, about the birth and about Helen's condition, the newborns' health, how big they were, *las mujercitas*, and oh, by the way . . .

What they really wanted to talk about was one family with four redheaded children. Because if the *partera* wasn't aware, people thought that redheads—

"Are bad luck? I am aware," Carrie said. "But I also know many, many people with red hair. I have an aunt and cousins with red hair, and there is nothing bad or evil about any of them."

Lupe did not hesitate to challenge Carrie's expertise, using her dimple and smile to soften what many would take as an insult. How many redheaded *tejanos* could there be? How many could Carrie truly know?

Carrie let out a small laugh. "Do you realize that in some parts of the world, red hair is quite common? Ireland and Scotland, for example. My father was a Scot." She stopped herself before she added that he had been dark haired.

One more glance between the sisters. Very politely, Consuela said, "Will you tell us about those countries sometime? Would people like us be allowed to visit there?"

Carrie bit back her smile. "It would be my pleasure. But for right now, do you know where Eli has got to?"

As it turned out, he had left her a note. A scrap of paper, and written on it a single word: *Witness*.

Carrie walked out of the house and stood in the road looking toward town. There was more of a crowd now, and great agitation was obvious even from this distance. As was to be expected. A riot, a public hanging, a slave auction: bloodletting and misery drew crowds in a way a fair or market could not.

With *witness* Eli meant to explain his reasoning and excuse what was, in Carrie's view of things, inadequate. He meant to defuse whatever anger she was feeling. And of course she could say without hesitation that Milo Garcia deserved a reliable witness, most especially in this situation. A well-respected, educated, sober witness. Eli had many friends among the Mexicans, but he was himself not Mexican. Then again, he was also not white.

The noise from town was building. Carrie told herself to go back and see to Helen, but a sudden, ungodly screaming rose up and up, and then came gunfire. First a stuttering: one, two, three, then a full rush and too many shots to count. Eli had been right; the mob from Fort Marcy was too impatient for a hanging.

With the last gunshot, silence fell, as if a faucet had been turned. It was something that surprised her, the way the fury of the crowd could suddenly abate. It wouldn't last, and in fact the crowd was already churning like a nest of wasps roused to defend the hive.

It occurred to her at this late point that there could well be people with injuries at the dispensary while behind her was a newly delivered mother, her first and primary responsibility. And of course there was the question that might not find an answer for some time to come. Eli could be alive or dead or a prisoner accused of treason. Those possibilities kept her where she was, unable to move, for a quarter hour or more. It took tremendous effort to turn her mind back to the newly delivered mother and her newborns, but she could do nothing for Eli while Helen might well need her. Helen did need her. She was turning back toward the house when she caught sight of a familiar figure running toward her through the deepening night.

He was moving fast, sure and steady. The blood running down his shirt shone black where it caught the moonlight. Then Eli came to a sudden stop in front of her. He was breathing hard, but if he was in pain, he kept that hidden away.

"Just a graze," said her husband. "It's already stopped bleeding."

Carrie gave him one long look and walked away back to her patient.

64

Just past midnight they walked home through the deserted plaza.

Carrie was struggling, but she was resolved to keep her anger to herself, for the moment at least. That meant she could not talk to Eli about anything of real importance. She would attend to practical matters, and started by sending him off to do her bidding.

Would he be so kind, she asked, as to light the biggest three lamps and bring them into the kitchen? And a bucket of clean water would also be welcome. Then the water would have to be heated, something he could do even with a graze on his head.

He raised a brow—still crusted with blood—but did as she asked. Then he stood in the kitchen in the light of the lamps and, without a word, stripped off his shirt. He sat on a stool, his hands fisted on his knees.

Carrie took up the examination of his stubborn and bloody head. The bullet had plowed neatly along the side of his skull just above the ear, five inches of a bloody trench that had not, as far as she could tell, touched bone. She used her fingertips, her face turned away, to trace his skull and found no evidence of a crack. Tonight and tomorrow he would have a headache. He might be deaf on the left side for a good while. She said none of this, because she didn't trust her voice. Instead she went on, listing for herself the things that needed to happen.

Carrie examined the wound again, and began the work of cleaning it. She was thorough, washing away dried and clotted blood, and using a scalpel to dig hair and grit out of the gash. Through all that, Eli sat quietly, made no complaints, and asked no questions, and Carrie felt another flush of anger.

She washed his entire head with a diluted solution of lye soap and clean water. Then she poured a liberal amount of her precious distillation of winterbloom and slippery elm into every inch of the wound, and paused until his tensed and twitching muscles relaxed.

"I suppose I should have warned you," she said. "It does sting. And now what to do with your wound. Pardon me, your graze. That's the question."

He cleared his throat.

Eli could deal with almost any pain, but he had a morbid fear of needles. This was one of the things Red Rosa had told her about her husband, a little nugget of information that she might not otherwise discover for a very long time. The older woman seemed to consider herself a kind of coach, her goal to provide the new wife with the information she would need to arm herself. There was a story behind his horror of needles, but she hadn't heard it yet and was glad, in this moment, that she'd never found a good opportunity to ask.

So, stitches. She could tell him he needn't worry; in this case, with a shallow wound that had been very thoroughly cleaned and would be cleaned multiple times a day, stitches weren't strictly necessary. For no good reason at all, she said none of that. Instead she said, "Six or maybe nine stitches should be enough."

He swallowed so hard she heard the muscles in his throat flexing.

Carrie studied the cup of his ear, where she had missed some dried blood. She asked herself how far she would push this very infantile, very rewarding small act of retribution.

"I'm thinking that maybe the stitches should wait until tomorrow," she said. Casually. "I'd like Dr. Benenati to have a look before I close it. And I'll need the bigger needle from the dispensary, though it is a little dull. But you're equal to that, I think."

He stood so abruptly that the stool went flying, then turned, and Carrie found herself lifted by the elbows until they were eye to eye and her feet were swinging.

"Just how long do you plan to torture me?"

Carrie met his scowl with one of her own. "Until I can put what you did behind me."

His grasp on her tightened. He brought her so close that she smelled the damp astringent on his scalp.

"I wrote you a note."

"Oh, please." She pulled herself out of his grasp and backed up until she hit the wall. "You were planning the whole thing from the minute we walked into the plaza. If not before. And for your trouble you've got a bullet wound."

"It's a graze!" Bellowing now, and she was glad of it. She knew how to respond to a man's bellow. She stepped toward him and lowered her voice to a hiss.

"A half inch closer, and it would have opened your skull and killed you. Are you so eager to be free of me?"

His breath caught. He turned away and then back, advanced so that she retreated, but he came on, until he lowered his head and she felt his breath on her brow.

"Carrie."

She waited.

"I have no intention of ever leaving you."

After a long moment, he said, "I'm sorry I scared you."

Carrie ducked away and left the kitchen. Over her shoulder she said, "We'll see about stitches in the morning."

The groan that came up from his gut was, she had to admit at least to herself, tartly satisfying.

———

THE NEXT DAY Carrie rose before first light and dressed quietly, hoping that Eli would sleep on. His morning would not be pleasant; the wound on his scalp meant a severe headache would soon make itself felt. And she was still angry, too angry, to sit across from him eating breakfast, but less angry than she had been. She was hesitant to put herself—or him—to the test. Better to wait and see him at midday. By then she could school herself not to react when his battered head came into view.

In the dispensary there was no one in the waiting area, but she heard men's voices from down the hall. Calm tones, no agitation, and still two newly built coffins stood leaning against the wall. She wondered if these were the last or if they would have to send for more.

"There you are." John Edmonds leaned around a doorway. "Could you possibly lend a hand—"

Carrie could, and did. She assisted Dr. Benenati as he straightened a broken leg and bound it; she dug dirt out of cuts and scrapes, cleaned and dressed them. A boy no more than fourteen had caught a bullet that drilled through his upper arm without causing major damage, but infection was a real threat and he would have to be monitored. His mother, her face immobilized by anger, sat next to the bed John had made for him, and would tend to his needs. If she didn't kill her son first.

For the rest of the morning, Carrie had no opportunity to rest or to find something to drink or even to think. Instead she heard the story of what had happened from a dozen men, some eager to talk, others compelled to confess, it seemed. Lucho Cabrera described for her how ten mounted men had come thundering out of the military reserve. Five had dismounted to force their way into the jail, while the rest served as a barrier to the crowd.

"They pointed their rifles at us. We have no weapons, but I swear some of them wanted to shoot us. They were just looking for an excuse."

This was one of the Juarez brothers, eager to tell her about Emilio Garcia's end.

"The soldiers, they didn't care who got in the way of the bullets. Eight men sitting there behind bars without even a stick to defend themselves, and the *esos malvados bastardos* kick in the door and start shooting. I can't believe only four died. The blessed Virgin must have been watching, that's the only explanation—" His voice broke.

"Do you know, have any more died?"

If she lied to him, he would never trust her again, but she didn't have the information he wanted. "Not all the injured are here," she said. "So we can't know how anyone is doing. We might never know how many died, in the end. The ones who are here, who found their way here, they will stay and get the help they need until they are ready to go home."

Joserra Barquero, an old farmer with cataracts that would soon rob him of the rest of his sight, was philosophical about the whole episode. Carrie wrapped a swollen wrist while he voiced his opinion.

"Milo was a good man. It's hard to be a good man, a good Mexican, here, where they treat us like animals. We can't even bury our people in the church graveyard. *Los diezmos son demasiado.* Who can afford the tithes?"

She heard about this last insult from many of the men. The dead would be buried ten or twenty or more miles away, where priests were more interested in people than pesos. In this heat they would be buried within a day, but justice and satisfaction would be a far longer wait.

In one way the territorial government, the army, and the Roman Catholic Church stood shoulder to shoulder: they depended on one another and were happy to overlook each other's sins, small and large. And all three ruled by degradation. Carrie had read everything she could find about the bloody uprising at Taos ten years before, and understood that Kearney's army had done everything possible to demean the Pueblos and Mestizos and Mexicans. All this time later they were still congratulating themselves, as if one battle in one war had ever put an end to the struggle for freedom or domination. They seemed to believe that the nations they had conquered, many hundreds of years older than their own, were incapable of rising again.

She was thinking about this as she pulled splinters out of the shin of a farmer who had got caught up in the violence. His name was Yayito Fernández, and he had come twenty miles to protest. Running across the plaza with the cavalry on his tail, he had been knocked to the ground. His serape got tangled in the wheels of a cart, and he was dragged halfway across the plaza before he had been able to free himself. In the end, most of his clothes were ripped away, leaving deep lacerations on his arms and legs, the kind of ugly wounds that invited infection, blood poisoning, and amputation. Even that might not be enough to save the man's life.

While she cleaned the muck out of his open wounds, he kept his misery to himself. Whether he was especially stoic or deaf Carrie couldn't tell at first. Not until she began to explain to him the nature of his injuries and the way he would have to treat his wounds. If he wanted to go home, he would have to be very diligent about keeping the wounds clean.

He blinked at her, shrugging as if she were telling him about a recipe for apple pie.

"*¿Me entiendes, señor?*"

"Sí," he said on a sigh. "Yes, I understand."

Carrie explained again, and again she got little more than a shrug.

There was just one thing that was perfectly clear: this dignified man who wouldn't flinch at having his wounds cleaned had no interest in whatever she wanted to say. There were many reasons this might be the case. Maybe he had lost friends during the riot and was overcome by sorrow; maybe her accent was too strong and he couldn't understand Spanish as she spoke it. And of course it was also possible that he—like many men here and everywhere—did not know how to take advice, much less instruction, from a *tejana*.

At one point she realized Josefa had come in and was waiting to talk to her. From her expression it seemed she had been observing for a good while. When Yayito waved off Carrie's attempt to explain once again, Josefa suddenly snapped to attention. She leaned over Yayito and spoke directly into his face, showing all the exasperation and frustration Carrie was forced to keep to herself.

"Now you listen to me."

That got her his undivided attention. She went on, brows lowered, in a rapid Spanish that Carrie was barely able to follow.

Was she, housekeeper to the doctor, to understand that he, Yayito Fernández, was ready to die? Because if that was his intention, he should start walking. Given his injuries it would take him until morning to get twenty miles, but once at home he could make arrangements quite easily and die in his own bed. Which would make a bed here in the dispensary available for someone who wanted to live. If in fact he did want to live, then he would listen to the *enfermera*'s instructions, and follow them exactly. Or his limbs would rot off.

Carrie appreciated her help, but it was hard not to make things worse by laughing at Josefa's closing statement: *"No seas tan testarudo."*

Testarudo was one of the first words she learned when she arrived in Santa Fe. Hardheaded.

Josefa was satisfied with his reaction, but told Carrie she couldn't wait. "They need me in the kitchen, and you're not finished. Can you find me after dinner?"

It was Carrie's firm intention to do just that, until an older couple brought in their son. Temo Sanchez was just twenty years old, a promising *cibolero*, still unmarried but interested in a particular girl, according to his mother. He would be the next person to die because a white man's pride had been injured.

The cause was plain to see: a deep purple-and-black bruise in the shape of a hoof that stretched from nipple to nipple. Broken ribs, punctured lungs: there was nothing even the best surgeon or hospital could do to save him. Carrie could not cure him, but she could provide answers to his parents' many questions, make sure that they had food and drink and a place to rest, and send for family members to mourn with them. And she could sit with them while he struggled to breathe. Until he stopped struggling.

SHE FOUND BOTH Josefa and Lulu in the magpie garden, just before siesta. Lulu sat away, back turned, building towers out of stone. She glanced at Carrie, her eyes swollen and red, and then she asked a question in an oddly dampened voice.

"Is Eli going to die?"

Carrie started. "You saw him at noon, didn't you? Did he look sick to you?"

She pursed her lips, dissatisfied. "He didn't eat with us."

Before Carrie could decide whether she should be worried, Josefa stepped in.

"He stopped by to say he was on his way to fix a pump at the convent. As a favor."

Lulu gave a very adult, very cynical snort while Carrie's mind scrambled for footing. Who had come to fetch him? When? How long? Then she settled on the important point: He wasn't lying dead at home; he hadn't collapsed in the plaza. He was out repairing a pump. She cleared her throat and talked to Lulu directly.

"He won't die of what happened to him last night. Someday he'll die like everybody dies, but not anytime soon."

A brow raised and hovered, the very picture of doubt. "Unless he's in an accident. Or somebody actually shoots him. You know, Carlos said he saw Eli get shot."

Josefa made a low growling noise in her throat. "That's not what Carlos said, Lulu. You remember better than that."

Her tone was sharp, but the girl either didn't notice or didn't care. She stood her ground.

"Maybe not," she said, chin lifting to new heights. "But that's what Carlos was thinking."

Carrie steadied her voice. "Whatever Carlos saw or said or thinks,

Eli is in no danger of his life." Perspiration was trailing down her nape, and she shivered with it. "He has a bloody gash in his scalp, but that is not something that will kill him. If he takes care of it properly."

In an effort to cut this distressing subject short, she turned to Josefa.

"Did you want to talk to me?"

"I wanted Lulu to talk to you," Josefa said. "She needs to tell you the story she told me."

"About Aunt Coyote," Lulu provided.

If Carrie wanted to hear what Lulu had to say, she would have to resist the urge to correct the girl. She pulled a stool over and sat down so that she could see both Josefa's and Lulu's faces.

"I'm listening."

Lulu's lower lip was sticking out, as a much younger child might do when she was reluctant or frightened.

"Go on," Josefa said. "Just start, and it will come on its own."

The little girl shrugged once, twice, and then she lay down on the ground on her belly, her face turned away. Josefa shook her head at Carrie, asking for her patience.

A full three minutes later, Lulu said, "It's about Hitty. Mama's cat."

Carrie made an encouraging sound. "Your Mama had a cat when she was a girl?"

"She wouldn't let me have one, but she did. She had a *gata mermelada* called Hitty. Marmalade. You know about marmalade cats?"

Hitty, Lulu explained, had long ginger fur and blue eyes and was smarter than all the other cats in the world. She would chase toys and bring them back and wait for them to be thrown again. And Hitty talked. Cat talk, but still, if you said something to her, she answered.

"Hitty sounds like an excellent cat."

Lulu sat up to tell the rest of the story.

"One day Mama woke up and Hitty had kittens. She had them right on the cushions, six kittens. Two marmalade, two white, and two *calicó*, that's white and marmalade and brown. Hitty was very proud of her kittens and so was Mama."

Josefa's attention was fixed on her work, but it seemed to Carrie that she was tense.

"Did your Mama keep all six of the kittens? That would have been a lot of work. And fun too."

Lulu turned to look at Carrie directly.

"No. She didn't keep any of them. Because they all died. And Hitty too. And that's why Mama said I couldn't have a cat, because no matter how careful you are, you can't keep them safe from mean people."

Saliva pooled in Carrie's mouth. Her first instinct was to walk away, but she needed to hear the rest of this story. "Somebody hurt Hitty and her kittens. Is that it?"

"Somebody killed them all. Somebody killed them all with a knife."

Lulu was watching, her eyes narrowed. This was a test that Carrie had to pass to be trusted. She kept her attention and concentration on Lulu and never looked in Josefa's direction.

"That's upsetting. Did she tell you who hurt Hitty and her kittens?"

Lulu sagged, as someone might do when she had put down a burden, and didn't care to pick it up again.

Carrie said, "*Lulu, no tienes que decir nada más.*" You don't have to say anything more.

Shifting to Spanish had an effect. Lulu sat up, her hands fisted in her lap.

"She said her big sister did it. She said her sister did it and laughed. Mama told her father, and he didn't believe it. And Mama said that she never spoke another word to her sister after that day, and never would speak to her so long as she lived because some people are too mean and evil and that I should stay far away from people like that. Like her. Aunt Coyote."

All emotion drained away from Lulu, leaving her as smooth and blank as the doll she had lost to her mother. She got up and slipped quietly away, back straight, shoulders squared. That narrow, slender back held so severely erect was a sight Carrie would not soon forget. For a long moment she sat and thought.

"Josefa, tell me. When did Lulu tell you this story? Was it yesterday midday?"

"Yes. When she ran away from the table, that was the start of it. Mrs. Chatham was more than she could handle."

This made sense to Carrie. A young girl who had just lost both parents, aware of violence in the town, and still no word from the family members in New York who were supposed to take her in. To all of this an aunt had arrived, one she was supposed to fear.

"I think you're right," she said to Josefa. "But to have told a little girl such an awful story. It's hard to imagine, even if Mrs. Markham thought she was protecting Lulu."

A small magpie settled on Josefa's knee and she whistled to it, for once unable or unwilling to look at Carrie directly. She seemed to be debating something with herself, and unsure about sharing it.

"Mrs. Markham," she said slowly. "Mrs. Markham was troubled, but not in the usual way. Women who come from the East, especially the ones from wealthy families, they never tire of complaining about being here."

"That's true." Carrie had to smile. "Some keep it to themselves, for the most part, but I can't think of one emigrant who believes she's better off here than she was in the East. Reizl may be the exception to the rule, I suppose."

Another magpie joined the one on Josefa's knee and began to squabble with the first, a noisy exchange that stopped their conversation. When Josefa had had enough, she shooed them off. "*Pájaros bobos.*"

"They may be silly birds," Carrie said. "But they amuse me, and I need some amusement just now."

Josefa's smile, rare as it was, gave Carrie some courage to continue.

Carrie said, "Women who grow up in wealthy families in the East generally like to talk about what they've left behind. What they've given up. Their sacrifices."

"That's how she was different," Josefa said. "Mrs. Markham never talked about her family. Did you not notice?"

"I did," Carrie said. "But more than that, I wondered why she chose to marry Dr. Markham. A marriage that meant leaving everything familiar behind her. She gave up the comforts many consider crucially important. That she missed. But why? Because she fell in love? She was young when she met Sam Markham, certainly, but I can't imagine her—even as a girl—so much in love that she would walk away from everything she valued."

"Unless she was desperate to escape an older sister."

They were silent for a moment, both considering what this would mean. Casual cruelty between sisters was nothing out of the ordinary, but the slaughter of pets, that was madness.

Carrie tried to make the many pieces in this puzzle come together, something she had been doing for weeks without success. But there was something new to add to the equation.

"So she gives up her life to escape her sister and possibly her father. She marries, comes here, and finds out—what? That her husband isn't trustworthy? That he visits prostitutes? That they are in debt?"

Josefa spread her hands over her lap. "*Las heridas se ensucian y supuran.* I don't know the English."

After a moment the words ordered themselves in Carrie's mind. "'Wounds worsen and fester,' I think that would be the translation. I was thinking along the same lines."

"Fester," Josefa echoed. "Yes, if a wound is not aired, it festers. My mother was here last night, did you know? In case any of our people needed help."

"I didn't know. I'm sorry I didn't get the chance to meet her."

Josefa tilted her head, and it seemed just then that she was tempted to smile.

"While she was here, she talked to Lulu, for quite a long time."

Carrie waited for Josefa to order her thoughts.

"She talked to me later, not so much about Lulu as Lulu's mother. She said to me that Mrs. Markham loved her daughter and wanted her to be safe, but she didn't want Lulu to *feel* safe."

She looked more closely at Carrie.

"You don't understand, and I didn't, either, not at first. But I think I do now. Mrs. Markham grew up in a family where she never felt safe. She needed to know her daughter was like her, and that meant Lulu would have to suffer as she had suffered. That's why she told her daughter this story about the dead cats. And maybe other stories. In time she may find the courage to tell us."

"I will have to work up my courage when that day comes," Carrie said.

"I'll go check on her now," Josefa said.

EVA HAD BEEN gone for a few days, off to visit her father-in-law and fetch Beto home after a long stay with his grandfather at the Pontevedra Hacienda. Carrie liked Beto and looked forward to seeing him, but today she was glad to find out that he hadn't been able to wait for siesta and had fallen asleep over his dinner.

Sitting with Carrie in the small shaded garden behind the *cacharrería*, Eva explained. "It's always difficult for him, leaving me to go there, and leaving his grandfather to come home again. He finally keeled over and he'll sleep now, if the fates are kind, until early morning."

"Lulu has been at odds and ends too."

Eva raised a brow. "I knew there was something up with you. Is there news about Coyote Chatham?"

At this point, Carrie recognized that she had no choice but to surrender quietly to the silly nickname. The insulting nickname, which might also be accurate. If only it were something to laugh about. Carrie sat up very straight, folded her hands in front of her, checked the door, the hall, and the windows for Beto, who was a master at finding spots to hear what he should not.

"According to Lulu," she began, "Indira Markham had a cat when she was a girl. In Richmond. This was a point of contention between them because Lulu desperately wanted a cat, but her mother refused and would not explain."

"I don't like where this story is going," Eva muttered.

"Your instincts are good, I'm afraid. The cat had kittens, and all of them, cat and her kittens, much adored, were butchered with a carving knife. By the older sister. That would be the person you call Coyote Chatham."

For once she had managed to truly shock Eva, who pressed a hand to her mouth.

"Do I understand correctly that Lulu recognized her aunt on the basis of nothing more than a few stories told by her mother?"

It was a comfort to Carrie to have rational, reasonable questions to consider.

"I don't know. There hasn't been time to get more background or even to ask questions. But I think her mother must have told her more. Other stories. Josefa has some interesting thoughts on all this."

"If I can get away this evening, I'll go talk to her. Any idea how best to proceed from here?"

"I'll tell you what keeps me awake," Carrie said. She leaned back in her chair and looked into the sky. "What if Lulu is wrong? How would we know if she just misunderstood?"

This was, of course, a crucial question—and neither of them had an answer. Eva wrapped her arms around herself and closed her eyes. Carrie wanted to caution against assuming the worst, but could not.

"My God," Eva said. "What an evil woman."

On her way home, Carrie realized that she wasn't sure which of the Ewell sisters Eva had been talking about.

65

Eli was still out when Carrie got home, but she refused to worry. She would not be a simpering, fearful woman watching for her husband. It was siesta; she would take a nap. She meant to take a nap, but it was very hot and she couldn't make Martha go away or keep quiet.

"You know," said her dead sister, "I would be the right one to talk to Lulu. I could reassure her that you like cats and don't even have a carving knife."

With that Carrie woke, drenched with perspiration, to find Eli asleep beside her. She was truly happy to see him, but for the moment she was satisfied with the chance to watch him sleep. He was dreaming, his eyes moving back and forth behind closed lids. Later, she decided, was time enough to talk about the argument of the night before. Maybe if they slept for another hour she'd be able to reason out for herself what came next. Apologies? Confessions? Vows of nonviolence in word and deed? It would take some finesse to sort it all out, and finesse was in short supply just now.

And she wasn't done for the day, not quite. Now, instead of waiting for Eli to wake and a long, easy talk over supper, just the two of them, she would have to get up, wash and change, and go out to see how the deliveries she had attended in the last week were faring. Generally, she liked visiting new mothers and their infants, and she would be glad to know that all were well. But it had been a long day.

Eli stopped her before she could put a foot on the ground.

"Running off again so soon?" He waggled both brows suggestively. "Don't you want to look at my graze first?"

Carrie rolled toward him and took his head in her hands. In fact, the dressing did need to be changed, and she would do that before she went out again. She told herself that he didn't deserve a smile just yet.

"Come on, then." She sat up, or tried to. He had captured her attention and intended to keep it.

"Hold on," he said. "Come talk to me."

The sound of horses coming to a stop at the front door robbed them of the opportunity. Carrie was no happier about visitors at this moment than Eli was, but she stayed behind to change, and he went ahead to see who it was. By the time she came into the hall, there was no sign of him, but she heard him talking to strangers outside. Men whose voices she didn't recognize, and why should that worry her? She went out to meet them.

The visitor was a Francesco Segura-Maldinado, who traveled with a groom who was heavily armed. Señor Segura was well-dressed and barbered; he rode a beautiful mare, one that advertised both his judgment and wealth; and his manners were without flaw. He seemed to be—or meant to be—a person of consequence, but Eli's face told her something else. Her husband wore a blank expression that meant he didn't like or trust the man in front of him.

For her part, Carrie saw something very familiar: a man who was looking for a midwife. Slightly dazed, anxious, trying hard to maintain his dignity. His wife or daughter or sister was in labor. He stepped forward to introduce himself to Carrie, in a very correct but heavily accented English.

"My wife is very young. It is her first child. Her mother's family sent a trusted midwife weeks ago, but she never arrived. The pains started at dawn. Will you attend?"

She invited him to come in and wait in the *placita* while she got her things organized. Eli stood behind her when she made this offer, which spared her his reaction. Whatever his concerns, he would find a way to tell her before she was ready to go.

When he came inside, she didn't hesitate. "Eli, tell me why you dislike Señor Segura. But remember please that I still have to attend his wife, even if he cheats at cards or is less than generous with his workers."

She regretted her flippant tone soon enough. Segura, Eli told her, was the son and heir of an old Criollo family who owned many mines to the north. Then he stopped talking, as if he was unsure of what to say. This was so unlike Eli that she turned to look at him. He wore an expression she didn't see often, something of almost begrudging capitulation.

"I can't tell you what to do." His voice was low and rough. "But I'm not letting you out of my sight. I'll go saddle the horses."

She stopped him with a question.

"Do you have reason to suspect I won't be safe?"

A muscle in his jaw flexed. "I'll tell you about it later. That's the best I can do."

Carrie put on her moccasins; changed again, this time into clothes suited to riding in the hot sun; wrote a note for Dr. Benenati; and went outside, where three men were waiting: Señor Segura; his somber, scowling guard; and Eli.

Whatever was wrong, she could put it aside as long as she had a patient who needed her help.

THEY RODE HARD, too hard, really, for the horses, given the temperature. Too hard for people too. Heat licked at Carrie's throat, wiggled underneath the brim of her hat, and slicked along her scalp. Damp clothing chafed, and leather was even worse. *What canna be changed maun be tholed*, she could almost hear in her father's voice. And Amelie's: *This and more will be demanded of you.*

The Segura hacienda came into sight with the sun hovering over the mountains. They would be here overnight, at the very least, and Carrie was glad that Eli had insisted on coming along, because there was something dismal about this impressive holding in the foothills of the Sangre de Cristo Mountains.

After the first sighting of the hacienda, they rode past great flocks of sheep watched over by young men on horseback and dogs as big as ponies. The hacienda itself—or maybe it should be called a rancho, Carrie was still confused about the difference—stretched for miles.

The main house took her by surprise, but Eli had described these very old fortlike adobe main houses: no windows on the ground floor and no door that she could see. It wouldn't be quick or easy to force a way in, and that had been the point when it was built. All around the house was an acre or more of garden that suffered in the heat.

This, her Cousin Jennet would say, was a place under a dark spell. She would make up a half dozen stories on the spot.

Two men held wide doors open, and they rode into a walled court-yard to dismount. There were a dozen or more people here, servants and ranch hands who stood quietly, arms crossed and heads bent together as they talked in tones too low to be heard.

Señor Segura moved with such speed that Carrie didn't realize at first that he had already disappeared into one of the rooms that opened off the courtyard. Somewhere nearby women began reciting the rosary.

"Go on," Eli said. "I'll be right here if you need me." He tried to smile, but it was a battle.

IN DEATH, SEGURA'S wife looked so very young, it robbed Carrie of speech. The women of the household had washed her, changed her linen, and folded a shroud around her, perfectly pleated. It was a beautiful piece of linen, edged with lace and embroidery that must have required many hours of work with silk and needle. Had it been here, waiting for the next death in the family? Had she sewn it herself as part of the linen a girl gathered for her trousseau? The newborn was wrapped in a simpler shroud of pure white linen.

A very young woman—no older than the one who had died—crept up to drape herself over the foot of the bed, resting her head on Mrs. Segura's still form. In the quiet Carrie could hear every breath, every sob and wail, and each apology.

In other circumstances, when there was no physician to attend, the family might have asked Carrie to examine the deceased. If it were in her power to give them any peace of mind, she'd have done it without hesitation. But someone had made the decision to prepare her for burial, and the attendants had done that work carefully and well. Her hair had been combed and lay plaited against her shoulder. There was a rosary in her hands, and coins rested on her eyelids. Death had claimed her so completely that there wasn't the slightest hint of the person she had been, even an hour ago. Carrie wondered if she had lived long enough to see her child, and hoped she had not.

He rested beside her, the small face as round as a full moon, mottled with bruises under a misshapen skull. Carrie could never remember which poet had written of nature, red in tooth and claw, but the phrase came to her in these situations.

The women who had tended the laboring mother would explain what had happened, if Carrie asked. They would even welcome the chance to explain, and so Carrie sat on a straight-backed chair and spread her hands out, ready to listen to a familiar story, shocking, devastating to those she left behind, but nothing out of the usual. The mother was too young and slightly built; she bled so heavily that it was thought that her uterus must have torn away. The child was just crowning in a river of blood when she simply looked up, as if listening to someone in the next room, and died.

"We had to get him out. We had to try to save him, the *patrón*'s heir. But it was so hard, it was—"

"Too late, yes. You did everything you could for both of them. All of you."

When the talking was done, one of the older women spoke to Carrie of food and a room to rest and led her away to a dining room, where Eli was waiting for her.

Carrie had no appetite, but she ate anyway, thinking of the ride ahead and the troubles with Lulu. Troubles she had not yet told Eli about. At this moment she couldn't imagine raising the subject of dead cats ever again.

Eli leaned toward her and spoke softly, and in English. "You provided real comfort, I heard from people who sought me out to say so."

Carrie wanted to think that was true, and that it would still be true in the weeks and months to come.

THE GUEST ROOM was good-sized and sparsely furnished, with brightly colored woven blankets, Navajo in design, if Carrie had it right. Compared to the temperature outside, the room was almost cool.

"The one thing I wish I had right at this moment—"

"A bucket of cold water to pour over your head?"

"It's vaguely disturbing that you knew what I was going to say," she told him.

She crawled onto the wide bed, unlaced her moccasins, dropped them, and fell asleep as soon as her head met the bedding. When she woke, no more than an hour later, his gaze was fixed on her face.

She stretched and yawned and wondered if she would be able to wash before they started for home. Eli didn't move a muscle or look away.

Carrie said, "I hope you slept for a while at least."

He jerked a shoulder, which meant that the question she put to him was a distraction he preferred to ignore.

"Mostly I've been thinking about what to tell you about Segura."

Carrie realized now how silent the hacienda was. In a household as big as this one, and with a wealthy owner, preparing for a burial would be complicated. The list of things to do must be pages long, from digging a grave to calling in a priest and getting the house ready for mourners who were probably already arriving. They would need beds and food for days, and the kitchen workers would be running flat out. But she heard nothing at all.

Eli's thoughts had gone in another direction, and his next question took her by surprise.

"Was this the first loss for you since you came to Santa Fe?"

It was a reasonable question, even if it struck her as odd at this moment.

"Do you mean stillbirth? Or maternal death, or both? I didn't have a chance to see this young woman alive at all."

After a moment's thought, she added, "Since I came here, I've delivered two stillborns, and there were two who died within a few weeks of delivery. Why do you ask?"

Carrie wished for a way to reclaim the calm of sleep, but they would have to get on the road again fairly quickly if they were to reach Santa Fe by full dark. She sat up and began to straighten her clothing.

He let out a sigh. "The horses won't tell tales, and it would be better to talk about what I know someplace else. I'll go tell the household we're leaving."

IT WAS THE right thing to do, Carrie felt that clearly, and at the same time leaving the Segura hacienda struck her as inappropriate. She couldn't remember leaving a birthing room so quickly, no matter the outcome. Then Eli started talking, and her worries about the household in mourning slipped away.

Eli said, "Segura has been married at least four times. He married as a young man, but she died within months. So he left and went to California to work with an uncle there."

She turned toward him, waiting.

"Then his father died and everything came to him, so he didn't have much choice but to come back. In the five years or so since he's been here running the family businesses, he's been married three more times."

He started talking faster, trying to get to the end of a story he hadn't wanted to tell.

"The first of those three marriages happened really quickly, but it didn't last a year. The baby came too early and they both died. Not a year later he married one of the Romero girls. She couldn't conceive— I heard this from Red Rosa—and so he sent her away. The story—one of the stories—is that she went to live with family in Mexico and died within a year."

Carrie thought for a moment. "And now another loss."

He ran a hand over his head and winced. Carrie would look at his wound when they got home. Better to bide her time while he told the story.

"The one who died this morning, do you know her name? Did anyone mention it to you?"

No one had, Carrie realized. She hadn't noticed, but should have, as this was an issue she thought about a great deal. In the East a married woman's name was usually shortened to a kind of possessive proclamation. Carrie's mother had been in Manhattan for years now and had many friends, but if you mentioned her by name—Lily Bonner or Lily Ballentyne—you would get blank looks. Lily Bonner Ballentyne existed solely as Mrs. Quinlan, an appendage to Harrison Quinlan. That was all you needed to know. When the Ballentynes first came to Manhattan, Carrie had found this disturbing for reasons she couldn't put to words.

"Her name was Carina Griego-Lopez," Eli said, his tone neutral. "I never met her, but her family is well-known. The hacienda south of Socorro, not far from the border."

He slowed to look at something on the horizon, his head tilted. Carrie followed his line of sight and saw the churning of dark clouds.

"We've got time," he told her. "I'll tell the rest of it. I think Carina was thirteen when she married Segura. The first two I know of were both about that age, thirteen or fourteen. I can't say what drew him to Carina, except that her mother had a house full of healthy kids, and so did both grandmothers. He liked the odds, I guess."

She said, "So he wanted someone to bear him children, first and last. I suppose he cared for her as much as he cares for—" She stopped herself, but Eli followed.

"A prize mare. That's probably the best way to put it. But you know how men who love horses sometimes lose perspective. Not all of them, but it's an itch for somebody like Segura. There's always a mare even more beautiful than the one he has at home."

And now she understood why Eli hadn't wanted her anywhere near Segura.

THE STORM SLIPPED by, leaving Santa Fe dusty and wind tossed, but dry. In the distance there was a low grumbling of thunder as it moved, on the prowl. Carrie lay in bed beside her husband and tried to quiet her mind.

"Ask," Eli said. "Or we'll never get any sleep."

She turned on her side. "Why would the parents agree to such a marriage? It makes no sense, not if they felt any affection for her."

He hummed, an almost mournful sound. "You can't imagine what it was like after the Treaty of Guadalupe Hidalgo. Everything familiar and safe suddenly gone. For a lot of people, Mexican people, it was like the end of the world. Men with business interests in Mexico had to scramble. A few of them managed to keep afloat, but most of them went under. For a while at least.

"Carina's father got hit hard, because he was loyal to Mexico and he sent his sons to fight under López de Santa Anna. He sent four, and two came home."

"Then Mexico loses the war." From her Mohawk cousins and aunts, she understood something of the constant battle for survival, the way it wore people down and robbed them of all hope.

"Mexico loses more than three hundred thousand acres and suddenly the Griego-Lopez family isn't Mexican anymore. The treaty says the States has to give citizenship to all the Mexicans on this side of the new border. Not that it happened easily."

Very softly Carrie said, "Imagine the screaming matches in Congress. They were obliged to grant citizenship to dark-skinned half Indians, and that didn't go over well. Not even for three hundred thousand acres."

Eli shifted one way and then the other, as if the bedding were making him uncomfortable.

"Griego was sure that if he could get his business up and running again, he could turn the situation around. Never happened. The faster he ran, the slower he moved. Then Segura comes into the picture."

He told the rest of the story in quick, dry sentences. A rich businessman from a prominent family, polite, observing every gesture required by custom, pays court to Griego's daughter and then asks for her hand. He never asks about a dowry, and instead he has a contract to offer the family business that will turn everything around. The fact that he's more than forty doesn't concern Griego. Rich men take a while to settle down, is how he explains it to himself. Of course, the man needs sons. He wanted sons. There are stories, sure, but there are stories about every rich man.

Eli stopped to collect his thoughts, but Carrie interrupted.

"Brokered marriages are nothing unusual, not anywhere in the world. Women are often not even asked. They find themselves in front of a priest or judge marrying a stranger because the connection will be a good one for the family."

Carrie didn't know how often such marriages were successful—she didn't even know how she would define a successful marriage, except by example in her own family—but there was an element here that buzzed in her gut like an agitated wasp.

"What worries me," she began again, more slowly, "is that he married three children, one after the other."

She caught up a breath, and Eli raised his head, waiting.

"I made a connection I should have seen before. Those girls he married, they are *genízaras*. Children claimed as slaves, following the old Spanish system. Isn't that so?"

Eli inclined his head.

She drew in another deep breath and asked a different question. "What if he does it again?"

That was the question, Eli agreed.

"I think we will have to wait and watch. You know how things work."

What he didn't say, a truth so obvious that it need not be put into words, was simple: A rich man who put some thought into it might go on all his life without ever being called to account, no matter how bloody his crimes. He could marry one small, barely mature girl after another. More girl than woman, never to be any older. Whether or not he truly hoped to get an heir from one of these young brides was not a question that could be answered, probably even by him.

A thought came to Eli that he couldn't hold back.

"Did I tell you too much about Segura's history?"

To this she summoned up an awkward smile and an easy denial.

"I asked you about him," she said. "And you told me." Nothing of accusation or disapproval in her voice. She still held tight to the things that angered her most, but he had the growing sense that would change, and soon.

Now he wished he had kept quiet, because she was suddenly fully awake. She sat up, and the moonlight caught the downward curve of a frown.

"I have to tell you," she said, yawning. "It really can't wait. About Lulu's Aunt Chatham and the slaughtered kittens."

When she had finished the story and she noted again how odd it really was, she said, "We don't know what's true, what was only imagined or misheard. It's enough to make me want to pull my hair out."

"Never that," Eli said. "But we need to put an end to the coyote woman's tricks."

66

DEEP IN THE night Carrie woke to rain on the roof. A pulse, a drum-beat, a familiar, comforting sound; it coaxed her back into a deeper sleep, and then she found herself in front of Waverly Place.

For most people, dreams slipped away. Nightmares were just as fluid. A nightmare might leave behind vague memories of regret, fear, or anger, but Carrie rarely remembered even that much. This time was different, because she knew, somehow, that she was dreaming.

She found herself standing across the lane from Amelie's cottage. The sun was hot on her shoulders, and the garden was dense and deeply green and ready for harvest. The garden smells she loved best were all there: tomato plants in the sun, ripe raspberries crushed underfoot, peppermint. Then she was standing just inside the door in Amelie's kitchen.

Amelie sat at the table across from a woman Carrie didn't know. A woman weeping as if her world had ended, and it might have. Many women came here, where they were free to mourn what others would not even acknowledge. Pregnancies went wrong so often that there was little tolerance for disappointment and no patience for tears. A lost child was not the only reason women came to the midwife for comfort, but Carrie knew from the way her cousin sat, bent forward, that this stranger was in mourning.

Carrie couldn't make out the things they said to each other, not until she realized that they were speaking Spanish, and that sitting across from Amelie was La Llorona, the weeping woman, the empty vessel with her broken heart and a fury big enough to fill the world. Her appearance here was not unusual. Amelie had known many ghosts, and was not surprised when another came to seek her out.

Carrie asked herself why La Llorona should look so familiar, and saw her mistake. This was not the weeping woman but Yatzil Morales, the young prostitute who brought her newborn to the dispensary during Carrie's first week in Santa Fe. Yatzil, who did not dare give her son a name until she could be sure he would live long enough to know it.

There were other women in the garden, Carrie realized. All of them here to speak to the midwife. Mrs. Perry, still without a child. Mrs. Meier, who miscarried three times and was pregnant again, her arms wrapped around her middle. Jo Cady, who ran a small bordello and paid Amelie to see to the health of the women she called girls.

And Mrs. Markham. Mrs. Markham sat at the table across from Amelie, the doll she had taken from her daughter bound to her chest by a bright red rebozo.

The room filled with her smells. Dark earth and disappointment and the grave, and a rebozo full of dead kittens. Anger coursed through Carrie, but Amelie was standing behind her now, and she caught Carrie by the upper arms.

"No," Amelie said, her voice hoarse but firm. "No. Look again, cousin. Look closely. Those are not kittens."

CARRIE WOKE SUDDENLY, breathing hard. Eli ran a finger down her arm, once and twice and more, until she stopped shuddering. So rudely wrenched from sleep, but he held back questions, and that was the greatest gift he could give her just now. While the dream faded away. The nightmare.

In the darkness Carrie said, "I almost never dream. I can't remember the last time I had a nightmare."

He had never asked for the rest of her own story. Eli would wait another week or year or decade without complaint. His generosity was a very deep well. The most precious things, things without dimension, things that couldn't be bought or sold, were available to her whenever she had need of them. His arms were always open to her.

In theory she had known that, but it wasn't until this moment that the truth settled down and down, into blood and bone. The truth was that Carrie had failed to meet Eli's generosity with her own. She held back the things that hurt the most.

He rested beside her. A breeze moved through the room with the hush of rainfall. Carrie closed her eyes and let the story go.

67

"GRANDDA DIED IN the fall of '43, and Grandy Elizabeth followed, not long after. Then the Sacandaga took our Da. That was the final stroke for Martha. Those three losses twisted her up, and she turned into somebody I didn't want to know.

"It was just Ma and Nathan and me at Seven Bells that summer.

"Martha was at the Red Dog, and Blue was at the millhouse on the other side of the Sacandaga. But Blue came every day with food. She kept up with chores and sat with Ma. We were all worried about her. Ma was sleeping a lot and losing weight, and she hadn't picked up a sketchbook for months, and people took note.

"Then Uncle Daniel showed up one day to put a stop to all that. He told Ma that they were starting up family Sunday dinners again. All the Bonners and Ballentynes and Savards, the Wolfs and Freemans. No excuses, no exceptions. He looked Ma right in the eye and said that if she didn't show up at Downhill House on her own, he would carry her.

"I asked Ma later what she was going to do, and that surprised her.

She said that one of the advantages of a family like ours is, you can never get so lost that you won't be found. So the next Sunday, we got up early to bake pies, and at midday the three of us walked to Down-hill House.

"Most of the older cousins were gone to Albany or Manhattan or even further away for work or school, but there were still enough of us to make noise. The cousins let out a yell when we came into the clearing, and whooped and hollered and shouted out questions and stories. Nathan was so excited he got the hiccups.

"There's really just two things you need to know about that afternoon. The first was, Ma sat in a circle with the aunts and their grown daughters, and her color came up. She smiled, and that made me want to tell Uncle Daniel that he had been right, this was the best way to help Ma. The second thing was, Martha came, too, and brought the girls. But not her husband.

"We were glad to see Martha, as difficult as she could be, but the girls, that was the real surprise. Greg Fisher didn't want them spending time with us. But he was away that day, and Martha did as she always did: she suited herself.

"Her twins were plain happy to be there. They climbed all over Ma, they laughed and sang. Not even two yet, but they threw themselves into the middle of whatever was going on. The sight of them running after older cousins, legs pumping, their hair streaming behind them, that memory I'll have forever.

"We had a good dinner on plank tables, with lots of teasing and laughing and talk about whose recipe for blood sausage was best, who would be going to Johnstown for supplies in the coming week, with the winter coming on. I was just sitting there, full of good food and relaxed, listening to Jennet tell a story about Cousin Jay and a raw egg, with him protesting and challenging every word, so I didn't even notice at first that Martha was standing up at the head of the table. She looked at Uncle Daniel, and when he realized what she wanted, he shifted out of her way. Then she just waited until everybody noticed her.

"Aunt Susanna was the first to speak up. She smiled at Martha and called down the table, asking if she had some news to share.

"Martha always did. She started with complaints. How hard things were, how many hours she had to work. Keeping track of the girls and seeing to the laundry and the marketing and the hired help. She said she was angry that nobody had ever explained to her what her life would be like. And with that she had used up all the goodwill she had coming.

"It was Ma's youngest sister who stood up to talk next. Curiosity had a sharp tongue, and she didn't hold back. Did Martha hear herself? Whining and complaining, what would her Da say?

"I was watching Ma, how the color was draining out of her face, but Hannah put a hand on her shoulder to calm her, and she stood up. She didn't yell or make threats. It was her measured voice, the one that made everybody stop and consider.

"Aunt Hannah asked Martha what it was she thought we owed her. Everybody in the family spent time with her, helping out. Every day.

"Martha stood very straight, shoulders back, all wounded pride, and her head swiveled down one side of the table and up the other.

"She said, 'You are my family. You have to help me.'

"Then Uncle Gabriel crossed his arms and got this stubborn look on his face as he got to his feet. He echoed Hannah's question and Curiosity's: What exactly did Martha want? To set up housekeeping on her own? Come back to Seven Bells? Or was she thinking of taking off and leaving the girls for her Ma to raise? Or maybe she was just realizing why nobody wanted her to marry Greg Fisher.

"Martha hated it when people criticized her husband. She said she would keep him, and gladly. All she wanted from the family was—"

Eli caught her eye. "She wanted you."

Carrie nodded because her voice had cracked. She swallowed and tried again.

"Yes."

"She wanted you to what end? As a maid? A nurse? A cook? A stable hand? A servant for her husband?"

Carrie shrugged. "All those things. She wanted me to come live with them at the Red Dog."

He gave a curt nod. "Everything. She wanted you to leave your Ma and Nathan to fend for themselves at Seven Bells. You refused."

She swallowed. "I did. Martha laughed at that, as if I had told a joke. As if Ma and Nathan were beside the point. As if I was talking foolish. She said, 'Da has been gone for months. Months. Da is dead and I'm alive and so are my girls, and I need you more than Ma does.'

"I don't think anybody was surprised, but to hear those words said aloud, and with such—venom, I have to say, was a shock. There was an almost empty silence that hung in the air. Then Uncle Daniel stood. He got up slow, and his expression was ice-cold. He said, 'Your sister is not anybody's mule. Certainly, she's not your mule. She can't solve your problems for you.'

"She didn't seem to hear him. She turned to me and smiled her beautiful smile, saying there was just one more thing she needed to tell me. She had made up a room for me, and didn't I want to come along now, today? The girls would be so pleased."

Carrie had been determined not to weep, but tears ran down her face.

"That was the most shocking part, the way she used the girls to get what she wanted. It just about broke my heart."

She turned to look at Eli directly.

"You know, I've thought about it every day for years, and it always feels to me like a light going dark. Or a door closing. I couldn't imagine how we'd go on, how we could still be a family. And I knew that Martha would keep pushing."

Eli leaned toward her. "That was the start of the battle?"

"That's how it started. It didn't end until Martha and her girls were in their graves. Let me tell the rest of it.

"Martha was slow-witted in a lot of ways, but not in every way. She could be sly, especially when she thought her own people were trying to hold her back. It took weeks before she gave in and acknowledged that nobody was going to take her side. Nothing anybody said to her made a difference, no matter how gentle or angry. She could turn off her ears like everybody else can close their eyes.

"But she didn't give up. She stopped talking to everybody but me. Blue would bring her kindling or soup or preserves, Aunt Susanna did the sweeping and the girls' laundry, everybody continued helping as they had been helping. It didn't matter. She ignored them.

"Every morning I came by to get the girls fed and dressed, and every morning she would start trying to change my mind as soon as I came in the door. Sometimes she tried her kind of logic, sometimes she just lost her temper and let it run wild."

There was a low creaking in Eli's voice. "Where was Fisher?"

"Mostly he was away tending bar, but sometimes he was right there. He ignored me but he'd talk to Martha. He told her that of course her family should be helping, and that maybe they should sell out and find a place to live where people *ain't so tightfisted.*"

The memory made her stomach clench, Greg Fisher condemning the family.

"For once Martha realized that they had shocked me, and she tried to explain.

"She said, 'He doesn't understand why you haven't moved in here yet. I need you. The girls do too. He's getting impatient.'

"The last two weeks in October were hard, Martha confessed, as if an accounting of her failures would convince me. She called herself a poor housekeeper, a terrible cook, unable to keep books. By that time I didn't let myself be drawn into conversations. If she had said she had hidden an elephant behind the inn, I wouldn't have commented. I said nothing unless the girls were nearby. I tried to quiet their fears by being my usual self, but it was getting harder.

"I hated the Red Dog by that time, but I couldn't bear the idea of the girls going hungry, and Martha wouldn't let anybody else in.

"Then on the last day, she confessed the worst of her sins. 'I'm not nearly as good as you are with the girls. I worry about them when they're alone here with me. Don't you worry about us?'

"I bit my lip and turned my head away, but she had put a crack in my armor, and she knew it. She knew I would have to respond. Jean was sitting right there, but it didn't seem to matter to Martha. She would have her fun.

"'Jean,' she says to her daughter. 'Jean, will you feel safer when Auntie Carrie comes to stay? I hope she doesn't decide to abandon us.'

"So I sent Jean out to play and then I turned to Martha, so mad that my hands shook.

"'Sister,' I said. 'Shame on you. Shame on you for using your girls like poker chips. You are heartless and selfish and cruel, and I want nothing more to do with you. You cannot simply hold your breath until you get what you want.'

"She blinked at me, and her eyes went big and round. Then came the twitch at the corner of her mouth.

"'Silly Carrie,' she said. 'That's how I've always done it. That's how I get my way.'

"And she was right. Most usually she got her way, but I swore to myself that this time she would not. I would not give in. When I left, I turned to her and said, 'I am ashamed to call you my sister.' And those were the last words I ever said to her.

"I woke up to a foot of new snow the next morning and an inch of ice on the water bucket, and mostly what I wanted right then was to burrow down deeper into bed and sleep and forget the things I had said to my sister.

"But the girls needed me, so I got dressed and ready to go. The sky was clear and cold and so full of light reflecting off the snow that I had to wait until my eyes stopped watering.

"It was a beautiful morning, but I trudged along imagining the things Martha would say. The only hope I had to avoid another fight was the frosty air. Martha would stay abed as long as she could manage. She'd stay abed all day if she could get away with it. Sooner or later she would have to stoke the stove, one chore she couldn't avoid now that the winter had come. The air was sweet cedar and hickory and applewood smoke.

"Then I realized that the chimneys at the Red Dog stood cold against the sky. No sign of smoke.

"I ran the rest of the way. But there was no one at the Red Dog. No Martha, no girls, no Greg Fisher. Beds still made, no sign of a fight. So I went out to the stable to see if the wagon and team were gone, but everything was just where it was supposed to be. That meant that Greg had to be somewhere nearby. Martha and the girls might be with him. That was frightening, too, but I didn't let myself think about what it might mean.

"From the stable I saw that a window in the girls' room was cracked open and so that's where I went next, to close it so the house didn't get any colder. And that's where I found the feathers. Just a few, but on the ledge. The door of the cage stood open too."

Eli's brows rose in surprise. "They kept birds?"

"Just two little sparrows that got separated from their nest in the spring. The girls were diligent about nursing those birds and would never have let them out into such weather. Up to that point I was anxious, but the sight of those feathers stuck in the snow on the ledge made my heart sink.

"I stuck my head out the window to whistle for them, but the birds were gone, and the girls were gone too. There was no sign of any living thing. All of Paradise seemed to have gone silent in the snow. I stood right there trying to make sense of the empty house, the silent village, wondering if it was time to fetch the uncles. Daniel, Ben, Gabriel, Blue-Jay, Henry. Time to call the aunts. Hannah, Martha, Curiosity, Susanna, Annie. Time to tell Ma. What to tell her, how to tell her.

"I thought of walking away. I could make a nest for myself in the caves behind the falls and hide there. In time someone would come to tell me that Martha and the girls were home safe. That idea was still in my head when an eagle landed in a pine tree, sending a shower of snow down to the ground.

"I knew every tree in the village. We all did. From the window, I could make out the pine where the eagle perched and just then, a flash of color. Just a hint of green in a world of greens, but still it got my attention. A bright, almost fragile spring green that didn't belong here, not until late March or April. The same green as Martha's winter cape and shawl.

"I was strong and fast and frightened to the very core of my soul, and so I ran. Through drifts of snow, tripping and falling and launching myself up and away. The only sound I could hear was my own heart wound to the point of hammering its way free of my chest. By the time I reached the trees, I was huffing like an old lady, but I didn't stop. Not until I found them, propped against the wall of the old icehouse.

"Martha was sitting between her girls, all of them perfectly still, as if listening to music coming from far away. They looked so peaceful, leaning against Martha, snowflakes and ice crystals sparkling from their eyelashes. Martha's eyes were wide open, but there was nothing in her expression of fear. Not for herself or for her daughters.

"I wanted to draw the girls into my lap, but I imagined them cracking and shattering. So I sat with them until my hands and feet were numb with the cold. In the end I got up, stumbling a little before I could regain my balance, and I turned back to the Red Dog.

"Greg Fisher was standing at the window in his daughters' room, watching me, watching his wife and daughters. Perfectly still, utterly calm. A half-eaten apple in his hand.

"I stopped at the door before I went back into the inn, I think because I wanted to believe that I had imagined the man standing at the window. Greg Fisher was somewhere far away, keeping bar in Johnstown or on a ship bound for Manhattan. The law might want him, but I did not.

"But there he was, still standing at the window where his daughters had slept, when I came to the door. Greg Fisher, who was once my brother-in-law, my sister's husband. Now a widower. Twice over a widower. Alone now, without wife or children. Suddenly he was nothing at all.

"He glanced at me over his shoulder, his gaze running up and down my body. He smirked. That's the only word I can find to describe the way he looked at me.

"'I'm just about to fetch the constable,' he told me. 'Or maybe you'd like to do it? Distraught as I am, it would make sense if you bring him—and your family, of course—news of this horrific tragedy.'

"He slipped a slice of apple into his mouth. His teeth snapped it in half, and he paused to swallow. Then he took up another apple and started to peel it, working patiently until a twist of peel fell to the floor. It was a dull dark red, but the flesh was brilliant white, and its sweet smell moved through the room.

"'A tragedy, really, what other word to use? The childish and weak-minded are especially prone to overreaction. She felt ignored and put-upon, you know that. Betrayal was more than she could bear.'

"'Yes,' I told him. 'You betrayed her.'

"He shrugged. 'Certainly, but not just me. You did as much. So did the whole family. And she felt betrayed by life. You knew she would never be content here, didn't you? No one should be surprised that she chose to depart the world this way. Or to take the girls with her.'

"The pure venom of his claim jolted me, and then a flutter of movement at the window made me look in that direction. The sparrows were back, bright-eyed, none the worse for wear. Waiting to be let in. I stepped toward the window, but Greg Fisher put himself between me and the waiting birds.

"'Let it be,' he said, almost jovially. 'You're free now of all this mess. Let it be.'

"He tossed the apple core onto the table where the girls played games and painted and drew. It landed on a stack of drawings of the sparrows, some as small as an apple seed, and on the same page, drawings of a magpie, an owl, a shrike.

"Beside the apple core was the knife, still with peel wound around its handle. I had used that knife almost every day since Martha married and moved into the Red Dog. Cooking for her and for my nieces. My thoughts had to be plain to read from my face and the way my hands trembled.

"'I picked the wrong sister,' he said. 'You're the one with some fire.'

"He took up the knife and studied it with a puzzled half grin. The morning light reflected off the blade to his face, and it was not kind to him. He was growing old, this man who Martha found so handsome, so wise and kind.

"His gaze shifted back to me, wide-eyed and curious, as if a game had just occurred to him.

"'Tell me, little sister. What would you do with this knife if I handed it over?'

"Do it," I told him, my voice coming from some other place, outside myself. "Give it to me and find out."

CARRIE SAID, "TELL me what you're thinking."

Eli knew that to hesitate would feel to her like a judgment, and so he told her. "I'm wondering if you even know what happened on that day."

"I know what the court decided."

"There was a hearing?"

"Four days long," she said. "I testified for a full day. Did you know that as a witness you can only answer the questions you're asked? You can't volunteer anything. Not even the truth. So I confessed."

Eli's gaze moved across her face. "You confessed. To what?"

"I confessed to resenting my sister. I confessed to being cruel and unkind and impatient. I confessed that I didn't know who was responsible for the events that led to her death, but that it could well have been my fault.

"And then I lied. Under oath I lied and said I didn't know where Greg Fisher had been that night, or where he might be right then. I withheld the truth when I said nothing of my aunts, who took me away from the Red Dog, or of my uncles, who cared for Martha and her girls.

"If the judge had asked, I could not have told him where the uncles had buried Greg Fisher, because I didn't know. And I still don't know today."

CARRIE FELL ASLEEP like a man who had fought a battle that he had never expected to survive. Eli was glad of it, though sleep was still far off for him. He went out to sit in the *placita* and think through Carrie's story.

The simplest truth was that he was relieved to know that Carrie felt no guilt about Fisher's death. Now he better understood the visits from the dead sister, and wondered if Martha would be content to go now that her story had been told. And he wondered, too, if Carrie would be glad to see the last of her sister.

That thought was still in his head when she roused from sleep and came to find him.

"Come to bed," she said, swaying on her feet. "Come or I won't be able to sleep."

"Got to check the horses, then I'll be right there."

When he came to their bed, she was in the deepest sleep. A healing sleep. He would make sure that it was just the first of many.

Eli slept, too, and without dreaming.

IN THE MORNING Carrie was determined to carry on as usual. They talked of everyday things as she dressed and put food on the table, as they ate, and wiped the dishes. Ready to leave for the dispensary, she had paused at the door and smiled in a way that made her seem very young and unsure. He saw her draw in a breath and square her shoulders, and then she was gone.

Eli saddled the horses and went out to see to his own work, where the Santa Fe River met the Mississippi. This was familiar territory, given endless disputes about boundaries and land claims. It was past sunset before he got back to town, and he came in to find Carrie at the table, sound asleep with her cheek pressed to a piece of paper. The quill was there, too, dribbling ink, but he was as tired as she was, and it was time to sleep. He put the cork back in the ink bottle and leaned down to pick her up.

"*Querida*," he said in a low, calm voice. "You'll sleep better in bed."

Her head jerked up to display one reddened cheek with a tracing of ink. It made him think of facial tattoos, but this was a distinctly *tejana* version, and he found himself almost smiling. Carrie saw the almost smile and was not happy about it. Her eyes narrowed as if he had done something rude. Before she could tell him his sins, he was halfway to bed.

"Too late."

"For what?" She was scowling. "For what is it too late?"

"Anything. Everything. Whatever you want to scold me about can wait till tomorrow."

It seemed his logic was enough to convince her, because she fell back to sleep and stayed there while he stripped her out of her clothes.

For days they carried on just the same way. They spoke of work and errands and friends, visits they should make, people they might invite. Mostly, Carrie kept her worries about Aunt Coyote to herself and resisted the urge to ask again when the circuit judge would come to Santa Fe.

On a particularly humid Friday morning, Eli came in from his chores and found Carrie putting out bowls of *chaquegüe* for each of them. It was one of his favorites, a gruel made from blue cornmeal that Carrie had needed a good amount of time and discussion with Josefa to master.

"You're still half-asleep," he told her.

Her whole face contorted. "I am not."

"So you mean to put more salt on your *chaquegüe*?"

She closed her eyes, pushed the salt box away, and shook her head. "Why are you so even-tempered? You could be a little grumpy now and then, just a little, so I don't look so awful in comparison."

Eli knew that any comment, whether he agreed or disagreed, was unlikely to distract her. Instead he would listen to her monologue—they were often quite entertaining—until she realized that she was going to be late getting to the dispensary and ran off, fully awake.

"Perfection," she was saying, "is a myth. No one is perfect, you know that, but you show a perfect face to the world. It's downright dishonest, and I think—"

A knock at the door made her jump to her feet. She stood just like that while the door opened and José Bilbao shouted a message down the hall.

"Los necasitan en el dispensario. La chamaca dice que deben apurarse."

Carrie was good at identifying people by the way they talked, even if they were trying hard to disguise their voices. This time she didn't recognize the voice at all. An older man, short of breath. A man who liked *punche*, the strong tobacco locals grew to wrap in corn silk and smoke. She could smell it from the next room.

Early morning was not the best time for Spanish language immersion, but Carrie caught most of it.

When he had gone, she asked Eli for a translation. She said, "Who is *la chamaca*, and why do we need to hurry to the dispensary?"

Eli's widest grin was a sure sign she had misinterpreted Spanish in a way he found amusing, but her anxiety was climbing fast, and she just wanted an answer.

"*Chamaca* isn't a *who*," he said. "It's a local word for a boy or girl. *Chamaco* or *chamaca*. An Indian word, though I couldn't tell you from which tribe. So it's Lulu who's sending for us. I wonder what it's about. I hope not Coyote Woman first thing in the morning."

She tried to smile but couldn't really manage.

"I've been thinking about the whole mess," Eli said as they walked across the busy plaza. "You really think Mrs. Markham agreed to marry Dr. Markham and come live out here just to get away from her sister?"

"I don't know," Carrie said, sounding more fretful than she liked.

He said, "So if we take it at face value, Mrs. Markham was so worried about this sister showing up, she decided the only way to prepare Lulu was to scare her half to death. Doesn't seem right."

And what was there to say to that truth? She decided to say nothing at all.

There were raised voices in the *placita* when they came through the corridor from the dispensary. Lulu pleading, then Lulu demanding, back and forth, by turns shrill and then roughened by tears.

Carrie heard her own name and then Eli's, and a deep unease slid down her spine.

Dr. Benenati was saying, "I understand, but we must and we will wait for Mrs. Ibarra to open her own mail."

It was an odd juxtaposition. Dr. Benenati and Josefa stood at the table opposite Lulu, who was on the very edge of reason.

FROM THE SIDE garden came an agitated screeching from the magpies, who were taking part in the disagreement.

Carrie said, "Do I understand there's a letter for me?"

There was a great scramble while Lulu grabbed a small basket from the table and darted to Carrie to press it into her hands. Both Josefa and Dr. Benenati watched without comment, most likely, Carrie thought, because she had worn them down already.

"There are other letters," she said. "But this one on the top is the most important one."

"Nobody else has important letters? Just Carrie?" Eli asked.

"We don't know exactly what came in the post." Dr. Benenati said this lightly, with the vaguest touch of frustration.

Lulu might not understand her own actions, but he seemed to be very much aware of her fragile state of mind. She was not to be reasoned with, and was focused still on her goal.

Determined, she spoke directly to Carrie and repeated herself. "This letter—" She pointed. "Is the most important."

This was a child who had been pushed far enough, a child on the verge of collapse. Lulu could no more retreat from this demand she was making than she could stop breathing.

Carrie looked at the letter, and she began to understand. "It's from Mrs. Colby, in Manhattan."

Lulu said, "My Aunt Colby."

Carrie nodded. "Did you want me to—"

"Yes. Read it aloud, right now. Please."

Josefa pulled the girl close to put an arm around her, but Lulu held herself stiffly. She desperately wanted this letter to prove that she wasn't alone, but she had prepared herself for the worst. She anticipated a long explanation gently worded, the words grown-ups used to excuse themselves when they didn't want to be questioned or criticized. The letter would say that Lulu wasn't welcome. She expected the disappointment and could not hide her fear.

Children unsure of their place in the world turned inward to protect themselves. It was physically painful to watch Lulu as she struggled to do that.

Carrie cracked the seal and unfolded the letter.

"It was written just over a month ago, and sent by express mail." Everyone knew how very expensive it was to send a letter express, even Lulu, who began to chew on her lower lip as Carrie started to read aloud.

"The letterhead reads 143 East Seventeenth Street in Manhattan. I have been to the Colbys' house on two or three occasions. Later I'll answer any questions you might have about their home. And now I'll read."

Dr. & Mrs. Michael Colby
143 East 17th-Street
Manhattan, New York

Miss Carrie Ballentyne
The Markham Dispensary
Santa Fe, New Mexico Territory

Dear Miss Ballentyne,
We have just had the terrible, tragic news about my brother and his
wife in a letter from a Mr. Bixby. For the next few days things will
be hectic while we make ready for the trip west, but I take the time
to write to you now for Lulu's sake. It is very hard for young
children when everything familiar is suddenly gone, and there is no
certainty about what will come next. My heart breaks for all three
of them, but especially for her. We want her to understand that she is
not alone, and that we are coming to get her.

In his letter Mr. Bixby explained the terms of my sister-in-law's
last testament, and of course we will do as she asked of us. Please
impress on Lulu that we are coming for her as quickly as we can. I
believe she will find things to like here. There are cousins and
neighbor children to play with, and we have a collection of household
pets that the children love and care for. She will have a room of her
own that looks out over our small but very lovely garden where
we have our meals in the warmer months. When she is comfortable
with this new place and a big city, and with her uncle and me, we
will sit down with her and make plans about her schooling.

I was often very frustrated with my brother and his—shall
we say—vulnerabilities, but he was dearly loved, as was his wife,
who suffered greatly far from all of us who would have gladly helped
her. The least we can do to honor them is to provide a loving,
attentive home where Lulu will be safe and find comfort, if not
quick relief from sorrow.

While I write to you, my husband writes to Mr. Bixby. If you or

*the other people who have a part in Lulu's daily life would like to
know more, Mr. Bixby has our permission to discuss our plans and
progress with you.*

   *This note is simply to acknowledge that you have taken on a
tremendous responsibility without preparation, and that we will be
there as soon as the roads and weather will allow. You have now
and will always have our deepest, most sincere gratitude.*

   *When you answered Sam's call for a nurse and midwife, I was so
pleased. Now, given this tragedy, I am tremendously relieved to
know that Lulu has you to care for her and see that she is safe until
we can bring her home to New York. Again, with thanks I remain*

   Yours most truly,
   Aurelia Markham Colby

It took just a short burst of tears and comforting before Lulu raised her
head, eyes rounded, and said something Eli should have predicted.

   "Mr. Bixby has a letter too," she said. "I want to know what Uncle
Dr. Colby wrote to him."

   She would have rushed out on her own if Carrie and Eli hadn't
volunteered to walk with her to Mr. Bixby's office.

   Eli was as happy for Lulu as he was relieved for Carrie. Assuming,
he reminded himself, that Mrs. Chatham could be stopped. With any
luck Dr. Colby's letter would resolve all the unclear points.

BIXBY WAS A good man but a disorganized one; he had put down the
mail delivered by the postal rider and couldn't remember where. Lulu,
her jaw set hard, began to search for it without discussion. She tossed
everything she had been taught about manners and privacy and other
people's belongings aside. No one tried to stop her. People knew what
a rising storm looked like.

   Lulu set aside a newspaper covered with coffee splashes to find the mail underneath. Then she stood, a muscle jumping in her cheek until Mr. Bixby unfolded the letter and adjusted his spectacles.

Dr. & Mrs. Michael Colby
143 East 17th-Street
Manhattan, New York

Mr. Thomas Bixby, Esquire
Attorney at Law
Santa Fe, New Mexico Territory

Dear Sir,
My wife and I are in receipt of your letter with the shocking and tragic news about my wife's brother and his wife. We are devastated and terribly concerned about our niece. There are many questions, but most of those will have to wait until we can meet with you face to face.

From the documents that came with your letter we understand that the midwife Carrie Ballentyne has been entrusted with caring for Lulu until we arrive to take her home to New York. I know Miss Ballentyne and have a very high opinion of her, as do all my colleagues at the New Amsterdam Charity Hospital, where she trained and was employed. My wife is especially thankful to know that Lulu is being looked after by someone who is both kind and experienced in dealing with tragedy.

We—and by this I mean all of my family (my parents are still living, as are two brothers who have large families)—insist that we waste not a day in fetching Lulu home. Please tell her how eager we are to have her with us. To that end, I hope that we will be able to depart for Santa Fe within a week's time. We will travel by rail to St. Louis and then we will hire experienced transport men to get us to Lulu as quickly as possible. Still, I fear it will be September before we arrive.

Please accept our heartfelt thanks for your many kindnesses and for your excellent legal aid in sorting out the estate, and securing Lulu's safety and comfort. We will, of course, assume all financial responsibility for Lulu, and will see to it that your fees and expenditures on behalf of the estate are paid in full.

With sincere thanks and all our gratitude, we remain yours truly, Dr. and Mrs. Michael Colby

LULU STOOD, HER arms crossed, studying the floor. The three adults waited, wondering what was coming next. Or, Eli realized, Carrie knew what was coming, because she fished a handkerchief out of her pocket.

"They want me," he heard Lulu say, her voice clogged with tears. "I didn't think they would."

68

LULU WAS NOT alone in her relief and pleasure with the letter from New York. They now had something to present to the judge that would verify what Mrs. Markham had written in her final statement. Because the Colby family was ready and able to take Lulu in and raise her, Mr. Bixby thought that there was little chance the judge would give Mrs. Chatham anything she was asking for.

Little chance, but Carrie still worried. So she turned her attention to her patients.

It was always an excellent distraction, listening to the stories women brought her. She made notes in what was now her third daybook since she came to Santa Fe, dispensed medication and teas for everything from heat rash to morning sickness to costive bowels, and consulted with Dr. Benenati. When she wasn't in the dispensary, she visited newly delivered mothers and their children, the thing she liked best about her work.

In Carrie's experience, every meeting with a patient started the same way: worries were voiced, questions answered, and a plan agreed upon. The difference in her work at home and here was subtle, and she wondered if Eli might understand. Since they had come to an agreement and married, Carrie had recognized that they would not always be able to understand each other. He seemed to regard her work as a matter of hard-won skill; she was a mechanic, of sorts, but one who saw beyond the surface challenges.

For her own part, Carrie knew that she still didn't understand why he had been dishonest the night of the riot. He had misled her, fully aware of how angry she would be once the trouble was over. They had talked about this at length, and found little common ground. Eli believed he had done what needed to be done, and thought that Carrie, raised with tribes on the New York frontier, should accept his decision.

"You thought that if you told me what you planned to do, I would forbid you. And then what?"

Eli had studied her for a long moment. "I would have gone anyway. I had to go."

They had learned to stay clear of the subject. Until something similar happened. Carrie hoped she could be more rational when the time came.

"SOMETHING ODD," SHE told him later that day. "I was checking in on Helen, and I heard Consuela say something about me."

He raised a brow, and for a moment she wished she hadn't decided to ask his opinion. But there was no going back now.

"She said, *La tía lo sabrá*. Why would she call me aunt? I don't understand."

Eli's smile was almost wistful, and he had to clear his throat before he could answer her.

"She didn't call you aunt, she called you *the* aunt. *La tía*. She said, 'The aunt will know.'"

"Maybe I am being dense," Carrie said, "but I don't see a difference."

He was on his way out to see the surveyor general, and in a hurry. "Take it as a compliment," he said, waved a hand, and was gone.

"Very helpful!" she called after him from the door. "I'll find somebody else who happens to speak Spanish. It may be a challenge, but I will persist!"

In the few minutes it took her to walk to Eva's *cacharrería* on the plaza, Carrie's common sense reasserted itself, but too late; Eva had already seen her and was moving toward the door. She scanned Carrie up and down as if she expected to see a wound of some kind.

"I don't mean to bother you," Carrie said. "I can come back—"

"Don't be ridiculous. Come in."

"I just have a question. Just a simple question."

Eva bit her lower lip as if she wanted to laugh, and then nodded solemnly. "I'm listening."

To CARRIE'S SATISFACTION, Eva was both surprised by the story and very willing to explain.

"It's not all that complicated. You have aunts, yes? You have mentioned them."

Now Carrie couldn't help smiling. "Many aunts, yes. And uncles and cousins."

"So when you're talking to your brother or your cousins about family, what do you call them? Would you say, 'Oh no, the aunts won't like that'? I'm guessing that you do, it's the logical way to talk about a group of people who have something in common. So you have an Aunt Hannah . . ."

Carrie finished the list for her. "Aunt Martha, Aunt Birdie, Aunt Susanna, Aunt Jennet, Aunt Curiosity. Jennet is gone now. Aunt Annie—why do you ask?"

Eva held up a hand. "Which aunt do you think of first when something good or something bad happens?"

She answered without thinking about it. "Aunt Hannah. And then her daughter, Amelie."

"There you go. You have many aunts, but Hannah is *the* aunt. Just think about it for a bit. Every family has that one aunt in particular, and somehow they decide who the aunt is without ever discussing it. And if they don't agree, if there are two aunts who claim precedence, there will be thirty or more years of trouble."

"But, Eva," Carrie said, her tone strained now. "I'm no blood relation to any of the women here. How can I be 'the aunt' to them?"

"It's simple," Eva said. "You are becoming *la tía* to the women of Santa Fe."

WALKING BACK HOME, Carrie considered. Hannah was, without a doubt, the matriarch of the extended Bonner-Savard-Ballentyne-Freeman-Wolf family. Everyone went to Hannah with their worries and disagreements and secret hopes. She kept the family history in her head and, if asked, could pull a second cousin three times removed from memory and tell you how it was that he sailed away to Japan and never came back. She had survived so much, and lived a long time.

In fifty years Carrie might know as much about Santa Fe as Aunt Hannah knew about Paradise and the extended family. It might take that long for her to figure out how she felt about it.

At home Carrie found that Lulu was waiting for her, with more questions. Lulu's mood was much better since they had heard from her aunt and uncle, but she was no less anxious. She would follow Carrie around, skittering from subject to subject and always sure she had forgot the one thing she really needed to know, which only Carrie could explain.

Today Lulu had questions about spending whole days on a train. She needed to know if there would be a necessary, and if there was not, how did people last all day without peeing? This was an important question because she would be traveling with her Uncle and Aunt Colby, and she wanted to be prepared.

Carrie was struck by the girl's serious expression and her almost desperate need to please these relatives she had never met.

"I can tell you about trains, but I have to go visit Mrs. Culpepper just now," she told Lulu. "You can come along with me and we'll talk on the way."

Disappointment blossomed on the girl's face, unmistakable.

"Mrs. Culpepper?" Her nose wrinkled. "But why?"

"She had her baby last week, didn't you hear? A big healthy boy. I'm curious to learn what they decided to name him."

"Well, I can tell you that. They'll name him after his father. Joe Culpepper."

Carrie hesitated. "It's my work. You know that, Lulu. Things have been very busy and I'm falling behind. I have three more patients to see today, after Mrs. Culpepper."

"Too many babies."

She shook her head as if she found the very idea of infants distasteful. Carrie decided to approach from a different angle; the girl might be old enough to understand.

"Lulu, the way things work in a healthy, strong family is that women care for each other. Especially when it comes to birth, we care for mother and child and family too. It would be a very hard life if we didn't. So I'll see Mrs. Culpepper and make sure she is healing as she should, and I'll examine the new baby as well."

Lulu turned her face away. "You mean, make sure that the baby is real."

She plopped down on the *banco* in the hall, and after a moment, Carrie sat beside her.

"What do you mean when you say that babies might not be real?"

A fine trembling now in the girl's voice. "You know. Sometimes babies aren't real people."

Carrie had been waiting for the day this subject would come up. Insofar as she knew, Lulu had never talked about the doll her mother had insisted was a healthy newborn. Her own newborn, a second daughter. A sister to Lulu.

She said, "Lulu, your sister was real when she was born, and then she died."

All the color left the girl's face. "No. She wasn't ever *real*. She was a *baby doll*." Every word distinct, her tone rising syllable by syllable.

"Well," Carrie began slowly. "I'll tell what I saw when I first got here. There was a doll that your mother called Imelda, but she was, as you say, a baby doll, not a real baby. Things sometimes get confused in the mind of a woman when her baby dies at birth. That's what happened with your Mama. In her mind she couldn't accept that your sister had died, so she convinced herself that Imelda was alive."

Lulu turned her face away.

"People can convince themselves of almost anything," Carrie went on. "People in terrible pain are really good at convincing themselves of things that are simply not true. I know a very old woman back home, her dog died last year, but she refuses to believe it. If you ask her, she'll say, 'I don't know what you're talking about. He's sleeping under the apple tree in the garden. He had tripe for his breakfast.' Arguing with her made her mad, but it never changed her mind about that old hound dog.

"So," she went on. "I remember your doll. She had blue eyes and pink cheeks and beautiful hair, just about the same color as yours. That doll was made from china or porcelain, I think. What was her name?"

The answer came in a whisper, as if Lulu feared being overheard. "Corabelle."

Carrie took a moment to quiet her own breathing, and then she stepped very carefully.

"When I was little, I shared a doll with my sisters. We called her Jane because it was the only name we could agree about. I think Corabelle is a lovely name for a doll. What happened to Corabelle, can you tell me?"

And this was the hardest blow. Lulu shook with it as a flood of tears erupted.

"She was my doll! Corabelle was mine. She never belonged to anybody else, not until Mama stole her from me in the night. She changed

Corabelle's name to Imelda and yelled at me when I wouldn't pretend. Until I did pretend because—because I had to. I gave in and called her—called her— And now she's in the grave with Mama."

Carrie was weeping, too, out of compassion for a little girl who was overwhelmed by anger and resentment. Angry at the mother she had adored, because her mother had left her for a grave that she would share with a doll.

To be so angry at someone you loved, and to have that person choose to die, that would leave a wound that might never heal.

"You are breathing funny." Lulu's eyes narrowed, as if there were a message on Carrie's face she couldn't quite make out.

"Like somebody who has got sunstroke and is about to keel over," she went on.

"You're right." Carrie's voice wavered and cracked. "Give me a moment to catch my breath and I'll tell you why, if you want to hear."

Lulu, ever curious, nodded.

"When I was little," Carrie began, "not quite so young as you are now, I had a sister called Martha. She was the prettiest girl in Paradise, but so stubborn and quite selfish sometimes. She did some very bad things, and I was angry at her. I was so angry at her that I turned my back when she asked me for help."

A long pause as the girl considered. "And then?"

"Then she died. I was angry at her, but I didn't want her to die."

"You feel guilty," Lulu said. "You feel guilty because she needed help and you said no."

"There are many things I feel guilty about."

This was not a conversation she could have, and she hoped that Lulu, as intuitive as she was, would understand.

There was a longer silence, almost companionable.

Lulu said, "Do you know about La Llorona? The wailing woman, they call her, or sometimes the weeping woman. A ghost always looking for her lost babies. I wonder if Mama is La Llorona. She could never get the baby she wanted."

———

WHEN LULU LEFT for home with Chico at her side, Carrie started out to call on Mrs. Culpepper. The path took her along an *acequia*, a canal lined with trees that touched overhead, making a shady tunnel. It was as peaceful and pretty a spot as Carrie had ever known, and still she was aware of La Llorona, who followed. If she were to turn around, she would see her, deep in conversation with Martha.

The Culpepper baby, the third child and first son, was, as Bonner women liked to say, in rude good health. Young Daniel Culpepper went to the breast enthusiastically whenever it was offered, slept for stretches of five hours, and had yet to show his family a bad mood. But he was not without fault, she was to understand.

"He poops a lot," one of the sisters reported. "Stinkiest poop ever."

Carrie excused herself before she could get drawn into the sisters' argument about relative stinkiness of infant poop.

By the time she had finished with the three additional visits she had slated for the day, she was dripping sweat. She started for home, thinking of cool water and the shady corners of the *placita*, and trying not to think of Lulu or La Llorona or Martha.

There were delays, as there often were when she walked through town. Nachín Justo stopped to ask her opinion about a swelling on his wrist; Alba Abeyta, a potter, had a spider bite on her thigh that just would not heal; and the young nun everyone called MaLucia asked about a rash that was spreading through her classroom. It was a challenge to remain polite and kind when she was so worn out, but she did her best, which in all three cases meant only that Dr. Benenati would have to be consulted. Tomorrow, at the dispensary.

At home Eli seemed to be reorganizing his clothes. He greeted her with a wide smile, which fell away almost immediately.

"You need an hour in a dark room," he said. "Go lie down, I'll bring you water."

Confused, on edge, Carrie looked around herself at this project of his. She could make no sense of it.

"An hour," Eli said. "And then I'll explain."

WHEN SHE WOKE, Carrie wanted to go back to sleep but she also wanted water and food, and she still needed to talk to Eli about Mrs. Chatham. Mr. Bixby seemed to think that Mrs. Chatham's plans could not survive the letters from Dr. Colby, whose claim was far more legally sound. That was enough for the lawyer; he assumed she would simply withdraw.

For her part, Carrie was sure Mrs. Chatham would not. She imagined the woman sitting in a corner somewhere, going over a different plan. Any plan to get control of Lulu and, more importantly, Lulu's inheritance.

She hoped Eli had a plan, because Carrie had no idea how to stop Coyote Woman.

She found him in the kitchen pouring a bucket of water into the almost-filled hip bath.

"I forgive you," she said. "For anything and everything."

Eli was grinning in that particular way that was not alarming, but it did put her on alert. As did the fact that he was wearing clothes she hadn't seen before. For the moment the bath could wait.

"Didn't know I own a fancy suit, did you?"

She cleared her throat. "That's you—your—"

Eli looked down at himself. "Yup, this is me. Who else?"

Carrie crossed her arms and leaned against the wall. "When I saw you last, you were in buckskins and an old field shirt with split seams and ink stains."

"You don't like me cleaned up?"

A small sound, harrumph-like, issued from deep in her throat, a habit that she had been trying to break because Nathan had said she was practicing to sound like an old lady. But Eli's mouth had curled in a grin, the one that seemed to say he had caught her in a joke or surprise.

Eli's clothes were practical, suited to the rough work he did. She still thought now and then of the night he had stopped outside the Westport hotel in driving rain and let all three horses stand while he looked at her standing in the window of her room. His hat, broad brimmed and low crowned, the brass-studded leather gloves with high gauntlets: now all that gear for traveling in bad weather was just down the hall, hung on hooks in the storeroom off the stable with tack and saddles and tarps. His clothes were well-made, and much mended, all of them out of canvas, denim, cotton, leather, doeskin, or linen. He had a pair of good breeches and a shirt he kept for meetings with officials and wealthy patrons who might hire him.

Nothing she had seen of his clothes compared to what he wore now. He stood before her, clean-shaven, barbered, and dressed like a banker.

No, she corrected herself. Not a banker. Maybe a merchant, one who sold expensive tools. A mill owner. A corn broker. That image almost made her laugh. She gestured with her hand for him to turn in a circle, and he did that, arms extended.

He wore a double-breasted vest and trousers of brushed cotton, both a deep chestnut in color. The trousers had riveted buttons of polished silver to anchor a pair of suspenders that still hung at his sides. The shirt, off-white with a faint tan stripe, had a standing collar. On a hook near the door, he had hung a sack coat of what looked like herringbone tweed. For the final touch he wore a string tie, neatly knotted.

Then she saw he wore moccasins, and she smiled. The moccasins gave her back her equilibrium.

She said, "What have I forgotten? Is the president in town?"

"Nobody that big," he said. "Bixby came by to invite us to supper at the fonda, to meet with Ford."

All her irritation seeped away. "Judge Ford?"

"That's the one. He got into town this afternoon. Told Bixby he'll listen to the whole Coyote Woman story before he decides what to do about the complaint she filed. But first things first, aren't you going to look at my . . . head?"

Eli bent low and turned so that she was looking directly at the wound. Her hands were cool and her touch steady as she traced it from one end to the other, looking for tender spots or blood or corruption.

No, he told her, it hadn't bled at all today. No trace of pus or discharge. Yes, he told her, it was tender to the touch, but at the same time he could report that the headache was gone.

"Satisfied?"

He knew it was odd, but he liked the way she delivered an entire sermon with a single glance. The twinging in his scalp reminded him that she had cause to be angry.

She was eyeing the hip bath. "I take it that's for me."

"I had one an hour ago," he said. "But if you don't want a bath—"

Carrie stepped in front of the bath, as if she planned to defend it from hostile overthrow. "I'll need a half hour," she said. "To bathe and change."

Eli would have stayed, but she chased him off.

"I'm not letting you near me in the bath," she said.

"Ever?"

Her mouth quirked. "Ever again when there's a chance of somebody walking in."

So he waited, pacing back and forth while he listened to her wash. He heard her humming under her breath, and knew she was feeling better.

He did follow her when she went to sort through clothes and get dressed for the meeting at the fonda. Generally, it seemed to him that she wasn't as fussy as many women were about clothing, but it took her a few minutes behind the curtain where she kept her things.

Finally, she backed out with her arms full. Over one arm she had the blue dress that he had seen in St. Louis at the wedding party, before things got started between them. Over the other was a rippling pile of sage green silk.

She managed a grim smile. "My choices for a meeting somewhere as fancy as the fonda are limited. Do you have a preference?"

He hadn't expected the question, and it took a moment to come up with an answer. "I'd like to see you in that flowery one again, but—"

Her head came up sharply. "When have you seen me in the periwinkle?" And: "Oh, that night in St. Louis. You were dancing with Eva. I thought she was your wife, did you realize?"

"Not right then, but Eva made me aware."

Through layers of sage green silk sliding over her head, her voice came muffled. "Of course, Eva took note. Was she shocked?"

"Eva? She told me that I shouldn't let you get away."

Some more swishing of silk, and she shook out the gown so the skirts settled.

It surprised Eli how well the sage green silk suited her. The shimmer somehow brought out the red in her hair and drew attention to the otherworldly blue of her eyes. He didn't know how to say something like that without sounding foolish, but he gave it thought. It would make her blush to hear such a compliment, and he liked making her blush.

She was looking over her shoulder at her back.

"All these buttons. Would you mind?"

He sat on the edge of the table and pulled her to stand, backward, in the V of his spread knees. The buttons were small and set close together, but the room was filled with evening light, and his eyes were sharp. And still he hesitated.

"Something wrong?"

"Hold up." His voice came hoarse.

He knew her body, but somehow the sight of her back framed in sage green silk robbed him of breath.

It wasn't all she wore, of course. There was a chemise of tissue-thin fabric that was hiked up to her ribs, waiting to be straightened and smoothed. Below her waist her petticoats gleamed white, and in between, naked Carrie. It startled him still, how skin never touched by the sun would be so warm in color, white, yes, but tempered by blue and rose shadows and as smooth as buttermilk. Her spine ran down like a path of polished stones he was tempted to follow. He drew in her smell, and it made him a little dizzy.

They were expected at the fonda. He focused on that fact and started with the lowest buttons, where the swell of her hips began. He had to lean closer to match buttons to buttonholes, and she shivered.

"Cold?"

An almost ribald laugh. "Hardly. Your breath on the small of my back startled me."

"Really?" He leaned close and huffed another soft breath. This time she shivered fiercely and leaned back, just very slightly, into him.

"I've been meaning to ask you," he said, his voice steadier than he expected. "Is there a name for these divots?"

He pressed his open mouth to the dimples at the small of her back, and she jolted.

"Eli—"

She turned, or maybe he turned her. It didn't matter. He was standing now, their bodies pressed together. His hands sliding down her exposed back, down and down to cup her buttocks.

Her mouth opened against his with a soft sound. Carrie had a way of drawing in her breath that pulled him apart into a thousand pieces, every one of which he must press into her until they were melded together. The sweet heat of her mouth and the touch of her tongue were his last coherent thoughts for some time.

CARRIE SAID, "I don't know that my sage green silk will survive such rude handling. Lord knows I might not." And she laughed. Spread open underneath Eli, stripped naked, she felt all her worries melt into nothingness and, in their place, laughter. She arched up, and Eli groaned, his attention shifting once again to the place they were joined. She saw this happening and began to pull away, rapped the heel of her hand against his scalp to get his attention, and remembered the wound too late. He winced and rolled away, but he was grinning.

"Finally," he said. "I was wondering when you'd get around to beating me."

THE FONDA COULD hardly be more than a hundred years old, from what Carrie knew of Santa Fe's history. The buildings showed some wear, but on the whole there was both style and dignity, and evidence of an imagination in the way things were arranged as well. Carrie was reminded of a vainglorious, very correct grandmother with a wicked past.

The portico was lined with pots full of geraniums, bold reds and oranges and purples against somber green foliage. Just beyond was a sculpture of a woman holding a working lantern. She sat in the middle of a broad clay basin that had been planted with ivy. The vines wound around the naked form, leaving only her face, part of one leg, a shoulder, and one breast free. In a place where public art was strictly Roman Catholic, this seemed a daring departure, and Carrie wondered if maybe she had assumed too much—or expected too little—of the people who owned the hotel.

In the reception area a small crowd of people stood together talking. In the early mornings when she walked past the Palace of the Governors, Carrie saw many of the same men waiting for the territorial offices to open. These were the people who believed anything and everything was for sale in a territory where the U.S. Army protected their rights and, as they saw it, owed allegiance to no one else. She had very little to do with any of them—she only rarely saw their wives and daughters, but their sons sometimes came to the dispensary when their piss began to burn like the fire of hell. They might not like the old Italian doctor, but he knew the business, and while he was gruff, he never betrayed a patient, no matter how many gold mines or how many acres his father might own.

Carrie was simply overlooked, which was exactly what she expected in a setting like this one. Eli was better known and had many business contacts, some of whom acknowledged him with a nod and a half smile. Then a waiter came to show them to their table.

He bowed politely, but there was a curl to his lip that made his dislike obvious.

"Please." He made a sweeping gesture with one arm. Then he hesitated, and a small but distinct sound came from his throat, like the snapping of a twig. With that he said what he couldn't hold back. His Spanish was strained and awkward.

"El señor Bixby ha estado aquí con el juez Ford por casi media hora."

A public insult was not so unusual, but in a formal setting like this one, and from a waiter, that was remarkable. A young man who dared to scold a patron of the hotel for making his dinner companions wait was either very sure of his position and his social standing, or he was foolhardy.

Eli had gone very still, but he smiled, and that was clue enough about how he would respond. It wasn't a smile Carrie saw very often, and it always surprised her when she did.

His gaze fixed on the waiter while the younger man fussed with his cuff and straightened his vest and did his best to look unconcerned. He did not regret insulting them, and wanted Eli to know that.

Eli's voice went low and rough.

"Manuelito."

In time—it seemed a long time—the waiter met his gaze. When that happened, Carrie understood that this young man wanted and even needed to show Eli contempt, but common sense and fear were gaining the upper hand.

"Manuelito," Eli said again, almost crooning. *"Baboso malparido. ¿Nos regañas?"*

The waiter blanched. Later, Carrie would have to ask Eli for a colloquial translation, because everything that came to mind seemed unlikely. She would ask Eva, too; Eva would not hesitate to explain all the subtleties. Carrie was still thinking about *baboso malparido* when they arrived at the table.

Mr. Bixby and Judge Ford came to their feet, all welcoming smiles. Carrie let out a breath she had been holding, seeing now that the waiter hadn't been echoing the sentiments of the two men whose goodwill was so important to Lulu's future.

"It is very good to see you again, Mrs. Ibarra, Mr. Ibarra. Though I regret the circumstances."

Carrie blinked. "Regret?"

But Judge Ford had turned to Mr. Bixby and a waiter—a different waiter—to order food for the table. A great deal of food, and wine as well. All in good humor, nothing too serious in his manner.

When he turned back to Carrie, he held up both hands as if this would stop her from asking questions.

"*Regret* may be too strong a word. I thought we had the little Markham girl all sorted, but now Mrs. Chatham—"

He looked over his shoulder, scanned the room, and shrugged. "It seems she's left."

Under the table Eli's hand settled on Carrie's. It was a quiet reminder, and one she needed. She would step back and trust him to negotiate this maze.

Eli raised a brow in Bixby's direction. The lawyer's scalp was turning a bright shade of red under the sparse crop of white hair, and his eyes were rounded in alarm.

"It wasn't my doing," he said. He would have gone on, but Eli's smile—this time—was gentle, and Bixby relaxed.

"So you've met with Mrs. Chatham," Eli said to the judge, his tone casual.

"Oh yes." Ford picked up his wineglass and sniffed. "They wasted no time seeking me out."

Eli tilted his head. "They? She wasn't alone?"

"Didn't you know?" the judge asked. "She's got a sweetheart." He was trying not to smirk.

Mr. Bixby was ill at ease, but prompted, he told the story.

"I just learned, not an hour ago, that Mr. Whiting has been showing her attention. Serious attention. They are here for dinner and supper almost every day."

"The postmaster." Ford shrugged. "Besotted with her. Hangs on her every word. I thought the man had better taste, to speak plain. But there they were, waiting for me. I didn't have much time to give them. I wouldn't be surprised if she knocks on my door in a couple hours."

When the food came, there was little talk at the table. Carrie hadn't thought she'd be able to eat, given the events of the day, and then found she couldn't ignore the dishes, unfamiliar to her but enticing. They were served *escamoles* fried in butter and wrapped in corn tortillas, a salad of tiny avocados, a vegetable called *huauzontle* that had reminded Carrie of broccoli when she saw it being sold in the marketplace. The broccoli she knew had never been prepared with such imagination, she was sure: *huauzontles* were stuffed with cheese, deep-fried in an egg batter, and came on a pool of a sauce that tasted of cilantro, chilies, and cream. Finally, when she could not take another bite, a tureen of *pozole* was brought to the table, full of roasted pork and tomatillos, chilies, and *maíz cacahuacintle*, the huge white kernels of hominy that were so loved.

Her appetite had been conquered before anyone else's, and so she sat quietly and watched the other diners. She wondered if Mrs. Chatham was nearby with Mr. Whiting, and tried to imagine what they might be talking about. She could not think of two people more different, but she was also very aware, given the patients she worked with, that love was unpredictable.

Unless, of course, this was another one of Mrs. Chatham's schemes to win custody of Lulu. Maybe tomorrow they would finally learn what had really brought her so far.

In a lowered voice, Judge Ford was talking to Bixby about local events.

"So it was the cavalry?"

Bixby nodded. "They broke down the door and started shooting."

Ford shook his head. "Of course it was Jack Purdy's doing, all of it. One of his rages. I have warned McCall a half dozen times to take the man's blasted cane away from him, but—" He shrugged. "My guess is that he owes Purdy some favor or is otherwise beholden, because he never does anything about the man. No matter who he beats."

"I wasn't on the plaza," Bixby said. "But I've heard from men who were, including Mr. Ibarra, as a matter of fact."

Carrie's head came up at an angle, something neither the lawyer nor the judge noticed. Her attention was focused on a table on the opposite side of the room, where three officers from Fort Marcy were finishing a meal.

She cast a quick glance at Eli, and her gaze skittered back across the room to the officers.

"Yeah," he said. "That's him."

Purdy was in good spirits, tipping back a measure of whiskey and then laughing, openmouthed and in full voice, poking the man next to him until he was satisfied with the reaction.

Bixby followed Carrie's line of sight and agreed with Eli.

"Speak of the devil, as they say. No sign of a bullet wound on his shoulder now, is there. To his left is Major St. Pierre, the head surgeon. The third officer is one of the Sprague brothers—Josiah, if I'm remembering right. Captain in the Third Infantry. Those three spend a lot of time together."

"I'm sure," Eli said drily. "Discussing the lynch law and how it doesn't apply to them."

Ford turned a brilliant dark eye on Eli. "You think that the army's assumption of extrajudicial authority was not justified?"

"It was not," Eli said, never hesitating. "I would say that it almost never is. But in this case, when drunken soldiers kick their way into a jail and shoot unarmed prisoners who haven't been convicted, or even tried in a court of law? They should have been charged with assault and murder."

Carrie squeezed his hand, but her expression gave nothing away. He might have caused a rift with the judge that would never be mended, but after many days of thinking about the raid on the jail, she understood how close his anger was to the surface.

"Well," Ford said. He emptied his wineglass and set it down with a thump. "To that I can only say that I agree."

He was still smiling, but he narrowed his eyes, studying Eli more intently.

"Weren't you with the Whipple expedition back in '53–'54?"

"I was," Eli said.

"Rough time on the Colorado." Ford's tone meant he would not take offense if Eli chose to ignore the subject raised. In fact, Eli didn't speak often about the years he spent with the surveyors on the Whipple expedition. If she asked, he would tell her. She was certain of that, and a bit uncomfortable with her certainty.

"And now you have Mrs. Chatham to deal with," the judge was saying. "I'd guess the Colorado was less trouble. That woman's tongue is hung in the middle so she can flap it double time."

Carrie let out a squeak of surprised laughter before she could stop herself.

Eli said, "She may be irritating, I couldn't argue with you there. The question is whether she has any grounds for her claim on Lulu. Any grounds that might change your mind about how the girl is best attended to."

"I understand the aunt and uncle from Manhattan are on the way here," Ford said. "If that's the case, then Mrs. Chatham's claims are without merit. And there are questions—I hear from Bixby and others—about Chatham's motivations. I'd rather see the girl safely settled with family in Manhattan."

Carrie cleared her throat. "I see your point, Judge Ford. But if I may suggest, I think it would be very useful if you were to talk to Lulu yourself, and let her tell you what she knows. Some of it—" Her voice broke, and she paused to take a drink of water. "Will surprise you."

"Well," Ford said, holding his empty glass up for the waiter to see. "Let's agree to meet tomorrow. Not a hearing, mind you. Nothing official. But maybe I can give the little girl some peace of mind, and also get the Chatham woman to come out with some truths. My sense is, she hasn't provided many thus far."

AS THEY LEFT the fonda, Eli paused and looked toward the staircase that led to the guest rooms.

"What?" Carrie looked, too, and saw nothing that might have caught his interest.

"The idea of Whiting courting Chatham. There's something odd there. Something off."

"Do you have any specific suspicions?"

He shook his head. "But others might."

The walk home was quick, and they were both so lost in their thoughts that they said nothing more.

Some time later, after the chores were done and Eli had checked on the horses, he stopped in the doorway of the *placita*, where Carrie sat quietly, looking at the sky overhead.

"Ready for bed?"

"Not quite yet," Eli told her. "I need to run a quick errand. At most I'll be gone an hour."

"Should I ask what you're up to?"

His nose wrinkled. "Not yet. Maybe not ever. Go on to bed, I'll be back soon."

The question that plagued Carrie, one she couldn't just put aside, was whether she should have told the judge Lulu's story about the cat and her kittens.

She could imagine him dismissing it with a wave of the hand. A child's story about an event—a troubling event, yes, and so many years ago—would have very limited use in a court of law. But the images had dug themselves deep in her mind, and it didn't matter how the judge interpreted the story. The courts could ignore it all, but Carrie wouldn't be satisfied until Mrs. Chatham was called to account.

She went to bed determined to keep that goal foremost in her mind.

69

THE NEXT DAY Judge Ford sent a note telling them that the meeting had to be delayed until one in the afternoon. Eli was glad not to have to rouse Carrie, and relieved to see a second face at the door, a familiar one. Iñigo was nothing like Eli's father, but when they sat together and spoke Basque, he felt closer to home.

Eli managed to wait until they were sitting in the *placita*, but only because Iñigo's self-satisfied grin indicated things had gone well. He would have to swallow his impatience; the man was equal to almost any scheme, but he could not tell a story gracefully. A story Eli could tell in three sentences Iñigo could spin out for an hour. But not today; Eli would not wait any longer.

"Iñigo."

"*Sí, sí, sí*, you want to know about Coyote Woman's new sweetheart."

Eli would have winced at the word, but it would not be good to set Iñigo off in a different direction.

He nodded. "I do."

Iñigo returned his nod, very solemn.

"Well," he began. "Coyote Woman spends a lot of time with Whiting, the one with the long face who runs the post office. And he has spent the night in her room at the fonda, more than once. I got this from Gloria, one of the cleaning women. Do you know Gloria? Fidel's daughter, a fine strong woman, and observant. She sees everything."

This confirmed one of Eli's suspicions, but not the most important one.

"So then I knocked on John Edmonds's door. I like John, always have. Such a conscientious young man, and clever. When I told him what we wanted to do for Lulu, he didn't hesitate."

Iñigo in a leading role was a trial.

Eli started, "Iñigo—"

He held up a hand. "So, here's what you want to know. Usually Josefa keeps the boy fed, but this morning he made some excuse and went into the dining room to eat. He took the table right next to Coyote Woman, waited until she was finished talking to the waiter, and asked her about her plans for Lulu. He always looks so solemn, and those sad eyes of his worked on Coyote Woman. They got to talking."

"Makes sense," Eli said. "She thought she had a new witness who'd support her claims."

Iñigo nodded. "While he was doing that, I went to see what I could find. Took about a quarter hour, but then she didn't bother really hiding the loot."

He wiggled in his chair, really pleased to share this part of the story.

"A whole drawer full of mail."

Eli let out the breath he had been holding. "Addressed to?"

"Not to her." Iñigo grinned. "From what I could tell, they were all sent from the East."

Eli got up to pace the room and sat down again.

"What did you do with the mail?"

"I dumped it all in a pillow slip, knocked on Ford's door—just down the hall—and left the whole mess with him."

"And now?"

Iñigo shrugged. "The judge said he'd need the morning to look through it all and make some sense of it. Said he was going to consult with Bixby and Chucho. You're making a face. Did you want to read the letters first?"

"No!" Eli paced once again. "It's enough that Ford has them. If nothing else, Mrs. Chatham's guilty of mail theft, and that's a federal crime."

"Good news for Lulu." Iñigo rubbed his belly and got up to wander into the kitchen.

"Any food to be had?"

"Red Rosa will feed you," Eli suggested. "Just don't tell her about Coyote Woman until this mess is set right."

It was the hardest thing, but once Iñigo was gone, Eli forbade himself to wake Carrie, even with good news. He had hardly slept himself, but sleep was what she needed. Then she came through into the *placita*. A deep V had carved itself between her brows, a sure sign that she was displeased.

"Eli! We are missing our appointment with the judge."

"No, he delayed it a few hours," Eli told her. "Go back to sleep, *querida*. I'll warn you a half hour before we need to leave."

"Come lie down with me," she said, holding out a hand. "I want to hear one of your stories."

He said, "Have I ever told you about Iñigo's misspent youth?"

70

At noon, dressed in her periwinkle blue, Carrie left with Eli for their appointment with Judge Ford. There was no need to stop by the dispensary, he told her. Eva and Josefa, Violante and Iñigo, and even Chico would walk with Lulu. Dr. Benenati had also been summoned, but she was not to concern herself.

"I worry about your memory," she told Eli. "You do recall that I don't like to be managed, don't you? I have the strong sense that something is happening you aren't ready to tell me. Something about Ford or—she who should not be named."

His smile was quick, and the only answer she got. The plain fact was that Eli wouldn't give in to her bullying. It was a tremendous relief. This observation—a confession—she kept to herself, biting her lip to keep her smile hidden.

They met in Mr. Bixby's office, far too small for such a crowd. Just the people who came in support of Lulu would have been too many, but lined up at the back of the room were Chucho and three of his deputies.

"The sheriff?" Carrie mouthed the words to Eva, who looked just as confused and concerned as she felt.

Then Judge Ford came in, his expression so dark that Carrie's heart leapt into her throat.

"So," he said, when he had put a portfolio down beside him on the table. "This is turning out to be a story to tell my grandchildren. Let me start by telling you that there will be no hearing about the custody of young Lulu Markham, because the person who filed the complaint has disappeared."

The shifting and murmuring grew louder while Lulu climbed up on a chair.

"Is she dead too?"

"I'll let the sheriff address that question," said the judge. But he gave Lulu a kind look that said she had nothing to worry about.

Chucho cleared his throat and stepped forward. "We tried to locate Mrs. Chatham at the fonda at about nine a.m., and found she had checked out. A hired transport left town at about that same time, with two passengers. We believe the passengers were Mrs. Chatham and Mr. Whiting."

"Oh," Lulu said, as if it all made sense to her. "I guess he won't be looking for a wife anymore."

There was a strained silence, and then Eva crouched down to talk to Lulu in a whisper.

"Sorry," Lulu called out. "I'll be quiet now. But—"

She stopped herself, but the judge gestured with a cupped hand that she should ask her question.

"Why was Chucho looking for her?"

"To arrest her," the judge said. "On my orders. When she is found, she'll be brought back here and charged with mail theft, among other things. Together with Mr. Whiting."

Iñigo let out a huge, braying laugh that would have got a sharp reprimand in any other judge's office. Judge Ford tolerated it with a single raised brow.

"You will be wondering," he went on finally, "how I decided to charge them both with a federal crime. Very early this morning, evidence was surrendered to me. Some dozen letters that an interested party found hidden in Mrs. Chatham's room. Under normal circumstances such evidence would be considered suspect, but these letters all bore postmarks from cities east of the Mississippi, and were not addressed to Mr. Whiting or Mrs. Chatham, but to individuals in this room. Mr. Bixby can confirm this, as he examined the evidence too."

He looked to Mr. Bixby for comment, but Violante was too anxious to hold back any longer.

"Judge Ford," Violante called out. "She stole some mail, yes, I don't doubt you. People send money through the mail, and Coyote Woman is greedy. But what does that have to do with our Lulu?"

The judge took an envelope from his portfolio.

"I am glad you asked. There were only four letters that had been opened. This was one of them. Given the seriousness of the situation, I read it. It's addressed to you, Dr. Benenati. Postmarked Richmond, Virginia. With your permission I'll read it out loud. It will clear up a lot of the confusion."

Dr. Benenati lifted his arm and made a graceful gesture with his hand.

"You are sure, Doctor?"

"*Sí, sí.* Please, read it."

John Smithson, Esq.
Smithson, Smithson & Gardner
Attorneys at Law
Monument Avenue
Richmond, Virginia

July 5, 1857

Dr. Enzo Benenati
Santa Fe, New Mexico Territory

Dear Dr. Benenati,

You will wonder why you are receiving a letter from an attorney you have never met, but I hope I may have your attention for a short period of time without causing you alarm. I assure you that the matter I write about here does not impinge in any way on your person or any person in your family, to the best of my knowledge.

On the 10th November last year, a long-time client of mine passed on. Dr. Ewell was from a very old and respected Richmond family, and the last of his line. His elder daughter lives in Richmond and was at his death-bed. His younger daughter has been in New Mexico Territory since her marriage, about ten years ago.

Since Dr. Ewell's death I have written three times to his daughter Indira, the wife of one of your colleagues, Dr. Samuel Markham. None of my letters received a reply.

From my notes it seems that when you retired from medicine, you sold your practice to Dr. Markham. It is my hope that the Markhams are still in Santa Fe. I do not ask you to deliver the enclosed letter to them, but instead, to speak to their attorney, whose name I do not know. There are urgent matters to be addressed in order to resolve Dr. Ewell's estate, but to make that happen, I have to have word from his daughter Indira, or a certified document confirming her death. Her half-sister is quite sure that this is, in fact, the case, but the law is unyielding in such matters.

The doctor and his younger daughter were not on good terms, following from a disagreement at least ten years in the past. Nevertheless, Dr. Ewell's last will and testament specifically states that the entire estate—and it is very large—must go to whatever grandchildren he may have, divided into equal portions.

As I understand it, Dr. and Mrs. Markham have a daughter. He told me so when it was clear that he would not recover from his final illness. He did not tell me how he knew this, but was certain of the fact.

If he was mistaken, or if the granddaughter is no longer living, the estate will be divided between Dr. Ewell's two daughters.

There is one complicating factor that I share only because you may need this information to convince you to approach Markham's attorney on such a personal matter. Dr. Ewell's elder daughter, Mrs. Kanthi Chatham, a widow, is exceedingly anxious about the resolution of this matter. If word does not come soon from Mrs. Markham, I fear her half-sister will make ill-advised decisions on how to proceed.

This is an imposition, and I would never attempt so much if the matter were not of crucial importance. I thank you for any assistance you can offer in this matter.

Sincerely yours,
John Smithson, Esq.

71

ELI SAW THE transition happen in the blink of an eye. Carrie, relieved of her concern for Lulu so suddenly, had immediately turned her mind to the fact that Mrs. Chatham had robbed her of personal letters.

The very second Ford called the meeting to a close, she was on her way to the desk where the judge was sorting through papers.

"Judge Ford," she said, almost breathlessly. "A question." She paused to cast a stern eye over the others who were inching forward with questions of their own.

"Yes, Mrs. Ibarra?"

"Who were the stolen letters addressed to?"

He hesitated. "You understand that we are talking about evidence that will be used when Mrs. Chatham is tried? Evidence can't be handed around like sweeties, Mrs. Ibarra, without being rendered useless. You do want to see Mrs. Chatham tried, I take it, after all the trouble she has caused you."

Eli watched this exchange with some concern. Carrie seemed to assume the judge was being dense. His expression said the same of her.

"Judge Ford." Her voice cracked just lightly as she fought to control her tone. "It has been many months since I've had any word from my family. If there are letters addressed to me, I want them now. Immediately. Do not talk to me about evidence, I will not hear it. Can I not trust the experience and expertise of the members of the bar to prosecute Mrs. Chatham for her crimes, to the fullest extent of the law? Beyond the law, if you choose. But it must be done without my letters. Which were stolen from me, and which you are now withholding without sufficient reason."

"Mrs. Ibarra, I assure you—"

She leaned forward so abruptly that he stepped back.

"Judge Ford," she said, repeating his name very softly. "Do I need to remind you how U.S. mail addressed to me came into your possession?"

Surprise, confusion, and then dismay raced across his face. Eli could almost read his thoughts. Was he being accused of playing a role in mail theft? Impossible. No one would believe it . . . but then his gaze locked on hers, and he swallowed. Suddenly he saw Carrie for who she was, and realized he had underestimated her.

Eli had no idea what would happen here or if he could stop what might be coming. In this temper Carrie was a stranger to him. A very attractive, interesting stranger. Intriguing, but unpredictable and possibly dangerous.

Judge Ford's brows lowered and his face contorted. If Eli had not seen Ford make this exact face just before he lost a game of chess, he might have been truly worried.

CARRIE DEBATED HOW best to secure the letters—three of them— on the short walk home. Eli was watching her, she was very aware. She blew out a deep breath and handed them over.

He tucked them underneath his shirt and was about to say something, when his expression went blank. Carrie hadn't often seen Eli truly surprised, but that was the case now.

"What—"

He took her shoulder and turned her around.

"The judge meant it when he said he was sending trackers after Chatham and Whiting."

At first Carrie saw nothing unusual. People came and went on the plaza, headed home for dinner and siesta. Three men on horseback sat just opposite the Palace of the Governors. Post riders, she thought at first glance. Then one of them turned a sunburned face in her direction.

Rainey Bang took his hat off and waved with it, and shouted, "Look, boss, there they are. Ibarra and the nurse. Or I guess I should say Ibarra and Mrs. Ibarra."

Titus Hardy and Miguel Santos started toward Eli and Carrie at a leisurely pace, but Rainey Bang was already out of the saddle and shaking Eli's hand.

"Aren't you the sly one, never said a word about courting the nurse. I wondered why you wanted to ride with us."

Eli's mouth quirked at one corner. "Didn't want our business spread around before we worked out the details."

Rainey's face clenched while he worked through this, but Hardy, coming up behind him, didn't wait.

"What Ibarra means," he told Rainey, "is that you couldn't keep a secret to save your life. You got tongue enough for ten rows of teeth."

"Talk the hide off a cow," Miguel added.

"Now leave Rainey be," Carrie said. "There's no harm in him."

Both Hardy and Santos ducked their heads to hide their smiles.

Eli said, "What are you three doing here, anyway? I thought you was headed for Texas."

"That's an interesting story," Hardy said. "We came across one of the Turner boys—you'll have heard the name, a real talent for sneaking away with somebody else's *remuda* in the dead of night."

He seemed to realize he was talking too much and too fast, because he cleared his throat.

"We brought him here to collect the reward."

Rainey, his voice rough with excitement, tried to cut in. "And then—"

Hardy threw him a hard look, and the boy shrugged.

"And then," Hardy went on, "we ran into Ford, and he hired us on the spot. Soon as we get some grub, we'll be off looking for the postmaster and a lady—Miguel, what was her name?"

"All I remember is she wears fancy clothes and has the postmaster picking pockets for her."

"And she was after Lulu," Rainey added, scowling. "Judge Ford said so. And her newly orphaned."

"Enough reason to hog-tie her and drag her back here, whatever her name is," Hardy said. Miguel and Rainey grunted their agreement.

"That much information I can give you," Eli said. "Around here we call her Coyote Woman."

AT HOME CARRIE sat for a long time with her letters in her lap, her hands spread over them. She heard Eli moving around the other side of the house, and wondered what he had been thinking when the judge took the bundle of envelopes from his portfolio and offered it to her on an extended palm.

There had been the vaguest hint of a smile on the judge's face, but Eli had probably not seen it. They could debate about that smile, whether it was born out of frustration or embarrassment, but it didn't really matter. Eli had not been shocked or displeased. What she saw there was admiration. Through the whole encounter, she had felt him standing at her back, but he had never spoken a word or inserted himself in any way.

And after running into Hardy, he was in high spirits.

"Can't you just hear him and Coyote Woman snarling and snapping at each other? Almost worth riding after them to watch."

He threw up a hand to stop her objection.

"I'm not going anywhere, I promise. You've got more important things to think about." He walked down the hall to his office and left her there to consider.

The letters were still on her lap. It was clear that they had been opened, but she wouldn't let that distract her. She wanted a few quiet minutes to read them, but it was dim and cool in the *placita*, and she was content to sit quietly until Eli had stopped laughing at the idea of Hardy trying to get Coyote Woman back to Santa Fe. And she was exhausted, suddenly. She put her head down on her folded arms, meaning only to rest for a few minutes.

"Carrie?"

She startled awake, ten minutes or an hour later. Eli stood in the hall, dressed in his oldest work clothes.

"I thought you might want some time alone," he said. "I'll eat at Rosita's and then I've got some work to do for the Petit brothers. I'll be about six hours, if you think that'll be long enough."

Six hours to read the letters she had been waiting for. Of course it wasn't enough time. Of course it was far too much time to be without him.

"As long as you come back to me. Eli?"

He turned back from the door, head canted, and she managed finally what she had first wanted to do on the Missouri River.

She winked.

EPILOGUE

Jennet Bonner
The Strawberry Fields
Paradise on the Sacandaga

June 6, 1857

To my sadly absent but most beloved cousin Carrie,
I promised to write you with important family news, did I not? So
here we are. Though these bits and pieces may sometimes be very
dreary I shall do my best to entertain. To achieve my purpose I asked
aunts and uncles and cousins for the news they would want me to
include.

Uncle Blue-Jay wants you to know that Cousin Cam is soon to
graduate from Boston College in Philosophy, and also that his littlest
Grace will be married sometime this summer to a fine young man
from the Turtle clan at Good Pasture. Aunt Susanna wants them to
marry at Lake in the Clouds, but the happy couple are not so sure.

Grace is, as you surely remember, exactly stubborn enough to unsettle a gentle Quaker mother.

Aunt Annie says that she hopes you are getting along in New Mexico Territory and watching your back. She has high hopes for this year's corn. And Cousin Jay's Gabe has his own rifle and is determined to earn the name Hawkeye at the next turkey shoot. Uncle Gabriel thinks that his grandson may well manage to achieve this title.

Uncle Ben says to tell you that Georgia has had a fine foal, to be called Bayou. Also, they plan to take a trip to visit Amelie (and Aunt Lily and all the rest of the family) in New York City. His scheme, he confessed to me, was to travel on to New Orleans. It has been too long, he says, since he was there, and he doesn't think anyone will remember that in 1814 Andrew Jackson would have hanged him had he not left in a timely manner.

Aunt Hannah laughed at this but wouldn't be drawn into one of the you reimagine history to suit your sense of humor debates, which is what he wanted, after all.

We are all very concerned about Aunt Birdie. She carries on as always, racing from canker rash to sprained ankle to burns, almost in competition with Uncle Henry, who is just as busy with patients. Aunt Hannah worries that Birdie will not survive another miscarriage. She has been ordered to bed by both Hannah and Henry. I imagine that it is a difficult situation when one doctor must obey the dictates of two others, especially when one is an older sister and the other a husband.

Given the worries about Birdie, Anna's dimples are not often seen these days. She is still the oddest, cleverest child, full of riddles and questions. She is often with us, in the hope that the Fractious Five will distract her at least a little bit. She especially likes to sit with Liam, the gentlest soul we have to offer, enjoys arguing with Ethan, certainly the most aggravating. Just recently she told Ethan that she, Anna Savard, was not afraid of him and thought him silly. The rest of my brothers congratulated her heartily on her good sense.

When I told Ma about this she said (as you will guess), Oh those fractious boys. By which she means she is glad that they are being useful and looking out for Anna, but she isn't feeling generous enough to tell them so. And then Da said, Martha, they are boys to you but they are grown, in case you have lost track. Then it was her turn to scowl. With talk of another war, that is no surprise.

Uncle Luke is still in Paris with the same excuse: he wants to make sure that Cousin (Not-Your) Nathan, newly enrolled in advanced medical studies at the Sorbonne (I may have this wrong, but who can keep track?), is comfortably situated. Luke spends all his time looking at furnishings and apartments with Nathan's new wife. I don't remember if you've met Lucy, but you would like her. She won't put up with nonsense. Nathan is so busy that Luke worries that Lucy will be bored or lonesome and run off. That, I think, is the reason he stays in Paris.

Otherwise, all the aunts, uncles and cousins (scattered far and wide) seem to be thriving. For my own part, I still find great satisfaction in teaching the Littles. You feared it would be boring to work in the same school house where you and I once traded notes and plotted our oh-so-clever practical jokes. Before the Troubles took you away. But I am never bored as a teacher. To be a good teacher you must first be a good storyteller, that is the trick and the joy of it. I have told some of the original Jennet's stories in the classroom as a special treat. It is a way to honor her and keep her memory alive.

I've left the most surprising bit for last. I know you remember my brother Ethan's friend from Johnstown, Max Gallantin, because you asked me about him when I came to the city to visit last year. It seems everybody knew, even at that point, that Max was fond of me. But I truly did not know. (Don't write and suggest that fond is an insipid word to use. I know that, but it's hard enough to write about it at all.)

Just after Ice-Out Josh Fiddler hired Max to help with the razing of the Red Dog. You would have thought St. Nicholas was moving to Paradise, the way my brothers reacted. They all went down to welcome Max when he arrived, but I stayed home. You know how they can be when there's too much ale and too little common sense.

The very next day they brought Max home with them for supper, and of course I couldn't stay away from table. I was perfectly polite. So Ma just comes out and says, who is that sour-faced girl at my table? This I ignored.

Then last week Da says out of the clear blue sky that Max might as well take the extra bed in the loft because living in the tiny room Mr. Bee rents out will give him a sore back and try his patience. That this would try my *patience did not occur to any of them. I said to Ma, here I was hoping Liam or Ethan would marry this season so we'd have some peace in the house, and instead you let Da bring in another brother to plague me.*

My brothers can think of nothing better to talk about than Max Gallantin. His many fine qualities. His expertise with carpenter's tools. (He makes his own, don't you know. His spokeshave is a thing of rare beauty, Liam informs me.) His skills in the woods (a young Paul Bunyan, Michael claims). How helpful he is. How quick witted. How fast he runs, and his baggataway stick, the heft of it (imagine, if you are brave enough, Robbie wiggling his eyebrows suggestively). This list of accomplishments and talents is never ending.

It all came to a head yesterday evening. Da started it by reminding us that you can tell a really good carpenter by his feel for wood.

It was a relief that Max was not at the table, because Da carried on and on about him. A truly talented carpenter convinces the wood to do his bidding, Da told us, and Max Gallantin makes the most beautiful and elegant dovetailed drawers. Those words were still hanging in the air when he turned and looked me in the eye and said, you know, girlie (yes, he will not give up calling me girlie), we been in need of a master carpenter in Paradise for a good while now.

Carrie, you know that I can hold my own with my brothers, but when Da backs them up, I abandon all hope. I broke and ran for the kitchen, hoping Ma would put it all right.

She was cutting up a pie and went right on with it the whole time I was telling her that the Fractious (and Da!) were plotting to marry me off to Max Gallantin because he understands wood. She never interrupted and finally she put her hands on table and leaned toward me to ask what I was really mad about.

That question surprised me, so Ma gave me the answer. She said, it's true, they went about the whole business heavy-handed, but think, Jennet. Just think, you may as well marry the man. You'll never find anybody who suits you or the family better.

I said, Ma! What is it you think I should do? Just announce to the man he's going to marry me, like it or not, the Bonner men have declared it so?

She gives me that sideways smile (you know the one) and says, well, you could do it that way, but he's been waiting out on the porch for you for an hour. Trying to work up the courage. Might be more satisfying if you let him do the asking.

And he was. He was waiting on the porch, and he did ask me.

I never said they were wrong about him, please remember. Max is good hearted and generous and he has a sense of humor. He's hardworking and yes, an excellent carpenter. His faults are, first, he cannot carry a tune in a bucket; second, at his young age there is significant gray in his hair; and third, he has four unmarried sisters. That's the worst I can say of him thus far. To my own chagrin I must admit that we are suited. And now I can say also that he kisses with just enough enthusiasm and on closer inspection I like his beard. Aunt Lily made your Da shave his beard off when they were courting, but I think I won't make such a demand. At least not straight away.

I think I will take Ma's advice without arguing first. This does not sound like me, does it. Please write and tell me if I am being too much like Ma. I depend on you for the hard truths. And send me your news. I worry about you and my imagination is, as you have always claimed, too wild to indulge for very long.

Your loving cousin,
Jennet Bonner, perhaps soon to be
Jennet Gallantin

Amelie Savard
Knucklebone Alley
New York, N.Y.

May 18, 1857

Dearest Carrie,

I have two women in labor, one on Charles Street and the other at
Leroy & Bleecker, but they are both primigravida and so I sit down
to write to you.

All is well here. Your Ma and Step-Da are both in good health.
At more than fifty Lily still rushes back and forth as if a sedate pace
would be grounds for arrest. She denies arthritis in her hands, but I
see it, nevertheless. At some point I will talk to Harrison about how
to help Lily when she won't admit she needs help. He's dour at times,
but he is dedicated to your Ma.

My own people, Ma and Da, brothers and sister, are well.
I am told that your sister Blue is once again expecting, but in good
health. Birdie is in the same condition, but not quite so well.
Ma writes that she is some worried about her and she keeps close
watch.

They need another midwife in Paradise, as Ma is slowing down.
I have been considering who of my students might fit best. If there is
no other solution I will go home to take up the work but I am very
comfortable here in my cottage and garden and I have many good
friends I would miss.

Da wrote to me to say they are thinking of going to New Orleans
for a visit, and soon. The next war is not far off, and they don't want
to be stuck there as they were when Jackson had his claws in the whole
city. He suggests (strongly) that I come with them. I am considering it.

I think too about traveling west to see you. Someday I will do it,
I am firmly resolved, but I fear it will have to wait until after the
next war has run its course.

*Write to me when you are able, and know I will always be here
ready to listen, whatever it is you have to say. How I miss your
bright mind and helpful hands and sweet face.*

Amelie

Lily B. Quinlan
18 Waverly Place
New York, New York

June 1, 1857

E. C. Ballentyne
in the care of Dr. Samuel Markham
Calle del Convento Viejo de la Parroquia Principal
Santa Fe, New Mexico Territory

My sweet girl,
The letters you and Nathan wrote to us from St. Louis arrived this
morning. It was such a joy to see your handwriting, and as a result I
find I can't wait even a day to start a reply. This letter won't reach
you before mid July at the earliest, and I expect it will cross paths
with your next letter home. And still I don't care to wait.
You should know first that everyone here in Manhattan is well.
In Paradise John is building another extension to the Mill House
because (as you will have guessed already) your sister Blue is
expecting again. Hannah is satisfied with her progress. My own
sister Birdie is expecting again too, but in her case Hannah will
confess to some worry, which is unsettling for us all.
As predicted, there have been almost daily meetings of one or the
other abolitionist groups since the publication of the Supreme Court's
irrational and illegal decision on Dred Scott. Your step-father and I
attend as many meetings as we can manage and are planning a trip
to Oberlin next month to take part in a conference where Mr.
Douglass is scheduled to appear. A few days ago we had a visit from
Gerrit Smith, who has been in constant motion since this newest
affront to the Constitution and human dignity. As furious as we all
are, he finds there is some satisfaction to be gained when he sees that
even the most sanguine and even-tempered of our kindred spirits are

rising up in protest. That war must follow is now universally acknowledged, or there is no way to stop the spread of slavery across the continent.

The packet that should arrive with this letter or soon after includes (as always) some reading. First is the copy of Mr. Douglass's My Bondage and My Freedom *that you misplaced and asked me to look for (Mrs. Cobb had been using it to prop up a wobbly table leg, I'm sorry to report). Also enclosed is* A Plea for the Indians; with Facts and Features of the Late War in Oregon, *by John Beeson. He and my mother corresponded for a short while. I have my own copy of his study and will start reading it as soon as I can work up the courage.*

It is not likely that you have many newspapers there, and what does come will be delayed. Is that excuse enough for the clippings I've enclosed? Among the pieces is an editorial from the New-York Tribune *with this line which I like particularly: "It is most true that this decision is bad law; that it is based on false historical premises and wrong interpretations of the Constitution; that it does not at all represent the legal or judicial opinion of the Nation; that it is merely a Southern sophism clothed with the dignity of our highest Court." And now I will stop dwelling on these matters for a short while at least.*

No doubt you will soon have a letter from your Cousin Jennet, who has committed to keeping you informed about all the uncles and aunts and cousins from that side of the fire. No doubt she will make you laugh in the process. It took Martha and Daniel six tries to get a girl, but she was worth the wait. It's remarkable how closely she resembles the aunt she was named for, though they never met. With the Little People scattered from New Mexico Territory to Paris and beyond, it is a challenge to keep track of you all, but she enjoys a challenge.

From your account it seems that the first half of the journey went fairly smoothly, but I will continue to worry until another letter tells me that you are both safely arrived. I do wish the telegraph would hurry up and find a home for itself in Santa Fe. Why California should have that wondrous, time-saving invention before New Mexico Territory strikes me as illogical. And unfair.

When I left home to study painting in Montreal, the new war with England was just picking up steam and it was neither easy nor quick to send news over the border. Ma worried every hair on her head gray, thinking about your Uncles Daniel and Blue-Jay in the militia. In truth, she deserved more empathy than I could give her. You have been far kinder than I was, but still I worry.

And so here I am sending off a long apology to Ma by confessing to you. I imagine her sitting here in the parlor with Josie's new puppies in her lap and smiling at me. Your Grandy had the sharpest eyes and sweetest smile.

I miss you every day, but most intensely at breakfast, when it was just the two of us; Nathan too lazy to rise, and Harrison already off to see patients. Those are wonderful memories, even when we were at odds and couldn't come to a compromise. I did know, even then, that I was not always fair. I worried too much about Harrison's expectations and not enough about what you needed from me.

I think a great deal about the first years in this house, and how difficult the adjustment was for you. Nathan took everything in stride, but the city did not suit you. I hope now these many years later you have come to a peaceful place, but it has never been clear to me how resolved past events are in your mind and memory. I should have talked to you about all that, but my mouth filled with bitterness whenever I considered it. That was my mistake.

Two apologies in one letter I think will suffice, and so I will close. I hope and trust that you are settled in with the Markhams, but hear me, now: you are not bound or indentured to them. You have the freedom to choose, and too few young women can say as much because they are limited by poor education or training, by financial restrictions or responsibilities, by superstition or fear; you are not.

You remind me so of my Ma, and I know she would be pleased with you and proud of the choices you've made. As your Da, my sweet Simon, would be.

You are the daughter of strong women and equal to whatever challenges you meet. Missteps are inevitable, but you will find your way.

I miss you, day by day.

Your loving mother,
Lily Ballentyne

Author's Note

I WRITE BIG, long, detailed novels, and I am not quick. This novel took me longer than usual for a range of reasons. First, before I started writing *The Sweet Blue Distance*, I had only rudimentary knowledge of the period right before the Civil War. I knew some things about the southwest U.S., the Bleeding Kansas period, and the abolition movement, but had to invest some time studying the way colonialization affected Indigenous peoples in the West.

In one way research for this time and place was a little easier: many people wrote about their experiences, and firsthand accounts are worth a lot to a historical novelist. Gregg's *Commerce of the Prairies* was a treasure trove of (sometimes suspect) details on travel, trade, customs, and cultural assumptions. The lives of women who moved west were less well documented, but Sandra L. Myres's *Westering Women* goes a long way to fill that hole with her close reading of original materials.

PLEASE NOTE THAT Spanish was not an original Indigenous language in any part of North, Central, or South America. However, it was introduced, forcibly, by Spanish colonists so long ago that it has gained many characteristics of an Indigenous language. Further, Spanish as it is spoken today has changed a lot from nineteenth-century Spanish in New Mexico Territory. Where possible, I have drawn on historical language sources.

Because I cannot claim even a solid working knowledge of Spanish, I depended on the help of two native Spanish speakers. I'm very fortunate to have had the assistance of Cathy Chavez (Albuquerque, New Mexico) and Yvonne Miguez (Round Rock, Texas). They were both immensely helpful and, probably more important, patient with my endless questions. I depended on them for more than anachronisms and colloquialisms; their families and communities are embedded in the culture and history of the Southwest, and they were attentive to missteps that might be construed as offensive. Whatever infelicities show up despite their help are my fault entirely.

If you are familiar with my work, you may be aware that before I began writing fiction, I was a university professor of academic linguistics. My research revolved primarily around language ideology and the way people perceive language variation. Or, more to the point, how those perceptions are used to rationalize discriminatory policies and practices. I am very conscious of the way my characters use language or comment about language. In this novel, that was especially the case, given the mid-nineteenth-century legislation that legalized removing Indigenous peoples from their homelands and separating their children from their families. The phrase "Kill the Indian, save the man" was widely used when these policies were discussed.

The purpose of taking children from their families was to deprive them of their native languages, cultures, and associations. In fact, language is the glue that holds a community together, and the effectiveness of the approach was seen in the decimation of whole communities and tribes. Details on these genocidal policies are widely available in scholarly publications. You might find this a good place to start (available online as a PDF): Kimberly Johnston-Dodds and John L. Burton's *Early California Laws and Policies Related to California Indians*.

The important point is that in all my work, academic and fiction, I am keenly aware of language use and attitudes and do what I can to shed more and clearer light on those issues.

On the subject of the Native or Indigenous peoples of this continent, I should point out that this novel is different from the Wilderness series novels. In researching those storylines, I learned a lot about the Indigenous tribes of the Northeast, at a time when they had already been decimated by colonization and were struggling to stay afloat.

For *The Sweet Blue Distance*, I could not follow the same pattern, because the Puebloan nations in New Mexico and Arizona consciously, actively chose to restrict outside influences on Pueblo identity and culture. Some tribes are more exacting about limiting access; the Hopi, for example, are very protective of their language and religious practices. Their efforts have been largely successful.

I admire the Puebloan nations for their foresight and determination to reclaim and protect their political and cultural independence. I respect their right to limit access, and thus I chose not to visit any pueblos nor did I seek out any tribal members for interviews. I limited research on their languages to a handful of words, and did this through a nonprofit that supports Indigenous language vitality within the pueblos.

Everything I know about the Pueblo peoples comes from historical documentation (always tricky to interpret) and scholarly publications, some of which were written by Puebloans. Thus, the Puebloan nations are less thoroughly described in this work than my readers might expect. I included a major character who is half-Puebloan to attempt to portray at least some aspects of the life of the Indigenous in this time and place.

Military history of this period in New Mexico Territory is spotty at best, but the bibliography includes those works that were helpful in sorting out the details. The lynching of a Mexican druggist by soldiers is based on an actual event as reported in the *Santa Fe Weekly Gazette*, but has been fictionalized. Soldiers broke into the jail and shot many prisoners, all unarmed and behind bars, including the accused but not yet tried druggist, who was killed outright. The soldiers were never punished, insofar as I have been able to determine.

The political chaos of this period can hardly be exaggerated, and most of it had to do with slavery and racism. Kenneth Stampp's *America in 1857: A Nation on the Brink* would be a good place to start if you're interested in the way the Civil War became inevitable.

Books and studies about travel on the Santa Fe trail are an embarrassment of riches. I made close study of the maps especially and don't know how I would have coped without them.

Given the complexity of the time period and the many issues raised, I have included a bibliography that touches on subjects I think will interest my readers—for example, postpartum depression and its treatment in mid-nineteenth-century America, racism focused on Latinx and mixed heritage in this same period, and the background of the forging of the Santa Fe trail.

Also included is a glossary of Mexican Spanish words, which I hope will be helpful to those who are unfamiliar with Spanish more generally and regional Spanish in particular.

Acknowledgments

THIS NOVEL TOOK far longer than estimated to finish, for reasons many of you know too well. The pandemic slowed all of us down and stopped some of us altogether, the kind of mass traumatic event that will be felt for years. To that came the election and the insurrection, the surge in systemic and violent racism, relentless undermining of the right to vote, mass shootings, and, oh yes, murder hornets.

It has been a rough three years, but I had help of all kinds. Specifically:

- I am always reminded how fortunate I am to be working with Jill Grinberg, my super agent, and her staff. Sam Farkas and Denise Page deserve credit for all the times they've come to my rescue on matters small and large.
- I've had quite a few editors over the years. Now I'm working with Kate Seaver, and I appreciate her analytical eye. Working with thoughtful people makes all the difference.
- My sincere thanks to Sandy Sheehy and Charles McClelland, who kindly offered me the use of their Albuquerque home for two

weeks. I was overwhelmed by their generosity. Academics understand each other's compulsions about research. Thank goodness.

- Jason Schmidt is a writer and novelist, an insightful and sharp-witted sociopolitical commentator, and after all that, a lawyer. His support has been incredibly helpful from multiple angles, including buck-up emails, research on really fiddly historical bits, and his willingness to untangle complex historical legal issues in an effort to stop me from embarrassing myself. Mostly he succeeds, but on occasion I will still misstep. Blame me, please.

- The genealogy for this multilayered universe of mine was a complete wilderness, but Polly Edwards managed to tame it, inasmuch as that is possible. I have changed character names in ways that make sense for the story but may confuse you, at first. The family tree Polly put together online should be some help. You'll find it on my website at SaraDonati.com/sweetblue.

- Penny Chambers is my closest friend. I don't think I'll ever run into anybody else who combines the patience, curiosity, and generous nature it took for her to listen to this novel as it was written, chapter by chapter, month in and out. She also feeds me and takes Jimmy Dean for long walks. He is planning on eloping with her. I think she'll go for it.

- Many people have given me feedback on early chapters, among them Karen Shelby, Amie Rukenstein, and Patricia Rosenmeyer. And then there are readers who have hung on since day one—more than twenty years now. A lot of them stay in contact on the Sara Donati Facebook page. I try to show them my appreciation by sharing bits from my research and, on the rare occasion, an excerpt.

- Special thanks to Kristina Gruell, who has always been extraordinarily helpful and supportive. She had her own publication challenges and health issues and kid crises, but she managed the Facebook page and group with panache despite all that. She also provided valuable feedback on early drafts of *The Sweet Blue Distance*.

I am really fortunate that there are readers on Facebook who are willing to jump in and handle things when I can't. Kristina is top of this list, and sincere thanks also to Michelle Schwartz, Sally Ross, Misty Seidel, Katherine Knapp Keena, Angela Blundell, Karen Jean Grimes, and Rachel Gorham for help, past and present.

Finally, my people keep me going. It's all for the Mathematician and the Girl, every word.

Glossary

TERM	TRANSLATION
acequia	A community-operated, engineered watercourse or canal for irrigation. A mayordomo is responsible for maintenance of community *acequias* and decisions regarding water distribution.
adobe	Bricks made of clay, sand, water, and organic material. Adobe buildings are usually covered with a compound something like stucco. Adobe far predates the arrival of the Spanish.
agrimensor	Surveyor
alburera	A quick-witted, sharp-tongued woman who excels at clever (nonsexual) wordplay
alguacil	Sheriff, bailiff, constable (regional)
Argentinean Criollo	The native horse of the Pampas in South America (encompassing parts of Uruguay, Argentina, Brazil, and Paraguay) with a reputation for long-distance endurance, hardiness, and stamina. Originally the word Criollo referred to humans and animals of purebred Spanish ancestry who were born in the Americas.
banco	A bench built into a wall, usually plastered in place

bastón	A combat or fighting cane. Also *topil*.
bofetazo	A hard blow to the face
bravucón	Bully
burro	Donkey; distinct from *mulo* (mule)
cacharrería	Dishware and pottery dealer; fancy dry goods
cacique	A Pueblo chieftain
caderas	Hips
cantina	Café, diner, tavern. "Variable sanctuaries in which pathetic, comic, tragic, and melodramatic situations are frequent." (Carlos Monsiváis)
chamaco, -a*	Boy, girl
chaquegüe*	Blue cornmeal gruel
chinchudo	Literally "a big ugly bedbug," also a hot-tempered person who gets angry easily
cibola	Bison, buffalo
cibolero	A Spanish colonial, Mexican, or American buffalo hunter from New Mexico Territory
cordillera	A rural road with houses in a row along one or both of its sides
Criollo	The children and descendants of Peninsulares born in the Spanish colonies. In the colonial caste system, a Criollo was technically a Spaniard but of lesser rank than a Peninsular. See also *Mestizo* and *genízaro*.
curia	Ingenuity, skill; *ser de mucha curia*: to be fussy, meticulous, industrious, painstaking
Department of New Mexico	A department of the United States Army during the mid-nineteenth century. It was created as the Ninth (geographical) Department in 1848, following the conclusion of the Mexican-American War. In 1853 it was renamed Department of New Mexico. Its primary purpose was administering the defense of the geographical areas that are now Arizona and New Mexico.

diezmos	Tithes, as to a church
enfermera	Nurse
fanfarrón	Braggart
ferretería	Hardware dealer, ironmonger
fonda	Hotel, inn
gabacho, -a	Someone from the East, an emigrant; less pointed than *tejano, -a*
gaucho	An accomplished horseman and cattle herder; the term originally of the South American Pampas
genízaro, -a	As a part of the colonalization of parts of North America, Spanish invaders often abducted and enslaved Indigenous people (primarily Navajo, Pawnee, Apache, Kiowa Apache, Ute, Comanche, and Paiute) to keep as servants, sheepherders, and general laborers in Spanish settlements such as San Miguel del Vado. *Genízaros* were also sold and traded. Very young women were highly valued for exploitation. By the end of the eighteenth century, *genízaros* were estimated to comprise at least one-third of the entire population. The term was also used for the descendants of the original captives.
gutta-percha	A form of rubber extracted from the sap of the palaquium fruit tree, native to what is now Malaysia. Gutta-percha is waterproof and resistant to acids, salt water, and chemicals. In the mid-nineteenth century, gutta-percha cloth of different weights was used to make blankets, coats, cloaks, knapsacks, and dozens of other items that were put to good use by the military.
hacienda	The large, private landed estates in the Southwest that originated as land grants during the Spanish colonial period. The *patrón*, or owner, had both permanent and transient employees to tend and harvest crops, maintain property and land, and work pastoral estates where cattle, horses, sheep, and goats originally imported from Spain were raised. A smaller hacienda was generally called a rancho.

huipil*	A loose-fitting tunic, common everyday wear for Mesoamerican women for centuries. Sewn from two or three rectangular pieces of fabric. The seams are bound with ribbons, or fabric strips, with an opening for the head and, if the sides are sewn, openings for the arms.
kiva	A chamber dedicated to ceremonial usage in Puebloan culture. Usually round and often located below surface level, with a packed-earth floor and firepit in the center. Size varies from very small (twelve inches in diameter) to very large (eighty inches in diameter).
La Llorona	A ghost who wails in the night as a sign of danger or impending death. People believe La Llorona to be (1) the ghost of a woman seeking her children who died at birth, (2) a soul from purgatory atoning for its sins, or (3) the spirit of an Aztec goddess to whom babies were sacrificed and who is heard during the night looking for children to carry off.
maldito	Damned
malvado	Evil, villainous
Mestizo	A person of both European and Indigenous American descent. The term was used as an ethnic/racial category for mixed-race *castas* that evolved during the Spanish colonial period.
monte	A gambling card game that originated in Spain. In the nineteenth century, it was known as the national card game of Mexico.
mujercita	Baby girl
mustang	An American feral horse that is typically small and lightly built
¡No mentira!	No lie!
parroquia	Catholic parish, encompassing church, chapel, rectory, convent, schools, etc.
partera	Midwife

patrón	Property owner, chief. A *patrón* had both permanent and transient employees to tend and harvest crops, and maintain property and land.
Peninsulares	People born in Spain who held the highest ranking and class status in the colonies
placita	A residential private courtyard space. The *placita* is meant to be entirely enclosed by the residential structure.
portal	A covered entryway or porch-like structure leading into a home or building. Also may refer to a covered patio attached to a home.
pozole*	Traditional pre-Columbian soup or stew
prostíbulo	Brothel
pueblo	1. (English) In New Mexico, Arizona, and adjacent areas in the Southwest, a pueblo is a fixed-location communal tribal dwelling consisting of contiguous flat-roofed houses built of adobe mud, stone, and other materials. The dwellings were built around a central plaza and could be many stories high. Each pueblo is associated with a different tribe of the Puebloan nations, of which there are in the present day nineteen. A map of the Indigenous nations is included on the novel's website: SaraDonati.com/sweetblue. 2. (Spanish) Village
punche*	Native tobacco of the Rio Grande valley, wrapped in corn husks for smoking
querido, -a	Beloved
ramera	Hussy, loose woman
rebozo	A woman's garment (scarf, shawl, or infant sling) considered a symbol of Mexican identity. The rebozo is a long, usually rectangular piece of material made from patterned cloth, handwoven from cotton, linen, silk, or wool. A rebozo has a broad fringe. Rebozos were common in the precolonial period.
remuda	A herd of horses that have been saddle broken, from which ranch hands choose their mounts for the day

tejano, -a	A term applied disparagingly to a white stranger from Texas or from anywhere in the eastern U.S. Also *gabacho/a, gringo, bolillo, geracho*. "*Tejano* was a name of loathing and fright." (Erna Fergusson, *Our Southwest*)
tesgüín,* m.	A kind of homemade corn liquor. Also *tesgüino, tisgüín*.
testarudo	Hardheaded, stubborn
Towa	The Tanoan language spoken by the people of the Walatowa (Jemez) Pueblo
tutear	In Spanish, to speak to someone using the familiar rather than the formal pronouns and verb declinations. *¿Podemos tutearnos?* (Can we address each other as friends?)
Vallero, m.	A blanket with a complicated pattern of stars
vaquero, -a	A livestock herder, always mounted. The tradition originated on the Iberian Peninsula and further evolved in Spanish-held colonies in Latin and North America. Vaqueros were the first and original cowboys in the Southwest.
zaguan	An access hallway into an interior courtyard or *placita* of a traditional residence. These may be narrow or large enough for a wagon or horse cart to be pulled into the enclosure.

*a term from Nahuatl, an Indigenous language (Aztec)

Selected References

Arnold, Sam. *Eating up the Santa Fe Trail: Recipes and Lore from the Old West.* Golden, CO: Fulcrum Publishers. 2001.

Ball, Larry D. *Desert Lawmen: The High Sheriffs of New Mexico and Arizona, 1846–1912.* Albuquerque: University of New Mexico Press. 1996.

Baxter, John O. *Las Carneradas: Sheep Trade in New Mexico, 1700–1860.* Albuquerque: University of New Mexico Press. 1987.

Bender, Averam B. Review of *New Mexico in 1850: A Military View,* by George Archibald McCall, ed. Robert W. Frazer. *Pacific Historical Review* 38.2. 1969.

Bender, Averam B. "The Soldier in the Far West, 1848-1860." *Pacific Historical Review* 8.2. 1939.

Bergink, Veerle, Natalie Rasgon, and Katherine L. Wisner. "Postpartum Psychosis: Madness, Mania, and Melancholia in Motherhood." *American Journal of Psychiatry* 173.12. 2016.

Bills, Garland D., and Neddy A. Vigil. *The Spanish Language of New Mexico and Southern Colorado: A Linguistic Atlas.* Albuquerque: University of New Mexico Press. 2008.

Boyle, Susan Calafate. *Los Capitalistas: Hispano Merchants and the Santa Fe Trade.* Albuquerque: University of New Mexico Press. 2000.

Bucknill, John Charles, and Daniel H. Tuke. *A Manual of Psychological Medicine: Containing the History, Nosology, Description, Statistics, Diagnosis, Pathology, and Treatment of Insanity, with an Appendix of Cases.* Philadelphia: Blanchard and Lea. 1858.

Buhk, Tobin T. *True Crime in the Civil War: Cases of Murder, Treason, Counterfeiting, Massacre, Plunder, & Abuse.* Mechanicsburg, PA: Stackpole Books. 2012.

Burgess, Barbara MacPherson. "Journals, Diaries, and Letters Written by Women on the Oregon Trail 1836-1865" (master's thesis). Kansas State University. 1984.

Cohen, Dov, Richard E. Nisbett, Brian F. Bowdle, and Norbert Schwarz. "Insult, Aggression, and the Southern Culture of Honor: An 'Experimental Ethnography.'" *Journal of Personality and Social Psychology* 70.5. 1996.

Connelley, William E. "A Journal of the Santa Fe Trail." *Mississippi Valley Historical Review* 12.1. 1925.

Dadd, George H. *The Modern Horse Doctor: Containing Practical Observations on the Causes, Nature and Treatment of Disease and Lameness in Horses.* New York: A. O. Moore. 1854.

Dary, David. *The Santa Fe Trail: Its History, Legends, and Lore.* Lawrence: University Press of Kansas. 2012.

de Aragon, Ray John. *Padre Martínez and Bishop Lamy.* Las Vegas: Pan-American Publishing. 1978.

Dempsey, Terrell. *Searching for Jim: Slavery in Sam Clemens's World.* Columbia: University of Missouri Press. 2003.

Dunlay, Thomas W. *Kit Carson & the Indians.* Lincoln: University of Nebraska Press. 2000.

Egenes, John. *Man & Horse: The Long Ride Across America.* Dunedin, NZ: Delta Vee. 2017.

Etcheson, Nicole. "The Goose Question: The Proslavery Party in Territorial Kansas and the 'Crisis in Law and Order.'" In *Bleeding Kansas, Bleeding Missouri: The Long Civil War on the Border,* edited by Jonathan Earle and Diane Mutti Burke. Topeka: University Press of Kansas. 2013.

Etcheson, Nicole. "Labouring for the Freedom of This Territory: Free-State Kansas Women in the 1850s." *Kansas History* 21.2. 1998.

Faller, Lincoln B., and George Bent. "Making Medicine against 'White Man's Side of Story': George Bent's Letters to George Hyde." *American Indian Quarterly* 24.1. 2000.

Fenn, George Manville. *In the Wilds of New Mexico.* New York: F. A. Munsey. 1888.

Fierman, Floyd S. *Merchant-Bankers of Early Santa Fe, 1844-1893*. El Paso: Texas Western College. 1981.

Fitzgerald, Daniel. *Mad Money: The Steamboat Era on the Kansas-Missouri Border*. Palm Harbor, FL: Dan Fitzgerald Company. 2011.

Forrest, Earle R. *Missions and Pueblos of the Old Southwest: Their Myths, Legends, Fiestas, and Ceremonies, with Some Accounts of the Indian Tribes and their Dances; and of the Penitentes*. Cleveland: Arthur H. Clarke Co. 1929.

Foster-Harris, William, and Evelyn Curro. *The Look of the Old West*. New York: Skyhorse Publishing. 2007.

Frank, Curtiss. *Re-Riding History: Horseback over the Santa Fe Trail*. Sunstone Press. 2016.

Franzwa, Gregory M. *Maps of the Santa Fe Trail*. St. Louis, MO: Patrice Press. 1989.

Frazer, Robert W. *Forts and Supplies: The Role of the Army in the Economy of the Southwest, 1846-1861*. Albuquerque: University of New Mexico Press. 1983.

Gardner, Mark L. *Wagons for the Santa Fe Trade: Wheeled Vehicles and Their Makers, 1822-1880*. Albuquerque: University of New Mexico Press. 2000.

Gibbens, V. E., ed. "Letters on the War in Kansas in 1856." *Kansas Historical Quarterly* 10.4. 1941.

Gillespie, Michael L. *Wild River, Wooden Boats: True Stories of Steamboating and the Missouri River*. Stoddard, WI: Heritage Press. 2000.

Gilmore, Donald L. *Civil War on the Missouri-Kansas Border*. Gretna, LA: Pelican Publishing. 2005.

Gleicher, Sheri Goldstein. "The Spiegelbergs of New Mexico: A Family Story of the Southwestern Frontier." *Southwest Jewish History* 1.2. 1992.

Gómez, Laura E. "Off-White in an Age of White Supremacy: Mexican Elites and the Rights of Indians and Blacks in Nineteenth-Century New Mexico." *Chicano-Latino Law Review* 25.1. 2005.

Gregg, Josiah. *Commerce of the Prairies, or, The Journal of a Santa Fé Trader* [. . .]. Two volumes. New York: Henry G. Langley. 1844.

Hills, E. C. "New-Mexican Spanish." *PMLA*/Publications of the Modern Language Association of America 21.3. 1906.

Hodge, Frederick Webb, et al. *Fort Union and the Santa Fe Trail*. Washington, DC: Government Printing Office. 1912.

Holmes, Kenneth L. *Covered Wagon Women: Diaries & Letters from the Western Trails, 1854–1860*. Lincoln: University of Nebraska Press. 1998.

Horgan, Paul. *Lamy of Santa Fe*. Middletown, CT: Wesleyan University Press. 2012.

Horn, Hosea B., and J. H. Colton. *Horn's Overland Guide, from the U.S. Indian Sub-Agency, Council Bluffs, on the Missouri River, to the City of Sacramento, in California.* New York: J. H. Colton. 1852.

Isaacs, Judith Ann. *Guide to the Jemez Mountain Trail: A National Scenic Byway.* Jemez Pueblo, NM: Butterfly and Bear Press. 2018.

Jaehn, Tomas, ed. *Jewish Pioneers of New Mexico, 1821-1917.* Sante Fe: Museum of New Mexico Press. 2000.

Johnston-Dodds, Kimberly. *Early California Laws and Policies Related to California Indians*, prepared at the request of John L. Burton. Sacramento: California Research Bureau. 2002.

Kincade, Mackenzie. *The Writer's Guide to Horses: The Author's Essential Illustrated Reference to All Things Equine.* Self-published. 2019.

Kingsbury, John M., and James Josiah Webb. *Trading in Santa Fe: John M. Kingsbury's Correspondence with James Josiah Webb, 1853-1861.* Dallas: Southern Methodist University Press. 1996.

Legends of America. *Old West Lawmen.* Lenexa, KS: Roundabout Publications. 2012.

Lieffring, Christina. "Steamboat Travel Was Dirty and Dangerous, Especially on the Missouri River." *All Things Considered.* NPR. KCUR 89.3. 14 July 2015.

Loudon, Irvine. *Death in Childbirth: An International Study of Maternal Care and Maternal Mortality 1800-1950.* Oxford: Oxford University Press. 1992.

Loudon, Irvine. *Medical Care and the General Practitioner, 1750-1850.* Oxford: Clarendon Press. 1982.

Loudon, Irvine. "Puerperal Insanity in the 19th Century." *Journal of the Royal Society of Medicine* 81.2. 1988.

"Mark Twain at Large: The Mississippi River." Exhibit: *The Mark Twain Papers* of the Bancroft Library, University of California, Berkeley.

Marland, Hilary. "Disappointment and Desolation: Women, Doctors and Interpretations of Puerperal Insanity in the Nineteenth Century." *History of Psychiatry* 14.3. 2003.

Marland, Hilary. "Under the Shadow of Maternity: Birth, Death and Puerperal Insanity in Victorian Britain." *History of Psychiatry* 23.1. 2012.

McCall, George A., and Robert W. Frazer. *New Mexico in 1850: A Military View.* Norman: University of Oklahoma Press. 1968.

McKay, Robert Henderson. *Little Pills: An Army Story.* Pittsburg, KS: Headlight. 1918.

Merrick, George Byron. *Old Times on the Upper Mississippi: The Recollections of a Steamboat Pilot from 1854 to 1863.* Cleveland, OH: A. H. Clark Company. 1909.

Moorhead, Max L. "Military Transportation in the Southwest, 1848-1860."
New Mexico Historical Review 32.2. 1957.

Mora, Jo. *Trail Dust and Saddle Leather.* New York: C. Scribner's Sons. 1946.

Mueller, Edward A., and Harry G. Dyer. *Upper Mississippi River Rafting
Steamboats.* Athens: Ohio University Press. 1995.

Myres, Sandra Lynn. *Ho for California!: Women's Overland Diaries from the
Huntington Library.* San Marino, CA: Huntington Library. 2007.

Myres, Sandra Lynn. *Westering Women and the Frontier Experience, 1800-1915.*
Albuquerque: University of New Mexico Press. 1982.

Newell, Clayton R. *The Regular Army Before the Civil War, 1845-1860.*
Washington, DC: Center of Military History, United States Army. 2014.

"The New Mexican Mail." *New York Times*, 6 September 1860.

Nickens, Paul R., and Kathleen Nickens. *Pueblo Indians of New Mexico.*
Charleston, SC: Arcadia Publishing. 2008.

Nieto-Phillips, John M. *The Language of Blood: The Making of Spanish-American
Identity in New Mexico, 1880s-1930s.* Albuquerque: University of New
Mexico Press. 2004.

Oraibi, Qöyáwaima. "Mû'yingwa, Two Children, and the Humming-bird." In
The Traditions of the Hopi, edited by H. R. Voth. Chicago: Field Columbian
Museum. 1905.

O'Reilly, CuChullaine. *The Horse Travel Handbook.* Cosa Mesa, CA: Long
Riders' Guild Press. 2016.

Ortiz y Pino, José. *Don José, The Last Patrón.* Santa Fe, NM: Sunstone. 1981.

Pacheco, Ana. *Pueblos of New Mexico.* Charleston, SC: Arcadia Publishing. 2018.

Rael, Juan B. "New Mexican Spanish Feasts." *California Folklore Quarterly* 1.1.
1942.

Reedstrom, Ernest Lisle, and Gilbert Crontz, ed. *Historic Dress of the Old West.*
New York: Blandford Press. 1986.

Reinhartz, Dennis, and Gerald D. Saxon, eds. *Mapping and Empire: Soldier-
Engineers on the Southwestern Frontier.* Austin: University of Texas Press.
2005.

Richards, T. Addison. *Appletons' Illustrated Hand-Book of American Travel: A
Full and Reliable Guide by Railway, Steamboat, and Stage to the United States
and the British Provinces* [. . .]. New York: D. Appleton & Co. 1857.

Riddle, Kenyon. *Records and Maps of the Old Santa Fe Trail.* Revised and
expanded. West Palm Beach, FL: John K. Riddle. 1963.

Ritch, William G. *Illustrated New Mexico, historical and industrial*, 5th rev. ed.
Santa Fe, NM: Bureau of Immigration. 1885.

Russell, Marion Sloan. *Land of Enchantment: Memoirs of Marian Russell Along
the Santa Fé Trail.* Pickle Partners Publishing. 2016. Ebook.

Sando, Joe S. *Pueblo Nations: Eight Centuries of Pueblo Indian History*. Santa Fe, NM: Clear Light Publishing. 1992.

Sando, Joe S., and Paul S. Chinana. *Nee Hemish, a History of Jemez Pueblo*. Santa Fe, NM: Clear Light Publishing. 2008.

Santa Fe Trail Association. Interactive Trail Map. https://www.santafetrail.org/interactive-trail-map/.

Sayer, Chloë. "Traditional Mexican Dress." Produced as part of the exhibition *Frida Kahlo: Making Her Self Up*. Victoria and Albert Museum. 2018.

Segale, Blandina, and Therese Martin. *At the End of the Santa Fe Trail*. Columbus, OH: Columbian Press. 1932.

Sherburne, John Pitts, and Mary McDougall Gordon. *Through Indian Country to California: John P. Sherburne's Diary of the Whipple Expedition, 1853-1854*. Stanford, CA: Stanford University Press. 1988.

Simmons, Marc. *Spanish Pathways: Readings in the History of Hispanic New Mexico*. Albuquerque: University of New Mexico Press. 2001.

Slattery, John. *Southwest Foraging*. Portland, OR: Timber Press. 2016.

Stampp, Kenneth M. *America in 1857: A Nation on the Brink*. New York: Oxford University Press. 1992.

Stanley, F. *The San Ildefonso, New Mexico Story*. Privately published. 1969.

Stavans, Ilan. "The United States of Mestizo." *Humanities* 31:5. 2010.

Sunseri, Alvin R. *Seeds of Discord: New Mexico in the Aftermath of the American Conquest, 1846-1861*. Chicago: Nelson-Hall. 1979.

Sutton, Robert K. *Stark Mad Abolitionists: Lawrence, Kansas, and the Battle over Slavery in the Civil War Era*. New York: Skyhorse Publishing. 2017.

Taylor, Morris F. *First Mail West: Stagecoach Lines on the Santa Fe Trail*. Albuquerque: University of New Mexico Press. 1971.

Theriot, Nancy. "Diagnosing Unnatural Motherhood: Nineteenth-Century Physicians and 'Puerperal Insanity.'" *American Studies* 30.2. 1989.

Trimble, Marshall. "The Army Corps of Topographical Engineers." *True West*, 21 August 2023.

Twitchell, Ralph Emerson. *Old Santa Fe: The Story of New Mexico's Ancient Capital*. Chicago: Rio Grande Press. 1963.

Twitchell, Ralph Emerson. *The Story of the Conquest of Santa Fe, New Mexico, and the Building of Old Fort Marcy, A.D. 1846*. Santa Fe, NM: Historical Society of New Mexico. 1923.

Utley, Robert M. *Fort Union and the Santa Fe Trail*. El Paso: Texas Western Press. 1989.

Valenčius, Conevery Bolton. "Gender and the Economy of Health on the Santa Fe Trail." *Osiris* 19. 2004.

Walker, Ronald W., Richard E. Turley, and Glen M. Leonard. *Massacre at Mountain Meadows*. New York: Oxford University Press. 2011.

Webb, Walter Prescott. *The Great Plains*. Lincoln: University of Nebraska Press. 1931.

Wheat, Joe Ben, and Ann Lane Hedlund. *Blanket Weaving in the Southwest*. Tucson: University of Arizona Press. 2003.

Wied, Maximilian, et al. *Travels in the Interior of North America*. London: Ackermann and Co. 1843.

Williams, Samantha. "The Experience of Pregnancy and Childbirth for Unmarried Mothers in London, 1760–1866." *Women's History Review* 20.1. 2011.

Woloson, Wendy A. *Refined Tastes: Sugar, Confectionery, and Consumers in Nineteenth-Century America*. Baltimore: Johns Hopkins University Press. 2002.

Wood, Dean Earl. *The Old Santa Fe Trail from the Missouri River: Documentary Proof of the History and Route of the Old Santa Fe Trail*. Kansas City: E. L. Mendenhall. 1955.

Wooster, Robert. "'A Difficult and Forlorn Country': The Military Looks at the American Southwest, 1850-1890." *Arizona and the West* 28.4. 1986.